THE
BELL WITCH
SERIES

BOOKS 1 - 3

Written by Sara Clancy
Edited by Kathryn St. John-Shin

ISBN: 9781671502918
Copyright © 2019 by ScareStreet.com

Thank You and Bonus Novel!

I'd like to take a moment to thank you for your ongoing support. You make this all possible! To really show you my appreciation for purchasing this book, **I'd love to send you a full-length horror novel in 3 formats (MOBI, EPUB and PDF) absolutely free!**

Download your full-length horror novel, get free short stories, and receive future discounts by visiting www.ScareStreet.com/SaraClancy

See you in the shadows,
Sara Clancy

TABLE OF CONTENTS

THE
HARVEST

THE BELL WITCH SERIES BOOK 1

CHAPTER 1

The Winthrop Family

Nightshift at the Stonebridge State Hospital for the Criminally Insane always carried an expectant silence. Having done his training at a private mental hospital, Cadwyn had grown used to a constant white noise of rambling whispers, broken sobs, and an endless shuffle of restless bodies. It was different here. After a certain hour, the commotion faded into silence, leaving Cadwyn's footsteps to echo down the seemingly endless hallways. No one was deluded enough to think this calm meant anything good. There was always lingering anticipation. The staff could only wait with bated breath to see what the inmates would present them with next.

Rounding a corner, he braced one shoulder on the heavy iron door and waved lazily at the camera mounted near the ceiling. The deadbolt gave a heavy thunk and the magnetic locks disengaged with a droning buzz.

"You're supposed to check my identification card," Cadwyn reminded the head nurse as he pushed his way into the room.

From the outside, Stonebridge's floorplan seemed pretty straight forward; just a long rectangle of red brick. Inside, however, it was a nightmare. All four floors were divided up by a maze of hallways. Windows were scarce, making it hard for someone to orientate themselves and near impossible to hold onto any sense of time. Mercifully, the unbreakable plastic shielding the rows of fluorescent lights muffled their constant hum. Numerous nurses' stations speckled the building. They, more than anything else, marked the transition from one level of security to the next.

"I know who you are, Cad. And I could see from the numerous cameras that you were all alone," Michelle's voice drifted out from behind the sheet of bulletproof glass. "Of course, I'll make sure to check your credentials before you head into high security."

Cadwyn braced one forearm on the little ledge outside the glass. "Why would I be doing that? I'm on low-risk tonight, remember? First time in months."

A smile slowly stretched Michelle's freckled face. Cadwyn groaned.

"Can't I just have one shift where no one tries to spit on me?"

"Wrong profession, love." Michelle slipped a hand through the small gap in the window and proceeded to wiggle a specimen cup around. "It's time for Peter the Human Eater to have his checkup."

"How many times can one human being have a urinary tract infection?" Cadwyn asked.

"Maybe it's karma," Michelle mused.

"I think the punishment for consuming human flesh would be a bit more than a sore crotch." He snatched the cup away as his friend started to hit him with it. "And why do I have to get the sample?"

"You're on shift."

"So are you. And, according to that wonderfully useful board behind you, there are actually several people here tonight who are assigned to high security."

Michelle shrugged. "None of us are six foot."

"Sayid is."

"He can't do that scary thing you do with your eyes."

Cadwyn chuckled, "What thing?"

"Yeah. Not buying it. Stop looking at me and go intimidate the serial killer into pissing himself, please."

As Cadwyn turned, he noticed an amendment made to the whiteboard. It stopped him in an instant.

"You put Gould back on my rotation?"

Michelle sighed. "Come on, don't make this difficult."

"I told you I wouldn't deal with him."

"Look, I know he rubs you the wrong way. But this place isn't exactly filled with nice people. Besides, you're a nurse. You don't get to pick your patients."

"Michelle, I'm telling you this knowing full well you can have me fired, ruin my reputation, and possibly have my license revoked." He waited for a heartbeat longer than necessary to make sure he had the head nurse's full attention. "If you keep Gould in my rotation, I will kill him."

"Don't even joke like that."

He stared at her until she met his gaze again. "I will do everything in my power to ensure his wound festers. I'll help the infection spread to his bloodstream. I'll watch him die a slow and painful death without ever intervening. Do you understand me?"

At first, Michelle tried to stare him down. She soon gave up. Growling through clenched teeth and snatching a clipboard off its hook with more force than necessary did little to dispel her resentment.

"Fine. I'll take him off. But we never had this conversation. Do you understand *me*?"

"Of course, I do. You're very articulate."

She sneered at him, halfway between amused and enraged, and shoved the clipboard through the narrow gap. A pen followed later for Cadwyn to begin filling it all out. The fact that every pen in the building had to be accounted for at all times really slowed down the paperwork side of things.

She swiped angrily at the board. "Okay, this time you're going to give me a dang answer."

"When have I not?"

"What is it with you and Gould?" she continued, her glare the only sign she had heard his comment. "It's not like he's the worst we've got around here."

Without looking up from his paperwork, Cadwyn replied, "My uncle once told me everyone has pressure points. Some you'll grow out of. Some you'll learn how to deal with. But there will always be something that cuts you right down to your soul."

Michelle scoffed. It was only once Cadwyn looked at her from under his lashes that she shrugged.

"I don't have any."

"My uncle would say you just haven't been tested."

Michelle looked somewhat offended by that but, instead of arguing the point, went back to her whiteboard.

"A wise man knows his weaknesses as well as his strengths," Cadwyn mumbled.

"Oh? Your uncle gave you that pearl of wisdom as well?"

"My grandmother," he answered.

"Right." She rolled her eyes. Scribbling on the whiteboard, she absently asked, "So, your point is that Gould pushes on one of your pressure points?"

Cadwyn cringed. "Cruelty to dogs and pulling teeth."

Michelle's marker left a streak of bright blue across the board as she whirled on him. "Are you kidding me? Teeth? Really? We've got three other patients in this wing alone who did unspeakable things with corpses, and *teeth* is where you draw the line?"

"There's no shame in having pressure points, only in denying them," Cadwyn said under his breath.

She stared at him. "Kimberly fed radioactive material to children."

"Which is horrific and disgusting," he replied. "This isn't a moralistic issue, Michelle. I'm not trying to say my personal pressure points are the epitome of evil. Think of it more like phobias. It's simply something you don't have any control over."

"Teeth?"

"Pulling teeth. Or breaking them. Anything along those lines." He let the conversation drop as his stomach began to churn.

Her frustration was starting to show. Shaking her head, she left her task and returned to the little window that separated them.

"What's any of this got to do with Gould? He's in here because he declared everyone at the IRS to be lizard people and tried to blow up the headquarters."

"Look up what he did to his pet boxer."

"Oh, it was the cruelty to animals button he pushed."

Cadwyn slid the paperwork back to his friend.

"It's cruelty to dogs in particular," he corrected. "And Gould hit both buttons."

Deciding that prolonging the conversation ran the risk of making him physically ill, Cadwyn held up the specimen cup in farewell and stalked down to the next door. With a sweet smile, Michelle refused to open the door until she had personally checked his identification card.

When at last he was through the first door, he quickly ran into the next. Several checkpoints turned the relatively short walk into a string of capsules. Some had a living guard to usher him on his way. At others, he had to flash his credentials to the mounted cameras and wait for someone in a distant room to hit the lock release. Having never worked at the general prison, he sometimes wondered how different their security was. They had hardened criminal psychopaths as well, after all. Although, he supposed the ones who called Stonebridge home were of a different breed.

Two burly guards met him at the last checkpoint. While Cadwyn was slightly taller than both Ted and Steve, each guard easily surpassed him in sheer muscle mass. Ted combined his impressive bulk with a standard issue military hair cut to look more imposing. Steve, on the other hand, achieved the same effect with the array of tattoos that seemingly covered everything but his face. Together, they were an intimidating sight, and that was the whole point.

"A urine sample? Didn't we just do this?" Ted asked, reviewing the notes on the monitor enclosed in the wall.

"It's a follow-up," Cadwyn said.

Steve scratched at the monotone skull tattoo that covered the right side of his neck. "If he throws it at me again, you owe me a beer."

"How is it my fault?" Cadwyn asked, positioning himself between the two men as they started down the long stretch of hallway.

"It ain't. I just want free beer."

"Stay classy," Ted mumbled.

Peter was one of the patients that had to be kept in permanent isolation. Unless absolutely necessary, he wasn't brought out of his cell and no one went in. All the guards hated the few occasions that made it unavoidable. Peter was an opportunistic predator and fond of blitz attacks. It made him unpredictable, volatile, and inclined to keep fighting until he was either sedated or unconscious. The paperwork those encounters created took hours to complete. Everyone hated dealing with Peter.

The final door opened with a loud buzz. Ted pushed the door open. Terrified screams rolled down upon them like a tsunami. Steve pushed Cadwyn behind him before they sprinted forward, silently instructing the nurse on exactly how far away he was allowed to venture. Ted used the radio from his belt to call in the disturbance. A protocol that guaranteed backup would be on the way while also ensuring the wing would go into lockdown. The large slabs of unbreakable glass set in each door allowed Cadwyn to see into each cell as they passed. Some cursed at them. Or spat. A few fed off Peter's panic, using it to fuel their own frenzies. Others hid. A flash of color streaked across his peripheral vision. The passing illusion of a child. A little girl dressed in green. Cadwyn lurched to a stop. *It's too soon.* The thought shattered as Steven bellowed at him. Breaking into a run again, Cadwyn soon caught up, repeating to himself all the while, *it's not midnight. I still have time. I didn't bring her here.*

Peter pressed himself against the door, his voice cracking as he shrieked, his hands smearing blood across everything he touched. The guards increased their speed, effortlessly falling into formation.

Ted positioned himself between the door and Cadwyn while Steve moved to the door. Cadwyn was forced to stretch his neck to see over the rounded muscles that lined Ted's shoulders. Peter hadn't left his position but the quickly thickening layer of blood made it harder to see him.

"Back away!" Steve growled, one hand clasping the hilt of his baton. "Back away from the door, now!"

"Let me out!" The words clashed together as Peter repeated them, becoming gibberish and mangling the few others he shoved in at random.

Dread burned behind Cadwyn's ribs. "Did he just say there's a girl in his cell?"

The guards shared a glance before they shifted into breach position. Going in with only two of them wasn't something either wanted to do. But they were quickly passing the point where what they wanted held any weight. Peter was working the whole ward into a frenzy and, judging by the amount of blood painting the door, was in danger of bleeding out. Ted rose up onto his toes, shifting slightly, seeking out a way to see through the few gaps still unstained by crimson. A visible jolt ran through his body. His broad shoulders tensed and, in a flash of movement, he had his baton at the ready and was snarling into his radio.

"Get here, now!"

"ETA in five minutes," came the crackling response.

"Inmate 364 has a civilian in his cell," Ted bellowed over the rising chaos around them. "Repeat. Inmate 364 has a child in his cell!"

"How is that possible?" Steve asked, pushing closer to the glass. The color drained from his face.

"Help me!" Peter's screams broke each time he threw his whole body against the door. "You can't leave me in here with her! Help me!"

The guards ignored the flood of questions that came across the radio to share a shocked glance. At the pause, Peter became more frantic, his actions feeding the confusion. Cadwyn's skin turned to ice when Peter shifted. It was just for a second, but he saw her. A little girl in green.

"Get him out of there," Cadwyn breathed.

The order, while softly spoken, was enough to snap the guards out of their daze. Neither of their extensive training had prepared them for this scenario.

"Let me out! Keep her away from me!"

Cadwyn stepped forward before he could stop himself, his hands balled into fists at his side. Guilt bubbled within his veins. *I didn't pay attention to the time. It's past midnight. I brought her here.* The guards shared a single nod. Steve grabbed the handle, swiped his key card over the sensor, and paused with his hand poised over the keypad.

"Opening in three, two, one."

The door was yanked open with enough force to spray the walls with blood. The sight of the bright red flecks whipped the trapped inmates into a frenzy, spiraling the situation further beyond their captor's control. The noise was deafening. Animalistic screams mingled with demented threats and the constant pounding against the walls. Caught in the middle of it all, Cadwyn was forced to remember just how dangerous the men around him were. He prayed the doors would hold as his muscle memory took over, making him back away, putting the solid wall to his back, and giving the guards room to grapple Peter to the ground.

"You're not listening to me," Peter wailed, thrashing against Ted's hold. "Get me away from her! You can't leave me with her!"

Ted pressed his knee between Peter's shoulder blades, pinning the man to the ground by weight alone.

"Hands above your head, now!" Ted snarled.

Peter's response was to throw his weight to the side, blindly throwing out blood-soaked fists. The noise around them grew impossibly louder.

"Cad!" Steve snapped from where he lay upon Peter's legs, trying to stop the madman from injuring himself. "We've got him! Check on the kid!"

A wall of guards powered down the hallway toward them. *Go now, before they see.* The internal command pushed him into motion. Cadwyn slipped around the three men, careful not to touch the bloody walls as he crossed the threshold. All the while, he prayed to find the child inexplicably inside.

"Cad? What's going on?" Steve asked.

Cadwyn swallowed thickly. "The room's empty."

"What? How? I saw her," Ted demanded in the same instant Steve latched onto one of Peter's arms and pulled it back, stopping only when the joint lingered on the brink of shattering.

"Where did she go?" Steve growled. "What did you do to her?"

The other guards finally joined them, allowing Ted the luxury of turning to catch Cadwyn's eyes.

"She has to be in there. Go and check."

Before Cadwyn could respond, the new arrivals began a chorus of reasons why a child could never get into the cell.

"I know what I saw!" Steve puffed out his barreled chest, challenging anyone to correct him again.

A constant clatter erupted amongst them. The inmates raged, the guards sniped at each other, and all the while, Peter pleaded not to be put back in the cell. 'Not with her.' The repeated demand was the only proof the two guards could point to that they weren't delusional. Until that moment, Cadwyn had held tight to the hope it wasn't *her*. But hearing the fear in the cannibal's voice, seeing the way he had shredded his fingers to the bone in desperation to get away from her; there was only one person he knew who could strike that depth of fear into someone like Peter Wallas.

"What did she look like?" Steve asked Peter, using the response as another shred of proof.

"Dark hair," Peter gasped. "Green dress. Her smile."

The description ended there. Becoming nothing more than broken sobs and endless begging to be taken away.

"That's her," Steve said.

Ted nodded, "That's who I saw."

Cadwyn noticed no one asked him. For the moment, he had been forgotten. It wouldn't last. Soon, they would calm down enough to need someone to tend to Peter's wounds. *Move now.* He had barely taken a single step into the room when he heard it. The arguments drifted away, replaced by the soft, metallic ting of an old music box. The tune was repetitive and simple. A lullaby he knew well. It had taunted his family line for generations. *Find it!* The cell was small and bare. There was nowhere in the blood-stained room for it to hide.

"Cad, get out here. We need you."

He didn't instantly recognize the speaker, but he turned toward the voice. Something solid knocked against his foot. A box about the size of his palm slid over the blood-slicked floor. Constructed from polished wood and glistening metal, it gave the impression of being a solid whole. But, as he watched, the variety of slates squirmed slowly around each other. A steady slide and clack. The timer had already begun its countdown. Cadwyn swooped down and snatched it up, palming it as best he could to keep it out of the guards' sight.

"I need the medic bay." *I can hide the box there.*

Steve and Ted grabbed Peter's arms. Together, they practically dragged him down the hallway, following close behind the lead guards. Two remained, impatient for Cadwyn to move. Before he could leave the room, a disembodied voice drifted to him. An aged whisper. Old and crackling and horrifically recognizable. *Come home, Winthrop. Come home.*

CHAPTER 2

The Crane Family

Willimina Crane. Reading her own name at the top of the college acceptance letter never got old. Each time brought a new little thrill. Pennsylvania State University wanted her. *Would have been better if it was 'Mina.'* She quickly chastised herself for the thought. What they called her didn't matter. Not until they were putting her name on her diploma, that is. *At least they didn't try and 'correct' it to Wilhelmina,* she thought. *Have to celebrate those small victories, too.*

She bit the insides of her cheeks to keep her growing smile from showing. The paper she held concealed under the table was proof she had achieved the second step of her Life Plan. Not only did she graduate high school with a 4.0 grade point average, but she also got accepted into the best Criminal Justice program in the country.

Then it's on to Harvard Medical School for my doctorate, she recited to herself. Admittedly, things got a little murky from there. She had repeated the question so many times it had almost become a time-killing game. *Practice medicine for a few years first, or head straight to the Federal Bureau of Investigation?* It was so easy to picture both options. Fingers tightening around her acceptance letter, she indulged in a few fantasies. *How long would it take to become a world-renowned surgeon?*

The question hovered in her mind as she glanced around the dining room. Generally, it was a rather large space, with ample room to fit the huge antique dining table her father took an inordinate amount of pride in. Now that almost every blood relative she had was crammed into the room, it suddenly looked rather tiny. The humid air was dense with all the lingering scents of their buffet.

A half dozen bowls still scattered the table top, allowing people to pick at the leftovers. The poker game taking up the far-right end of the table was entering its fourth hour and a *Jenga* tower clattered down to a chorus of cheers. Larger conversations had run their course and those still in the mood to chat were left with a steadily decreasing pool of options. Mina briefly listened in on her sister's argument with one of their cousins. It had been forty minutes and they were still at odds over who would win in a fight between a sasquatch and a leprechaun. She longed to leave the room for at least a little while, get some fresh air, and stretch her legs. *Maybe mom will let me go check on the kids*, she thought, eyeing the door to the living room.

The layout of the house kept the small herd of children in clear view. A cartoon played on the T.V., but no one was left awake to watch it. The few younger teens left to watch over the kids were preoccupied with their phones. Ready to graduate from high school, Mina had finally earned her place at the 'grown-ups' table. She was officially an adult in the eyes of her family and was expected to stay awake with them to see who The Witch selected. *The Witch*. The thought alone made her want to pinch the bridge of her nose. Somewhere along the way, her ancestors had decided the ghost of Katrina Hamilton was stalking them. *A ghost witch*. She mulled the concept over once again. *Yep. Still doesn't make sense.*

Admittedly, the Crane family had experienced some bad luck. Mina couldn't deny that. But a few accidents and a handful of coincidences didn't automatically mean the occult was involved. Mina had tried to prove this point a few times by dissecting the deaths most commonly used by the Crane elders as proof. It hadn't gone over well. No one wanted to be told they had spent their entire lives afraid of strange but completely natural phenomena. That everything they knew to be true was simply a product of mass hysteria and self-fulfilling prophecies.

So here I am, Mina thought as she scanned the room again. A small pang of guilt weaved around her stomach. It seemed ungrateful and even rude not to fall in line. Belief in The Witch was the only thing her family really asked of her after giving so much. *It was just one night of the year, after all. Like waiting up for Santa Claus.* She grimaced.

What kind of jerk makes fun of her loved ones' fear? Even as she reprimanded herself, Mina couldn't shake the thought that it was an accurate comparison. Sooner or later, someone would have to actually intervene to keep the delusion going. Her parents had to put the presents under the tree. And someone would have to make the selection. For the first time, she would actually be in a position to see who's in charge. They might even let her in on the way they helped the situation along. Butterflies flopped around inside her stomach. *That's going to be such an awkward conversation.*

The exaggerated sounds of the cartoon wafted into the dining room, creating a constant backdrop to the low murmur of conversations happening around her. It drew her attention back over to the couch. Last year, she had been one of the teens watching over the little ones. She knew they wouldn't have gone through all of the junk food they had been supplied with. Making a mental note to search through the wreckage on the way back, she resolved to take a trip to the bathroom. Standing as discreetly as she could didn't stop everyone in the room from instantly snapping around to face her. The silence was almost a physical thing.

"Sorry," she mumbled. "I'm just going to duck to the bathroom. I'll be right back."

"Take Jeremiah with you." Her mother's passing command brought life back into the room.

Everyone went back to what they were doing, their chatter sounding louder after the momentary silence. No one was paying enough attention to her to notice the slump of her shoulders.

Seventeen-years-old and I'm still not allowed to walk down a hallway without my older brother's protection, she thought.

Mina carefully kept her mind away from the world of awkwardness that awaited them once they were actually inside the bathroom. There wasn't any point. Privacy didn't exist during The Selection. For the entire twenty-four hours, no Crane by blood was to be out of sight for any reason. It left Mina grateful The Selection happened during the fall. California could be merciful in the summer and Anaheim wasn't too bad. But their air-conditioning had been broken for years, and everyone was always too paranoid to crack open a window on that day of all days. The only thing that could make the stifling heat of the dining room worse would be the collective body odor of her entire extended family.

Mina's hesitation drew her mother's attention.

"It's alright, dear. Jer doesn't mind. Do you sweetie?"

Jeremiah was already by the door, hands shoved into his pockets. "Nah, I wanted to grab my phone charger from my room anyway. We'll get it on the way back."

Whatever protest Mina might have been able to muster died the moment her mother grabbed her forearm and gave it a little squeeze. A fine tremble ran along the podgy digits.

"You'll be okay. Just be quick. Jer will keep you safe."

Mina summoned a small smile. *This is the year,* she told herself as determination rushed through her. The whole night, she had been torn between submitting to the demands of her family and taking another shot at inserting some sanity into the situation. But she knew she couldn't take this much longer. Every year, she helplessly watched her loved ones cower from shadows and legend.

I'm going to finish this tonight. I'm going to make them see the truth.

A voice in the back of her head reminded her facts and figures didn't matter much to those around her. *I'll have to catch them while they're planting the box.*

"Yo, Mina," Jeramiah snapped her from her thoughts. He swung one arm out into the hallway. "Do you have to pee or not?"

"Yes. Thank you for making that public declaration."

"Oh, no." Jeramiah flipped his head back to better show off the roll of his eyes. "Now people know you have normal bodily functions. The horror."

"It's called dignity. I know you're not exactly familiar with the concept."

Instead of a verbal response, he alternated between jabbing his thumbs down the hallway and clapping his hands like trying to coax over a puppy. *Don't swear in front of dad. Don't swear in front of dad.* The mantra helped her to hold her tongue as she crossed the room. Jeremiah had a skill for knowing exactly when she was on the brink and, of course, exploiting it.

"Who's a good girl?" He cooed as she came closer, careful to keep his voice low enough so their parents wouldn't hear. "You're a good girl. Yes, you are."

It was him pinching her cheek that pushed her over the edge.

"Oh, f–" She caught herself just in time to change it to 'forest green.'

In unison, the siblings turned to catch their father's reproachful gaze. The slip wasn't close enough to an actual swear word to bring down his wrath. But the warning was clear.

"So close," Jeremiah taunted in a whisper.

"Would you just go?"

"I'll get you next time."

Concentrating on his display of maniacal laughter left Jeremiah an easy target. One solid shoulder barge knocked him off his feet, leaving him to topple into the wall in a fit of indignation and hissed curse words.

"What was that?" their father snapped.

They fled into the hallway.

"Do you think we'll ever be too old to be treated like children?"

she asked.

Jeramiah barked a laugh. "I'll be coasting as soon as I hit twenty. You, however, will always be his sweet little angel."

"That's not fair."

"Sorry. You're the baby. It's the rules."

Mina scrunched up her mouth and busied herself folding her acceptance letter.

"When do you plan on telling them you got in?" Jeremiah asked.

"I've got it perfectly planned out," she said. "I'm going to yell it out of the taxi window on my way to the airport."

"Flawless."

While the hallway wasn't long, it was still enough to turn the noise of the family into a muffled murmur. Jeremiah began to cast quick looks over his shoulder. His smile remained, but the warmth was quickly draining from it.

"Are you okay?" Mina asked.

He nodded rapidly. "Yeah. Of course."

A few more paces and he abruptly paused. "Did you hear that?"

"Hear what?"

"Nothing," he rushed. "It's nothing. Let's just hurry up before mom starts to worry."

She studied him as they passed by the hall closet and reached the bathroom door. "You really believe there's a witch, don't you?"

His casual shrug didn't take the fear from his face. "Don't you?"

"No. Clearly not. Haven't you been listening to me at all?"

"Oh, come on. How many of us have to end up dead before you get with the program?"

"Accidents and coincidences."

"Yeah, well, there's a lot dad hasn't told you," Jeremiah dismissed.

Mina snapped around to look at him. "Like what?"

"Don't worry about it."

"Jer."

He shook his shoulders as if he could dislodge her suspicions. "Don't get all worked up. You're such a red."

Mina found herself trapped somewhere between annoyance and amusement. "Aren't we too old to be using colors as insults?"

"Says the one who threw some shades of green at me earlier."

A part of Mina wanted to bring the conversation back around. To push her brother a little harder and see just how deep his conviction in The Witch really went. But, seeing as how the banter was taking the tension from his shoulders, she just couldn't bring herself to follow the instinct. So instead, she poorly hid the word 'purple' in a forced cough as she led the way into the bathroom.

"Go orange yourself," he grumbled. "And you're just peeing. I'm not hanging around for you to fix up your hair."

"I wasn't going to."

"Oh." He pressed his lips into a tight line. "Right. Okay."

"What?"

"No, no. It looks good." He bared his teeth in a weird fake smile.

If she didn't start ignoring him now, she would have to prepare for a prank war. Something that was never advisable while using the facilities. So she bit back her pride, held her tongue, and set about her business. The downstairs bathroom was the only one used on the night of The Selection. It was far bigger than the upstairs one, thanks to the architect's whim of attaching it to the laundry room, and the extra square footage allowed the process to be a little less awkward than it otherwise would be.

There's no privacy tonight, she told herself. *Or dignity.*

Jeremiah closed the door behind them and rested his forearms on the top of the dryer, playing with his phone as casually as he could. It gave the illusion they couldn't still clearly see each other. Mina chewed on her bottom lip as she tried and failed to answer nature's calling. It was hard to be a Crane with a shy bladder.

"I've officially got a red bar," Jeramiah declared. "My phone is dying while you're doing nothing. You murderer."

"You're not exactly helping."

"Twelve percent!"

"All right, all right. Hey, order me a pizza, yeah? I've been craving some Hawaiian."

The proceeding argument as to whether or not pineapple belongs on pizza created enough of a distraction for her to do what they had come to do. Soon enough, they were back in the hallway.

"So, we agree," Jeremiah declared. "We get the charger and then order two large pepperoni."

"I said Hawaiian."

"Which is obviously insane, so I vetoed it."

Mina's ready reply shattered into a startled squeal. There was barely time to register the cool hand that had latched onto her forearm before it yanked her violently to the side. The folding door of the closet rattled open, revealing the gaping chasm that had replaced the rows of neatly folded sheets. Instinct brought her free hand up to brace herself for impact. But there weren't any shelves remaining to break her fall. The hand didn't release its iron grip until Mina hit the floor. Behind her, the door snapped shut with a sharp clatter. Her heart thrashed within her chest, beating with a sudden ferocity that left her breathless and dizzy.

"Jer?" Mina swallowed thickly to keep her mounting fear from her voice.

In the muted light, she kept a sharp eye on the walls and ceiling, reassuring herself they hadn't moved any closer. *Deep breaths,* she reminded herself. *Walls don't move. It's just in your head.* The doors remained closed, slicing the light into blurred bars.

"Jer, this isn't funny."

"I'm not doing it," Jeremiah replied.

The feeble doors shook as he yanked on the handle.

"Jer!"

"Mom! Dad!"

It wasn't Jeremiah's bellow that caught her off guard. It was the clear, razor-sharp fear that cut through each word. Scrambling up onto her knees, she threw her weight against the door, careful to drive her shoulder into the joints. The thin door shook but refused to budge. *It should open.* Logic and basic physics dictated it should. *Unless something's pushing on the other side.*

"Jeremiah, get off the door!"

"I'm not on it! Dad! Hurry!"

Snapping around, Mina checked the walls once more. *They haven't moved. Walls don't move.* In defiance of her thoughts, the walls shifted. Every time she looked away or blinked, they lurched closer. Afraid to close her eyes, she slammed both hands against the door, and burrowed her fingers into the grooves between the slats in an attempt to pry them open.

"Open the door!"

"Baby?" Her father's voice echoed toward her as if from a distant place. It was soon lost under the chaos of the others crowding outside the door and her own feral screams.

"Open the door! I can't breathe! Open the door!"

Blood rushed through her ears in a deafening roar. The air grew as thick as tar. What little she could choke down coated her throat and clogged her lungs. Her elbows bashed into the walls as she struggled.

They're too close. Too close.

Static devoured her mind. An almost living buzz, like a swarm of insects were scurrying over the paint and plaster. Cold sweat prickled along her spine. Her hands grew slick as she clawed wildly at the door. The sound of breaking wood was lost under the cries of her family. New slivers of light told her she had broken the slats. Fractured edges sliced into her fingertips as further proof. But the door wouldn't open, and the walls now pushed hard against her shoulders.

"Daddy!" she pleaded. "Please, get me out!"

Dust drifted upon the thick, musky air, barely seen within the muted light. Her vision blurred while her aching muscles became as rigid as stone. All the while, shadows shifted across the slats. Someone demanded they knock down the wall. It was almost lost among her own heavy breathing and the dozens of voices assuring her everything would be okay.

She spotted motion in her peripheral vision. Fingers. Needlelike fingers. Slender and covered with skin so thin the veins and tendons threatened to break free. Fear locked Mina's joints, completely immobilizing her as the impossible hands continued to grow.

Striking like a snake, they turned on her, wrapping around Mina and dragging her back. There wasn't anywhere to go. Her spine struck the far wall with enough force to crack the plaster. Dust gushed down like rain, further distorting the light and detailing the motion of invisible creatures. They scurried around her and then over her legs, crawling up the walls and out of sight. Each time Mina tried to focus on them, to determine their shape and size, the creatures would shake off the dust and completely disappear from sight.

It happened so gradually Mina didn't notice it at first. All the noise from outside the closet drifted away into a series of whispers and sighs. It made the sharp, metallic ping all the louder. The odd notes came without warning, making her jump and push harder back against the wall. It was impossible to move since the sides of the closest were now as narrow as a coffin. Separate notes sped up and joined, becoming a tune. The song of a music box. It drifted to her from the darkness as the ceiling loomed ever closer. The familiar lullaby coursed through her veins like ice water.

Hot, rancid breath gushed over her shoulder. "Come home, Crane. Come home."

Mina screamed. The door burst open, flooding the linen closest with fresh air and light. Thrashing, sobbing, and gulping for air, Mina realized she wasn't stuck in a makeshift casket. Instead, she had somehow crammed herself under the lowest shelf of the closet, wedging her body between the wall and a storage box.

"It's okay, baby," her father said as he grabbed her kicking legs and dragged her out. "Just breathe. You're out now. I have you. Just breathe."

Braced against her father's chest, the rest of her family came in all at once for a singularly crushing hug.

"I'm so sorry, Mina," Jeremiah sobbed. "I didn't see it coming. I'm sorry."

Mina was vaguely aware of her mother snarling, "I told you to watch her."

Her focus was on the music box. She had no memory of picking up the cube that she now clutched in her right hand. But it was there. Solid and real and still playing the lullaby.

"No," her mother whispered.

Jeremiah latched onto her wrist like she was going to be dragged away again at any moment.

"We'll take care of it," her father assured her. "Don't worry. I'll take care of everything."

CHAPTER 3

The Bell Family

Basheba tore off a chunk of her hamburger meat and tossed it across the car. Buck went for it instantly. The Rottweiler only had to bounce slightly in the front passenger seat to snatch the morsel out of the air. Still, it was enough to spray the interior with his slobber.

Basheba quickly twisted to protect her food. "Really, Buck?"

The words came out as a mixture of a whine and a laugh, which would have only confused the dog if hadn't been so fixated on chomping down his mouthful.

"I know you know how to swallow," she grumbled.

Too lazy to properly clean up the mess right then, she leaned back in her seat and flopped her foot about. She had learned during the past year that thick hiking socks were pretty effective at mopping long trails of drool off of dashboard vinyl. Once done, she left them up on the dash, positioning them over a heater vent. This was one of the benefits of being four-foot-eight. Cramped spaces didn't really make it difficult for her to get comfortable. Licking his chops, Buck shuffled closer until his massive head rested upon her thigh. It was hard for Basheba to be appropriately annoyed at the drool dampening her thermal leggings when he gazed up at her with his big brown eyes.

"You've had your dinner," Basheba dismissed.

It didn't dislodge her dog's head from her lap, but she did at least get to take another bite in peace. Savoring the taste, she relaxed a little more in her seat, eyeing the car's neon clock. *Almost midnight.*

It was hard to believe an entire year had passed since she had last been in Nashville. The area was pretty enough, especially when ravaged by the coming fall. Some trees stood like bare skeletons, their gnarled, twisted branches clutching at the chilled night air. Those that still had their leaves had shed their summer shades for the blazing colors of fall.

While it was bitterly cold, there was still no promise of coming snow. She cocked her head to the side to better study the sky. If they had any luck, the whole week would pass without so much as a flurry. The passing thought made her snort. *Whoever goes in will have a lot more to worry about than the weather*. A chill worked its way down her spine. She nudged the heater higher with her toe. The bounce of her thigh made Buck grumble with annoyance, and she rubbed him with her knuckles as penance.

Generally, she loved winter. Even sleeping in her car hadn't diminished that. All she needed was a good sleeping bag and Buck's body heat. It was just this one week that made her detest the cold— the 23rd to the 30th of October. She resolved to grab another sweater the moment she finished her meal. Stuffing an intact onion ring into her mouth, Basheba looked out over the parking lot.

It was a stroke of luck that her favorite burger joint also happened to be open all night. This way, not only could she get a decent bite to eat at midnight, but she could camp out for the night with little chance of being asked to move along. She rechecked the clock. *Not much longer now*. Soon, Katrina would make her selection. Either Basheba would crawl into the back seat and get some sleep, or she'd begin the forty-minute drive north. Back to Black River. To the place where it all started.

Anticipation prickled her skin like a thousand needles. She began to mindlessly eat, shoving the onions rings into her mouth faster than she could chew, her eyes constantly searching the horizon. Tonight, the environment was everything. She needed to make sure her setting was at least somewhat under her control. Somewhere familiar but not isolated. Populated and busy. Somewhere well-lit with little to obstruct her vision or escape.

She had carefully chosen the parking lot of the diner. Towering floodlights filled the nearly barren space, allowing her to watch the steady stream of people come and go. A mixture of stressed college students and people coming off late-night shifts. The bars were far enough away she wouldn't have to worry about any drunk idiots trying to get into her car. And, if things went bad, the open space would allow her to run for quite a distance before traffic became an issue. The car's windows were up, the doors locked, everything safely stowed away. Scratching Buck behind his ears, Basheba decided she was as prepared as she could hope to be.

Unable to resist the dog's pleading eyes, she gave him the last bit of her hamburger, keeping the onion rings for herself. Alternating between devouring her deep-fried treats and slurping down her soft drink, she continued to scan the area. The night pressed in on the edges of the lights, still and dark as coal. It made it impossible to miss the first light flicking off. The spotlight was situated on the far side of the carpark. Without it, the night rushed a few feet closer to her. It was barely anything, but her heart froze.

Buck's ears flattened as he sat up. His nose twitched and his eyes locked on the distant patch of shadows. They both watched as another light died with a low, electric hiss. The scent of ozone stained the air. Shadows rose up like a surging tide, silent as a serpent. It wrapped around the next light in the row and, with a heavy thud, it died, too.

Darkness rushed forward to claim new territory. It was so dense and complete that it looked as if someone had simply cut chunks of the world out of existence. Basheba watched. Waited. The few remaining floodlights kept her little car nestled within a warm orange glow. The neon sign of the burger joint buzzed like a swarm of bees. People continued to come and go, none of them paying the slightest attention to the abyss that existed about a yard from their feet.

Glancing away was her mistake.

The darkness crashed forward, consuming everything in its path, coming to an abrupt stop about a foot from the front of her car. Buck stiffened, shoulders hunching and a low growl rumbling within his broad chest.

"Steady," she whispered to him.

Obediently, he stopped squirming, although his growl remained constant, filling the empty air. Basheba craned her neck to see a little more. Everything was still. The shadows hung before her with razor-sharp precision. She squinted but couldn't find a single shape in its obsidian depths. Carefully, she reached down and turned the high beams on with her oil-slicked fingers.

The darkness peeled back, not fleeing from the headlights in long tunnels. More like a retreating tide, washing back until it revealed a child. Possibly no older than seven, the little girl stood with her hands loosely clasped in front of her, her shoulders down and relaxed, her feet together to give the overall appearance of delicate innocence. The hemline of her floral dress tapped her knees as it drifted in the evening wind. It was the crude mask covering her head that made Basheba cringe.

The dented, peeled dome was forged into a mangled jack-o'-lantern. A deformed smile separated the head. Gaping holes served as eyes. The mask hid all of the girl's features and left Basheba stunned. Buck's throaty growl served as her only anchor to reality. Sinking her fingers into his fur kept her from spiraling down into the throes of panic. It wasn't children in and of themselves that summoned an almost primal fear within her. But when paired with decrepit, old costumes, especially the ones that kept her from seeing their faces, she couldn't control her instinctual reaction. What terrified her the most, however, was there was only one person left in her life who knew of her rather unique phobia.

"Hello, Katrina," Basheba whispered, trying to keep her voice somewhat strong, defiant.

Buck erupted into a series of barks, the sudden noise snapping any bravado she had managed to summon. She jumped. Her startled scream transformed into a gasp as her icy beverage drenched her lap. The sensation stole her attention for only a split second, barely a flick of her gaze. But when she looked back, the child was gone.

Buck's growl was the only thing to break the silence. Gone were the other people, the cars, the general murmur of life that clustered around the all-night diner. The night had closed in while she had been distracted by the single child. It now pressed in around her on all sides, leaving barely an inch of visibility. Buck lunged up, awkwardly shifting his weight around the passenger seat, his nose twitching wildly as he thrashed about. His attention was drawn to each window in turn.

Long strings of saliva dripped from his jaws as his lips curled back from his fangs. His growls turned into savage barks. Leaping and lurching, he twisted around to try and see each window. Basheba turned with him. Despite her dog's frenzied outburst, it was still possible to hear the sounds drifting in through the locked car doors. Children's laughter came from the darkness. Pattering footsteps circled her like a shark within the murky abyss of the ocean depths. There was no longer just one, but dozens. Each running wild, making it impossible to track any of them by sound. They came with the fluttering snap of streamers.

The first strike against the window caught her off guard. A startled yelp escaped both her and Buck. Both of them whipped around to stare at the rear door but, in seconds, it was as if the skies had opened. The unseen specters burst free of the shadows to strike the car before disappearing once more.

Childish giggles rose louder than Buck's threatening snarls. Each child's head was covered with stacks that could barely be called masks, fitted with molded noses and grotesque frozen smiles. The patches, pale of color, streaked across her vision, followed by long trails of serpentine streamers.

Laughter rang in her ears as footsteps raced across the roof of her car. The vehicle trembled under the force, causing the suspension to squeal. She shrank back against her door, balling herself up tight, avoiding Buck's now aimless attacks. A hand came down against the glass just beside her head. Basheba spun around, her heartbeat choking her as she found a handprint of condensation marring the glass. A new wave of horror pushed everything else into the back of her awareness. Breathing hard, she reached out. Her trembling fingertip smeared the child's handprint. *It's on the inside.*

"Come home, Bell."

Basheba threw herself back from the small voice. Wedged against the steering wheel, the loud bellow of the car's horn broke the night. It covered the sound of the attack but did nothing to diminish the voice of the pumpkin-headed girl. She sat in the back seat, a small living cube of wood and metal set upon her lap, clasped between tiny hands.

"Come home."

The girl stretched out her hand, the box resting upon her fingers in offering. It wasn't possible for Basheba to reach it without moving from her seat upon the horn. Still, when she lifted her hand, the box appeared against her palm. Light burned her eyes. She flinched, and it was all gone. The night had returned to what it had been before, filled with people and cars and life as it had always been. All that remained was the box.

It was just large enough that she had to stretch her fingers to keep it in her palm, and it was cold to the touch. The polished sides were an intricate pattern of glistening metal. As if awakening to her touch, the pieces began to move, sliding and clicking into new positions. Basheba's eyelids fluttered closed as a slow melody filled the air, simple and repetitive, like a child's lullaby. Buck nuzzled his wet nose against her, whimpering with concern. The touch startled her. Suddenly the horn was blaring painfully in her ears. She shifted back into the driver's seat, one hand clutching the box while she rubbed at Buck's neck. He nuzzled into the touch, inching closer until his thick head was pressed against her neck.

"It's okay. We're okay," she whispered.

He didn't believe her. *Smart boy.* Feeling the eyes upon her, Basheba finally managed to take action. She secured the box carefully in the glove box, put on her seatbelt, and peeled the car out onto the main street. Buck kept his head rested upon her forearm as she took the exit to Black River. It was time to go home.

CHAPTER 4

The Sewall Family

"Ozzie?"

Osgood Davis glanced up from his phone as his mother opened his bedroom door, and froze, trying to look as innocent as humanly possible. It was hard to make the aesthetic look convincing after having been caught in clear defiance of her order to go to sleep. She arched an eyebrow and crossed her arms over her chest, her Manolo Blahnik pumps clicking loudly against the marble hallway floor. It was a clipped sound that had always preceded a grounding. He had always suspected that's why his mother insisted on wearing them in the house. It was all an intimidation technique.

"You were supposed to go to sleep an hour ago."

"I had homework," he declared.

The well-used excuse was his only shot, since his education was the one thing she would put above everything else. He could come down with the black plague and she would still be quizzing him on the periodic table.

"Can't let that fancy private school go to waste," he pressed with a smile.

Her eyes narrowed. "Osgood Davis, don't think for a second you're too old for me to tan your hide."

He blinked at her. It was always a little strange hearing Texas slang with a Korean accent.

"I swear, ma. I was turning in right now."

The tapping continued as she narrowed her eyes. "You better. Or

I'm taking away that phone."

"Got it."

"And your Porsche."

"What?" Ozzie snapped, springing up to give her an appropriately horrified look. "A bit much, don't ya think?"

She scowled. "Ya? Am I raising a yokel?"

"You," he corrected swiftly, barely squeezing the word in before she continued.

"I've never felt comfortable with you having that thing. It's too much power for someone just learning."

"Everyone else has got one, Ma."

"I'd rather you practice on the Mercedes," she dismissed. Releasing a long sigh, she smiled at him, seemingly forgetting all annoyance. "You haven't heard the scratching tonight, have you?"

The question instantly shifted the mood in the room. What had started as an annoyance had become something to keep him up at night. About a week ago, he had first heard the scratching, gnawing sound on the walls of the pool house. He hadn't thought much of it. Dallas, like any major city, wasn't really known for its abundance of nature. So it was pretty common for whatever wildlife around to make their way onto the Davis property, filling up the lakes and running about the spacious lawns. He hadn't thought much of it. That was until he had heard it against the living room wall, then just outside his window on the third floor. Then inside the walls.

They had hired three different pest control companies. None of them had found anything, and the sound had grown worse. Long scrapes that trailed from one side of the room to the other, that crossed above his head while he was trying to sleep.

It probably wouldn't have bothered him half as much if it wasn't for his parents' reactions. Cue a lot of whispering, skulking about, and heated shouting matches with an old family friend, Percival Sewall. That alone was strange; everyone loved Percival.

Ozzie shook his head, dread becoming thick in the pit of his stomach as he watched his mother sigh with relief.

"Good. That's good."

"What am I missing?"

His mother straightened and forced a smile. "Nothing, baba. Nothing but a good night's sleep."

"Do you think that sounds convincing?"

She jabbed one manicured finger in the general direction of his pillow. "Sleep. Now. Or no Porsche."

Ozzie dramatically leaped for the sheets. While the antics managed to coax a laugh out of her, she still didn't give him enough time to get comfortable before turning off the overhead light, leaving him to do the rest of his squirming by the glow emitting from the hallway.

"So you're aware, I will be randomly checking on you later. If I find you awake again, you will feel my wrath."

"Yes, Mom."

With a last parting smile, she closed the door. Ozzie waited until the sound of her heels had completely faded before getting up. The whole trip to the door left him feeling like an idiot. It didn't stop him, though. He cracked the door open, almost sagging with relief as a sliver of light broke into his room, turning the darkness into muted shades of gray. Just barely enough for him to make out the outline of the objects filling his room. It eased the knot in his stomach but didn't take it away completely.

He padded across the carpet, set his iPhone to charge, and got back into bed. After a few moments of staring at the bar of light, he eventually closed his eyes. Just as he drifted toward sleep, he heard it; the scratching of nails against wood. It trailed along the wall, never crossing close enough to the window for him to catch sight of what was making the sound. His heart stammered when the direction shifted. No longer outside. The long, slow scrape came from within the wall by his head.

Ozzie's fingers twisted up the sheets as he listened to it coming closer. Inch by inch. Stopping only when the thin layer of plaster and paint separated them. Then silence. Staring at the ceiling, he held his breath, straining to hear it again. When it came, it was far louder than before. No longer the chipping of wood but the tearing of fabric. It came from the underside of his pillow.

A scream ripped from his throat as he leaped from the bed. He sprinted across the room, snapping on the light in under a second. Panting hard, he stared at his bed, waiting for something to crawl its way out of the mattress.

"Master Osgood?" Maxwell, the family butler asked from somewhere down the hallway.

Ozzie couldn't find his voice to respond. The sound replayed in his mind as he struggled to find some other explanation. But there wasn't one. He knew what he had heard.

Maxwell called for him again from just outside his door. Ozzie huffed a breath and wondered just how much he'd cop from his friends if they ever heard about this. *Almost sixteen and still afraid of the dark.*

"I'm alright, Max. I didn't mean to worry you," Ozzie said, mindlessly swinging one side of the double doors open. "Can you get me some honey tea? I can't sleep."

Leaning back into the hallway, he sought to catch his butler's eyes. Ozzie's stomach plummeted. A few feet still separated him from Maxwell. Each pore of the middle-aged man's body stood out as a pitch-black dot. Every lumbered motion the man took made them split open. Tiny spiders scrambled out of his skin. Millions in number. Birthing only for a new egg to ooze into the vacated pore.

"Master." Maxwell rasped the words around the long, thin arachnid legs that flicked and squirmed past his lips.

The hatchlings flooded across the floor, the walls. They clung to the ceiling and consumed every trace of light as they scurried toward him. Ozzie screamed. The sound barely reached his ears as he turned and sprinted down the hallway. The cool marble floor bit at his feet as he ran. He barreled down the wide, twisting staircase, not daring to touch the railing as the spiders kept pace beside him.

"Mom! Dad!" The words left him breathless.

Missing a step sent him tumbling. The sharp edges of the stairs smacked against him as he rolled, hit the wall, and dropped the last of the distance to the foyer. Panic alone got him back up. Presented with the sprawling estate around him, he didn't know which way to go. Two wings, three levels, and endless corridors. The wrong choice could leave him separated from his parents by a living wall of arachnids.

"Mom! Dad! Help!"

"Master Osgood," Maxwell rattled behind him.

Tiny spiders scrambled over Ozzie's feet. All thought was severed. He sprinted for the door, driven by the single desire to flee, to get away from the monster constantly birthing the eight-legged monstrosities. He flung the front door open and instantly smacked into an immovable wall. Arms locked around him. The confinement sent Ozzie into a wild panic. He thrashed and screamed and struck the wall but couldn't move it.

"You made your point!" Percival yelled.

The sharp roar rumbled from the wall against Ozzie. Shock left him breathless as he snapped his head up. *What is he doing here?* Ozzie pushed the thought aside. It didn't matter why the old family friend was there. It only mattered that he *was*. That Ozzie wasn't alone with Maxwell anymore.

Percival didn't look at him. The balding man's gaze was locked on the staircase, dark eyes burning with hatred as well as fear. Ozzie struggled to get free as the clicking of spider legs echoed in his ears.

"You made your point, Katrina! He'll be there! Leave him alone," Percival continued

The clicking came to a sudden halt, replaced by the soft ping of a music box. Trembling, Ozzie chanced a glance over his shoulder. Maxwell and the swarm that had crawled from his skin were gone, replaced by a small girl who stood halfway up the staircase. She smiled down at them, cradling a cube of wood and metal between her tiny hands. Ozzie was vaguely aware of his parents coming into the room. Their gasps of shock. Their mad dash to get to him. But the little girl held his attention.

"Come home, Sewall." She disappeared but her voice still hovered within the cavernous room. "Come home."

Ozzie couldn't place the exact moment when it happened, but he found himself clutching the box, feeling it twitch as the melody continued to play.

Numb with shock, dizzy from his fading adrenaline rush, he could only think to mumble, "But I'm not a Sewall."

CHAPTER 5

Ozzie had no idea why his mother had insisted on making him tea. The only way the beverage was going to calm him down was if he used it for a makeshift lobotomy. Still, she insisted. So he sat in awkward silence with Percival as his father got him an ice pack for his head. It hadn't even occurred to him he was injured until his dad had started fussing.

"Ethan," Ozzie's mother said as she placed a mug before his father. She handed the second to Percival.

"Thanks, Ha-Yun," he smiled weakly.

She pursed her lips into a tight smile before going to collect her own mug.

Ethan placed a hand on his son's shoulder, drawing his attention, "Do you need anything for the pain?"

"I'm fine, Pa. Really. It's just..." He shivered and tightened his grip on the mug until his fingers ached. "The spiders. You know? Did you see the spiders?"

"Yeah, I did." Ethan's sharp cheekbones pushed uncomfortably against the top of Ozzie's head as he pulled him into a one-armed hug. "They're gone, son. I promise, they're gone."

Ozzie leaned into the embrace before the thought hit him. "Maxwell! Did anyone check on him?"

"He's okay," Ha-Yun assured, reaching out to squeeze his hand. "He was a bit confused why I had woken him up, but other than that, he's perfectly fine."

Ozzie nodded absently, barely aware of the motion. "Good. That's good."

It seemed as soon as one fear was eased, another question forced itself to the forefront of his mind. He lifted his eyes to meet Percival's dark gaze.

"That thing… Why does it think I'm a Sewall? Was it coming after you? I don't really see how it could confuse us."

He didn't need to do anything to draw attention to the obvious differences between them, but Ozzie still flopped a hand around for good measure. Aside from the apparent age difference and Ozzie's evident Korean heritage, Ozzie's jaw was square but soft, and his eyes carried the same dark shade as his thick black hair. Percival, on the other hand, was a bald, blue-eyed white man, with a short, graying beard and disproportionally dark eyebrows.

"Well, maybe we have similar eyebrows," Ozzie noted.

Percival wiped a hand over his face, but it didn't stop his chuckling.

"Don't get me wrong," Ozzie continued. "You're cute for an old guy. If I look like that at your age, I wouldn't be mad."

"Hahaha! Thanks for that," Percival's said, his voice gruff but soft at the same time.

It was the seriousness in his eyes that made Ozzie blurt out. "I'm not a Sewall."

"Actually," Ha-Yun began before sharply clearing her throat.

Her gaze darted between the two men surrounding Ozzie. Ethan repeated his wife's throat-clearing maneuver, took a deep breath, and turned to Ozzie.

"I'm a Davis," Ozzie insisted. "Osgood Davis."

"You are," Ethan said. Reluctantly, he added, "But not biologically."

Ozzie stared wide-eyed at his father before whipping around to face his mother. "You cheated on dad?"

"I would never!" Ha-Yun snapped.

"They had stopped dating before we got together," Ethan insisted.

"How did she end up with his baby then?"

"Ozzie," Percival soothed. "It's true I was with your mother. It was a summer romance, and I loved her. I still do. But we weren't *in* love."

"So you were happy with her hooking up with your best friend?" Ozzie shrieked.

"I'm the one who set them up," Percival chuckled. "Look at them. They're a perfect match."

"And we always told you that ours was a whirlwind marriage," Ethan continued.

"Did you know you weren't my father?"

"I am your father," Ethan said sharply. "Percival is your godfather."

"Did you decide that, or did you know?"

Ethan looked to Ha-Yun.

"We knew there was a possibility," she said carefully, looking at each man in turn as she continued. "And, after we all sat down and discussed it, we decided we didn't need to know."

"I protested that point."

"Percival..."

"Not because I didn't think you two would be the best parents for him. Hell, I'd be a horrible father. This is the exact reason why I wanted to do the paternity test."

"And it's the exact reason we didn't," Ha-Yun snapped before she caught herself. Deflating with a sigh, she rested her elbows on the table and rested her face in her hands.

"I thought you were insane," she admitted.

"In her defense, we both did," Ethan said. A small smile tipped one corner of his mouth.

Percival shook his head but couldn't keep himself from laughing. "Yeah. I must have sounded nuts. If I was a petty man, I'd be pointing out how right I was."

Unable to decide what to process first, Ozzie settled for

shrieking, "What is going on?!"

Percival put a hand up to quiet the other two and took the lead.

"You're going to have to bear with me here. This is information we tell Sewall children from birth. The only other time I had to tell the whole story to someone outside of the family, it obviously didn't go all that well. So, just listen to the whole tale first, okay?"

Ozzie reluctantly nodded, suddenly very grateful to have the mug. It gave him something to latch onto.

"In the early 1800s..."

"1800s? You're starting in the 1800s? How about you just explain what happened eighteen minutes ago?"

"What did I just say about interrupting?" Percival deadpanned, his dark eyebrows lowering over narrowing eyes.

"Sorry."

Hunching his shoulders, Ozzie bit hard on the inside of his lip and struggled to keep his silence.

"We're starting in 1812 in the small Tennessee town of Black River because that's when the Bell family first ran into Katrina Hamilton." Percival's eyes scanned the room as he almost whispered the name, as if he thought the muttering would conjure the girl. "It all started as a property dispute." He huffed a bitter laugh at that. "Katrina sold the Bells some barren land. They made it work. She declared they had swindled her and demanded they give her a percentage of their profits. Understandably, no one took her seriously. They probably would have if they had known she was a witch."

"A witch?" Ozzie blurted out.

"Did that look like a normal occurrence to you?" Percival challenged.

"Yeah, but, come on. Witches? It's just a religion or something, right?"

"Don't mix up witch with wiccan, kiddo. We're not talking about healing herbs or benevolent spirits. What we're dealing with is dark and satanic." He paused to take a sobering breath before continuing. "Katrina proceeded to torment the Bell family for two years. She tried everything she could to ruin them. Socially, financially, spiritually. Anything she could do to them, she did. For two years, she raged a war against them. If it wasn't for the aid of the Winthrop family, the Bells would have been destroyed."

"Okay," Ozzie prompted when Percival fell silent.

"In 1817, two young girls were helping with the fall harvest. Basheba Bell and Caroline Winthrop. Hearing a baby's cry, they looked up to see a cloaked figure taking the Bell infant into the woods. They gave chase, raising the alarm for the field hands to follow. The slaves testified they had the girls and the strange figure in sight until they passed the first line of trees. Then, they all just disappeared. Vanished."

Percival took a drink before continuing.

"Two days later, the girls returned. They accused Katrina Hamilton of witchcraft, and declared she had been stealing children from the town and sacrificing them to the devil in the forest. Now, this was two hundred years after Salem, give or take. Folks liked to think they were too smart to believe in witches anymore. And no one wanted the reputation of being the hick town that hanged a poor woman because of suspicion and hysteria. It was a hard sell. And if it had just been the Bell child, no one would have convicted her. It was the Winthrop girl."

He chuckled.

"That eight-year-old had steel in her blood. Many histories believe that it was her testimony that convinced the judge, appropriately enough named Justice Crane, of Katrina's guilt. She was hanged."

"Hanged?" Ozzie cut in despite his best efforts not to interrupt again. "I thought witches were burned at the stake."

Percival shook him off while simultaneously taking a sip of his tea. "No, we're in America, not Europe."

Ozzie blinked at him.

"They were burned in Europe. There were laws against it in America. Witches were hanged."

"But, the Salem Witch Trials. They burned two hundred people," he insisted.

"No, they didn't," Percival said. "Who the hell taught you history? Two hundred were *accused*. A few died in prison and one man was crushed to death during interrogation, but only nineteen were actually executed. And all of them were hung."

"Oh."

"The burnings happened in Europe. That was a whole different nightmare and, while Katrina was born in Germany, has nothing to do with what I'm telling you. So please, just shut up for five minutes."

Ozzie clamped a hand over his mouth to better illustrate his continued efforts.

"As I was saying, Katrina was hanged. That's when things got worse. It started as scratches."

He managed to keep from blurting anything out by shooting quick glances to his parents. They both avoided his gaze, guilt evident on their faces. *Percival told them it would happen.* The realization came with no trace of resentment. He had heard it, seen it right before his eyes. The box was sitting at the center of the kitchen counter to prove it. And yet, he was still having a hard time believing any of it. Ozzie couldn't imagine what it would have all sounded like for his parents. Just an old friend, an urban legend, and a request to jump on board with the insanity.

Percival continued. "It started on the outside of the farmhouse and, at first, they were convinced it was some kind of animal. Their slaves became concerned it was one of the strange creatures they had reported seeing in the surrounding woods. Then the sound moved inside. I've been told you've experienced something similar."

"Is that why you're here tonight?" Ozzie asked.

"I always keep an eye on you around this time of year. I know that sounds a little on the 'stalker' side of things, but let me finish and I'm sure you'll understand."

Percival took a deep breath and downed half of his quickly cooling tea before he continued.

"You've witnessed it doesn't take long for these kinds of things to escalate. For the Bells, it was moving objects, spontaneous fires, physical attacks, disembodied voices. And it wasn't just them who witnessed it. When word got out, people came from miles around in hopes of seeing proof of a ghost. Like they were some kind of sideshow attraction, like it was entertainment to see a terrified child being thrown across a room. And yes, incidents like that were common and well documented."

Seeing his friend struggling to contain his growing anger, Ethan cut in, "And they believed it was this Katrina Hamilton?"

The question jarred Percival out of his thoughts. "She admitted it. You have to understand the voice they heard wasn't just some distant, unintelligible whisper. It was clear. She held conversations with different visitors. By all accounts, she was also well versed in profanity, which she hurled at the Bells for hours on end. In time, Katrina's influence spread. She was still fixated on the Bell family, but the Winthrops, as well as the Cranes, started to report encounters. The torment continued for four years. Then, in the winter of 1821, she was strong enough to kill."

Ha-Yun lurched off of her stool and headed to the fridge. "I need a drink."

"I don't get one?" Ozzie asked as he watched her pour a generous amount of red wine into three glasses.

"You're fifteen."

"So I'm old enough to get haunted but not old enough to drink?" Ozzie ran a hand through his thick black hair, steadying himself to ask, "I still don't understand why she hates the Sewalls. Or the box." While the cube had mercifully stopped playing its lullaby, there was still life in it. The walls squirmed. Tiny irregular shapes slithered around each other before falling into a new position with a soft click. "Full disclosure; that box creeps me out."

"That's probably because there's a demon inside," Percival said before finishing half of his wine in one large gulp.

"What?" Ozzie shrieked.

Percival held up one finger as he finished off the glass and handed it back to Ha-Yun, who dutifully refilled it.

"Before we get into that... don't worry, we're close... I'll explain how we got dragged into it. Our ancestor, Abraham Sewall, was an old college friend of Justice Crane. Apparently, they were roommates or some such thing. He had just arrived in Black River to help make some sense out of the situation when Griogair Bell was murdered. Katrina probably should have done her research before playing her hand. Abraham had a lot of resources at his disposal. Enough to help the Bells, Winthrops, and Cranes all escape Black River, and Katrina's influence. For the most part, at least. She still got her revenge, still gets to play her games."

Twisting the stem of the wine glass between the fingers of his right hand, Percival reached out to tap one finger against the top of the box.

"We call it the Harvest. It's happened every year on this day since 1821. Katrina will select one member from each of the four families and present them with a demon box. See the way it moves? It's counting down. If nothing's done, it will open seven days exactly from when she handed it to you."

"And unleash a demon?" Ozzie said. "An actual, real demon?"

He nodded. "You'll see it around soon enough. While it's contained, it can't directly cause you any physical harm. But it will mess with your head; show you things, make you hear things that aren't there. Trick you into hurting yourself. Anything it can think of to try and stop you from finding the key and relocking the box."

"Relocking? I can keep it trapped in there?"

"That's the game, Ozzie. If you win, Katrina takes the box back, and you're left with the fallout."

"If I lose?" Ozzie asked.

"You die. Horribly."

Both of his parents crowded closer to him, eyeing the box with horror.

"It's okay," his mother soothed. "We'll help you. We'll find the key."

"We'll be with you every step of the way," his father promised.

"You can't," Percival said, nursing his second round of red wine.

Ha-Yun narrowed her eyes, her painted lips pulling back into a snarl, "I'm not just going to watch my son being tortured and do nothing."

"You don't get to watch, either. Only the selected four can go into the forest during the Harvest."

"What kind of rule is that?" she snapped.

A bone-deep weariness filled Percival's eyes as he replied. "One we didn't pick. Katrina's game. Katrina's rules."

"Well, we won't play by her rules," Ha-Yun said.

"Gee, never thought of that in the almost two-hundred years we've been forced to do this." Rage began to seep into his voice as he tightened his grip on his glass. "Despite what you might think, we do love our family members. None of us want this. We don't offer up our children, our parents, our siblings as sacrifices. We've fought back in every way you could possibly think of. And we've always failed."

"So you do nothing?"

"We teach them!" It was the first time Ozzie had ever heard the placid Percival shout in anger, and it made him jump. "We let them know this is coming and prepare them as best we can! I wanted to do that for him! You're the one who said no. Both of you did, so don't you dare put this at my feet."

The outburst made Ozzie jump. He watched his normally stoic godfather clamp a hand over his mouth, as if desperate to try and keep in everything else he wanted to say. The damage was done. Tears were already lining Ha-Yun's eyes, and Ethan looked so crushed by guilt that he could barely lift his head.

"Ozzie needs to go to Black River," Percival said at last. "The key is always hidden somewhere within the old Bell estate. The others will help him find it."

"The others? You mean the ones selected from the other families?" Ethan asked.

Percival nodded. Reaching across the kitchen island, he cupped a warm hand over Ozzie's arm. The touch was comforting, and Ozzie felt fearful tears start to burn the back of his eyes.

"Together we survive, alone we die. That is the only thing you can ever trust within the Witch Woods. They will be your strongest allies and surest weapons. She will do whatever she can to try and break that bond. You can't let her."

"What bond? I've never met these people."

"You should have." Percival spoke in a whisper, but his parents reeled as if they had been struck. "But the others will know about Katrina and you. You'll have to take a lot on faith and build these relationships as quickly as you can. I'll help you."

"How?" Ozzie asked.

Percival smiled slightly. "We can start by posting your selection."

"Posting?" Ethan asked.

There was warmth back in his voice as he casually revealed they had a website.

CHAPTER 6

Latching onto the chance to do something helpful, Ha-Yun rushed to retrieve her laptop. Within minutes, Percival was navigating his way to the website while the Davis family pushed tightly in around him.

Percival paused and lifted his head. "I'm not comfortable doing this with someone breathing down my neck."

"Put it up on the big screen?" Ethan suggested, remote already in hand.

A click of the button brought a plasma screen out of the wall. It almost consumed the space, and the group had only to turn around to view the details clearly. Ozzie had to admit it was far more comfortable. He could almost pretend he was just watching a movie play out. The soft tick of the box seemed to grow louder as if to mock him.

"This is the website?" Ethan asked when vibrant, cheerful colors filled the 103-inch screen.

Cute little cartoon characters bounded around the scattered links. Recipes, holiday reviews, fashion, and decorating tips. The place looked like a family run lifestyle page. A few clicks and a password brought them to a page simply marked 'The Harvest.' Below, the links were marked by the year concerned. They started in 1821. Ozzie's insides tightened a little more as Percival mindlessly scrolled down the list. Hearing this nightmare had been going on for nearly two centuries was one thing. It hadn't really had the same impact as seeing it laid out before him did. All the while, the box continued to scrape and click.

Finally, Percival selected a link and the screen changed again.

Not to another variety of links—rather, a picture of a man filled the screen. He was unmistakably older than Ozzie, hovering somewhere between his twenties and thirties. Old enough that wrinkles had forged around his warm brown eyes. The light in the photograph made it hard to tell if he was graying or just had some really pale blonde streaks in his floppy brown hair. High cheekbones, a strong jawline, and a wide, thin mouth gave him an almost rattlesnake kind of smile.

"Oh, thank God." Percival slumped forward, rubbed a hand over his scalp, and pulled back with a jerk. "Thank God."

"Who is he?" Ethan asked.

Ha-Yun shook her head, "I don't know if I trust him or not."

"That's Cadwyn Winthrop. Cad if you get on his good side. And we're damn lucky he got selected."

Percival finished a gulp of wine before he continued, his tone shifting into something clinical and sterile. That tone, more than anything else, told Ozzie just how difficult what lay ahead was going to be.

"This is Cadwyn's first time being selected. His brother, however, was in a Harvest and lost. Inexplicably, Abraham made it out of the woods. You have to understand the demons don't just like to physically torment you. Their goal is to destroy you mentally as well. One of their favorite ways to do that is isolation. They turn themselves into such a threat that family members have no option but to take a step back." Tears loomed in the back of his throat, making his voice crackle.

He's done it before. The fact locked into Ozzie's mind, leaving only the question of how many times he had been forced to pick his own survival over the wellbeing of loved ones.

"Cadwyn's a living legend. He never left his brother's side until his death."

"He managed to be a decent human being," Ha-Yun said. "That's how low the bar is?"

Anger flashed through Percival's eyes but didn't make it out of his mouth.

"You saw the opening act for these creatures. Imagine enduring that every day for close to a year, only it can touch you. And all the while you know the one you're enduring this hell for is going to die. Or worse."

"What could be worse?" Ethan asked, dumbfounded.

Percival took another mouthful. "It's been documented on numerous occasions that, once the demon has weakened its target, it can take possession of the body. If this situation isn't corrected, the demon can then use the body to kill those outside of the family."

"Corrected?" Ethan asked. "You mean 'killed,' right? It forces you to kill each other."

"Is that what happened to Cadwyn and Abraham?" Ha-Yun asked.

Percival saluted them both with his wine glass. "I can't go into details."

"What?" Ha-Yun asked, too shocked to look enraged.

"You're neither blood nor bride," Percival shrugged. "There're some things that aren't spoken of outside of the family. What I can tell you is I know Cadwyn. He's loyal, protective, intelligent, and a registered psych nurse."

"You've also just suggested he may have murdered his brother," Ethan said in passing, leaping up to begin pacing the room.

"What you need to know from the story is this: at twelve years old, Cadwyn played chicken with a demon, and the demon blinked first." He turned to Ozzie to add, "If I could personally choose who would go into those woods with you, Cadwyn would be in my top ten. Play to his protective instincts. Build a friendship with him. If you can earn his loyalty, he'll die for you."

"I don't want to manipulate anyone," Ozzie said softly.

"Don't think of it as manipulation. Everyone else has had a lifetime to build these bonds, you're just playing catch-up." With that resolved, he scrolled down.

Ozzie perked up at the next photo to grace the screen. The girl was around his age, maybe a little older, with large dark eyes that matched her hair, tawny skin, a warm smile, and a figure that could stop traffic.

"She's cute."

"This isn't a dating site," Ethan mumbled, only to have his wife swiftly remind him their son wasn't blind.

During all of this, Percival had reached for one of the forgotten glasses. It was the most Ozzie had ever seen him drink. He had never known the old man could handle his liquor so well.

"That's Willimina Crane. Mina," he corrected with a shrug.

Ethan eyed his friend closely. "Is she going to be a problem?"

Percival snorted, "She isn't exactly an assist. See, she's one of the babies of the Crane line, and her folks insisted on treating her like it. They've kept her as far away from all of this as they could."

"So, she's in the same position as me?" Ozzie asked.

Percival shook his head as he continued to drink. "No. She knows her history. The problem is she doesn't believe it. For years, she's been trying to convince people this whole thing is a string of bad luck, natural gas leaks causing hallucinations, and group hysteria. Basically, she's a coddled little princess." He puffed out his chest and woefully clicked his tongue. "Katrina's going to have fun with her."

"What do you mean?" Ethan asked. "Surely, if her selection process was anything like Ozzie's, she now knows it's real."

"Katrina tends to treat skeptics one of two ways; either she crushes them under evidence until they're blabbering messes, or she makes sure to foster their doubt. The point is to take them out of the game. Have the Harvest fighting amongst themselves instead of working as a single-minded whole." Taking a sobering breath, he glanced at her photograph again. "No one wants to go in with a skeptic."

"Are you saying she's going to get Ozzie killed?" Ha-Yun asked.

Percival flinched. "Mina's weapon to wield is her tenaciousness. The girl's like a cassowary…"

"A what?" Ozzie cut in.

"It's a giant bird, okay?" Percival said. "A very large, very aggressive bird that uses five-inch-long claws to murder anything that annoys it. The point is, the girl's relentless. Once she sets her mind to something, you can't stop her. If she gets on board, she could be a remarkable ally. If she doesn't, well, the group will have to handle that."

Before anyone could question exactly what that would entail, he moved the page down again. No one in the Davis family seemed to know how to react to the last member of the group. Even without a size reference, it was clear the girl was tiny. In combination with porcelain skin, hair like spun gold, and delicate features, she'd easily be confused with a doll.

"She's a child," Ethan said at last.

It was then they noticed Percival's silence. His eyes spoke horror, but a smile played across his lips.

"There's no age limit," he muttered absently, as if the response was a knee-jerk reaction. "The oldest selected was ninety-two. The youngest was three weeks."

As the family reeled from all the thoughts and images that piece of information summoned, Percival let a quick burst of laughter pass his lips.

"Who is she?" Ozzie asked.

"That's Basheba Bell."

"Like the story?" Ethan cut in.

"Don't worry, she's not the same girl. That's just one of the weirder aspects of the curse. No matter our intentions, we always repeat the old family names."

"That's stupid," Ha-Yun muttered.

"Probably. What was it you wanted to call your son again?"

"Park." Ha-Yun's eyes stretched wide, her jaw dropping as if it had just occurred to her that she never had any intention of naming her child Osgood.

Deciding his point had been proven, Percival saluted the image with a glass. "You know that top ten list I mentioned? Basheba would be in my top five."

Ozzie studied the photograph again, trying to see what Percival could possibly be talking about. There was a doe-eyed naivety about her. No matter how long he looked, Basheba seemed like the kind of girl who would be utterly mystified by bubbles.

"I give up," Ozzie said. "What's so special about her?"

"Most notably, this isn't her first rodeo," Percival said. "She was selected for Harvest two years ago."

"Is that allowed?" Ethan asked.

"The Bell family has dwindled over the years. The smaller the bloodline, the higher the likelihood of getting selected. There's only four of them left. No, sorry. Three." Percival's eyes clouded over as he made the correction. "There's three, now. Jonathan didn't make it out last year."

While his grief was never spoken, it still filled the room and made the air thick. No one disturbed Percival as his body stilled. For a brief moment, the man's eyes closed and a fine tremor raced over his shoulders. Ozzie was sure he was about to cry. But then, with a sharp intake of breath through his nose, he returned to his cool demeanor.

"Basheba knows first-hand what ya'll are walking into. Yeah, she's small and not much of a physical help. But she's quick on her feet, ruthless, and practical. She'll be willing to cut Mina loose if she's not going to pull her weight."

"Isn't that going against the group unity you keep talking about?" Ethan asked.

"Sometimes, you have to give up a lamb to save the flock."

The way Percival greedily shot the last of the wine like it was whiskey left Ozzie convinced that this, too, was something the older man had personal experience with.

"She's a good kid," Percival said at last. "But the last few years have left their mark. We'll have to be careful to win her over before you head out."

"What do you mean by that?" Ha-Yun asked.

He gestured out like the response was obvious. "Which one of them do you think is going to be excited by the prospect of going into the Witch Woods with a complete novice? No one wants to be stuck babysitting while fighting for their lives. We have to ensure none of them think of Ozzie as dead weight. Cadwyn's proven he's capable of mercy killings, Mina's nothing if not practical, and Basheba's seen too much to be kindhearted." He chuckled slightly. "This is the one time where being unpopular could actually get you killed."

Ethan nodded, his motion calm while his eyes blazed with panic. "What do you suggest we do?"

"First of all, we have to make sure we get there first." Not leaving any room for argument, Percival got to his feet, hurriedly swallowing down the last of the red liquid. "Each selected has exactly seven days from when the box is handed to them, so time is a factor. Dragging your feet with getting to Black River is an unforgivable crime. If we take a helicopter, we can make it there in about an hour and forty minutes. Traditionally, if we have the time, the selected spend a day setting out a strategy and getting a good night's sleep. Ozzie, you'll be picking up the tab for all of it. Everything. Without question. We Sewalls are still the best off financially, and we're going to remind them of our generosity. Understood?"

"Yeah." Ozzie cleared his throat and spoke again with something he hoped sounded like conviction. "Yes, let's do this."

"That's the spirit. Grab the box and let's go."

Ozzie hesitated. The box still sat on the middle of the kitchen counter, shining in the overhead lights. Popping and scraping as the pieces moved. He jumped when Percival placed a warm hand on his shoulder.

"No matter what happens, you can't lose that box," he said

gravely. "Your survival depends on it. Pick it up now, and don't let it leave your person until this is done."

Ozzie nodded. *I can do this. She's a dead witch. I'm a Davis. A Sewall. There's nothing that can get the better of me.*

For all his conviction, the box still lay there, untouched.

CHAPTER 7

Time didn't work the same in Black River as it did everywhere else. Nested within miles of untouched wilderness, the farming town seemed content with the simpler way of life. Plentiful crops of corn and wheat saw them through the summer. The winter harvest stood ready for the picking. Stalks with bulbous puffs of cotton, fields of plump pumpkins, and orchards full of crimson apples spread out over the undulating earth. The woods rose up sharply at the edges of the outlying properties. Towering old growths of oak and maple worked together to enclose the town.

The autumn night hung over the area, thick with chill and still as the grave. Basheba knew the instant she entered the town limits. Not by some shift in the forest or the sudden emergence of the crops. It was the moonlight. From Nashville, it had hung low in the sky, drenching the calm world with silver light. The moment she entered Black River, it died away, wilting until there was barely a trace of it left to touch the road before her.

Buck hadn't lifted his head from the crook of Basheba's arm. He had dozed on and off for the forty-five-minute drive, only stirring to growl softly at the glove box. She didn't try to move the object. Simply kept her focus locked onto the dark road as she weaved past the ancient homesteads. Her grip on the wheel tightened when she approached the last obstacle that properly separated the town from the surrounding farmlands.

There were numerous points where the river that gave the town its name thinned into little more than a babbling brook. Naturally, it was at these markers the first settlers had decided to construct bridges, and the town hadn't seen any reason to change that. Most of them hadn't even been upgraded and remained as little more than a few planks hastily nailed together. There were a couple that had been changed into covered bridges. She had purposefully gone a mile out of her way to ensure she managed to cross at one of these points.

A dull overhanging light bulb illuminated the opening and she set her gaze upon it, breathed deep and slow, locked her elbows, and pushed down the accelerator.

The car lurched forward over the gravel road. Her headlights flooded the elongated cave of the tunneled bridge and washed over the dark water. A broken cry escaped Basheba as she put her entire body weight down on the brake. The tires locked and skidded over the loose earth. With a final lurch that threw her against her seatbelt and sent Buck tumbling onto the cab floor, the car came to a halt.

"Sorry, sorry," Basheba whispered as Buck scrambled his way back up.

It took a concerted effort to loosen her death grip on the wheel. She gave him an apology scratch behind his ears.

"Sorry," she breathed one last time.

Don't look. Just don't look. It was impossible to listen to her own advice. The dark water drew her gaze. It shifted like liquid onyx around the stones that stood out like exposed bones. Her heart hammered painfully against her ribs, each beat rattling her small frame.

"It's only a few inches deep," she told Buck. "Only a few inches."

He grumbled, nose twitching wildly as he glanced around. Watching his fruitless efforts to find the source of her anxiety made her feel like an idiot. She gave him another scratch.

"I'm okay. You're with me, right boy?"

Buck plopped his butt down on the seat, straightening his front legs, a guard dog at its post. At least, that's what she liked to think of him as.

"All right. We're going to just shoot on through. It'll only take a second."

Not trusting herself to see through her conviction on the first attempt, she ordered the Rottweiler onto the floor in front of the passenger seat. Once he was safely stowed away, she put her manual car in gear, took a deep breath, and stomped down. She was forced to shift rapidly as the car picked up speed. Flimsy wooden walls kept the river from her view. Basheba locked her eyes on the end of the tunnel, racing toward it, the process only taking a few seconds.

A sudden jerk threw her forward. Her seatbelt tensed, crushing the air from her lungs before forcing her back. Buck yelped, the headlights died, and the roar of the engine was reduced to a hollow rapid clicking. Wincing, Basheba struggled to understand what had just happened.

Vaguely, she was aware that the abrupt stop had sloshed her brain around her skull. *Whiplash?* The thought was quickly dismissed. All the pain in her body existed in the single bar where her seatbelt had struck her.

"Buck, you okay, boy?"

Deprived of both high beams and moonlight, shadows strangled the world around her. Buck's fur was the perfect camouflage. She groped for the seatbelt, calling for him again when she first heard it. Something moving within the water. The door muted the sound but she recognized it instantly. Snapping into motion, she hunched forward, slipping her emergency bag out from under her seat. Leaning to the side, she blindly fumbled with the latch of the glove box. The instant she had the witch's music box in hand, she thrust open the passenger door and rolled out, calling for Buck to follow. A bark and scrape of claws indicated he was following.

Don't look back. Don't stop. The self-commands unbidden and unnecessary. Past experience had already sent a surge of adrenaline through her veins. Cold air burned her lungs as she sprinted for the far end of the bridge. The wooden slats rattled under her feet. Small gaps opened to allow the sound of rushing water to echo around her.

The unseen presence consumed the distance between them, slithering through the water with impossible speed. Water exploded through the slats like a geyser, drenching her as the scent of damp earth and decaying moss spewed into the air.

Buck yelped and snarled. Basheba gathered her strength and leaped forward. Still air struck her as she broke free of the wall of water. With a sharp twist, she managed to land hard on her shoulder and duck into a bone-rattling but effective roll. She came to a stop on all fours, snapping back around to stare at the bridge, fingers clutching both her bag and the music box.

Whatever force that had kept the water rising died with a low hiss. Gravity took hold, bringing the droplets back down like a pattering rain.

Panting hard, Basheba scanned the lonesome road, absentmindedly patting Buck when he ran forward to lick the river water off of her cheek. A few unseen night birds chirped from the treetops. The stream gurgled lazily against the stones. Buck's nails scratched shallow grooves into the dirt as he bumped and wiggled for her attention.

Basheba never stopped scanning the river as she crammed the enchanted cube into her backpack. Still refusing to look down, she patted the slick, waterproof material repeatedly, searching for the trademark shape. Only then did she rise to her feet.

A shift in the water instantly drew her attention. The dull moonlight caught the minuscule breaking waves more than the object that had disrupted the flow did. Her attention locked onto the curved blob, narrowing her focus until it was the only thing she could see.

Suddenly, twin orbs broke through the pitch darkness of the object. Eyes. Impossibly wide, burning red, and fixated on her. There wasn't time to process the sight before light shattered the darkness, rendering her blind.

Her car's engine roared like a wounded animal. The feeble planks of the bridge strained under the rapidly moving vehicle. Regaining all of its previously lost momentum, the car barreled toward her. She spun on her heel, calling for Buck to follow her as she sprinted away from the approaching high beams.

Gravel crunched and the engine whined behind her. Basheba lunged desperately for the tree line. Her feet got tangled and she dropped like a stone. Thorny bushes slashed at her as she dropped down behind them. A colossal cracking thud sounded before chipped bark sprayed over her back like shrapnel. She scrambled forward, ignoring the spikes of pain as she sought shelter. A nearby thunderous crack made her freeze.

She shivered in the resulting silence. Every ounce of pain she had ignored made itself known, leaving her breathless and whimpering as she freed herself from the tangled mass of spikes.

The night was dark once more. Scrambling, she pulled her phone from her pocket. A cobweb of fine cracks distorted the lock screen picture but the flashlight app still worked.

"Buck?" The first call was barely more than a whisper. But when she received no reply, it rose to a shout. "Buck!"

Basheba knew she was projecting when she decided his bark sounded relieved. The Rottweiler bound into the glow of her phone.

"Good boy," she gushed while fighting her way back onto the road. "Smart boy."

He reared up as she approached, balancing his front paws on her shoulders to better lick her face. She almost buckled under the extra weight.

"Are you okay, Buck? Did she hurt you?"

Logically, she knew he couldn't answer. So she rubbed his flank encouragingly while shoving him into motion. About half a yard down the road, her car was now wrapped around the thick trunk of a tree. Glass scattered across the ground, shining like diamonds in the flickering headlights. A thin string of steam curled up from the now dead engine with a serpentine hiss.

Basheba eyed the tree as she closed in on the totaled vehicle. "A witch elm? Really, Kat? It's a little on the nose, don't you think?"

Yelling into the darkness only made her feel better for a moment. After that, the gnawing dread ravaging her stomach forced her into action. She checked for the box once more, slipped her backpack on, and headed down the road in a lurching jog.

***

Cadwyn eased up on the brakes and pulled his motorcycle into the gas station. The 2016 Triumph Thruxton's primal growl echoed over the open slab of concrete. In anticipation of the Harvest, he had slept as much as he could. It didn't really matter, though. Stonebridge and Black River were separated by a seventeen-hour drive. With a full shift on top of that, there was no way to avoid the effects of sleep deprivation. He clung to the hope that the others arrived promptly, allowing them the luxury of a full night's sleep in a proper bed.

The leather of his riding gear crackled as he swung a long leg off the bike. He stumbled. The extended ride had turned his muscles into stone. Pain sparked under the waves of pins and needles that covered his skin.

Cadwyn swallowed a few curse words and carefully stretched out his legs, his back, his arms. *Caffeine.* The reminder made him turn toward the door. Halfway there, he recalled he also needed to fill up his Thruxton. At least the extra pacing helped to work the blood flow back into his legs.

That done, he retraced his steps back to the gas station, ignoring the few people who were watching him. The dawn was pushing against the horizon, giving the gas station a thin but steady flow of early risers on their way out and people just coming off of night shifts.

He remembered entering the doors. Then everything was covered in a fog, clearing after he had been staring at the drinks fridge for who knew how long. It would put his organs through hell, but he gathered up a half dozen energy drinks, the kind loaded with enough caffeine to put an elephant into cardiac arrest. Cadwyn guzzled down one of the cans as he made his way to the counter.

"Hey," the bored clerk said.

Cadwyn forced a smile in greeting and held up the can he was working on to make sure they added it to his bill. The others, he dumped on the counter.

"Pump five, thanks."

"Long night?" The clerk chuckled.

"It's going to be a long week," he replied, glancing up as he started to count out a couple of bills.

A looming abyss reared up behind the man, a dark shadow the overhead lights couldn't touch. It was thick and wide and lunging toward Cadwyn. He jumped back, knocking over a display and scattering candy bars across the floor.

"Hey!"

In the space of a blink, the shadow dissolved, leaving only a confused minimum wage employee.

"Are you all right?"

"Yes." Cadwyn rubbed a hand over his face, digging his knuckles into his eyes. "I'm fine. Thanks. Sorry."

He had just begun to gather up the bars when the clerk came around and helped him.

"It's okay, I've got it."

"I'm really sorry," Cadwyn said.

The clerk took the bars and studied Cadwyn carefully. "Are you okay to drive?"

He nodded rapidly and got to his feet, making sure to leave the change as an apology tip. Another of the energy drinks was gone by the time he had returned to his bike. He could feel it strumming through him like a live wire. It still wasn't enough to drive the dry, aching feeling from his eyes. A few swift smacks and the cool air helped a little.

Call someone. The thought seemed to come from a distant echo chamber. It took a few seconds for him to realize what his own mind was telling him. The Bluetooth in his helmet would allow him to keep a conversation going. The question was who he would call. His clouded mind dredged up the answer that left him cold. *Rudolph.*

Crushed under a wave of guilt and grief, he didn't notice the first patters against the high metal awning. It was only when it picked up speed and became a downpour of hail that he paid it any attention. A moment later, his brain caught up with why.

It doesn't sound right.

A lighter tinkle. A different pattern. The morning sun drove back the shadows, illuminating the tiny objects falling from the sky.

His stomach clenched, almost forced the sugary drink back up his throat. Clamping a hand over his mouth, he swallowed rapidly and fixed his eyes on the ground. Soon enough, the constant stream of falling teeth bounced into his field of vision, their jagged ends encrusted with withered flesh and stained with blood.

She's trying to stop you. They're not real.

Knowing that didn't make it any easier. After stowing away the drinks, he shoved his helmet on. Teeth scattered around his feet as he threw a leg over his bike.

Through the tinted visor, he caught sight of the downpour once more. Fine tremors shook his hands, remaining even while he twisted his grip around the handles. His stomach rolled, sloshing the minimal contents of his stomach and threatening to bring it back up.

Falling teeth caught on the wind, swirling as they fell until they completely covered the ground. Cadwyn squeezed his eyes closed to block it out. Before he could calm his rapid heartbeat, sleep reared up within him, and he was forced to open them again. Forced to watch the unnatural rain, to hear the tiny patter as they skittered across the ground.

He gagged.

You have to go. You have to keep moving. You're running late.

The motivation gave him enough strength to stomp down and

bring his bike roaring to life. The familiar sound covered the worst of the noise, but there was still the sight to deal with. *It's just hail.*

Instead of the phone call, he turned on his music, pushing up the volume until he couldn't hear the teeth crunch under the wheels of his bike. Clenching his jaw until it ached and unable to quell the tremors that racked his body, he peeled out. *Just get to Black River.*

CHAPTER 8

Ozzie couldn't get over the fact that the whole forest looked like it was on fire. He'd seen autumn leaves before, but nothing like this. Endless shades of red and yellow stained the foliage. They blazed in the morning light and shimmered with the slightest breeze. It was hypnotic, and he found himself staring unblinkingly for moments on end. *The lack of sleep probably isn't helping*, he thought, blinking rapidly to remoisten his dry eyes.

Being forced to wait for the rest of the world to wake up had been its own kind of torment. Logically, they knew the wait was worth it. Chartering a helicopter would get them to Tennessee faster than taking a standard flight or driving. But knowing that didn't make the wait any easier. Ozzie's parents had paced endlessly across the gravel entrance to the airfield, literally creating a trench. It was small and mostly consisted of high heel marks, but Ozzie had decided it counted.

Percival had tried to keep them all distracted, regaling them with stories of past Harvests and all those who had survived. While Ozzie had done his best to listen, his attention had always been drawn back to the box. It had shone like molten gold in the first few rays of daybreak. Every now and then, he was sure he could feel something moving inside of it.

Stifling a yawn, Ozzie scrubbed a hand through his thick black hair and leaned against the window. *It's actually kind of pretty,* he thought as he watched the scorching colors pass by. He had thought, once he had the moment to think, he could do just that—explore his deepest soul and bring the chaos of his mind into a coherent order once again. It just seemed like something he should be doing.

It hadn't worked out that way.

He had tried to think, put the full force of his mind and determination into it, about what was waiting for him. He tried to think of different ways he could win the others over, or even about all the things that had forever changed now that he knew all that paranormal stuff was real. But he couldn't keep his mind from straying. A few times, he had taken a run at the easiest topic before him.

How do I feel about being a Sewall?

He adored his family; loved his life in general. Only a few hours ago he had learned it was all a lie.

Not to mention my godfather is genetically my dad.

It felt weird to even think of it. All his life, his mother and Percival had been like siblings. Emotionally close, sporadically annoying each other, and with zero romantic tension. It was just gross to think they had been together like that, let alone produced him.

And no one cared! At least, not enough to let me know.

That was about the limits of his organized thought process. Over and over, his brain crumbled the moment he reached that point. He tried to grasp the thoughts, force himself to lead them to their inevitable conclusion, but never could. Everything always brought him back to the same point.

The image of Maxwell with spiders burrowing out of his flesh.

Not Maxwell, he told himself. *It just made itself look like him. Maxwell is fine. Spiders don't do that.*

Images of twisting, hairy spider legs flashed across his mind. Bile burnt the back of his throat as his stomach roiled. The helicopter rotated at the same moment. Sunlight found the box again, glinting off it to create a blinding glare that jerked him from his spiraling thoughts.

Instinctively, his fingers tightened around the box until his bones hurt. He began to slowly twist the cube back and forth, letting the sunlight dance off the polished sides. His brow furrowed when he noticed that the constantly moving puzzle pieces never pinched his fingers. A small quiver rattled the innards.

Was the demon I saw the same as what's trapped inside this thing?

Ice entered his stomach as another question tore its way into the forefront of his mind. *It's 'trapped,' but it can do that. What else can it do?*

What scared him was the possibility that, at some point, it could have all been real. Physically real. That he could have touched that grotesque sight. *That it could have touched me.* With a visible flinch, he forced his gaze back to the sea of foliage, desperate for some distraction.

There's so much of it. The woods stretched out to the horizon in every direction. A thick blanket disrupted only by the deep grooves left by passing streams. Without warning, the dense trees gave way to farmlands. Fields of crops and cattle zipped by within an instant, and they were left hovering over the small township of Black River.

The thick stream the place was named after divided the town in two. Even from above, the conscious effort to keep the town's rustic aesthetic was evident. The few undeniably modern buildings scattered about tried their best to camouflage themselves amongst the antique architecture. An old chapel still held the place of pride atop the only distinctive hill in the area. Made of black wood and spearing the sky with a single steeple, it was the largest building in the whole town.

Ozzie's pilot had to circle the area twice before he found the small patch of land subbing for an airport. Black River didn't have a real airport. What they had was the local sporting ground that hadn't had anything else going on that day, and was grateful for the large donation. Lush green and well-tended, the short grass whipped violently as they landed. With Percival settling things with the landowners, and his parents handling the final matters with the pilot, there was nothing for Ozzie to do but get out and study the alien surroundings.

Black River wasn't like anything he had ever seen. While his parents liked to travel, it had always been to places like Italy, Rome, Las Vegas, or the Bahamas. Places designed to meet their needs and entertain them with an endless array of wonders. This place, while having a quaint charm, was about as far away from his norm as he could imagine. It left him feeling both larger than life and insignificantly tiny at the same time.

With a sudden rush of clarity, Ozzie realized he was completely out of his depth.

I have no idea what I'm doing. I've never even been camping! They're all going to know I'm useless. I'm going to get everyone killed.

Ozzie turned, instinct demanding he get back onto the helicopter and get out. A lump of pure dread crystalized in his stomach as he was left to watch the helicopter rise into the clear sky.

"Where's the car?" Ethan asked over the sound of the chopper's blades, then caught sight of his son.

Concern wrinkled his brow as he studied Ozzie's face. He didn't say anything, though, just placed a hand on his son's shoulder and gave it a reassuring squeeze.

The harsh wind died and the retreating engine left them to the mercy of the early morning silence that lingered over the town. Time seemed to hover, broken only by a breath of wind that made the distant leaves whisper. Ozzie shivered and inched closer to his father.

Percival stalked over, casually adjusting his overcoat. "What was that?"

"The car?" Ha-Yun prompted.

"I didn't hire one," Percival replied. Noticing the looks of his companions, he added, "Black River doesn't have the infrastructure to handle the influx of the four families. Not to mention the tourist season. It's just quicker to walk."

Ozzie hurried to fall in step alongside the much taller man. *Can't wait for my dang growth spurt.* The passing thought caught him off guard. It was strange to think that, even while his brain was breaking under the weight of the new information, there was still enough room left for his regular self to slip through. In a strange way, he found it rather comforting. It was a small bit of normalcy that he desperately clung to.

"This place has a tourist season?" Ozzie asked.

The short look Percival threw him made him stammer.

"I'm not saying your hometown isn't pretty. It's nice. I'm sure there's a crowd who would love to come out this way. I hear a lot of people like to travel to see the leaves change color. I mean, that's," he paused as he winced. *We've talked about this Ozzie. If you don't know how you're going to end a sentence, don't start it.* "A thing," he stammered.

Percival's tense expression was softened by a smile he fought to smother. "I wasn't born here, Oz. Even if I was, I'd still hate this place."

"Oh. Then, what's up with…" Again, he didn't have a way to end it, so he swirled a finger out to indicate Percival's vanishing smile.

"As a Sewall, it's our duty to hate the tourist trade here."

"Why?"

"No one's coming here to see the autumn aesthetics, Ozzie."

It still wasn't clicking in Ozzie's head, and he glanced back to his father for some help. Ethan fell into step on Percival's other side and asked the question.

"Then what's the real reason?"

Percival kept his gaze locked straight ahead. "The Witch."

Ozzie longed to be able to meet his parent's eyes and see if they were just as confused as he was. Unfortunately, he also didn't want to be so obvious about it as to jog forward and peer around his godfather, so he was stuck doing nothing but shifting his fingers over the box.

"People come to see Katrina?" Ha-Yun asked.

Percival paused mid-stride. Instantly, he had everyone's unwavering attention.

"Don't call her by name. Not around here."

Ha-Yun's eyes widened and she leaned closer to whisper, "Does it heighten her powers?"

"No," he snorted. "She's essentially a serial killer who's specifically preyed on our families for close to two centuries. Hearing her name, well, for the people you're about to meet, it'll be like moseying into Waterloo and bringing up John Wayne Gacy."

"But she's a tourist attraction?" Ethan asked.

"Her legend is," he replied, evidently bitter. He started walking again. "In and of itself, her life wasn't much to write home about. The whole world is full of psychopaths systematically ruining random people's lives. After death, however, The Bell Witch became one of the most documented cases of poltergeist activity in the world. To this day, there's barely a case that measures up to the number of eyewitness accounts, collected evidence, and spirit photography."

"They had cameras back then?" Ozzie asked.

Percival was so caught off guard by the question that he forgot to cover his laugh.

"What? No, they didn't. But people came out here after cameras were invented. They *still* come out here. I–" He choked on his own words and shook his head. "How is this confusing you?"

Ozzie shrugged, keeping his mouth shut. Eventually, Percival went back to what he had been saying.

"She's also a witch. Some folks are into that kind of thing. That interest has allowed Black River to build a tourism industry somewhat like Salem. Or the Amityville Horror house, depending on who you talk to. Some come for the tragic history while others just want to see a ghost."

It didn't take long for the group to be confronted with numerous examples of what Percival was talking about. Halloween had invaded the town. Old fashioned decorations clustered around the buildings and lined the streets. None of them were the flashy, plastic things Ozzie was used to. Draped sheets fluttered in the crisp morning air, looking like formless ghosts. Scarecrows released small creaks and groans as they swayed on their spikes. The bulbous sides of fat Jack 'o' lanterns distorted their frozen grins into sinister smirks. But it was the witches amongst them that sent stray shivers down Ozzie's spine. They clung to the lampposts, filled the windows, and dangled from the skeletal arms of the trees.

Ozzie protectively cradled the box to his stomach as they continued down the street. The further they went, the more evidence he found of the town embracing their home-grown urban legend.

It seemed every street corner had a folding board advertising a different ghost tour or Witch Wood's hike. Most of the businesses they passed were a play on puns or direct references, most notably the distant café called Witch's Brew. The lampposts had originally been fashioned to look like the old gas burning kind. At some point, someone must have suggested that changing their tops into pointed black witch hats would be hilarious. Even the town's library had a few cackling, black hatted crones pushed up on their windows.

Black River wasn't a town that opened up their Main Street early. Most of the businesses remained closed and dark as they made a beeline to the Witch's Brew. The welcome sign was still switched to 'closed,' but the door wasn't locked, and Percival didn't hesitate to push his way through.

Nighttime shadows lingered within the café. Chairs were stacked upon the rounded tables and, every now and then, Ozzie caught the sterile scent of floor cleaner. A small silver bell affixed above the door announced their arrival. It didn't take more than that soft tinkle to have the unseen back doors slam open.

An instant later, the swinging door behind the counter opened to unleash a flood of people. Their chatter filled the space like an approaching storm. In seconds, they were surrounded. Everyone was talking at once. Introductions came hard and fast until Ozzie couldn't recall a single person. All he knew was they were all Sewalls. *My relatives.* It was overwhelming. Crammed into this room alone were more relatives than he had ever had with both of his parent's families combined.

Swept up in the retreating tide, they were ushered around the corner and out the back door. Working together in a whirlwind of limbs and well wishes, they bundled him through the kitchen and out the back door. Somewhere along the line, he was handed a glass of lemonade and a plate piled high with chicken fresh off the grill.

The sudden shift in both mood and location left Ozzie stunned. He found himself constantly looking back over his shoulder to make sure he hadn't been transported somewhere.

We were just on Mainstreet.

He was sure of that. And the building itself wasn't too large. Crossing its innards wouldn't have brought them back out to the woods. It seemed he was standing in someone's rural backyard.

It was spacious, with the curve of the road behind them mirroring the bend in the river. A flat patch of earth separated the back of the building from the riverbed, with enough room to comfortably fit a bonfire and numerous large tables. Strings of lights hung in scalloped rows from tree branches that were heavy with bright foliage. They dangled loosely, offering a rather useless glow that couldn't compete with the early morning sunlight.

There were more leaves on the ground than trees to account for them. They created a thick and squishy mulch blanket.

The Black River lived up to its name even while drenched in sunlight. It was impossible to judge its depth. Here and there, the glassy surface broke against a stone, giving the appearance the stream couldn't be more than a few inches deep. At other points, the still, dark waters seemed bottomless. It lay like a sheet of polished oil stretching out for about thirty feet before giving way to the woods. A heavy stone, covered in orange moss and evergreens, jutted out toward them from the far side. Ozzie hated the sight of it.

The people who had welcomed them soon bled into the swirling crowd. It looked as if they had just walked in on a celebration. Tired but happy faces. Drinks still flowing from the night before.

Ozzie clutched his music box tight, jabbing it against his stomach and twisting his wrists into painful angles in an attempt to cover it as much as possible.

Was this all a prank?

Before him was an ocean of happy faces. Laughter and the scent of barbeque hung heavy in the air while children ran about in giggling swarms. Confronted with all of this, it was hard to think it was anything but a sick joke. Ozzie desperately tried to pinpoint which of his more ridiculous but organized friends could pull something like this off.

"What is this?" Ethan demanded, his voice sharp but his volume low.

"This is my family. I told you they'd all be here waiting."

"They're having a party?" Ha-Yun asked.

Percival tipped his head to the side. He seemed to find that more dignified than a shrug. "Wouldn't you?"

"If everything you've told us is true," she stressed, "then all of these people know someone could die."

"And they know, at least this year, it's not them."

Ethan stammered. "So they celebrate? That's sick."

"What would you have us do? Ensure the last few hours the Selected gets to spend with their family is full of dread and tears? To send them off into hell with the knowledge that no one expects them to return? That's sick, my friend. We make sure they have a few more happy memories to cling to when things get bad. This isn't supposed to be a funeral. It's a celebration of life and displaying absolute confidence the Selected will make it through."

"Still." Ha-Yun shivered and inched closer to Ozzie. "Don't you see this as a little twisted?"

No one had expected Percival to laugh at that. "My family has had this curse hanging over them for generations. And we're still here. Broken. Defiant. Flourishing. And sane. A huge part of the reason for that is that we embrace life. We celebrate it. Especially when things are bad."

Ha-Yun opened her mouth, but Percival quickly cut her off.

"When your family has been cursed for centuries, you can decide how you handle it. This is a Sewall matter. And you're not a Sewall."

A delighted squeal announced the arrival of a woman an instant before she threw herself into Percival's arms. After a tight hug, the questions started to flow, quick and random. She barely had confirmation this was, in fact, 'the' Osgood before she was asking about kitchen renovations and the state of affairs in Washington. Every so often, she would bounce back to Ozzie. But she never lingered. The moment her straying eyes fell upon the cube Ozzie kept tightly gripped in his arms, she would jerk away and force a smile.

"Don't take it personally," Percival whispered to him as the woman retreated, checking once again to make sure they weren't following her. "Some find it harder than others to deal with the reminders."

Ozzie swallowed thickly. Everything he wanted to say got trapped in his throat when he noticed the pain that quickly crossed his godfather's face.

"So, the hair loss situation is a family thing, huh?" Ozzie asked with as much playfulness as he could muster.

A loud bark of laughter escaped the older man. Ozzie wasn't ready for the pat on the back Percival gave him and lurched forward with the contact.

"Sorry. It's in the genetics."

"Great."

"Hey, a lot of people think it looks dignified."

Ozzie had just straightened himself again when another person knocked him from behind. This time, the box almost slipped from his hands. His heart lurched as he struggled to keep his fingers around the smooth surface.

"Basheba, sweetie, aren't you still underage?"

Ozzie jerked straight again. The speaker held no interest for him. Every ounce of attention he was capable of latched instantly onto the girl in front of him. Having pushed past him, Basheba had intercepted the beer an older man had brought for Percival. Condensation trickled from the beer bottle to clean thin trails on her mud-streaked skin. She didn't pause in guzzling down the amber liquid, only lifting one finger to keep the questioning man at bay for a little while. It allowed Ozzie a few moments to try to get his thoughts in line. Despite his effort, the first thing that popped into his head was, *she's tiny.*

She was at least a foot shorter than him. Her face had grown a little plumper than it had been in the photograph, and her legs were a little too long to be called stocky. The flannel shirt she wore was basically a dress. It hung limply over the miniscule frame, torn, muddy, and stained with blood. Leaves clung to the knot of hair bundled on the crown of her head. The layer of dirt wasn't enough to dull the golden sheen, though. Only after she had swallowed the last drop did she suck in a deep breath and address the man.

"Why, yes, Lucius, I am," she said, her voice as sweet as honeysuckle. "Do you have another?"

"I don't think your uncle would like that," Lucius replied.

Basheba smiled. A pretty expression on a pretty little face. But there wasn't even a hint of warmth to it.

"And, of course, his happiness is the sole focus of my existence."

Lucius opened his mouth, closed it, and turned to Percival for help. A single nod was all it took to send the man scurrying back toward the picnic tables. Basheba watched him go, her expression unchanging but ice forming within her gaze.

"How are you, Basheba?" Percival asked it like it was completely natural for her to show up in such a state.

Apparently, that was the correct move, because her mood instantly shifted. She looked like the living embodiment of a spring day as she said, "The Witch is a bitch."

Percival snapped his fingers, "I've had my suspicions for years."

"She totaled my car."

"Horrible woman. Are you injured?"

Basheba's lower jaw jutted out to the side as she suppressed her brewing rage. "I'm this close to going around town burning everything Katrina-related."

Percival flinched at the name but held his tongue. With that, Ozzie had reached his limit. It was all too much to suppress simultaneously.

"Why do *you* get to say her name?" he blurted out.

Basheba took a moment to look him over from head to toe before answering. "Who's going to stop me?"

"I just mean, well, Percival said it was like mentioning a serial killer to their victims."

He wasn't prepared for Basheba to roll her eyes and mutter about how she wanted another drink. It had never taken so little to make him feel like a complete idiot.

Pursing her lips, she let out a sharp whistle. The answering bark was instantaneous. The actual appearance of the dog took a little longer and was preceded with startled squeals and breaks in the crowd. Ozzie didn't understand until he saw the animal for himself.

The Rottweiler was massive. A hundred and twenty pounds of muscle and fangs. It circled around Basheba to tap its nose against her left hand. From paw to shoulder, the dog had to be two feet tall, at least. Straightening its front legs, it dumped its rump onto the mushy leaves and stared at her with unwavering intensity. Side by side with her pet, Basheba looked as breakable as glass.

"That's a big dog." Ethan struggled to sound casual while simultaneously attempting to gather his family closer to him. "I assume he's well trained?"

Both Basheba and the Rottweiler ignored him. She jerked a chin toward one of the ice buckets.

"Fetch."

The dog's lower fangs shone like polished marble before it was suddenly sprinting across the field, massive paws kicking up mud and leaves. That done, she returned her attention to the group before them.

"Quick question; who the hell are you?"

"Oh, um," Ozzie glanced helplessly to Percival. "You didn't check the website?"

"I was a little busy avoiding vehicular homicide. You might remember me mentioning that."

Ozzie blinked at her, "You were serious?"

It seemed like she wanted to glare at him, but her angelic face didn't allow for such an expression. It ended up as more of a pout, which Ozzie found unsettling.

How am I supposed to get a good read on her if she can't express things properly?

It was like playing poker with someone who had just left a Botox party.

Ozzie shuffled his feet and fought the urge to look at Percival again. *I can handle a conversation on my own. I can make her like me.*

"I just thought the witch couldn't do anything physical until–"

"Oh, you're Osgood." She said it as if the mystery had really been bothering her.

"Ozzie," he corrected with a shrug, only to be ignored.

Her attention was stolen by the immense black dog's return. One side of its lips was bunched up around the beer bottle it carried. Without prompting, it dropped the bottle into Basheba's waiting hand and graciously accepted a neck rub as reward.

"Good boy," she cooed as she read the label.

The animal melted into the touch, plastering itself to her side and looking up at her with utter adoration.

"Very good boy." Twisting open the top, she smirked at Percival. "He's even learned my brand."

Ha-Yun's motherly instinct couldn't be denied. "You mentioned earlier you were underage."

"I'm twenty," Basheba said slowly.

"Still," Ha-Yun pressed gently. "That's not twenty-one."

The blonde couldn't contain her giggle. "You're new here, aren't you?"

"Ha-Yun." Percival cleared his throat, seemingly sharing Basheba's amusement. "By now, you must realize being a member of the four families comes with a certain degree of stress. Everyone here has developed a tactic for dealing with it. Admittedly, some are healthier than others, but it's considered polite not to draw attention to them. Let alone criticize."

"So, you just ignore illegal activity that could be damaging her developing brain?" Ha-Yun turned back to Basheba. "What does your mother say about this?"

The younger woman stopped nursing the bottle to mumble around a full mouth, "Katrina killed her five years ago."

Ha-Yun instantly deflated. "Oh. I'm—"

"And I might die tomorrow," Basheba chirped.

In that moment, Ozzie found the small pixie of a woman incredibly creepy. It was in the smile. The brilliant, pristine smile matched with dead eyes.

Like a shark sensing blood, Basheba continued, her pleasant smile frozen in place.

"I'm for sure going to be tortured, both mentally and physically. Katrina might even let me see my father's death. She showed me my mother's two years ago. And brother's. Both my sisters'. Countless cousins. At this point, it'll be kind of mean not to let me know if my daddy died screaming or not. Like ruining a set."

Slowly, deliberately, she rose the bottle back to her lips. The tendrils of hair that hung around her face began to sway. It was the only hint she was trembling.

"I'm sorry." She tipped the bottle. "Does this bother you?"

"No," Ha-Yun said softly. She didn't appear to know what she wanted to express, and her face restlessly shifted through countless emotions. "No, it doesn't. I'm so sorry."

"Don't worry. I'll pace myself." She turned fully to Percival. "Where's Cadwyn?"

"He hasn't arrived yet."

"So, um," Ozzie lurched into the conversation, desperate to find a way to claw onto a better standing point with her. "Do you prefer BeBe?"

"What?"

"You know, Basheba Bell. BeBe. Or do you just go by your last name?"

"I prefer Basheba."

"Really?" He snorted.

Big mistake, he realized when her eyes narrowed again. She didn't say anything, just glared at him as she took another slow sip.

"I like your dog," Ozzie blurted out.

Stupid. Stupid. Stu— His trail of thought shattered as he watched her face light up. Until that moment, he had been half-convinced she wasn't capable of making a real smile.

"His name is Buck. And he's the best boy who ever existed. Ever. I will fight you on that."

A smile and a joke? Ozzie almost puffed out his chest with pride. *Now we're getting somewhere.*

"Well, obviously he is," Ozzie chuckled.

"Does he bite?" Ethan asked, trying to keep the light tone.

"Well, obviously he does," Basheba said. "But only when I tell him to."

Okay, two jokes. One's a little dark, but that's still a good sign.

His hopes were confirmed when her smile grew, and she tilted her head to the side, her tangled gold hair spilling over one narrow shoulder.

"He's a guard dog. Very well trained."

"I see," Ha-Yun said. "He looks like a lovely animal."

She beamed, one hand lovingly rubbing the dog's neck. "Yes, he is. And beautifully brutal."

Percival took half a step closer to her and lowered his voice, almost as if he was trying to keep everyone else from hearing them.

"I didn't get a chance to say it last year. I'm very sorry for your loss."

Almost instantly, her pale eyes brightened with threatening tears. She bit her lips and nodded rapidly.

"Johnny was a good man. He was the best of us."

"Yes." Life came back to Basheba. Her cheeks warmed, and she concealed every trace of emotion behind a tiny, ever-present smile. "He was."

Ozzie had the distinct impression he was missing some integral piece of information; something important that would explain the way she locked her gaze onto Percival as she took another mouthful. He had never seen the man look so unsure. He shuffled his feet but was kept from having to come up with a response when she abruptly scanned the crowd.

"So, you finally got to bring Osgood–"

"Ozzie." He regretted correcting his name when Basheba turned her attention back to him.

One blink and she went from staring him down to looking like the most approachable person he had ever met. *Is it possible to get emotional whiplash?*

"Ozzie. Right, sorry, I'll get it. Don't you worry. So, what finally brings you onto our little farm of crazy?"

Ozzie cleared his throat. *Is there a way you're supposed to say it?* Not thinking of one, he settled for holding up the music box.

"Ah. I was hoping you were holding that for a friend."

"Nope. Just me."

"How old are you?"

"Almost sixteen."

Her eyelids fluttered closed, effectively keeping any other trace of emotion contained. There was just that smile. *The creepy, creepy doll smile.*

"Well." Her eyes opened, and she said it so delightfully, Ozzie could almost hear bells chiming in her words. "You're going to die. Enjoy your last day on earth. Well, last without all the nightmare-inducing stuff."

With a salute of her bottle, she was gone, disappearing into the crowd as a stranger appeared behind Ozzie.

"Don't worry about my niece," the man replied. He was pretty much just a scrawny frame topped with wire rim glasses and wrapped in a tweed coat. "Go on, get some sleep. The others won't be here for a while yet."

The reassurance flooded Ozzie's insides with warmth. As small as it was, it was the first hint from someone outside his family that everything was going to be okay. He desperately wanted to believe it. But there was something in the way Percival lifted his chin that made him hesitate. The tiny motion spoke volumes to Ozzie. *He doesn't trust this man. There's real hatred there.*

"Oh, thank you," Ha-Yun stammered.

Ethan rushed forward to grab the man's hand, shaking it almost violently in his gratitude. Only afterward did he recall that they were lacking some introductions.

"I'm sorry. I'm Ethan, this is my wife, Ha-Yun, and our son, Ozzie."

Ozzie's stomach tied up in knots as he watched his parents stammer and gush their gratitude on the stranger. He had never seen them this desperate. The truth sliced into him like a knife. *They're terrified. They don't think I'm going to survive. They think I'm going to die here.* Suddenly, the air seemed too thin to breathe.

"Oh, Percival has kept us well apprised of all of you," the man smiled. "I'm Isaac Bell. Have you met my daughter yet? A sweet girl called Claudia?"

"No, we've just arrived," Ha-Yun said.

Isaac's smile grew warmer while the tendons in Percival's neck pressed against his skin.

"You must be exhausted. I know my home won't be up to your normal standards, but it's close, warm, and yours to use as you wish."

"That's very kind," Ethan said. "Thank you. But I don't think any of us can sleep right now."

"You'll be surprised. Come, I'll introduce you to my daughter, and we'll get you comfortable. I'm sure Percival has a lot he needs to get in order."

"Thank you. But we really should be talking to Basheba," Ha-Yun said.

Isaac dismissed the protest with a wave. "She'll protect your son. I'll make sure of it."

It hadn't occurred to Ozzie how desperate his parents were for any kind of reassurance until he watched them both gush gratitude onto the stranger without any further prompting. Ozzie lingered back as Isaac herded his parents across the open field, waiting for them to be far enough away so they wouldn't hear his whisper to Percival.

"Why don't you like this guy?"

"Because he's a horrible human being," Percival whispered back. "He has absolutely no control over his niece, by the way. I don't know what he's angling for, but there's no way he can deliver on what he's promising."

"So, I should still be trying to win over Basheba?"

Percival mulled the question over before giving a quick shake of his head. "No. We can't, now. Any attempt to play nice will be tainted by Isaac."

Ozzie's stomach dropped. "What do we do then?"

"We need Cadwyn."

CHAPTER 9

Sheets of iron had replaced Cadwyn's eyelids. Muscle memory had long since taken over, keeping him upright on his bike even as he played with the brink of sleep. Reckless speeding hadn't been one of his best ideas, but it had shaved a few hours off his journey. The noonday sun had started to push into the afternoon by the time he reached the outskirts of the town.

The long, monotonous roads didn't help to keep his attention, but it did make it easier to ride. Looming trees shaded him from what little warmth the sun held. Combined with the air whipping around him, he was pretty sure he had fallen into a mild state of hypothermia. Although, that could've admittedly been a trick of his sleep-addled mind. While the demon had abandoned its trick of raining bloodied teeth upon him, the damage was done. His leather gloves crackled as he tightened his grip. It wasn't enough to stop his fingers from shaking.

Reducing his speed, he weaved through the cavernous jaws of the covered bridge. Chipped wooden planks, weather-worn and eaten away by burrowing insects, rattled under his wheels. The sound became a steady rhythm that mingled with the hum of his bike as he crossed over the babbling brook. Sunlight poured in between the old slabs of lumber that constructed the walls, cutting across the bridge in solid bars and flashing against his helmet's visor. The strobe light effect rendered him blind, leaving him to navigate by feel alone.

His bike growled in protest at the slower pace, but he didn't speed up. The ancient bridge was only large enough to accommodate one car at a time. If he was going to career headfirst into a farmer's truck, it wasn't going to be at full speed. The sound of vibrating wood gave way to the crunch of dead leaves and the even feel of concrete. A twist of the wrist let him burst back out into the light. A small incline later, he was finally able to leave the river behind. *In the home stretch now.* The looming promise of sleep kept him moving. A few rapid blinks brought his eyes back into focus.

His brow knotted as he approached the first curve that marked the twisting road to come. A Witch Elm tree stood proudly in the arch of the bend. Its cluster base had been a formidable match for an old Chevrolet hatchback. The whole front of the car had crumbled like paper against the thick trunk, leaving glass scattered over the damp road and the weak headlights fighting against the shade cluster under the canopy.

Cadwyn slowed again, staring at the sight, trying to get his sluggish brain to make sense of it all, or at the very least, tell him why the sight left dread gnawing in the pit of his stomach.

1979 Chevrolet Chevette Hatchback. The information drifted across his mind before the meaning followed. *That's Basheba's car.*

Cadwyn gripped the brakes. The soft layer of leaves caught his wheels, making him skid and slide as he brought himself to a sudden halt.

Look around you! The thought tore free of the foggy haze that filled his skull. Still straddling his Thruxton, he tore his eyes off the mangled steel to survey his surroundings.

The forest stood tall and still around him. No witch. No demonic force. No Basheba. The kickstand struggled to keep the still rumbling vehicle upright as he leaped off and raced to the driver's side door.

No body. No blood.

The disjointed thoughts left Cadwyn sagging against the gaping hole of the window, trusting his thick leather jacket to protect him from the shards of glass that protruded from the frame like broken teeth.

She's not hurt.

He stared at the front seat, trying to understand why he cared about the scattered shrapnel. *It's undisturbed,* he realized at last. There was no sign anyone had been in the driver's seat at the time of impact. Gripping the door with both gloved hands, he cast a look down the road. It twisted out of sight after only a few yards.

Well, go, a voice in his head whispered, almost as if his inner self couldn't stand his sleepy stupidity for a moment longer. *If you hurry, you might be able to catch up with her.*

Before he could turn away, a clear bag of yogurt pretzels caught his eye. The combination of a long torso and a long reach made it easy for him to snatch up the bag from the back seat. *What on earth?* Vibrant green icing filled two of the pretzel holes, each glop topped with candy eyes to make them look like little aliens. A little ribbon kept the bag together and he twisted the attached tag around to read it.

"Intergalactic Truck Stop. Best stop on the Milky Way Highway," he read aloud. A soft chuckle rolled around the inside of his helmet. "Basheba, the places you go."

Struck with the sudden urge to try one, he pulled back away from the car. It wasn't until he was plucking at the drawstring that his situation dawned on him. This had all the makings of a trap.

Shoving the bag into one of his jacket pockets, he scanned the area with more concern. The tint of his visor muted the vibrant woods around him. It saved his eyes from the glare, but swelled the shadows, letting them gather beyond the initial tree line. The normal sounds of wildlife that would fill the woods were lost under the constant rumble of his bike. Robbed of both sight and sound, he retreated back to the road, constantly watching for any signs of movement.

Adrenaline ripped through his veins like wildfire, burning away any trace of fatigue and leaving his hands twitching. A few quick strides and he was back on his bike, gunning the engine until it howled like a wounded beast.

Nothing rushed from the undergrowth to prevent his escape. He didn't know if he should find that a comfort or a dark omen, but it didn't matter. All he wanted was to get to town.

Picking up his speed turned the slow, meandering curves of the road into dangerous turns. The road slashed at his knees as he leaned into them, stripping away the leather of his biker pants to grind against the internal padding. Bit by bit, it came closer to reaching his flesh.

A straight stretch allowed him to push his engine to its limits. Frozen air lashed at him. Shadows danced across his eyes, some coming from outside his visor while others seemed to be within his helmet. Decomposing leaves and mud spewed up from his wheels as he barreled down the foliage-covered road. The earth trembled, the trees thrashed violently, and, with an explosion of shattered twigs, a massive beast lumbered free of the tree line. Two swift strides brought the creature to the center of the road. Cadwyn jerked, forcing his bike into a skid and almost losing control entirely as he slid a few yards to an abrupt stop.

A fair distance still separated him from the beast, allowing him to see the colossal creature in its entirety. It had the body of a man, if the man was a gigantic bodybuilder. Swollen muscles twitched beneath skin stained with blood, mud, and sweat. Its shoulders were broad enough that its bull head wasn't out of proportion. Unknown muck matted the short fur that covered the minotaur's head and neck. Black eyes bulged from the brown fur, undeniably bovine, but still somehow conveying dark malice. Trails of steam worked its way from flaring nostrils, coiling in the chilled air before dissipating around its curved horns.

The minotaur hunched forward, dislodging the clumps of flesh previous kills had left clinging to the deadly peaks, allowing the putrid chunks to fall onto the earth between its feet. Cadwyn's heart hammered painfully against his ribs as the minotaur carefully lined its horns up for attack. Its bare, mud-encrusted feet scraped over the ground.

Cadwyn jerked hard on his heavy bike, balanced himself on the foot bars, and forced the acceleration to its breaking point. The back tire spun wild, forcing the whole bike to fishtail before it found traction and suddenly shot forward. He desperately searched for a way around the minotaur but found nothing. A part of him wanted to turn back, to take one of the other roads into town. But there was something heavy in the back of his mind that whispered he wouldn't make it across the stream again. Katrina wouldn't let him slip her trap so easily.

Demons can't touch you. His own thoughts sounded like they came from the far end of a tunnel. *Not until the box is open. The Witch is just trying to waste my time. Get to town.*

Heat pulsated from the motor as the bike snarled. The minotaur snorted, gushing clouds of steam into the air.

It can't touch you.

The bull charged forward to meet him. Its wild baying cut over the sound of the machinery. Impossibly large muscles bulged as it braced for impact. At the last moment, the minotaur swept its head out, ducked lower, and drove one huge horn into the Thruxton's front wheel. There wasn't time to feel the sudden jolt before he was airborne.

Crushing steel and the dying gasps of the bike clashed somewhere in the back of his awareness before he hit the ground. His helmet absorbed the worst of it and allowed his muscle memory to take over. Tucking in his limbs, he allowed himself to roll.

Leather ripped. His helmet snapped against the road until his visor was little more than a few shards of Perspex plastic left scattered along the path he had taken. At least, the momentum had drained away. Cadwyn rocked onto his shoulder but there wasn't enough energy behind him to complete the rotation. He flopped onto his back. A solid thud that pushed the last of the air from his lungs. It was a small relief to let his arms drop from his chest.

Nothing's broken.

He would have laughed if he had had breath to do so.

Writhing in pain, he felt his brain slosh around the inside of his skull. Pushing himself up onto his elbows, sucking in a deep breath, he glanced back down the road.

The minotaur thrashed wildly, working the remains of the bike off its horns. Frozen in horror, Cadwyn watched, witnessing the creature's strength as it hurled the mangled bike into the woods without ever placing a hand upon it.

With a thunderous bellow, it turned back to Cadwyn and charged. Cadwyn forced himself up. Every joint in his body screamed in pain. Blood oozed through the places the leathers hadn't been able to properly protect. Cadwyn ripped off his helmet, keeping it gripped tightly in his arms as he sprinted to meet the creature.

At the last moment, the bull once again lowered its head. Cadwyn dropped lower. Due to the beast's colossal size, he was able to pass between its legs. With every ounce of force he had within his power, Cadwyn drove his helmet into the minotaur's crotch.

A pained sound cracked through the silence. Its legs wobbled, its balance thrown off by the abrupt strike and resounding pain. While it toppled forward, Cadwyn got back up onto his feet and spun. The beast was already reaching for him, forcing him to retreat instead of striking its throat as he had intended.

Avoiding one arm brought him into contact with a horn. The razor-sharp tip easily severed his protective leathers and slashed across his chest. Cadwyn ignored the pain and latched onto the horn, forcing the entire weight of his body against it, trying to push the bull's head down. The minotaur merely stretched its neck. But he had his opportunity again.

Grasping the horn with both hands, he drove his knee up. What remained of the protective padding added to the blow and muffled the feel of the beast's crunching larynx. Steam spilled from its mouth to fill the air. It thrashed wildly, easily tossing Cadwyn aside as it choked.

Get up. Get up.

Cadwyn took the blow and scrambled to his feet, desperate not to miss the opening, knowing he might not get another chance. He swung the helmet with both hands. This time, it cracked against the minotaur's eye. The resulting spike of pain and disorientation bought him another few seconds.

Don't let him get off his knees.

Cadwyn shrank back to avoid the wild limbs before surging forward. The combination of his body weight and the creature's confusion helped him bring it down. It took every muscle Cadwyn had, straining to the point of breaking, to crack the minotaur's skull against the road. But the first victory gave him an opening for the next.

Fall back. Strike again.

It was a method that had been trained into him to bring down the people he worked with, but never with this violence. The first streams of blood made Cadwyn gag. His natural instincts told him to stop each time the wounded beast released an animalistic cry.

Fall back. Strike again!

The solid crack of bone became a wet crunch. Blood, brains, and hunks of furry flesh clung to his skin. Pain and fatigue made his arms wobble, forcing him to release the horns in favor of the helmet. Cadwyn hit the beast's skull until it lost all shape, and then continued until his helmet cracked and splintered into useless shards. He hit until he was physically incapable of lifting his arms again.

The minotaur had long since stopped moving by the time Cadwyn flopped back. Thin wisps of steam snaked up from the fresh blood that pooled around him. It was impossible to tell which one of them it belonged to. Adrenaline faded, pain returned, and he found himself barely able to link together a single thought. All he could do was breathe.

His unfocused gaze stared at the canopy above them; blood red leaves shivering against a covering of dense grey clouds. At first, he didn't notice it. Then he absently assumed it was a misfiring of his obviously bruised brain. Red and blue light danced around him, flashed across the trees, and tainted his view.

It wasn't until he heard the crunch of footsteps that it occurred to him it could be on the outside of his malfunctioning brain. He blinked and the feet came to a stop by his skull. He had to squint in order to bring the police officer into view.

"What the hell happened here?" The officer asked.

Cadwyn's mouth jerked into a half smile. "Hi, Trevor. How're the kids?"

CHAPTER 10

Mina sat at the small table by the window. Sunlight streamed through the polished glass, giving her all she needed to study the box in detail. It was the first time she had been able to get a good look at it. Tradition dictated the cube was to be instantly sealed within a thick iron box, the kind used for radioactive material. She had always been told the Selected was allowed to take it back out once they were far enough away from the children. However, that didn't seem to be the case. Her father had refused to even let her near it until they were within the town's café, curiously named Witch's Brew. He had disappeared out the back with her other relatives shortly after they had arrived, leaving Jeremiah with strict instructions to keep her from opening the container. That had lasted only as long as it took for her to reach across the booth.

After studying each side in turn, she had come to one conclusion; she should have bought that magnifying glass keychain she had seen in the store before. Suddenly, it seemed completely practical, and not dorky at all. Growling in frustration, Mina sat back and thought, then shot a question at her brother.

"Do you have your phone on you?"

Jeremiah jolted at the sudden address. "Don't you?"

"It's charging in my bedroom."

Cautiously, her big brother slipped off the distant table and inched his way across the room.

"Don't you dare take the box," she warned him.

"I don't want to touch that thing."

He fished his phone from his back pocket and held it out with the tips of his fingers, keeping himself as far away from the table as he could without throwing his birthday present. Mina struggled to keep from rolling her eyes.

"Can you open it for me, please?"

After unlocking it, he presented it in exactly the same way as before.

"Thanks." She pulled the phone away and quickly clicked off a few photographs.

"What are you doing?" Jeremiah asked.

"I need a magnifying glass."

"You're taking photos," he said.

The stress must be getting to him.

"So I can magnify them," she replied.

He still wasn't getting it. The box held the full focus of his attention, his eyes wide and his breathing shallow.

"You know, zoom in."

"Oh, right," he mumbled absently.

Mina picked up the box to shift the angle of her photographs.

"Do you have to keep touching that thing?" He still had enough sense to keep his voice down.

Neither of them wanted to know just how mad their dad would be to learn that the box was outside the container.

"I want to get a better look at this pattern. It keeps moving."

"What pattern?"

"These squiggles." She zoomed in on one of her photographs to show him what she meant. "See, here? Under the shifting metal bars."

Jeremiah craned his neck to see the screen but didn't dare come any closer to the box.

"Oh, yeah," he murmured.

"At first, I thought they were just decoration. But there's no repetition. The same symbols, odd spacing, not repeating," she thought aloud.

"What are you babbling about?"

She finally looked up. "I think it's a language."

"A language?"

"A language hidden under moving elements on a box with no seams." She couldn't help but feel a bit impressed. "Who would go to this much effort for a prop?"

Jeremiah glared at her. "Are you kidding me? You still think this is fake?"

"Not fake exactly," she admitted. "But exaggerated."

"You were locked in a closet with her."

Mina threw herself back in her seat, remembering just in time not to toss his phone across the room, even if it would have been dramatically fitting.

"I have claustrophobia. You know that. Being in that closet..." She shuddered under the memories that began to prick at the corners of her mind but forced herself to continue. *You need to appear strong if he's going to take you seriously.* "In those circumstances, it would be completely normal for someone with my condition to exaggerate certain things, or even outright hallucinate."

Jeremiah slumped down on a nearby chair. Then, deeming that wasn't enough, smacked his head down against the matching tabletop.

"Everything I experienced can be explained," she insisted.

"What about the box?!" he bellowed to the ceiling, raising his hands for good measure.

She scoffed. "Obviously, it was in the closest before I got there."

Jeremiah released a sound akin to a dying animal as he began to smack his head upon the table repeatedly. Before he could gather himself enough to actually speak, the door to the kitchen swung open and a short girl rushed in.

Mina eyed the Rottweiler that trotted at the girl's side rather than the girl herself. There was something about the gigantic canine that put her on edge. The door smacked open again, letting a boy follow her.

"Basheba! Hey, wait up," the young Korean man called.

The girl in question slowed her pace but didn't stop. "Can you be quick? I've got to go run an errand."

"Well, can I come with you?" His initial nervousness evaporated behind a brilliant smile. "I just thought it would be cool if we could hang out for a bit. You know, get to know each other."

"Why would I want to do that?"

The question left the boy stuck in a state of stunned sputtering. Basheba didn't wait around for him to gather his senses. She was opening the door when she noticed Mina and Jeremiah on the far side of the room.

"Oh, hey!" The boy beamed. "You're Mina, right? I'm Ozzie. We're going into the woods together. Part of the creepy box club. I can mention that in front of him, right?"

"You really can't handle awkward silences, can you?" Basheba asked, watching him from the corner of her eyes.

Mina decided it was best to ignore the snide comment. "This is my brother, Jeremiah. And, yes, he knows all about it."

"What are you doing with your music box?" Ozzie asked, clearly desperate to keep the conversation going.

"Examining it. Would you like to join us?"

"Sure," he said before casting a quick glance to Basheba, almost like asking permission.

"You go right ahead," she said, pulling the door open wider.

"Who's going with you?" Jeremiah asked quickly.

She tilted her head to indicate the dog.

Jeremiah looked to all of them in turn before stammering. "You're one of the Selected. You can't be alone."

"Buck's way more loyal than anyone else around here," she dismissed. "But if it makes you feel better, I'm on my way to pick up Cadwyn."

Ozzie perked up at the name. "Cad?"

"Yeah."

"Picking him up from where?" Mina asked.

"Local jail." She wiggled her mobile phone in the air. "Apparently, they're refusing to let him go without proper supervision."

"You count as proper supervision?" Ozzie asked while Mina inquired about the charges.

Basheba rolled her eyes.

"I'll come with you," Ozzie said.

It took Mina a second to make a decision. Each one of them had a box, so she wouldn't lose the opportunity to study it. On the other hand, being able to question the other Selected like this was likely to pass her by if she stayed. Soon enough, they'd be hiking through the backwoods. *Not an ideal environment to get the truth from anyone,* she determined. Additionally, her parents wouldn't be around to interfere.

"I'd like to stretch my legs."

"Mina," Jeremiah whispered sharply.

"Aren't I supposed to work with them? Isn't that an integral part of this?" she argued.

"But–"

"I'll be okay."

"You say that."

She held up one hand in the Scout's honor salute. "I promise I'll stay with the group at all times."

Jeremiah chewed on his inner cheeks. "Okay. There and back. Give me my phone and if anything happens, have Basheba call me. Got it?"

"Got it." Mina stood up and took a few steps toward the door, before it occurred to her. "Don't tell dad."

"I might not be book smart like you, but I'm not a complete idiot."

To offer him a small measure of reassurance, she closed the radioactive metal box and took the music one with her. Absently rolling the phone over and over between his hands, he offered her a weak smile and watched her go. They had barely gotten a yard away from the café door before Jeremiah raced after them.

"What's wrong?"

Jeremiah drew her into a crushing hug, his arms shaking as badly as his stammered breaths.

"Just come back, Mina. Okay? Come back."

"I will. I promise." *None of this is real,* she told herself sharply. And she meant it. Every word. But that didn't stop her from returning his hug with matching intensity. "Just keep dad out of my hair for a bit, okay?"

"Yeah. And I'll keep the tide from going out, too," Jeremiah snorted.

Finally, he let go and rushed back into the café. A cold chill swept down her spine when he was out of sight. *It's nothing. You're just being paranoid.* Righting her thoughts, she crammed the box into her jacket pocket, forcing the seams to their snapping point. Ozzie gave her a warm smile when she finally looked away from the Witch's Brew.

"So." She tried to sound as casual as possible. "Where's the police station?"

Ozzie's thick dark eyebrows knitted together.

"I only found out this place existed yesterday," he chuckled nervously. "I thought you'd know the way. I mean, I know you haven't gone into the woods before, but you come here every year, don't you?"

"No. This is my first time in Black River."

"Oh."

For a split second, the warmth in Ozzie's dark eyes flickered like a small flame in the wind. It allowed her to see the fear he had kept hidden beneath. A sharp breath and the warm was back.

"Neither of us should be in charge of the map, huh?"

Rattled by what she had seen, Mina struggled to return his smile. "I guess so."

"Hey, Basheba?"

They both turned to discover the short girl was already halfway down Main Street. They had to run to catch up. Mina had to hand it to Basheba. It took a certain level of commitment to remain completely oblivious to two people standing only a few feet away. Ozzie's first few attempts to draw her into conversation fell flat and he was soon grappling for topics.

"Looks like she's been here a bit," Ozzie said to Mina. "We should definitely give her the compass."

Basheba turned down a side street, absentmindedly giving her dog a playful nudge and smiling at his overreaction.

Mina took pity on him and decided to take a run at Basheba herself. "I was told you've been in the woods before."

The dog paid more attention to them than its owner did.

"Have I done something to upset you?" Ozzie asked.

"No," Basheba replied.

While she didn't turn around, she did manage to sound honestly confused as to how he could have come to such a conclusion. Mina and Ozzie shared a glance, each clearly hoping the other would somehow know how to handle the small woman.

Before they could sort out a plan of attack, they had reached the police station. A reception desk separated the small waiting area from the larger back. A few scattered desks filled the space, topped with more books and takeaway containers than paperwork. A row of thick black bars turned the back corner into a series of holding cells.

"You can't just walk back there," Mina whispered harshly.

It wasn't a surprise that Basheba didn't listen. She pushed through the low swinging gate and into the back office. Her dog leaped the aged wood to follow.

"Ladies first?" Ozzie said with a shrug.

It was getting harder for Mina to keep a tight grip on the frustration growing inside of her. "This is how people get shot."

"Huh. Hey, what do you think will happen if we were shot before we have to go into the woods?"

Mina fled from that question by grudgingly trailing along behind the older girl, leaving Ozzie to follow. Almost in unison, they entered the restricted area and the staff bathroom door flung open. Ozzie jerked back a step, as if contemplating outrunning the law enforcement officer. Holding up one hand to steady him, Mina straightened her spine and fixed a gentle but polite smile upon her lips. Before she could speak, however, Basheba greeted the man with an energetic and almost childish glee.

"Trevor! I missed you!"

She raced to the man. Instead of surprise, the taller man scooped down and caught her around the hip, lifting her clean off her feet. One quick spin, and he placed her back down.

"Oh, look at you. You must have grown half a foot," Trevor beamed, ruffling her hair. His skin seemed a dozen shades darker against her golden hair.

"Does he know she's in her twenties?" Ozzie whispered in Mina's ear.

Mina shook her head, captivated by the sight before her, "I don't think he does."

"Now, what are you doing here?"

Basheba giggled and clasped her hands behind her back, twisting her torso like a proud child.

"I'm here to pick up Cadwyn."

Trevor frowned, "He called you?"

"Why wouldn't he?" Basheba pouted.

Suspicion crossed his face, and she matched it. However, she kept a certain adorable charm to her glare, which soon had the man chuckling.

"I'm sure you know what you're doing, little poppet," Trevor dismissed.

Crouching down, he called the dog over. The move effectively hid his face from Mina's line of sight and kept her from getting a good read on the man. The towering beast of a dog wallowed happily in the officer's attention, tongue lolling out the side of its jaws and tail whipping about as he leaned into the body rubs.

"Who's this gorgeous boy?"

"That's my dog, Buck," Basheba beamed with pride.

Mina managed to catch Basheba's gaze over the distracted officer's shoulders. The innocent façade slipped like a mask to reveal a small smirk. No more than that. But it spoke volumes and made a slither of ice coil in the pit of her stomach. The front door burst open, allowing a very loud elderly woman to come waddling inside. Trevor's head snapped up and Basheba instantly resumed her performance.

"I've got to go take care of that."

"Okie dokie," Basheba chirped.

The officer barely hesitated before holding up his hand, the cell key dangling from one finger.

"You need to give this back to me before you go."

Basheba nodded rapidly, sending her hair flying. "I will. Cross my heart and hope to die."

"Good girl." He placed the key in Basheba's cupped hands and headed off to the front of the station.

The second his back was turned, Basheba's smile dropped, her eyes grew cold, and she stalked toward the cells.

Mina rushed to catch up. "Exactly how old does he think you are?"

"No idea," she dismissed. "If I ask, people start looking at the details and it spoils the illusion."

Ozzie joined the group. "I always hate it when people think I'm a kid."

"You are a kid," Basheba said.

"And why tell the truth when the lie lets you manipulate a police officer?" Mina added.

For once, the blonde paused and turned toward her. "You disapprove?"

"I do."

Basheba hummed thoughtfully. "It's a good thing I don't care about your opinion then, isn't it? Otherwise, you might have actually hurt my feelings."

"What is it people say about burning bridges?" The voice drifted groggily to them from the furthest cell. The one tucked into the corner.

"That it makes good kindling?" Basheba replied.

The roll of her eyes wasn't enough to hide her smile. It was small but honest and instantly spiked Mina's curiosity. She decided to keep her mouth shut and watch the interaction unfold.

A mound that Mina had mistaken as blankets heaved as a man worked his way out from under it. Rich brown hair flopped over his forehead in sweaty strips. A fledgling bruise had started to claim the sharp peak of his right cheekbone. The remains of a nosebleed stained his upper lip and dried blood coated his shirt. Finally succeeding in freeing his long legs, he hunched forward and braced his elbows on his knees.

"What happened to you?" Ozzie asked.

"I beat a minotaur to death with my helmet," Cadwyn grinned. "How was your morning?"

"A real minotaur?" Mina snapped despite herself.

"You killed it?" Ozzie asked.

Basheba straightened, "Are those my pretzels?"

CHAPTER 11

"Wait, you weren't arrested?" Ozzie asked, squinting as they left the station and reentered the sunlight. He kept glancing over his shoulder, sure Trevor would chase them down. "I thought you were arrested. Don't you have to sign something or talk to someone?"

Cadwyn smiled as he stretched his arms over his head. His teeth were long, sharper than the norm, and slightly stained pink with blood. Ozzie averted his gaze to the Halloween decorated streets, trying to quell the queasy feeling steadily trickling into his stomach.

"Trevor wouldn't dare cross me after what happened last time," Basheba commented.

Ozzie's gut tightened. "What happened last time?"

Cadwyn stifled his humor to give him an actual answer. "She's just messing with you, Ozzie. Which is mean."

He clearly said the last sentence in reprimand of Basheba. She ignored him.

"I wasn't arrested," Cadwyn continued. "Trevor was just letting me sleep in the cells until he could hand off responsibility of me to someone else."

"Responsibility?" Mina pushed.

"Black River doesn't have a hospital, and the local doctor is a quack. I refused to see him."

"I don't get it," Ozzie said.

"Having found him, Trevor would have a duty of care over Cadwyn," Mina explained. "Cadwyn has a right to refuse medical treatment, of course. But can you imagine the legal and ethical nightmare Trevor would find himself in if he just let Cadwyn wander around and die of his injuries?"

Ozzie gave that some thought. "So, Trevor's covering his butt? Why couldn't you just say that?"

Mina takes herself too seriously. The glare she threw Ozzie's way made that little bit of information blatantly clear. Shrinking away from her annoyance, Ozzie found his attention drawn to Cadwyn's blood-soaked shirt.

The man's biker gear had protected most of his body, but it gaped in the front where it had been slashed open, allowing glimpses of the bandages wrapped around his torso. The majority of the material was still pristine, white as snow against the midnight black of his leathers. But blood had started to seep through to the surface. Little crimson dots that seemed to grow before Ozzie's eyes. The vibrant color filled his vision.

"Maybe we should take you to the doctor," Ozzie said before swallowing thickly.

Cadwyn made a sneak attack for Basheba's yogurt pretzels. It earned him an elbow to the ribs. Not hard, just enough to make him jerk away. The motion must have reopened the wound because fresh blood pushed against his bandages.

"You're bleeding," Ozzie said weakly.

"It's just a little seepage. Completely normal for new stitches," Cadwyn assured.

The comment drew Mina's attention. "Trevor knows that kind of first aid?"

"No," he chuckled. "I did it myself."

After being rebuffed from the snacks, Cadwyn began rummaging through the bright red bag he had retrieved from Trevor's desk before they left. Ozzie had dismissed the fat backpack as Cadwyn's luggage, but now, as the older man searched through the numerous pockets, he caught sight of the medical symbol embroidered on the top. *A medical bag,* he realized. Ozzie found himself strangely disappointed. *It doesn't look like the ones they use in the movies.*

With a grunt of victory, the nurse pulled free what he had been searching for. A beaten-up pack of cigarettes.

"Maybe we should still take you to a doctor," Ozzie said.

"Why does no one take my degree seriously?" he mumbled around a cigarette, already fumbling with a lighter.

"They do," Basheba said. "They just don't take *you* seriously."

One well-practiced strike of his thumb got his Zippo to work, and he glared at her over the steady flame.

"Thanks for the clarification."

"Anytime." Basheba's smile faded when the tall man managed to snatch a handful of the pretzels out of the bag.

"I will burn you," Basheba declared. "Don't try me."

The threat made Ozzie's chest tighten. He didn't doubt for a moment that she meant it. Cadwyn, however, only chuckled. Even though he towered over the woman beside him, the nurse still tilted his head back to blow a lungful of smoke into the air.

Mina cocked her head to the side, "You're a medical professional."

"So I know exactly how bad this is." With the slender cigarette nipped between two fingers, he took a long drag and blew the smoke above them once more. "Don't smoke kids."

While his words remained playful, there was an undeniable shift in Cadwyn's tone. Something colder. Almost bitter. *Don't judge their coping mechanisms.*

"I need either a nap or a coffee," Cadwyn said, gingerly rolling his shoulders. He exchanged his cigarette with a pretzel. "These things don't have enough sugar to keep me awake."

"If we survive, you're buying me a new pack," Basheba grumbled.

"A minotaur ran you off the road!" Mina's enraged outburst made everyone flinch.

Their small group stopped in the middle of a residential street and turned their attention to her.

"That's right," Cadwyn said.

Mina's jaw dropped. "You expect us to believe that?"

"Why would I lie?"

Don't bring me into this, Ozzie silently pleaded. It didn't stop Mina from turning to him for backup.

"Can't you see none of this makes sense?"

Ozzie winced, not sure what to say, or whom he was better off isolating.

"Where do I even start?" she declared.

Cadwyn took another deep draw of his cigarette and said, "Throw them at me in any order."

"All right." Planting her feet, she crossed her arms over her chest. "How did you survive a bike crash with only minor injuries?"

If Mina was expecting a reaction beyond a smirk, she was disappointed.

"Everyone in the four families should know how to fall. Not that the additional training didn't help."

"Someone trained you?" Mina asked. "To fall?"

"Fall, absorb impact, take the pain and keep going," he nodded.

"That's some strange training for a nurse, isn't it?"

Basheba didn't stop chewing as she cut in, "He's a psych nurse at a hospital for the criminally insane. Don't you know violence against medical professionals is a real problem?"

"Besides that, bikes are death traps. No one should ride one unless they know how to crash them." Almost as if he had momentarily forgotten about Mina, he turned to the short girl beside him. "Now that your car's totaled, are you going to get a bike? Maybe a side cart for Buck? Ginger's expanding *Ride or Die*. She'll have room for you in the program."

"I sleep in my car."

"It sounds so sad when you say it like that."

"You should give Ginger a call. She might make you her poster boy." Basheba raised her hands for emphasis. "My program kept this idiot alive."

"Slightly hurtful."

Mina's frustrated groan brought the pair back into her interrogation.

"For the sake of argument, I'll concede you know how to fall and that was enough to save you. It's a long shot, but okay."

"That's clearly the sound of conceding," Basheba noted.

"How did you kill it with your bare hands?"

"Determination and a deep reservoir of resentment," Cadwyn mumbled around his quickly disappearing cigarette.

"From what I remember, minotaurs are heavily muscled beasts," Mina pressed. "It's a little unbelievable someone like you could kill one with your bare hands, don't you think?"

As subtly as he could, Ozzie inched a bit further away from Mina's side, not wanting to get caught up in the dark looks that were now being sent in her direction. Especially since Basheba started that creepy smiling again.

"And what do you think I can kill?" Basheba asked.

Mina ignored the question and switched tactics. "And your whole story goes against the established legends. I've always been told the demons can't cause physical injury until the box is opened."

Basheba laughed. A sweet little cackle that held an edge of mania. It was Cadwyn who replied.

"We're in Black River, Mina. I was passing by the Witch Woods."

"So?"

Instantly, Basheba's humor fell away. "You have to be kidding me. Didn't your daddy teach you anything?"

"The Witch Woods is Katrina's home turf. She can do things there that she can't do anywhere else."

"With all due respect, Cadwyn, what does that mean?"

"It means if you can't wrap your brilliant mind around the idea of a guy with a bull head, you're not going to last," Basheba said, her humor flooding back into her voice.

Mina bristled, the muscles in her jaw twitched as she met

Basheba's cool gaze.

"Cadwyn," Mina said, still staring at the small girl before her. "You killed it. Then Trevor found you. Is that right?"

"Yes."

"Then Trevor must have seen the corpse. He didn't strike me as a man who has just seen a mythical beast brought to life."

It clearly enraged Mina that Basheba lazily selected another pretzel. She shifted her weight from one foot to the other, her pretty face growing taut.

If Basheba noticed, she didn't care. "It's almost as if it's not the weirdest thing he's seen around these parts."

"Then where is it?" Mina snapped. "There has to be a corpse. He wouldn't have just left it on the road for anyone to find. So where's the body, Basheba?"

"Because that's something she would know," Cadwyn cut in.

Basheba grunted, took her time swallowing, then said, "Funeral home."

Doubt crossed Mina's face for the first time. "I'm not sure I follow."

"Well, let's use logic," Basheba said, paying more attention to her dwindling rations. "There's no hospital around these parts. The funeral home is the only place decked out to take care of a corpse if they felt like holding onto it. If they don't, the crematorium and graveyard are nice and close."

Nonchalantly, she stared at the woman and continued munching.

"I'm just guessing this last bit, but I'm envisioning this thing as being really buff. Heavy. Not something you can shove into the back of a police cruiser. So that big old hearse the funeral home has would be pretty convenient for transportation." She turned abruptly to Cadwyn. "These things are making me thirsty, have you got any water?"

He quickly produced a bottle and handed it over. "You know,

that's a pretty good idea."

Somehow, she managed to hum quizzically while chugging half of the bottle's contents.

He lowered his voice to elaborate. "They do have a distinct lack of practical experience."

Once more, Ozzie found his thoughts spiraling beyond his control. All that toppled out of his mouth was, "I can see it?"

"Funeral home's right around the corner," Cadwyn said cheerfully.

Basheba released a disgruntled humph.

"What else have you got to do with your day?" Cadwyn asked.

"Sleep, mostly."

"Damn, that does sound good."

"No, this will be very educational," Mina cut in. She smiled up at the towering man. "Please, show me the minotaur."

It then turned into a staring contest between the two girls, each one daring the other to back down. Eventually, Basheba smiled. Small and sweet and with a predatory edge.

"You know what? Let's go. There is no foreseeable way this could go wrong."

Mina's unspoken confidence only grew when Basheba turned on one delicate heel and stalked off, Buck trotting along beside her.

Cadwyn cringed as he watched her go. "That right there is the air horn of warning signs. We probably should change our plans before we see what she's thinking."

"I'd like to see it," Mina declared.

Keeping her spine rod straight, she stomped off after Basheba. Ozzie wasn't sure what he was supposed to do, so he was grateful when Cadwyn patted him on the back of his shoulder. He offered him a warm smile.

"I guess we should catch up with them before they get themselves into trouble."

He couldn't argue with that. *We have to get them on the same page,* Ozzie thought desperately as he followed behind the girls. But no matter how hard he thought about it, he couldn't come up with a way to get them to that point.

Basheba cut across the road, rounded a corner, and followed the new street until the forest blocked their way. A quaint white house stood alone to their right. It was pressed slightly into the woods, making room for the graveyard that started before them and rolled up over a nearby hill. Gray stones dotted the frost-bitten grass. Most were chipped and dulled by centuries of storms and had sunken into the earth to stand at strange angles. A few still held their original polish. It was easy to pick them out when the sun peeked from behind the gathering clouds to make them glisten.

People milled around the gravestones, some following tour guides in brightly colored coats while others made their own way around. A few graves in particular seemed to draw their attention. They clustered around the stones, posing for photos before swarming in like bees. Ozzie was too busy trying to figure out what they were doing to notice that Basheba had stopped walking.

"Sorry," he mumbled after colliding into her back.

Basheba didn't acknowledge him. A deep flush steadily crept into her cheeks as she watched the flow of tourists. It looked like she was going to scream. The illusion ended when she choked down a staggered breath.

She's trying not to cry, Ozzie realized.

"What are they doing?" he asked aloud.

"A few of our relatives are buried up there," Cadwyn said.

Ozzie looked from the people to Basheba and back.

"I don't get it."

"We're a tourist attraction," Cadwyn answered in a whisper. "The cursed lines of the Bell Witch."

"Are they putting chalk on one?"

The older man held off answering until he had snubbed out his first cigarette and lit a new one.

"That's Katrina's grave," he said, once again blowing the fumes above their heads. "Recently put up, of course. Convicted witches weren't buried on hallowed ground."

"Are they leaving a mark?"

"Oh, that's new, too. Leave a mark and get a wish. I haven't got a clue who came up with that."

Suddenly, Basheba burst into motion. Only Buck had anticipated it and she was entering the graveyard gates before the others thought to follow. They somehow managed to lose her within the thin crowd.

"There!" Mina said.

She pointed up the hill. It was easier to notice Buck's black coat than the blonde.

"What's she holding?" Mina asked.

"A rake?" Ozzie suggested.

Cadwyn broke into a sprint. "She found the gardener's shed."

A tour had just started up the hill, the meandering guests blocking Ozzie and Mina's path and slowed them down enough that they only got halfway up before chaos broke out. Shouts of protests and demands for answers were covered by Buck's menacing snarls.

Mina abruptly grabbed Ozzie's wrist and brought him to a stop. Side by side, they watched as Basheba attacked a gravestone with the metal teeth of the rake, chipping off pieces with every swing. Cadwyn swooped in to block off the few people brave enough to risk Buck's wrath. Eventually, she drove the tip of the rake into the soft earth by the base of the headstone. It took all of her weight bearing down on the opposite end to leverage it out.

With a few startled cries, the stone toppled, flopping down the hillside with heavy thuds. Basheba wiped the sweat from her forehead, tossed the rake aside, and started back down to the main gate as if nothing had happened.

She walked over the fallen stone and made it back to Mina and Ozzie before the crowd caught up with her. Buck and Cadwyn still tried to hold them back, but it was an impossible task. Now that they were close enough, Ozzie could pick a few sentences out from the general, belligerent noise.

"What the hell is your problem?" A woman screamed, pushing aside Cadwyn's arm to get a few steps closer. "I'm calling the police."

"Fine," Basheba dismissed.

"Who do you think you are?"

Ozzie couldn't pinpoint who had spoken, but Basheba whirled on them like an angered snake, reared up and ready to strike.

"That bitch doesn't get to be buried near my family!" Each word cracked like thunder. Far louder than her small form would give credit for.

The stunned silence didn't last. Like coming rain, the questions were sporadic at first and then joined into a sudden downpour. Some wanted to know which of the four families she belonged to. Others asked for a photograph, while even more amongst them moved about the phones they were recording with to try and catch her face. Basheba shouldered past Ozzie and Mina.

"Let's go."

It was Buck more than Cadwyn who kept the crowd from following them from the graveyard. With fang and threat, he blocked the way until the group had reformed by the funeral home. The door wasn't locked. Basheba flung it open before whistling softly. Buck yelped in acknowledgment and raced toward them, paws kicking up clumps of earth and head lowered with dedicated purpose.

"Good job!" Basheba bent over and opened her arms wide, welcoming the slobbering, excitable dog into her embrace. Her voice was light but crackled around the edges. "Who's the best boy in the whole wide world?"

"Is it me?" Cadwyn asked as he closed the door behind them, fixing the lock just in case anyone thought to follow.

"You're lovely and all." She dropped into baby talk and cupped Buck's floppy cheeks. "But how can you compete with this face? Look at it. Look at his beautiful face."

"Well, you have me there."

She wrapped her arms around Buck's neck. The dog accepted the embrace, standing strong like a sentinel as Basheba progressively looked smaller. Ozzie shuffled his weight and locked his eyes onto the floor. The small sign of vulnerability was obviously not meant to be viewed by anyone, least of all a stranger like him. *I wonder if her dad's grave is up there.*

"That was a crime," Mina declared, breaking the uneasy silence. "You can't just destroy property like that."

Basheba rolled her eyes. "Who's going to stop me?"

Mina crossed her arms over her chest. "You might have to spend the night in jail."

"Good," she responded. In response to their startled looks, she said, "What? I don't want to stay with my uncle and the hotel doesn't take dogs. The cell is kind of my best option."

It was the first opening Ozzie had found to make himself useful, and he latched onto it. "I'll make sure the hotel takes you and Buck in. Don't worry about it."

"Exactly how can you do that?" Mina challenged.

Ozzie shrugged one shoulder. "If all else fails, I'll buy the place."

"I always forget how rich you guys are," Cadwyn noted. "If we're going to see the bull, we probably should get moving. One of those guys is definitely going to call the cops."

"We can't just walk down there," Mina said.

Basheba smirked and stalked across the room. "Again, I ask, who's going to stop me?"

"Whoever locked the door," Mina replied.

Both Basheba and Cadwyn broke into laughter.

"That's so cute," Cadwyn said. "You think people lock their doors around here. Did you not notice how easy it was to get in?"

It bothered Ozzie that, once again, Basheba knew exactly where she was going. She had no problem finding the back door that opened up to the basement, or the light switch inconveniently placed a few steps downs.

The stench of chemicals wafted out. It was only faint traces, but it burned his nose and lodged in his throat like sharp stones. He reeled back, smacking into Cadwyn who was hurriedly snuffing out his cigarette in a nearby pot plant.

"What is that?" Mina asked, one hand gently covering her nose.

"Formaldehyde," Cadwyn said. "The sweet rotten apple undertone is most likely glutaraldehyde."

"I'm failing chemistry," Ozzie said.

Burying his cigarette butt under a handful of potting soil, he elaborated simply. "Embalming fluids. Highly flammable embalming fluids. That we shouldn't be able to smell so strongly from up here."

The last sentence was directed at Basheba. Still standing a few paces down the staircase, she hesitantly turned to look at him, like she didn't want to turn her back on the stark white tiles lining the walls of the basement. Ozzie clamped a hand over his nose and pushed closer.

It wasn't hard to look over her shoulder. The lower floor looked exactly how Ozzie had imagined. Sterile and clean, with metal surfaces that gleamed under the harsh glare of the overhead lights. He tried not to look at the array of scalpels and bone saws arranged on the table. *Why do they have a microwave? What are they cooking?*

He could barely catch sight of the far wall, the one pressed up against the graveyard. The vast amount of sunlight promised there was a window there, but all he could see were rows of heavy metal shelving crammed with bottles. A single silver table stood in the middle of the room. It was empty.

Ozzie barely stifled his yelp when Cadwyn latched onto his arm and roughly yanked him back, throwing him against the opposite wall. Before he could understand what had just happened, Mina was slammed against his chest, forcing the air from his lungs. Cadwyn braced one arm against the doorframe as he reached for the short blonde.

Buck's attention was locked onto something unseen down the stairs. Shoulders hunched and teeth bared. Basheba turned. There was just enough time to see the fear in her eyes before the door slammed shut.

CHAPTER 12

The fluorescent lights buzzed like hornets as they flickered. Basheba pushed herself back against the door, feeling the wood rattle as Cadwyn fought to open it. She assumed it was Cadwyn. *The other two have no reason to bother.* Buck's claws scratched at the stairs as he staggered back and forth, desperate to attack, but awaiting her command. Rattling metal hinted at movement below. Something large and unseen.

"Basheba!" Cadwyn screamed.

Her hands began to shake, her heart picking up pace until she could barely breathe around it.

"Basheba!"

The scrape of flesh on tile drew closer. Shadows moved and merged as something lumbered ever closer to the bottom of the stairs.

"What's going on?" Cadwyn bellowed before striking the door in anger. "Talk to me!"

Darkness engulfed the foot of the stairs. A wall of shadows that only slightly dissipated in the staggered light. The thick body of the minotaur blocked the entire width of the stairs. It dwarfed her. Thick bands of muscles covered its chest, swelling with every snorted breath.

Most of the damage was to its skull. Spikes of bone protruded through matted tufts of fur, severing the flesh and leaving it to hang in strips. One horn still protruded proudly from its temple while the other was twisted back to resemble a goat. An eye dangled alongside its mangled snout, twisting in its steaming breath.

Basheba pressed harder against the door but there was nowhere to retreat to. The minotaur took a step closer.

"Get them out," Basheba stammered.

Cadwyn instantly replied, "What?"

Buck's snarls turned wild and savage, a ferocious sound that she felt down to her bone marrow. Basheba balled her fists until her arms trembled and her knuckles threatened to pop. She tried to draw in a deep breath and found herself choking on the chemical stench.

"Get them out!" she bellowed.

Cadwyn paused, slammed against the door again, and shouted back, "Stay away from the chemicals, Basheba!"

The sentence would have made her laugh if the scent of formaldehyde wasn't lodged like a dagger in her throat.

Will it kill me?

On the other side of the immovable wood, she could catch traces of movement; mumbled words she couldn't understand and pattering feet.

They're gone. I'm alone.

She had asked for it, and yet, the reality gutted her. The first bitter sob forced her to double over, one hand pressing tight against her stomach as if to keep everything from spilling out. Buck raged as the bull staggered forward, taking its first step onto the staircase.

Amongst the chaos, the sound of the music box rang out, filling her ears and leaving her cold. Decades of hate rose up to meet the sound, filling her with a visceral rage that left her trembling.

"Buck." Her whisper silenced the dog. It waited for her command. Glaring at the deformed face of the bull, she spoke one word. "Kill."

Nails slashed over timber as the colossal dog burst into motion. Halfway down, he launched himself at the monstrosity, wide jaws seeking flesh. The bull-man swung out a thick arm. But it underestimated both Buck's agility and his ferociousness.

Taking the blow to his torso, Buck twisted around and latched onto the beast's arm. Blood gushed from between his fangs. Bones cracked and flesh tore into strips. The minotaur thrashed and jerked in a desperate attempt to dislodge the Rottweiler.

Basheba ran for the small gap between the colossal beast and the wall. It was barely anything, but her tiny form didn't need much. The minotaur twisted just as she threaded herself through. Pain exploded across her back as a mammoth arm struck her spine and sent her careening through the air. She didn't have time to suck in a breath before she hit the far wall. Medical tools scattered around her as gravity dumped her on the bench. Sparks raced along her veins, exploding behind her eyes and whiting out her vision. A pained yelp made her head snap up.

Built from dense muscle, Buck weighed far more than she did. He flew through the air as a dark blur but landed short of the wall, sliding the rest of the distance to the side of the cabinet. No sooner had he hit the floor than he was up again, shaking blood from his muzzle, baring his fangs as he attacked.

The minotaur bellowed in fury and charged forward, trying to catch Buck with hand and horn. The dog evaded each attack, circled the beast, snapping and snarling for the minotaur's neck. The sight pushed Basheba into action. She scrambled off of the bench and snatched up a scalpel. A small plastic sheath protected her fingers from the razor tip.

Now that she was on level with the beast, its size was overwhelming. It was three times her height, broader than her entire length.

She dropped to the ground, uncapping the scalpel as she rolled under the examination table in the center of the room. It only took a few seconds for an opportunity to present itself. Basheba lashed out from her hiding place, one hand cupping the front of the humanoid shin while she raked the deadly tip across the back of its ankle. The Achilles tendon snapped with a sudden gush of blood and an agonized wail.

Basheba flung herself back under the table. Buck roared. Blood slicked the tiles. Metal squealed and crumbled as the minotaur stuck the top of the table.

Tiles turned to shrapnel under the twisted metal. Basheba scurried back, barely getting a foot away before the minotaur grabbed the edge of the table and ripped it back. Fear locked her joints. She couldn't move as the mutilated, mammoth creature loomed over her.

Buck surged forward, exploiting the distraction to leap off the exposed underside of the table and latch onto the minotaur's throat. His paws dangled as the beast staggered back. Basheba didn't know if it was the added weight, the sudden attack, or the snapped tendon, but the result was the same. The minotaur buckled. The ground shook as it dropped onto its knees. Buck thrashed his head, opening the wound and turning everything crimson.

It'll get his arms around Buck.

The thought propelled her up. A few steps and she was at the metal rack. Chemical bottles filled the shelves with a narrow window clearly intended for ventilation mounted in the wall above it. Bottles toppled as Basheba scaled the shelving. One hand shoved open the window the minotaur must have closed. Fresh air rushed in, its touch making her remember the steady burn in her lungs.

She jumped back down and scanned the shelf. *Formaldehyde.* With the heavy plastic bottle in one hand and the scalpel in the other, she sprinted back to the dueling animals. It had just gathered enough sense in its mangled mind to reach for the Rottweiler as she approached.

"Buck!" she commanded in a rush. "Release!"

Instantly, he let go. Without his grip, he dropped, narrowly avoiding the minotaur's groping hands.

The side of the scalpel pressed against the palm of her hand as she latched onto the twisted goat horn. Yanking hard, she tried to knock it off balance and buy herself another few seconds. But, with a wet, sucking sound, the horn ripped free of the scalp.

The monstrosity bellowed and struck blindly. Retreating, Basheba called for her dog and thrust a trembling hand to the window.

"Up."

He obediently bolted for the window, leaping from one shelf to the next until he could work his body through the gap. Once outside, he spun around and resumed barking, calling for her to follow. Gathering the last of her courage, Basheba held the bottle between both hands and drove it down upon the remaining horn with all of her strength.

The tip easily pierced the bottom of the bottle. A glug of liquid burst out and the air became unbreathable. She gagged and sputtered, her eyes watering and the skin around her nose burning. It looked like water. It burned like acid.

The bull-man's scream shook the walls. It was a broken, animalistic, tortured wail that twisted up her gut. The outburst of pain wasn't enough to quell the fire burning in her veins. She wiggled the bottle to widen the hole, leaping back to avoid the increased flow. There was no escaping the fumes.

Holding her breath rather than fighting for it, she darted around the flailing arms of the melting minotaur and sprinted for the bench. Without pause, she tossed the scalpel into the microwave and set the dial. It wasn't until she hit 'start' that she realized she had no idea how long it would take for the sparks to start.

Panic made her run faster than she ever thought possible. The shelves rattled wildly as she scrambled up, wiggling the bolts that attached it to the wall until the concrete chipped away. She clung to the window's edge as the shelving toppled from under her feet. Buck latched onto the back of her shirt, dragging her faster than she could crawl.

"Run!" Basheba's scream was broken by hacks and coughs. She could barely breathe.

Forcing herself up onto all fours, she was finally able to get her feet under her.

"Run!"

Through the tangle of her hair, she spotted Cadwyn and the others rounding the building. She could tell the exact moment that he caught the stench of mixing chemicals.

"Up the hill!" he bellowed, waving his arms to urge the gathering tourists to back up.

None of them listened. She didn't bother to stick around and explain. Weaving through the first thin layer of onlookers, she followed Cadwyn's advice and set her gaze on the crest.

Two more failed attempts to get people to move and Cadwyn decided to switch tactics.

"Toxic gas!"

His words incited panic. The flames that spewed from the windows of the building like it was the pits of hell caused a stampede. Explosions ripped the funeral home apart, creating fiery comets that rained down upon them. Black smoke billowed up from the points of impact, blurring her vision, leaving her unable to see the headstones before she was inches from them.

Weaving around the camouflaged obelisks and bashing into people, Basheba lost track of everyone around her. Heat filled the air as the inferno built upon itself, fed itself, grew into lapping flames that yearned to spread to the neighboring woods and shake the ground with new blasts. The hill seemed insurmountable until she broke free of the lingering smoke and the peak came into sight.

Her legs grew heavier with every step. Fire rippled down her throat and her eyes felt like embers. There wasn't anything left within her when she reached the top of the hill. She dropped, propping herself up against the nearest headstone, and tried to steady her breathing.

I just need enough to whistle. Buck will come when I whistle.

Each attempt turned into ragged coughs.

"Basheba," Cadwyn said as he dropped to one knee beside her.

"Didn't I say to leave the chemicals alone? I distinctly remember telling you to leave the damned chemicals alone."

"I knew I forgot something," Basheba croaked.

She flinched as he placed a small plastic dome over her nose and mouth, pulling the attached elastic back to keep it in place. *Oxygen tank,* she realized as breathing became easier. *He comes prepared.*

"Buck," she whispered.

"I'll get your dog in a second," he said. "Just stay still."

Basheba didn't see Mina but heard her clearly over the crush of noise around her. "You set it on fire."

"You are clever," Basheba said, suddenly too tired to keep her head up.

She dropped her head back against the cool gravestone and surveyed the chaos around her. Some people screamed, grasping at fresh wounds, while even more stood in shock. Beside her, a man with an accent she couldn't place was trying to gather people to go back down and fight the flames. In a clean leap, Cadwyn stood on the rounded top of a gravestone.

"Shut up!"

He roared the words, filled them with such authority the crowd quieted down to listen. Thrusting his bright red medical bag up over his head, he continued.

"Does everyone see the medical seal? That means I'm in charge! No one is to go down the hill!"

"We have to put the fire out," the accented man argued.

Cadwyn was having none of it. "That's a funeral parlor. It's chock full of corrosive chemicals that create poisonous gas. Here, we are upwind and have clean air flow. Down there, the fumes will either kill you, or help you develop a lot of cancer later in life."

The group shuffled anxiously but didn't speak of going down again. Softening his tone, Cadwyn continued.

"I need all the able-bodied people I can get to help me tend to the wounded." He crouched down and placed a hand on the man's shoulder. "Help me. Please."

Basheba couldn't understand how the forced contact actually calmed the man down. But that, matched with Cadwyn's beseeching gaze, was enough to get the entire group of men to agree. Straightening once more, he allotted tasks to the tour guides. The first was to call the police and the other the fire department. Both of them had strict instructions to explain the dangers of the fire.

"Hands up if you're a local!" He gave them a second to comply. "Call your family, your friends, that weird neighbor. Every number you have. Tell them all to get downwind. As far north as they can. Get in a house and keep all the doors and windows closed. Make sure to tell them to take their pets and any children they're particularly fond of."

Basheba watched with no small sense of awe as the crowd obeyed his commands.

"Everyone else, we're going to set up a triage. Anyone who's wounded but conscious goes by the Leanna Winthrop grave. Head injuries by Rebecca Bell. Anyone unconscious we're going to move above the gas line. Work together. Be gentle. Then have someone sit next to them and put a hand up. I'll come as soon as I can. Oh, and if anyone with minimal injuries gets in my way demanding immediate treatment, I will make sure you never feel pain again. Understood? Okay, let's do this."

He jumped down and, before setting to his tasks, grabbed Ozzie by the front of his shirt. "Stick close to me."

"Yes, sir," Ozzie nodded without hesitation.

Bag gripped tight, Cadwyn stalked away, throwing the order over his shoulder. "Mina, take care of Basheba."

Mina stammered but slumped down on the damp earth. After a long moment, she shook her head and muttered.

"You set the place on fire."

Basheba pulled the mask back enough to mutter, "Yeah, I know."

Mina made no attempt to smother her scoff and Basheba didn't bother pretending to care. Taking as deep a breath as she was capable of, she pursed her lips and blew. Still no whistle.

"And the minotaur?" Mina asked abruptly.

"I doubt it got out."

"Convenient."

"Not really. I almost died, you know."

Finally, she was able to force a weak but full whistle. She held her breath until she heard the answering bark. An instant later, Buck was licking her face, leaving smears of minotaur blood as he tried to crawl onto her lap.

"You're not going to get away with this," Mina noted. "Destruction of property, arson, releasing poisonous chemicals in a residential neighborhood. All of it with witnesses. You're getting arrested. You know that, right?"

She chuckled, "Okay, Mina. Sure thing."

"Do you really think you're this untouchable? That a whole town will turn a blind eye?"

Smiling bitterly, Basheba rested her chin atop Buck's head. "Welcome to Black River. Where no one locks up the human sacrifices."

CHAPTER 13

Madness or mass corruption? The question had kept Mina up all night. Even now, as the four families overwhelmed the small parking lot, it replayed in her mind. She couldn't understand how Basheba had been allowed to walk free after what she had done. But no one had cared. At most, she had been chastised like a child and sent on her way. Leaning against the side of her father's rental car, Mina examined her memories again, searching for any hint of an answer.

Black River's fire department was astounding. They had swarmed over the burning funeral home in moments, their top of the line gas protection masks reflecting the dancing flames. Organized, well-funded, and highly trained, there hadn't been a moment of hesitation. They instantly knew what to do with the chemical fire, and they all played their parts to perfection. The building was lost, but the flames hadn't spread to the woods mere feet away.

Not exactly a volunteer rural service, she thought, one finger absently tapping against the music box in her hand. Glancing around at the dense forest surrounding the parking lot, she thought she probably shouldn't have made that assumption. *One burst of wildfire would wipe this place off the map.*

It seemed particularly unfair Basheba had escaped with fewer injuries than a lot of the innocent bystanders. The burning shrapnel that had rained down upon them had left many with broken bones and third-degree burns.

Evacuating the worst cases to the nearest town with a hospital hadn't done much to lessen the demands on Cadwyn and the local doctor. It hadn't taken long for Mina to insist she switch tasks with

Ozzie. In part, because she couldn't stand the utter indifference Basheba had for the misery she had caused. Mostly, however, she didn't want to let such an opportunity slip away.

It wasn't often an aspiring medical student could have such practical experience. On that hillside, she had learned Cadwyn was brilliant at what he did, Ozzie had the weakest stomach she had ever seen, and Basheba was most likely a sociopath.

It was hours of blood, bone, and misery.

She had never felt such a sense of purpose.

The memories brought the emotion back and she found herself smiling. Whatever traces of doubt she had still carried about her future had been obliterated. She was going to be a doctor.

Have to get through this first.

Lifting her gaze, she watched as the members of the four families continued to trickle into the tiny parking lot.

There wasn't enough room to accommodate them all. Most had been forced to leave their cars along the single narrow street that had brought them there. Kids scrambled over the remaining vehicles like ants while the adults talked amongst themselves. Tension still filled the air, but it was nothing compared to the sheer panic they had brought to the graveyard.

But it wasn't the explosion that bothered them, Mina recalled. They had been terrified one of the Selected had been killed. It begged the question; *what do they think will happen if the Witch's chosen ones die before entering the woods?*

Mina carefully stowed the thought away for later examination. Right now, she needed to understand how an entire town could experience something like that and not care. It went against all logic that Basheba was here with them, casually rechecking her camping supplies, and not in a holding cell.

Basheba had a skill for knowing when she was being watched. The moment Mina fixed her gaze on her, the blonde looked up and met her eyes. Just as quickly, she dismissed her and went back to rearranging the contents of her bag.

Mina bristled, infuriated by the brush-off and disgusted by the way the blonde continued to treat her family. Basheba's uncle had been trying to talk to his niece since they had arrived. Two hours later and Basheba had yet to say a word in response. She just walked away, leaving the little aging man to follow behind.

He keeps trying, Mina thought. *No matter how many times he's rejected, he never gives up on her. It's more than she deserves.*

"You'll be okay," Mina's mother said for the hundredth time that morning. She pulled her once more into a tight hug, pulling back only to cup Mina's cheeks with both hands. "Listen to Cadwyn. Keep him close."

"I'm so sorry." That had become her father's mantra. Something he repeated while refusing to look her in the eyes. This was the first time in her life he had failed to keep a promise to her and the shame of it seemed to weigh on his shoulders.

"It's all right, dad. Everything will be fine, you'll see."

"I should have got you out of this. I should have found a way."

We could just leave. She didn't dare voice the words. Family pressures and tradition were hard things to break.

You don't have to fix it. I will.

She wouldn't admit it to anyone, but there had been moments in the past few days when doubt had started to build up. *Pebbles of doubt can build a battlement if you let it.*

Being here didn't help. There was just something about the ancient woods that made her uneasy. Seeing her strong, proud parents broken like this did more to dispel her fears than any reassurances could have. Their tears hardened her resolve to end the charade.

Prove the hoax and set them free from this insanity.

"I'll be fine, really," Mina insisted, squeezing her mother's shoulders once more.

"Don't underestimate the Witch Woods," her father warned. "It's a dangerous place."

"I think I'm taking the greater danger with me," Mina mumbled, barely able to keep her gaze from darting over to Basheba. She wasn't sure how she felt about sharing a tent with a girl who played with her dog as people burned.

Her father's quizzical expression broke into a boastful smile. "That's the attitude, darling. Give her hell. But come back to us."

"I will."

Her mother's hand grasped her wrist, squeezing until Mina gasped in pain.

"Mom?"

"You have to come back."

"I will. I promise."

Lowering her voice to a whisper, her mother met her gaze with an unblinking stare. "You must come back. Do whatever you have to. But come back."

Nails dug through the layers of Mina's jacket to reach her skin. The small spike of pain made her mother's meaning clear. *Whatever it takes.*

"It won't come to that," Mina insisted as she pulled her arm free and forced a smile. "We'll work together."

"The Witch can take the rest of them. But not you. Give her what she wants, you have the stomach for it, I know it."

Mina glanced to her father for help but found only a matching conviction.

"I'm not going to hurt anyone," Mina said.

"They don't have to suffer. Make it quick. In the bottom of your bag, there's a container of belladonna leaves. You only need one leaf for each person. Put it in their food. It'll be over before they know it."

Mina's skin went cold. Her blood stopped flowing in her veins, and the earth crumbled from under her feet.

"I'm not a murderer."

The words passed her lips as a whisper. She was afraid to say it out loud. Terrified to confirm that the woman who had raised her with gentle hands and kind words had just ordered her to kill.

"Listen to your mother."

The weakness was gone from her father's voice, replaced with something dark and cold. Mina didn't have time to pull back. Someone unseen blew a horn, making the entire crowd fall into a tense silence. One more long bellow of the Viking-like horn and Mina noticed Cadwyn cutting through the crowd. He smiled and waved to his weeping family until he stood before the man with the horn. Basheba and Buck joined them on the little patch of grass that separated the parking lot from the start of the hiking trail.

"You have to go now," her mother said. "Remember what I told you."

Mina nodded. In her shock, she was barely able to mumble, "I love you."

Turning, she was captured by Jeremiah's arms. He hugged her until she couldn't breathe.

"I'll walk with you," he whispered.

The walk itself was too surreal for Mina's brain to understand. Everything came in small pieces unrelated to the others. The crunch of gravel under her feet. Whispered well wishes as the crowd parted before her. The weight of her camping bag. Sun-warmed skin and the morning dew sinking into the hem of her jeans. Within a blink, Jeremiah had fallen away, and she was standing next to Ozzie. She looked over her shoulder to find her brother again.

With the same disorientation, she followed Cadwyn and the others into the woods. The trees welcomed them with outstretched arms, quickly shielding them from the morning sun and shrouding them in a damp chill. The trail twisted rapidly, sharp turns that weaved around the thickest of the old growth and quickly cut them off from the rest of the world. The rising sunlight made the leaves glow. Birds fluttered about overhead, preparing for the coming cold and a cluster of squirrels chased each other across the path before them. A lazy stream, unseen but heard, bubbled past to stir the silence.

"Did that man have a Viking horn?" The question cracked out of Mina before she realized she had formed it.

Cadwyn shrugged. "It's tradition."

"How?"

Her question overlapped Ozzie's own.

"This is actually kind of nice. Is the whole walk like this?"

Both Ozzie and Mina turned to Cadwyn for a response. He looked to Basheba, wordlessly reminding them both that this was his first time as well. Refusing to pause for the conversation, she took the lead, Buck trotting by her feet. The dog had been outfitted with a backpack of his own and Mina was struck with the sudden curiosity to know what was in it.

"We're not in the Witch's Woods yet."

"Huh?" Ozzie said.

"A nature preserve butts up against the Witch's Woods," she explained. "We're just cutting through here so we can stay out of her territory for as long as possible."

"So, when exactly will we cross over?" Mina asked.

"You'll know."

With that, Basheba settled back into silence. It didn't matter what the rest of them discussed, she refused to engage, only acknowledging the presence of her dog.

They started at dawn and paused for lunch at noon. Already, Ozzie's new boots were making his heels blister. Cadwyn tended to them and rearranged the bags between the four of them, trying to lighten the boy's load. Mina's stomach had squirmed as he had riffled through her pack, sure he was going to discover the poison her mother had supposedly given her. Despite her best efforts, he still noticed her relief when he handed the pack back. In a small mercy, he mistook it and smiled.

"It'll be a bit lighter for you. Let me know if you need me to change it around again."

Mina said she would, but she knew she wouldn't, not until Basheba showed any sign of discomfort. Mina hated the fact that the smallest, weakest one amongst them was struggling the least.

Three more hours of hiking, and she started noticing the warning signs nailed into the trees that lined the path. *No trespassing. Turn back. Do not enter.*

"Should we be walking here?" Ozzie asked. "Maybe we took a wrong turn."

"We're just off the Witch's Woods. The police put them up to try and deter people from entering," Basheba replied.

Mina eyed the next sign she passed, a brightly colored one that urged the reader to turn back and had a suicide hotline scrawled across the bottom. A chuckle escaped her lips unbidden.

"What is with this town? If they really think the Witch is a threat, why don't they do anything about it?"

Basheba pointed to a nearby sign as she stalked past it.

"Signs? That's the best they can do?"

"What exactly do you want them to do?" Basheba countered. "Arrest her for being an illegal witch?"

"Haunting without a license?" Cadwyn offered with a small smile.

"Maybe they could do an exorcism," Ozzie suggested. "You know, bless the woods and force her out."

"They tried that when this first became a problem," Cadwyn said.

Basheba snorted, finally stopping and calling Buck over. "It's not their problem."

"Of course," Mina said. "Why on earth would they care about people dying?"

She had known Basheba would reply quickly but hadn't been prepared for her response.

"The harvest."

"I'm sorry, what?"

"Haven't you noticed that for a nothing little town, this place looks really good? Nice cars. Nicer houses. Nothing that should be within their budgets. Pick any farm at random, and you'll find it brimming with produce. Not just produce. *Perfect* produce. Walk through an orchard, and you won't find a single apple that's misshapen or rotten."

Mina blinked. "The Witch bribes the townsfolk with plentiful harvests?"

"Yeah. I think she does."

Again, Mina didn't mean to laugh. It just came out. "That's what you meant about human sacrifices? What are they? Ancient pagans?"

"Sure. Because they're the only people ever, in the history of the world, to think human sacrifice was a good idea," Basheba deadpanned. "And no one ever does anything monstrous for personal gain or a belief in the greater good."

"The whole town is pretty obsessed with the Witch," Ozzie mumbled.

"And Roswell is obsessed with aliens. That doesn't mean they exist."

"I'm confused. Are you saying Katrina is a real threat and the police should intervene? Or that she's just a local legend and not worth anyone's time?"

Mina found herself staring at Basheba, unable to answer.

"Well, this has been productive," Cadwyn cut in. "How about we have a look at the map?"

Basheba pulled the map from her pocket, unfolding it as she knelt down. Cadwyn helped her trap the edges under small rocks to keep the wind from taking it. Yellow highlighter marks pointed out the essential places; where they came in, where they'll turn off, the far off point that Mina assumed was their destination. Ozzie wasn't afraid to ask questions and had Basheba explain each one.

"What's this place?" Mina asked, pointing to the line of pink dots that arched between the yellow marks.

"Potential campsites," Basheba said.

"And these two black marks?"

Tension filled Basheba's shoulders. "Two things I was hoping to avoid. Unfortunately, we're running too far behind. We're going to have to cut between the two of them."

"But what are they?" Mina asked.

Cadwyn leaned forward to tap one of the marks. "I know that one's the Devil's Tree, right?"

"What's the Devil's Tree?" Ozzie asked.

"It's the tree they used to hang people from," Mina said. "My grandma used to tell me legends about it. Apparently, it's cursed. If you get too close, the ghosts will grab you and lynch you up with them."

"Yet another thing you're too smart to believe?" Basheba muttered.

"I have no doubt horrible things happened there, and that it was used as a suicide spot for many people. That doesn't make it supernatural."

Basheba grunted.

"I would ask you for evidence, but you tend to set that on fire," Mina added.

"What's this one?" Ozzie blurted, the words clashing together in his haste to get them out.

He shot nervous looks around the group before Basheba answered in a flat tone.

"Bell's Brook."

"Your family found it?" Ozzie asked, clearly hopeful for a conversation change.

Basheba smiled, her eyes dead and cold. "My namesake drowned in it."

Ozzie instantly deflated and stammered out an apology.

"How were you to know?" Basheba dismissed, busying herself with the pockets of Buck's saddlebags.

"Bare bones history," Cadwyn cut in. "Basheba Senior was gathering berries with her friends. She went to cross the brook and fell in. After laughing for a bit, her friends realized she hadn't come up and waded out to help her. It was then they discovered the brook was only three inches deep where she disappeared. Her body was never found."

"I don't go near that water."

Basheba spat the words out as she finished fastening the last belt of Buck's new harness. He still carried the saddlebags, but now they sat upon armor instead of fur. The thick harness covered his chest and spine with sharp two-inch spikes. With a matching collar and what could be best described as a tactical dog helmet, he looked ready for war.

"Where did you even get that?" Mina mumbled without thinking.

"Same place I got these."

Basheba tossed a small bag to each of them. A collar and twin cuffs of the same make were inside. It didn't click in Mina's head until she saw both Basheba and Cadwyn putting theirs on.

"You want us to wear these?"

"They protect your most exposed arteries. Neck and wrists. Also keeps people from choking you." Cadwyn ended with a warm smile and a passing, "It's tradition."

Once everyone was outfitted and Basheba had safely tucked the map away, they swooped under the metal bar that separated the main trail from the Witch's Wood.

For the first hour, everything remained the same—a crisp autumn day with all the beauty a day like that could hold. During the second, things changed. It started gradually, so Mina didn't notice at first. A dulling of color, a dip in temperature, a thickening of trees. The mist lacked such subtlety. Mina watched in shock as it rolled toward them as a wave, swooping around the tree trunks and leaving a thin layer of frost upon everything it touched.

None of them managed to smother their gasped cries. First

contact was like submerging their feet in ice water. Numbing to the point where it almost felt like fire. A thousand needles driving through her boots to find her flesh.

"I hate this stuff," Basheba muttered, pausing to angrily rip open one of the pockets of Buck's bag. Again, she brought enough for everyone.

Mina caught hers with both hands. "Feet warmers?"

"They start working upon contact with air," Basheba said. "Put them in your boots. They're horrible to walk on, but you won't get frostbite."

As Mina ripped open the pack, she heard Basheba add in a whisper.

"Hopefully."

"This happened to you before?" Ozzie asked as he hopped around, unwilling to sit in the airborne frost to put on his shoes.

"It's part of her game."

Ozzie stopped, growing motionless as a weak smile curled his full lips. "I'm really glad you're here with me."

For a moment, Basheba was held in stunned silence, staring at him like a deer caught in a car's headlights.

"Sure," she said at last. "Don't mention it."

Cadwyn straightened his spine, drawing himself up to his full height to look around. Distracted by the conversation and the cold, Mina had missed the greater implications of the fog. It covered the path. And, without it, she was lost. The dense trees all looked the same. The more she looked, the less she saw, until nothing looked real anymore.

"Basheba?" Cadwyn said, pulling a compass from his pocket as he inched closer.

She waited until she had put little socks on Buck's feet before retrieving the map from her back pocket. The instant it was free, the dog reared up. It latched onto the paper and ripped it from her hands. A sudden breeze claimed it before Basheba could snatch it back. The paper flapped, toppled, and danced on the air, weaving through the bare branches and luring them further from the path. They all knew it. But the need for the map forced their hand.

Running until sweat dripped down her spine, Mina lunged for the paper. It spiraled around her arm, staying just beyond the reach of her fingers, before soaring higher. Lunging after it, she burst into a barren meadow.

The grass was brown and brittle, crumbling with the slightest amount of pressure. It was the first time since dawn she had been able to glimpse the sky. The clear blue was gone, choked behind heavy clouds that pressed down upon the canopy. A single gnarled tree stood in the middle of the dead earth. Swollen and bare and formed like a hand reaching toward the sky. Mina heard the others join her but didn't look at them.

"I take it that's the Devil's Tree," she whispered.

Cadwyn nodded.

"Up there!" Ozzie's outburst made everyone turn to him before they realized he was pointing to the top of the tree. Tangled around the highest branch, the map flapped like a flag.

Relief bloomed behind Mina's ribs, barely stifled by the weary expressions the others wore. She stripped off her pack and placed it at Ozzie's feet.

"Cadwyn, can you give me a boost please?"

His eyes widened.

"It's lucky for all of us I'm a good climber," she smiled.

Basheba stepped closer, "You don't have to. We have the compass."

"Yeah, you're not the least bit convincing."

She flinched back. "Did anyone else bring a map?"

"This is mostly stuff Ozzie bought me," Cadwyn said.

It was the same story for all of them. Frustration brewed on Basheba's face until she bit savagely at her lips.

"I should have bought more than one. It was stupid of me. I

meant to get more yesterday."

"It's okay, Basheba. I'll just go get it." When soothing didn't work, she added somewhat playfully, "Yell if anything weird comes close."

The group cautiously edged closer to the tree. Cadwyn braced his back against the trunk and cupped his hands, transforming himself into a human ladder. Grabbing his shoulders helped her to balance.

"This is a trap, you know," he whispered. After a moment's pause, he added, "If anything happens, jump. I'll catch you."

"Thanks," she said, because she felt like she should respond, but didn't know what else to say.

One firm push and an awkward stomp on his shoulders allowed her to reach the lowest branch. She scrambled up, her new hiking boots scrapping away the bark. Focus was her strong suit. She used it now, fixing her attention on the map, surging toward it, letting everything else fade away.

Branches thinned as she got higher. Some cracked and threatened to snap under her weight. Higher and higher, until she was straining, her fingers trembling and her shoulder threatening to pop from its socket. One final surge and the paper was in her grasp. Her landing broke the branch. It crashed down to the earth as she scrambled to keep from following. How she managed it, she had no idea, but she ended up swinging around the trunk and landing hard on another, far sturdier branch.

"Mina?" Cadwyn called.

Pressing her forehead against the trunk, she thrust her hand out. "I've got it."

As she straightened herself, she heard it. A low, steady buzz. Shifting and living and swarming. *Bees.* Her heart skipped a beat and jammed itself into her throat. The map ripped on the bark as she grasped the tree with both hands, trying to hold her panic at bay.

"Cadwyn?" It came out as a whisper. She cleared her throat and tried again. "Cadwyn?"

"I'm right here. Right under you. Just fall back."

"Where's the hive?" *He must see them. That's why he sounds like that. God, they're so loud.*

"Listen to me, Mina," Basheba said. "Close your eyes and fall to the left. We'll catch you, okay? Just close your eyes and fall."

Just tell me where the hive is!

"Mina! Just do what I'm telling you!"

Her body reacted to the direct order, but not in compliance. Twisting her head to the right, she forced her eyes open. There, dangling from the nearby branch, she found the hive. Fat insects of black and yellow squirmed and swarmed. Crawling over each other as they delved into the honeycomb labyrinth they had created in the hollowed-out eye socket. The hanged man dangled from his noose, decayed and bloated, riddled with bees as they burrowed under his flesh to create their home.

"Mina!" Cadwyn roared.

A scream ripped out of her chest. The corpse twisted, swaying as the bees burst free from his body, their numbers blacking out the sun.

CHAPTER 14

The Devil's Tree convulsed violently, lurching from side to side. Half frozen clumps of earth hurled out in every direction as the roots ripped free of the soil. What started as a slight hum confined to the open, dangling corpse grew to a deafening roar. He could barely hear himself as he screamed for Mina to jump. Stubborn to the end, the girl hadn't listened. She had looked.

"Jump, Mina!"

Her answering scream came with a thunderous crack of splintering wood. The top branches exploded, releasing a wild swarm that blanketed the sky. A wall of stinging insects hid her from his view.

Cadwyn braced himself to catch her, but the impact didn't come instantly. The droning hive covered any sound that might have given him a hint of where she was. They rushed at the group, raining down upon them like fire. He could feel the bees' venom swell under his skin. Grinding his teeth against the pain, he forced his arms to remain outstretched, waiting. She still hadn't come down.

The tree rattled. Thick branches dropped through the living cloud, slamming into the earth and making it tremble. Mina's scream almost went unnoticed. He shifted toward it at the last moment. The impact sent them both sprawling across the brittle earth. Mina's elbow drove into his mouth and blood splashed his tongue. He didn't know which one of them it belonged to. Rolling to the side as best he could, he tried to bundle the frantic girl close, tried to shield her from the attack. The insects went straight for their eyes, their mouths, crawled under the necklines of their shirts in a hunt for tender flesh.

"Up!"

Bees crawled over his lips, trying to squirm down his throat, piercing his gums and tongue. Cadwyn swiped at his mouth and spat, attempting to clear his airway.

But there were always more.

A thousand needles stabbed him all at once and flooded his bloodstream with venom. Trembling with pain, he looped an arm around Mina's waist and dragged her to her feet. Mina kicked and screamed, too far beyond the point of reason to even try to calm down. He swooped low, tossed her over his throbbing shoulder, and sprinted across the open field.

Breaking free from the heart of the swarm and clawing at his eyes, he was able to catch a few fleeting glimpses of the others. Basheba had haphazardly wrapped her thick knitted scarf around her head to leave only her eyes exposed. It did little to keep the insects at bay. Running didn't dislodge the layer of bright yellow and black that covered her arms.

She latched onto Ozzie's shoulder with one tiny hand and kicked hard at the back of his knee, driving him to the ground. He fought the touch until she yanked his scarf up over his head to bring him some small measure of relief.

"To the woods!" Basheba bellowed.

The dead earth crumbled under their feet as they stampeded for the tree line, revealing tangled roots and potholes to catch them. Half blind, Cadwyn ran until he felt the sharp twigs slash across his face and rip at his arms. Pain radiated from the stings to mask any damage the plant life caused. He kept running, trying to keep Basheba and Ozzie in sight through squinted eyes, unable to leave the swarm behind completely.

Each insect he knocked aside was replaced by a dozen more. Shrubs and fallen trees caught his legs. Coupled with Mina's constantly shifting weight dragging down one shoulder, he stumbled and tripped. The pain was the only thing that kept him moving. Pain, and the simple plan to follow Basheba's retreating back.

"Left!" Basheba screamed.

He jerked around obediently, following her voice until the ground gave out from under him, and he fell. It was a short drop with rocks and icy water at the end. He tried to soften the impact for Mina, twisting around to take as much of it as he could, but there was little he could do. The stones found every newly forming bruise and stoked the fire the bee venom had ignited in his skin. He cried out in agony. Bees swarmed the instant his mouth opened.

Then he hit the river's surface. Icy water flooded his mouth and sent the insects into a wild panic. He spat and choked as his throat swelled.

Cadwyn forced his head under the water, gaining a few seconds reprieve while using the current to force the insects from his mouth. He stayed until the need for air made his lungs burn. A sharp tug on his backpack jerked him back up. Blinking the water from his eyes, he flung an arm back. Bees squished between his skin and the slender wrist he latched onto.

Basheba. It's too small to be anyone else.

She wrenched her hand free of his fingers and jerked at his bag again. Only after she had found what she was looking for did it occur to him that she was trying to fight her way inside his medical pack.

A deep whoosh covered the sound of the droning hive. Blistering heat washed over him and scorched the fine hairs on his neck. He flattened himself into the water but the river wasn't deep enough to let him escape the flames. Then, just as suddenly as it began, it all faded away.

Rearing back, he gasped for air and tried to peer through his swelling eyes. His vision cleared just as Basheba turned to face him, an aerosol can of antiseptic spray in one hand and his Zippo lighter in the other. Shock coursed through him as he watched her bring the items together. The spray caught the flames and released a guttural whoosh.

She wielded the makeshift flamethrower with focused determination, systematically setting the swarm alight, turning them into burning embers that spiraled through the air and fell like ash.

Cadwyn choked on a breath as she suddenly shifted, bringing the flood of fire barreling toward him. Snapping one hand up, he gripped the back of Mina's head and forced her down into the water. There was barely any depth for her to retreat into.

Her screams bubbled and gasped as the icy stream flowed around them. His front froze while his back burned. Mina never stopped fighting him, forcing him to tighten his grip and bring her to the brink of drowning. His head was spinning and his limbs felt like lead when Basheba finally pushed the flames aside.

His arms trembled as he forced himself up onto all fours and dropped to the side, gasping for air, relishing the swell of his lungs even as his throat throbbed with agony. Mina sputtered but couldn't stop sobbing. Propping her up against his shoulder, he looked downstream, searching for Basheba again.

She stood only a few feet away. Her small chest heaved and her raw hands trembled. But her eyes blazed with focused fury as she glared toward the riverbank. Cadwyn desperately searched for Ozzie before catching sight of him around Basheba's legs. The boy was beaten, shivering, too horrified to move from his seat within the Arctic stream, but alive.

Cadwyn braced his hand on a submerged stone and rocked himself into motion. But before he could get his feet under him, he recalled that Basheba was staring something down.

A man stood on the banks. Thick and sturdy, several feet taller than Cadwyn himself. The surviving bees crawled over him, clustered into a squirming flesh of ebony and brilliant yellow. The only part of the man's actual body that was visible under the swarm was his eyes. Catlike, putrid yellow, and terrifyingly familiar.

For a split second, Cadwyn felt himself thrown back in time, back to when he was just a boy and something demonic had slithered under his brother's flesh.

It can't be the same one.

An almost humanoid shape stared them down. Waiting. Glaring at Basheba with a hatred that matched her own.

Basheba snapped her hands up. Before she could reignite the spray, she dropped. Her last act before disappearing under the surface of the water was to toss the two items she held into the air. Ozzie's shout snapped Cadwyn from his shock. The teen had thrown his entire body forward, managing to catch both the lighter and the aerosol can, keeping them in the air and sending them toward Cadwyn, leaving him no way to break his fall.

Ozzie body-slammed the jagged stones, the impact sending up a wall of water. It struck Cadwyn like liquid ice as he lunged for the items. They fumbled across his fingertips until he was able to pull them into his grasp. Holding them tight, he glanced over to find Ozzie half submerged; his head and torso lost within the sloshing water as his legs restlessly searched for a nook to lock his toes in.

A sharp drag pulled them deeper into the impossible sinkhole. Slick stones clicked against each other as they toppled out of the way, leaving Ozzie with nothing to hold onto. Cadwyn started toward them just as Mina screamed.

Whirling around, his limbs moved before his conscious mind could catch up. He released the flammable antiseptic spray and lit it. The heat of the flames pulsated against his river-numbed fingers, the glow stung his eyes, making his already limited vision ripple.

The human hive burst at the first contact with the flames, shattering apart into a million tiny insects that swept around to encase them. He raked the fire back and forth. Years of muscle memory warned him the can was becoming too light. It was going to run dry.

Ozzie reared back, his face barely breaking free of the frothing water. "Mina!"

The boy trembled with the strain it took to bring Basheba up. It took all of his strength to lift her enough for her to gasp once before the unseen force caught her again. Whatever had her, dragged her down with enough power to almost claim Ozzie as well.

Cadwyn shifted, trying to carve a clear path for Mina to reach the others. Only when Ozzie cried out again did Cadwyn realize Mina hadn't moved. He glanced over to find her where he had left her. Curled into a tight ball, she screamed and whimpered, clawing frantically at herself until blood stained the shallow pool she sat in.

"Mina! Help!" Ozzie pleaded.

Her screams became a string of nonsense.

Cadwyn looked from her to the others, and realized he was trapped. If he moved to help Ozzie, Mina would be left unprotected. If he didn't, the young boy might drown along with Basheba.

While Cadwyn hesitated, Ozzie brought one hand out of the water, bracing it on the rocks to push himself high enough to bellow.

"Buck!"

The dog didn't come to the stranger's call. Ozzie slid forward a few inches until his mouth was barely above the dark inky liquid.

"Buck!"

Cadwyn twitched with the need to run to them. He turned back to Mina, a desperate plea on his tongue. All he needed was a split second to know there was nothing he could do. Her panic attack had a tight hold on her that only time could release. Seconds passed in a blur, each one bringing him to the point of no return. If he didn't choose who to save, they were both going to die.

The swarm's drone diminished Ozzie's half-wild cry while the whoosh of fire and Mina's whimpered sobs crowded into Cadwyn's skull.

Make the call.

An abrupt bark spared him. Head low and back protected, Buck sprinted through the wall of swarming insects with single-minded determination. Reaching Ozzie's side, he barked and paced the edge of the pit. Ozzie flopped out his one free arm to try and catch the dog.

The swarm took Cadwyn's attention and, by the time he looked back, Ozzie had twisted his body around to plant his feet against the stones on either side of the pit. All his efforts barely managed to drag Basheba up. It was more her backpack than her actual body, and he almost lost his grip when the bees clustered.

Cadwyn swung the flame around to drive off the onslaught. The brilliant glow filled his vision for an instant and, by the time it cleared, Ozzie had hooked one of Basheba's bag straps around a spike protruding from Buck's armor. A swift smack to the dog's rear sent the Rottweiler plowing forward. The soaked material snapped taut while the water frothed. A few of the stitches popped. Buck's muscles trembled. Ozzie scrambled up to help and then, just as quickly as it had begun, it all stopped.

The bees vanished. The pain they had brought lingered even as the stings dissipated. Basheba didn't shoot free from the pit. Instead, the riverbed simply returned to its original form. A shallow brook barely large enough to find her torso.

Now, without the resistance, Ozzie was flung to the ground and Buck took off at a sprint. As she coughed up a lungful of water, Basheba managed to croak out a command for him to stop. The dog's obedience was instantaneous, and she was left to flop over the sun-warmed stones.

In the sudden stillness, the heat pressing against his hands was brought to the forefront of Cadwyn's awareness. He hissed, dropped to one knee, and, after sparing a second to toss the items onto a nearby stone, he dunked his hands into the frigid water. The chaos of noise that had filled the forest was now reduced to sporadic gasped breaths, Mina's sobs, and the soft trickle of water flowing over the rocks.

Cadwyn pushed aside his confusion and brewing panic to call out. "Ozzie? Are you okay?"

"I don't know."

"Is anything broken? Can you see bone?"

There was a brief pause. "No."

"Take care of Mina."

With that, Cadwyn jumped up and ran to Basheba. The heavy waterlogged pack kept her on her back, each mouthful of water she spat up sloshing over her face. Carefully, he rolled her into a recovery position, barely able to assess the damage as Buck nuzzled her with concern. Her lips were blue, her body shook, and her chest heaved as it tried to work the icy liquid out of her lungs.

Get them somewhere warm and safe.

The simple thought played across his mind as the sun began to sink behind the dense forest and the shadows crept in.

CHAPTER 15

"But I felt them," Mina whispered to herself.

She pressed her torso against her thighs and stared at the ground before her, willing herself to concentrate, to dislodge the fog that had wrapped around her brain. *There has to be an explanation*, she told herself. *A logical explanation. I just have to think.*

The distorted face of the hanging man filled her mind's eye. She could almost smell the honey the hive had gathered within the rotting skull. Her stomach convulsed. Throwing herself to the side, she retched. Bile and spit splattered over the dead leaves.

"Really, Mina?" Basheba sighed. "In the middle of the campsite? You couldn't have walked a few feet in literally any direction?"

Her fingers shook too hard for her to wipe her mouth with any kind of dignity. *Think, Mina. Find the answer. There has to be an answer.*

The fire Basheba had started did little to fight off the gathering shadows, but it did work to ease the ice that had encased her bones. Mina had been the only one to lose her backpack. If Cadwyn hadn't had the forethought to put a thermal blanket in his med-pack, she would have been left naked with only the fire to warm her. No one had a similar size.

The looming threat of nightfall had shifted everyone's priorities. Darkness and hypothermia seemed more important than making peace with the madness they had just experienced, especially when thin snow had started to fall, gathering with the lingering mist to leave them all shivering. There was no shelter in sight. Only an endless stretch of bone-white trees and shadows. They wouldn't last the night without the sleeping bags Cadwyn had stowed in her bag when he had redistributed the weight amongst the group. So the boys had hurriedly changed into somewhat dry clothes and set off to retrieve her pack, leaving them to set up camp.

Basheba hadn't waited for them to be out of sight before she instructed Mina to just sit down and keep out of her way. There was a practiced efficiency in everything she did, a quiet confidence in how she performed her tasks. From picking the perfect location amongst the trees for the tent, to how she constructed the fire. In those few moments that Mina's mind strayed away from the problem before her, she watched Basheba.

Her first action had been to start the fire. A healthy, fat teepee of flames that reminded Mina of family bonfires. The tent had gone up almost instantaneously under her skilled manipulations, and she had been busying herself ever since with tasks Mina couldn't name. She had never really been into camping.

Mina's thoughts returned once more to all her unanswered questions and dwelled there ever since. She studied her hands. The firelight turned her skin copper. There wasn't a single welt.

"But I felt them," she mumbled.

"You know what's a fun game?" Basheba said abruptly. She sat back on her heels; forearms smeared with mud from the pit she was digging. "Silence. Let's play silence."

The words swirled in Mina's head until they fell into some kind of meaningful order.

"What are you doing?"

"Building a fire."

"We have one."

"A cooking fire," Basheba said, stocking small twigs into the pit. "Dakota holes are also good for drying clothes."

"Dakota holes?"

"Large hole for fire. Smaller hole for the chimney. Link the two with a tunnel. You get concentrated heat without exposed flames."

Basheba rattled off the facts while unpeeling a few tampons she had retrieved from her pocket. Noticing Mina's glance, she smiled and wiggled them in the air. "They're great for tinder. And come in handy as waterproof packs."

She reached into the pit, her slender shoulders shifted slightly, and a bright orange glow emerged from the hole. Smiling contently, Basheba took a moment to warm her hands. It was the only time she had been still since the boys had left.

"You taught yourself all of this?"

Basheba closed her eyes and huffed. "What happened to playing the silent game?"

"Do you have a problem with me?" Mina asked.

"Several," she replied with an almost playful shrug.

Anger trickled into Mina's stomach, twisting with her fear until she had to clench her jaw to keep from screaming. Taking in a sobering breath, she schooled her features and forced her voice to come out calm.

"We should talk about that."

Basheba barked a laugh, pausing in her activity to spare her one fleeting glance.

"Why?"

"It seems important that we get along."

"We're never going to get along," the blonde replied airily, busying herself with twigs and leaves once again. "We're born to be at odds, little girl."

Mina rolled her eyes. "Why? Because two women can't work for a similar goal without a cat-fight breaking out?"

Basheba blinked at her, a smile creeping across her face. "Wow. You just full-on channeled your daddy there, didn't you?" She shrugged. "I guess the arrogant, self-righteous fruit doesn't roll far from the tree."

Mina couldn't stifle her snort. "Those are two qualities you're in no position to be accusing others of."

Basheba's smile carried all the venom her dead eyes were incapable of. Mina tightened her arms around her knees and forced herself to meet her expressionless gaze.

"You really want me to tell you why we can't get along? Because you're clearly not going to get it on your own." Feeding the submerged fire made light dance across her pale face. "We want fundamentally different things. And since we're both goal-driven, we're bound to clash. I can't get on board with your hero complex. Or the superiority one for that matter."

"Both better options than your Napoleon complex," Mina shot back.

Basheba giggled. It wasn't the reaction Mina was aiming for.

"Yeah, I suppose you have me there," she dismissed almost wistfully. "My point is that you want to save the world. You want to be the one to fling open the gates and save the poor, inept, ignorant villages from their self-imposed dark ages."

Mina squirmed but lifted her chin. "And what do you want?"

She hummed pleasantly. "If I had all the money in the world, I'd build a wall around all of Black River. A large, impenetrable wall."

"Okay." Mina frowned in confusion. It wasn't what she had been expecting.

Light danced in Basheba's eyes. "And then I'd lock the gate and set it all on fire. The town. The forest. Just sit back with a beer and watch it burn."

"What is with you and fire?"

"I don't know. I just think it's neat." Poking a stick into the concealed flames coaxed flickering embers to drift up and dance across the night sky. She watched it all with a dreamy smile. "I'd love to see how many of those fine townsfolk chose to burn with their crops. They're more than willing to see us die for them. Bet they'll have a different view on human sacrifice when they're the ones on the altar, though."

"Wait," Mina cut in as her stomach rolled. "In your fantasy, you'd locked all those people in when you burn the town?"

Utter confusion scrunched up Basheba's face. "Duh. Otherwise, what's the point?"

Is she really this twisted, or is it just a show? A self-defense mechanism?

Either way, it left a sour taste in Mina's mouth. It was the contentment in Basheba's eyes that scared her the most. The glassy, doll-like orbs finally had some life in them. Something that, until now, only Buck had managed to accomplish. But even as dread gathered inside her like a coming storm, she couldn't fight off her exhaustion. It sunk down to her bone-marrow and pulled at her eyes. She would have probably fallen asleep where she sat if it wasn't for her constant shivering. Hard, rattling shutters that left her breathless and were impossible to stop.

Mina wanted nothing more than to end the conversation. She knew now nothing good could come from long discussions with Basheba Bell. But each time she kept her silence, she felt panic sparking along the edge of her awareness. Without a distraction, she'd fall back into hysterics. Already, she could almost hear the bees again. If Basheba was her only option to keep control of her brain, she'd take it.

"Why do you hate them so much?" Mina asked.

"Really? They allowed the complete slaughter of my entire family because they were given apples, and you wonder why I don't like them?"

She's insane, Mina decided. A loud buzz passed behind her and she flinched, twisting around to study the woods.

"Did you hear that?"

"It's the woods at night," Basheba said, already working to construct a rack out of twigs. "There's a lot to hear. Care to be a tad more specific?"

Mina pulled the thermal blanket tighter around her shoulders. "Bees."

Basheba stilled and stared lifelessly in front of her. "Nope."

The silence that followed worked on Mina's nerves. She needed conversation.

"Not your entire family."

Already arranging the makeshift clothesline over the fire pit, Basheba sighed dramatically. "I know I'm going to regret asking this, but what are you babbling about?"

"You said the town killed your *entire* family. That's not true."

"They killed all the ones who mattered," Basheba dismissed.

"Why do you hate your uncle so much?"

Basheba jabbed the rack into place and began arranging the damp clothes to dry. As calm as her body was, her face was in constant motion. Shifting rapidly between a manic smile, a furious snarl, and a tearful sob. Eventually, her features settled into a smile completely devoid of any emotion.

"Now, that's a bit personal. We haven't even braided each other's hair and talked about boys yet."

"If it's too personal, you don't have to tell me."

"Yeah. That's kind of what I was getting at. But nice try making me feel guilty about not opening up. Smooth attempt at manipulation."

"I wasn't trying to do that. I'm just trying to have an actual conversation with you. Maybe even understand you a little. Are you always this paranoid?"

Basheba smiled again, small and tight and with a bitter amusement in her eyes. "I'm not paranoid. I just don't like people. Everyone who's worth anything is dead, anyway."

"You like Cadwyn," Mina pointed out.

"He follows me on Instagram." Basheba turned to her, one delicate hand placed over her heart. "That's a sacred bond."

Frustration piled up inside her until she was teetering on the edge of screaming again.

"What happened to you to make you like this?"

All traces of humor were swept from Basheba like a flash of wildfire, leaving only smoldering embers burning in her pale blue eyes.

"It must have been nice to be so utterly protected from reality," she said slowly. "You must have known your family members were dying. What did your daddy tell you? Did he say they were in car crashes? Maybe freak accidents? You'd think that eventually, you'd get a little suspicious you weren't getting the whole story."

She didn't get louder or throw her arms about, but it was clear Basheba was fueling her anger. It was growing and bubbling inside her. Mina was suddenly very aware that she was alone in a dark forest with a volatile, unpredictable, and possibly sadistic girl.

"My earliest childhood memory is of this place," Basheba continued, abruptly taking on an almost dreamy tone. "My older sister had been selected. None of them returned. When that happens, we form search parties to find the remains. I volunteered."

"The police let you? How old were you?"

Basheba flopped back onto the earth. Apparently, rolling her eyes wasn't dramatic enough. Bathed in the dancing light of the nearby fire, she stared up at the canopy, letting the tiny flakes of snow drift onto her face.

"You're so dumb it's physically painful." Basheba chuckled. "About a century in, the Black River police admitted to themselves there wasn't much they could do. Admitting there was a killer in the woods only put pressure on them to catch said killer. So, instead of being forced to hang innocent people to prevent riots, they decided to take a step back. Sure, they'll come and take statements and photos and tick all the boxes necessary to make sure the paperwork's in order. But anything more just leads to the deaths being exploited. We become entertainment. Promote Katrina's legend. Draw more people into the woods. Not exactly what they're going for. So, we take care of our own. We send them in and we go and find them after."

"But why your parents would let you do that? If they truly

believed in all of this, why expose you to it?"

"Because I'm a Bell. It's my responsibility to look. To know. And to fight on anyway."

Mina had a suspicion she was quoting someone but didn't dare to ask who.

"We found her," Basheba continued. "Not too far from here, actually. Just a couple of miles. Katrina had used their bodies like art supplies. She cut them up, nailed them into trees. Let their organs drape down like Spanish moss." She suddenly bolted upright. "A totem pole! *That's* what she was going for. How did it take me so long to get it? Well, now I just feel dense."

Mina kept her silence, twisting her numb fingers together until they hurt. The laughter that slipped past Basheba's lips made her cringe. It didn't last long, though.

"That was the first time I saw my dad break. He couldn't handle seeing his little girl like that. Mom was waiting for us at home. I didn't want her to go through that, too. So, I volunteered to climb up and pull out the nails. I never knew how many organs were in a human body. It took forever."

Mina watched the emotionless girl for a long moment. "How old were you?"

"Are you actively trying to miss the point?"

Before Mina could reply, the smaller girl continued.

"Let me spell it out for you. No matter how bad you think of me, your family is worse. Your daddy *chose* to keep you ignorant. He did that. And then he had the balls to get enraged when I reminded him I'm not just cannon fodder for his crotch goblin's survival."

Mina bristled but picked her words carefully. "You don't seem to have this opinion of Ozzie."

"You and Ozzie are in completely different situations. It was his mother's intervention, not Percival's choice, that kept him ignorant. Also, he just saved my life. That kind of endears me to him a little bit."

Suddenly, Basheba turned to her. Being the sole focus of the smaller girl's attention made Mina's insides twist sharply.

"You know what you're like? You're like that jerk who has never been assaulted, but thinks he has the knowledge to educate rape survivors on how they should handle their trauma. The kind who refuse to admit they're wrong no matter how much evidence is piled up before them."

Basheba lifted her hand to keep Mina silent. "We've barely known each other for forty-eight hours, and you don't hesitate to ask me incredibly personal questions. What? Like it's my job to educate you? To convince you? God, you are like your father. But what really gets me is the fact that it doesn't matter what I say, you're never going to believe me. Even now, after everything you've seen, after everything I've told you, you've still got your cute little nose up in the air. Just biting at the bit to explain to me that I'm just too stupid to understand what's really going on."

Chest heaving and color filling her cheeks, Basheba blinked thoughtfully. "Huh. That makes you more repulsive than me, doesn't it? I mean, I set a high bar, but you might have just climbed over it."

Mina hadn't realized she was hugging herself, twisting her arms around her torso until they crushed the air from her lungs. She could feel her brain melting into slush under the weight of Basheba's accusation. The horrors she had seen. The sound of bees still lingering in her memory. Under the blonde's watchful gaze, Mina felt everything she knew about herself dissolve into a putrid ooze, dripping away to better mirror Basheba's opinion of her. She didn't know if she'd ever see herself the same way again.

***

Why won't they stop shaking?

Ozzie's gloves had been too wet to wear. But, without them, his fingertips had long since gone numb, leaving nothing behind but a deep, throbbing ache. He stared at his hands, ordered them to stay still. It didn't do any good.

Just stop shaking!

Stumbling over the stones and through the underbrush must have disturbed Cadwyn because the older man inched closer to his side, approaching him like he was a startled animal. After a moment of hesitation, he placed a hand between Ozzie's shoulder blades. He knew the contact was coming but still couldn't stop himself from flinching. Ozzie shoved his trembling hands deep into his jacket pockets, not wanting the older man to see his weakness, but knowing it was too late.

"I'm not afraid," Ozzie blurted out.

"I am," Cadwyn replied. "The last thing I want to do is go back to that tree. I'm glad you're keeping me company."

Ozzie tried to narrow his eyes but couldn't help smiling. "Yeah, I bet you're glad it's me."

"Why wouldn't I be?"

He shrugged. "No offense, but I'd feel safer with Basheba. She might actually be crazier than this place."

Cadwyn chuckled, "Yeah, she might be."

"Think we're all going to be like her after this?"

"I don't think anyone is like Basheba," he replied. Cadwyn left his hand on Ozzie's back as he stooped over slightly, trying to catch his gaze.

"You handled yourself really well today, Ozzie."

Balling his fists didn't stop his hands from shaking. He just wanted them to be still, even if only for a second, but his body was determined to out him as the coward he was. Cadwyn's eyes were as kind as his smile. He gestured loosely to Ozzie's pockets.

"It's the adrenaline. Though, that swim probably didn't help."

Having his joke fall flat didn't diminish his smile. He patted Ozzie's shoulder.

"You'll feel better when you're warm and dry with a good meal in your stomach."

I don't think I'm ever going to feel better. Ozzie kept the thought to himself as they continued to trudge over the slush of decaying leaves and gathering snow. All the while, his trembling grew steadily worse. Memories taunted him, playing like twisted home movies in his mind's eye, never dwelling on any single horror but shifting between all they had witnessed. Each flash broke his resolve a little more.

Keep it together Ozzie. Breathe. Don't let them know they're stuck in the woods with a completely useless child.

It was all for nothing. Tears gathered behind his eyes. His throat swelled shut, forcing each breath to break into a snot clogged sob. Holding his breath, he tried to smother the sound. It only made it all the more noticeable when he finally gasped for air.

The first sob hurt the most. Those that followed toppled out of him as an unrelenting force, shaking his shoulders and making his chest ache. Cadwyn quickly pulled him into a hug as tight as their injured, aching bodies would allow. The wall of body heat left Ozzie painfully aware of how cold he was. There was something about that silent, warm comfort that made the tears come faster. Cadwyn didn't comment. Just rested his head on top of Ozzie's and rubbed his back in soothing circles.

"I'm sorry," Ozzie mumbled between his broken wails, shoving his face hard into Cadwyn's chest to try and smother the sound. As if there was still a chance Cadwyn hadn't seen what a complete mess he was. "I'm so sorry."

"Hey, none of that. You did great."

Great? The word rattled around Ozzie's skull, laughing at him as it clashed against the truth of what he must really look like. A blubbering child clinging to the closest thing that would pass as a father figure. Stripped bare of what he thought he was, Ozzie could only confront what lay at his core. He wasn't strong. Wasn't brave. Wasn't invincible and ready to take on the world. He was useless.

Pathetic.

I'm going to die here. I'm going to take them all with me.

Cadwyn tightened his arms around Ozzie's shoulders and brought one hand up to cup the back of his head. "I know seeing a demon can be overwhelming the first time. I can't say it gets easier, but it won't be so bad. The shock wears off after a while."

He went through all of this when he was just a kid.

The knowledge mocked him. To know a child confronted the same thing with more bravery than he could now summon. Percival's voice replayed in the back of his head. *He played chicken with a demon, and the demon blinked first.*

"I'm sorry," Ozzie stammered. "I'll get better. I promise. I'll get better, somehow."

"You saved Basheba's life. Your quick thinking and quicker hands made sure we could keep fighting. How much better do you want to get?"

"You don't have to humor me." Ozzie pulled back, roughly wiped the tears from his eyes, and snorted down a few breaths. "I know how stupid I am."

"You're not."

"It was the first challenge and look at me! She broke me, Cadwyn!"

His voice remained calm and serene. "So what?"

Ozzie used the back of his hands to rub at his eyes again. No matter how many times he wiped the tears away, there was always more to take their place.

"What do you mean? Isn't that bad?"

"Ozzie, Katrina and her demons, this is all they think about. They spend every day thinking about ways to hurt people. Of course, she broke you. We're all going to break. Probably more than once. That part doesn't matter."

"What part does?" Ozzie asked meekly.

He hadn't realized he had lowered his gaze to the ground until

Cadwyn cupped his shoulder and gave him a small shake. Just enough to make him look up and resume eye contact again.

"What matters is what you do with the rubble. She has no say in that."

He sniffed, "Huh?"

"The Witch can break you, but she can't take anything from you. My brother taught me that." He waited until he knew he had Ozzie's full attention before continuing. "If you don't think you can make it as you are, take the rubble she reduced you to and rebuild yourself into someone who can."

"How do I do that?"

"Let's start by taking a second and getting those tears out, all right? It'll do you a world of good."

At Ozzie's hesitation, Cadwyn nudged his shoulder. "Hey, crying doesn't mean you're weak. It means you gave a damn."

"Your brother tell you that, too?"

"Nah. Basheba's sister." A small, sad smile flicked across his face, but he quickly hid it behind unrelenting kindness.

There was no mockery in it. He wasn't looking down on him or trying to prop him up for his own gain.

"You're just a nice guy."

Cadwyn's eyebrows jumped, and Ozzie realized he had said that last part out loud.

"Sorry, it was passing through. I didn't mean to sound weird or creepy."

"Ozzie," Cadwyn chuckled. "Do you remember where I work? That's the least creepy compliment I've had in a while."

"What's the creepiest?"

"They mostly revolve around my teeth."

Ozzie sniffed. "They are nice teeth."

"Thanks. They're fake."

The short burst of laughter reopened the dam of tears waiting to be released. He crumbled, both mentally and physically, trusting

Cadwyn to catch him. Without a word, the taller man held onto Ozzie and let him cry.

CHAPTER 16

The sudden thrashing of a nearby bush shattered the silence that had fallen over the girls. A startled scream escaped Mina as she scrambled toward the teepee fire. An instant later, Basheba was crouched by her side, a hunting knife clutched in her delicate hand. They shared a quick glance before refocusing on the shaking plant life. Mina's heart hammered against her rib cage as she tried to steel herself for what was coming for them next.

The bush ripped in two as Buck leaped through it, a bloody mass clutched in his jaws and tail wagging with victory.

Basheba was grinning before Buck's paws hit the ground. She reached out for him, drawing him closer with a rush of praise and excited baby talk. The studded armor was still strapped to his muscular body, but he didn't seem to feel the weight. Bouncing around like a boastful puppy, he rushed over and dumped his prize at Basheba's feet. Blood instantly began to trickle from the broken mass and pool around the mangled corpse, catching the snowflakes as they drifted down. Basheba reached past Mina to stab the lump.

"What did you bring me, baby boy? Huh?"

It hung limply from the long blade, twisting slightly as she lifted it up to the firelight for closer examination.

"Is that a rabbit?" Mina asked.

"New England Cottontail. We're going to eat well tonight." Her voice took on an almost giddy tone as she pulled Buck into a one-armed hug, either expertly avoiding the spikes or ignoring their sharp bite. "Who's the cutest, smartest, best boy in the whole wide world?"

"Okay, now I know that's got to be me," Cadwyn said as he

stalked out from the gathering darkness.

"Nope," Basheba dismissed.

He jabbed a thumb to the shorter boy trailing a step behind him. "Ozzie?"

"No. But I do like him more than you at the moment."

Ozzie's chest puffed up a little. Or perhaps it was just that he straightened out of his miserable, defeated slump.

"You do?" he asked.

"You saved me. And you got the bag."

"Hey." Cadwyn tossed the pack to Mina. "I helped."

Basheba slipped past the tall man to her carefully organized cooking utensils.

The boy noticed the clothes warming on the makeshift rack and gratefully changed. It wasn't easy changing under the sleek thermal sheet without losing it, but Mina was determined to make it work. While the rest of the group shuffled and hopped awkwardly about, Basheba busied herself retrieving a pair of latex gloves from Buck's saddlebag, yanking them on, and examining the rabbit.

Mina paused.

Is it okay to eat a rabbit from the Witch's Woods?

"You guys even warmed our socks?" Cadwyn said happily.

"You are awesome," Ozzie said, sighing with contentment as he pulled on the thick wool.

The leather of the collar and cuffs had worked with the river water to rub Mina's skin raw. Still, she didn't dare to take them off as she struggled to pull her sweater on. Somewhat sheepishly, she mumbled.

"That was Basheba. She set up everything."

By the time they had all gathered around the flames, Basheba was ready to reduce the once living creature into a meal. Mina wasn't a squeamish person. She had proven that to herself on the hillside with Cadwyn. But, for some reason, seeing Basheba cut into the little bunny churned her stomach.

The older girl had cleared a stone and stretched the rabbit out on its back with its ears pointed toward her lap. The ever-present mist was somewhat held back by the fire and, as the others crowded around for warmth, she went about her work with clean, efficient, confident motions. The first small cut into its stomach brought a weak beading of blood and a puff of steam. Mina couldn't look away as Basheba worked her fingers in to pry the wound wider. It wasn't because the scene horrified her, but because the fresh kill must still have had some warmth to it. Her frozen fingers ached with jealousy.

Basheba plucked out some small organs and brought them closer to the flames, turning them over with the utmost care, studying them intensely. Eventually, she smiled.

"And to the victor goes the spoils," she said and offered them to the grateful dog.

It was the gulping wet smacks that finally drew both boys' attention. Ozzie's jaw dropped. Mina had never so clearly seen the color drain from someone's face. It didn't matter that he instantly looked away. His nose wrinkled and he started making small, gulping noises.

"Ozzie?" Cadwyn asked in a whisper. "Are you feeling okay? You look pale."

"Why are you killing a rabbit?" Ozzie asked just shy of a whimper.

Basheba didn't pause in her motions, "I'm not. It's already dead."

"But we have other food," Ozzie protested.

Confusion crossed Basheba's face and her hands finally stilled, if only for a second.

"No one told you?" Shrugging off her own question, she gestured a bloody finger to the backpacks. "Check the food."

Curiosity put Cadwyn into motion, the other two following. It didn't take long for him to pull out a clear bag of mixed nuts. He weighed it in his palm for a moment before the lines in his brow deepened and he threw Basheba a quizzical glance.

"Give her a second," Basheba dismissed. "She must be feeling a little lazy."

Opening the pack, he tipped a few cashews out onto his palm, shifting them about with his thumb.

"They look completely normal," Mina said. Plucking one up, she popped it into her mouth.

It turned to sludge on her tongue. A thick, tacky slime coated her mouth, ensuring the taste of rancid meat would linger even after she spat it out. Beside her, Cadwyn made a few disgusted grunts, signaling to her that the other nuts had rotted the same way.

Focused on gouging the innards out of the rabbit, Basheba didn't bother to look up as she spoke. "That's one of her favorite tricks."

"Then why do we keep bringing food along?" Ozzie stuck out his tongue and scoured it with his fingernails after tasting one himself.

Finding her water bottle in her pack, Mina rinsed her mouth out and passed the bottle to Ozzie.

"Wishful thinking, I guess," Basheba shrugged.

Cadwyn dangled the bag in front of his face and poked at the still intact nuts. "She doesn't do this all the time, does she?"

"Katrina likes to mix stuff up," Basheba said.

He frowned and eyed the rabbit with suspicion.

"Will that be safe to eat?"

With a wet squelch, Basheba pulled the rabbit's skin off. "As long as it's not something she created. Its organs looked fine."

Those few words brought hope fluttering into Mina's chest. *There are limitations,* she realized. *If there are limitations, there has to be an internal logic.* It felt like the earth had once again become solid beneath her, no longer crumbling in spontaneous chaos or shifting around her like a dream. There were limits to Katrina's abilities. That meant, even here, in the Witch's Woods, logic existed. Rules existed. Perhaps they weren't the same biology and physics rules the rest of the world had to abide by, but they prevailed in some form, and even Katrina couldn't change that. *If I can figure out what they are, I can find a way to end this.*

Mina clamped her mouth shut before the words could topple free. She couldn't be the first one to ever have these thoughts. Spouting off about them now would only antagonize Basheba and derail their conversation. And she needed Basheba to keep talking.

It struck Mina that she hadn't really been listening. When people spoke, she had been too distracted by her search for cause or reason to simply take in the information. *Observation. Hypothesis. Experimentation.* It had seen her through before, and it would see her through now.

"How can she do that?" Cadwyn asked, studying each of the food bags in turn.

"That isn't the strangest thing that's happened today," Ozzie grumbled, his voice slightly muffled as he crouched low and hung his head between his knees. "I'm still trying to figure out why she stopped with the bees. Why did she let us go?"

Mina's arms curled protectively around herself at the mention of the swarm. Between Ozzie's heavy breathing and Basheba's steady dissection of the rabbit, no one noticed.

"That one's easy," Basheba chirped as she slopped the empty skin aside.

Ozzie gagged.

"There's only so long your 'Thinking Brain' can handle being afraid. After that point, it switches over to 'Caveman Brain,'" she continued.

Cadwyn braved the spitting embers to sit closer to the flames. His obvious fatigue couldn't keep an amused smile from tipping his lips. "I'm going to need you to elaborate on that."

The blonde girl scoffed and started to hack off the rabbit's limbs.

"You can't keep someone in a point of terror forever. If you try, we'll eventually face the threat like our caveman ancestors would have." One solid swipe severed a leg and made the blade clash against stone. "We grab something solid and beat it until it stops moving.

That's why she gives us breaks and switches to soft torture methods."

"Soft torture methods?" Cadwyn almost chuckled.

"Right. Sorry. We're supposed to call them 'advanced interrogation techniques,'" Basheba said. "No sleep, hunger, the cold. All that stuff designed to break us down mentally and make the next horror hurt all the more. Katrina likes to alternate between the two."

"That's not comforting," Ozzie mumbled, the firelight making the fine layer of sweat on his face glisten.

"It wasn't meant to be."

"Are you okay?" Cadwyn cut in. "I'm serious. You look really pale."

The teen pressed his lips tight and shook his head, all the while keeping his eyes locked on the dirt between his feet.

"Talk to me," Cadwyn urged.

"Is it the blood?" Basheba asked innocently.

To test her theory, she rocked up onto her knees and reached out, pushing her blood-slicked fingertips into Ozzie's peripheral vision. The boy reeled at the sight, retching violently.

"Blood? Really?" The question slipped Basheba's lips before she huffed gently. It wasn't an unkind sound. "You were fine in the graveyard."

Ozzie swallowed several times in a desperate attempt to stifle his gag reflex.

"Those were burns. It's different."

He barely got the words out before he retched again. Cadwyn was there to rub his back and offer him sips of water. *The aftertaste won't be helping*, Mina thought. It wasn't doing her any good.

"You're okay." Cadwyn's voice was surprisingly soothing. "Just take deep breaths."

Ozzie nodded weakly and obeyed as best he could, spitting a few mouthfuls of water onto the dirt. Keeping his smile bright for Ozzie, Cadwyn swung an arm out loosely toward his medical bag, clearly asking someone to grab it. Basheba raised her eyebrows and her blood-covered hands. Firelight danced off her knife, drawing more attention to the thick liquid that drenched it and the pale skin. Ozzie made the mistake of glancing up and moaned pitifully.

"Sorry," Basheba said and quickly brought her hands back down.

Mina hurried to grab the pack and bring it over. It was a small container of vapor rub that he was after. He instructed the teen to smear some of the sharply scented gel under his nose.

"To block the smell."

It seemed to help a little bit. At least enough that Ozzie was able to sit upright and not look like he was about to faint.

"The smell's the problem? Hold up."

She set the rabbit to cook, messing with the coals to swell the flames. That done, she yanked up a few handfuls of some tall grass. Without shaking off the sticking snow, Basheba used it to clean her hands and tossed the matted mess into the teepee fire. A sweet scent Mina couldn't place quickly tainted the smoke. Ozzie breathed deep and drew one knee up to his chest.

"I'm sorry," Ozzie mumbled. He attempted a weak smile. "I guess I've lost my hero status in your eyes, huh?"

"Start pulling teeth and you'll see me in a worse state," Cadwyn assured him before Basheba could respond.

"Bees," Mina rushed, hoping to distract him and hold off the smaller woman's response. "I'm terrified of bees. Any flying, stinging insect, really."

"Oh. Well, that explains why you were so terrified." Ozzie's eyes widened and he rushed to add. "Not that you didn't have reason to be scared. Anyone would have been in your situation. I just mean..." He stammered for a second before sighing. "I hope you're feeling better."

"Thank you," Mina smiled.

"Drowning," Basheba stated. She barely glanced about the group before fixing her attention on cleaning her hunting knife.

"You're afraid of drowning?" Ozzie asked.

Basheba shrugged one shoulder but it was a tense, jerking

motion. "Girls with my name don't do too well in deep water."

Drowning. The word repeated in Mina's head, bringing with it a thickening trail of guilt.

"You handled your fear a lot better than I did." She felt obligated to say it out loud; to publicly admit her weakness.

I'll do better next time. God, I hope there's not a next time.

Basheba's dismissive snort snapped her out of her thoughts.

"That's just practice. And it didn't hurt that I knew it was coming." Using the back of her wrist to push the hair from her forehead left a smear of blood behind. "You won't have such a high opinion of me when she brings out the kids."

"Hold up. Did you just say 'kids'?" Ozzie asked.

"They're terrifying," Basheba said with a shudder. "Especially when you can't see their stupid little faces."

Ozzie glanced around the group, looking about as confused as Mina felt.

"Just to clarify," Mina said as gently as she could. "You're scared of children? Human children?"

"I have a logical aversion to tiny little psychopaths with no impulse control and a limited understanding of empathy."

"So, smaller versions of yourself?" Cadwyn smiled.

She paused, looked at him over the flames, and held her blood-stained hands out in a helpless shrug.

"Terrifying, right?"

***

Curled up on his side, Cadwyn stared at the wall of the tent and tried to decide if it was worth leaving the warmth of his sleeping bag to sneak a cigarette. The heavy snow had set in just as they started their dinner of charred rabbit and apples Buck had brought back from the surrounding darkness. He never thought he'd eat a piece of fruit that had recently been inside a dog's mouth but, by the time

Basheba had roasted them over the hot coals, hunger had won out. In all, it hadn't been a bad meal.

Cadwyn had new gratitude for Basheba's nomadic lifestyle. There was fierce independence in everything she did. It allowed him more than enough time to check and treat the numerous small wounds everyone had received, and fix some of his stitches that had popped free. The only chore she had delegated to anyone else was cleaning the dishes. She had kept them far away from any significant body of water. But there was a small trickling stream close enough to glisten in the firelight. It was maybe six inches wide and two inches at its deepest, but Basheba refused to go anywhere near it. No one pushed the issue. The two teens had leaped at the chance to make themselves useful. It took them fifteen minutes to warm their fingers back up after they were done.

Even while she took care of them, Basheba retreated in on herself, ignoring their physical presence as best she could. The only one she never failed to respond to was Buck. He was her constant shadow and, without prompting or reason, Basheba would stop whatever she was doing to lavish the dog with affection. The moments ended as abruptly as they started and were so random that it didn't take long for the remaining three to begin betting on when it would happen next.

Rolling over onto his back, Cadwyn watched as the falling snow deepened the shadows atop the tent. The increasing downfall had brought them inside the tent shortly after dinner, and it hasn't stopped since. It worked with the creeping fog to chase off any trace of warmth. He made a mental note to thank whoever was in charge of selecting the sleeping bags. Heavy-duty thermal was a good choice. It made it all the harder to get up, though. He had forgotten about his cigarette craving as soon as his legs started to cramp. The three-person tent was a tight squeeze for their party. Not at all helped by Buck taking up almost as much room as Basheba did.

He glanced across the row of sleeping bodies. Cadwyn and

Basheba had taken to the walls, ensuring the younger two remained protected between them. Buck had coiled around his owner, allowing her to use him as both a pillow and a blanket.

Cadwyn wasn't too proud to admit he was jealous. A big furry animal would be a welcome relief from the ever-deepening cold.

Basheba had stocked the teepee fire just before they had retreated to the tent, and the passing hours hadn't done much to deplete the lashing flames. It made the tent walls glow and accentuated every passing shadow. The idea of having someone keep watch had been tossed around the group but came to nothing when Basheba crawled into her sleeping bag without comment. After a bit of prompting, she murmured that they could do whatever they wanted. *It wouldn't make any difference.*

That comment had lodged into Cadwyn's brain like a splinter, keeping him awake and restless long after the others had fallen asleep.

Does she mean that Katrina will come for us, and we're doomed no matter what we do? The pop and crackle of the flames answered the distant scurrying of rodents. It seemed every sound was sharpened by his clustering thoughts. *Or does she mean that Katrina will keep her distance and let our anxiety get to us?*

Letting his head roll to the side, Cadwyn studied the line of sleeping figures again. He hoped it was the last option simply because it obviously wasn't working on anyone else but him. A small smile pulled at his lips as he watched the others. The fragile peace helped ease his mind. Adrenaline and determination could stave off sleep only for so long. Eventually, staying awake was really no longer an option. The body did what it needed to do and, as his eyelids grew heavy, he realized just how grateful he was for that.

Cadwyn drifted, never fully awake nor truly sinking into oblivion. The cool air invaded his lungs on each breath and trailed down his neck like icy fingers. Small creatures scurried through the undergrowth, and birds let out low, dreary calls. The fire hissed as snowflakes melted against their touch, releasing a woody scent combated against the lingering odor of wet dog.

Tension steadily slipped from his muscles until he felt like he was melting into the frozen earth. He sunk. A distant snap made him flinch, forcing his eyes open, leaving him blinking owlishly at the tent ceiling.

Nothing had changed.

Not sure if he had just dreamt the sound, he looked around while moving as little as possible, not wanting to risk stirring the others. The others breathed slow and deep. Buck whimpered in his sleep, his paws shifting over the tent floor to produce a muffled scrape. Holding his breath, Cadwyn strained to hear anything that didn't belong.

All traces of sleep left him when he caught the distant trace of cackling laughter. His heartbeat kicked up so fast he could barely breathe. Craning his neck but careful not to lift his head, he looked at the others, hoping at least one of them had stirred. Mina and Ozzie had curled up together in a desperate bid for warmth. They effectively blocked his view of Basheba.

Blindly, he slowly stretched one arm out, slipping it over the top of the sleeping teenagers with the intent of tapping Basheba awake. Buck's low growl made him pause. After a moment, he continued. He still couldn't see her or the Rottweiler. The high-pitched laughter came again, far closer than it had been before, and he whipped around to stare at the tent wall behind him. He almost yelped at the first touch. Tiny, chilled fingers crept around his palm, slow and sluggish, the motion of someone still half-asleep.

"Basheba?" he whispered.

She shushed him. The sound barely louder than the chirp of cicadas and the crackling campfire. Her thumb rubbed circles against his palm. That small point of human contact changed everything. All the monsters he had created in his head turned back into shadows. The laughter died away and the placid calm returned. At last, he was able to close his eyes again. Cadwyn curled his wrist so he could take a better hold of Basheba's hand. A branch snapped from somewhere close by. He jerked his head up.

"Did you hear that?" he whispered.

Again, she shushed him. A long, quiet push of breath through her teeth.

Right, don't wake the others.

A part of him wanted to get them up. If something was coming for them, it would be better for all of them to be alert and ready to face it.

Or run.

In the back of his mind, he wasn't entirely convinced he wasn't just being paranoid. The more he questioned himself, the less certain he was that he had heard anything at all. Basheba squeezed his hand reassuringly, and he nodded to himself.

She's been here before. It was a small point but left her in a far better position to survive Katrina Hamilton's Harvest.

It struck him with renewed force just how much security he found in her presence. It didn't matter that he was oldest, biggest, and undoubtedly the strongest physically in the group. Every time he thought of Katrina, he was hurled back through time to become that scared little boy watching helplessly as monsters devoured his brother, mind and soul. Suddenly, he was hyperaware of the music box in the sleeping bag with him. Its pointed edges dug uncomfortably into his spine, but he didn't try to move it. He knew what was gestating inside it, and that knowledge was driving him mad. It left him jealous of the others, Ozzie and Mina in particular. They had had so many years of blissful ignorance.

A sharp snap made him jump, jerking him from his thoughts and thrusting him back to reality. He couldn't pinpoint the exact moment he had dozed off, or how long he had been out, but Basheba's hand was still in his. Soft, cool skin that left him feeling like a giant.

"Basheba?"

Again, her only response was a low shush. Drawing a deep breath through his nose, he forced himself to lay still, and locked his gaze onto the top of the tent. Beside him, Mina rolled closer to Ozzie who groaned at the disturbance but didn't wake up. The air seemed to thicken as he breathed. Tightening his grip on Basheba's fingers, he forced his eyes closed and tried to calm his mind. But the demon's eyes were there, waiting for him in the darkness of his mind. Basheba squeezed back, and he was able to choke down a staggered breath.

Leaves crunched. Tension turned his muscles to stone and his eyes snapped open. *It's just outside.* Keeping his head locked into place, he lowered his gaze to the zipper. The tent walls seemed to pulsate in the firelight, shifting and moving with the collecting shadows. He tightened his grip on Basheba a bit more. Something shuffled outside, and he flicked his eyes to the side, wishing he could see the small woman. Another crunch of dead leaves and a shadow cut over the tent. A dark, dense, foreboding strip of ebony that severed the tent in two. Cadwyn went to lurch up but Basheba's grip kept him down.

"Shh," she whispered on a breath.

Has she been through this before? Did Katrina come do this to her? Does she know what's out there?

Questions sizzled through his panicked mind as the shadow washed over them.

Growing larger or coming closer? He couldn't tell.

His core began to shake, the tremble working into his lungs, forcing him to hyperventilate. Basheba didn't move. Her hand was solid as stone and cold as ice. The small bit of contact was the only thing keeping him from running, from waking up the others, and fleeing from whatever was slowly creeping toward the opening of the tent. It blotted out the firelight, shrouding their shelter in murky darkness as it crept ever closer, each step announced by the decaying plant life. Cadywn clenched his jaw, and held his breath. The silence accentuated every hint of sound. The footsteps stopped right outside. The fabric rustled. His heart slammed against his ribs until his whole body shook with the blows.

Get the kids up! Get them out! Save them! The orders were a deafening scream within his skull, but Basheba's hold on his hand kept him in place. Her stillness became his.

Trust her plan, he told himself. *Whatever it is.*

The zipper rasped as it slowly pulled open. Firelight showed through the opening, seeping around the suddenly diminished figure, washing over the two sleeping teenagers captured in the center of the tent. The shadowy figure loomed inside, and Cadwyn snapped. Slipping loose of Basheba's grip, he jerked upright, a startled scream bursting from his lips.

Ozzie and Mina jolted awake. Buck snapped and snarled. Basheba flung the tent flaps back to fill the space with light and drifting snow. Cadwyn blinked against the glare while his brain struggled to comprehend what was standing before him.

Basheba stood in the entrance, her short stature barely filling the opening even while it cast a colossal shadow. Buck shoved his snout between her legs, still growling, clawing at the dirt as he looked for what had caused the startled cries. Cadwyn snapped around to look at the far side of the tent. Basheba's sleeping bag was empty.

"What? What's wrong?" Mina stammered.

In the same moment, Ozzie also asked what was wrong and Basheba snapped a few profanities.

"What is it? Why are you yelling like that?"

He could only look back and forth between where she stood and where she had been lying only a few seconds ago.

"Cadwyn?" Basheba said sharply. "What's wrong?"

"You were outside?"

Her brow furrowed. "Yeah. Nature called." After a second, she sighed. "I took Buck with me and didn't go far. Promise."

"You were outside," Cadwyn said.

"Yes," she said somewhat sharply. "I'm sorry if I scared you."

Swallowing thickly, he looked down at his hand. He could still feel the chill from her touch. "Whose hand was I holding?"

Basheba awoke with a jerk. The scent of winter hung heavy in the crisp air and the chill nipped at her nose. Buck's cheeks wobbled as he grumbled in protest. Instead of getting up, he repositioned his head on top of hers and pretended to be asleep. It took a few moments before she could recall where she was. Blinking her eyes open, she found herself the focus of everyone in the tent. Mina and Ozzie looked miserable as they sat side by side to share the warmth of a single sleeping bag. Dark shadows lined Cadwyn's eyes, highlighting the wrinkles that seemed to have deepened overnight. He clutched a mug of tea with both hands and stared at her over the rim.

"Well, this is in no way unnerving," Basheba said softly.

"How were you able to sleep?" Mina countered.

She shrugged, the small motion enough to have Buck protesting again. He looped one paw over her to keep her in place.

"It's a natural bodily process," Basheba offered.

"But, after everything? And then what happened with Cadwyn?" Mina shook her head rapidly like she could fight off the thoughts haunting her.

Basheba gently shoved her pet off her and tried to sit up. Buck had other thoughts and, by the time they were done, he was lounging across her lap, effectively pinning her to the ground with his body weight. Shivering in the chill, she released a jaw-cracking yawn. In truth, it hadn't been much of a conscious decision. She had more collapsed than settled in for a nap.

No good could come from clarifying that now, she reasoned.

Absently, she patted Buck along his snout and resolved not to threaten their fragile morale. Or her own. She looked so much braver when she saw herself through their eyes.

"Katrina's coming for us either way. Might as well nap while you can." Basheba turned to Cadwyn with a smile. "Don't suppose you have another cup of that tea?"

"It's just hot water," he admitted with a small pout. "The teabags have gone moldy."

"There's some spruce trees out there."

He blinked at her, and she explained during another yawn.

"You bruise the needles and leave them to soak for ten minutes," she smiled. "Rich in vitamin A and C."

"How do you know this stuff?" he asked.

She scrunched up her face, "I read. Honestly, it's not that hard."

Breakfast was tense and packing up the camp was not much better. The snow slowed things down considerably. The others tried to help but their lack of experience was almost as bad as the snow. She couldn't believe she was the only one who had ever gone camping before. It seemed like they had missed out on a necessary part of childhood.

Or maybe I was being trained.

The thought bubbled up in the back of her head, bringing with it a thousand different memories.

They had made sure I'd be comfortable in the woods, she realized. A mixture of gratitude and sorrow mixed up her insides until tears pricked at her eyes.

"Basheba?" Cadwyn asked softly as he helped her stow away the tent. "Are you okay?"

"Yeah. Just thinking."

"It'll all be okay."

"I was thinking about good things," she assured him as she pulled Mina's bag closer and started packing things away. "Some good things have happened to me, you know."

"Like what?"

Pushing a sleeping bag down with determination, she lifted her chin. "I got a puppy."

"Okay, I have to give you that."

Basheba's attention wavered when her fingertips brushed against some soft plastic. *More food?* Her stomach rolled at the thought of her sleeping bag getting drenched in the repulsive stench of decay. Yanking it out, she froze, her eyes locked on the little ziplock bag nestled against her palm. *Belladonna.* Katrina hadn't touched the leaves, leaving them crisp and vibrant green. Anger bubbled in her stomach. *Bloody Cranes.*

"Basheba?"

Her head jerked up and her hand closed in a tight fist around the baggie. "Yeah?"

Concern danced in Cadwyn's eyes. "Are you all right?"

"Just missing my morning coffee," Basheba forced a smile and shoved the bag of deadly foliage into the deep pockets of her waterproof hiking pants. "Were you saying anything important?"

"I was just..." He trailed off, the smile on his lips as fake as her own. "Did I cross a line asking about your father?"

Basheba couldn't recall him mentioning any of her family. It didn't matter, though. She wasn't about to tell him anything about her family in detail. There wasn't a lot she had left of them. Just some memories, and a half dozen photographs her uncle hadn't been able to collect first. Logically, she knew sharing these things wouldn't deplete what she had. But logic didn't have much sway over grief. She wasn't about to take the risk. Her memories were her own. Just as her body and her mind were. *And if I can't have them, no one will.*

"Basheba?" Cadwyn asked again, his voice softer than before. Kinder and with distinct hesitation.

"We're wasting daylight."

Brushing aside the gathering snow, she hurriedly zipped up Mina's bag and called the girl over to collect it. Basheba made sure to have her own pack in place and was several feet away before the girl was near. A low whistle brought Buck to her side and she stalked into the woods, leaving the others to catch up if they were so inclined.

The small cluster of leaves in her pocket felt as heavy as lead. It wasn't that she was surprised. It wouldn't be the first time the Crane family had come into the Harvest with this kind of game plan. What niggled at the corners of her mind was how easily she would have ingested the poison. Thinking back, she recalled several times she had accepted bottled water from the Crane girl during last night's dinner alone.

Just because they want to live doesn't mean they care if you do.

She stumbled as the past warning slipped to the forefront of her mind. It had been two years to the day since she had learned that lesson. Sweeping her eyes across the near identical rows of trees, she wondered how close she was to where it had all gone down. Long, silenced screams echoed around her. The coppery scent of blood pricked at her nose.

If I move the leaves, would the blood still be there? There was so much of it. It must have stained the soil red.

"Hey." Ozzie's voice shattered the memories that had shackled Basheba's mind.

She twisted around to watch the group coming closer, still repositioning their packs and organizing their winter gear. Each step came with the crunch of snow and the crackle of frost. Ozzie's blisters had grown enough to give him a small but noticeable limp. *He'd be in a lot of pain if it wasn't for the numbing cold.* A smile pulled at her lips. *Thanks, Katrina.*

Mina eyed Basheba's smile, suspicion plain on her face. "What's wrong?"

"I just need to check the compass," Basheba replied smoothly. "Cadwyn?"

The older man dug into his pocket as he approached and pulled out the small compass disk. It didn't take more than a glance to notice the needle never set on a single spot but spun around at random.

Ozzie sucked in a sharp breath.

"Katrina?" Mina asked.

"Magnetic field," Basheba replied. "But I'm glad you're getting into the swing of things."

Ozzie frowned. "What magnets?"

She tried not to laugh at how adorably confused he looked. *Like a little puppy.*

"The hills are filled with nickel," Basheba explained. "Nickel messes with the magnetic fields compasses use to work."

Fear sparked in the depths of Ozzie's dark eyes. "So, we're lost?"

"No."

"I don't mean to argue." Mina's voice sounded a little tense as she spoke the blatant lie. "But we are now without a map or a working compass. How are we not lost?"

"Well, for one thing, the giant mountain that's messing with the compass can help with orientation," Basheba dismissed.

While Cadwyn smiled, he shook his head in a sign of annoyance. "Do you know which way we should go now?"

Basheba pointed in two opposing directions.

"Now you're just trying to be irritating," he said.

"We all need hobbies," Basheba dismissed. "There are two ways to get to the ranch house from where we are now. We go this way," she said as she pointed up the gradually increasing incline, "we'll have to climb up a cliff face that will put an extra day on our trip."

"Why would we take that path?" Ozzie asked.

"It avoids the orchard," Basheba said, stubbornly forcing down the memories that tried to bubble to the surface.

The three people looked at each other and Mina asked, "What's wrong with the orchard?"

Memories pushed hard against her mind's eye. She clenched her jaw and balled her hands in a desperate attempt to keep them out.

"The fruit," she whispered. Swallowing thickly, she carefully bottled the wildfire burning within her soul and searing her mind.

Calmer now, she tilted her head to the side, allowing her matted blonde hair to sweep over her shoulder. "No offense, but I don't think you two will do well going that way. Better to fall to your death. Quick and simple."

"That's the way you went before?" Mina asked.

Basheba nodded.

"You survived."

"I was prepared."

Mina smiled. "But we have you and Cadwyn."

"And there's nothing we'd rather do than deal with two teenagers having mental breakdowns in the middle of haunted woods." Basheba watched the girl's polite smile slip. "Sounds like fun."

"How many days do we have left?" Mina asked. "If the detour is going to put at least an extra day onto our trip, how long will we have left?"

Basheba shrugged. "Two. Maybe one, depending on Katrina. The closer we get to the house, the more she can mess with the daylight hours. It makes it harder to keep track of time."

"That's cutting it rather close, isn't it?" Mina asked.

Lifting her chin, she stared at the girl.

"Again, I'm not trying to argue. I'm trying to understand," Mina insisted. "I don't know how long it generally takes to find these keys. Is a day enough?"

She shifted her weight between her feet. "It depends on how well she hides them."

"I suck at hide and seek," Ozzie blurted. "I'm not going to be good at this. I'll need more time."

Cadwyn slipped closer to Basheba's side, hunching over to whisper to the far shorter woman. "I'm not so sure any of us can make it up a sheer cliff face."

Avoiding his gaze, she refrained from commenting.

"*I* won't get up it. Not with this cut on my chest," he continued in a whisper. "And definitely not while carrying Buck's weight, if that was your plan."

Her eyes instantly lowered to the loyal dog sitting patiently at her feet. Leaving him behind wasn't an option.

"I'll take you to the orchard," Basheba said. "But I take no responsibility for what happens there. You all get to carry that yourselves."

Chapter 18

The sun couldn't penetrate the thick blanket cloud cover, leaving the world in perpetual twilight, allowing shadows to shift amongst the trees. Time had turned the fog into a constantly churning mist. Weak enough to see through, cold enough to leave a thin layer of ice over everything it came into contact with. The snow never stopped. Random snaps rang throughout the woods as the overloaded branches cracked from the trunk and crashed down around them.

Despite Basheba's insistence that their ignorance would lead to their demise, she wasn't in any rush to educate them. Mina had struggled to hold her tongue as she watched Cadwyn try and fail to draw the small girl into a conversation. The task was made all the harder since she couldn't get a firm read on Basheba's motives. At first, Mina had been confident Basheba harbored a real and honest fear of the place. But, as time passed, and she still refused to talk, Mina started to suspect it wasn't the only reason. Nor was it just another example of her frigid nature. *Something's changed.* Mina couldn't pinpoint what it was, exactly. But her gut told her it was significant. And that worried her.

Time passed slowly. The cold and her gathering hunger made the trip all the more uncomfortable and, by the time Basheba started to slow down, Mina was glad she wasn't facing a climb at the end of the trudge. Just when she thought she couldn't walk another step on the frozen stumps that were once her feet, Basheba let them take a break.

Ozzie dropped into the mist, slumping onto his back like an upturned turtle. While his antics made both Mina and Cadwyn chuckle, neither decided to join him, and instead found a large stone that could keep them above the mist. Basheba gave her spot to Buck, using his elevation to more easily scrub at his neck in a playful way. The dog's muzzle was white with frozen slobber.

"How deep is the snow?" Basheba asked Ozzie without looking at him. "Just show me with the length of your finger."

Obediently, Ozzie shoved his hand down. "Goes up to the middle of my palm." Repeating the motion a few times, he decided to stand beside his first declaration.

"Good. Take off your bag."

Ozzie flicked his gaze to Cadwyn, waiting for the older man to give an approving nod before he started to struggle free of his pack.

Does he feel the change, too?

In a small act of mercy that she felt endlessly grateful for, Mina found her water bottle hadn't frozen over. She took a few mouthfuls before offering it around. Basheba eyed the bottle for a second before meeting Mina's gaze. Without a word, she turned back around and resumed working on Ozzie's pack, sliding the tent's collapsible metal poles free.

Confused, Mina wondered what the woman's problem was. Basheba's expression had seemed to hold some kind of meaning, but she didn't know how to interpret it. Then it dawned on her. She had been messing with Mina's bag earlier, putting their supplies away. Was there really belladonna there? Had Basheba found it? It would certainly have explained the woman's preoccupation.

But perhaps I'm reading too much into things. Maybe she's just distracted by the forest and being her antisocial self.

Still, Mina couldn't shake the suspicion and waited fretfully until Cadwyn was busy checking Ozzie's blistered feet to move over to the smaller woman.

"Is something wrong?" she asked quietly, almost dreading the answer.

Basheba glanced up at her, her face scrunched up and brows knitted.

"I mean, you seem tenser."

"Do I?"

"Is there anything you want to tell me?" Mina tried again, wanting to get the confrontation over with but dreading it at the same time.

A tiny smile tipped the edges of her mouth. "Like what?"

The conversation was broken as the boys came over. There wasn't much left to eat, and they quickly went through the few berries Basheba pointed out. With that done, it was wordlessly agreed that they wanted to get moving again, to get the horror over with. For once, it was Basheba holding them back. She finished tying the poles to the side of the bag. Then, she worked to loop the ends around the spikes on Buck's armor.

"Shake."

The dog flopped around, successfully knocking the poles aside.

"Good boy," she cooed, completely ignoring everyone else so she could focus on her dog.

"What are you doing?" Ozzie asked when no one else did.

"I'm not going to let him get stuck with your pack if things go wrong," Basheba said.

"He's taking my bag?"

"It won't bother him." She finally paused in her gushing affections to throw a glance over her shoulder. "You can barely walk."

The small act of kindness caught Ozzie off guard. "Thanks, Basheba."

The tiny woman scoffed. "Buck's the one doing the work. Aren't you, pretty boy? Such a good boy."

The group used Basheba's distraction to check in with each other and drink a little more. Eventually, the blonde remembered what she was doing and set off. Once again, it seemed she didn't care if anyone noticed or followed. Buck trotted happily alongside his master, unconcerned with his armor, or the heavy pack now attached to it.

"Were you planning on switching our bags later on?" Ozzie

asked, hurrying to clarify. "Cadwyn and Mina could probably use a break as well. And you, of course."

"I think Mina will want to keep hold of her bag," Basheba said with a light giggle.

The guys threw her some questioning looks, but she shrugged, attempting a confused nonchalance. Mina suddenly felt queasy.

She found the belladonna. She had to have. I can't believe my mother actually put it there. She honestly wanted me to poison these people.

Mina wasn't sure what made her feel worse; her parents pushing her to murder, or Basheba believing she was capable of going through with it. *Oh god,* the knowledge was a punch to the gut. A burst of pain that left her breathless. *Basheba thinks I planned to kill her.* Images of the graveyard flashed across her mind. The blonde had almost poisoned the town population because she *thought* they *might* be turning a blind eye. *What would she do to someone whom she thinks is a clear and present threat?* Gulping down the blossoming fear, she followed the others in silence.

The tiny woman always knew where she was going. She wove their way amongst the trees, working over the rolling hills and across moss-drenched creeks as if she was following a map only she could see.

A deep, bone-aching exhaustion had taken hold of Mina by the time Basheba let them rest again. Keeping to the base of a hill kept them somewhat protected from the snow and growing winds. Without discussion, Mina, Ozzie, and Cadwyn clustered closer for warmth. To absolutely no-one's surprise, Basheba favored her dog, instead.

Hunger bit at her insides like a wild animal. Mina spent the vast majority of her break trying to find the perfect way to ask Basheba to send Buck on a hunt. She didn't know how much time had passed but they seemed to have plenty of daylight left. Even if she was wrong, she would be deliriously happy to simply spend a few moments beside a fire.

Before she could decide how best to ask, Basheba let go of Buck and started fussing with the bags again. This time, she retrieved a thin cord from the tent and proceeded to slash her mud-stained shirt into strips.

"Okay, we're going to kindergarten the hell out of this," Basheba said abruptly. "Everyone holds onto the cord. You do not let go of the cord. You do not stop walking."

Oddly enough, it was their silence that finally made her look at them. The large hunting knife in her hand added an extra unsettling element to her glare.

"Am I talking to myself?" Basheba asked.

The three of them hurried to retroactively agree with the requirements. Cadwyn was the only one who ventured to ask questions.

"What's going on with your shirt?"

"Well, I can't trust any of you not to look. So, I'm making blindfolds."

His brow furrowed. A silent sign of confusion that somehow earned him Basheba's full attention.

"I already know what's on the other side of the hill. You don't have to. So, just hold onto the cord and trust me to lead you through."

"I don't like the idea of making you face whatever this is alone," Cadwyn said. "That's the only good thing about this whole setup. We'll all come out with *shared* trauma."

Basheba straightened and passed him the far end of the cord. "Oh, *now* you're all about sharing? Once the pretzels are gone?"

"Are you still not over that?" he asked, taking the cord more out of reflex than conscious thought.

"Cadwyn, years from now, when you're old and gray, and on your deathbed, I will still be berating you over those pretzels. Your poor grieving wife is going to be so confused."

"Huh," Cadwyn said. "You'd think she'd be used to you by then."

"You'd think. But she's very slow. Pretty, but slow."

Cadwyn shrugged. "Can't wait to meet her."

With that, he began to get everyone into position. Basheba, Ozzie, Mina, with him at the rear. Mina wondered if he had noticed Basheba's increased dislike of her and wanted to keep them separated. She was a little surprised when Basheba trusted everyone to tie their own blindfolds.

"Can we at least get up the hill before we put them on?" Ozzie asked. "I'm not that great walking in snow. And if I fall now, I'm taking you all with me."

"We'll go slow," Basheba promised. "Don't worry. It's not for long. The ranch house is right on the other side of the orchard."

Since that was the closest Basheba seemed to come to offering actual reassurance, no one was quick to brush it aside. It was Cadwyn who checked their blindfolds were set in place before Basheba started to walk.

True to her word, she went slow, inching their way up the hill at half the pace she had been forcing them to adopt all day. That changed once they were down the other side. Unable to see heightened Mina's other senses. The wind bit her harder. The crunch of frost and snow was louder. She finally noticed the increasing lingering stench.

The ground had been flat under her feet for a while before the sound of rustling leaves once again surrounded them. Here, however, the sound was riddled with the creak and groan of swaying branches. Her nose wrinkled as the air grew sweet and musky at the same time. The combination brought to mind rotting meat and mothballs.

Even though they all walked in a singular line, it was easiest to keep track of Buck. His makeshift sled created a tell-tale scrape. Everyone else faded into nothing more than footsteps.

Lingering between sensory deprivation and overload, Mina could almost feel her curiosity welling up inside of her, filling her skin and drenching her mind.

They kept walking. A single, slow line trailing through a self-imposed night. The smell grew stronger while the sound of struggling branches became numerous and loud. Mina twisted her hand around the slender cord. Resentment seeped into her curiosity to create a thick sludge in her lungs. It made it hard for her to breathe. Paranoia pricked at her thoughts, whispering that there was nothing around them, that all of this was just Basheba's way to punish them for whatever unknown crime she was blaming them for.

What can she stand to see that I can't handle? Her hand twitched with the desire to take a quick peek of her surroundings.

No one would know. Just one little glance. She pushed it aside only to have a voice whisper, *how do we know she's not leading us to the Witch? She was the only survivor of her last group. Maybe this was how she did it. Offered everyone else up, and killed them herself. It's what my parents wanted me to do after all. She might not be any different.*

The gathering thoughts got the best of her, and she hooked one thumb under her blindfold and peeled it back.

Sunlight, as weak as it was, blinded her for a moment. She squinted around, trying to make sense of what she saw. Everywhere she looked, tall apple trees stretched out to the horizon in perfect rows. One after the other, each loaded heavily with bleeding lumps. A heartbeat later, she understood what she was seeing.

Bodies.

They dangled by their feet, plump and discolored, soft and malleable, like rotten fruit. Snow clung to the blood that dripped from them to create small pools of red around the trunks. A soft groan drew her horrified gaze. One of the nearest bodies twisted in the breeze to bring its rotten, distorted face into view.

Shock hit her like lightning. Death hadn't distorted the face enough that she couldn't recognize her own cousin. Once she had seen one, there was no way to stop seeing the others. One after another, then all at once, she saw the faces of her missing relatives.

The ones she had heard whispers about. Those who had come to the Witch's Woods and had never been seen again. And the others. Those whom she had never met before but could *feel* the Crane blood lingering in their veins. And still others who weren't of her blood. Somehow, she could instinctively pick them out. Winthrop, Seawall, Bell. They all crowded the branches. Hundreds of people. Thousands. Twisting and swaying in the snow-speckled breeze.

Mina's jaw dropped but she didn't scream until her cousin's eyes snapped open and focused upon her.

Chaos broke free.

Cadwyn and Ozzie tugged off their eye masks. The added attention woke the corpses. Death rattles filled the air as, one after the other, the bodies turned toward them. Rotten hands clawed at the air in a desperate attempt to reach them. Buck went wild, his thrashing dislodged the pack from his spikes. Basheba tugged harshly on the cord only to have it slip through their hands.

"Run!" she roared.

Hard shoves sent them into motion, but the damage was done. The writhing bodies around them were already tearing themselves free from the trees. Most couldn't stand. Crippled and riddled with decay, the corpses dragged themselves along the ground, moving to cut the living off as they sprinted down the narrow path between the rows. Blood bubbled up from the ground, staining the snow and shining through the mist. Ozzie's panicked cries gave way to panted breaths and whimpers. Mina grabbed his hand and urged him on as the orchard disintegrated into a bloody mush. His hands squeezed hers to the point of snapping bones. When he fell, he took her with him.

CHAPTER 19

The drop was short and came to a sharp end with a sickening snap and an explosion of pain. Ozzie clutched his arm, instinctively drawing it closer to his body. He could feel his right collar bone shift, the broken edges scraping together, and almost blacked out with the spike of agony. Mina landed on top of him. She rolled away quickly, and he got his first good look at the world around him.

The orchard was gone, replaced by a dark tunnel gouged into the earth. Holes riddled the roof, allowing snow and blood to drift down into the abyss. The screams of the others came down with the debris. He couldn't see them, but he was sure Basheba and Cadwyn hadn't followed them into the pit.

Buck's head emerged over the rim above his head, barked a few times, and then disappeared. He was about to call him back when he noticed Mina's whimpering. It had been lost under the carnage of other sounds above him. Peering into the murky light, he caught sight of her huddled in the shadows. Curled into a tight ball, she pressed her forehead against her knees, clenching her muscles tight to try to stop herself from shivering.

"Hey, Mina, are you hurt?"

"I shouldn't have looked," she whimpered.

Ozzie had barely gotten a glimpse of the hanging bodies before everything had gone to hell. He forced himself not to think about it now, sure that whatever was lurking on the edges of his conscious awareness would cripple him. *What would Cadwyn do?*

"Mina, can you walk? We need to keep moving."

Almost instantly, evidence of this toppled down from the sky.

The living corpses had found the openings in the earth and, compelled by their desire to reach them, had hurled themselves into the open air. Their sun-bleached bones shattered as they landed and destroyed their decomposing flesh. It only slowed them down.

Ozzie gripped Mina's shoulders, remembering a moment too late the amount of pain the motion would cost him. "We have to move. We have to get back to the others."

Mina lifted her head, her eyes widening when she saw what surrounded them.

"What is it? What's wrong?" he asked.

"It's too small."

The space was narrow, but not crushingly so. It was almost the same as walking under the low, hanging trees in the forest. But the walls changed everything. They pressed in on them, deepening the shadows and making everything seem smaller.

"Mina, it's a trick." Hearing his own voice made him cringe. Even he wouldn't believe that lie.

She looked at him, though, so he pushed on.

"It's the Witch, Mina. She's just messing with your head. This place is huge."

"Huge?"

The bodies were piling up, creating writhing, festering mountains that inched ever closer to them.

"Godzilla could stroll through without having to duck."

Dead fingers gouged at the soil by his foot.

"Mina, we have to go. I need you to move." He shook her slightly, forcing her to finally look him in the eyes. "Please, Mina."

Her wide eyes locked onto his. While the panic remained, her body stilled. Sucking in a deep breath, she clenched her jaw, nodded once, and got to her feet. A hand latched onto Ozzie's ankle, gripping tight enough that its fingertips popped like rancid grapes. Frantic screams ripped out of him as he kicked his leg back, desperately trying to dislodge the hand, but only succeeding in dragging the corpse along with him. Mina darted forward. She stooped down, driving the heel of her boot into the brittle bone and snapping it in two.

Ozzie snatched the limb up, narrowly avoiding the other hands that burst free from the squirming pile of flesh. The crude weapon felt light and feeble in his hand; nearly worthless, but better than nothing. Tucking his injured arm protectively against his stomach, he lashed out, swinging the limb like a club. He couldn't put the strength he wanted behind the attacks; his body wasn't capable of it. Still, the severed arm collided against the others with a resounding, reassuring crack. It didn't stop the encroaching tide of bodies. Knocking back one only left room for more to follow.

"Can you see a way out?" Ozzie asked Mina, stomping and kicking and swinging.

Mina's back bumped against his as he retreated. She had collected a leg bone from the mush and, together, they carved out a few feet of clear space.

"Maybe if we can get to the top," she said. "Can you climb?"

The thought alone brought a spark of agony.

"I don't think so." Bones shattered under his feet as he kicked a corpse back. "Maybe I can try."

A swift kick from Mina's boot severed a head and sent it soaring into the distant shadows. Watching the motion brought their attention to the clumps of dirt that toppled down from the opening. The horde of corpses fell into such sudden, intense silence that Ozzie heard each clump squish as they landed. He glanced to Mina, barely catching her eyes before the light began to die. They both snapped their heads up to see what had blocked the light.

Spider legs slipped around the edges of the hole, the tips sinking into the raw earth as its colossal body rose up and blotted out the sun. The opening was nearly ten feet in diameter, large enough for an elephant to fall through. Yet the earth ripped away in clumps as the spider surged down, its bulbous abdomen sealing the hole like a cork.

Ozzie knew he was screaming. His legs gave out, and he fell upon the still corpses. Tears scorched his eyes. But it all felt beyond him—a distant notion that he could never really be a part of.

Only the monstrous spider was real.

Its exoskeleton clicked as it scraped and struggled. Eyes like glistening black orbs filled his vision. The air became saturated with a choking chemical smell as venom seeped from the spider's sword-like fangs to splash over the corpses. They bubbled and melted upon contact. Weak sunlight blinded him as the creature reared back. The earth fell like rain as it threw itself back down, its large abdomen striking the rim again.

"Ozzie!" Mina cupped his head with both hands. He couldn't see her. "Ozzie!"

She jerked him sharply, nearly tearing the tendons of his neck but forcing him to meet her gaze.

"Stay with me," she begged him. "I can't do this without you."

A shower of dirt rained down on them; the spider was a few feet closer. They threw themselves away from the flailing limbs that shredded through the clustered bodies. Bone, flesh, and rotten organs joined the airborne mud, becoming shrapnel that slammed into their backs and tripped their feet, bringing them back down. Ozzie screamed as he landed hard on his shoulder. Mina's gloved hands caught his face again.

"It's okay. It's okay," she repeated.

He tried to look at the charging spider, but she held his head in place, forcing him to see only her.

"I can't," he whimpered.

"It's like the bees. Just an insect."

"We're trapped."

Cracks snaked through the earth, connecting to the nearest hole and threatening to bring it all down upon their heads.

"It's just a bug." The words left her mouth with a robotic edge. It was something she had obviously repeated to herself until the words had lost all meaning.

What would Basheba do? The answer slammed into him with a physical force.

"Bugs can die."

Mina's eyes widened as she realized what he was suggesting. One trembling hand left his face to wrap around the severed leg she had used as a weapon once before.

"We go for the underbelly," she whispered.

He could barely see her through his hot tears. They dripped free when he nodded. A spider leg swung down and forced their hand. After scrambling away from the path of destruction, the world opened up and the spider dropped into the pit. Side by side, they charged, primitive weapons in hand.

The bulbous end of the spider slammed against the walls as it tried to turn and strike. Each motion ripped apart the dirt confines. Ozzie jammed the broken bones through the small gaps between the exoskeleton. Mina slipped past to do the same to another limb. The dual attack forced the arachnid to sway and slam against the wall of the pit.

Feet slipping through the mud, Ozzie rushed forward, spotting Mina in his peripheral vision. The spider countered and struck; forced them to retreat and reposition. Terror exploded within every cell of his being but he forced himself to go in over and over again. His mind fell away. There was no time for thought.

Suddenly, Mina stabbed its abdomen with the broken edge of the bone. The shell cracked, releasing a green sludge. The spider whipped around, fangs splashing the walls with venom, and struck out at her. Ozzie lunged forward, adrenaline giving him the strength needed to sink the splintering bone into its underbelly.

Mucus rained down upon him. The spider trembled and reared. Droplets of venom sloshed over his wounded right arm and instantly began to eat away at his jacket, working down to his skin. He stabbed again. Again. Cracking the outer shell until he could tear it apart with his hands. Fire burned through his collar bone as he tore out chunks. Mina appeared beside him, adding to his efforts, creating a downpour of sludge and innards. Something sleek and metal brushed against his fingertips. Ozzie caught the briefest glimpse of a wrought iron key before, with a final tremor, the spider collapsed on top of him.

***

Basheba's lungs burned as she sprinted toward the ranch house. Buck ran before her, snapping and snarling, carving a path through the corpses for her. Beside her, Cadwyn endlessly searched the landscape.

"I can't see them," he panted between breaths. "We have to go back."

"Keep running!" she ordered.

The orchard was crumbling around them. Massive trees toppled, their roots spewing blood as they were ripped out of the trembling earth. Bodies scattered the path. The living corpses crawled over the heaving ground. Immense sinkholes turned the earth to honeycomb, swallowing trees and the dead alike, drawing ever closer to their only path out of the orchard. Cadwyn's arm looped around her waist, wrenching her off of her feet and bringing her along with him as he leaped forward.

He forced them into a roll after the first, solid impact. Encased in his arms, Basheba was somewhat protected from the following jolts, but there was no way to prevent her head from smacking against the ground. Stray stones slashed at her scalp and released hot blood to trickle over her forehead.

When they, at last, came to a stop, the world stilled along with them. Their panting stirred the silence. Calm snow drifted down upon them while heavy clouds muted the surrounding colors. Everything was reduced to dreary smears of their former luster. That, more than anything else, assured her she was back.

Peeking out from under Cadwyn's arm, Basheba stared up at the broken ruins of the Bell family home. Time had stained the white walls a broken, dirty gray. Burrowing insects had eaten away the base, and the ceiling was more moss than tile. What had once been a front patio had long since sunk into the earth, leaving only a few splintered ends to split the ground like ancient tombstones.

"I'm home," she whispered.

Cadwyn's weight lifted from her. An instant later, he yanked her up, his hands drifting over her hairline, causing sparks of fire. She swatted his hands aside.

"You're bleeding," he told her.

"I'm fine." Her legs felt weak but held her weight. "Where's Buck?"

"And the others," Cadwyn pressed.

She ignored him as she began to whistle. There was no response. Dread turned her organs to stone. Licking her lips, she whistled again, louder than before. She could feel hysteria digging its hooks into her flesh. Once more she whistled. Silence answered her.

"Buck! Come here, boy!"

"Basheba."

She slapped aside the gentle hand he placed upon her shoulder.

"He made it out with us, right? Did you see him? I need to go back." Biting her lips couldn't stop her ramblings. She called for him a few more times, each repetition growing increasingly desperate. "Buck!"

Warmth flooded her chest at the answering bark. Her weak knees dropped her onto the muddy snow and she lifted her arms, welcoming the Rottweiler into a tight embrace. She took care to spare the dog from her spikey collar and wrist cuffs. His own similarly fashioned armor drove into her skin, but she didn't care. Any amount of pain was worth it to feel him safe and warm within her arms again.

"Are you okay, boy? You had me worried." She sniffed and kissed his snout, unintentionally coaxing him to lick her face.

"Is he all right?" Cadwyn asked.

"Of course, he is. He's the best boy." Her skin felt too tight as she pulled her music box from her straining pocket. Presenting the hated object to him, she instructed the dog to sniff it and gather its scent. "Fetch."

His paws churned up the snow and dirt as he sprinted toward the house.

"You trained him to find the keys?" Cadwyn asked.

"Well, I haven't been able to test it. But he does well finding my favorite beer. And my socks."

Shoving her box back into her pocket, she stripped off her pack and searched for her hunting knife. Cadwyn called for her just as she wrapped her fingers around the handle. The area around the house was a barren patch of dead earth. An empty expanse covered in dirty snow. Knife in hand, she stood, and they suddenly weren't alone.

Children surrounded them. Two near identical rings of prepubescent girls, their dresses as black as midnight, their bonnets as white as the falling snow. She staggered back until Cadwyn took hold of her shoulders and drew her close. Constantly readjusting her grip on the handle of the dagger, Basheba watched as one girl stepped forward. She was the only one who was different. A familiar face in a green dress.

"Katrina." Basheba hated that it came out as a whisper.

A smile stretched the girl's lips as she lifted a hand. A string looped over her palm, leaving a wrought iron key to dangle and sway. Basheba eyed it carefully.

"You're just giving it to us?" Basheba scoffed.

"Only one," Cadwyn whispered.

Katrina's smile grew to impossible lengths.

"You're letting *one* of us go," Basheba said. Using the tip of her knife, she hooked the string and plucked the key free of the witch's grasp.

Katrina let it go, watching the two with obvious anticipation.

Passing it blindly to the man behind her, Basheba heard some shuffling and a tell-tale click. *His key.* Her stomach twisted tight. Biting hard on the inside of her cheeks, she tried to keep her face unreadable.

"Go, Cadwyn," Katrina said. "Our game ends here."

Cadwyn shifted slightly, bringing his large frame into Basheba's field of sight.

"And what about everyone else?"

"What does it matter to you?"

His shoulders heaved as he sucked in a deep breath. "I wouldn't be able to live with myself."

Katrina tilted her head. The barely noticeable motion signaled the girls to take a step in, choking off any escape route.

"Can you live with yourself knowing you murdered children?"

He stared at the cube in his hand. It had fallen silent, the pieces now locked in place. Squeezing it until his nails turned white, he spared Basheba a glance before replying.

"You're not kids."

The children surged forward as a pack. Swarming over them, tearing into their flesh, dragging them down to the cool earth.

Basheba didn't hesitate to slash at the little monsters, cleaving large clumps of flesh from bone and leaving the snow stained with blood. She released a sharp whistle, calling for Buck as she struck the nearest child.

At first, Cadwyn tried to keep from hurting the children, shaking them off instead of striking them. But their unrelenting attack soon drained him. His eyes were squeezed tight the first time he used the box as a weapon. He brought it down upon a girl's skull, the sharp edges cracking through skin and bone, leaving a gaping hole for her brain matter to seep out. His fight for life chipped away at his moral hesitation until he struck with a savage brutality that matched the children's.

Sweat gathered under Basheba's thick winter clothes. Her

already exhausted muscles struggled to do what she demanded of them. A child latched onto her hair, dragging her down, trying to pin her to the soil, covering her with grasping hands. Buck lurched from behind the wall of children. They buckled under his crushing weight as, instead of pushing through the crowd, he crawled his way over the top of them. Ice replaced Basheba's blood when she lost sight of him. An instant later, she was brought down to her knees. She swung the blade up, driving it into the soft underplate of the nearest attacker.

Cadwyn's screams became muffled. Through the tangled limbs, she spotted him. He had been forced onto his back, his body pinned into place by the combined weight of multiple children, his jaw pried open by the girl upon his chest. Her tiny fingers wiggled into his mouth. A sharp yank and blood poured from between his lips.

With a giggle, the girl examined the tooth she had just retrieved, tossed it over her shoulder, and giddily swooped back in to snap out another. Screaming in agony, he thrashed with renewed force, using the spikes on his wrist cuffs to gouge at their skin. It didn't keep them back for long.

Hands worked under her clothes, clawing at tender skin, searching for her music box. The children had piled on her, grinding her into the now-red snow, ripping out handfuls of her hair and gouging at her cracked lips. The crowd thinned for the barest second as Buck plowed through them. Blood gushed from the girl he held in his grasp. Vicious shakes opened the wounds. The fragile bones of her neck cracked as he tightened his colossal jaws.

Basheba lunged up, taking advantage of the momentary distraction. Slick with blood, the children struggled to keep their hold, and she burst free. They were on her before she could get to her feet, dragging her down again and keeping her on her knees. Every muscle in her body trembled as she forced them to their full strength. With a solid thrust, she grabbed the bonnet of the girl sitting on Cadwyn's chest, wrenched her back, and sliced her throat.

Use had dulled the blade but it still sunk deep enough to sever the artery, baptizing them both in her blood. Before she could see if it was of any help, a heavy weight landed upon her spine and drove her down. Hands pulled at her fingers in an attempt to pry them from the knife handle.

Buck charged. Lowering his head, he used the spikes as a battering ram, forcing the girls back just enough to drop a severed head on Basheba's hand. The soft squish came with a sharp clack against her knuckles. She snatched it up as Buck shredded the crowd. His armor held strong, preventing the small bodies from gouging at his head or back. There was nothing they could do to counter his attack of fangs and pure muscle.

Rolling the head over to look at the mauled flesh of the neck, she discovered a slip of metal protruding out of the cracked spinal column. Prying it out with the tip of her knife, she rolled closer to Buck, using his protection to retrieve the box from her pocket. Sliding pieces exposed a small lock. Bone marrow gathered around its edges as she pushed the key inside.

The lullaby came to life, hollowing out her mind until it was all she could hear. Deafening. Endless. Echoing within her bones. Hands grabbed her arms, trying to pull her away. She twisted her wrist. The key flipped the lock and silence claimed the world.

An arctic chill rushed to meet her flushed skin. The blood remained while the rest of Katrina's creatures scattered like ash. Buck leaped about to snap at the floating particles, endlessly frustrated that he couldn't sink his teeth into any of it. She called him over as she crumbled. An arm around his shoulders kept her somewhat upright. She could barely lift her head as she called out for Cadwyn. Waiting for his reply and hearing nothing sent her adrenaline coursing again. She snapped upright to find the man sitting a few feet from her side. His arm held out before him, his eyes wide and unblinking under a layer of dripping blood.

"Cadwyn," she said gently as she shuffled to his side. Carefully, she placed a hand on his arm. "They weren't really kids. They weren't human."

"We have to wash off before Ozzie finds us." His voice was distant and flat. All the screaming came from his eyes.

Mina's voice broke over his soft ramblings. Snapped from their daze, they looked up to see the two teenagers sprinting from the orchard. Both were covered with thick mucus, but it was the way Ozzie clutched his arm that made Cadwyn shoot to his feet. Ozzie skidded to a stop when he saw them. Basheba was slightly impressed when, after a moment of hesitation, he forced himself on.

"He's hurt," Mina panted. "His shoulder. We found a key!"

Cadwyn shrugged off his winter jacket, turning it inside out to hide the blood before fastening it around him as a sling. With Ozzie in shock and Cadwyn fixated on his task, it fell to the girls to catch each other up.

"You climbed up a dead spider to get out of the pit?" Basheba asked when Mina had finished filling her in.

"That's the part you're stuck on? We found a key!"

"*Ozzie's* key," Basheba explained. "Every box has its own."

It struck them all at the same moment that Mina was the only one left unaccounted for.

"We'll find it," Ozzie promised, pain pulling the muscles of his face taught. "We have a bit more time."

"I don't suppose you want to give us a hint," Basheba screamed to the barren world around them.

She hadn't expected a reply, but one came swiftly. Pain exploded behind her left eye. A blinding, crippling fire that made her knees buckle and her mind sputter. Cadwyn was by her side in an instant, slowing her decent to bring her gently to the ground. His fingers were warm and smeared with blood as he pried her hands back from her face.

"What is it? What's wrong?" Ozzie asked, and offered his good hand to Basheba so she'd have something to hold onto.

"I can't see anything," Cadwyn whispered, clearly not sure if he wanted her to hear or not.

Basheba meant to calmly state that she could feel something pushing against the back of her eye. The words came out as a feral scream that had Buck restlessly pacing beside her. She reached out blindly to soothe him, and he nuzzled her palm. The gentle touch served as an anchor, allowing her to croak out.

"The key."

"She put it behind your eye?" Ozzie asked. "Can she do that?"

"We need to get her to a hospital," Cadwyn said.

"My box hasn't been locked," Mina cut in. "Is it safe to travel through the orchard again if my demon hasn't been properly sealed?"

"I can't handle another spider," Ozzie stammered.

A deep growl left Cadwyn's throat. "I can take her down the cliff."

"I thought you said you couldn't climb it before," Mina said.

"Not with Buck on my back. Basheba weighs a lot less. I can get the key and come back."

"Do we have time for that?" Mina asked.

"You want us to wait here?" Ozzie said. "With the Witch?"

Grinding her teeth Basheba snapped a hand out to grab Cadwyn's wrist. "I'm not leaving Buck."

"It'll just be for a little while."

They all knew it wouldn't be, but it was Mina who voiced the points one after another. Basheba was the only one who knew her way through the woods. They had no supplies. With the incoming storm, the stream Basheba had mentioned could freeze over. Crossing it with an injured girl on his shoulders could be suicide.

"Cut it out." Basheba's order brought tense silence.

Cadwyn stammered until she dug her nails into his arm. The waves of pain had weakened to a near constant but tolerable ache.

"You have your med-kit," Mina said. "Cut the key out and put an end to this."

"In the middle of the woods? While I'm covered in mud and blood? With no anesthetic? And, at best, two days away from proper medical care? Are you insane?"

"You can pop it out." Mina rushed on when Cadwyn glared at her. "You won't have to cut anything."

"But her eye will be outside of its socket!"

"There's every chance she'll keep her vision," Mina argued.

"I'm not putting her through that much pain because you can't be patient."

"You know what's coming," Basheba cut in. "Let's end it here."

Cadwyn shook his head, "This isn't up for debate."

"Is it up for extortion?" Basheba countered. "You pop out my eye, or I'll stab it out."

"We can make it back to town. I know I can do it."

"Cadwyn," she groaned. "The demon isn't the only reason I want to do this."

"What's the other?"

"Spite. Katrina did this because she doesn't think I'll go through with it. She thinks I'd rather leave Mina to die than lose my eye. Well, screw that."

"You can't just do things out of spite."

"It's the only reason I do anything," Basheba countered. Clutching Buck close, she tried to settle herself against the snow, as if this would all be easier if she could just get comfortable. When she shifted her gaze to Mina, she could feel the metal edge rubbing against the back of her eyeball. "You want to be a doctor, right? If he won't do it, try and stop the bleeding."

For once, Mina kept her silence and only nodded.

"Ozzie, don't watch."

"I want to be here for you, Basheba."

"And I don't want you to throw up on me," she replied with a weak smile she hoped was encouraging.

He tried and failed to return the gesture. Swearing constantly under his breath, Cadwyn rummaged through his med-kit for sterile wipes and cleaned his hands as best he could with them.

"You'll have to stop holding the dog," he grumbled.

"If I let go of him, he's going to go for your throat," Basheba said.

Instinctively, she closed her eyes to try and prepare herself for what was to come. Her gut churned when Cadwyn instructed her to open her eyes again.

"I'll do my best."

"I trust you," she whispered.

His hands were shaking as he placed them by her eye. She tried one last time to reassure him with a smile. It didn't work, but he began, anyway. Pain swept through her, consuming her, boiling her within her own skin. Buck struggled against her, trying to break free and save her. She felt the pop just before darkness washed over her and dragged her into oblivion.

CHAPTER 20

Locking the final box had changed everything. The oppressive cold that had been there since they first stepped into the Witch's Woods was gone. There was still a chill, strong enough to have them huddling together during the night. But the mist had lifted and, without it, the harshest bite of the air had been soothed.

They had lost most of their camping gear at the Bell homestead. When Basheba was conscious, she had instructed them as best she could, but they had all agreed to let her sleep as much as possible, so they were often left to work things out for themselves.

The two-day hike passed in a blur, fatigue, pain, and shock each playing their part to keep their minds dulled. Every time Mina tried to think, all her brain could linger on was the incredible sacrifice Basheba had made for her. A part of her was quick to believe the woman's explanation. Hatred and spite were strong motivators. But in the somber aftermath, with each of them nursing their physical and psychological wounds, Mina didn't think that was the case. Nor was it the noble desire to keep the demon from being unleashed upon them. By the time they had left the Witch's Woods to rejoin the cleared recreational path, Mina was sure Basheba had been motivated by grief. Mina had seen the orchard and felt their lineage. She knew how many Bells hung there.

Reaching the parking lot felt like stepping back in time. Everyone looked exactly as they had left them. Comfortable. Healthy. Safe. Once more, the four families had crammed themselves into the limited area. This time, however, the scent of hamburgers drifted on the air and a few tents had replaced the cars. It looked like a tailgate party.

They were ready for a long wait.

It was impossible to tell who in the mob spotted them first. One cry set up the next and soon enough the clearing was full of life. The excitement only grew as it became clear all four had survived. A few poppers were set off; sharp cracks that rained colorful streamers down upon them. Others threw flower petals; pink and white roses that flipped and twisted before settling on the fine layer of speckled snow.

It's like they're welcoming home heroes.

Mina looked to Basheba, trying to see if this was the standard practice. A yellowed gauze patch covered one eye. The other held more sorrow than fire.

They hadn't reached the parking lot before people flooded up to meet them. Ozzie had to brace his good arm over his wounded one to keep from getting jarred by the flood of relatives he didn't really know. Cadwyn welcomed his mother, holding onto her even when his stitches started to bleed again. Mina looked up in time to have her father and mother almost knock her off her feet.

"Are you hurt?" Jeremiah asked as he joined the group.

Mina shook her head.

"That's my girl," her father boasted, raising his voice louder for the others to hear. "To hell and back with barely a scraped knee!"

Cheers rang out, sounding like an army after the two days of near silence. Mina slowly pulled away from her parents to wrap her brother in a tight hug.

"What happened out there?" he whispered.

"I'll tell you later." She leaned back enough to catch his eyes, wanting him to know the full weight of her words. "You and the others. No more secrets."

He shushed her. "Don't let mom and dad hear you say things like that. We have our traditions."

A booming voice rang out over all the other mirth, drawing

Mina's attention. Across the parking lot, Basheba stood with her uncle before the couple Percival Sewall had brought along.

Ozzie's parents, her mind corrected.

The uncle was boasting. Understanding his actual words weren't necessary. It was clear by position and gesture alone that the Bell was raining praise down upon his niece. But he never looked at her. His attention was fixed on the rich couple.

Every muscle in Basheba's body locked tight as her uncle began to play with her long blonde hair. Twisting the strands around his hand until each rhythmic clench of his fist made her arch her neck back. It almost looked like an absentminded sign of affection. An innate desire to maintain some kind of physical contact with the relative he had almost lost. But there was something in it that left Mina unsettled.

She felt it like a coming storm; the moment when Basheba snapped. Mina anticipated that she'd push the older man away. Slashing at his face with her hunting knife wasn't something anyone had seen coming. Shock and horror washed through the crowd. Only four people stood undisturbed.

Four people and a dog.

While the knife had made contact, the man had jerked away in time that the cut on his face wasn't deep. He belatedly hurried to move out of his niece's reach as someone handed him a shirt to press to his face.

"I need to get Basheba to a hospital," Cadwyn cut in smoothly, before the small woman could do more.

"I have a helicopter," Ozzie cut in. "If you guys want a ride."

"Thanks," Basheba smiled, her attention diverted from her uncle.

"I'm coming, too." Mina got three paces before her father tried to pull her back. "Someone's got to hold Buck. I'll meet you at home."

The whole time in the woods, she had wanted nothing more than to be back with her family. Now, she felt like she couldn't breathe.

They knew. They knew about all of this, and they said nothing. Nothing but lies my whole life.

She pushed down the thought just as she had a thousand times before and hurried to catch up. A voice drifted from the woods before they could leave. A sweet, whispered voice that left everyone in tense silence. The voice of the Bell Witch.

"Goodbye. I'll see you next year."

* * *

SACRIFICIAL GROUNDS

THE BELL WITCH SERIES BOOK 2

CHAPTER 1

Campfire smoke and forest pine lingered in the warm Spring breeze. Only a few months ago, Mina would have found it a pleasant smell. Now, each breath threatened to summon a flood of memories she would sooner forget.

Tales of the Bell Witch had filled her childhood. She had never believed them. Even now, she was sure that superstition and fear had mutated individual 'facts' beyond recognition. But she could no longer doubt there was far more truth to it than she had ever suspected. She had lived through the Harvest; those last days of October when the Bell Witch selected a person from each of the four families she had damned, and lured them back to where it had all started. The backwoods of Black River, Tennessee. The Witch Woods.

A screaming child sprinted across her field of vision. Mina jerked, her shoulder slamming against the side of Basheba's car as the child cut across the campsite. Basheba glared at the kid until it jumped into the nearby lake and disappeared within the turquoise water.

"I hate Spring Break," Basheba muttered as she returned to prodding the campfire to make the flames grow.

They were the first words Basheba had spoken in the last twenty minutes and Mina was eager to extend it into a full conversation.

"Because of all the kids?"

Basheba arched an eyebrow but went back to tending her fire without a word. Under five feet tall, blonde, and with skin like strawberries and cream, Basheba Bell looked like a porcelain doll, not a woman in her twenties with a violent fear of children. Even the leather patch covering her left eye couldn't change that.

"How's your eye?" Mina asked, studying the eyepatch with a mix of awe and guilt.

The Bell Witch hadn't been the only one to underestimate Basheba and the lengths to which she was willing to go. Mina had thought herself as good as dead when the Witch had manifested the key behind Basheba's eye. Everyone else had already locked their demon boxes, and the two girls had clashed from the beginning. But Basheba hadn't hesitated. There, laying in the snow and muck, covered in blood and without anesthetic, she had ordered Cadwyn to cut out her eye.

Over the months, Mina had thought of that moment so often she could recall every second in detail. Cadwyn Winthrop was a career psych nurse in a maximum-security prison. It was kind of a waste. He had the hands of a surgeon. With only a basic medical pack, he had skillfully removed Basheba's eye, retrieved the key, and returned the orb to its socket without causing any lasting damage. His expertise didn't end there. Somehow, he had managed to keep infection at bay for the entire two-day hike back to town. If Mina hadn't been afraid of Basheba before, the fact that she walked the whole way without a word of complaint would have done it.

"Had a check-up this morning," Basheba answered at last. "I've got to wear the patch for a few more weeks. After that, I'll just have to do the odd exercise to keep the muscle strong."

"Any visual damage?"

"None." A small smile curled the edges of her lips. "I knew Cadwyn could do it. I'm not going to lie; I really want to rub it in Katrina's smug face."

Mina flinched. When people spoke of the Witch, it was always by her title and with a certain degree of reverent fear, like she was some malicious god. For Basheba, however, the Witch was nothing more than a pathetic hag with delusions of grandeur. She called her by name. Either spitting it out with undiluted contempt or lingering on it with mockery. Mina couldn't decide if she found it unnerving or comforting. *Maybe it's different for the Bells*, Mina thought. *They've lived with her the longest.*

Katrina's obsession with the Bells had been her destruction. It had exposed her as a witch and brought about her execution. But even death hadn't been enough to stop her. She hated them with a rage so potent it had bled out to consume four bloodlines for two hundred years. She was The *Bell* Witch.

"My first year of college has been fun," Mina blurted out. Basheba might be immune to awkward silences, but she wasn't. "Busy, but fun."

"Criminal Justice, right?" Basheba asked absently.

"Yeah. It's a huge workload, but I was prepared for that. It's the extracurriculars. Between moot court, volunteering at the hospital, and the soup kitchen, I barely have time to think."

Basheba paused and turned to her.

Mina shrugged. "I need a free ride to Harvard Med. The competition is intense. You need to stand out."

Basheba's brow furrowed but she quickly hid her reaction. "You have a free ride now, right?"

"Full scholarship," Mina beamed, puffing up a little with pride.

Mina had written down her life plan when she was in kindergarten. From there, no matter how hard she worked, it felt like she was just waiting for her life to begin. Now she was on track. Her Criminal Justice degree was in sight. She'd use it to secure her medical degree. Then it would be straight to the Federal Bureau of Investigation.

"And that covers dorm room?"

Mina deflated somewhat. "It did, but I'm staying with my cousin."

"Why?"

"My parents offered to pay for my living expenses if I did. I don't have time for a part-time job. It only makes sense."

Basheba opened her mouth as if to speak, but then seemed to decide in the last moment to keep it to herself and went back to tending her fire, waiting for her kettle to boil. Buck, Basheba's colossal Rottweiler, grumbled as he shuffled closer to Mina's knees. His slick tongue flopped out to lap at his jaws. There was something in the motion that Mina took as a threat. Buck adored Basheba and rarely ventured more than a few feet from her side. This unwavering attention felt like he was obeying a command. In the woods, she'd seen just how savage he could be for his mistress.

The Witch had preyed on Basheba's odd fear of children, conjuring demons that looked just like them. Buck hadn't hesitated to rip through them in a storm of fangs and blood. Even if she had been spared the sight of the horrific aftermath, the sheer size of the Rottweiler was enough to leave people on edge. Mina watched families come and go, pulling up into the camping spaces next to Basheba's, only to move again after catching sight of the monstrous hound.

Barbeques were lit while Basheba worked on her tea, adding the scents of sizzling sausages to the lingering aroma. People played in the lake, splashing and squealing, while others wandered about, taking photographs of the surrounding mountains.

"This is a gorgeous spot," Mina said, hoping to reignite the conversation. "Have you been here before?"

"I don't go to the same place twice," Basheba dismissed, poking at the charred wood. It split with a pop, spewing embers up around the kettle.

"Nowhere?" Mina asked.

A few distant shrill screams of delight and the crackle of the fire was the only response Mina received. *My back is starting to hurt from carrying this conversation*, Mina thought with a small measure of bitterness. She had come here with a purpose, and couldn't broach the subject until she got Basheba into a good mood. *Maybe I should have started with Cadwyn.*

She frowned as she studied Basheba's car. A dented, old copper-colored Chevrolet hatchback that should have gone to the scrap heap after the Witch had totaled it. Apparently, Basheba had put a lot of the money Ozzie Sewall had given her into restoring it.

Davis, Mina corrected herself. Up until a few months ago, the poor guy hadn't even known he was biologically a Sewall, or of the curse he had inherited. His whole life, he had thought that Percival Sewall was his godfather and that he had been born a Davis. It was a lot to deal with, but the fifteen-year-old had held it together in the woods.

"Have you heard from Ozzie lately?" Mina asked.

It might help somewhat. Basheba had warmed up to him a bit.

"Yeah. His arm's fine."

"I thought he gave you money for a new car."

"My car works just fine. I used that for travel, instead," Basheba shrugged. "I don't think he'll mind."

"As the heir to *two* of the wealthiest families in the world, nah, I don't think he will," Mina giggled.

Basheba's brow furrowed slightly.

"They both made it onto the Forbes Top 100 list last year."

"Really?"

"I know, it's so weird, isn't it? I always thought people that rich were obligated to be jerks."

"No, I mean, you read Forbes Magazine?" Basheba shook her head in bafflement. "Weird."

Mina pressed her lips into a tight smile to keep from sighing. *This isn't going well.* She had memorized a few topics of conversation before approaching Basheba. It hadn't been an easy task. Four days in the woods alone and she still didn't know that much about the shorter girl. It was easy enough to tell what she hated. She never hid her rage. Against the families, the Witch, her uncle. Her disgust was bearded for all to see. But Mina wanted to put her in a good mood. That was harder. Beyond travel, the only things that brought a smile to her face were Buck, Cadwyn, and fire. *She brought up travel. Follow up on it.*

"Where did you go? With the extra cash?"

"Florida. I wanted to see the Everglades and go to Disney World." At last, the blonde smiled with real warmth. Not at Mina, but at Buck.

"Disney World?" Mina pressed, trying to regain the girl's attention.

Basheba hummed. "I prefer Dollywood."

"They let you on the rides with your eye in that condition?"

"No."

"Why didn't you wait? I mean, if you never go back to a place, it seems a bit of a waste."

Basheba stared at her like she was slow. "If I waited, my eye wouldn't have looked so gross."

"Yes, that's right," Mina said, still confused.

Basheba sighed heavily and pinched the bridge of her nose. "Well, they wouldn't let me bring in my service animal if I looked okay, right?"

Mina stammered as the kettle whistled. She studied Basheba carefully as the blonde poured out two cups of tea and came to sit beside her.

"You managed to convince them Buck was a service dog?"

It was a level of bravado Mina hadn't thought anyone was capable of reaching. The trunk of the hatchback car had been converted into a bed and, once she was seated upon the mattress, Basheba's legs were too short to reach the ground. She swung them absentmindedly as she handed Mina a mug.

"We've got under seven months until the next Harvest, and I wasn't about to go out without getting a pic of Buck and me with Cinderella."

Blindsided by another unexpected statement, Mina numbly took the mug. "Cinderella?"

"She's my favorite."

"*You* have a favorite princess?"

"Yeah."

"And it's *Cinderella*?"

"The girl was willing to walk on broken glass just to give the middle finger to her lifelong emotional abusers," Basheba sighed wistfully. "If only I could be that badass."

The memory of Basheba using a lighter and a can of antiseptic spray as a makeshift flamethrower flashed across Mina's mind.

"Personally, I find you terrifying." Mina hadn't meant for the words to slip out but was glad to see Basheba's growing smile.

"Aw, that's sweet. Drink your tea."

Warmth beamed from her smile even while her eyes remained as cold as a grave. It made Mina's skin crawl. *She's up to something.* Forcing a matching smile, Mina cupped the hot mug with both hands and nodded her thanks.

"Blow on it first. Don't want to burn yourself," Basheba chirped.

Mina took a tentative sip. It took a moment for the heat to fade and leave a sweet, lingering taste.

"This is nice," Mina said.

"Oh, good. I was worried I wouldn't brew it right," Basheba said. "I had to do your favorite blend justice, right?"

"Favorite blend?" Mina raised her mug to sniff at the steam. *Sweet berries.* But she couldn't place which kind.

"I just assumed it was," Basheba continued pleasantly, adding when Mina took another exploratory sip. "Why else would you bring the leaves into the woods with you?"

Mina lurched forward, spraying the contents out over her hand and lap. *Belladonna. I just drank Belladonna.*

"Too hot?" Basheba asked.

She glanced up at the blonde, absently wiping at her mouth. Basheba smiled.

"Drink your tea, Willimina."

"Basheba, that was Belladonna."

"I know."

"Deadly Nightshade," Mina pressed. "It's toxic. Have you been drinking this?"

"Of course not," Basheba chuckled. The sound came and went in a second, replaced by an icy glare. "Drink your tea."

What? "It's poison."

"Well, yeah. I'm murdering you. Honestly, how is it taking you this long to catch on? You're supposed to be smart."

For a long moment, Mina could only stare at her, brow furrowed and jaw hanging open. A thousand thoughts raced through her head, but she could only manage to stammer.

"You can't do that."

"Who's going to stop me?" Basheba said with clear amusement.

"I won't drink it."

"That's your choice," Basheba shrugged. "It's what I would do. But then, I always take the hard way."

"What?"

She got her answer when she stretched out her arm, ready to tip the contents on the grass. Buck's lips curled back as he released a low, rumbling growl. Long, pristine fangs glistened in the noonday light. Mina froze. She didn't expect the sharp lurch he took toward her. Forgetting about the cup, she threw herself back to escape his snapping jaws, making the steaming liquid slosh over her hand.

"Hey, don't wet my bed," Basheba protested.

Gathering her wits, Mina chuckled nervously. "You almost had me there. I honestly thought you were going to kill me."

"I am," Basheba replied. "Well, me or Buck. But there's no 'I' in team. A kill for one of us is a kill for both."

"You can't do this!"

"You keep saying that," Basheba dismissed.

Mina grappled for understanding, her heart racing and Bucks growling ringing in her ears.

"We're in public."

"So?"

"Dog attacks draw attention. People are concerned by that sort of thing."

"Yeah. And when people are concerned, they make sure their loved ones are safe first. Keys are in the ignition. It won't take long for him to rip out your throat. I think we can get away while they're trying to help you."

"You'll have to leave everything behind," Mina blurted.

"They're just things. All replaceable."

"We're not in Black River. Crimes have consequences here. You'll go to prison, and Buck will be put down."

Basheba tilted her head, seeming to consider that. At last, she shrugged. "We're five minutes from the state border. You'd be surprised what you can get away with just by crossing jurisdiction lines. Drink. Or stand. Your call."

The reality struck Mina like a wall of ice. Basheba Bell was completely willing to kill her. Here and now. After they had been chatting idly for at least twenty minutes. *Think,* she commanded herself as sweat beaded along her hairline. *Stay calm and think.*

"I never used it," Mina said, trying to buy some time for her mind to work.

"You didn't have time to," Basheba countered. "That doesn't count. You brought it along. One leaf for me. One for Cadwyn. One for Ozzie. None for you. The intention's pretty clear."

Cadwyn. A small idea blossomed on the edges of Mina's brain. She shuffled as if to get comfortable, the motion making Buck growl again. It was just enough of a distraction that she was able to slip closer to her purse.

"I didn't bring it. Someone put it in my bag."

It was Basheba's turn to look completely baffled. "You were holding it for a friend?"

"I didn't pack it. I only knew it was there just before we set out."

"You didn't get rid of it."

"I didn't see a reason to. It wasn't weighing me down."

The blonde was silent for a moment, too consumed by her thoughts to notice Mina's slowly creeping hand. The latch of her purse brushed her fingertips.

"All right," Basheba said, startling Mina and making her freeze. "Who put it in your bag?"

Mina's stomach dropped. "Why?"

"Why do you think?"

A fresh wave of ice replaced her blood. Mina's mother had always been gentle. A quiet, reserved, dignified kind of woman. She was the solid foundation Mina had built her identity upon. To hear she expected her daughter to kill had shaken everything she knew about herself, her mother, her world.

"I'm not going to tell you that," Mina said, holding her gaze as she slipped her hand into her purse.

The motion went unnoticed.

"Why not?" Basheba asked pleasantly.

Mina saluted her with the mug, exaggerating the motion to keep the blonde's attention diverted. "Why do you think?" Mina glanced down to the muscular dog currently glaring at her. "I'm not going to let you kill my family."

"I have no plans to."

"Right."

"Honestly, I didn't even plan this. It's all in the spur of the moment. My brother used to call me impulsive."

Slivers of sorrow shattered the hard stone of Basheba's glare. The blonde dropped her gaze. A small motion that instantly drew Buck's concern. He stopped growling to nuzzle at Basheba's hand, receiving a smile and a scratch in return. It was barely a few seconds of distraction and Mina used them well, snatching her phone out of her bag and hitting the speed dial. Basheba sighed and rolled her eyes.

"Really? This will all be over before the police arrive, you know that, right? And my uncle, the good one, the dead one, taught me how to live pretty much off the grid. With Ozzie's funds, no one will find me."

The phone buzzed. "I'm not calling the police."

"Oh, Daddy Crane? I'm terrified," Basheba huffed.

"Not him," Mina said, internally praying for the call to connect before Basheba grew bored. "I'm calling the one person whose opinion you actually care about."

Understanding dawned on her face. Within seconds, she went from surprise, to annoyance, to childish guilt, like she had been found sneaking cookies before dinner.

"Mina, what a surprise."

Cadwyn's voice was calming. Smooth and deep. Like smoke and honey. With a flurry of fingers, Mina switched the call to video chat and flipped the screen around. Forcing Basheba to look at the man who was, in all likelihood, her only friend.

"Basheba's trying to kill me."

"I'm sorry," Cadwyn said. "I think I misheard that."

Basheba opened her mouth, closed it, then slumped back against the side of the car, all the while glaring at Mina.

"You tattletale. See, now I really want to kill you."

Buck lurched forward, bracing his paws on the tow bar and snapping for Mina's leg. She retreated back as Cadwyn demanded to know what was happening and Basheba dismissed the whole thing. Heart in her throat, Mina knew she wasn't going to get a better time and blurted out over the commotion.

"I want to kill the Witch!"

Silence followed.

"Say that again," Cadwyn said slowly.

"You know she's already dead, right?" Basheba added.

Trying to summon some measure of dignity, Mina lifted her chin, carefully positioning the phone in an attempt to make sure they could all see each other.

"I want to go back. Now, in the Spring, when she won't be at the height of her powers. I want to end this."

Basheba shared a look with Cadwyn, both keeping their silence for a long time.

"Have you got any idea how to do that?" Basheba asked.

"Let me live and I'll tell you."

"You can always kill her later," Cadwyn said. "And, since this is something to be discussed in person, we can hang out for a bit."

Basheba pursed her lips in thought. "I still don't know if it'll be worth it."

"I'll pay for lunch," Cadwyn said.

"Deal."

Mina didn't know if she should feel blessed or insulted by such a low ransom but pushed on anyway. "Where would you like to meet?"

"Ozzie was just about to pick me up," Cadwyn said, a small smile playing on his wide lips. "We'll come to you."

CHAPTER 2

"I'm sorry about Emma," Ozzie said before glancing up from his phone. "Take this left."

They had to wait for a few kids to pass by on their bikes before they could set off down the road. The rental car hummed quietly over the narrow, well-tended streets. Wide sections of gravel bracketed the road, gradually giving way to long stretches of uninterrupted grass. Each of the houses had its space, with no fences or real driveways to speak of, and seemed to be hybrids of urban homes and rural ranch houses. Plain, comfortable, and oddly distinctive. The small town had a laid back, almost lazy feeling to it.

Ozzie checked the directions on his phone again before he added, "She's actually really nice."

"And a minor," Cadwyn said.

"I didn't know she was going to hit on you," Ozzie said. "Though, looking back, I probably should have. She's got this thing for motorbikes and older men. So, your entrance sealed the deal there."

"This whole conversation makes me very uncomfortable."

"Right. Sorry." He moved in his seat to face the older man. "You don't have to worry, though. She lost interest pretty quickly once I told her that you're a nurse."

Cadwyn looked at him from the corner of his eyes and bit back a smirk.

"No offense. I still think you're cool."

"I'm not offended at all."

Ozzie clicked his tongue and looked out the window. There wasn't much to draw his attention.

"Have you ever heard of cognac eyes?" Ozzie blurted. "Oh, straight through this stop sign."

Cadwyn slowed, carefully checking the deserted street twice before continuing on.

"Once or twice. Why?"

"Emma got prissy about it. Insisted your eyes are *cognac.*" Ozzie puffed out a breath. "They're brown. She sounds so pretentious sometimes."

"And I'm uncomfortable again," Cadwyn said before pressing his wide mouth into a thin line.

"Change the subject?"

"Please." Before Ozzie could think up another topic, Cadwyn picked one. "I didn't know they let fifteen-year-olds have pilot licenses."

"I'm sixteen now, remember?"

"Right. Sorry."

"Anyway, you can begin flight training at any age. Now that I'm *sixteen,*" he said, exaggerating the word until Cadwyn chuckled, "I can fly solo. I won't be eligible for a private pilot certificate until next year, though."

"You weren't flying solo. You had your instructor," Cadwyn hid his cringe to add, "and some passengers."

Ozzie shrugged sheepishly. "Dallas to Massachusetts is a long flight and my friends wanted to keep me company. They've all had Spring Break in Texas before and got bored."

"I understand." Of course, he had no idea. Cadwyn wasn't a Sewall or a Davis. He had no idea what it was like to be insanely, almost insultingly, rich. It just seemed like the thing to say.

"And when they heard I was coming to pick you up—"

"Wait. They were interested in meeting me? What have you told them?"

Ozzie nodded once as if that answered Cadwyn's question and continued on. "Anyway, it was good we had Kai tagging along, now that we've changed our plans and are staying here. Her family has a plane here in New Jersey, so they won't all have to fly commercial to New York."

"I'm glad we could help them escape such a horror," Cadwyn chuckled.

"Emma's allergic to public transportation," Ozzie replied.

"That's not a thing."

"She says she breaks out in hives."

Cadwyn's laughter grew. "As a medical professional, I'm telling you, that's not how allergies work."

"Oh. So, I've just been flying her around for nothing?" He deflated slightly. "Yeah, that figures."

"How long have you been flying?" Cadwyn asked, his voice warm and comforting, easing Ozzie's wounded pride.

"We've always had a private jet." Looking purposefully out of the window, he quickly added, "But I only started taking lessons in November."

"After the Harvest."

Ozzie cringed. There was no reason for him to be embarrassed, he knew that. He just hated the fact that he seemed to be the only one affected by their time in the Witch Woods. Cadwyn had gone right back to working with the criminally insane, casually dealing with serial killers and cannibals. The girls had picked a wooded, rural area to meet up. Ozzie broke out in a cold sweat just going into his backyard now, and that was just a few yards of trees to give the deer something to wander through. When he chanced a glance at the older man, he found Cadwyn was grinning, his teeth straight and perfect.

"You're laughing at me?"

"What? No, of course not. I'm proud of you."

"Huh?"

"It's easy to wallow in your own pain. Believe me, I know. But you decided to improve yourself." Deep lines fanned out from the corner of Cadwyn's eyes as he looked at Ozzie again. "That takes a lot of strength. I'm impressed."

"Oh." Fire prickled Ozzie's cheeks. "Full disclosure, I don't know how to respond to that."

"You don't have to say anything."

"I'm uncomfortable," Ozzie teased.

"You didn't have a minor hitting on you for an hour!"

Cadwyn looked so dramatically traumatized that Ozzie couldn't help but burst into laughter.

"At least she's pretty."

"I'm in my thirties!"

"When you say it like that, you do sound like a creep."

"I didn't do anything," he protested.

Ozzie laughed harder. No matter what the Witch had thrown at them, Cadwyn had always been calm and serene. A man in complete control of himself and his emotions. Ozzie was honor-bound to mercilessly exploit this sudden weakness.

They ended up talking over each other, their rapid-fire words bleeding into each other, and almost missed the diner. With a slight curse and a sharp turn on the wheel, Cadwyn cut across the gravel road and lurched into a parking place. He cut the engine and turned fully to Ozzie.

"Do *not* tell your mother I did that."

"She's going to swear at you a lot," Ozzie grinned. "But it'll all be in Korean, so you won't understand most of it anyway."

"That doesn't make it better."

Out of the car, with the sun shining brightly over the treetops and the scent of fries in the air, Ozzie finally felt brave enough to ask.

"Did Basheba really try to kill Mina?"

"Yeah. But she's over that now. Don't worry about it."

Ozzie's thick eyebrows jumped to his hairline. Always observant, Cadwyn paused midstride and sighed.

"They had an issue between the two of them. It's handled now."

"Does she always try to kill people?"

"Not always," Cadwyn shrugged.

"How is this not freaking you out?"

Rounding the front of the car, Cadwyn gently placed his large hand on Ozzie's shoulder, careful to avoid the newly healed break.

"Basheba's lived with the Witch longer than any of us. That affects you."

"You're older," Ozzie noted.

"I've only been selected once," Cadwyn said. "The Witch singled her out twice. And she's been in more search parties than anyone else alive. That much time in the Witch Woods does things to you."

"So, we let her try and kill people?"

Cadwyn's lips moved soundlessly, but his eyes remained sure.

He'd let her, Ozzie thought.

"You wouldn't do something like that. And a demon tortured you for months." Ozzie regretted the words as soon as they left his mouth. The moment he saw Cadwyn flinch. *Good going, Ozzie. Bring up the demon that killed his brother.*

"I've never known her to do anything without provocation," Cadwyn said smoothly.

"What about her uncle? She slashed his face because he touched her hair."

"That's just what you observed. We don't know what was going on between them." Cadwyn continued before Ozzie could say anything else. "Whatever happened between the girls, it's done. No good will come from you opening that wound. Understand?"

"Yeah."

Ozzie's recent growth spurt still couldn't compete with Cadwyn's lofty six feet. The older man ducked his head until he could catch Ozzie's downcast gaze.

"She's not going to hurt you."

"She might hurt other people, though."

He hesitated, clearly choosing his words in his head before letting them slip past his lips.

"Basheba has survived this long because she doesn't let threats to her safety go unpunished. The Cranes know that. They knew the consequences of their actions, and decided to threaten her anyway. I'm not saying I think Mina should carry the blame for it. I don't. I told Basheba. She listened. And she agrees with me."

"But—"

"It's done, Ozzie. Don't bring it up."

He nodded numbly and followed the towering man to the diner door. Cadwyn opened the fly screen, holding it a while to let Ozzie enter first. Shadows lingered in the old box-like structure. Preoccupied with his thoughts, Ozzie didn't notice the creature until it was looming over him. It had large, unblinking eyes and fangs longer than his hand. Its big, leathery wings were stretched wide to blot out the overhead lights. A startled cry ripped from his lungs as he staggered away. He slammed into Cadwyn's chest and his sneakers slipped over the polished wood floor. If the older man hadn't gripped him by the shoulders, he would have fallen to the ground. A frantic heartbeat passed, and Ozzie realized the creature wasn't coming for him.

"It's a statue," he mumbled, heat pulsating against his cheeks.

"I'd say it's taxidermy," Cadwyn said.

"What animal?"

Cadwyn hummed thoughtfully. "Well, those legs are obviously from a horse. And maybe a Doberman's head, though the muzzle is too wide. The claws look bird-like. Ostrich, maybe? I have no idea where they got the wings from."

Hearing Cadwyn verbally dissect the monster made Ozzie feel steadier. Which, in turn, left him feeling like a moron for shrieking like that in a public place. Sheepishly, he glanced around. The person behind the counter was laughing at him, and there was a man in a distant booth who seemed just as amused. Thankfully, the place was otherwise deserted. The back doors opened up to a grassy patch speckled with picnic tables. It gave him a clear view of Mina jogging toward them.

Only two years separated them. It was hardly anything. But he always felt like a little kid around her. She was just so put together. Sophisticated, or stylish, or something he couldn't put his finger on. It made it harder to ignore the fact that she was gorgeous. Huge ebony eyes, tawny skin, hair with that loose curl thing that some of his friends spent hours at the salon to get. *How can someone who's just been poisoned look so pretty?* He remembered not to stare just as she passed the threshold.

"Hey, guys," she beamed. "I am so glad you're here. I hope it wasn't too out of your way."

"Don't worry about it," Cadwyn said as he slipped around Ozzie to greet her.

They shared a quick hug before he slipped a penlight out of his back pocket and clicked it on. "How are you?"

With a nod, Mina casually rattled off the symptoms. "I had a slight fever that broke about an hour ago. Still suffering a bit of dry mouth. Sweating and increased heart rate are starting to even out."

First, she looked at the penlight he shone in her eyes, then lifted her gaze to the ceiling when instructed.

"What's your name?"

"Willimina Crane."

"And his?" He jerked one thumb toward Ozzie while he checked her pulse.

"Osgood Sewall. I mean, Davis. Sorry. Hi, by the way."

"Hey," Ozzie said with an awkward wave he quickly regretted. "And either way's fine."

Cadwyn's expression remained carefully neutral as he surveyed the girl. "Where are you?"

"Devil's Diner in New Jersey."

"And why are we here?"

"It's where Basheba Bell chose for our meeting place."

"Oh, no. That wasn't one of the health check questions," Cadwyn said with a smile. "I just don't get why she picked here."

The squint of Mina's eyes made it clear she knew Cadwyn was just trying to break the tension.

"Apparently, there've been sightings of the New Jersey Devil in the woods out back. She's hoping she'll catch a glimpse before we go."

"The things that girl gets up to," Cadwyn mumbled, more amused than frustrated. Straightening, he clicked off his light. "How much did you drink?"

"Just a sip."

"Any hallucinations?"

"No."

"Still peeing?"

"Cadwyn," Ozzie whispered sharply.

Cadwyn looked confused for a second, as if he didn't see how asking a girl that question in public was strange.

"Inability to urinate is a sign of Belladonna poisoning." Turning his full attention back to Mina, he added, "But you don't have to answer. I was just doing my due diligence. All the evidence suggests you're fine."

"Are you sure?" Mina asked.

"You're not flushed. No memory loss. You're not slurring your speech, or having seizures." He listed off. "I'm guessing you didn't ingest anywhere near enough to be worried."

"Isn't any dose deadly?" Ozzie asked.

Cadwyn laughed until he realized that he was serious. "No. It's used a lot in medicine. For a young woman in otherwise good health, the amount she took shouldn't be a problem."

"Good thing I called you, then," Mina sighed in relief.

"Nah, you would have talked her around."

"You grossly overestimate how much affection she has for me," Mina dismissed as she turned. "Come on. She's out this way."

Cadwyn caught her arm. A gentle touch that forced her to pause all the same.

"You think Basheba changed her mind because we're friends?" he asked with all seriousness.

"Of course. What else am I supposed to think?"

A frown curved his lips, his brow furrowed, and his eyes clouded with something Ozzie couldn't define.

"I'm going to give you the same advice I gave her when she was your age," he said at last.

Mina snuck a quick glance at Ozzie. "Okay."

"Anyone who says, 'if you love me, you'll do this,' doesn't love you. They're trying to emotionally manipulate you."

Mina pulled her arm free of his grip. "I don't get where this is coming from. But, sometimes, people say that because they know what's best for you. Sometimes, you have to do things you don't want to for the people you care about."

"Caring about someone demands you respect them enough to listen to them. Truly listen and think about what they tell you. It doesn't necessitate obedience. Anyone who tells you that it does isn't thinking about what's best for you. They're thinking about themselves."

The muscles around Mina's eyes pinched tight. She bit her lips like she was trying to keep her response to herself. But the moment passed quickly, and she soon pulled herself to full height, hiding her discomfort behind a smile.

"I'll keep it in mind. Thank you. Any other words of wisdom?"

There was a sharp edge in the last sentence that Cadwyn deliberately ignored. "Never trust someone when they tell you their spouse 'just doesn't understand them.' My Grandma told me that one."

Mina blinked. "Was that ever useful to you?"

"My first boss said that to me word for word, actually."

"Right." Her mouth hung open as her brow furrowed. "Right. Well, come on."

Ozzie waited until Mina was a few steps ahead before he

whispered to Cadwyn, "You told Basheba that?"

Cadwyn nodded.

He chuckled. "I wouldn't think she'd need to hear it."

"I know it's a radical concept, Ozzie, but she is human. Just like the rest of us."

CHAPTER 3

Buck almost barreled Mina over as he rushed past her, making a beeline for Cadwyn. It was hard to tell which one of them was more excited at being reunited. Cadwyn dropped to one knee to let the colossal dog balance his two front paws on his shoulders. A nice gesture that left them both toppling onto the grass. The more Cadwyn laughed, the more Buck attacked with licks and yelps.

"I missed you, too, buddy," Cadwyn said between gasps.

Seemingly satisfied by that, Buck turned his attention to Ozzie, who was a little more apprehensive. Eventually, once both boys were covered in a layer of slobber, the Rottweiler turned and bounded back to the far picnic table. There was barely enough room for him underneath, but he crammed himself in there anyway. Basheba kicked off her shoes to rub her bare feet against his side. The table rattled as Buck tried to roll in the confined space. Through sheer determination, he ended up on his back so Basheba could absently rub his belly. All the while, the blonde stared at the woods. She only acknowledged the group at all when Cadwyn slipped onto the seat opposite her. Between the table's lack of room and Buck's presence, he opted for keeping his legs in the open.

"Hey," he smiled.

By now, Mina had been around Basheba for half of the day. This was the first time the blonde flashed a real smile.

"Hey, you made it. I got a gift for you."

"Is it being exposed to your sparkling personality?" Cadwyn teased.

Basheba was already searching through the backpack she kept

with her almost all of the time.

"Nah, I'm horrible."

"I'll take your dog," Cadwyn offered.

"I will literally stab you."

Cadwyn brushed off the threat with a one-shoulder shrug. "Sounds about right."

Mina and Ozzie joined them just as Basheba leaned across the table and yanked a huge, fluffy, wolf head beanie over his dark blonde hair. Flaps that ended in pompoms flopped over Cadwyn's ears to brush against his collar bones.

"Perfect," Basheba said.

Cadwyn bit back a smile. "I have questions."

"I went to a wolf reserve," she said, looking somewhat smug at her gift. "Feel free to eat it."

"Are you still going on about those pretzels?" Cadwyn asked. "That was one time."

"They were *alien* pretzels. You can't get them just anywhere."

"You abandoned them."

"It was still my food, Cad," she hissed.

He pulled the beanie off of his head so he could study it. "You have to let it go."

"There's no statute of limitations on food theft!"

The flash of anger and the accusatory jab of her finger only made Cadwyn burst into laughter. *Does he honestly have no fear of her?* Mina wondered. *Or does he think she'll never turn on him?*

The thoughts were a welcome relief from what had been cluttering her head. Cadwyn's passing words had burrowed into her mind like woodworms. Conjuring up all the thousands of memories of all the times her family had repeated almost that exact configuration of words against her.

You're our daughter. We love you. You'll do this for us, right?

Sucking in a deep breath, she pushed the thoughts aside and rested her hands on the table.

"Can we get this meeting started?"

"I can't listen to you without food," Basheba said before she made purposeful eye contact with Cadwyn. "As I was promised."

"Yeah, yeah."

"I'm hungry."

"I'm going," he shot back. "Don't sink your teeth into my leg just yet."

Basheba scoffed, "But you have such good thighs."

After a long moment, Cadwyn asked with muted seriousness. "Should I be flattered or disturbed?"

"Depends how long you take to bring me my food."

"Right," he straightened and swept a hand around the table. "Burgers all round?"

While Cadwyn jogged back to the building to place the orders, Ozzie took a seat next to Basheba. The tension in the teenager's shoulders quickly melted away as they caught each other up about their injuries and the legend of the Jersey Devil. By the time she presented him with his own gift, Ozzie was all smiles and laughter. The fuzzy blue plushie only made him laugh harder.

"An octopus," he chuckled. "Which aquarium did you go to?"

"That's a replica of the dreaded kraken of Thunderbird Lake, you uneducated plebian."

"Yeah, definitely too cashed up to be a plebian, but roll on," Ozzie grinned.

Watching Basheba laugh and smile, it was hard to believe what had happened only a few hours ago. *She's a good liar,* Mina thought, recalling the police officer in Black River. Basheba had managed to convince him she was a child so she could get away with a lot more. It would have been impressive if it wasn't so insidious.

Finally, Cadwyn returned with a handful of cups and a jug of pop. He poured a glass for everyone and handed Mina hers. It was a small, wordless gesture that carried a world of reassurance. *This is safe to drink.*

"Thank you," Mina said, clutching the cup protectively to her stomach. "Does anyone mind if I get started now? While we're waiting?"

"I'm interested," Ozzie chirped while Cadwyn plucked the plushie out of his hands to better examine it.

"Do I have time for a cigarette?" Cadwyn asked absently.

The question drew Basheba's attention. "I thought you only smoked in October?"

Cadwyn scrunched his mouth up. "It's like Pavlovian Conditioning. Going into Black River? Put some tar in your lungs."

Basheba absently sipped at her drink. "Just throwing it out there, but I'm not a huge fan of the smell. Do you mind sitting downwind?"

"I just got comfortable." He drummed his fingers on the table as he thought it over. "It's too much trouble. I just won't. Okay, Mina. You have my full attention."

Mina had watched the interaction carefully, studying their dynamics. Her normal approach to befriending the blonde hadn't worked all that well. So, Mina had decided to fall back on what she knew—the scientific method. *Observation. Hypothesis. Experimentation.* Cadwyn was the only person Mina had seen Basheba interreact with in a solely positive way. It now seemed that understanding why, and successfully emulating that relationship, was important for her survival.

"Mina?" Ozzie asked.

"Right." Mina drew in a deep breath and pulled her bag out from under the table.

Buck didn't so much as lift his head. Resting it on the edge of the table, she opened it and pulled out a handful of books and maps.

"I want to kill the Witch," Mina said.

"I love the enthusiasm," Basheba said. "I just don't fully understand how you plan to do that."

Ozzie looked around the table. "Can you even kill a ghost. Like, is it possible?"

"Kill might not be the best word," Mina said as she placed the books and papers on the table, and stowed away her bag again. "But it achieves the same thing. I want to cut her off from this world and send her to whatever comes after it."

"Again, I ask *how*." Basheba played with the beading condensation on her glass with one fingertip. "I'm sure you've heard all the stories about people trying to do just what you're suggesting. None of those stories have a happy ending."

"I know. I've done my research." Mina placed her hand on the small mountain of notebooks. "I found out it's been over half a century since someone last tried. There's been a lot of advances since then. And, between us, we have two distinct advantages that none of the other groups had."

"If she says, 'friendship and a can-do attitude,' I'm going to try and kill her again," Basheba whispered to Cadwyn.

Her tone was light and teasing, but there was iron underneath; something that promised that she wasn't joking.

Mina cleared her throat. "I meant you and Cadwyn."

The two people in question shared a mutually confused glance before Cadwyn ventured.

"I'm not sure I follow."

"Well." Mina had practiced the speech to perfection, but now couldn't remember how it started. "My family keeps records. Diaries. I looked into them all, and then found what I could about the other members of the, for lack of better phrasing, Witch-hunting groups. Those who survived continued their diaries and, after reading a few of them, it became clear they lacked enough knowledge to be prepared."

Cadwyn drew in a deep breath as if steadying himself. "And I've lived with a demon."

While his face remained calm, Mina knew she had to tread carefully. "What happened with your brother was horrible, and I don't want to bring up bad memories. But the experience would have offered a different kind of education. You know how they think, what to expect, and it's left you rather unflappable."

Cadwyn only stared at her. Just when she was sure she had lost and offended him, he ran his hand roughly through his hair, bringing his bangs into disarray.

"Well, you've got me there."

Now came the harder part. Meeting Basheba's eyes, Mina reminded herself to keep to the facts.

"You're the only person alive who the Witch has selected twice."

"I'm starting to think Katrina has a crush on me," Basheba dismissed, although it was clear she had no small measure of pride over her survival rate.

"And you've been to the woods more times than that," Mina continued, hoping to take advantage of her good mood.

"A few times," Basheba confirmed.

Ozzie snapped around to face her. "Wait. You have? Why?"

"It's tradition. We create search parties to go on and find the bodies of those who didn't make it out. All the families pitch in."

"How old were you when you…? The first time, I mean."

"Five or so. I don't really remember."

Ozzie looked horrified. "What? Why would anyone do that?"

"Because I'm a Bell," she cut in, fire crackling along the edges of her words. A small warning that he was getting far too close to insulting her family. "That always comes with a certain degree of guilt. If Griogair Bell had just given her the property back, given her a cut of his proceeds, bent to the irrational demands of a vile woman, all of this wouldn't have happened. Making sure the murdered get a decent burial is the least we can do." Within the space of a second, she was all smiles while she brought the glass to her lips. "Isn't that the stupidest thing you've ever heard? Talk about victim blaming."

"So, they took you to find dead bodies?" Ozzie asked, still not satisfied.

"Dad used to bring me around the edges of the woods, show me the weird creatures Katrina had created," Basheba said, a nostalgic warmth filling her gaze. "He was so proud I was never afraid."

"Never?" Ozzie asked softly.

"He had these big hands, my dad," Basheba whispered, more to herself than anyone else. "When he held my hand, I couldn't even see my fingers. I thought he was a giant."

The moment shattered and Basheba snapped her head up. She almost looked stunned that she had said any of it aloud. Snatching up her glass, she mumbled something about being hungry before draining and refilling her cup. No one knew what to say, not until Cadwyn broke the silence.

"Your dad was five-five."

She smacked her glass down. "I was really little at the time. He seemed bigger."

"Yeah," Cadwyn grinned, tipping his glass toward her. "Larger than life."

"From womb to tomb," Basheba recited and clinked her glass against his.

While Mina didn't understand the reference, she knew well enough not to ask. Basheba had only mentioned her father a few times. But each time, it was with adoration and raw love. It was clear she had idolized the man. Mina had come to suspect that Basheba was more volatile with love than with hate. She wasn't going to even approach the topic until she knew she was on firm ground.

"You know Katrina," Mina ventured. "At the very least, you obviously tick her off. So, between the two of you, we have more knowledge than any of the other groups that have gone before us."

"And what do you bring to the table?" Basheba asked.

"Relentless determination."

"Yet everyone calls me stubborn as an insult," Basheba muttered.

"How about history, then? The Cranes are the largest surviving family of the four. We keep records. I can tell you the tricks the Witch has used in the past. The assault methods that failed—"

"Have you ever been to Black River outside of the Harvest season?" Basheba cut in.

"Well," she stammered. "No."

"It's not just Katrina you have to worry about. It's the cult."

"There's a cult now?" Ozzie asked.

Cadwyn caught the teenager's eyes. "That's how Basheba addresses the locals."

"I address them like that because they're a dang cult," she snapped. "Or at least a percentage of them are."

Ozzie tipped his head in question. "What percentage?"

"Forty-three," Basheba answered without hesitation.

Cadwyn almost choked on his drink. "Show me the math."

"What is your obsession with math and evidence?" Basheba accused.

"What do you mean by 'cult'? No one told me about that," Ozzie cut in.

Feeling she was quickly losing control of the conversation, Mina rushed to assure him. "There's no cult. It's just Basheba's theory that the townsfolk are working with the Witch."

His face scrunched up. "Why would anyone do that?"

"Because their entire livelihood depends on her," Basheba dismissed. "And it doesn't matter if you believe me or not. All of you have bigger things to worry about."

"Oh no. Now what?" Ozzie said.

"My uncle owns Witch's Brew. You know, that café we all meet at each year? If we enter town, he'll eventually find out, and then the phone calls will begin, and the Kings will descend."

"Kings?" Ozzie asked.

"Oh, right, you're new." Basheba drew in a deep breath. "Being haunted by a dead witch makes people close ranks and cling to what they know. A fascinating trend that happened to each one of the four families is that they became kind of a monarchy. A very patriarchal, power restrictive monarchy. They call the shots, and they don't like anyone going to town without their knowledge or permission. Because heaven forbid we aggravate our personal serial killer."

"That's not true." Mina rolled her eyes.

"My cousin Jeffery is the Winthrop family leader," Cadwyn said.

Basheba snapped her fingers and pointed to him. "That's what they call it to soften the blow."

"I've heard Percival call his brother 'family leader,'" Ozzie said with a frown.

"Zachariah Sewall," Basheba nodded. "King of the Sewall line."

Ozzie turned to Mina. "Who's your family's king?"

"We just listen to our elders. As is respectful."

"Her daddy," Basheba chirped. "Mina, our little princess."

A flash of anger twisted up Mina's mouth. "So your uncle is your king? He's the only man left."

Basheba laughed outright and reached across the table. Mina flinched back before she realized the blonde was only going for the map.

Spreading the map of Black River out before her, she explained, "Pregnancy is a horror show I will have no part in. And my uncle would never let his precious virginial daughter be sullied by the touch of a man. Which works out pretty well, because she's incredibly gay. There's no one left."

"What about your uncle?" Mina cut in. "He still capable of having children?"

"I live in dread of the day he realizes he can be a sperm donor," Basheba admitted. "Luckily, the only woman who could tolerate him left him decades ago. He's not popping out any more kids. Our line is dead. Can't really be a king if you have no subjects."

"That's one way of looking at it," Cadwyn said into his glass.

Basheba quirked an eyebrow. For once, Cadwyn hesitated.

"Jeffery thinks—and I can't stress enough that this is *his* opinion, not mine—that if you refuse to acknowledge Isaac as your leader, then the remaining Bells should be brought into the Winthrop family."

"Does he now?" Like snow melting in the Spring, every trace of emotion melted from Basheba's face. "'Brought in' meaning I'd be under Jeffery Winthrop's control?"

"Well," Cadwyn cleared his throat. "Ah, there would be an expectation that you would turn to him and the other Winthrop elders for advice. Yes."

"Just advice? Or that I'd follow through on his orders?"

Cadwyn was too busy drinking to reply.

"So, by your cousin's thinking, if I refuse to bow to my blood relative, I should bow to him, instead?" The muscles in her jaw twitched. "Isn't that interesting."

"You've made a reputation for yourself, Basheba," Cadwyn tried to soothe. "I got the impression that all of the families want control over you."

"Control," she repeated.

"I'm sure that's just a bad choice of words," Ozzie cut in with a nervous laugh.

"Don't bother, Ozzie," Basheba said. "I've known for years they don't see me as an equal."

"I'm sure that's not true," Mina said.

"No, it is." The smile the blonde gave was sharp and full of venom. "Every one of them is beneath me. Mom taught me that well enough."

Sensing the dangers of any follow-up questions, Cadwyn cut in before the others to stress, "I want it stated for the record that I don't agree with Jeffery's plan or thought process."

Basheba nodded, her gaze unfixed. "The record acknowledges the protests of Cadwyn Winthrop."

Cadwyn licked his lips. "He's just worried your coup will spread."

A burst of laughter passed her lips. "My coup?"

"Well, you are rebelling against your rightful king," Cadwyn said, refreshing Basheba's glass as if he wanted to distract her.

Basheba hummed, her gaze turning dreamy. "I would look good in a crown. But then I'd have the world's stupidest subjects. Doesn't seem worth it."

"Would they really try to stop us?" Ozzie asked.

"You're not coming," Cadwyn said.

Ozzie bristled. "Why not?"

"You're *sixteen*," Cadwyn replied.

"I went into the woods when I was fifteen."

"We didn't have a choice, then. We do now."

"Shouldn't I have that choice?"

"You're a minor," Cadwyn said. "You can't even vote yet."

"We need him," Mina said. It was a little unnerving to suddenly have their undivided attention. "At least, we need his credit card."

"Explain," Cadwyn snapped.

"Well, I thought we'd get a hotel room to serve as our base of operations before heading out. Making sure we're well-rested and such."

"What's your point?" Cadwyn asked.

"You need to present identification to book a room. If Basheba's right, we're working against ourselves to use our well-known names. Everyone there knows Sewall. No one knows Davis."

"You know what?" Basheba suddenly declared. "I've got nothing else to do this weekend. I'll join your suicide mission."

"Me too," Ozzie declared before Cadwyn could respond.

He glared at the teen and Basheba in turn. Ozzie avoided the gaze but Basheba just smiled.

"Couldn't just back me up?" he asked her.

Basheba giggled, leaning back as the food arrived. "Vive la Révolution."

CHAPTER 4

Apple blossoms coated the apple trees white. Pristine petals drifted over the rural road like snow, twisting in the air and gathering in the lush grass. The vibrant oranges and reds of the Fall seasons had been replaced with an explosion of green. A blanket of wildflowers covered the rolling hills, pushed back only by the small farms of the same vibrance. Morning light cut through the thick foliage to flash against Basheba's aviator sunglasses. The crisp morning air churned in through the driver's side window as she drove, toying at her hair and carrying the scents of the countryside into her car.

The thirteen-hour drive had proven too much for the others and, one by one, they had each fallen asleep. Mina and Ozzie shared the mattress that filled the trunk and back seat, with Buck happily snuggled between them. Cadwyn sat in the front passenger seat, his head propped up on the window and generally too big for the space. He had taken the wheel until they stopped for dinner the night before. She had protested at first, but he had stood firm, insisting she needed some time to sleep and that he could easily drive while she dozed.

Like I haven't driven way farther on less sleep before.

It hadn't taken long for the others to pick his side, refusing to be in a car with such a 'fatigued' driver. Basheba had caved when Ozzie started offering to buy their flights. Leaving her car behind was a far worse option than letting Cadwyn drive it for a few hours. And they all refused to leave without her.

Knowing she was defeated, and that they might have a point in regard to road safety, didn't make the reality any easier to accept. It had only been for a few hours but the damage was done. Even now, hours after she had regained control of the driver's seat, she felt the shift. It was different now. The gentle rumble of her parent's car sounded the same. The sense of freedom and safety she had always felt within its metal body was still there. But it was different now. It all felt further away. *He* felt further away.

Her father hadn't had much to leave her when he died. There was the car, though. And she had the knowledge that she had been the only one to drive it since his death. She had been the only one to sit where he had sat. To touch the stick shift and wheel. Her feet had pressed the pedals and it felt like she was following in his footsteps. For two years she'd had that. A silly, sentimental little thought to keep her connected to the dead. Now, Cadwyn had been in the driver's seat and that link was severed. Never to be fixed again. The tradition was over. *What do I have left?*

Taking one hand from the steering wheel, she pulled at the twine looped around her neck. A few tugs and the numerous wedding rings slipped free of her shirt. They clattered against each other and against the single locket that dangled from the middle of the group.

They were the only true mementos she had of the dead, and she guarded them with savage ferocity. The few photographs she had were incomplete. There was always someone missing. Her uncle had taken everything else. In the beginning, no one had been bothered. It had been easier to leave one person in charge of dividing up the estates since any legitimate will would demand a death certificate. Lawyers would ask too many questions. Isaac had his own business. No one else wanted to waste their limited lifespans on paperwork. He was setting up high-interest trust funds, growing what little they had to supply for the next generation. It was her mother who had started the tradition of keeping the rings.

A small smile crept across Basheba's lips as she recalled the first time she had come back from a body retrieval to find her uncle waiting for her. He had crouched down before her, one hand stroking her hair as he asked if she had found her great-grandmother's engagement ring. Basheba had nodded, and her uncle's smile had spread.

"What a good girl you are," he had said, patting her hair with renewed strength. "Hand it over."

Basheba's gloved fingers hadn't been quick enough to fish it out of her pocket before Basheba's mother had swooped down upon them, shoving Isaac into the dirt. It was as if Isaac always forgot the Bells, including himself, weren't all that physically imposing. Their family tended to be small, fragile, and about as visually intimidating as a newborn fawn. At six-foot-three, Basheba's mother had towered over him, no matter how he puffed himself up. But that day, in that moment, was the first time Basheba had seen Isaac for what he really was—a scared little man cowering in her mother's shadow.

"Baba, keep the ring in your pocket, okay?" Her mother had instructed.

Basheba almost teared up at the memory. It had been over two years since anyone had used her nickname.

"Gwen, be reasonable," her uncle snarled from her memory. "She's a child. She'll lose it."

"She managed to bring it out of the Witch Woods just fine."

Isaac's voice had turned into a whisper. "It's worth ten thousand dollars."

It was the first time Basheba had ever heard her mother cuss someone out. She hadn't understood most of the words at the time, but now they made her laugh.

"I knew you've been selling them, you son of—"

"I have them appraised," Isaac had insisted. "That's the intelligent thing to do."

"Where are the—"

"You can't think Basheba is responsible enough. She'll lose it."

When she next spoke, it had been with an icy calm. "Interrupt me again. I dare you."

Isaac had slinked off into the safety of the grieving crowd, leaving

Basheba to be scooped up into her mother's arms. No one had ever had hair as soft as her mother's. It had been the perfect place to hide her face when she cried.

"Shh, little lamb. You didn't do anything wrong." Her mother's eyes had sparkled when she smiled at her. "I want you to keep the rings, keep them safe until I ask for them, okay? Can you do that?"

"Daddy told me to give them to Uncle Isaac."

"Daddy doesn't always know what's best."

The tip of Basheba's nose tingled with the memory of her mother tapping a finger against it. Still smiling, she baaed like a sheep, coaxing Basheba to return the gesture until they were both giggling.

A stray beam of light slipped under Basheba's sunglasses and struck her eyes, making her flinch, severing the memory. She released the rings long enough to wipe a stray tear away. Unthinkingly, her hand drifted back, this time finding her great-grandmother's ruby ring. *I wonder if uncle knows I still have them.* The notion that he did made her smile again. A sharp intake of breath made her jump and she snapped around.

"What are you thinking about?" Cadwyn asked with a yawn.

She shoved the cluster of rings into her top. "Nothing."

Lines creased his forehead as his eyes tracked the movement.

"What are you looking at?" The words came out as a snarl, fueled by her irrational fear that sharing any of her memories would somehow make her forget.

"Nothing," he said cautiously.

"Oh? Nothing? Really?"

His gaze flicked between her shirt and her eyes, clearly searching for a way to extract himself from the situation.

"I'm just inappropriately staring at your chest," he offered.

Basheba bit the inside of her cheek to keep from smiling. Watching his face turn red as he held back his laughter made her crack. Their chuckling made the others stir and they were all awake as she took the turn, leaving behind the main road and cutting through the flower drenched fields. Mina and Ozzie spent most of the remaining drive checking in with their parents, both blatantly lying about where they were. Ozzie was in New York with his friends, who were apparently confirming the lie on their end. Mina, on the other hand, was in Cambridge, taking a Harvard campus tour with her friends.

"Okay, dad. I've got to go, one of the lectures is starting." Mina caught Basheba's amused gaze in the review mirror and twisted slightly, seeking the privacy that she couldn't possibly achieve. "Okay. Love you, too. Bye." She hung up and sighed. "Okay, let's hear it."

"I've got a Harvard jersey in the bag back there if you want it. Help sell the lie."

"Why would you have a Harvard jersey?"

Basheba forced herself not to look back at her. "I got it when I went there."

Mina jolted as if she had been struck with a cattle prod. "You went to Harvard?"

"The tours are open to the public," Cadwyn cut in. "Don't tease her, Basheba."

"Don't judge my hobbies," she shot back.

"For the record, as a responsible adult, I'm not on board with everyone lying to their parental units," Cadwyn said, speaking loud enough for everyone in the car to hear.

Basheba watched him out of the corner of her eyes. "Are you going to do anything about it?"

"And have you call me a tattletale?" he asked, aghast. "I'd never survive that kind of emotional assault."

Basheba's reply lodged in her throat as she made the final turn and entered the apple orchard. It was something beyond words or sensation. Something bone-deep. As they traveled down the narrow gravel road, the gnarled limbs of the tree arching above them like clutching fingers, their clustered flowers blotting out the sun, a little voice deep inside her soul whispered the truth. *We're home.*

Silence took the car as they traveled the last few miles, surrounded by the perfect rows of trees, each brimming with too much life to see far beyond them. Barely anyone worked the fields. Mostly, it was just younger kids who had clearly been roped into helping their relatives over the school break. One or two looked up at the passing car, but most just went about their work erecting scarecrows.

"We should pick a different spot," Basheba said, her voice barely rising over the hum of the old car's engine.

"This is the only place that met all of your demands," Mina huffed. "A bed and breakfast on the outskirts of town. Few rooms, with minimal bookings. Easy access to the highway with no environmental barriers to hinder escape. It took me ages to find this place."

"They're putting scarecrows up in an apple orchard," Basheba said. "Clearly, they've signed up for Team Katrina."

"Apple orchards don't use scarecrows?" Ozzie asked, reaching into the front seat to nudge Cadwyn's shoulder.

"I don't know anything about farming."

"Their website used the term 'rustic aesthetic' so much it's lost all meaning to me," Mina said. "It could just be decoration."

"When are you guys going to learn that I'm never wrong about these things?" Basheba demanded.

"Okay, say you're right, where do you suggest we go?" Mina might have kept her tone rational and pleasant, but Basheba knew the girl was luring her into a trap. "Any neighboring town is going to take hours out of our day just getting back and forth. All the other places are closer to main street Black River and don't take dogs. Our only other option is camping out, and I'm not good with that."

"I'm not either," Cadwyn chimed in. "I'd prefer a sturdy door I can lock."

Basheba drew in a long, deep breath, trying to buy herself some time to think. But they had long since exhausted their options before the previous day's dinner. *There's nowhere safe for us in Black River,* she thought. She gripped the wheel to keep from seeking out her parent's wedding rings again.

"All right," she said at last. "But I retain the right to tell everyone 'I told you so.'"

Cadwyn caught Mina's gaze over the back of his seat. "That's as good as you're going to get. Take the win."

"All right," Mina said, somewhat bitterly.

It made Basheba smile. But that soon faded when the apple flowers parted just enough to bring the two-story farmhouse into view. Its baby blue siding blended harmoniously with the meticulously tended garden surrounding it. The bushes hung heavy with blooming flowers and the open yard was a field of lush grass.

"I hate to say it. But this looks nice. Like something out of a fairytale," Ozzie said.

"Appropriate, given the wicked witch lurking about," Mina mumbled.

They kept quiet as Basheba slowed the car and inched up the last of the driveway. Someone came out onto the front porch as they approached. She waved them closer, a warm and sunny grin on her face.

"Who's that?" Ozzie asked.

"The owner, I suppose," Mina said.

"Huh," Ozzie said. "Not gonna lie, I was expecting more of a grandmother archetype."

The woman's lipstick matched her blazing red hair and 50's era dress. It was hard to tell her age but she looked to be younger than Cadwyn. Basheba stopped the car but didn't turn off the engine. Not until the morbidly obese woman coaxed them over with a heavily tattooed arm.

"Welcome!" she beamed. "Come in, come in."

"I don't like this," Basheba muttered. "Nothing good ever comes from someone being that happy to see me."

Cadwyn leaned toward her and whispered, "We're paying her to be nice to us."

"Right. Hospitality. Everyone get out of my car."

They all piled out, each one only having a single bag of belongings. Buck was the only one excited to be free of the vehicle. With a delighted yelp, he bounded around the yard, trying to jump on and sniff everything at once.

"My, what a big boy he is," the hostess said as she came down from the patio.

"He's a sweetheart," Basheba said. "I'll clean up after him. Oh, you're talking about Cad."

She turned to find the woman beaming up at a very nervous looking Cadwyn. Forcing a polite smile, he glanced to Basheba for help. *He'll face down a demon without blinking,* Basheba thought as she hurried over to close ranks. *But someone shows him some physical interest and he's terrified.* She would have walked over to save him, but the hostess quickly became distracted with Mina, so she took her time wandering closer.

"Aren't you just the prettiest thing?" she said, snatching up Mina's hands and drawing them out wide to get a better look. "How exotic. I bet all the boys swoon over you. Hawaiian?"

"Filipino," Mina replied.

The way Mina managed to keep both her polite smile and tone left Basheba rather impressed. The woman spent a moment gushing on about Ozzie before noticing Basheba. Leaning forward and bracing her hands on her knees wasn't enough to bring them to the same height.

"Hello, sweet angel. I'm Whitney. You are?"

"In my twenties," Basheba replied with a sugary sweetness. "Did you not see me driving the car?"

Whitney's expression soured. "Right."

"I apologize," Cadwyn cut in smoothly. "It's been a long drive."

"I understand." Though she had smiled warmly to Cadwyn as she answered him, her expression cooled when she looked back down to Basheba. "It would be a sore spot for me too."

Cadwyn gripped Basheba's shoulder. If Whitney noticed, she didn't say anything.

"All right. So, why don't we get you all checked in, I'll give you a tour, and then we can have some tea?"

Basheba smiled. "Oh, I know the perfect blend."

CHAPTER 5

Bunches of dried lavender hung about the room, filling the air with their scent and stealing what little headroom Cadwyn had. The whole building, while quaint and beautiful, was designed for people closer to Basheba's height.

Ozzie giggled from the other twin bed. "You're not going to fit on that thing."

"I have noticed that, thank you."

The door opened and the girls rushed in.

"Whitney is already riding my last nerve," Basheba said.

"What a surprise," Mina replied.

Basheba turned around to eye the woman as Buck launched himself onto Cadwyn's bed, kicking and squirming until every item on the mattress had been knocked to the floor. But it was impossible to be mad when the dog confronted Cadwyn with those big brown eyes.

"Who was the last person you got along with at first sight?" Mina asked.

The response was instant, "Buck."

The dog yelped and bounded over to his owner, where he promptly sat and waited to be lavished with attention. She didn't make him wait long.

"Did you guys get the bigger room?" Ozzie asked.

Before they could respond, Whitney called them back down the stairs and the tour began. The layout was simple, with the dining room taking up most of the lower floor. First, Whitney took them to the extension attached to the back of the house. A long dining table, already set with fine china and decorated with fresh flowers, filled up most of the space. The far wall was exposed brick, broken up by a large hearth. A few overstuffed chairs and a low bookshelf made it a sitting area. Cadwyn was grateful to enter the sunroom, hoping to escape the overwhelming scent of lavender, and was struck with the aroma of daisies. He rushed forward to hold the door open for everyone, desperate for some fresh air. The others took it as an act of a gentleman and he wasn't inclined to tell them otherwise. As before, Buck sprinted out. His paws dug into the earth as he brought himself to an abrupt stop.

"Buck," Basheba called to him instantly.

Instead of turning to her, his attention remained locked on the distance. Following his line of sight, Cadwyn noticed rows of small white boxes. The wind changed and brought with it the scent of honey and the steady drone of bees.

"Are those beehives?" Mina asked, her face paling.

If she hadn't already had a deep phobia of bees, her time in the woods would have been enough to change that. The Witch had forced her to confront a hanging man half gouged out by a swarm. Cadwyn had been on the ground during the incident and still had memories of it. Wordlessly, he slipped closer to Mina's side. Not crowding her, but making sure he was in arms reach should she need it.

"Yes. We like to keep things as natural as possible, so we cultivate several hives to pollinate our orchard," Whitney said, sweeping an arm out toward the white boxes as if she was a game show host. "You'll be able to taste their honey with your afternoon tea. Oh, beautiful, are you feeling all right?"

"I'm allergic," Mina said smoothly.

Smart girl, Cadwyn thought to himself. The Witch already knew their deepest fears but no good could come from broadcasting them to the locals.

"Don't you worry, darling," Whitney assured. "They're very polite. They'll keep to their business if you keep to yours."

"As most insects do," Basheba mumbled.

Whitney's hospitable smile slipped as she glared at Basheba. She soon remembered, though, and fixed it back into place.

"Let me give you a tour of the gardens."

"Thanks," Ozzie rushed to say, glancing over at Basheba to see if she would go along with it.

She's going to want to know the layout, Cadwyn thought just as Basheba slipped into her sweet little girl persona. The one she pulled out when she wanted to butter people up. The one that had the local police thinking she was a child.

"Oh, all the trees look so pretty. Can we go down this way?" she asked, pointing off in a seemingly general direction.

They shuffled off and Cadwyn threw Mina an encouraging smile. She barely noticed him as her eyes remained locked on the beehives.

"I'm okay," Mina assured.

Cadwyn gently touched her arm and said, "That changes, I'm right here."

Suddenly, she snapped her gaze up to meet his. "Thank you."

"Anytime." He gave her forearm a gentle squeeze. "Come on, let's get the hell away from those things. They give me the creeps."

In an attempt to make her laugh, he presented her with his arm. She rolled her eyes at him, but he figured that was close enough. He'd take what he could get. Looping her arm around his, they hurried to catch up with the others. After a few feet, he realized one of their party had yet to move. Buck remained rooted to the spot, his head still high and alert, his ears twitching with every slight sound.

"Buck, come on, boy." When he didn't respond, he attempted one of the whistle's he'd heard Basheba use in the past.

"What was that command?" Mina asked when Buck ignored them.

"I don't know."

She looked at him like he was an idiot. "You remember that he's trained to maul people, right?"

"Clearly, I forgot that," Cadwyn said before raising his voice. "Buck! Heel!"

For an instant, Buck's obedience training took over and he ran a few paces toward them. When he realized it wasn't his beloved Basheba calling him, he locked his legs, and skidded to a stop. All the while, his gaze was fastened on the bees.

"That can't be good," Mina whispered.

Cadwyn twisted around and discovered they were alone. "We need to catch up with the others. Now."

"We can't just leave Buck. Basheba will kill us if anything happened to him."

Cadwyn couldn't say exactly when or how they had assumed responsibility for the dog, but he wasn't about to argue the point. Basheba would probably murder everyone in the tri-state area if anything happened to Buck.

"Come on, let's go!" Cadwyn said, trying to keep the desperation from his voice.

A low whistle drifted from a distant point. Buck took off toward it in a dead sprint, pushing past them, and leaving them alone in seconds.

"Why do I feel betrayed?" Cadwyn asked, watching the dog disappear into the trees.

Mina tugged hard on his arm, trying to pull him out of his thoughts and make him move. They had just passed the first row of trees when they heard it. The low, drowning buzz rushed toward them, filled the trees, lingered in the air. A swarm of thousands. Mina clutched his arm, tightening her grip until even his shirt couldn't protect him from her nails.

"We're okay," he whispered, urging her to move. "Just stay close."

They hurried deeper down the path, hoping to catch sight of the others, but there was no relief from the constant buzz. It was always waiting for them. Surrounding them. Growing stronger until it drowned out every other sound. Movement drifted across the corner of Cadwyn's eyes. He gripped Mina's shoulders tight and brought them both to an abrupt halt.

Panting hard, she moved to throw him a questioning gaze. Even without looking at her, he could tell the instant she saw it. The trees shook as something moved behind them. Its milky skin blended in with the surrounding trees, making it impossible to get a proper grasp of its size or shape. But, by the shake of the trees, he knew it was far bigger than either of them. And it was circling them. Gruff snorts and bovine bellows drifted through the ever-present sound of the bees. Not taking his eyes off of it, Cadwyn arched his spine and whispered in her ear.

"When I say run, you go, and don't stop until you find Basheba."

Mina nodded. He allowed them just long enough to draw in a steadying breath. Then he made the call. They both broke into a sprint, pushing themselves until their lungs burned and their legs struggled to keep up the pace. Cadwyn kept a step behind the teenager and glanced behind.

Thick trees slashed and swayed as the creature barreled past them in pursuit. It closed in fast, consuming the distance between them until the shredded remains of the branches rained down upon them like shrapnel.

Cadwyn pushed Mina's back, forcing her to go faster even though he knew they weren't going to outpace it. With a startled scream, she dropped to the earth. He looked down at her, horrified that he might have tripped her up, and didn't notice the fence she had avoided until he slammed into it. Unrelenting wood slats collided with his hips, while his momentum flipped him forward over the fence. The grass softened the blow, but he still landed hard enough to knock the air from his lungs. Pain exploded along his spine as he rolled up.

The thick wood planks of a white running fence separated them now. Mina was on all fours, her eyes wide as the orchard ripped itself apart behind her.

"Go," he ordered.

It seemed she had been waiting for his permission. Pushing up like a sprinter, she followed the fence line, glancing back once to make sure he was following. The orchard exploded, the trees shedding their blossoms to create a wall of white between them that completely severed her from view.

"Go!"

Shielding his eyes, he fled away from the onslaught, further from the fence and Mina, praying that she had listened to him. Then it all stopped. The shaking trees, the noise, the hailstorm of plant life. The mangled leaves and flowers drifted down to blanket the earth around him, allowing him to see for the first time where he had wandered to. The orchard stood to his left. An empty field stretched out to his right. Then, looming like a beast on the horizon, were the woods that surrounded the town. The ones that butted up against the Witch Woods. Just the sight of it made a chill course down his spine.

Mina was somewhere out of sight. He hoped she had found Basheba. Jogging a few feet along the fence, he eyed the orchard. The space between the rows was completely empty. It gave him enough courage to try jumping back over.

A thunderous snort pushed against his back. He turned in time to see the horns slicing down toward him. Flinging himself to the side, he narrowly missed getting gorged.

The pristine, white bull surged on a few more feet before it managed to bring its tremendous bulk to a stop. Its hooves gouged at the earth. Steam billowed from its snout as it turned its massive head, locking its eyes upon him. Cadwyn bolted for the fence. The bull whirled around with the agility an animal of its size shouldn't be able to possess. With a colossal bellow, it charged after him, easily cutting him off from his escape route. He scrambled back as the beast threw its head about, barely managing to get his foot out of the path of the horns. The tips drove deep into the soil. Hard enough that, for the briefest moment, the bull was locked in place.

Cadwyn took advantage of the moment to throw himself up and start running again. Clumps of damp earth splattered his back as the bull ripped itself free. He forced himself to go faster, knowing there was no real escape. Hot, humid air pushed against his neck. He hurled himself to the side, hitting the ground hard. White-hot pain cut across his thigh, whiting out his vision and making his leg tremble. Blood soaked his jeans, spilling from between his fingers even as he grasped the wound.

Choking on his screams, he looked up to see the bull slowly circling him. Its dark eyes locked onto him as it lowered its head, swiping it back and forth as it paced, hooves clawing at the earth; taking its time as it lined up to charge again. Adrenaline flooded his veins until he was vibrating with it. Cadwyn leaped up, barely feeling the wound as he sprinted across the field. The bull lunged and pulled back.

He realized too late that the animal wasn't trying to kill him. It was herding him. Pushing him closer and closer to the forest wall. He tried to move around it, to slip back to the relative safety of the orchard. The bull cut off his every attempt. He lost ground. All too soon, he had been forced into the long shadows of the towering trees.

The bull's attacks had slowed. It no longer needed to force him to run. Now, it simply paced closer, steadily forcing him to back up, driving him deeper into the shadows. He pried his eyes off of the bull long enough to glance over his shoulder, checking to see how far he had gone. Something stood amongst the trees, its skin darker than the shadows that shrouded it. Twin horns curled out of its forehead to brush against the foliage. While he couldn't see its eyes, he knew it was watching him. He knew beyond a doubt that this was what the bull was driving him toward.

The knowledge froze him in place. Snorting hard, the bull surged forward. An ebony blur streaked across his vision. It launched itself at the bull, latching onto his leg and giving a violent shake. *Buck.* Blood spurted free as the Rottweiler thrashed, widening the wound it had inflicted. The bull bellowed in both fury and agony, slashing at Buck in an attempt to stab him. Buck pulled back but didn't retreat. Blood-stained saliva dripped from his fangs, and he snapped and snarled at the bull.

"Cadwyn!" Basheba's scream dragged his eyes from the standoff before him.

He looked over to find Basheba sprinting across the field, her hair glistening golden in the light, and her lips curled in a savage snarl. In that moment, be it because of desperation or blood loss, he had the strongest urge to cheer her arrival.

"Move, you idiot!" she bellowed.

Snapped from his shock, he raced to catch up with her. Chaos grew behind him, but he refused to look back. His eyes were set on the far gate, the orchard beyond, and he needed to get there before the bull escaped Buck's attack. There was a sharp, pained yelp from somewhere behind him. In an instant, rage replaced the determination on Basheba's face. She reached behind her as she picked up her pace, slipping her hand under her jacket. With a sharp jerk, she pulled free her hunting knife. *How long has she been carrying that?* The thought barely had time to race across his mind before they clashed.

Basheba threw herself at the beast that was running him down. Cadwyn caught her mid-air and attempted to keep going. Simply keeping hold of her proved to be almost impossible. She thrashed and snarled, as ferocious as her dog, and knocked him off balance. They fell and she slipped free of his grasp. Before the bull could strike, Buck attacked from the opposite side, coaxing the bull to swing its head around. Basheba took advantage of the opening, lunging forward to slash her blade across its muscular neck.

It reared back, bucking and kicking its hooves wildly. Cadwyn tackled her out of the way before it could stomp her head. Buck went for its exposed underbelly, forcing it back again. Clasping her hand tightly, Cadwyn ran for the gate again. It took a few hard pulls to make her follow. And, even when she did, her eyes never left Buck.

"It's a trap," he spat out between panted breaths. "We need to fall back."

Basheba licked her lips, desperately trying to force out a whistle and signal her dog, but she was breathing too hard to make it work.

"He'll follow!" Cadwyn snapped.

They raced back, Basheba clutching his hand. Each rumbling growl made her look over her shoulder. He had to continually pull her forward to prevent her from going back.

"He'll follow," he repeated.

When they finally got to the fence, Ozzie and Mina reached out to help them over. Whitney had been slower to come but struggled a bit faster once she realized her bull was injured. Cadwyn looped an arm around Basheba's waist and unceremoniously dumped her over the fence. By the time he was working his long legs over, she had already scrambled back onto her feet and was in the process of climbing back into the paddock. He shoved her hard on her shoulder to keep her out.

"It hurt him!" Basheba roared, her one good eye glaring at the bull with bloodlust. "I'm going to turn it into hamburger!"

With his feet once more securely on the ground, Cadwyn had to pick her up again to drag her away.

"You attacked my bull?" Whitney stammered.

"It attacked me," Cadwyn tried to placate.

The woman wasn't having it. "You shouldn't have been in his field. Call your dog back before he does more damage."

A bellowing bark proved the order to be useless. Buck was already on his way back, muscles rippling under his fur as he ran at a staggering speed. He outpaced the injured bull and hurdled over the gate with ease. Cadwyn glanced back across the field. All the fury had left the bull. It now limped lazily across the grass, licking at its injured leg, and looking utterly confused. Cadwyn searched the tree line beyond it, trying to find a trace of the inky black shadow he had seen before. The adrenaline that had kept him upright faded away and he dropped with a broken cry.

"Are you okay?" Basheba asked breathlessly. "You're bleeding."

"I'm okay," Cadwyn assured as he gripped his wounded thigh. Then it hit him. "You're talking to Buck."

The size difference between Buck and Basheba made it completely unnecessary for her to kneel down to hug his neck. She did so anyway, lovingly patting him and tending to the small, barely visible scrape on his side. The Rottweiler winced.

"I'm sorry, I'm sorry," Basheba said swiftly. "Cadwyn, he's injured. Can you have a look at him?"

"Seriously?"

When she looked at him, he lifted one bloodied hand to prove his point. Mina knelt down beside him, having already ripped the sleeves of her shirt off. She checked the wound.

"Is it deep?" she asked.

"I'll need stitches," he said, gasping sharply as she tied the tourniquet tightly around his thigh.

"Basheba," Ozzie said. "Give me the keys, I'm going to get the car."

Basheba tossed them over to the teen as she moved closer to check on Cadwyn.

"How's my hero?" Cadwyn smiled.

"I'm fine." She paused and smirked. "Oh, you're talking about Buck."

"You should get a tetanus shot," Mina cut in. "I wouldn't trust what's on that bull's horns."

"Oh, he's very clean," Whitney said. "You will be paying for his vet bills, of course."

"Sure thing," Basheba said, her voice tight. "Quick question: where did you get that thing that almost killed my friend?"

Cadwyn could almost see Whitney's mind churning, trying to figure out if she was in any legal trouble. Still, she answered.

"He's a gift from the woods."

Mina whipped around to face her. "What do you mean by that?"

Whitney laughed lightly. "It's just a local saying. You'd be surprised what wanders out of those woods."

Cadwyn glanced back to the shadows on the far side of the field. The creature was gone, but he could still feel it watching him. A cold, gut-twisting glare that left him breathless.

"Yeah. You'd be surprised by what stays inside it."

CHAPTER 6

The last time she had been in Black River, Mina hadn't had the opportunity to meet the local town doctor, but she understood from Cadwyn that he wasn't very good at his job. Even when he had been sitting in a jail cell, nursing the wounds from both crashing his bike and from a minotaur attack, he had still preferred to stitch himself up without anesthetic, rather than deal with the man.

Prepared for him to argue once more against getting medical treatment, Mina pushed the issue, even as Cadwyn insisted he had everything he needed in his medical kit to stitch himself up. Basheba hadn't been of much help, taking Cadwyn at his word that he had the situation under control. Ozzie, however, had aided Mina in reaching the level of nagging necessary to get the man into the car. In the end, it was probably Whitney's presence that made up his mind.

The woman had trailed them to the gravel road where Ozzie had the car waiting, screaming the whole while about the wellbeing of her animal and the necessary vet bills.

Basheba might have hit the woman if Ozzie hadn't positioned himself rather unsubtly between them. In a desperate attempt to get the hostess to back off, Mina mentioned that Cadwyn had the grounds for a negligence lawsuit.

"Your website said we would have full reign of the property, and you failed to mention both the killer swarm, and a clearly dangerous animal behind a flimsy fence," she had argued.

Whitney's cheeks almost went as red as her lipstick.

"He went into the bull's paddock."

"Unlabeled paddock," Mina had snapped, "holding a white bull that easily camouflages with the apple blossoms. After you left us unattended, and unaware."

Mina had thought the woman would back off. Instead, she had thrown herself at Cadwyn, desperate to appease the injured man. After two minutes of that, Cadwyn had crawled into the back of the car himself.

He had spent the drive cleaning and packing the wound with the items from his medical kit. The only thing that stopped him from stitching it up on his own was Mina pointing out that he needed a tetanus shot. And the doctor would insist on looking at the wound before giving it to him. It hadn't taken long for them to reach the doctor's office. In keeping with the town's aesthetic, it had been converted from a two-story historical home. Painted midnight black, it almost seemed superimposed upon the vibrant colors of the treelined street.

In a last attempt to get out of it, Basheba had argued that the second he put his name down, word of their arrival would spread through the town like wildfire. Cadwyn had latched onto the idea. But, at last, the threat of infection from a bull that clearly dug its horns in filth, was enough to silence their protests. At least for a while.

The waiting room was mostly empty. Their only competition for the doctor's time was an elderly woman who looked to be in her nineties, a child with the sniffles, and a farmer who had fallen from a ladder. They moved swiftly into one of the waiting rooms in the back, only to have things lag from there.

After five minutes of waiting in the cramped office, Cadwyn began to fuss. His tourniquet had slowed the bleeding and, with nothing left to do, he began to feel the pain. It also couldn't have been comfortable to be sitting in his underwear, a paper-thin sheet the only thing protecting his modesty, while surrounded by fully dressed people. Every small squirm crinkled the plastic sheeting covering the low table.

"I could have been done by now," Cadwyn muttered.

He tried in vain to find a reclined position that wouldn't leave his legs dangling over the edge. Basheba had claimed what little area was left. She perched on the very end, her knees pulled up to her chest, and her back pressed up against the wall.

"And it would be cheaper," she mentioned. "Unless you have a good health plan."

"I have great coverage," Cadwyn said.

The blonde arched an eyebrow. "Really?"

"I work for the government, Basheba."

She absently ran the tip of one finger around the rim of her eyepatch. "I should get health care. It's just so expensive. I've only got the income from my Instagram sponsors."

Both Mina and Ozzie leaned forward, follow-up questions on their tongues, only to have Cadwyn cut in first.

"We'll get married," he said. "I'll claim you as a dependent."

Struggling to keep a straight face, Basheba jabbed a finger toward the door. "Should we head to the chapel now?"

"Nothing's going on here. Just let me stitch this up and I'll be all set."

Mina sighed loudly. "That has to be the most elaborate way I've ever heard of to get out of something. You'd get married just to do your own stitches?"

"They weren't really going to do it," Ozzie said, for some reason whispering even though there was no hope for privacy.

"Basheba would go through with anything just to prove a point," Mina countered.

"I actually would," she shrugged. Patting Cadwyn on one of his feet, she added, "Not that you wouldn't make a great hubby."

"I'd be perfect for you," Cadwyn said. "Most of the time I'd be in a completely different state. And, once a year, on our anniversary, I'll give you food."

Basheba placed a hand against her heart and made a sweet 'aw' noise that sounded far too strange coming from her mouth.

"We're waiting for the professional," Mina said firmly.

"I'm a professional, too," Cadwyn noted.

Mina leaned against the wall, her arms crossed over her chest, eyeing Buck where he lay curled at Basheba's feet.

"I will admit to having some apprehension over whether or not dogs are allowed in the office."

"Hey, he's cleaner than you are," Basheba snapped. "And if anyone asks, he's an emotional support animal."

"I do feel like he's rooting for me to pull through," Cadwyn smiled. "My new fur step-son."

Ozzie sat on the chair by the door, playing with a rainbow slinky he had found in the toybox. He looked up, frowning slightly.

"What did Basheba mean by 'cheaper?'"

Mina shared some confused glances with the others, not quite sure she had understood the question.

"Ozzie, you know you have to pay to see a doctor, right?" she asked gently.

His face scrunched up. "You do?"

"You came to the hospital with us for your arm," Cadwyn reminded.

"Yeah, that was a weird experience. Normally, Doctor Jenny comes by my house for stuff like that."

Basheba's jaw dropped slightly. Mina had never seen the blonde look so utterly confused. "You've been paying for my medical bills. What did you think that was for?"

"Your eyepatch."

"The bill's over $3,000! You didn't think that was excessive?"

Ozzie shrugged. "How much do eyepatches cost?"

"I got this one for $15."

Ozzie nodded once and pointed to her. "Huh. Yeah, that does seem a bit over the top now that you mention it."

The door opened, severing the conversation and drawing

everyone's attention to the nurse who had just entered the room. Mina noticed it was the same woman who had been at the reception desk and wondered how many people were actually working at this practice.

"I'm sorry, the doctor's a little backed up. He sent me in to check on you."

The moment the nurse closed the door, Buck was on his feet. While he didn't growl, it was clear he was agitated, and the change instantly made Mina tense up.

Basheba seamlessly slipped into her darling pre-teen persona, the one that had convinced the woman to let the dog into the room in the first place.

"Buck," Basheba cooed.

The dog dumped its rump onto the floor but kept his deadlock stare. The nurse eyed him with cautious suspicion as she inched around him to reach Cadwyn's side. She eyed the blood-soaked remains of his jeans, which had been left in a tangled lump in the nearby sink. The moment the nurse placed her clipboard down to examine his thigh, Cadwyn snatched it up and quickly read through it.

"The wound looks clean," she said.

"Yeah. I got bored." Cadwyn looked up from the paperwork with a charming smile. "I can do the rest myself if the doctor's busy. All I need is a tetanus shot, and I'll be out of your hair."

"Oh, you're a doctor now?" she teased.

"Nurse," he corrected. "Specializing in psychiatric and emergency care."

The nurse shifted her weight onto one foot and tucked some strands of brunette hair behind her ear.

"That's impressive, Mr." She paused to take the sheet from him and recheck his name. "Winthrop? As in the Bell Witch Winthrops?"

Cadwyn squirmed, struggling to keep hold of his polite smile.

"I guess you could put it that way."

"You're kind of a celebrity around these parts," the nurse said. She placed a hand on his leg casually, keeping the clipboard to her chest. "Did you know that?"

"I've heard rumors."

The nurse inched closer and Cadwyn tensed, his eyes darting to Basheba. The blonde didn't notice his soundless plea for help. But she was paying attention. Patting the back of Buck's head with one hand, her eyes remained locked on the nurse. Mina searched the blonde's face carefully but couldn't catch on to what she was thinking.

"Would I be able to get the supplies, please?" Cadwyn asked, his voice carefully smooth.

"I suppose I can make an exception," the nurse said with a sly smile. "Just this once."

"And the shot?" Basheba asked.

The nurse jumped as if she had forgotten there was anyone else in the room.

"I'll just go grab that, shall I?"

"Please," Cadwyn said, his eyes crinkling around the edges.

The second the door closed after the nurse, he dropped the expression and bolted upright. He instantly caught Basheba's gaze.

"You saw that, right?" he demanded.

"Yep," Basheba chirped, her attention now fixed on the door.

"She was flirting."

"I noticed."

"That's three times now," Cadwyn said. "Three times in two days that strangers have made a pass at me."

"Why does that worry you?" Ozzie asked. "I mean, you're a pretty good-looking guy. In an unconventional way."

Cadwyn's arched an eyebrow and Ozzie waved a hand about his face.

"I think it's your mouth. It's a little too wide. Something's off about your teeth, too."

"They're fake," Cadwyn said, not sure if he should be offended or not.

"My point is that people will want to hit on you. Back me up, Mina."

She glanced at Ozzie, surprised at being brought into the conversation. "I don't see why you two are so tense. It's unprofessional but —"

"Cut and run?" Basheba cut in. The question was clearly directed at Cadwyn alone.

"Pass me my sweatpants."

"What is going on?" Mina asked. "You need medical care. We all agreed on that."

"Oh, my God, you are supposed to be smart." Basheba sighed, pinching the bridge of her nose and squeezing her eyes shut tight. Jumping down from her perch, she flung her arms out. "In this town, when something feels wrong, you don't stick around to see how the situation will shake out. You set something on fire, and you run."

"We're not burning down the doctor's office," Cadwyn said calmly.

She glared at him, her annoyance somewhat lessened as she watched him awkwardly struggle his way into his pants without aggravating his wound.

"Well, if you want to be lazy about the situation," she grumbled.

"Everyone, just stop," Mina snapped. "This is insane. Flirtation doesn't equal a death threat."

"And besides," Ozzie added. "We weren't anywhere near Black River when my friend hit on you. The Witch's influence can't reach that far." His dark eyebrows drew together. "Can it?"

Basheba huffed and proceeded to ignore them both, leaving them with only Cadwyn to turn to for answers. His focus was on getting the drawstring of his pants tied up. Frustration bubbled inside of Mina. *If the Witch could manipulate people from such distances, surely she would have before.* Years of research washed through her skull, dredging up a term from the depths of her mind—*Folie à deux; madness shared by two.* It was clear that the more time they spent together, the more they fed into each other's paranoia. For a moment, another term threatened to distract her. *Folie à famille; the psychological theory that a family can share a madness.* It had been one of her first exploitations for her family's belief in The Bell Witch. That each generation had taught their children to fear the monster in the dark. *Things had been simpler then.* Still, she wasn't ready to give up on common sense altogether.

"Can we at least try to use logic here?" she asked.

Basheba huffed louder. "Fine, Mina. What do you suggest?"

"We at least steal the meds we need before we leave. You know, so he doesn't die of infection in the Witch Woods?"

The blonde blinked at her then grinned broadly. "Am I starting to like you?"

"That's a terrifying thought."

"I can leave some money, you know, so they won't call the cops," Ozzie offered.

"Yeah, okay, I suppose," Basheba said. "Sucks all the fun out of the situation, though."

Not wanting to deal with that conversation, Mina headed for the door. "I'll go grab the shot."

"Do you know what you're looking for?" Cadwyn asked.

"My cousin got it a few weeks back. I remember what it looks like." For once, her habit of latching onto every possibility to increase her knowledge of medicine was going to come in handy.

"You can't go by yourself," Cadwyn said.

"I'll be fine," Mina assured.

"He means you're going to need someone to distract the nurse," Basheba said. She rolled her good eye. "She's getting the shot, or is supposed to be, so there's a high possibility you're going to cross paths. Have you never stolen anything before?"

"I'll go with her," Ozzie said, hopping up and leaving the slinky on the chair.

"We'll meet you out front," Basheba said.

"Be careful," Cadwyn added.

Basheba smiled. "If you mess this up, just yell for Buck. He'll hear you."

Mina was surprised by how comforting she found that notion. Trying not to show it, she cracked open the door and slipped out into the hallway, Ozzie close behind her. The layout of the converted house made sneaking around a lot easier. Since the living room served as both the reception area and waiting room, they had a wall and some distance away from any prying eyes. Mina jerked her head down the hall and Ozzie took off first, as silent as a ghost. Leaving the door slightly ajar, Mina followed.

Doors lined the hallway. Ozzie paused at each one to press his ear against it, checking for any traces of noise before opening the door enough to glance inside. Mina copied the process on the other side of the hallway. She wasn't sure what the nurse had meant by having a backlog, because it seemed like every room they checked was an empty doctor's room.

At the very end, the hallway diverged into a T-intersection, leaving one room on each side, both without doors. Ozzie took the right and Mina the left. Moving unintentionally in unison, they both pressed themselves against their assigned wall and carefully craned their necks to peek around the corner. She was disappointed to find a dimly lit laundry room. Just a slab of cement, a few machines, and a back door with rusted hinges. Slightly discouraged, she turned to tell Ozzie and found him darting across the narrow corridor, his eyes wide and his arms flying about with barely contained frantic energy.

She didn't have time to ask the question before he barreled her into the laundry room. They scrambled to cram themselves behind the small strip of wall beside the door. There was hardly enough room to hide them both. They froze as footsteps shuffled out of the opposite room and disappeared down the hallway. Ozzie slumped and whispered.

"Exactly how illegal is this?"

"So far, we're just trespassing," she replied. "But I'm sure our lawyer can argue that we just got turned around."

Ozzie's eyes remained wide as he nervously chewed on his bottom lip. Several moments later, he curled slightly to look out into the hallway, checking to see if it was empty. He nudged her with his elbow, and she moved so she could see what he saw. The same nurse from before disappeared into the waiting room. An instant later, she rushed back out, heading to the reception desk. They barreled across the hallway and into the medical supply closet. Without a word of discussion, Ozzie took a sentry position by the threshold, allowing Mina to search the array of glass door cabinets. She ran her finger along the glass, tracing the bottle's labels, slightly horrified to feel the door rattle under her fingertip.

"She didn't even lock it? That's insane."

"Mina," Ozzie hissed. "Just take the win."

"Right. Sorry. Hold on, they don't even have a door for their drug room? That's got to be some kind of medical malpractice."

"Mina," Ozzie said through clenched teeth, his eyes almost bulging out of his head.

"Sorry, sorry," she stammered and forced herself to refocus.

Perusing the cabinet and the array of medications, it struck her that the vast majority of the vials were slender single-use tubes. *Doesn't anyone get sick in this town?*

"Mina," Ozzie's voice barely carried over the hum of the distant air conditioner.

She sped up her search, scanning the neat rows, searching for a green edged label that matched her memory.

"Mina," Ozzie repeated, his voice becoming ever softer.

"Hold on," she whispered back. She could barely contain her squeal of joy when she pushed up onto her toes and spotted the matching colored label. "Found it."

Thrusting open the glass door, she reached deep into the back of the cabinet and plucked out a half dozen vials.

"Mina."

Flushed with victory, she turned to answer him and saw the pure fear on the boy's face. His gaze was locked on a spot beyond her left shoulder.

A cold gush of air washed across the back of her neck. She froze, tightening her grip around the vials until her fingers ached. All of her focus narrowed down upon the singular task of controlling her breathing. As if she could master everything around her if she could only slow her breathing.

Her attempts to think were derailed the moment the thumping began, erratic, dull, and heavy. Something was slamming hard against the wood sides of the cabinets behind her. The vials rattled against each other with a metallic click.

Curiosity ate at her insides. The muscles in her neck strained with the urge to turn and see what was behind her. Ozzie yelped with surprise as she suddenly bolted for the door. Unable to get out of the way, she crashed into him and they both tumbled onto the hallway floor in a tangled mess of limbs. Still clutching the vials, she rolled off of the stunned boy. Somehow, Ozzie was the first one to his feet, already tugging at her arm as the thudding sound grew louder.

Getting her feet back under herself, she couldn't resist the temptation to look back. The cabinet that had been behind her was scraping across the floor, pushed from behind by a clustered array of pale limbs. Thin and pale under soggy clumps of dirt, the arms clawed and thudded against the cabinet walls. Their nails cracked in their desperation. It was as if several children were trapped behind the thick piece of furniture. The cabinet legs scraped against the tiled floor, releasing a wild squeal that cut through the increasing thuds. The vials rattled violently as the cabinet loomed over her.

"Mina!" Ozzie cried, snapping her out of her shock.

His hard tug forced her to her feet and she staggered to keep from falling onto her face. She dug in her heels and threw her weight back, forcing him to trip backward.

"Back door," she said.

They sprinted away just as the cabinet reached the threshold of the closet. Filthy limbs lashed out, scraping at the thin carpet and trying to trip them. A voice called them back. Mina didn't look to see if it was the children or the staff. They darted through the laundry room and slammed through the back door. Once more, no one had thought to lock it. Hands battered the frosted windows that speckled the back of the house. Their touch left smears of dirt and blood.

Still clutching each other's hands, both Mina and Ozzie staggered to a stop. She wanted to go right, him left, and they were left stranded just beyond the door. It was as if being drenched in warm sunlight tricked their brains into thinking they were safe. The door suddenly wrenched open. Limbs filled the space. Squirming, writhing, clutching at the frame until the plaster and wood cracked within their grip.

Children. They're all children. The thought speared Mina's mind, a spike of fear hurling her from her shock. Ozzie felt the same impulse and they shoved at each other, each deciding to go the way the other had suggested. Legs and faces began to squeeze through the mass. Ozzie released Mina's hands and began to push at her back, shoving her hard to the left. The limbs followed them as they fled around the corner of the building. Every window was filled with limbs. Drowned, gargling shrieks filled the air around them. Ozzie's hands became a constant weight against her spine. The contact seemed like her only tie to reality. The only thing she knew was real.

Basheba already had the car idling at the curb, with the hatch trunk and the front passenger door open wide. Ozzie jumped into the front passenger seat while Mina scrambled into the back, careful to avoid clashing with Buck or Cadwyn as she did so. The moment both doors were closed, Basheba pulled out into the street, barely checking for traffic.

"What happened?" Cadwyn asked, one hand protectively

clasping his wound.

Mina presented him with the vials she had protected so carefully. It hurt to relax her fingers.

"I'm pretty sure Katrina knows we're in town," Ozzie said between heavy, panted breaths.

"I told you so," Basheba replied in a sing-song tone.

Even Cadwyn was stunned into silence by the reaction, leaving enough silence for her to add almost cheerfully.

"I'm hungry. Who wants breakfast?"

276

CHAPTER 7

Cadwyn had learned long ago to never go anywhere without an impressively stocked first aid kit. It didn't matter where he was going, he always had his bag close at hand. Most people he knew in his day to day life assumed he was either a hypochondriac or a doomsday survivalist. Anyone with knowledge of The Witch thought he was responsible. In truth, it was his safety blanket. But that didn't keep him from taking a great deal of pride in his kit. Adding the numerous, stolen vials of Tetanus vaccine to the kit made him brim with pride. He felt like a collector with a new prized piece.

Basheba pulled up into the town's supermarket parking lot and killed the engine while he was still fussing over his new addition. She twisted around in her seat and chirped with a smile.

"Need any help?"

"You just want to stab me repeatedly," he replied.

"Damn, foiled again."

He chuckled at that, awkwardly stretching out on the mattress Basheba used as a bed to slip his sweatpants down. His long legs got tangled up in Basheba's sleeping bag. That, combined with the position of the wound, made the whole process painfully difficult.

"Can I help?" Mina asked, barely able to contain her excitement.

He frowned at her.

"The stitching, I mean. Not the pants," she clarified. "For medical practice."

With one last yank, he managed to free himself from his sweatpants. "Have you even sutured an orange before?"

"No," she admitted sheepishly.

Heaving a sigh, he tossed the pants behind him and jerked his chin to the overstuffed medical bag. "Sanitize your hands."

"Seriously?"

"I'll let you do the needle," he clarified.

She was a good nurse. Attentive, sure, and with an iron stomach. Although, he knew that already. Their last encounter during the Harvest had given her more than enough opportunities to prove herself. From the firestorm of poisonous gas of Basheba's making, to the wounds inflicted upon them by The Witch. Her thirst for experience and knowledge was something he could indulge. It was a tether that he felt could solidify into a real bond, if nurtured correctly.

Only a few days before, he had managed to get his hands on a local anesthetic, a gift from a doctor friend who could legally buy it. It kept him from having to steal some from work. He allowed Mina to prepare the syringe, watching carefully as she followed each of his instructions to the letter. Completely focused, she slowly inserted the needle into his flesh. He flinched. She froze.

"Sorry, did that hurt?"

"You're stabbing his open wound," Ozzie said, his suddenly pale skin looking clammy under a fine sheen of emerging sweat. "I don't think it's going to tickle."

"You're doing fine," Cadwyn assured her while effortlessly threading a needle with his gloved hands. "Just keep your hand steady as you take it out."

Mina nodded. Returning her laser focus to the task at hand, she kept her hand as still as stone as she pushed the plunger. Slow and steady, she pulled the needle out. The pace allowing him to feel the movement. It didn't waver at all.

"You're going to be a good surgeon," he said.

"You think so?" She grinned happily. "Thanks for letting me do this."

He dismissed that with a wave of his hand. "How else are you supposed to learn?"

"Most people would say in a classroom?" Mina chuckled.

Cadwyn paused, once more realizing how far some of his life experiences were from others. It was so easy to forget when surrounded only by the families.

"I suppose that's one way."

"How did you learn?" she asked, voice still warm and tickling with laughter.

Cadwyn didn't have it in him to ruin it, not if she was smiling after what had just happened. Basheba made a different decision.

"I'm guessing by doing it on himself," she called from the front seat.

Cadwyn shot her a glare. For once, it was enough to make the blonde look somewhat remorseful.

"Sorry," she mouthed.

"On yourself?" Mina asked.

It was possible to see the exact moment she recalled the tales of his childhood. Stories of the last man standing. He didn't blame his family for eventually leaving his brother's side. Each of them had other people they needed to protect. Or they couldn't witness him slowly being torn apart, body and soul, by Katrina's demons. He could understand it. But he could never have done it. No matter what it cost him, he couldn't have left his brother alone. *Not until the end.*

"Oh, I'm sorry. I didn't mean —"

Cadwyn nudged her with his good foot to break off her stammering.

"My brother taught me how to do this. It's a good memory. One I'm happy to revisit. Now," he said as he held up the needle with one hand and smacked his thigh with the other, "drugs have taken effect. So, hand me the tweezers and watch closely. We're doing a simple continuous stitch."

The bull's horn had been sharp enough to leave a straight, clean-edged cut. Coagulation had done its part, slowing the flow of blood from a constant pour to a trickling weep. He allowed Mina to clean the smears left behind by the gauze and pinched one side of the wound. The flesh offered little resistance for the needle and offered a small droplet of blood to slick its passing.

A low, sickly moan made him freeze. He snapped around, unable to see Ozzie in the front seat as he doubled over, desperately trying to stifle his gag reflex. *He's scared of blood.* In all the chaos, Cadwyn had completely forgotten. Guilt trickled, thick and hot, into Cadwyn's stomach at his utter lack of care for the teenager. Before he could think of anything to say, Basheba had already sat up, forcing a very disgruntled Rottweiler to crawl over Ozzie's back. The teen's whimpers cut sharply into gasps for air against the dog's weight.

"Well, I'm officially hungry. And since I'd get dirty looks if I didn't get food for everyone, I'm going to need someone to carry the bags. Ozzie, you up for it?"

The teen lunged on the face-saving excuse to leave and was out of the car before Buck had time to get off of his back. Basheba somewhat gracefully crawled into the driver's seat again.

"If anyone has an allergy or dietary restrictions, say it now or go hungry. I'm not doing two trips."

"Nothing deep-fried, please," Mina said.

"I hate coconut," Cadwyn reminded.

At the wave of her hand, Basheba coaxed Buck from the car. "Deep-fried, coconut. Got it."

Cadwyn smirked, tipping his head to catch sight of Ozzie through one of the windows. Color was already coming back to his cheeks.

"Thanks, Basheba," Cadwyn said.

Half out the door, she gave him a furrowed look. "Yeah, I was trying to provoke a different kind of response."

She slammed the door.

"I know you're a good person," he called out, trying his best to mimic her previous sing-song tone.

Her muffled voice drifted through the partially open window, "You can't prove a thing."

Chuckling to himself, he held out the needle and tweezers to Mina.

"I'm in a good mood," he said. "Give it a whirl, Crane."

***

Ozzie rushed to the supermarket's automatic doors, only stopping when they opened and a wave of chilled air smacked him in the face. Basheba wasn't about to jog to catch up, not until Buck decided they were racing. Then she broke into a sprint, pushing herself until her lungs were burning, even though she never had a chance of winning. The dog spent the extra time waiting for her by body slamming Ozzie for attention. One of his leaps made the door open again and he trotted inside.

"Is he allowed to do that?" Ozzie asked.

Basheba shrugged as she crossed the threshold. "Who's going to stop him?"

While the store wasn't crowded by any measure, there were enough people milling about that she was able to track the path Buck had taken. The people he passed all stopped to glare in his general direction, clearly not sure how to react. A short snort escaped her.

"Like a dog in a store is the weirdest thing they've seen in this town," she muttered to Ozzie.

When she didn't get a reply, she lightly patted him on the back.

"Stop beating yourself up. So you don't like seeing someone getting jabbed. So what? Otherwise, you did well today."

"I didn't do much," Ozzie grumbled.

"You got the meds, didn't you?"

"Mina got them," Ozzie said, somewhat distracted as he watched Basheba get a shopping trolley.

It's probably the first time he's ever been grocery shopping.

"And you got Mina out," she countered. "Don't brag about things you didn't do, but don't be afraid to claim the things you did."

Basheba pushed the cart toward him. While he looked at it like it was alien technology, he soon got the hang of it and followed her into the low aisles.

"Why do you think I got Mina out?" he asked.

"Because she's a Freezer," Basheba scoffed.

"A what?"

"A Freezer." She walked sideways to better watch his reactions. "You know, like how everyone has a default 'F?'"

"I've got no idea what you're talking about."

"Survival instincts," she said. A few gasped cries let her know that Buck was still lurking nearby. "Flight and Fight get the most screen time, but there's also Freeze and Friend. Each has its perks and drawbacks depending upon the situation. My uncle, the good one, the dead one, he had this theory that everyone has a default 'F.' And you've got to know yours if you're going to master your reactions."

"How was I supposed to know that?" Ozzie dismissed the question and quickly asked another. "Mina is a Freezer?"

"I think it's because she's an analytical thinker," Basheba said, tossing a few bags of chips into the cart. "She can't react to anything until she's convinced herself she's actually seeing it."

"And you're a Fighter," Ozzie said carefully, as if he wasn't quite sure how Basheba would react.

"Bold and impulsive," Basheba chirped. "It's not a bad thing. None of them are."

Ozzie's gaze lowered to his hands. "It seems better to be a Fighter."

"Yeah, it's great when you're confronted with demons from the depths of hell determined to rip your soul apart. Not so much when it turns out they're just a family trying to celebrate Billy's sixth birthday."

Basheba cringed at the memory.

Ozzie's eyes grew wide. "What did you do to Billy's family?"

"Don't worry about it," she dismissed and picked up her pace. "My point is, I'm pretty sure whatever shook you guys up at the doctor's office had Mina standing like a deer in the headlights. If you weren't there, she probably wouldn't have gotten back to the car. Whatever else happens, you can be proud of that."

The metal wire of the shopping cart was cool against her hands as she gripped it and hopped up onto the front rail. After she had crawled over the edge and stood in the main barrel, she was tall enough to grab the box of cereal she had wanted from the top shelf. She tossed it in with the chips and didn't bother to get out.

"What would you classify Cadwyn as? A Fighter, right?"

Basheba should have expected the question. It was pretty obvious that the teenager had a bit of a man-crush on the older nurse. *I wonder if it'll develop into a bromance or hero-worship?*

"According to my awesome dead uncle," Basheba said, coaxing Cadwyn to turn the corner. "He was born with the *friend* impulse."

"Friend?" He sounded a little disappointed.

"Approach your fear with compassion and restraint," Basheba recited the words her uncle had told her so long ago. Memories consumed her mind until her nose filled with the phantom aroma of s'mores and overcooked hot dogs. She could feel the heat of the campfire against her cheek, hear his voice that always seemed to grumble like a bear. "Then try to understand them and give them what they need."

Ozzie's question snapped her back to reality. "Who actually reacts that way to anything?"

My uncle. "The bravest people I know," she said instead. "To confront your fears without panic. To try and find something good about the thing that terrifies you. I've tried, a lot, and have never once succeeded in pulling it off."

"But he was pretty active in the woods," Ozzie protested, as if still slightly offended on Cadwyn's behalf.

"Your first impulse isn't your only one. You can learn to

challenge it and Cadwyn's done just that. Actually, I've never even heard of anyone being able to fight their defaults the way he does." Her spike of pride faltered as she recalled, "But I guess he learned the hard way."

"What do you mean?"

"A Friend's strength is either in finding compassion and mercy, or outlasting their fear until it gets bored and slithers off somewhere. You can't befriend a demon. And they don't get bored. Oh! Down this aisle, I want some granola bars."

Ozzie's footsteps slowed.

"How can you talk about this stuff so easily?" Ozzie asked.

"Fear theory?"

"The demons," he said in a sharp, low whisper.

She shrugged one shoulder. "Oh, that. It's just practice, Ozzie. Live with us long enough and you'll get the hang of it, too."

Buck's yelp drew her attention to the end of the aisle. She tossed some instant noodles into the cart as her large Rottweiler rounded the corner and hurried over, his nails frantically clacking upon the tiles.

"Hey there, beautiful," she grinned, leaning over to pat him.

"Are you its owner?" The sharp voice came from a woman who was clearly trailing after Buck. The woman jabbed a finger accusingly at Buck while also trying to soothe the screaming toddler perched in the shopping cart's seat.

"I'm not a fan of the whole 'master-pet' dynamic," Basheba replied, balling her hand into a fist and holding it by Buck's snout. It didn't take him more than a second to understand that command, and he batted her hand with the back of his paw, almost like a fist-bump. "We're just really good bros."

"But he is yours?" the woman snapped.

For a moment, the woman turned her full attention to her toddler, allowing Basheba an opportunity to squirm a little further away from the approaching screaming lump of fat and drool.

"You can't bring your animal in here," the woman said at last.

"Why not? You brought yours."

Horrified outrage twisted up the woman's face. "Charles is a *baby.*"

"Buck is housebroken," Basheba countered. "Seems like that's the better option."

The woman puffed up her chest. "You can't have dogs around food."

Admittedly, Basheba was having a bit too much fun antagonizing the stranger. *Any opportunity to ruin the day of a Black River native.*

"Everything is packaged. It's fine."

"What about the fresh produce? He'll drool all over them."

Heaven forbid something tarnish the local crops, she scoffed internally. "He drools less than your crotch-goblin. Any chance you could get it to shut up some time soon?" For added emphasis, she patted the head of her obedient and silent pup.

"I'm going to call the manager on you."

"Oh, no," Basheba droned lazily.

"And I'm going to call the police."

"Okay."

The lady stomped her foot in frustration and pulled her mobile phone from her purse. "I'm calling them right now. What's your name?"

Basheba leaned forward, resting her arms on the edge of the railing and making sure she had a perfect view of the fallout before she answered the question. As expected, the woman's eyes grew wide when she recognized the last name.

"Bell?"

Basheba nodded happily. "That's me."

Without a word, the woman turned her cart around and rushed off back around the corner, picking the quickest route to get out of Basheba's sight.

"What just happened? I thought we were celebrities," Ozzie said.

"For some," she said. "For others, we're a living Chernobyl site. There's no safe place around us."

Glancing down, she grinned at her dog and patted her thigh. He leaped into the cart without hesitation. If it wasn't for Ozzie's death grip on the handle, it would have toppled over. As it was, Basheba ended up squeezed into a corner, helpless prey for Buck's attention. He licked her face without remorse.

"We should probably get some drinks, and maybe some fruit," Ozzie said.

"Canned fruit is the next aisle over."

"What about real fruit?"

"From this town?" Basheba scoffed. "Why not just take a cyanide tablet? At least that way you'll get to feel like a Soviet spy."

"I ate food here last time."

"At the family barbeque?"

He nodded, eyes a little too wide.

"Yeah, the Sewalls put on a good spread," Basheba noted. "They bring everything in from out of town."

Whatever comfort Ozzie might have got from that faded away when they rounded the corner and entered a more open setting in the supermarket, where the fresh produce butted up against the fridges. It made it impossible to mistake that they were now the center of attention. A cold lump forged in the pit of Basheba's stomach as she surveyed the gathering before her. Some only snuck quick glances. Others stared without restraint.

"Maybe we should just get the drinks and go," Ozzie whispered. "I'm sure Cadwyn and Mina are getting hungry."

"Yeah," Basheba replied. Abruptly, she shook off the creepy feeling and turned around to check. "You're paying, right?"

"I can," he stammered, somewhat confused.

"What?" She put on the Tennessee twang that constant travel had dulled over the years. "I might be cheap, baby boy, but I ain't free."

Ozzie scrunched up his nose and rolled his eyes. But there was also a smile in there and she figured that was a good sign. *At least he's not afraid. Now I just have to make sure he stays that way until we're back out in the open.*

Perched in the shopping cart, she used her extra height to scan the building as best she could. While they had people's attention, no one ventured too close, giving Ozzie a free path down the last aisle. They didn't stop. Basheba just tipped the bottles into the cart as they passed. Buck grumbled in protest and propped his front paws on the railing, nudging Basheba aside to make more room for himself. Barely any time had passed before they were approaching the checkout.

Basheba straightened abruptly when she noticed it. The silence. No talk or chatter to dull the scrape of the shopping cart wheels. Even the ambient music pumped through the old speaker system had died away. The baby had stopped its squalling. Everything was just suddenly still.

Basheba twisted around, checking to see if Ozzie had noticed it, too. As she locked eyes with him, the first note rang out. A metallic twang like an old music box that resonated off the barren walls. The first strike didn't have time to fade away before it was met with another, and another, all clustering together to create a tune she had known since childhood. It was Katrina's music box. The gift she gave to each of her chosen few, marking them for selection, drawing them back to the woods. Her music boxes with demons lurking inside.

Ozzie had only heard the music for one season, and yet it struck him instantly. His hands gripped the handle of the cart so tightly his knuckles threatened to split the skin. Buck began to growl, long and low, the sound barely rising above the twang of the music box's melody.

"Don't suppose you're up for just running with the food," Basheba said.

287

"We have to pay. I mean, we have time, right? It's just a few things. Better than security snatching us up and making us sit in an office for a while."

She rolled her eyes. *Bloody Sewalls.*

"Fine," she grudgingly accepted. "But we're doing this fast or I'm leaving you behind."

His hard swallow seemed to echo over their silent audience, "That sounds fair."

Without warning, Ozzie sprinted for the counter. The sudden lurch caught both of the cart's passengers off guard. They stumbled back, throwing their combined weight against the side of the shopping cart and knocking it out of Ozzie's control. They sideswiped a display of nail polish remover bottles, sending them scattering across the floor. Making no attempt to gather them up, Ozzie pushed on to the counter, apologizing profusely every step of the way. Buck leaped from the cart as Basheba gathered their shopping up into one armful and dumped them onto the counter. The checkout clerk eyed them suspiciously from under his dark mop of hair.

"Instead of scanning each one, how about we just shove an obscene amount of money at you, and you keep whatever's leftover as a tip?"

He scoffed. "How will I know what's the tip if I don't put them through. You're not that bright, are you?"

Basheba pressed her lips into a tight smile. "Too bad. He's loaded."

Unimpressed, the clerk started to scan the items, deliberately going a little slower than necessary. All the while, the music played. Each 'ping' of the machine interrupted the flow of the song that was now playing in earnest through the old speakers. Basheba restlessly tried to keep track of everyone surrounding them.

It was the anticipation that killed her. Helplessly waiting for Katrina to make her move. Restricted to reaction instead of action. The weight of her hunting knife against her spine was a constant and comforting pressure. Her hand twitched to reach back and touch it. Still, the music played. Basheba took note of the volume, determined to bolt if it got any louder. There were too many aisles, too many places for things to hide. Too many people. But the song still hadn't grown louder by the time they were halfway through checkout. It wasn't comforting. Tension twisted around her gut like barbed wire.

Katrina wouldn't let a chance like this slip past. Basheba scanned the room, her fingers twitching with the desire for action. *So what's the go, Katrina? Are you going to make your move? Are you too weak after the doctor's office?* The thought made her smile, even though she couldn't bring herself to believe it.

Scanning the room again, she noticed the man working his way toward the door. It was impossible not to. He was a giant minotaur of a man. Big and broad, with biceps that threatened to split his shirt sleeves even as they hung loosely at his side. His heavy brow lowered like a cliff ridge over his dark eyes, casting them into shadows as he glared back at her. A cluster of other men started to drift out from the depths of the building, gathering like waterdrops in front of the only exit. The large man nodded to the clerk, and the boy's movements slowed to a crawl.

She caught Ozzie's gaze. He had been too pre-occupied with completing the task before him that he hadn't yet noticed the gathering men.

"We need to go," Basheba told him in a whisper. "Now."

Ozzie nodded once, tossed Basheba his wallet, and started gathering up whatever items had already been processed.

"I haven't finished yet," the clerk said when Basheba thrust a credit card into his face.

"We don't want the rest," she replied.

The worker didn't take the card.

"You wanted me to ring you through," he said. "I'm going to ring you through."

"No. We're checking out. Now."

He stared down at her, clearly expecting some kind of social protocol to kick in and have her back down. *Politeness has killed too many of my relatives for me to care, buddy boy.* When it dawned on him that she wasn't going to give way, his gaze flicked over her shoulder. Basheba slammed her hand down on the countertop, creating a loud thwack that resonated through the building. The clerk jumped along with Ozzie.

"Who is he?" Basheba asked.

"Just a friend."

Basheba bit a smile. "Your friend's blocking the door."

"It's a free country."

"It's a democracy," Basheba corrected. "If it were free, I'd be able to do whatever the hell I wanted without consequences."

She ignored the look Ozzie threw her way.

"Aren't you Bells used to that sort of thing?" the clerk asked.

Basheba tilted her head to the side. The clerk arched an eyebrow in challenge.

"You're a Bell, right? Basheba."

When Basheba didn't reply, the clerk smiled like he had won a small victory.

"Well, Bells are used to getting their way. Historically, I mean."

Basheba's continued silence irked him.

"With Katrina Hamilton," he pressed, fishing for a response.

She couldn't help but bite. "You must have failed so many history classes."

"I know the real history. Not the lies and misinformation your family spread."

"Oh, you're an idiot," she said as if she had just solved a puzzle. "Ring us out. Now."

The clerk bristled at the dismissal and snatched up the card. He didn't process it through, however. "Katrina Hamilton was just an old widow. A healer working with herbs. The Bell's swindled her out of her land, and when she stood up for her rights, you accused her of witchcraft."

"My *ancestors* accused her," Basheba cut in with a bitter smirk. "Supposedly."

"There's not supposedly about it. They're called facts."

Basheba laughed. "Quick note. By your version of events, she died an innocent woman. Then, while dead, learned witchcraft and came back as a ghost. What an overachiever."

The clerk's smug smile curled into a bitter frown. "After what she endured, I'm not surprised."

No matter how many times she encountered it, Basheba was never fully prepared for the complete lack of doubt present in the Black River citizens. There was no discussion about the reality of ghosts. No hesitation to believe. Pushing aside her momentary surprise, Basheba tipped her head to the men at the door again.

"And what about those guys? They part of your little delusional cult as well?"

"What cult?" the clerk asked.

"Basheba." Ozzie's warning made her realize just how many people were around them now. Still at a distance, but undeniably staring. Enough men had now gathered by the door that they blocked the only exit. They whispered amongst themselves, the words lost under the music box's melody.

Basheba felt the pressure building inside of her, as if her blood was suddenly too thick for her veins. The tune played on, an endless loop that worked on her nerves and made her feel the eyes upon her all the more. Carefully, she took in the room, noting the people who had changed their positions. At the remains of the toppled tower of nail polish remover bottles, a small group had gathered, including the woman from before. Her child continued to wail. Red-faced and weeping, it threw its whole body into each gasp and shriek. Basheba couldn't hear any of it. *What else are you changing, Katrina?*

"You got the bags, right, Ozzie?" Basheba asked.

He stammered that he did as she smiled encouragingly.

"Good." Making sure she sounded as pleasant as she could, she reached over and plucked a lighter from the display on the countertop. "This too. Put it through."

The man hesitated and Ozzie snatched the card back, exchanging it for a handful of bills.

"Oh, and this," Basheba added as she bent down and scooped up one of the large plastic bottles of nail polish remover.

She swiped it over the scanner herself then turned on her heel and stalked to the door. Buck was quicker than Ozzie to fall into pace beside her. Already an imposing sight by size alone, Buck lowered his head and bared his teeth. The first traces of doubt rippled across the men's faces, their expressions growing as Buck's low, steady growl rumbled around the room.

Adrenaline flooded her system, growing in intensity as confusion rippled through the group. *It's their turn to wait and see what I have planned.* She put the butt of the lighter into her mouth and uncapped the bottle. Working swiftly, she took the sturdy weight of the industrial-sized bottle in hand and swung it like a bat. Clear liquid splattered over the row of men. The air was instantly thick with the pungent odor. They staggered back, more angered than concerned. That changed the moment she tossed the bottle at the center man's feet and retrieved the lighter from her mouth.

"Do any of you boys know how flammable nail polish remover is?" she asked.

One click, and a small flame danced at the tip. Her smile grew until her cheeks hurt when she saw it dawn upon them. *Step aside, or I'll light you up.*

The following seconds lingered, filled only with the sounds of Katrina's lullaby and the soft gurgle of the still-leaking jug.

"What the hell is wrong with you? Put that out!" the colossal man bellowed.

He loomed over her, his dark eyes blazing with rage as liquid dripped down his sleeve.

"Basheba," Ozzie pleaded. "We should go. We should go right now."

"What do you think I'm trying to do? These guys are blocking the way," she said.

"So you don't ask us to move?" someone she didn't bother to try to pick out of the crowd demanded. "Put the flame out, you psycho!"

Buck snarled and snapped, bracing his paws wide and lowering his skull. Basheba lowered her hand as if to drop it into the clear puddle at the men's feet.

"Your call," she said. "Move or burn."

"You threw it everywhere," a man screamed amongst a string of profanities.

"This is the only exit. The whole place will go up! You'll be trapped in here, too!"

Basheba could barely hear the man over the rising chaos behind her. The other shoppers had realized what was going on. Those who looked prepared to make a run for the door were held back by those who were terrified of her dropping the lighter.

"Are you insane?" someone screamed amongst the flood of whispered demands.

Another person called for someone to call the cops.

"I'd say it's more apathy," she commented. *Or a greater knowledge of how fires spread.* "And boredom. My arm's getting sore boys. Time to choose a side."

Life or Katrina. Which one do you love more? The men all turned to their muscled leader in the center, searching for a sign of what to do next. Wordless, the huge man took a step back. The others followed suit, parting down the center to let Basheba and Ozzie pass. Basheba kept the lighter flame burning as she strode forward. The slick liquid splashed under her hiking boots. She refused to take her eyes from the door, refused to give them any sign of weakness or fear. The men loomed over her like the battlement walls of a dark castle. As hard as she tried, she couldn't miss just how outmatched she was.

Inch for inch. Muscle for muscle. Pound for pound. Buck closed in on her left side, Ozzie on her right.

With a soft beep, the automatic doors swung open and they were engulfed by the warm spring air. Her new focus became the car. And, while she let her arm drop to her side, she didn't let the lighter flick off just yet. When they were halfway to her car, she broke into a wild fit of giggles.

"What?" Ozzie asked breathlessly.

"I was so sure I was going to slip in that nail polish remover."

"You might actually be insane. Like, clinically," Ozzie said in a rush. He constantly checked over his shoulder and scanned the parking lot. "We need to leave. Now. Faster. Walk faster."

Sneaking a glance over her shoulder, she saw that, while the men now lingered by the door, none of them had moved to follow.

"We're fine."

"They called the cops," Ozzie hissed.

"So?"

"So, you threatened to burn people alive, Basheba! People who didn't do anything to us!"

"You heard the music."

"No one else did."

"They're in bed with Katrina."

"Maybe they are. What I'm asking is: how do you intend to explain any of that to an authority figure?"

"I recognize no one's authority but my own," she replied, finally letting the lighter flicker out.

A bit of his heat left his voice when she glared at him. "Okay, sure. But, the security cameras and numerous witnesses will say you went up to a group of people without warning and threatened to murder them, and courts of law exist."

Basheba opened her mouth to argue. Nothing came out. Mina and Cadwyn started to slip from the trunk to help with the groceries. Ozzie waved an arm at them, the cluster of grocery bags smacking together.

"Get in the car. We're leaving. We need to leave right now."

Clearly confused, they sank back in and awkwardly closed the hatch door. Ozzie ordered Buck in before dropping into the passenger seat, bags piled up in his lap, and almost slamming his foot in the door in his haste. The instant Basheba opened the driver's side door, Mina bombarded her with questions.

"I may or may not have done an impulsive thing," Basheba admitted.

"A crime, Basheba," Ozzie snapped, his voice increasingly inching into a squeak. "You committed a crime."

"Some people might have misjudged the situation."

"You! *You* misjudged."

Basheba clicked her tongue. "Mistakes were made."

"You threatened to set them on fire." Ozzie said each word as if it was a complete sentence.

"What is with you and fire?" Cadwyn asked casually.

She glared back at him. "What is with you and getting your butt whooped by bovines?"

"Can we leave now, please?" Ozzie pleaded, practically vibrating in his seat.

As Basheba closed the door, she noticed the sudden twist in Cadwyn's lips. His eyes were locked over her shoulder and, following his gaze, she spotted her Uncle Isaac storming toward them.

"Oh, damn it," she said in a whisper.

"Basheba!" Isaac bellowed. "We need to talk! Now!"

"I'm really getting tired of people telling me what I need to do," she mumbled before heaving a heavy sigh.

Everyone in the car stared at her, none of them voicing the questions that were clearly written on their face. Her uncle reached the edge of the parking lot and screamed for her again, ordering her out of the car.

"I'm going to have breakfast with my family," Basheba said.

"Anyone want to come along?"

CHAPTER 8

Mina watched as Basheba settled down by a gravestone, resting her back against it while she munched on some dried apricots.

"This isn't exactly what I thought she was suggesting," Mina whispered to the boys, not wanting to risk her voice carrying the few feet separating them from the blonde.

Cadwyn's brow furrowed. "You thought it was more likely she would willingly be obedient to her uncle than that she'd want to eat in a cemetery? Seriously?"

Ozzie used a spork to scoop out a dollop of peanut butter and then proceeded to lick it off the spoon like a lollypop, talking around it. "Yeah, that was pretty dumb of you."

Mina turned to Cadwyn for support and only got a shrug in return. The older man offered her some salted peanuts.

"Did she get anything that's an actual breakfast food?" Mina asked, sorting through the array of bags and bottles. "Or fruit?"

"She doesn't want to eat anything from the locals," Ozzie said around his mouthful.

Heaving a sigh, Mina picked up a breakfast bar she wasn't familiar with, flipping it over to read the nutrition label.

"Wow, that's a lot of sugar."

"You know you might be murdered in the next few days," Cadwyn said.

"That doesn't mean I want to spend the rest of the time I have left feeling disgusting," she said, tossing it back into the pile.

At least the granola bar has some nutritional value, she reasoned and began picking one apart. It had to be approaching noon and the warm sunlight was heating the grass they sat upon. The air was filled with the scents of a dozen different flowers, some growing wild, and others left in remembrance for loved ones. At the top of the hill, overlooking the rustic town and surrounded by sprawling fields and woods, it was easy to forget where they were.

Only two points of destruction kept the place from looking like a postcard. The first was the funeral home, which had yet to recover from Basheba's last visit. The other was the memorial headstone for Katrina Hamilton, which had been re-erected in their absence. Basheba had kicked it back down the hill before she settled down to eat with her relatives. They were out in the open. With the high ground and a clear view of every direction. No deep shadows. No way for them to be crept up on.

Mina watched Basheba as she rested her head back against the cool, grey stone and tipped her face up to the sunlight. Buck napped with his head in Basheba's lap. The sight struck a chord in Mina. *This is the only time I've seen her relaxed.*

It made Mina think about her own family. *The flock of Cranes.*

More than two hundred smiling faces filled her mind's eye. Holidays and birthdays. Weddings and graduations. Thousands of little moments that had filled her life with warmth and companionship. An army of people ready to catch her if she fell. For the briefest moment, she tried to imagine what it would be like if every single one of them was in the ground.

"Does she really have no one?" Mina found herself asking.

Cadwyn hesitated to take a sip of his water bottle. "In the Winthrop family, we're always told to fight to the very end. Sometimes, when I look at Basheba, I think that's a stupid idea. At least the dead don't have to mourn."

"But she has to have friends?" Mina pushed. "She went to school, right?"

Cadwyn shook his head. "They were always traveling. She was homeschooled."

"College?"

"I don't think she ever went," Cadwyn said, chewing thoughtfully. "Hold on."

He rocked onto his side and pulled his phone out of his pocket. Wincing slightly, he sent a quick text to reassure his parents, as they all had been doing for the last hour, and started scrolling.

"What are you doing?" Ozzie asked.

"Pulling up her Instagram page," Cadwyn said, idly munching on a handful of nuts.

"Hey, we should all follow each other," Ozzie declared with a smile. "I tried to find you guys but couldn't."

"I'm *Nurse The Worst*," Cadwyn said absently. "My patients have access to the internet, so I can't use my real name. Basheba's tag is *Buck's Road Trip Adventures*."

Ozzie's enthusiasm was infectious, and they were all soon sitting with their phones. Mina wasn't surprised to find that Basheba ran her page like it was Buck's. Lots of photos of him at landmarks and tourist traps. And an admittedly cute one of him gazing lovingly at Cinderella. *Can dogs be partial to blondes?*

While there were a lot of followers, a lot of opportunity to engage with other people, Basheba didn't respond all that much. Even here she didn't want human interaction. The more she thought about it, the more Mina's sympathy became stained with fear. *She really has nothing to lose. Only Buck.* Bile splashed the back of her tongue as it sunk in. Basheba hadn't been bluffing. Not with her, not with the men at the store.

"Basheba!"

The sharp name cracked their comfortable silence. Despite his injury, Cadwyn was the first on his feet. Isaac was still at the bottom of the hill. He stormed halfway up before he noticed Cadwyn had positioned himself directly in his path, his towering form more than enough to block any view of the small girl.

"Step aside, Cadwyn. This is between me and my niece."

299

Mina looked between the two men. It was hard to think that the short twig with wire-rimmed glasses was any kind of threat to Cadwyn. *I bet people think that about Basheba, too.* Mina's gaze traced the thin scar that crossed Isaac's face, the one Basheba had left behind only a few months ago. Not completely healed, it was still puckered and red, and promised to be a dull grayish-white in the future. *That's never going away.* Mina thought. *You'd think it would be enough of a warning to keep your distance.*

"Isaac," Cadwyn sighed. "Just walk away."

"You're protecting her? Do you know what she did just now? She's going to ruin everything!"

"I'm protecting you," Cadwyn cut in. "She's not in the mood to tolerate you right now."

"I can handle my niece."

"There's some evidence that you can't," Ozzie said, shyly wiggling his fingers in front of his face.

Rage made Isaac's face redden, highlighting the scar all the more.

"This doesn't concern you," Isaac spat out.

"May I point something out?" Mina didn't wait for him to reply before continuing. "Basheba has proven in the past that she's willing to be violent with you. Are you sure you want to confront her in an isolated cemetery?"

Isaac jabbed a finger at her. "And your father sings your praises. You're no better than that ungrateful little wench."

Cadwyn shook his head in bafflement. "Did you just call her a— you know what? Never mind. Just leave. Take a breather. Give her a call once you've calmed down."

Isaac neither left nor came forward, just lingered there at the base of the hill, glaring at them each in turn, clearly trying to decide his next course of action.

"I'll be calling your father, too," he snarled at Cadwyn.

"I'm in my thirties, but okay."

Buck was the one that ended the stand-off. The dog emerged from behind a tombstone like a hellhound, head low, eyes fixed on him, fangs flashing as a deep threatening growl rumbled his sides. Isaac backed up and, with a final glare, stalked off with the same intensity with which he came.

Basheba whistled, light and sharp. Instantly, Buck perked up and bound off like a puppy, leaping over the headstone to get back to Basheba's side, where he was instantly lavished with affection and praise.

Cadwyn sighed. "We should move again."

"Why?" Ozzie asked. "He left."

"To contact everyone. My dad's not going to take these newest developments well," Mina answered.

Ozzie helped them pack everything back into the bags, his forehead scrunching up every so often as he thought about something.

"What did he mean by ruin everything?"

"He buddied up to the cult a long time ago," Basheba said, swooping in to snatch up some bags and head down the hill.

The painkillers must have been wearing off because Cadwyn's pace slowed as he went down the hill. Mina lingered with him, allowing Basheba and Ozzie to pack the car. As much as she didn't want to come here, Mina now found herself reluctant to leave. It seemed as if they were always getting pushed from one place to another. *If we can't get a good footing here, how are we going to survive in the woods?*

The question hovered like a fog on her brain, dulling her perception until she was barely paying attention to anything around them. She didn't even notice the woman approaching the hill until she was nearly at their car. From a distance, she looked remarkably like Basheba. It was a difference of inches. A few in height and a few around her waist. Wearing a bright summer dress, and leaving her golden hair free to trail down her back, the stranger had embraced the Disney Princess appearance Basheba downplayed with flannel and plaid.

"Oh God, no," Cadwyn said, picking up his pace.

"What now?" Mina said.

None of this was going as she had planned.

Cadwyn arched an eyebrow. "You don't know who that is?"

"I'm now guessing it's Claudia, Basheba's cousin," she said, giving him her arm to lean on as he developed a heavy limp. "Any chance she likes her more than her uncle?"

Cadwyn only laughed.

"That's not a good sign," Mina mumbled.

If she hadn't personally seen what the small woman could do when unleashed in the forest, Mina would have cut her loose by now. She was starting to hate that, despite everything, Basheba was still worth keeping around.

The ground leveled out and Cadwyn was able to move a bit quicker. They were still too late to intercept Claudia before she gained Basheba's attention. *At least she has the common sense to stay out of arm's reach*, Mina noted. They couldn't have been more than a few sentences into their conversation and already Basheba's face had settled into a neutral expression. *Another warning sign.*

"Hi," Mina cut in with a cheerful smile. "I don't think we've been introduced. I'm Mina Crane."

"Yes, of course." Claudia's smile lit up her round face, making her look all the kinder. "I'm so sorry I didn't get to meet you before. I wanted to thank you for helping my cousin. You could never know how much it means to me."

"I'm her shield," Basheba said. "As long as I'm alive, she's got less chance of getting an invite from Katrina."

Claudia flinched. "Must you call her by name?"

"Yep," Basheba chirped.

"And you know I love you," Claudia pressed on, as if Basheba hadn't spoken.

Basheba rolled her good eye. "Shows."

"It hurts me when you talk like that."

"Good."

Claudia jolted, fine lines creasing the skin between her eyes.

"They're insults, Claud," Basheba said with frustration. "I am intentionally insulting you. For the sole purpose of hurting you. How do you not get that by now?"

The larger blonde shook her head, already looking close to tears. "Don't you ever get tired of being so hateful?"

"No," Basheba smiled happily. "I find it pretty fun."

"Everyone needs their hobbies, I suppose." Claudia's voice remained kind and as gentle as a summer breeze. But Mina noticed that her watering eyes had suddenly gone dry. *She might have a bit more in common with Basheba than her father.* The idea alone scared Mina.

"Daddy is still upset about the way you treated him."

Basheba looked close to gagging. "Could you not call him that? It's so gross."

"You called Uncle Jonathan 'daddy.'"

"Couple of things," Basheba said, bracing one hand against the car as her mouth pulled tight. "Firstly, I was little. Secondly, my dad wasn't a humanoid-shaped pile of fecal matter that just *Frosty the Snowman'd* his way into consciousness. And third, you mention my dad again and this interaction is going to get real ugly, *real* quick."

"Violence is not always the answer," Claudia said.

Basheba shrugged one shoulder. "But it's always an option."

"Perhaps it would be best to get to the point," Cadwyn cut in, adding in a lighter but pinched tone. "We're all a little tense."

"Yes, of course," Claudia smiled. Puffing herself up with a deep breath, she reluctantly turned back to her cousin. "While I love you, your unscheduled visit is causing problems for a lot of people."

Mina watched the smile spread across Basheba's face and knew the girl couldn't have said anything worse.

"Aw, you're so sweet," Basheba said.

Claudia shifted her weight from one foot to the other. "You need to leave. Today, preferably."

Basheba burst into a stream of giggles. "Are you trying to run me out of town? You? Yeah, Buck should be scared of a squirrel."

"What are you even trying to achieve?" Claudia snapped, her arms flying wide and her mask of gentle perfection slipping.

"Mina wants to kill Katrina. And, you know me, I'm always up for a witch hunt."

A variety of emotions flitted across Claudia's face. All the while, her mouth hung open and her arms fell limply to her side.

"What?"

"We're going to kill Katrina."

So much for keeping a low profile, Mina thought. *Although, I guess that idea was destroyed a while back.*

"You can't do that." Claudia cleared her throat and continued. "You can't kill a ghost."

"Call it an exorcism, then."

"You can't."

Basheba giggled. "Oh, you're worried. Afraid your daddy's cult isn't going to take it well."

"Lord in heaven, Basheba, there is no cult! You and your conspiracy theories. You can't spend your whole life hunting Bigfoot and aliens."

"Watch me."

"Aliens?" Ozzie perked up.

"She used to force us all to sit outside for hours searching for UFOs," Claudia said. "Uncle Jon—"

She didn't get the whole name out before Basheba's fist cracked into her jaw. The tiny girl leaped to do it, throwing her whole weight into the blow, somehow summoning enough strength to force Claudia to the ground.

"Say his name again," Basheba hissed, her eyes full of burning fury. "I dare you."

Claudia cupped her jaw, her eyes wide and lined with pained tears. Thin trails of blood trickled from the corner of her mouth to drip into her golden hair.

"Let me look," Mina said, moving to crouch down beside the struck woman.

"Don't touch me," Claudia snapped.

She lurched onto her feet, using the few inches she had to tower over her smaller cousin.

"How dare you."

"Oh, go cry to your daddy," Basheba dismissed. Her eyes lit up as something occurred to her. "And tell him something for me, would you?"

Claudia kept her silence, her hand still protectively covering her reddening cheek.

"I thought he'd get this on his own, you know, like a sane person. But it looks like he hasn't. So, let me make this clear." Basheba took a step closer to her relative, Buck close at her heels. Despite being physically tiny, Basheba appeared to be the biggest threat. "I was *never* afraid of him. I kept my silence to protect my father. To spare him from knowing what kind of man his brother was. Now, dad's gone. And there's nothing left to protect him from me."

"What are you talking about?" Claudia whispered. "Daddy never did anything to you."

Basheba laughed, bitter and cold. "How can you function being this stupid? Just repeat that word for word to him, okay? You've pushed me too far. Come near me again, and I'll show you exactly what I did to the others."

Shoving Claudia hard in the chest, Basheba turned on her heel and stalked toward the driver's seat. Before Mina could make sense of what had just happened, Cadwyn was already steering her toward the back of the car. Claudia watched them drive away, confusion mixed with fear on her face as she hugged herself tight.

CHAPTER 9

The day passed slowly as they sat crowded in the boys' room. The beds were smaller, but there were two of them. And, since Basheba only traveled with one backpack, it was easier for the girls to move. The idea of fleeing the town while they still could had swirled amongst the group. The Witch knew they were here and Basheba's paranoia of the supposed cult had spread to Ozzie.

Everyone was on edge. No one felt in control anymore. Mina couldn't have been more surprised that Basheba had backed her up in her argument to stay. The element of surprise wasn't ever in their favor anyway. They had to be on their guard, but little had changed. If anything, Mina took this as a sign that The Witch was concerned. *Why else try to scare us off?* She couldn't shake that it was all hopeful thinking.

With the girls resolved to stay, there was no chance that Cadwyn was going to leave them. He didn't have it in his nature. Ozzie hadn't spoken much during the discussion and had simply gone along with the decision of the group. It left Mina feeling a little guilty. He was so young. She couldn't shake the idea they were manipulating him. *He shouldn't be here at all.*

They had briefly discussed heading into the woods now, escape the town, and whatever The Witch had planned next. That had died the moment Basheba shook her head. "There's not enough daylight left to get past it," Basheba had said. No one had the guts to ask her what 'it' was, leaving her to continue.

"We're better off getting as much sleep as possible and setting out at dawn".

So they had hunkered down in the bed and breakfast, all crowded into the same room, waiting for night to fall. Hours had passed slowly. Marked only by the changing light and the sporadic calls from their near frantic family members. Oddly enough, Ozzie was the best at placating them. He was always calm and collected. *His parents don't know how much danger he's in*, Mina thought as she watched him expertly turn the conversation to the dramas of some family friends.

Accustomed to long car rides, Buck didn't grow restless until the sun had dipped enough to give the light a honeyed glow. They left as a group, crowding down the narrow hallway and only pausing to let everyone use the restroom at the top of the stairs. Buck seemed to understand the shift in the air and had kept closer to his mistress than he normally would have. He had refused to even leave the porch until Basheba came down to the grass with him. Cadwyn had taken to the swinging seat, watching over Ozzie and Basheba as they played a quick game of fetch with the energized dog. Mina remained on the threshold.

The sunset painted the white apple blossoms an array of pinks, purples, and blues. The air smelled sweet and clear. Try as she might, she couldn't catch the faintest trace of a motor. No planes flew overhead. No cars rumbled down the distant road. There wasn't even a tractor to break the pristine silence.

"It's like time stopped here," Mina said.

"Yeah," Cadwyn said with a sigh. "It's ruined country getaways for me. When things get peaceful, I remember this place."

"I could see myself getting a weekend home here someday," she said, curling her fingers in the soft knit of her cardigan. "You know, if it wasn't for the murderous witch."

"She does drive down real-estate prices."

Mina smiled but she couldn't shake herself free of the melancholy that had settled into her bones. Everything about her was quaint. Beautiful. And yet, the air itself was oppressive. She felt trapped. Barely fifteen minutes had passed before they headed as a group back to the room. Mina was left unsettled by how grateful she was to retreat to their room. As a lifelong claustrophobic, small rooms had obviously never held much appeal to her. Now, it felt like safety.

Her mobile blared to life as they reached the top of the stairs and she reluctantly glanced at the screen.

"It's my dad," she said softly.

Ozzie lingered beside her as the others started down the hallway.

"Are you going to dodge him again?" he asked.

"I can't keep doing that."

Biting the inside of her cheek, she hovered her thumb over the screen, not brave enough yet to answer the call.

"Mina?" Cadwyn asked, lingering halfway between the top of the stairs and their bedroom door. "Are you coming?"

And take the call in front of Basheba? Mina thought, cringing internally.

"I'll take it in the bathroom," she said.

Ozzie straightened slightly. "Do you want me to wait?"

"No, that's okay. I'll only be a moment."

"We're not supposed to be on our own," Ozzie pressed. "I can stay outside the door. You'll have your privacy."

Cadwyn shuffled a little closer, clearly about to offer switching places with the teenage boy. Even that small movement made him wince, coaxing Mina to cut off his question before he could ask it.

"Thanks, Ozzie. I'll keep the door open a bit." She turned her smile to Cadwyn. "I'll be quick."

The older man nodded once and disappeared into the room, leaving them alone in the hallway.

"It'll be okay," Ozzie promised.

"You are so sweet," Mina said, one hand on the bathroom door handle.

He chuckled. "Just what every guy wants to hear."

"Just take the compliment," Mina said as she slipped into the

308

room.

Alone in the bathroom, there was nothing else for her to do but answer the insistent cry of her phone. She pressed the button, licked her lips, and brought the phone up to her ear.

"Hi, dad."

"That's how you start this conversation?" her father said, his voice cold and slow. "I'm sure you meant to start with an apology."

"Dad—"

"For lying to us. For running off across the country without permission. And now Isaac is calling me about this insane plan to go against The Witch. All of these you should be apologizing to me for."

Mina instantly grabbed at the one point she thought she could actually win. "I'm in college now, dad. I'm all grown up. I don't need your permission to go anywhere."

"I am your father," he snarled. "You'll never reach an age where you don't need my permission."

For a moment, she was too stunned to talk. Her father continued on in her silence.

"You're going to destroy everything Isaac worked so hard to create. Did you even think about that?"

"We've avoided his café. If he's telling you anything else, he's lying."

"I'm not talking about his pitiful little business," her father said, his voice still slow but solid. "Did you ever stop to consider how difficult it must have been for him to establish himself in that town? The truce he would have to cultivate to maintain that peace?"

Mina's stomach dropped. "Are you saying that he made a truce with The Witch?"

Basheba can't be right. Not again. Not about this.

"He's done the impossible to keep his family safe."

"He's joined up with the woman who's killed generations of his family," Mina corrected. "God, no wonder Basheba hates him. You can't come back from that kind of betrayal."

"Basheba only cares about herself. She has no idea what kind of pressure comes with being a family leader. And her refusal to breed didn't give him many choices."

"Breed?"

"Don't snap at me about semantics. When you're older, you'll see that you don't get to pick and choose which obligations to fulfill."

"No one should be forced to have children."

And she's terrified of them.

"She shouldn't have to be forced," her father said. "As a woman born into the four families, she came into the world with that burden. Ignoring it is selfish, especially when her line is dying."

"By that logic, why aren't you mad at me? I'm going to school instead of having kids. Aren't I going against the family?"

"Don't be confrontational," he signed bitterly. "You're a Crane. There're enough of us that you can have the luxury of time."

Mina stammered, "Well, while we're on the topic, I don't know if I want kids. I'm going to be busy with my career."

"We'll talk about it later," her father dismissed. Before she could press the issue, he continued, "What matters right now is that you come home before you do any more damage."

"I can't do that."

Ice entered his words. "You will, Willimina. Right now."

"Dad, I need to do this. I can do this. We can be free. You should be here helping me."

"Helping you commit suicide? You have no idea what you're dealing with."

"Because you never told me," Mina cut in, startled by the anger in her own words. "You want to talk about obligations to the family? Let's start with the fact that you keep the kids willfully ignorant."

"I tell them what they need to know."

"Stories about the Boogieman under the bed is a world away from telling them the truth about a serial killer stalking the family. They have a right to know what's coming for them. The real, brutal truth. I had a right to know."

"You're coming home, Mina."

"When I do, I'll tell them everything."

"You will keep your mouth shut!"

It was the first time in Mina's memory that she could recall her father raising his voice at her. It left her speechless.

"This is Basheba's doing. I knew she'd be a horrible influence on you," he snarled with real rage in his voice. "Mina, this is what you are going to do. You will hang up this phone and leave. I've already told Isaac to expect your arrival. He'll take you to the airport and put you on the first flight home."

"No." She could barely make the word louder than a whisper. Still, she knew he heard her because the phone line when silent.

Her hands shook as they tightened around the phone. The bathroom was too small for her to pace out her restless energy.

"I'm going to pretend I didn't hear that."

"I'm sorry, Dad, but I can't come home. Not yet. I need to do this."

"You'll die."

"Can't you just trust me?"

"Get home now, Mina."

Her heart rammed against her ribs hard enough to leave her breathless. Licking her suddenly dry lips, she stammered, "No. I'm sorry."

"You say that word to me one more time, and you won't be going to your little school anymore."

"You can't do that."

"I'm your father."

"And you don't pay my tuition. I got a free ride, I earned that."

"I pay for your rent and living expenses."

Mina froze mid-stride. "You were the one who insisted I should focus on my studies and not get a job. Was that just so you'd have something to hold over my head? Oh God, Dad. Do you hear what you're saying?"

"I hear it. I'm a father telling his wayward daughter to get back in line."

Realization settled on her mind like a branding iron. All this time, he wasn't being supportive. He wasn't proud. *He was only making sure he remained necessary to me.*

"I have to go."

"And pack your bag," he finished for her.

"Whatever you say, Dad," she said, tears pricking her eyes. Even the half-truth left a bitter taste in her mouth. "I love you."

"I love you, too. I'll see you soon."

"Yeah."

"You'll understand one day, Mina. I only ever have your best interests at heart. And I know best."

"I love you," she repeated again just to hear him repeat it back. There was a risk that she might never hear him say it again. "Goodbye."

Hanging up the phone, she braced her hands on her hips and hunched forward. Her dark hair fell around her, blocking off her view of the bathroom. A few tears dripped free as she struggled to breathe. She had never gone against her father's wishes before. *Because I've never seen this side of him before*, she reasoned to herself.

Sucking in a few deep breaths, she washed her face and raked her hands through her hair, trying to work herself back into something resembling presentable. More than once, she had to pause to collect herself. Once she was sure that she didn't look like she was on the verge of tears, she opened the door. Ozzie scrambled up onto his feet. With a soft smile, he shoved his hands into his pockets.

"Are you okay?"

"Perfectly fine," Mina said.

"You know the bathroom isn't soundproof, right?"

Mina swallowed thickly, feeling the burning lump of tears that threatened to break free.

"Don't tell Basheba any of that."

"Why would I?" he asked. "I just want to make sure you're okay."

"I'm fine," she assured. She huffed a breath and pulled a hand through her hair again. "None of this is turning out like I thought it would."

"Are you still sure we can do it?" Ozzie asked directly.

She gave it some real thought, balanced the chances, and shrugged. "Yeah. I do."

"Then I do, too," Ozzie said. "So, let's go prove it."

Warmth rimmed her eyes. Before she could overthink it, she pulled Ozzie into a tight hug.

"Thanks."

Ozzie hugged her back. "Anytime. Do you want to take a second? It's okay if you cry. It just means that you care."

Pulling back and wiping her eyes with the tips of her fingers, she smiled. "I'm good. But thanks."

"Back to the room?"

"Yeah," Mina said with a determined nod.

They turned in unison and the last flush of sunset painted the walls. Within seconds, the once dull hallway was a brilliant yellow. The buzzing started softly. Barely more than a whisper that crept from walls. It steadily grew louder, becoming a constant hum as the wallpaper began to shift and bulge. Mina's nose wrinkled at the new scent that drenched the air. *Honey.*

Ozzie latched onto her hand and tugged her forward. He didn't hesitate to break into a full out sprint. They only got a few paces before the walls began to rot. The wallpaper became brittle, flaking away in patches to create a patchwork of holes. Bees writhed within the gaps. Crawling over each other as thick honey wept from the gaping honeycomb wounds.

Mina's chest squeezed tight until she choked on her suddenly rapid breathing. Sweat prickled her hairline and she clutched tight to Ozzie's hand.

"Just keep moving," Ozzie said.

The swarm poured out of the walls. Honey drenched the floor, creating a puddle that made them fight for every step.

"It's okay, we're almost there," Ozzie assured, tugging her forward again. The buzzing increased, covering every trace of thought that crossed her mind. All she could do was follow where Ozzie led her as the world around them became a gigantic hive.

She slammed into Ozzie's back as he abruptly stopped short. Panting hard, she crowded into him and balled her free hand into the back of his shirt. Only then was she brave enough to glance over his shoulder and see what horror could compete with the nightmare around them. A dark figure stood at the other end of the hallway, with their bedroom door between them. There was barely enough room for its looming stature. But it was also broken. Its limbs hung limply, and it struggled to hold its head up, flopping it from side to side as if its neck was broken. Throwing its shoulders back, it lulled its head up so they could see its face.

"Mina," Ozzie whispered. "You see a scarecrow, too, right?"

"Yeah," she whispered.

Moving in jerking lurches, the scarecrow dragged itself free of the honey-covered floor. It crawled onto the walls. Each touch shattered the decaying honeycomb. Bees rallied against the intrusion and poured out of the gap, their numbers so large they looked like billowing smoke.

Mina's scream covered Ozzie's own. They both staggered back, trying to escape the onslaught. The scarecrow clawed faster toward them. Each touch upon the honeycomb wall released a new flood of insects. They swarmed toward them and Mina realized they were being driven back. Either to the bathroom or back out of the house.

"She's trying to separate us." The fragment of thought toppled out of her mouth.

Ozzie's eyes were wide, his breathing quick, but he tightened his grip on her hand and asked a silent question. The bees surrounded them, their stingers sinking into their flesh and creating a flash of pain that cleared her thoughts. She squeezed his hand back and they both raced forward. Into the swarm. Closer to the scarecrow. Pain exploded within every cell of her body. She couldn't hear anything beyond the never-ceasing hum.

"Basheba!" Ozzie screamed. He tried to call for Cadwyn, too, but the swarm attacked his mouth, making him choke and sputter.

His pace faltered and he tripped. Mina released the back of his shirt to wrap her arm around his waist, dragging him forward. Through the swarm, the shadow of the scarecrow clawed closer. Its fingers ripped chunks from the walls. It was racing them to the door.

"Hurry," Mina sobbed, trying to pull Ozzie back into a regular pace.

They reached the door and scrambled for the handle, barely able to see or breathe while the swarm attacked her face. "Basheba!"

The door ripped away from her hand. She didn't wait to throw herself inside, slamming down upon the floor and bringing Ozzie down with her.

"Close the door!"

It was a waste of her breath. Cadwyn had already slammed the door shut, holding it in place with his body weight.

"The box!" Mina gasped, thrusting a hand toward her backpack.

She had already crawled out from under Ozzie and staggered to her feet by the time Basheba tossed her one of the containers Mina had brought with her. With swollen fingers, she ripped the box open and staggered to the door. The bees that had invaded the room with her swarmed with renewed force. Fire burned under her skin, boiling her alive, making her hand tremble as she poured the salt in a line across the threshold. She had to shove Cadwyn's legs out of the way to complete the trail. Half of the bees attacking her decayed into dust while the last grains of salt completely covered the threshold.

"Bloody hell," Basheba mumbled, swatting at the remaining insects. She clapped her hands and Mina threw the box back to her.

In quick order, Basheba sealed the windows. Mina scrambled to her back, retrieved another box, and did the same for the fireplace.

The world fell silent. The pain ebbed away. Mina flopped down on the floor, breathing hard and resisting the urge to curl herself into the fetal position. They were gone but she could still feel them. As if they covered her. Crawling and squirming and piercing her flesh.

"I swear people have tried salt before," Cadwyn said numbly.

"It's my own blend," Mina said, pulling her aching body into a seated position. She noticed them staring at her. "I did some research on ancient European methods. Salt repels ghosts, iron wards off evil spirits, and sprigs of mistletoe were used to keep witches out of homes. I hypothesized that a mixture of all three wouldn't diminish the effectiveness of each individual component."

Basheba stared at her, jaw hanging wide. "Am I actually starting to like you?"

"I'm not sure I want that," Mina replied, a weak smile pulling at her still stinging lips.

The fragile peace shattered when the knocking started.

"Cadwyn," a soft voice whispered. "Cadwyn, open the door."

CHAPTER 10

"Cadwyn."

Years had passed since Cadwyn had last heard the voice whispering to him through the thin, wood door. Still, he recognized it instantly and it left him reeling with shock.

"Cadwyn, please. Open the door."

"Who is that?" Ozzie asked, still sprawled across the floor at Cadwyn's feet.

Staring at the door, Cadwyn tried to respond, to form the name that screamed within his skull. Nothing came out.

"Cadwyn, I'm scared. Let me in."

Long dormant instinct kicked in, forcing him to reach for the door handle without conscious thought. Basheba's small hand latched onto his wrist and stilled him. Numbly, he stared at her fingers for a long moment, not seeming to understand why his arm had stalled.

"Do not open that door," Basheba commanded.

"I have to."

"What?" she asked.

"Open the door. I'm scared," the voice whispered with urgency.

Cadwyn snapped around to the door, "Abraham."

Basheba squeezed his forearm, the nip of her nails drawing his attention back.

"Abraham died," she said, strong but gentle. "His music box opened, the demon was unleashed, and it killed him."

Tears burned his eyes, falling free as he trembled.

"I killed him," Cadwyn said. "I did that. When he couldn't take it anymore."

"That's not on you. Katrina forced him into a horrible situation. You did what you did, what you had to do, to set him free," Basheba said.

Cadwyn turned to the door, and she squeezed his arm again.

"He's dead, Cadwyn. Whatever thing that is, it's not your brother."

Swallowing thickly, he asked in a whisper. "What if death doesn't release us? What if she gets to keep the souls?"

"She doesn't," Basheba answered swiftly.

"How do you know?"

"Because if I let myself think anything different, I would go insane," Basheba said. "We die. We're free. That's it."

"Cadwyn, I'm scared."

He jerked toward the door. The short girl threw herself between him and the wood.

"She can only do cheap imitations, Cad," Basheba snapped. "And they're always messed up *Frankenstein* monstrosities. Whatever that thing out there looks like, you don't need to see it."

He didn't mean to move toward her. Or loom over her tiny frame with his shoulders squared and anger curling his lips. Cadwyn couldn't recall how he got into that position, but he found himself staring down at her with a volatile mixture of fear, rage, and pain.

"It's all I can do," he choked out. "That's how it always was. That's all I was able to do. Watch."

"You don't owe the dead anything," Basheba said.

"I owed it to him when he was alive!" Cadwyn snarled. "No matter what I did, it never let me take the focus off of him for long."

Basheba softened her tone, "It wasn't your demon to endure."

"I was the one who could take it!"

The words burst out from the depths of his soul. He could feel the damage reverberate through his bones and scrape along the underside of his skin. Holding his breath was the only way to keep himself from breaking into a fit of sobs. And still, the voice of his brother called to him, begged him, pleaded to be allowed to come inside.

"I have to see what she did to him. I just have to."

Basheba caught his arm again. "Do you want them to see it, too?"

She gestured with her free hand to Mina and Ozzie. The teenagers had backed as far away from the door as the limited space would allow. Fear still radiated from them. In their eyes and the quickened pace of their breath. The fine trembling of their hands, and the way they subconsciously clutched handfuls of the other's shirt.

"Katrina's been playing with them all day. You're going to let her go for another round?" Basheba pushed. "Go on, ask them. Let them vote on if you should open the door or not."

Cadwyn narrowed his eyes on her even as his anger slipped away.

"It's all I can do for him," he whispered.

"You've done all you can do." She stepped closer to him, her tone softening until her words almost flowed like a lullaby. "He fought as hard as he could for as long as he could, and now he gets to rest. You do, too. If you let her do this to you, she wins. I'm not going to let Katrina win another round."

The barest hint of a threat weaved its way into the last sentence. Cadwyn didn't question how far Basheba would go to 'win.' It didn't matter. All of his focus was on the teenagers that had, in turn, seen too much, and nowhere near enough. It ripped him apart, but he let his arm drop.

"Cadwyn?" The voice called.

Balling his hands, he lowered his head, riding out the crushing waves of guilt and terror that raged within him. *I'm not betraying him. I'm not leaving him alone. He's gone. I have to protect the living.*

"Cadwyn, please. Don't leave me with her. I don't want to die alone."

Cadwyn squeezed his eyes tight, feeling a few tears slip free. "He didn't. I made sure he didn't."

Silence was his response. Basheba slipped her hand to the middle of his back and pushed him forward.

"Go hug Buck. He makes everything better," she said.

"Cadwyn? Cadwyn! Let me in!"

The door shook violently as something large slammed against it. Clawing and scratching and screaming with wild fury. Abraham's voice cracked as he howled, twisted up with something dark and primal until the sound alone left ice in his veins.

"You coward," it snarled like a feral beast. "You swine. You murdered him, Cadwyn. Tell yourself whatever you want, but you butchered your brother."

Slowly, he twisted around to face the door.

"Cadwyn?" Basheba said slowly.

"I know that voice," he whispered. "It's the same demon."

It can't be. It's not the Harvest season. He had always been taught that Katrina's demon could only walk the earth during Katrina's Harvest. A few days in October, that's all they were supposed to get.

"None of the music boxes opened," Cadwyn whispered to Basheba. "It shouldn't be here. It shouldn't be able to be here."

"Oh, I never left," the demon purred in its militated voice. "I couldn't go without you, Cadwyn."

"Hey, Mina, I don't suppose you brought earplugs," Basheba called out.

"I saw you in the forest," the demon continued. "I was so sad we didn't have time to play together again. Don't you worry, Cadwyn. We will. We'll have days together. I promise you that. Make it easier on yourself. Let me in."

"Go back to hell," Cadwyn snarled.

Cracks riddled the door as the demon pounded against it again, more violent than before. It ranted and raged, spewing out profanities and weaving elaborate tales of things it would do to them once it got inside. Cadwyn staggered back from the door, absently reaching for Basheba for some human contact. Something to ground him and reassure him that he was okay, that he was safe. That he wasn't back to being a skinny twelve-year-old boy alone in a cheap hotel with his brother and the demon that tortured them both. Basheba latched onto his hand and squeezed it.

"Did you get dentures, Cadwyn? Or did they find a way to root those fake chunks into your gums? I hope it's the gums. I want to rip them out again, one by one. Do you remember the pliers, Cadwyn? Do you remember the way you screamed?"

Basheba squeezed his hand until pain shot up from his palm. It grounded him in the here and now. *I'm not a kid anymore. I'm not alone.*

"I remember what you did," Cadwyn called out. "Do you remember me sending you back to where you came from?"

The taunt brought more fury than Cadwyn had expected. The walls rattled with the blows.

"Now, I'm back. And I want your teeth. I'll get them when I rip that tongue of yours right out of your mouth!"

Plaster rained down upon them from the cracking ceiling.

"I'm coming for you, Cadwyn! I'm going to get you! You never escaped me! You never will!"

Cadwyn's whole body began to shake. Childhood fears and the terrors that still lingered in his nightmares crushed down upon him. He crumbled under the weight of it, but the attack didn't stop. An onslaught of grotesque desires filled the air, screamed out by a thousand voices until everything else faded away.

Basheba tugged hard on his arm, making him stumble forward. He couldn't recall when he had started crying, but he wasn't sure if he could stop. She shoved him onto one of the beds and searched through her bag.

The building shook around them, adding to the falling dust. He looked up, worried the old structure wouldn't hold, and jumped when

Basheba shoved a set of headphones onto his ears. Even at its highest volume, Basheba's mobile phone couldn't drown out the screaming demon, but it dulled the other sounds. Made them manageable.

He sucked in a deep breath, vaguely aware of the two teens crawling into bed beside him. They followed Basheba's example, each pulling out their own mobiles and pumping music into their ears. Seeing them tremble with terror forced him to focus. There wasn't much he could do. No escape. *Don't force them to watch,* a voice whispered in the back of his head. He got up and, with one long stretch of his body, he snatched up the comforter from the other bed.

Ozzie and Mina curled up against his left. Basheba and Buck crammed themselves onto what little space remained on his right. Cadwyn settled the blanket over them, creating a dim cave that cut them off from the rest of the room. The dust still fell. The door still barely stood against the onslaught. And the demon still screamed from only a few feet away. But they no longer had to see it. *We can wait it out,* Cadwyn told himself, cradling the teenagers closer. *Katrina's never had the stamina. The demon can't get in.* He squeezed his eyes shut and focused on the pounding beat of the music. *We can wait them out.*

***

It took Ozzie a while to master how to leave it all behind. His flesh, the noise, everything that his reality had become. Focusing on the music allowed him to slip away, to drift within his skull on the tide of music and rhythmic beats. A small ping jerked him back into his own skin. Sitting up made both Cadwyn and Mina stir. They both sent questioning looks at him, exhaustion and fear clear on their faces. Ozzie checked his phone and held it up for them to see the 'low battery' warning.

Slipping off the bed to get his charger, he almost fell flat on his face. Hours must have passed since they had huddled under the blanket and he had moved little since then. His muscles protested the motion to the point that they felt as if they were snapping apart under his skin. He ended up lunging out of the bed. After hours in the confined space, the night air hit him with an icy chill. Dust billowed up with every step he took, choking the air and diffusing the moonlight into a misty haze. Instantly, he wanted to climb back under the blanket. *I could just listen for a while. How bad could it be?* Then he spotted Cadwyn peeking out from under the blanket to watch him and he steeled his spine.

He knew Cadwyn wouldn't think any less of him if he showed his fear. Somehow, that made him want to hide it all the more. Cadwyn had been the one to see Ozzie fall apart in the woods. Had held him tight and told him it was okay to cry. *Let her break you. And build yourself into something stronger with the rubble.* Cadwyn's words rolled around his head, and Ozzie forced himself to give a reassuring smile. Knowing he couldn't hold it for long, he turned his back to search through his backpack.

It was moments like these that Ozzie found the hardest to deal with. Adrenaline saw him through the attacks. The need to attack or, at least, react kept his mind occupied. But when there was nothing left to do except wait, Ozzie felt as if his skin was crawling over his bones. He couldn't keep his hands from shaking. A thousand 'what ifs' battled with the exhaustion that came with his adrenaline crash.

Finally finding the charger cord and adapter, he straightened and began his search for an outlet. Cadwyn slid one hand out from under the blanket and pointed to the lamp on the bedside table. It took Ozzie a moment to realize that he was telling him to follow the lamp's cord to find it. *Right. Logic.* Mentally kicking himself for being so stupid, Ozzie crawled over the foot of the bed. He didn't want to go near the door if he didn't have to.

Scrambling ungracefully with locked muscles, he made it to the far side of the bed, then froze solid. Childhood fears of monsters lurking under the bed bubbled up from the forgotten recesses of his mind. A part of him didn't want to look. Didn't want anyone in the room to see him give in to such childish fears. *They already think of you as the baby.*

In that moment, all the extravagance of his sixteenth birthday felt ridiculous. His parents had played up the importance of the age, as if being sixteen made him more of an adult than he was at fifteen. It all felt absurd now. No one considered him any more competent than they had before. *Just put your feet on the floor and walk.*

Still, he couldn't bring himself to do it. *There are real monsters in the house. It's not stupid to check a logical and accessible hiding place. What if they can come up through the floor?* By the time he had finished his pep talk, he truly believed that something was hiding just below the mattress. Slowly, he let his arms lower himself down and lay flat upon the end of the bed. He didn't know when each tremble of the building had stopped releasing new dustings of plaster. All he knew was the air felt cold and almost solid against this spine.

Tipping over the edge of the mattress, he noticed the comforter had fallen to brush against the floorboards, effectively blocking him from seeing anything that might be waiting for him. Carefully, he began to gather up the length of material. Inch by inch. Like if he moved slow enough he might not disturb the lurking monster. Once it was done, he slid forward, took in a sobering breath, and tipped forward. All of the images he had created in his mind faded in a flash of reality. *Nothing.* Just the floorboards and a couple of dust bunnies.

The tension that had wrapped around him snapped, leaving him to sag forward. *Idiot. I'm such an idiot.* Not brave enough to look up and see Cadwyn's gentle, encouraging smile. Without looking, he knew the older man would already be peeking out over the top of the blankets to keep an eye on him. Ozzie crawled off the bed and went in search of the outlet. It was in this last bit of motion that he accidentally knocked the lump that was Buck. He grumbled his protest but seemed to give up halfway through and went back to sleep.

Wish I was him, Ozzie thought.

Once more, he stopped abruptly. Basheba was curled up on the very edge of the bed. Dust coated blonde hair fell across her face in streaks, stirring slightly as she breathed. *Is she asleep?* Against himself, he checked with Cadwyn, as if the older man could make sense of how the only one amongst them without headphones had managed to nod off. Cadwyn followed his gaze and grinned, the blankets covering his broad shoulders jostling slightly with his barely contained chuckling. *Yeah, she's asleep.*

A few moments of silence separated the songs on his phone. In those seconds, he was exposed to the full weight of the demon's perverse words. *At least it's not screaming anymore,* Ozzie thought, trying to make his own words loud enough within his skull to drown out everything else. The relief that came with the new song renewed his focus to find the outlet.

Moving silently so as not to wake Basheba, he found the lamp's cord and followed it to the wall outlet. It was situated under the window, giving him something to balance against as he squatted down, his muscles screaming as they stretched. Eventually, he was able to fumble everything into place and his phone began to charge. Only once everything was in place and he had struggled his way back up into a standing position, did he realize he was now, essentially, tied to the wall.

For the briefest moment, he eyed Basheba, wondering if he could get away with nudging her out of the way. Cadwyn seemed to read his mind and arched an eyebrow. Somehow, that tiny motion carried a complete message. *Remember how she's not a morning person?* Ozzie pressed his lips tightly together and nodded swiftly. *Bad idea. At least I'll be able to stretch out my legs a bit.*

Really, he didn't want to. He wanted to crawl back into the bed with everyone else and try to forget about everything. To seek out the comfort and safety of the group. For all of that, he was too afraid to face the world without the shield of his music. So he waited. Nervously stretching out his legs and searching for anything to keep his mind occupied. Bit by bit, his phone began to charge, and he found himself gazing out of the window. The night was thick and heavy. A shroud of velvet ebony that allowed the town to glow in the distance and the stars to shine like a stream of diamonds.

He looked out over the orchard. Drenched in the moonlight, the trees almost looked like clouds. If he tried, he could imagine he was flying. Ozzie almost smiled at the thought. The decision to learn how to fly had been a result of his last encounter with the Witch. He had yearned for something to help him feel in control again. Something he could master and hold before him as proof that he was better than he had been before. Stronger in some way. He had wanted to prove to his parents that he was okay. To Percival, his biological father, that he could make a good Sewall. And, to Cadwyn, that he had managed to make something worthwhile out of the rubble the Witch had left him as. *It seems kind of stupid now,* he thought. *Wilderness survival would have been smart. Maybe something physical, like parkour. How long does it take to master jumping across rooftops?*

His thoughts were disrupted by a flicker of light. It came and faded so swiftly, he doubted he had seen it. Leaning closer to the glass, he peered into the shadows, tracing the lines and curves of the thick orchard trees. Another flash of light forced him even nearer to the window till the tip of his nose pressed against the warmed glass. Two points of burning light trailed across the horizon, flickering as it passed through the foliage, steadily growing larger and multiplying. Ozzie frowned as the small orbs became a long trail.

Silence cracked down upon them, heavy and complete, thickening the air more than the lingering floating dust did. Ozzie leaped back from the window, his earbuds ripping free to clatter against the wall. Near frantic, he reached over and shook the bedpost, hissing at the others to wake up. Cadwyn and Mina bolted upright. It seemed to be their sudden movement more than anything else that woke both Basheba and Buck.

"What's going on?" Basheba grumbled.

"We don't know," Mina whispered.

The blonde snatched up a pillow and, after thumping it a few times, flopped down upon it. "Wake me when there's something for me to stab."

"Um, guys," Ozzie said. He didn't know why he kept his voice low, but he couldn't seem to raise it much louder than Mina's whisper. "There might be something going on outside."

"Like what?" Mina asked.

"Ghost orbs, maybe?"

Even wounded, Cadwyn's long limbs allowed him to easily climb over Basheba. He limped slightly as he rushed to Ozzie's side. By the time Ozzie turned back to the window, the floating fireballs had emerged from the darkness. *Not ghost orbs,* Ozzie thought with a sinking dread.

The wide expanse of the front yard was filled with people. They strode toward the house, flaming torches held high above their heads, eyes fixed upon the house. Ozzie's breath caught in his throat as he noticed the huge man from the supermarket leading the charge. Cadwyn and Mina crowded around him to stare out the window.

"Hey, Basheba," Cadwyn called.

"Napping," Basheba grumbled.

"Basheba. Up. Now."

Grudgingly, she flopped the blankets back and sat up. "If all of this is just to give that drama queen Katrina more attention—"

"There's an angry mob on the front yard," Mina cut in.

"The cult?" Basheba kicked the blankets the rest of the way off of her legs.

"And you might get to stab someone," Ozzie said numbly, pointing down at the man now standing next to the living mountain. "Isn't that your uncle?"

CHAPTER 11

Basheba's boots shielded her feet from the chilly floorboards. Stifling a yawn, she padded over to join the others, adjusting her eyepatch as she went. *Sleeping with it on isn't a good idea.* She barely remembered to keep to the shadows. Tomorrow would be the full moon and the plump disc was already emitting a startling amount of light. Grudgingly, Basheba had to admit that the timing had been a good choice on Mina's part. There wasn't anything worse than being in the Witch Woods during a new moon. After a few groggy blinks, Basheba realized the light was growing. *Firelight,* she thought, her interest pricked. She half-slumped against the wall and craned her neck to glance outside. A sea of burning torches steadily seeped from the shadows to pool on the front lawn.

As they watched, their numbers grew, allowing the combined glow of the flames to illuminate their faces. The stark contrast of light and shadow rendered them almost unidentifiable. Still, it barely took more than a glance to find her spindly uncle amongst the larger locals. *So this is the cult.* Seeing them all set out before her, she realized she should have been able to pick them out of the general crowd long ago. *It's all about the excess.* Everyone before them was weighed down by either extra fat or muscle.

"Livestock," Basheba whispered, the last traces of sleep draining away.

"What did you say?" Mina asked.

Basheba jerked her chin to gesture to the crowd below. "Don't they look like livestock to you? Slaughter-ready hogs and prized draft horses. Here I thought Katrina would consider her cult a, well, cult. I forgot how proud she was of her livestock. She never stopped cultivating her animals. She just switched species."

"They're a mob," Mina whispered. "But we have no proof they're a cult."

"They look kinda cult-ish," Ozzie commented, his voice softer than the others as he skittishly eyed the crowd. "But shouldn't they be wearing masks or something?"

Basheba eyed the teenager from the corner of her eyes, not quite sure if he was serious. "They plan on murdering us all."

Ozzie cringed back from the window.

"Livestock," Cadwyn pondered. "That makes sense." He elaborated once he noticed the looks Mina and Ozzie were giving him. "Her slaves? Honestly, how watered down is the history they taught you? A vast amount of the Witch's wealth came not from the land, but from the slaves she, for lack of a better word, bred. Hers were renowned for being obedient and strong."

"I thought she was impoverished and that's what started this all," Ozzie said. "When she had to sell off her property to the Bell family, and got jealous that they knew how to make the land work."

Cadwyn's eyes flicked restlessly, trying to get an idea of just how badly they were outnumbered. "Black River had a smallpox outbreak about five years before the Bells arrived."

"A highly infectious disease in cramped slave quarters?" Mina looked sickened and sorrowful at the thought. "They never stood a chance."

"The financial hit was why she had to sell the property to the Bells," Cadwyn concluded. Abruptly, he snapped his face down to frown at the youngest two. "I'm sorry, this is bothering me. Are you saying that no one ever mentioned to either of you that the Witch was a slave master?"

"My family's stories kept more to what happened after her death," Mina admitted. "I'm only starting to realize just how much they've been keeping from me."

"You're only getting that now?" Basheba scoffed as she returned to the bed to retrieve her backpack. "You're such a slow learner."

"As long as I learn," Mina said, her eyes narrowing with annoyance.

Basheba could only shrug at that, a reaction the teenager obviously wasn't expecting and didn't know what to do with. Which only made the whole thing more satisfying on Basheba's end.

"Is anyone else worried that Mina's salt mixture doesn't actually work?" Ozzie asked. "I mean, what if the demon could get in this whole time but it didn't really try to? What if it just wanted to make sure we didn't get out? Not until they came."

Basheba's gut gave a painful squeeze. Her motions slowed as she caught Cadwyn's eyes. "Boy's got a point."

She let the others discuss the matter in dreaded whispers while she pulled out her collars. It had long since become an unofficial tradition to wear them during the Harvest sacrifices. Thick, leather bands, studded with sharpened, metal spikes, polished to a high sheen that shone like quicksilver in the weakest light.

Fastening the collar first, she then worked on the cuffs as she mentioned to the still arguing group, "Is someone keeping an eye on the cult?"

"Right," Ozzie stammered.

As the one closest to the window, he took sentry point. "There's more of them."

"How many?" Basheba asked, tossing the drawstring bag that held the other cuffs and collars at Cadwyn's feet.

It landed with a loud clatter of metal. Ozzie counted in a soft murmur.

"About twenty."

"About?" Mina asked, working on her collar.

"It's dark down there. I can't tell if anyone's lurking in the trees."

Basheba called Buck over to her. He grumbled while getting out from under the warmed blankets, pausing to stretch and release a jaw-cracking yawn.

"I know, buddy," Basheba cooed. "They always pick the worst times to try and kill us."

When she had decided to attend the Medieval Fair, she had only been looking to see some guys on horseback slamming into each other. Discovering a man who created custom body armor for dogs was a special delight. It had cost her a small fortune, but it was worth it. Knowing Buck was protected was worth any price. He took the weight of the metal scales like it was nothing. Getting the helmet on was always the hardest part. He wouldn't stop trying to lick her face and chew the straps.

"There," she said, rocking back onto her heels. "Such a handsome boy. You ready to raise some hell?"

He barked once and plopped his rump on the ground.

"Um, Basheba," Ozzie said. "Your uncle is talking to that big guy from the store."

"I knew it," she chimed before standing up and walking over.

When she took Ozzie's position, he awkwardly backed up, letting Cadwyn put the last collar on him. She studied the group.

"Yeah, that's too many people. We need to lure them into the woods."

Mina jerked. "The woods?"

"I saw a demon waiting for us on the other side of the bull's paddock," Cadwyn said.

"There's one waiting outside the door," Basheba countered. "And a cult down there. At least in the woods, we'd only have the demon to deal with."

"Unless they follow," Mina said.

"They won't," Basheba said. "No locals ever go into the Witch Woods. Their loyalty to Katrina doesn't give them safety in her home. Either they'll stop following us, or I'll have an eventful evening with considerably fewer participants."

"That's quite an assumption," Mina noted.

Basheba heaved a sigh and held her arms out to better display her tiny stature. "I operate by killer doll rules, okay? My upper body strength is a joke and most people can drop kick me. In a one-on-one fight, I'm useless. But give me some guerilla warfare tactics and the element of surprise, and I'm lethal."

Mina stared at her for a moment before realization dawned on her and her jaw dropped.

"They're human," Mina said.

"We know," Ozzie said in confusion.

Mina ignored him. "We're not killing them."

"I doubt you'll be doing much of anything useful," Basheba countered.

"Basheba?" Ozzie asked in a squeak.

She sighed, fighting back the first traces of guilt. "Do any of you actually believe we're going to get out of this situation without bloodshed?"

"But," Ozzie stammered, finally catching on. "They're human."

"Don't worry about it," Basheba dismissed. "I'll do all the heavy lifting. Just like always. All you have to do is get your stuff and make sure you're ready to run."

"We'll cut through the bull's pen; create a bit more chaos for them to pursue us," Cadwyn said.

Basheba paused for a moment and eyed him carefully. "Are you okay to run?"

"Give me a minute to take another dose of painkillers before you make things worse?"

"You better hurry," she smirked. "I've been struck with the sudden urge to make life utterly unbearable for people."

With practiced ease, he administered the shot and finished getting the others in order, making sure they weren't about to leave anything valuable behind.

"So, what do you plan we do for the distraction?" Ozzie asked, pulling the strap of his bag higher onto his shoulder.

"Haven't decided yet."

Mulling their limited options over wasn't any help. Long-set plans weren't exactly in her wheelhouse. *That's more Mina's thing*, she decided as she jumped up onto the narrow window ledge. There was just enough room for her to stand upright, and she kept on her toes to make sure she didn't disturb the line of salt. Unhooking the metal latch and ignoring the questions from the others, she swung the window open wide.

"Hey, Uncle!" She leaned back against the window frame and beamed down at the crowd. "Did Claudia pass along my message?"

Isaac stopped talking to the bull-man and tipped his head back to glare up at her. "Yes, she did."

"Surprised to see you here, then. Didn't think you'd have the guts to be in the same state as me."

"Look around you, Basheba. You don't seem all that threatening at the moment. Surrounded. Scared. With the use of only one eye."

She let all the venom she felt for the man seep into her smile. "And I could lose a lot more and still be more competent than you. We're going to have to have a long talk once this is over."

"You're only getting through this night with my help," Isaac sneered. "I'm here to try and save you."

"From what? The walking fire hazard?" She turned her smile to the bull-man. "I hope you boys washed up properly. I'd hate for a stray ember to light you up like a Roman candle."

The bull-man's face scrunched up with sharpened rage. "You're not welcome here."

His voice effortlessly boomed through the still night air.

"Yeah," Basheba shrugged. "I've been picking up on that vibe. You guys are always so subtle."

"Must you antagonize them?" Mina whispered harshly.

Basheba scrunched up her eyebrows. "What did you think I was going to do?"

"Maybe not get us killed," Mina said.

After a snort, Basheba returned her attention back to the mob.

"Okay, let's move this along. Hit me with it," she called down to them.

The bull-man frowned. "Excuse me?"

"I'm sure you practiced it in your head all the way over here, just to make sure that it sounds appropriately scary. So, let me hear it."

The man's brow furrowed, and, for a moment, it almost looked like he was going to check with Isaac to see if she was serious.

"Oh, don't be shy! I'm sure it's great!" She crossed her arms over her chest, lifting one hand to roll a wrist while adding. "It's going to be stereotypical as hell, but that's fine."

"What is wrong with you?" Isaac snapped.

"What? He's undoubtedly got an evil-guy threatening speech. Watch, I'm calling it now. His spiel is going to contain a reference to Katrina, something about the greater good, and a general threat to my person."

"Do you think your petulance will save you?" the bull-man bellowed.

"No, I think a vast amount of violence will do that," Basheba smiled.

The air shifted against Basheba's back as Cadwyn slipped a little closer. "Are you sure about this?"

"I'm halfway to certain," she whispered back, her mind still skipping over their dwindling options.

At least the morons are keeping to the front, she thought. Although there was no way to tell how many people were circling around the back, she was relatively sure her blatant disregard for the situation was enough to distract them, keep them pooled together instead of spreading out. *We need to speed this up. Force them to make their move before they're ready*. There was only one way she knew to force someone to bite. And that was to get them too blind with rage to think clearly.

"You brought this upon yourself," the man continued, his voice solid enough to invade the room and roll off the walls. "Did you honestly think you could invade the Witch's territory and not have her retaliate?"

"Oh my God. Seriously? You guys can't even call her by her name?" Basheba shouted down. "How does it feel to be her pet?"

"You've angered her. All that you have done has put the entire town at risk of her vengeance."

"Is that covered by your homeowner's insurance?" Basheba said, adding for good measure, "I'm curious. When you knew you'd have to form a cult and get on board with human sacrifices to appease a long-dead witch, how did you not think, 'maybe I'll move?'"

The taunting worked enough that the man began to seethe. He glared up at her, his beefy hands clenching hard enough to make his arm tremble. *Come on, just be stupid already.*

"Come out here now. Meet your doom, and we'll let the others live."

"Bingo!" Basheba declared, throwing her arms in the air and cheering.

"This is serious, Basheba," Isaac snapped. "What are you playing at?"

"Oh, hey! I got Bingo!" Basheba declared, counting it off on her fingers. "Katrina namedrop, mentioning the greater good, and a personal threat. And in only a few sentences, too. What do I win?"

"You will die screaming!" the bull-man roared.

"And you're going to die tonight," she countered, a large, victorious smile stretching her lips wide.

It was that expression, she knew, that finally broke the man below her. His hand clutched the base of his flaming torch until the wood crackled apart. Moving as a mound of trembling fury, he surged to the front door and out of sight, leaving the confused crowd behind him.

"About damn time," Basheba muttered to herself as she leaped down from the ledge. "Okay, guys. Here's the game plan. Lock the door after me and be ready to run when I—" The sentence stumbled to a stop on her tongue as she realized she still hadn't settled on a plan. "When I do whatever it is that I'm going to do."

"That man's going to get into the house," Ozzie stammered, his eyes wide with fear.

"That was the plan," Basheba said. "I need at least one of them."

She checked that her hunting knife was still securely strapped to her lower back and grabbed one of the salt boxes for good measure.

"You can't go out there alone," Ozzie insisted.

"I won't be. I'll have Buck."

Her dog perked up at the mention of his name and he began to wriggle with anticipation.

"What do you intend to do?" Cadwyn asked, eyeing her with suspicion.

Basheba shrugged, "Don't worry about it."

"How are we supposed to know when to run in when we don't know what you're doing?" Mina asked.

"Don't worry. I'll make it so obvious that even you won't miss it."

During the conversation, Basheba had retrieved a reusable plastic bag from her backpack, dumping the hair ties it contained into the depths of her bag and refilling it with a bunch of the salt mixture. She nuzzled the open end under the door and reached for the handle. Ozzie stopped her.

"Time is a factor here, buddy," she chirped.

"I want to help you," Ozzie said. "I want to come with you."

A giggle left her mouth before she realized the boy was serious. Cringing slightly at the teenager's embarrassment, she schooled her features and tried to salvage his pride.

"My grandma used to say, 'there are times when we need violent people to do wicked things.'" She paused to glance around the room. "And, since I'm the only naturally violent person here, this stuff is kind of my responsibility. Not yours. Not Cadwyn's. Not Mina's." She smiled at him brightly and knocked her knuckles against his shoulder. "Step off my turf, Sewall."

"But—"

"The best way you can help me is to do what Cadwyn tells you to do, and stay out of my way." Before he could argue, she slipped closer to him and whispered. "There's going to be blood. Probably a lot of it."

As hard as he battled to keep his determined expression, he couldn't hide the way his face paled at just the mention of it. Below them, the door crashed against the wall, announcing that someone had entered the house.

"Okay, Buck." She beamed at the Rottweiler, her attention alone enough to make him grumble and squirm with barely contained delight. "You got your war face on?"

Reaching behind her back, she pulled her hunting knife free and raised her foot. In that moment, reality became merely a suggestion on the outskirts of her awareness. Everything inconsequential fell away, allowing her focus to narrow on the course she had set herself. All that mattered now was the dog by her side, the weight of the knife in hand, and the mysteries lurking on the other side of the door.

"Ya ready, boy?"

He yelped and nosed at the doorjamb, scratching at it hard enough to peel away the paint. Settling her side against the door, she took a deep breath, the motion of her chest causing the rings around her neck to sway and thump against her sternum. It wasn't the jewels that grabbed her mind's attention, but the slightly sharp crown of the Irish Claddagh ring. The tarnished and withered gold was the oldest remaining artifact of the Allaway line. She couldn't help but smirk. *And the four families think they have a twisted backstory. They've got nothing on the Allaways.*

"Come on, Buck," she almost giggled. "Let's go do some violence."

CHAPTER 12

One solid stomp on the edge of the bag sent the salt mixture under the door in a sudden whoosh. In the same moment, Basheba hurled herself against the door, surging out in the hall with Buck tucked close to her side. Mina slammed the door shut behind them, smothering the light from the hallway, and leaving them with only the glow seeping through the windows to see by. Basheba kept running as her eyes adjusted to the sudden darkness. Whatever had terrorized Mina and Ozzie had left its mark. A heavy stench filled the air, thick and gut-wrenching, a mixture of sulfur and rotten meat. It was a combination that hovered in the Witch Woods when *they* were around. It marked the presence of a demon.

Her heart thudded against her rib cage with renewed strength. She pushed herself harder, sprinting down the hallway until there was no way for her to slow down for the corner. She skidded across the threadbare carpet and slide-slammed the wall. Far more agile, Buck bounced off the wall, using it to surge forward and barrel down the stairs before her. The sound of his nails against the wooden floorboards faded into the depths of the house, and she was left alone in a smothering silence.

Basheba slowed to a cautious creep upon reaching the final few stairs. Adrenaline turned her pulse into deafening thunder in her ears, almost completely drowning out the soft creak of the stairs underfoot. Moonlight streamed through the front windows to pool over the scattered rugs. The yellowed glow of the cult's flaming torches flickered over the walls, casting strange shadows over the portraits, illuminating the white paint of their eyes more than anything else. While it left her feeling watched, she couldn't deny that the firelight soothed her. A familiar comfort in an alien environment.

Basheba kept to the walls, wading through the lagoon of dark shadows that remained gathered there. The unreliable light distorted the details of the rooms, but she recalled the simple layout well enough.

The silence unsettled her. It was thickened with the promise of the stories Isaac could have been feeding them. For whatever else he was, he was a Bell. He knew how she was trained to survive because he was trained in much the same way. Her mind's eye filled with an image of him stopping the men coming to kill her at the door, giving them some last-minute instructions. *Lure her out. Force her to come to you. Don't let her keep familiar ground.* Her fingers worked around the hilt of her knife. *You're not just a Bell,* she told herself. *You were trained to hunt, not just survive.*

Crouching low to keep from casting a shadow herself, she slipped under the window and reached for the lock on the front door. While she still hadn't settled on an actual plan, she knew she needed at least two bodies for it to work. Painful experience had taught her well enough that one dead body rarely served as sufficient warning. Still, she wasn't delusional enough to think she was in any position to fight the whole cult on her own.

The lock latched with a dull thud that resonated around the empty rooms. Her fingers roamed endlessly over the knife's hilt, adjusting and readjusting her grip while she strained to hear the slightest sound. Even Buck's movements were lost to her.

Crossing the room, she scanned it, keenly aware of any shift in the shadows. She almost jumped out of her skin when Cadwyn shattered the silence. The walls muffled his words, but the tone was clear enough. He was attempting to come to some kind of agreement with the cult. *Negotiator to the end,* she thought with a strange mixture of pity, jealousy, and amusement. A small part of her wondered what she could have been if she had been born a little bit more like him. *Dead, probably,* a voice whispered in the back of her head. *You'd be dead right now.*

Careful and cautious, she made her way through the house like a ghost. The conversation outside became a steady murmur, making it harder to pinpoint where the natural creaks and groans of the house were originating from. Random floorboards groaned in the distance. Coming and going too swiftly for her to lock eyes on the source. Restlessly, she tightened her grip on the knife, adrenaline making her palms prickle with sweat. Her heart hammered but she kept her breathing slow and steady.

She inched into the dining room. The glass doors allowed the moonlight to cut the room into a ladder of silver and shadows. Moving silently, she followed the length of the massive dining table, creeping from one dark patch to the next. A dark shadow lurched across the pools of moonlight, and she spun around to face the source. It wasn't the bull-man. Someone of a similar build, but a far shorter stature. And vaguely familiar.

Her heart stammered with a fresh rush of adrenaline. *Hunting formation. One acts as a distraction while the other circles around.* It was a tactic she'd used more than once.

"Hey, you're one of the guys from the store," Basheba noted as she kept herself in motion, gaze flicking around, trying to track down the other man.

Clearly expecting a more terrified response, the man hesitated, seemingly not quite sure what to do next. He soon recovered and addressed her with a snarl.

"I'll give you a chance to make this easy. Although, I can't promise it'll be painless."

A dark mass crept out of the abyss, slowly pacing along the floor just behind the man. Silent and swift.

Basheba smiled, "Oh, this is going to hurt a lot."

Buck's growl broke the relative silence. His exposed fangs glistened in the minimal glow while his dark fur allowed him to blend into the gloom. The man turned, his eyes widening as the savage growl neared him. Buck's sharp snap shook him out of his daze.

"You're never—"

Basheba cut him off with a simple command. "Kill."

Buck lurched forward, combining his muscular strength and sheer weight to offset their would-be attacker. The man threw up an arm to fend him off, and the dog's jaws latched onto it. The sharp crack of bone echoed under the man's screams. The slick shredding of flesh joined with it. Buck didn't relent. Each time he was torn free, he simply found a new pound of flesh to sink his teeth into. The man's screams barely covered the jarring crack of his bones.

The grotesque noise covered the sounds of the man charging toward her until it was too late. Basheba turned just as the bull-man swung his massive fist. It caught her under her jaw and sent her flying back. Blood splashed across her tongue as she slammed into the wood floor.

"Call him off!" The bull-man bellowed.

Stars danced across Basheba's eyes and she realized she had hit the back of her head against the floor. Vaguely, she became aware of the knife still clutched in her hand.

"Call your mutt off!"

The bull-man leaped over the table with startling agility. He landed on top of her, his hands instantly going for her throat. The razor-sharp spikes of her collar sunk effortlessly into the tender flesh of his palms. Hot blood gushed over her neck as the man pulled back, howling with pain and fury. Basheba thrust herself up and, without hesitation, plunged the knife into the man's stomach, pushing in until the hilt pressed against his skin. He roared again, doubling over and throwing his fist down. Basheba slid herself back over the floor, narrowly missing the blow.

The screaming stopped as she got to her feet. Buck released his grip and the corpse dropped, motionless and silent.

Blood dripped from his snout as he turned to the bull-man.

Shoulders hunched and head low, he prowled closer, snarling all the while. The bull-man pushed himself up onto his feet, trying to keep both Basheba and Buck in sight at the same time. At last, he glared at Basheba.

"You bitch."

She smiled, trying to hide how vulnerable she felt without her weapon in hand. Whatever injuries she had given him didn't seem to take away his strength. Buck's constant growl offered some reassurance. Enough to keep her spine straight and her head raised.

"Flattery isn't going to change things now," she said. "You could leave, get some medical attention."

With a feral smile curling his lips, the man slowly pulled the blade out. Blood bubbled free to stain the front of his shirt. In the dim light, it looked as black as tar and as polished as onyx.

"I'm going to murder you slowly," he promised.

"Now, that's just lazy."

Rage mangled his face as he charged toward her. Buck lunged at the same moment, landing on the man's back and latching onto his muscle-swelled shoulder. Basheba backed up a step. Everything within her skin went cold when the man lurched back. There was a heavy thud, a pained yelp, and Buck was tossed away. He slid across the dining table and off the other side, knocking over and breaking the chairs when he landed on them.

"Buck!"

She was so focused on her dog she almost missed the man's approach. Far smaller than him, she was able to dive under the table and roll out the other side. Buck was slumped amongst the wreckage of the chairs.

"Buck," she whispered.

With a savage grunt, the bull-man latched onto the end of the long table and hurled it to the side. The show of strength affected her more than she cared to admit. She longed to run. But the sight of Buck sprawled out made her turn on her heels and face her attacker.

"You hurt my dog!"

"I'm going to kill it right after I kill you." The bull-man grinned, brandishing the knife for her to see.

Rage ignited within her like a flashfire, scorching her fear and turning it to ash. She moved first, keeping low to force the man to bend is injured torso if he was to attempt another attack. He turned, trying to position himself, and swung the blade down. It sliced into her backpack, forcing her lower, knocking her off balance but giving her the opening she needed to rake her deadly wristband across the back of his ankle. The sharp spikes cut through his pant legs and into his flesh.

A pained cry left him and he buckled a bit, but the wound wasn't as deep as she had wanted. *Cut the Achille's heel. Bring them down.* The instructions she had been given so long ago had always served her well. She knew her size, her weakness, and how helpless she would be if she didn't get the upper hand somehow.

In a burst of motion, she gripped the side of the toppled table and leaped over it. The bull-man came for her swiftly. He slashed, bringing the blade a hair's breadth away from her face. Basheba struck out at his retreating hand, slicing his wrist open. He bellowed and hunched over the table, trying to reach her, spraying blood from his wound in his fury. A pained gasp for air left the man's lungs as Buck bounded onto his back. The dog latched his jaws around the back of the bull-man's neck.

Basheba burst forward. With the weight on his back, the wound in his gut, and the jaws locked onto his neck, there was no way for him to escape the coming blow. Basheba swung with all the strength her small body was capable of, driving her arm up and embedding the spikes of her wristband into the man's eye.

A wave of hot blood washed out over her skin as the man trembled and screamed, then dropped her knife. It came and went in a moment. The growing puddle of blood caught her feet and she slipped and tumbled to the ground. Buck was beside her in an instant, nuzzling her with concern and licking the sweat from her brow.

"Are you okay?" she asked, patting whatever patches of fur she could reach under his armor, offering reassurance while looking for any injuries.

He was just stunned. She almost wept with relief.

"You had me worried, you drama queen," she whispered into his fur as she hugged his neck.

A raspy, gargled sound pierced the stillness. She lurched back from Buck, grabbing the discarded knife and ready to strike. The bull-man remained slumped in the crumpled heap Buck had left him in. The stark white of his bone jutted through the tendons and flesh of his neck as blood pooled beneath him. He dragged in another breath, releasing the ghastly sound once more. Muscles twitched and strained in his jaw, but he couldn't work his head off the ground.

"I can't move," he rasped.

Basheba slowly got to her feet, eyeing the spinal cord that glistened with ebony blood in the hazy glow. Fire crackled outside and the cult restlessly stirred, but no one came to help. *They assume these guys can kill a little girl on their own.*

Basheba sucked in a breath through her teeth and winced. "Yeah, your neck is broken. I don't think you're getting back up." She scanned the room to reassure herself that no one else was lurking about. The corpse of his companion and the liquor cabinet helping to forge a plan in the back of her head.

"This is awkward," she cut in over the man's snarled threats and curses. "But I kind of need you dead. You only have yourself to blame, so I don't want you getting bitter about the whole situation."

His remaining eye rolled up to glare at her as she approached.

"You don't have it in you."

"Oh," she hissed. "Now it's more awkward. You're not my first. Sorry."

The knowledge settled on the man and he began to thrash as best his broken body could. It was little more than a shark toss of his head.

"You'll die for this!"

"Don't be bitter," she dismissed, crouching down next to him.

"They'll come for you."

"They're not even coming for you," she countered. "I think I have pretty good odds against a bunch of cowards. They'll probably take care of themselves once they see you're dead."

The man's blood-stained teeth flashed as he chuckled, deep and cold. "You little idiot. There are others to take my place."

"I did view you as expendable."

"You best hope she doesn't take control," he said, grinning to himself. "You think I'm bad?"

"Not particularly," Basheba said, only to be ignored.

The man was determined that his last words would carry the threat.

"The one who takes my place is so much worse than me. Blood-thirsty and savage. She'll destroy you all. She'll rip your soul to shreds."

His laughter grew, echoing off the walls even as his lungs began to fill with blood. Basheba patted the back of his head gently with one hand before driving the hunting knife deep into his remaining eye. His laughter cut off into a violent trembling, his nervous system spasming with the last throes of his dying brain. It only lasted a moment and then they were left in silence. Jerking her blade free, she rocked back on her heels and glanced at Buck. His nails scraped over the floorboard as he squirmed with barely contained energy.

"We're going to need rope and that broken chair." A new thought struck her and she bit back a smile. It was long past time for Uncle Isaac to learn just what he was messing with. "It's a special occasion, Buck. Let's go for some shock and awe. Go fetch the whiskey."

CHAPTER 13

Cadwyn lingered by the window, watching the cult members squirm restlessly. Their anxious energy bled into the room, making Mina pace back and forth while Ozzie sat on the bed, completely at a loss for what to do with his hands.

"It's taking too long," Mina said, twisting around on her toes to retrace her path. "Everything went silent fifteen minutes ago. Something has obviously happened to her."

"Just breathe," Cadwyn said absently. He was too busy trying to keep Isaac in sight, to pay much attention to her anxieties.

Every so often, the older man would feel the weight of Cadwyn's attention and tip his face up to glare at him.

If the situation were different, Cadwyn would have laughed. Compared to the sheer murderous fury Basheba effortlessly wielded in her eyes, the man's scowl had the air of a toddler's temper tantrum.

"Do you think she's okay?" Ozzie asked.

"I have every faith that she is," Cadwyn reassured.

In the corner of his eyes, he watched Ozzie look up at him, his fingers wringing in the comforter.

"How can you be so sure?"

"Because it's Basheba," Cadwyn said with a wry smile. "You only ever have to worry about the people in her way."

"What did she mean?" Mina mumbled.

"Are you talking to us or yourself?" Ozzie asked.

The question startled Mina. She paused, looking at them both in turn before elaborating on the thought that had slipped from her mouth.

"I was just thinking about the message Basheba passed on to Isaac. 'Come near me again, and I'll show you exactly what I did to the others,'" she quoted. "What did she mean by that? What did she do?"

Cadwyn frowned, rapidly reaching the limits of his tolerance for the girls' feud. "Are you sure that's what you should be focusing on at the moment?"

Mina shrugged as she wrapped her arms protectively around her torso. "We've been here for fifteen minutes. I've already obsessed over my father, my ignorance of my family dynamics, the demon, the flaws of my plan, and the cult outside. This was just the next thing on the list."

Ozzie's heavy brow inched up his forehead. "You've already worried about all that?"

"Of course. Haven't you?"

"I'm still stuck on the cult," he said, awkwardly gesturing to the window.

She turned to Cadwyn for backup.

"I've been rather busy keeping watch," he said.

Mina deflated somewhat and returned to her self-soothing habit of pacing. "Jeremiah always tells me I worry too much."

"That's your brother, right?" Ozzie asked.

Mina nodded rapidly, her gaze already clouding over with unspoken thoughts.

When the room fell once more into unbearable silence, Ozzie tried again to break the tension.

"How's he doing?"

"Good," she mumbled absently. "He's dating someone, but hasn't mentioned it to the family, yet." Pausing again, her head perked up. "Why are they hesitating? They could just storm the place."

Cadwyn looked out the window again, once more making eye contact with the incensed Isaac.

"Because they know there's a demon in here."

"Well, that's a good sign, right?" Ozzie said, hands fluttering as if he could somehow grasp a silver lining. "I mean, it backs up Basheba's theory that they won't follow us into the woods."

"Great," Mina mumbled, pacing again. "The wolves won't follow us into shark-infested waters."

"You sound like your dad," Cadwyn mentioned absently.

He could feel Mina staring a hole in his back.

"How much do you know about my father?"

"Enough to lean more toward Percival's perspective of him than yours."

Ozzie's fingers drummed against his knees, latching onto the passing hope for a change in conversation. "You're friends with my godfather? Um, father. Wow, that's still really weird to say."

"I wouldn't say we're friends," Cadwyn said. When Ozzie's shoulders slumped, he quickly added, "He's a man I greatly respect, we just don't run in the same circles."

For the briefest moment, Ozzie seemed content, proud to know that his lifelong friend was held in high regard. It struck Cadwyn anew just how much had been thrust upon the boy. Cadwyn didn't have any first-hand knowledge about Percival Sewall's relationship with the Davis couple. Rumor had it, he had dated Ha-Yun before they all came to the mutual conclusion that she was better suited for Percival's best friend, Ethan.

The whirlwind romance that followed had seen the new couple married, with Percival as their best man, before they even knew Ha-Yun was pregnant. Somehow, they had all stayed good friends despite what had to be an awkward situation. Seemingly the only sticking point of the dynamic was that the Davis family refused to tell Ozzie who his father was, and all the connotations of having the blood of a Sewall. But the Bell Witch had known. She had given him her music box and selected him for her Harvest the previous autumn. In the space of three days, Ozzie's entire world had crumbled down around him, burying him in the smoldering wreckage. Cadwyn still found himself in awe that the teenager had managed to crawl his way out.

"What did she do?" Mina mumbled to herself, breaking Cadwyn free of his thoughts.

"I don't think it matters right now," Ozzie said as tactfully as he could.

Mina continued her pacing, one arm still wrapped around her torso while her other hand tapped the ends of her hair against her bottom lip. Cadwyn had never known that such a move could look thoughtful.

"It is, so long as Isaac's leading the charge," Mina said. "Did you notice how they only said they wanted Basheba?"

"They were obviously lying," Cadwyn said.

"Perhaps they were, but I don't think Isaac was," Mina said.

Ozzie's hands rubbed his legs again, a helpless search for reassurance.

"What do you mean?" he asked.

"I don't know what the message was about, but it was clearly a threat. And suddenly, here he is with a mob for backup. I think, for him at least, this whole thing isn't about appeasing the Witch. I think he's trying to eliminate Basheba before she can follow through on her promise."

Cadwyn was the first to dismiss it, saying, "None of that matters."

"I don't want to get drawn into a family feud unaware."

"Why not? We've all been into your family business," Cadwyn said.

She bristled. "What do you mean by that?"

Sucking in a deep breath, he closed his eyes, kicking himself for opening that particular Pandora's box. A series of shouts caught them all off guard. Ozzie and Mina rushed to the window, crowding in front of him to press against the glass. He was easily able to look over their heads but wasn't all that excited with them being in clear view of the people below.

Cadwyn's muscles tensed when the first person pointed toward them. In the space of a heartbeat, he realized they weren't looking at them, but at the rooftop. Like a rising tide, more in the mob lifted their heads to focus above them. It churned his stomach to wonder what they were looking at. Cautiously, Mina pushed the window open a crack. The scent of smoke and apple blossoms flooded the room. Murmured voices became sharp and clear. The combination left Cadwyn inescapably aware that there was no real separation between them. No safe place to hide.

As the first spike of fear subsided, his brow furrowed. "Where's their leader?"

Mina and Ozzie both threw him a questioning look before reexamining the crowd. Frustrated murmurs rippled through the group, growing in fever as the people twisted and turned, searching the crowd just as much as their three prisoners did. The bull-man didn't return. Cadwyn's mouth quirked into a smirk.

"She got him," he whispered.

A sharp bar of tension loosened, allowing him to take a deep breath.

"You seem proud of her," Mina said.

"Aren't you?" Cadwyn asked. "The woman has talents."

She tipped her head, trying for a shrug, but too tense to pull it off.

"I guess my perspective is off," Mina said, "having been on the receiving end of her talents."

"You didn't die. Don't exaggerate," Cadwyn said with a growing smile.

The lift of Mina's chin resembled the princess she was at heart. "You sound like Basheba."

His grin was lost when the girl didn't turn to see it. What little amount of levity he had managed to cultivate was shattered when Isaac stormed to the front.

"Basheba!" Isaac snarled. "Why must you make everything difficult?"

"Boredom, mostly."

Cadwyn released a long breath to hear his friend's voice. He had never considered that she wouldn't be able to handle herself, but it felt good to know she was unscathed enough to maintain her sass.

Isaac stewed in his inept rage before Whitney made her way from the crowd. Basheba's past observation lingered in Cadwyn's mind. It startled him slightly to know he wasn't the only one contemplating the theory.

"If she's right," Mina mumbled to herself, "and an excess of fat or muscle is proof of the Witch's favor, then Whitney's one of her favorites."

"She's not that heavy," Ozzie defended.

Cadwyn and Mina both looked at him with raised eyebrows.

"She's 300 pounds, minimum," Cadwyn said. "That's morbidly obese."

Ozzie cringed. "Yeah, maybe, but you're not supposed to talk about stuff like that."

"I'm a nurse," Cadwyn reminded. "Noticing and remarking on possible health problems is literally part of my job."

"Yeah, okay, but…" Ozzie lowered his voice to a strained whisper, as if the woman below might overhear them. "It still feels mean to say it, though."

"She's actively trying to murder us," Mina noted. "I don't give a damn about her feelings."

Once the mob noticed Whitney's movements, they parted for her, allowing her to strut to Isaac's side. The firelight from the nearest torch cast her face in dancing shadows but couldn't diminish the vibrancy of her lipstick. Her mouth was pulled as taut as the skin around her eyes as she glared up at the rooftop.

"Where is Timothy?" Whitney demanded.

"Who the hell is Timmy?" Basheba shot back. "Nah, I'm just

kidding. I don't care."

"Everything is a joke to you, isn't it?" Whitney snarled.

"You most certainly are," Basheba said.

Cadwyn chuckled, the sound bristling over his nerves, and whispered, "She walked into that one."

Isaac didn't share Cadwyn's amusement. Growling out a sigh, the older man shoved his wire-rimmed glasses higher up on his nose.

"I suppose it was too much to expect you to face the consequences of your actions with any amount of dignity."

"Have I disappointed you, Uncle? Oh, please, come in so we can discuss this face to face."

Cadwyn didn't need to see her to know the feral smile that accompanied her words. Still, he leaned forward slightly, cautiously, trying to catch a glimpse of her. Isaac bristled, squaring his shoulders and clenching his jaw. All his posturing to look strong only highlighted his desperation.

"He's always seemed like a jumpy guy to me," Ozzie whispered.

"This is different somehow," Cadwyn said, eyeing the man carefully.

Mina made a sound similar to a bitter snort. "His crown's slipping. Father said he made 'arrangements.' I'm guessing he asked for quite a lot in exchange for handing over Basheba."

"It's remarkable how little that man learns from his mistakes," Cadwyn said.

"But, what did he ask for in return?" Ozzie squeaked.

A flood of horrible options flooded Cadwyn's mind but there wasn't time to contemplate any of it.

Isaac collected himself and stormed a few feet closer to the house, still cautious to keep out of striking range. *At least he's smart enough to know she won't be unarmed,* Cadwyn thought.

"I think it's clear we don't see eye to eye!"

"I despise you with every fiber of my being," Basheba cut in casually. "But go on."

"But you are family! The Bell blood flows through your veins as much as mine! For the love of your father, of all those we have lost, I beseech you to listen to reason!"

"Let them kill me?"

"It has to come to an end," Isaac bellowed. "You have to have known this day would come! You can't deny your nature forever! You're a Bell woman, Basheba! If you had merely acted in accordance with the demands of your ancestors, all of this could have been avoided! Don't make it worse. For the memory of your father, my beloved brother, do what you were born to do!"

Heavy silence followed, broken only by the crackle of the open flames.

"That's some blatant emotional manipulation," Mina muttered.

Ozzie's mouth scrunched up in disgust. "What a scumbag."

"Go get your things," Cadwyn said with as much calm as he could muster. They hesitated, and he nudged their shoulders. "Now."

Too late. Basheba's voice, cold as an arctic breeze while still sweetly pleasant, drew everyone's attention.

"You're right, Uncle."

A smirk pulled at Isaac's lips.

"I should follow the example of my ancestors. But I'm not just a Bell."

Cadwyn jerked at the first high-pitched scream. An instant later, a colossal shadow streaked across the window. The noose wrapped around the man's neck brought the body to a sudden jolt. He only realized Basheba had split open the man's stomach when the jolt spilled the man's innards. The screams grew louder as the body swung back. Cadwyn barely had time to twist around and shelter the smaller two before the body crashed through the window. Shards of glass pattered against Cadwyn's biker jacket.

Shock rattled them all when they turned back to see the leader of the cult twisting on a noose, his intestines dropping from the wide hole in his stomach, a severed hunk of kidney slowly trickling down his legs. The next round of screams came a split second before the next body crashed through the other window, disemboweled and limp. The mob below worked into a fevered panic. Horrified and rattled to see the brutality they had wanted to inflict instead turned onto two of their own.

"I will eat your heart!" Basheba bellowed, her voice distorted with feral delights and bloodlust.

The wind changed, bringing with it the stench of whiskey. Cadwyn shoved the others away from the window just as fire sizzled down the length of the rope and reached the man's liquor drenched clothes. The fire wouldn't last long, he knew. But the initial flash was scorching and the first lapping flames impressive. The panicked screams turned to sorrowful wails, blood-chilling and shrill. Golden light filled the room, bringing with it the overpowering stench of burning flesh. Cadwyn answered the phone vibrating in his pocket without ever taking his wide eyes off the ghastly sight.

"That was the distraction, idiots," Basheba's voice was as calm and pleasant as it could ever be. "Do me a favor? I'm going to lure them around back. Can you get my hunting bow out of my car? It's in a compartment under the mattress."

"Hunting bow?" he asked numbly.

Shaking himself out of his shock, he turned and began manhandling the others, forcing them to get their stuff and head to the door.

"Yeah, I prefer my knife, but I think we're going to need it."

"I'll get it," he mumbled, barely aware that his mouth was moving.

"This is why I'm willing to marry you," she teased.

"Well, this and my great health care plan."

"Obviously," she laughed. "See you in the Witch Woods."

And with that, she hung up.

CHAPTER 14

Mina choked on her scream as the flaming bodies consumed her vision. Already, the flames were starting to dwindle as the alcohol burned up, but they still lashed violently, hot enough that it burned her eyes to see it. Ozzie grabbed her shoulder, yanking her out of her horrified stupor. She staggered along with his persistent pulling, only turning after she had been shoved out into the hall.

"Bathroom," Cadwyn commanded, closing the door behind them and locking it in place before sliding the key under the door.

Ozzie twisted his hand in the collar of her shirt, refusing to let go even as they ran together. Solid thuds echoed from the darkness downstairs. The house shook as the cult threw themselves against the front door, trying and failing to break it down. Cadwyn appeared at their backs, shoving them into the bathroom, barely able to close the door before the sound of shattering glass allowed the enraged voices inside.

Cadwyn swiftly locked the bathroom door and tied the shower curtain around the handle. Watching him, her thoughts began to emerge from the panicked haze of her mind.

"My bag," Mina mumbled.

"I've got it," Ozzie said in a whisper.

With numb fingers, she took her backpack from him, feeling the depth of her ineptitude like bitter bile on her tongue. Moonlight spilled through the high set window, turning Cadwyn into a looming shadow. He straightened from his task, his long arms stretching out to herd them like lost ducklings.

"Window," he whispered, his voice almost lost under the

rampage below.

He was the only one tall enough to reach it. After pushing it open, Cadwyn braced his back against the wall and cupped his hands, giving Ozzie the boost he needed to squeeze through the gap. He awkwardly fumbled before dropping out of sight. Mina's breath caught. It was a physical effort to keep her panicked cry silent, not wanting to draw the attention of the mob that was storming toward them.

"There's a landing," Cadwyn said, his hand roughly cupping the back of her head and yanking her closer.

They scrambled against each other, her awkward movements accidentally striking the wound on his thigh before she managed to find the cup of his hands. He jerked her up. She swung her bag out first and braced herself against the windowsill. Despite her best efforts, she still had to step on Cadwyn's shoulder to get the last of the way out.

The short drop onto the roof tiles didn't give her enough time to brace herself. Pain sliced through her bones as she smacked against the unrelenting surface. She slid a few inches down the slight slope before she managed to find purchase.

"Are you okay?" Ozzie asked.

She nodded once, clenching her teeth against the lingering pain. He skittered into the shadows. It took her half a second to realize that Cadwyn didn't have any helping hand. Pushing herself up, she twisted around only to find Ozzie retreating from the window. The sounds of the bathroom door being ripped apart followed Cadwyn out as he slipped from the gap with more grace than either of them had managed to summon. In a nearly impossible maneuver, he rolled across his shoulders, bringing the long expanse of his body to a stop by planting one foot against the roof tiles.

"How?" Ozzie whispered.

Cadwyn's bangs dropped into his eyes in a sweaty tangle. The moonlight made the fresh blood seeping through his pants look like oil.

"I've added parkour into my workout routine," Cadwyn spoke in a whisper as he ushered them up to the side of the building, forcing them into the shadows and out of the sight of the people still breaking down the bathroom door. "After our experience in the woods, I figured it would be a useful skill."

Mina knew he was only speaking in an attempt to keep them calm. A part of her resented being handled with kid gloves. A small, bitter part that detested her own weakness. Still, she couldn't help but cling to the small offer of normalcy.

Cadwyn kept them wedged between the wall and his own body, his black biker jacket allowing him to shield them like a shadow as they moved to the corner. Firelight from the burning men danced before her, far dimmer now than it had been before. The smell remained, though. Thick and heavy and nauseating. She tried not to think about what they were moving toward. Or the fact that they were effectively heading right back to the room they had fled. With terror twisting her gut and clouding her thoughts, she knew she wasn't in any condition to suggest an alternative plan. Instead, she focused on mimicking Cadwyn's light tread. It startled her to realize just how graceless she was.

When they reached the front corner of the building, Cadwyn pressed a hand against Mina's stomach to bring her to a stop. Straining his towering form in a way that must have been agony for his legs, he glanced around the corner.

"Go," he whispered. "Don't look."

The rhythmic thud against the door suddenly changed, signaling the cult had finally broken through. Cadwyn grabbed Ozzie by the back of his neck and hurled him around the corner first, following a step behind. All three of them pressed their spines against the wood, freezing in place and fighting their panting breaths to keep silent. Mina's full focus locked on the noises echoing from the bathroom. *They have to know we're out here,* she thought. Images filled her mind. Images of the cult dividing and spilling out onto the ledge to follow them. Half coming from the bathroom while the others clawed free of the shattered bedroom windows. *We're trapped.*

The rope released a low creak before it snapped. The smoldering corpse dropped like a stone, landing on the porch steps with a nauseating squelch. Mina squeezed her eyes closed and tried not to look, but her mind supplied a vivid image anyway. Every second pressed down upon her like heavy stones, crushing her lungs and thickening the air until she choked on each breath. The touch of the evening breeze reminded her just how exposed she was. Flickering firelight played across her eyelids like a spotlight. She flinched when she heard what she had dreaded. Harsh voices and heavy footsteps coming from both sides. Mina clenched her jaw and lifted her chin, trying to prepare herself for what was coming.

A bloodcurdling scream sliced through the night, making her jump so hard she almost lost her footing. As the sound ebbed away, Mina held her breath again, sure that even her heartbeat would reveal their position in the resulting silence. All at once, footsteps stampeded away, flowing back into the depths of the house and out of earshot. She slumped as she released her breath.

"Why didn't they come out?" Ozzie asked.

Cadwyn grinned, a brilliant flash of straight white teeth. "They're too big."

The relief in his voice was proof that all of it had been a gamble. Cadwyn refused to let them move until the night stilled, leaving only the crackling, sputtering fire to disturb the silence. Carefully, he skidded to the edge of the roof ledge. He crouched low to check that the coast was clear. While the drugs in his system took the edge off the pain, a fresh wave of blood seeped out. Enough that Mina worried he had pulled a stitch. He waved them over.

"When I lower you down, I want you to hide in the crawlspace," he whispered. "Wait there until I come for you. I have to do something for Basheba."

"Crawlspace?" Ozzie asked, clearly baffled.

Mina squeezed his hand, reassuring him that he just had to follow her. *I can lead the way. I can do this. Don't freeze.* Cadwyn sat down and dug his heels into the groove of the drainage pipe. Mina went first. They linked arms and, with his elbows locked against his sides, he slowly lowered her down. It was an impressive amount of strength, and she only jolted slightly, her feet blindly groping for porch fencing. She found it and scrambled down to keep watch while Ozzie was lowered next. His foot slipped on the railing and he fell backward into the flower bushes that lined the building. Mina had to crawl over the porch railing since the burning corpse was still on the stairs. She found him writhing in the foliage. Approaching sounds of footsteps made her heart jerk and she released the railing, dropping down out of sight.

Mina and Ozzie shared a wide-eyed stare as they waited. A heavy click and the door slowly opened. She shoved Ozzie's shoulder, using her other hand to point out the small gap under the stairs, the passage illuminated by the smoldering remains. The gap was just big enough for them to slither through.

Rich-smelling earth shifted under them as they clawed their way into the minimal hiding space. She hoped the relative darkness would be enough to keep the signs of disturbance from being too obvious. They were still situating themselves when the floorboards creaked. A shadow draped over them, cold and deep, while the fire's warmth pressed against her face. Ozzie's fingers found hers. Without a word, they clutched at each other, each tightening their grip until it hurt. The footsteps paused just above their heads.

Mina could feel her heartbeat in her throat. It was impossible to tell which one of them was trembling, but her arm shook with it all the same. Unable to take the tension squirming in her gut like live snakes, Mina glanced up, peeking between the floorboards. A scream ripped from her throat as the head of an ax drove down. Wood splintered in the wake of the deadly blade. Mina flattened herself against the earth, staring in horror at the deadly tip that would have cleaved her head in two if the thicker butt of the ax head hadn't become wedged in place.

With a sharp jerk, the ax was wrenched free, raining splinters down upon her face. Mina couldn't help but stare up at the man through the gap. Long, matted tendrils of hair framed his face, taking on the same hue of the firelight. The shadows did nothing to diminish the pure disgust that radiated from his pale eyes. She hadn't thought it would be possible for a complete stranger to hate her that much. It took her breath away like a vice squeezing her lungs. It was only when he reared the ax back for another blow that she was broken out of her shock. She slid over the loose earth and twisted around, scrambling on hands and knees to go deeper into the shadows.

The man's beefy hand slipped through the gap with the speed of a snake strike. Pain sizzled up the length of her leg as the man's tightening grip crushed her ankle. She kicked back with her free foot, blindly crunching her heel against the man's fingers. His hand retreated to be replaced with another strike of the ax, the blade narrowly missing her foot as she burst forward. Ozzie waited for her a few feet ahead, barely visible in the lingering shadows.

"Are you all right?" he asked, voice higher than normal and eyes wide.

"Yeah. Go. Just go."

The wood continued to crack apart behind them, but it didn't take too long for their attacker to realize he wouldn't be able to follow. Footsteps thundered above them, closing in, pausing above them once more. Ozzie and Mina rolled to different sides as the ax blade broke through the floorboard. This time gouging deeper, almost hitting the earth. Coming to a stop, Mina looked to Ozzie. A desperate attempt to form some kind of plan with him to keep them from being separated. Somehow, Ozzie interpreted the glance to be some kind of direction. He nodded and skittered forward. Mina burst into motion to follow. The ax blows continued to chop through the floorboards.

Sometimes, it was close enough to nip at their flesh, while, at other times, the blows landed far from them, offering them slithers of hope that the man had lost track of them.

"What are you doing!"

The sudden outburst made Mina flatten herself against the soil. A few feet away, Ozzie did the same. Panting hard, they shared a panicked glance before both tried to see through the flooring. It took her a moment to realize she recognized the voice.

'Whitney,' she mouthed to Ozzie.

His heavy brow furrowed before he returned his attention to the conversation happening above.

"They're in the crawlspace," the muscled mand huffed.

"So you destroy my place? Get out of the way!"

In a burst of movement, Ozzie scurried across the area of damage and rejoined Mina's side. Firelight washed through the ax holes. Together, Mina and Ozzie cringed away from the largest gap, trying to keep the growing light from touching them. A hard thud resounded just before Whitney's face filled the gap. A sweet smile stretched her face as she purred down to them.

"Hello, little darlings. Did Eddy scare you? He can be such a brute. Come on, now. Come out."

Ozzie leaned heavily against Mina's side, trying to get further away from the woman.

"Is she serious?" he whispered.

"We won't hurt you," Whitney continued in her sickly-sweet tone.

Her face shifted across the gap, trying to get a decent look at them.

"We only want Basheba," she continued. "Leave her behind and you're free to go."

"Why her?" Mina asked, half regretting making any conversation at all. But she had to know; needed to peel back the layers of lies and deceit that shrouded her life, and find the truth in something.

"You needn't concern yourself with that. Come on, now. I'll get you both some tea. I made a Bee Sting cake today. It's delicious."

Mina and Ozzie shared a bewildered look.

"Why do I feel like she's trying to plump us up to eat us?" he whispered.

Clearing her throat, Mina spoke with all the confidence she didn't feel. "I'm not going anywhere until you answer my question."

"You're in no position to make demands, little princess," Whitney said.

"Is it because of Isaac?" Mina pushed. "What did he promise you? The man's a notorious liar."

"You'll never understand, little princess. Let's get you back to your daddy. The Witch will take you when she wishes it."

"Whitney!" It was a voice that Mina didn't recognize, but the panic within it alarmed her.

She flinched again when something struck her on the back. Turning around, she hurriedly scanned the darkness, finding Cadwyn crouched by a small gap. He waved them over. Tapping Ozzie's shoulder, she sent him first, still straining to hear the conversation happening above.

"She's making her way to the bullpen," the stranger said.

"Good," Whitney said. "He'll take care of her."

"But," the man stammered.

"But what?" Whitney snapped. "She's one scared little girl. Kill the dog and she'll be nothing."

"She's already killed three of us," the stranger protested.

"The dog did."

"The dog didn't gut them."

Whitney's voice took on an icy edge. "Watch your tone."

"Of course," the stranger whispered. "I'm just saying, I don't think Isaac told us the truth about her. It makes me nervous as to why he's so insistent."

"The Witch wants her."

"So he says," the stranger added nervously.

Whitney was silent for a moment before she hissed out. "Kill her. And someone bring Isaac to me!"

Another clump of earth hit her. An impatient reminder that she had to move. She continued to strain for every word as she retreated to the opening. Cadwyn dragged her out the rest of the way the second she came into reach. Even the shadows couldn't hide his anger.

"The cult didn't pick Basheba as their sacrifice. Isaac did," she said in a rushed whisper.

Cadwyn's brow furrowed, the implication striking him like a physical blow. *Dad was wrong,* Mina thought. *Isaac isn't just following the cult in a desperate bid to survive. He has sway over them.* Shaking off the shock, Cadwyn lifted his head and jerked to the shadows of the driveway.

"I thought we were meeting Basheba in the woods," Ozzie said.

"We are," Cadwyn assured in a whisper. "But she's lured them that way. I can't get you both past them unseen. There're fewer people minding the road."

Once more, the older man positioned himself to be their shield. Mina absently noted the contraption in his hand. It looked too small for him. A mangled archery bow, the tips bending in at an odd angle and tipped with wheels. A cylinder was strapped across his back. It too looked like a child's toy as it rested against his broad shoulders.

The crunch of the gravel under their feet sounded like screams in the darkness. Voices murmured from the distance. Shouts and demands met with the low bellow of a bull. Adrenaline made her stomach roll and her hands shake. Her shoulder brushed Ozzie's as they clustered close to each other, both finely tuned to any change in Cadwyn's posture. More than once, he ushered them into the darkness under the tree limbs. The scent of apple blossoms hit her nose. A pleasant sweetness that engulfed them as they huddled in the shadows, waiting for the people to pass.

After the third time, Cadwyn kept them just behind the tree line, regardless of how it clearly agitated him. Despite the distance they put between them, the screams only grew louder. One shriek broke above it all. Agonized and feral and unmistakably female. Cadwyn whipped around at the noise, his jaw hanging low and his eyes wide. He forced them all to break into a run.

CHAPTER 15

Ozzie had thought it would be easier to keep up with Cadwyn in the woods, where the tangled mass of branches would work against the man's height. But Cadwyn's sure stride never faltered. His movements were clear and precise as he threaded his towering form through gaps in the foliage that Ozzie didn't even know were there. Every few yards, Cadwyn had to slow down and wait for them to catch up. Guilt trickled through his fear to pool in the pit of his gut.

I'm going to get better, Ozzie resolved. He clung to that determination to silence the little voice that questioned if he'd ever have the chance.

At last, they approached a clearing, noticeable only by the way it glowed. Leaves and flowers diffused the moonlight, painting the air with a silver haze. Cadwyn slowed at last, chest heaving and eyes darting. Ozzie found a moss-covered log and crouched low behind it with Mina. Both of them waited anxiously to catch Cadwyn's eyes and waved him over.

"How's your leg?" Mina asked when the older man crouched down beside her.

"I'll fix it up after this," he whispered absently. "Can you see her?"

Ozzie poked his head up just enough to see over the log. The brilliance of the meadow all but killed his night vision. "Where's the paddock?"

Before Cadwyn could point it out, the stillness around them was broken by the sharp rustle of snapping branches. Torchlight flickered through the clustered leaves. All at once, Basheba burst into the meadow, announced by an explosion of petals. A hulking woman stormed after her. Her outstretched hand clawed at Basheba's spine, unable to get a grip as the smaller girl suddenly leaped like a startled fawn and dropped to the ground. Ozzie lurched up to help but Cadwyn was quicker, grabbing his wrist and dragging him back down into the hiding place. Pain sparked through his knees as they collided with the earth again. The pain was forgotten when he heard a strange 'twang.'

A branch snapped around, swinging over Basheba's body to smack hard against the woman's chest. She took the impact and just stood there, branch flush against her breasts, her mouth gaping like a fish.

"Ozzie, look away," Cadwyn whispered.

He didn't understand why until he noticed the black stain working its way across the front of the stranger's shirt. *Blood.* Even the thought made his stomach roil. His heartbeat picked up, leaving his head spinning and his skin damp with cold sweat. Basheba jumped to her feet and started struggling with the branch. In the end, she had to wedge her foot against the woman's stomach and throw her weight into it. Basheba's hunting knife slipped from the stranger's flesh, dark and dripping with blood. That done, Basheba left the woman to slump lifelessly to the earth, more occupied with fussing in the shadows.

"She knows how to set up booby traps?" Mina muttered.

Cadwyn swallowed thickly but tried not to look disturbed. "Aren't you glad you're on her good side?"

Basheba whistled and Buck lunged from the darkness. After receiving a few pats, the ever-obedient dog took the order to drag the body back to his hiding place. Ozzie scrambled up again when he noticed Basheba turn away.

"Hey," he whispered harshly, not quite sure how many people he might attract.

It was still enough to make Basheba whip around. Ozzie's heart staggered, certain she was about to hit the tripwire. It didn't happen.

"Hey, you guys made it," she beamed, the mud streaking her face making her teeth seem all the brighter. Tipping her head to the side, she shook a few leaves loose from her hair. "I'm actually pretty happy you're all alive."

"Is that a booby trap?" Mina asked numbly.

Basheba looked behind her as if she had only just noticed it. "So it is. Huh. Strange." She shrugged. "Should we go? I'll get my knife."

"How did you learn to do that?" Ozzie asked.

"How many have you killed?" Mina said at the same time. She caught the strange looks and furrowed her brow. "That wasn't an escape tactic. She was *luring* people in."

"We can discuss this after we flee for our lives," Cadwyn said coldly.

Mina's shoulders hunched like a chastised child. Basheba bled into the darkness, returning an instant later with hurried backward steps. The trees rustled as a man emerged in hot pursuit. One thick hand grabbed her wrist while the other brought a handgun within an inch of her nose.

"Uh, uh, uh, little girl," he grumbled. "No more running. No more tricks."

Basheba quirked an eyebrow, seemingly completely unaware of the gun. "Don't suppose you feel like taking a step to your right?"

Cadwyn surged forward a step, hesitating when the gun was turned onto him, but only stopping completely when another man emerged from behind Mina, his rifle already high and at the ready. The men grinned wildly at each other, a few gleeful chuckles slipping their lips.

"You city folks should have known better than to take this fight into the woods," the man holding the rifle sneered. "You're not hunters."

"*They're* not," Basheba corrected, sounding as if she was discussing the weather.

The man squeezed Basheba's arm, jerking her close as if he wanted to rip her shoulder from its socket. The small blonde winced but refused to release any sound of pain. Cadwyn jerked, then kept still as the second man trained his rifle on him. Ozzie's hands started to shake uncontrollably.

"Oh, you're a big bad hunter, are you?" The man holding the tiny blonde grinned.

She tilted up her chin. "My whole family line was."

The man scoffed, moving the gun just far enough away that his face could take its place.

"Bells are nothing more than little rabbits running from the fox."

Basheba lowered her voice, drawing the man closer still.

"I'm not just a Bell. And ghosts aren't what I was trained to hunt."

The two men chuckled, sharing wide grins.

"And what do you hunt?" the man holding the rifle asked.

Basheba met their smile with one of her own. Gentle, shy, and every bit a Disney princess, she replied, "Long pig."

The movement was a blur. A dozen things happened at once, all overlapping and melding in Ozzie's head. Basheba lunged toward the man holding her. She stomped her right foot against his thigh to boost herself up while she drew her left knee to her chest, her shin pushing against the man's forearm. He fired blindly as his arm was forced wide. The single shot boomed like thunder.

Cadwyn spun around, ready to throw himself on the other attacker. A black mass bled from the abyss, silent and swift. *Buck.* The man fought against the enormous Rottweiler. But, with Buck's body keeping his rifle uselessly by his side, he didn't stand much of a chance. Ozzie turned, intent on helping Basheba, only to find she had locked her limbs around the man that had once held her.

The tiny woman dug her teeth deep into his throat. He bellowed. Another bite, along with a sharp shake of her head, and the sound was replaced by a gurgling rasp.

Blood gushed from his neck like a river of liquid onyx, frothing and spluttering from his mouth. It poured to the ground like grotesque rain. A spasm of shocked pain sent the gun toppling from the man's hand. He clawed and pounded at Basheba. With a wild growl, he wrenched her free and tossed her to the ground. Basheba bounced across the ground, kicking up the leaves and flower petals in her wake. Then she caught herself, arranging her limbs into a deep crouch, and time made sense again to Ozzie, ticking by at a normal pace.

Foliage swirled through the silver air, engulfing Basheba in a halo of shifting shadows. She drew herself up to her full height, the movement swift despite the blow she had taken. Blood poured from her lips, covered her jaw, and drenched her shirt. Steadily, she began to stalk, her steps silent but sure. The man grasped his neck but there was no stemming the flow of blood that spurted from between his fingers. It seemed that rage and fury were the only things keeping him upright. Ozzie was sure he would have charged at her, or leaped for the gun, if it wasn't for the throaty growl reverberating from behind him.

Basheba and Buck circled the man, calm and calculating, patiently waiting for the right moment to strike. There was no order given. The two simply moved as one. A single being of raw brutality. Buck latched onto his hip, clamping down until the bone shattered. Basheba went for his neck again, wrapping her limbs around the man's flailing body, sinking her teeth into the soft flesh of his jugular. The man thrashed and screamed as much as his broken body would allow, but all the effort was for nothing. Together, Buck and Basheba brought him down, unrelenting in their attack until the man lay motionless beneath them.

Basheba rocked back onto her heels. Panting so hard her shoulders rocked with the motion, she tipped her blood-soaked face to the sky. Absently, she wiped the back of her forearm over her mouth, only managing to smear more blood onto her pale skin.

"Cadwyn, Ozzie, you might want to look away for a bit," she panted, absently wiping some sweat from her forehead, leaving a smear of blood behind.

The words shook Ozzie from his shock. All at once, everything crashed down upon him. The sight, the chaos, the coppery stench that now hung thick in the air. Bile surged up Ozzie's throat with enough force to double him over. He braced against his knees as he wretched, spewing the limited contents of his stomach on the ground between his feet. Sucking in a breath made him throw up again.

Cadwyn was instantly by his side, one large hand rubbing his back in comforting circles. Ozzie barely straightened enough to catch a glimpse at the older man. It was enough to know he wasn't the only one sick to his stomach. Neither one of them were prepared for Basheba's sudden gasp of horror.

"What is it?" Cadwyn asked.

Looking out from under his eyelashes, Ozzie watched Basheba hurriedly patting her chest, each touch leaving a streak of blood on her flannel shirt.

"Basheba?" Mina asked.

"He broke the chain," Basheba gasped. She threw herself onto the ground, frantically clawing at the earth, blindly searching for something, her body violently trembling.

Mina took a step into the meadow. "Basheba?"

The blonde's trembling only grew worse as she began to pluck unseen items from the layer of matted leaves. Ozzie didn't get a chance to see what they were as the frantic girl cradled each one protectively to her stomach. Mina glanced at them, as if checking to see if either one of them was willing to take her place, but neither was in a condition to do so.

"Basheba, what's wrong? Maybe I can help."

"The rings," Basheba said, her voice cracking with tears, the words tumbling over each other. "There're twenty-six wedding rings. I need to find them. He broke the chain!"

The last words were spat out like a snarl, filled with enough rage that she paused her searching to kick wildly at the corpse beside her. They could hear her counting, over and over, the numbers increasing each time, but never reaching twenty-six.

"The Claddagh ring," Basheba muttered between heavy breaths.

By this point, she had gouged a deep groove into the soft earth, leaving clogs of dirt sticking to the layer of blood.

"The Irish Claddagh," she whispered. "I have to find it. Mom said I needed to take care of it. I can't lose it. She'd be so disappointed."

Mina crossed the last of the separating distance and knelt down before her. Concerned, Buck whimpered, nuzzling at his mistress's side in an attempt to get her attention. It was the first time Ozzie had ever seen Basheba ignore his attempts. All of her attention was fixed on the search for the missing ring. It was only disturbed by her compulsive need to recount the ones in her hand.

"It's okay," Mina whispered.

"It's not okay!" Basheba all but screamed. "That ring is all that's left. They took everything else!" Hyperventilating, she resumed her search, muttering over and over that she had promised her mother that she'd take care of it.

Moving carefully, as if worried any sudden movement would provoke Basheba's wrath, Mina reached into a clump of moss and plucked free a small loop that glistened in the light. Basheba froze. Suddenly, the blonde burst forward, wrapping a very startled Mina in a tight hug. Giggles broke the tension. At least enough that Ozzie was able to straighten somewhat, so long as he only breathed through his mouth.

"Thank you," Basheba grinned, the coating of blood making the sight grotesque.

She snatched up the ring and hurriedly counted her collection.

"Twenty-six," she breathed.

All tension instantly left her body as she slumped down against Buck, at last giving the dog the attention he craved. They cuddled together, a cozy image of gore, as Basheba's giggles became mixed with sobs.

"Twenty-six."

"Basheba," Mina said gently. She waited patiently for Basheba to quieten.

With a snort, the blonde tried to wipe the tears from her eyes, but only succeeded in covering the last patches of clear skin with gore.

"We need to go," Mina said. "Can you lead the way?"

Basheba sniffed, blinking her water-logged eyes. "Yeah," she breathed. Like a flash of lightning, the raw grief vanished, and she straightened. She eyed the corpse. "We'll have to wrap up the leftovers. I've got a thermal blanket in Buck's armor."

"What?" Mina asked, subtly checking with the boys.

Cadwyn looked as baffled as her.

"Well, we need to take at least one of them," Basheba said. Carefully, she stored all the rings in her pocket, shoving them down until there was no chance of them slipping out. Then she retrieved the folded thermal blanket from Buck and tossed it to Mina.

"What's this for?" Mina asked.

"Whichever body you pick, we're going to have to keep it warm," Basheba replied, hurrying to retrieve her knife while seemingly keeping the booby trap in place.

Mina glanced from the thermal blanket in her hands to the bodies scattered around the meadow. "Why do we need them warm?" Mina asked.

"Because it's past sundown and we have to go through its territory," Basheba replied. "We're not getting past it without a distraction and the only thing that distracts it is human flesh. So, pick a corpse, or offer up a limb."

Once more, Mina looked to the boys. Ozzie wished there was some measure of comfort he could offer. In the end, he couldn't even bring himself to help wrap up the man's body.

CHAPTER 16

A strange silence filled Mina's head, as if all of her competing thoughts had somehow combined to create an all-consuming white noise. She followed beside Basheba, her fingers aching from carrying the dead weight for so long. In the end, it had taken all four of them to carry the makeshift body bag over the uneven earth. There had been little discussion amongst the group once they had set out, as if everyone had assumed that Basheba would instinctually know the way. The silence of the mob faded away, replaced by their soft, shuffling footsteps and the distant bubbling of a stream. Basheba angled them toward it.

Mina bit her tongue as she trudged along. *Organize your thoughts*, she told herself. *Plan it out.* Even now, she clung to the scientific method like a talisman against evil. It was her only way to organize and understand the world around her. Experience had taught her well to be careful of how she approached Basheba. By now, she knew the smartest course of action was not to voice her questions at all. Unfortunately, she also knew it wasn't her nature. Especially not now that her entire world order was crumbling down upon her head.

Dad knew. The single whisper slashed to the forefront of her mind, bringing with it a wave of sickening vertigo. Her father and mother had been the very foundation of her life. Everything she was, everything she thought, was built upon the unshakable knowledge that they always had her best interests at heart. Anyone else could be wrong. Everything else could change. But their love and regard for her were set like stone. She saw herself through their eyes, and had structured her entire personality to match. *And it was all a lie. They never believed in me. Never thought me destined for great things.*

Mina eyed Basheba out of the corner of her eyes, sick with the growing suspicion that the blonde might have been right about her. That she was nothing more than a pampered little princess with no understanding of the world around her.

Whitney's voice taunted her from her memories. *You'll never understand, little princess. Let's get you back to your daddy.* The woods opened up, revealing a narrow stream that glistened in the moonlight. It filled the warm night air with the clean note of fresh water and musky moss.

"Okay," Basheba said, her voice soft enough to blend in with the silence rather than disturb it. "Five-minute break."

She dropped her corner of the body bag, the jerk forcing the material from Mina's grasp. The corpse hit the ground with a dull thud. Not much of a noise, all things considered, but it made Mina cringe all the same. Basheba was in good spirits and she spun around and threw a smile in Cadwyn's direction.

"Need help with your leg?"

Cadwyn swallowed thickly, his eyes a little too wide, and the tendons in his neck pressing against the skin.

"Did you have to use your teeth?" he asked, the question almost making him gag.

"It wasn't exactly a planned thing," Basheba protested. "If it helps, I didn't even chip a tooth."

Cadwyn drew in a deep breath through his nose. "Actually, that does help a little."

"But still incredibly gross?"

"If that's your nice way of saying utterly horrific."

"You handle blood on every other part of the human body," she pointed out.

"And you handle kids swarming around Disneyland. Wanna babysit?"

Basheba jerked a thumb over her shoulder, "I'll go wash my mouth out."

"I would appreciate it," Cadwyn said, still keeping his distance.

It looked as if every joint in his body was locked in place with tension.

Ozzie gagged and avoided all eye contact. "Thanks."

"I didn't lose any teeth, if that helps," Basheba said.

"It does," Cadwyn said softly.

Absently, he ran his tongue over his teeth. Mina had the sneaking suspicion he was counting them. *He was just a kid,* Mina thought. Images came unbidden to her mind's eye, of a lanky little pre-teen trapped under a demon, helpless as the monster pulled his teeth out one-by-one.

His brother was possessed. The thought sent a shiver down her spine. *Did the demon wear his brother's skin while he hurt him?* Squeezing her eyes shut, Mina forced the thought away in favor of focusing on the more pressing issue. Namely, she was now in a haunted wood with a woman who had quite literally ripped a man's throat out with her teeth. But first, she carefully watched Cadwyn for a moment.

He dropped the body with the bare minimum of care, just enough to be considered respectful, and shuffled to one of the larger boulders that speckled the riverbed. Ozzie trailed beside him, jittery with unspent adrenaline and his eyes constantly searching the tree line. Basheba picked a spot by a rocky outcrop rather than the stream itself. Even by the moonlight, Mina could see she was cleaning the blood off more with mud than with water. The sight brushed aside Mina's thoughts enough to recall, *she's terrified of water.*

Basheba's namesake had been one of the small children that had brought the Witch to the noose. One of the first to be tormented by the vengeful ghost. *And for all she survived, she drowned in a few inches of water.* During their last visit, the Witch had left no doubt that she was well aware of Basheba's fear. If it hadn't been for Buck and Ozzie, Basheba would have drowned in the very same river her ancestor had died in. *And I did nothing.* Mina curled her arms around herself, forcing herself to endure the wave of shame that crashed down upon her, and all the memories that still haunted her nightmares.

Icy water rolled against her skin. The buzz of the bee swarm covered every sound. She closed her eyes and could still see the hive that had hollowed out the hanging man. All of her life, she had heard of what it was like to be terrified. None of it had prepared her for the soul-shattering actuality of the emotion. Or how she would react to it. *I just froze.*

Mina snapped her eyes open and drew a deep breath into her lungs. *Crying about it isn't going to change anything.* The words were an echoing memory of her own, spoken gently by her parents, more as a comfort than a chastisement. Her gut hurt just to think about them. And how her relationship with them was never going to be the same. She hadn't realized she had once again fallen into self-pity until she heard her mother click her tongue. *Mina, whatever you're looking for isn't going to be on your shoes. Chin up.* Her spine straightened without her conscious decision and she strode over to Basheba.

"Can we talk?" she asked as she approached, not wanting to startle her. "I have a few questions."

The silence that followed the request highlighted how much chatter had been going on before. Basheba paused, a handful of mud cupped in her hand and a rattlesnake smile curling the corners of her mouth.

"I'm not trying to be provocative," Mina said in a rush.

Shadows robbed Basheba's eyes of their blue shine, but not their intensity. "What are you trying for, exactly?"

"An education."

Basheba's eyebrow jumped up her mud streaked forehead. Mina bit her bottom lip hard, forcing her eyes to remain on Basheba. *Chin up.*

"I know we don't get along."

"What?" Basheba drew the word out mockingly.

"But you've always been honest with me. Brutally so." Mina huffed a small laugh when the truth of her next words sunk in. "You're the only one I can trust to be unequivocally honest with me."

After a moment of contemplation, Basheba seemed pleased by the words.

"All right, little princess. We've got a few minutes to kill while Cadwyn patches himself up. What do you want to know?"

"Everything," Mina said. "But I think we should start with more pressing matters."

"Makes sense."

"Why is Isaac so afraid? What did you do?"

Basheba barked a laugh. "And here I thought you were going to ask about *it*."

"Yes, that's important," Mina admitted. "But I trust that you have that well in hand. I need to think about what comes after."

"And my uncle comes after?"

Mina's eyes lowered despite her best efforts. "My father hinted that he knew some things about Isaac's relationship with the cult. I don't know to what extent. But..."

"But he made it clear he was in Isaac's corner?" Basheba finished for her.

"Yes," Mina mumbled.

She wasn't sure how she expected Basheba to react. Laughter wasn't it.

"Yeah, that sounds about right. You know, my great aunt used to say that, when people are scared, they cling to their status quo. Unfortunately for us, Katrina came along in a pretty bad time for women. And our families haven't moved on from there. Not really. They put on airs, say the right things, and swear up and down that they consider women their equals. But apply a little pressure and, well, they run back to their status quo."

"My father's not like that," Mina said on reflex.

The moment the words left her mouth, she found herself questioning them. She flinched when Basheba's smile turned into sweet poison.

"Isn't he?"

"He's always taken care of me." Mina's voice softened with each word as her doubt grew.

"Wow, your education is seriously lacking. Let me impart some wisdom my momma taught me." Her smile fell, her face became relaxed, but her eyes retained their fire. "Only weak men seek to control strong women. And strong women will never bow to weak men."

Mina bristled at the not so subtle jab against her mother but held her tongue on that account.

"Did Isaac try to make you bow?" Mina shifted under Basheba's gaze. "I just want to know what war zone I walked into."

"Fair enough."

"Really?" Mina asked.

"You're right. This does concern you now, so you might as well be in on it," Basheba said. She took to playfully tussling Buck as she spoke. "The Allaway line has a lot of traditions. Some even regarding a girl's first period. I got a party. Complete with cake, a pearl necklace, and an octopus hairpin."

"An octopus hairpin?" Ozzie said, puzzled.

"A kraken. They're the unofficial family sigil. The pin was the kind that sits on the back of your head. And you thread a sharp little barb through its tangled tentacles to keep it in place." Her gaze grew unfocused as her memories dragged her under. She pulled herself from them violently. "The Bells had their own tradition regarding periods. You're officially a woman, so you better start popping out the crotch-goblins. Only Isaac still believed that when I came around. And he was very vocal about my responsibilities and obligations."

Cadwyn made a disgusted sound. "You would have been, what? Twelve?"

"Nine, I was an early bloomer."

"And he was talking about babies?" Ozzie squeaked. "That's gross."

Basheba smirked, "You should have seen his face when I told him that I had no intention of *ever* having a child."

Mina almost smiled at that, recalling how frightened the blonde was of children. It may have come across as disgust, but it was terror.

"And that's why you're at odds?" Mina asked.

"No, this is the background necessary to understand how we got where we are. Just shut up for a few more minutes," Basheba said. "Where was I? Oh, right, my period party. The next day, we got word that Claudia was sick. No one knew what was wrong with her, but Isaac was beside himself and begging my parents to meet him at the hospital. It was all last minute. My sisters got to stay with some friends and my brother and I were left at home."

"Your parents left two children home alone?" Mina asked.

"We were independent kids," Basheba dismissed.

Buck playfully chewed on her hand. Mina suspected it was the only thing keeping her from slipping into her memories.

"It was the first time we had a home to be left in. We built it ourselves. This little one-room log cabin in the Alaskan wilderness." She bit her bottom lip to keep in a chuckle. "No running water. No heat. No electricity. No neighbors for miles. We had grizzly bears and moose cutting through our front yard and, in the winter, I used the aurora as my nightlight. Heaven couldn't be more beautiful."

"How do you use the restroom if there's no running water?" Ozzie whispered to Cadwyn only to be shushed.

"My brother used to love to fish. We spent the whole day on the frozen lake before we were forced inside by an approaching snowstorm. I remember going to sleep with him making shadow puppets on the walls." Her smile fell. "I woke up with a stranger looming over me. He smelt like sour milk and had the roughest hands. They felt like sandpaper against my skin. One clamped over my mouth, the other pulled at my clothes."

Mina's stomach rolled with dread and disgust. *Nine, she was only nine.*

"He hurt you?" Cadwyn whispered when Basheba fell silent.

She stirred. "Turns out my little hairpin was sharp enough to puncture a man's neck, if you swing it hard enough. I must've gotten the artery because he bled out on top of me. It took both me and my brother to shove him off."

"Basheba, I'm so sorry that happened to you," Mina said. "But I don't understand."

Basheba paused; Buck grumbled at the sudden loss of attention. "Is it really that hard for you to think that family could turn on family?"

"Isaac sent him after you?" Cadwyn asked, his voice taking on a deep growl.

"Them, Cadwyn. He sent *them* after me."

"I don't understand," Mina repeated.

"It was the third guy who was too much of an idiot to cover his tracks properly," Basheba continued. "He had printed out the webpage. Can you believe that? Looking back, that guy's death was just natural selection at work. I'll spare the minor of the group the gory details. Just think of it as an advertisement. Calling all creeps, there's a little girl alone in the woods. Do what you want with her."

"Isaac tried to have you killed?" Cadwyn asked.

"Worse," Basheba said, pulling Buck closer for a hug, careful of the spikes that covered them both. "The only restriction was that I was to be left alive. Well, alive enough to bring the resulting child to term." A bitter laugh cracked out of her. "And before you ask how I know it was him. Only Isaac is stupid enough to think my parents would force their underage daughter to give birth to her rapist's kid. Honestly, I don't know what he thought would happen. It's bothered me for years. All I can think is that he was hoping I'd be too mortified to tell my parents about the assault. That I'd keep it a secret until it was too late for an abortion."

"Oh, my God," Mina whispered, her arms wrapping around her torso.

Basheba scoffed. "Yeah, he's always hated me. Way more than any of my siblings. I mean, he never tried anything like that with them, or anyone else, as far as I've heard. I don't know what I did to tick him off so much. Admittedly, it probably didn't help that I cussed him out with a rather extensive vocabulary when he presumed he had a say over my womb."

"What did your parents think happened?" Ozzie asked. "I mean, how did you explain away the dead bodies?"

Basheba laughed, good-natured and warm. "I was nine. Mom had long since taught us how to hide a dead body."

Mina's brow furrowed. The confusion increasing when she noticed how baffled Cadwyn was. *It's not a skill taught to the four families.*

"Why did she teach you that?" Mina ventured.

"Tradition," Basheba said with a small, secretive smile. "Anyway, after the first couple, my brother and I took the fight outside. It was the two of us and the Alaskan wilderness against some morons who couldn't track an elephant. They never stood a chance against us," she chuckled, her eyes softening. "*Us.* That's how my brother always worded it. He never put the blame on me. It didn't matter how they came at us. He never wavered."

Basheba released Buck only long enough to wipe at her cheeks.

"You never told anyone?" Cadwyn asked.

A look of horror twisted up her face. "And have my father find out? I couldn't do that to him. My dad was a good man. It wasn't his fault we share DNA with the human equivalent of a stomach flu. And I'd be damned if I let him suffer for it." Shaking her head, she stared off into the distance. "I decided Isaac and I would sort it out ourselves, when the time was right."

"So, when you said that you'd do to him what you did to the others…" Mina prompted.

Basheba flashed her bloodied teeth. "Yeah, Ozzie's still too innocent to hear any of that in detail. And, honestly, I still don't entirely trust your law and order mentality. There's no statute of limitations on murder, after all."

"Who would believe me?" Mina asked, trying to keep her words light.

Basheba took the words as intended and smiled. "I've got that working for me at least."

"So, let me get this straight," Mina thought aloud. "From his perspective, he sets you up. Probably expecting a frantic call from two scared kids. But that doesn't happen. You and your brother never say anything, and he can't bring up the subject to see what happened."

"Isaac had the good sense to avoid direct conflict with either of my parents," Basheba said, once more curling up with Buck. "They both intimidated the hell out of him."

"And that's why he's so aggravated," Mina murmured with sudden realization.

She glanced around only to see confused frowns.

"I'm starting to get an idea of the way Isaac thinks, and I'm sickened to realize we have something in common. We're both planners."

Basheba cocked an eyebrow.

"I didn't say we were *good* at planning," Mina clarified, physically sick by the truth in the words she spoke. "Just that, it's what we do. We overthink things. And that can lead to a lot of mistakes, especially if we start with a misapprehension."

"He mistook Basheba's silence for fear," Cadwyn offered, still somewhat apprehensive to follow where Mina led.

"He assumed he would have Basheba's backing as soon as he took his place as head of the household. And, with her, he'd have all the things he doesn't have amongst the four families."

Basheba lifted her hand and waved it to get attention. "What's that? I'm not exactly popular."

"But you are respected." Cadwyn added with a smirk, "Sometimes, grudgingly so."

"My parents outright detest you, and even they admit you're the best at this," Mina said.

Ozzie followed Basheba's example and lifted his hand. "Percival actually thinks the world of you."

"Aw, that's sweet," Basheba preened.

"My theory is that Isaac watched you earn respect and influence, and he built his plans around the assumption that, one day, that would be his own," Mina continued, absently tapping the ends of her hair against her lower lip as she thought. "But I think Whitney is in charge of the cult, now."

"Oh, so *now* it's a cult," Basheba muttered under her breath.

It was easy enough for Mina to ignore the comment as her mind raced.

"I overheard them discussing a deal they had with Isaac. And my dad suggested that Isaac has worked hard to come to an arrangement with them." She rushed on as all three of her listeners perked up at that information. "I'm thinking he was using Basheba as leverage. Perhaps threatening to unleash her on the town."

"Unleash me? I'm not an animal."

"You did blow up a morgue, and you carpeted the town with poisonous gas," Cadwyn deadpanned.

"The minotaur started it," Basheba protested.

"You threatened to set them on fire," Ozzie said.

The blonde huffed. "That was *hours* ago. Stop living in the past."

"You gutted two men," Mina noted absently. "And ripped someone's throat out with your *teeth*."

Basheba's mouth opened and closed a few times. "Yeah, okay, you got me there."

"If Isaac overplayed his hand, Basheba's behavior would risk everything. He's supposedly head of the family. If he can't get her in line, then everyone will see him for what he is."

"A weak, petty man," Basheba noted.

"He'd be desperate to prove he has power over you. Killing you might be the only way he has left to do that."

Ozzie meekly put up his hand again. "I don't mean to sound like a jerk, but why is any of this relevant? I mean, relevant *right now*?"

"Because my father made it clear, in no uncertain terms, that he agrees with Isaac," Mina said. "I don't know if he's aware just how deep Isaac's sunk, but the situation concerns me. Not to mention all the spy implications."

"Spy implications?" Ozzie said, barely suppressing his amusement.

"The families talk amongst themselves, right?" Mina asked.

Cadwyn looked as if he had just been struck. His hands paused as he packed away his med-kit. "There is an unofficial council of family elders."

"And I'm guessing they'll all talk rather freely," Mina said. "I don't feel easy knowing every family secret can work its way back to the cult, if not to the Witch herself."

"Is that how she knew how to find me?" Ozzie asked.

Cadwyn patted his shoulder in an offer of comfort but didn't say anything, leaving the question hanging over the group.

"In the spirit of full disclosure," Mina continued awkwardly, not sure how Basheba would respond, "when I received my music box, my parents both assured me they would 'fix' it. Before anyone jumps to conclusions, I have no evidence that *anyone* can sway the Witch's Harvest selection."

"But you think he can?" Even as Basheba carefully stripped all emotion from her words, she couldn't hide the spark of fire burning within the question.

"I have a habit of overestimating my father," Mina replied. "And

I'd like to point out, if Isaac has somehow wormed his way into a position where he can have that power, my father wouldn't be the only one he's pimped it out to."

"He set my father up to die," Basheba snarled. "He's choosing who gets to be the human sacrifice."

"We don't know that for sure," Cadwyn said, swiftly adding, "but the possibility is enough to worry me. I'll look into it once we get back."

"I can ask Percival," Ozzie offered. "I know I can trust him with my life. And he's made it pretty clear he thinks Isaac is a creep."

"I love your dad," Basheba grinned.

"Don't worry, I won't tell him anything you've told us."

Basheba chuckled. "I'm actually kinda hoping you'll tell a lot of people. I've always told myself I'll hold this truce so long as dad's alive and Isaac keeps to himself. Now, he's actively tried to kill me. So, I'm going to burn his entire world down around him. You know, when I have a free five minutes. Speaking of time restraints, we should get moving. That thing," she said as she jabbed a finger toward the corpse Mina had blissfully forgotten about for fifteen minutes, "is going to draw *its* attention. We want to keep moving."

CHAPTER 17

Basheba kept a close eye on Buck as they made their way over the uneven forest floor. The thick blanket of wildflowers masked the steadily increasing slope. Basheba's legs throbbed and her arms trembled from carrying the weight for so long. *Why are dead people always so heavy? It's just so inconsiderate.* As the hours stretched on, she was forced to confront the fact that she was the smallest, weakest one within the group. This made her all the more determined to outlast the others. She would be damned if she was the first one to ask to rest.

They struggled to the top of the precipice and awkwardly began to shuffle down the other side. Buck trotted on before them, idly sniffing at everything within reach. Basheba tripped more than once by not looking where she was going, but still didn't take her eyes off of Buck. He would be the first one to know *it* had found them.

Conversation had dwindled soon after they had started off. Whatever curiosity they had dwindled under their growing anxiety. Paranoia hung thick in the floral drenched air. The night encased them, with only their own footsteps and the stray hoot of an owl to disturb it. By the moon peeking through the canopy, Basheba estimated it was past midnight when Mina couldn't keep her mouth shut any longer.

"What is *it*?"

Much to Basheba's relief, Ozzie took that as a cue that they were stopping and dumped his portion of the bag. Cadwyn followed suit and promptly slumped his weight against the nearest tree.

"There's been a lot of speculation over the years," Basheba said.

"*It's* the reason we go through the hiking trail's parking lot."

Mina huffed slightly, pulling her arms over her chest to release some of the knots in her muscles. "That doesn't tell me much."

"You don't know enough about cryptozoology for it to make any sense," Basheba countered.

"I'm sure you're up for the challenge of explaining."

Basheba smirked, oddly amused. *She might actually be tolerable if she got her ego under control.*

"Personally," Basheba said, "I always thought of it as a *Mahaha*."

Ozzie perked up. "Did you just fake laugh?"

"No, that's what it's called," Basheba said.

His dark brows knitted with suspicion. "I might not be able to see the punchline, but I know this is a setup."

"The *Mahaha* is a creature of ancient Inuit legend," Basheba said.

"It's a monster that tickles you to death," Cadwyn said cautiously, as if dredging up a distant memory.

"Look at that, Mr. Winthrop, you finally managed to impress me," Basheba said.

"I've saved your life on numerous occasions."

"Yeah, but you're a nurse," she teased. "That's not impressive, that's just being competent."

"I'm sorry," Mina cut in. "It *tickles* you to death? How is that intimidating?"

Basheba suppressed a shiver at the memories her mind's eye started to play like an old movie. Instinctively, she looked for Buck as she spoke.

"It has these ten-inch-long nails. Strong like silver. Sharp as a scalpel. You'll hear it before you see it. It giggles. I've never heard anything laugh like that. It's just…" She bit her lips, trying to steady her breathing. "Sadistic. Gleefully sadistic. I don't know how it works, but you'll laugh when it 'tickles' you. When its nails slice through your flesh like hot steel through soft butter. You'll laugh as it turns your stomach to mush. You'll be smiling while it eats you."

Jerking herself free from the past, she crouched down, whistling for Buck. He trotted over instantly, presenting his rump for a rub. Not an easy task, given his armor. The brush of his fur beneath her fingertips chased away the horrors of the past.

"Then why are we going this way?" Ozzie asked after a length of tense silence.

Basheba shrugged. "It's faster. If we can keep up the pace and cut across the river, we'll be there just after dawn."

"It takes three days from the hiking trail." Mina didn't say the words as an accusation or complaint. She spoke them with fear. "We willingly spend two extra days in the Witch Woods rather than face the *Mahaha*."

"That's why we've got our friend in tow." Basheba smiled, unable to resist giving the corpse a swift kick.

Despite her nonchalant tone, Basheba was already regretting staying in one place for so long. Being found by the monster was an inevitability. *Where* they came into contact was somewhat under their control. And she wanted to make sure that it was on the edges of his territory, not in the heart of it.

"Break's over," Basheba declared, giving Buck a parting rub.

Trained as he was, it didn't take more than that for him to return to his vigilant stance. The others were somewhat more reluctant to return to their task. Each one of them was now paying far more attention to the dark woods.

"Katrina knows we're here," Mina said.

Basheba scrunched up her face as she hefted the dead weight back onto her shoulder. Short as she was, she needed to hold it a lot higher simply to be level with the others.

"But she hasn't sent anything after us yet," Mina added, casting a quick glance at Basheba. "That's a lot of faith to put in her *Mahaha*. Is that faith earned?"

"I survived it," Basheba said.

The scars on her ribs burned with the memory, and she could taste the crisp river water that had saved her.

"How many didn't?" Mina asked.

Gripping the thermal sheet tighter, Basheba jerked forward, forcing the others into movement.

"Don't worry about it," Basheba said, adding under her breath, "so long as there's a body of water around."

"What?" Mina asked.

"You know, I love it when you're silent," Basheba smiled.

Mina took the not-so-subtle hint and turned her full focus to lugging the body forward. The wild bouquet grew thicker and higher. For the others, the flowing stalks brushed against their hips. Basheba's tiny stature allowed them up quite a bit higher, and the combined scents made her head spin. The tiny pink bulbs of bleeding hearts hooked on the buttons of Basheba's flannel shirt as they entered into a wide meadow. In the darkness, it took her a few moments to notice what other flowers were there to greet them. Stopping just on the precipice of the meadow, she dumped the weight, retrieved her phone, and swept the weak flashlight across the area.

"I'm going to need my bow," she muttered to Cadwyn, adrenaline flooding her veins.

The bow and quiver caught on his broad shoulders in his haste.

"I'm not intending to annoy you," Mina said.

"And yet you always manage to."

"Are you able to shoot that with any kind of accuracy?" Mina pressed on.

Basheba glared at her. "I'm a good hunter."

"I'm not questioning that," Mina said, waving a finger to indicate Basheba's eye patch. "I'm just thinking your depth perception might be a little off right now."

Not willing to admit that Mina had a point, she snipped, "I promise not to shoot you. Now, can I please focus on saving your life?"

Mina's expression hovered somewhere between satisfied, chastised, and irritated, but she nodded anyway.

"What's wrong?" Ozzie whispered.

Basheba risked sweeping the light once more over the meadow, annoyed to find that not one of them understood. Clenching her teeth against a frustrated groan, she elaborated.

"They're all warnings."

"The flowers?" Cadwyn asked.

Mina asked at the same time, "Warnings?"

"Ozzie's an arachnophobe and Cadwyn has a thing about teeth," Basheba said. "That purple one by your hand is called *spiderwort*. The little white ones are *toothwort*."

"I don't know much about flowers, but aren't they both native to Tennessee?" Cadwyn asked, inching closer to pass her the bow and quiver.

"They are," Basheba admitted. "But you see those ones a bit further in? The white ones that look like spiked-up corn cobs? That's *asphodel*. It's not supposed to be in these woods, and it means 'may regrets follow you to the grave.'"

She opened the quiver and fished her hand into the internal pocket to retrieve her hand guard.

"I can also see some *dog rose*, which means 'pleasure and pain.' And I'm not keen on these guys." She paused to pluck a stalk of tiny green cups. "*Bells of Ireland.*" Basheba held it out for Cadwyn to take, a small smile on her lips.

"Bell," he said with an understanding nod.

She set the quiver in place and tugged until the strap was flush against her chest. It was awkward to put her backpack over the quiver, but she had grown used to the lopsided weight. "They also mean 'good luck.' Oh, and the whole meadow is surrounded by *witch elms*."

"I'm sorry," Mina said, clearly struggling to come to terms with everything she had just heard. "You know flower meanings? Really?"

"I like to know when someone's threatening me. And the woods are Katrina's preferred method of communication." She grudgingly added, "And I find it amusing when people thank me for giving them bouquets that passive-aggressively insult them."

"It's even harder to imagine you being *passive*-aggressive," Ozzie said, inching closer still to the group, his eyes restlessly searching the shadows.

Basheba smirked. "My parents were big on family unity. It forced us to be creative in ways to insult each other."

"My brother and I use colors as swear words," Mina said.

Basheba studied her out of the corner of her eye, her face mostly hidden in shadows. "Well, peach. Let's go fuchsia up Katrina's day."

The thick leather of her hand guard quickly warmed to her skin. Well used, it now fit her fingers and wrist like a second skin, making it easy to notch the end of her arrow into the bow. A low series of whistles brought Buck around, commanding him to be prepared and alert. She gave the others time enough to organize the dead weight between them and began to lead the way into the meadow.

"Can't we go around?" Ozzie asked.

"I'm not keen to see what's waiting for us in the shadows," she whispered back. "If they want us, they can come out into the open and get us."

There was nothing to gain from informing the poor boy that Katrina loved to act as if the trees had been named after her. Or from letting him know about any of the things Basheba had found nestled in the clustered needles that consumed their trunks. *Let him keep some measure of innocence,* she thought.

The moon brightened as they moved, letting the shadows deepen until its light almost seemed to die just beyond the tree line. Basheba kept her steps light, and her hands ready upon the bow, her gaze snapping toward every trace of movement. A cool breeze came out of nowhere to rustle the trees and towering flowers. Basheba hunched low, almost completely hidden by the shifting petals. Behind her, the others followed suit as best they could, barely able to keep from dropping the corpse.

Buck's growl rumbled through the sudden silence of the woods. His lips pulled back from his fangs as his gaze became locked on a spot just to their right. Readjusting her grip on the bowstring and arrow, she tracked her pet's line of sight. Moonlight flared into an unnatural silver glare that all but destroyed her night vision. Cursing under her breath, she narrowed her eyes, peering through the dancing flowers.

Ethereal strips of ivory pushed against the darkness before disappearing once more out of sight. Under her watchful gaze, another path of the illusive white emerged like a shark from the ocean's depths, stretching out to form a gigantic smile. Basheba moved on reflex. Flower petals scattered in the wake of the arrow, carving a path across the field. The journey barely took a second. Still, the smile disappeared long before the arrow struck home, leaving the shaft to be swallowed by the darkness.

"Damn it," Basheba hissed, readjusting her displaced eye patch.

Low, giggling laughter drifted on the night air, swirling around them, brushing against the back of her neck like tickling fingers. The sound had echoed through her nightmares for years and yet she still reacted to it like the first time. Swallowing hard, she tried to force her heart out of her throat and retrieved another arrow. Lowering her weight onto one shin allowed her to completely hide within the wildflowers. The laughter returned. Louder than before and rolling like mist.

"Stalk," she whispered to Buck.

Instantly, his nose went into the air. Almost immediately, he had the scent, and he whirled to the left. There wasn't a drop of bloodhound in him, but his paw went up all the same. A clear and decisive point. Sliding across the damp earth, Basheba positioned her bow over Buck's outstretched paw and fired. The swaying plants swallowed the arrow almost instantaneously.

"Did you hit it?" Ozzie asked.

"You can see more than I can, Ozzie," she hissed, already getting to her feet, a new arrow in hand. She turned to find them all just staring at her. "Now's the time we run."

Cadwyn gripped the body's wrist, pulling it free of the bag to hurl the dead weight over his shoulders. The heavy weight almost dragged him down. Sheer determination allowed him to straighten. With clenched teeth, he commanded Ozzie and Mina to run. They followed the order without question. Basheba settled herself between the two teenagers and Cadwyn, an arrow at the ready and Buck by her side.

The laughter returned. As if every blade of grass and suspended leaf carried the sound. Buck kept his nose high, sniffing the air, searching to catch the scent again. Suddenly, Buck locked his legs. His claws ripped up chunks of dirt as he slid to a stop, head lowered, teeth bared, and one paw outstretched before him. Once more, Basheba dropped to one knee and fired blind. The laughter rose into a shrill delirium. The petals shattered to release a man into the air. Gravity didn't hinder him. Arms and legs rose as he loomed over her, his long talons glistening, shark-like teeth cutting down from his parted lips. Basheba fell onto her back, grappling for another arrow.

Buck streaked across her vision. A creature of ebony and fury. He sunk his teeth into the *Mahaha's* arm. Pure fear crashed through Basheba as she watched the deadly talons sweep down toward Buck. Forgoing the arrow, she cupped the bow with both hands and swung it like a bat into the *Mahaha's* haggard legs. The metal cracked against bone and the *Mahaha* stumbled back into the flowers. Basheba was on her feet before Cadwyn could try to help. He shifted the heavy weight across his shoulders, freeing one hand to place it against her back.

"Are you okay?"

"Yeah," she whispered.

Ozzie called to them, sharp and panicked, and she realized the teenagers had already made it to the tree line. Still, she refused to move until Buck responded to her sharp whistle. Pulling another arrow free, she knocked it and began to run. Even with the weight bearing down upon his shoulders, she knew Cadwyn could have easily taken the lead. Instead, he remained in step with her, refusing to leave her behind. *Noble, but stupid.*

The flowers slashed and swayed in two clear trails. A telltale sign of two creatures carving their way through the underbrush. Laughter bounced around the meadow, rolling over itself to grow into a deafening roar. Panting hard, Basheba forced another whistle. Buck barked as he emerged from the crush, a dark, undefinable shape closing in behind him. The other trail picked up speed as it bore down upon the two unprotected teenagers.

"Drop it," Basheba ordered.

Cadwyn tossed the corpse onto the ground, the impact resounding with a heavy thud. Basheba whirled on the body, her free hand tugging her hunting knife free.

"Hey!" she screamed as she drove the knife into the body's gut.

A sharp slice, a solid stomp, and the stench of cooling blood burst into the air. The trailing creature stopped short. Without the movement, it was impossible to tell where the giggling *Mahaha* was. Blood soaked her once more as she reached in and cut free the first organ her fingertips found.

"Basheba?" Cadwyn whispered.

She handed him her hunting knife, using her now-free hands to stab the kidney onto an arrow, hefting it to hurriedly judge the added weight. Behind her, Cadwyn flipped the knife in his hand with surprising skill, readjusting his grip to the back of the knife, so that the blade ran down the length of his forearm.

The breeze died to leave the coppery stench of blood pooling around them. All trace of movement stilled. Basheba licked her lips and glanced over her shoulder to meet Cadwyn's gaze. He nodded once, wordlessly agreeing to follow wherever she would lead him.

Hopefully, it's not to the grave. The thought came before she could completely lock her emotions down. Silence lingered.

"Grab some of the organs," she instructed Cadwyn in a whisper before she called out, "Buck! Clear 'em out!"

Duck hunting had solidified the command. His snarls shattered the silence. The grass thrashed wildly, two trails cutting back and forth, entwining around each other and leaving no way to tell which was which.

"Come on, Buck," she whispered, her heart hammering against her chest.

Anxiety sparked under her skin, trying to make her restless. She forced her body to become stone, ready and alert, waiting for Buck to flush the *Mahaha* out. A streak of black bounded through the moon-drenched meadow. Half a heartbeat later, the sickly gray monster followed. Basheba seized the opportunity, angling the bow slightly higher to compensate for the weight of the organ. The bowstring snapped taut, hurling the arrow across the space. The *Mahaha* snapped a hand up, catching the arrow before the point could penetrate its flesh. But the allure of the organ was too enticing for it to ignore and it began to gnaw on the piece.

"Now," Basheba said.

They broke into a sprint. Plants crushed under their feet, pummeled into the soft earth. The wind picked up, howling through the witch elms to create a ghastly wailing howl. Mina screamed for them to hurry as Ozzie restlessly squirmed beside her.

"Cross the river!" Basheba bellowed.

Mina nodded, grabbed Ozzie with both hands, and dragged him away. Buck growled even as he sprinted, frothing at the mouth and hackles raised. Needing no instruction, Cadwyn scattered the organs with wide sweeps of his arm. Each bloody clump of flesh landed with a wet thud; a sound that was met with a rustle of reeds. They were short distractions that offered them only a few extra seconds. Both Basheba and Cadwyn exploited them all as best they could, running until their legs ached and their lungs were replaced with burning coals.

Laughter followed them, broken on occasion by the slick squelch of teeth ripping into raw meat. But each time it returned, it was closer than before, trailing behind them as if it were a game. Cadwyn quickened his pace, his long legs making it an easy task, and entered the forest first. He slowed just beyond the first twisted branches, catching his breath and frantically searching.

Without enough air to speak, Basheba shoved him with both hands, forcing him to move. The clustered trees made it nearly impossible for them to travel side by side. If it wasn't for Cadwyn's remarkable skill at finding openings within the foliage, they would have been forced to travel single file. Buck leaped over a fallen log and plowed through the leaves, leading the way as he hunted the others down.

Basheba's backpack slapped against her spine. Sweat made her hand slip over her bow's handgrip. Her eyepatch, slicked with her body heat and sweat, shifted and itched against her skin. Still, she kept running, keeping Cadwyn in her peripheral vision and tracking the destruction of Buck's pursuit. She ran until her legs wobbled and she staggered to the side.

Without warning, the trees she relied on for support disappeared, leaving her grasping at air. The laughter had covered the sounds of the river. Basheba locked her knees, trying to slide to a stop before she toppled into the small ravine. She clawed at the rocky surface, her legs dangling over the edge, the damp moss soaking her jeans.

"Basheba!" Ozzie called from the other side of the riverbank. The froth of the rapids would have hidden him completely if it wasn't for the way he waved both of his arms.

Cadwyn didn't see the edge, either. But he threw himself into the fall, leaping forward as far as he could as ivory nails closed in around him. The wide sweep of the *Mahaha's* arms slashed through the night air. Blood splattered from the deadly tips as the *Mahaha* tightened its grip, narrowly missing its prey as Cadwyn dove into the river. The monster's nails created sparks against the stones as it dropped onto all fours to watch Cadwyn fall. It laughed until the moment he hit the water and disappeared into the rapids. Then it turned its burning eyes onto Basheba.

Basheba scrambled onto her feet to leap over the side, hoping to clear the rocks that clung to the bank. Razors slashed her torso, effortlessly cutting one strap of her bag. The current took her the second she hit the water. Battered against the stones and desperate for air, she could do little against the tide. She clawed at the moss drenched boulders. Her backpack slipped from her shoulders and was lost to the waves. She refused to lose her bow, too.

Basheba's breath was forced out of her lungs as the river's current crashed her into a boulder. She dragged herself up, gasping and sputtering, and bodily hugged the rock. Rushing water crushed her against unmoving stone and dulled her senses. Relief left her weak when she spotted Cadwyn crawling his way out onto the far bank, Buck huffing as he tugged at the half-drowned man. A surge of water rushed over her, a black wall that filled her with terror and dragged her down once more.

CHAPTER 18

Cadwyn's feet sunk into the mud as he dragged Basheba's motionless body out of the river. Buck pushed past him to nuzzle her hand and gently chew on her fingertips. She didn't respond. Whimpering anxiously, the large dog nudged her head, the spikes of his helmet scraping her skin. The river had taken her eyepatch, leaving the livid bruise on full display. It appeared stark against her pale skin.

"Is she breathing?" Ozzie gasped, half failing in his attempt to help get her out of the water.

Cadwyn dragged Basheba into his arms and hiked past the rattled teenagers, seeking out solid ground.

"I need some light," he snapped.

Mina could only gape at him, "The water ruined all of our phones."

Spotting a rock in the dim moonlight, he hurried to it, ordering Mina to untangle the limp girl from the bowstring and quiver.

"Where's her bag?" Ozzie asked somewhat breathlessly. "She never goes anywhere without it."

"She's bleeding," Mina noted.

Cadwyn ignored them both as he gently laid Basheba out on the stone. His hand went to the ever-present medical-kit he so obsessively carried everywhere. The familiar weight reassured him that they had everything they needed. Buck braced his front paws on the stone and began to lick Basheba's face, growing desperate to get a reaction.

"Ozzie, take care of Buck. Mina," he said as he tossed his med-kit against her chest, "get ready."

Mina nodded rapidly, tugging on a pair of gloves while Ozzie strained to pull the massive Rottweiler away from his owner. Cadwyn placed the side of his head against Basheba's chest, willing himself to hear a heartbeat, a breath.

"Goddamn it, Basheba," he hissed through clenched teeth.

With well-practiced ease, he began chest compressions, rocking her tiny body with each push. *She can't drown,* he told himself. *After everything, she can't go out this way.* Memories mocked him. A thousand stories of her namesake. A little girl that defied a witch and died in a shallow brook. The thoughts scattered when he reached thirty compressions and focused on tipping her head back. All of his focus was on watching her chest rise and fall with his borrowed breaths. She didn't breathe on her own, so he repeated the compressions. Droplets of water beaded from his hair and dripped onto her face. She still didn't stir.

"Do you know CPR?" Cadwyn asked Mina, perhaps too sharply as he kept count in his head.

"Yes," she replied. "I'm here the second you need me."

Two more breaths. Still nothing. *Don't let her die like this!* his brain commanded.

"Come on, Basheba," he whispered. "For once in your life, don't be stubborn."

Two more breaths. Another round of compressions. Each second jabbed a knife into him. *Six minutes,* the treacherous voice whispered in the back of his head. *The brain starts to die after six minutes. How long was she in the water?* He dipped down, sealing his mouth over hers to fill her lungs again. The first gurgle caught him off guard.

"Basheba?" Mina asked.

Ozzie staggered forward, dragged by Buck's renewed determination. Cadwyn rolled Basheba onto her side, settling her into the recovery position as bone-cracking coughs rattled her body. River water pulsated out of her in steady gushes, far more than her lungs should have been capable of holding. She began to gag. The pale light revealed enough to see the color changing in her cheeks but not what was choking her.

Cadwyn hooked two fingers into her mouth. A squirming mass pressed against his fingertips. He jerked back as the first of the infant snakes squirmed past her lips. More and more followed until it seemed like hundreds of them came pouring from her mouth. Each one writhing against the others as Basheba's coughs vomited the reptiles onto the stone. The growing mass pushed out into the moonlight and he noticed the scale pattern—a tell-tale speckled cross band that even he could recognize.

"Cottonmouths!" He threw an arm out, urging the others back from the venomous snakes, hurriedly bundling Basheba into his arms.

Her constant choking made it nearly impossible to hold her in any stable position. The snakes continued to pour from her, a writhing puddle that glistened in the dying moonlight. Slithering out into the world with a determination that unsettled Cadwyn.

Cadwyn cautiously backed up, terrified that he would trip and bring them both into a sea of venom. The snakes followed them into the trees, slithering into the thick foliage and out of sight. Buck threw himself against Ozzie's hold, half-wild with the impulse to protect his clearly distressed Basheba.

Her first deep breath sounded like a death rattle. It left Cadwyn both relieved and concerned as he sought the high ground. There wasn't anywhere they could go where the snakes couldn't follow, if so inclined. Mina helped Cadwyn scramble up onto a boulder, Ozzie and Buck close behind. What little light peeking through the canopy created a haphazard pattern on the forest floor that was barely enough to see by. Basheba's pained gasps covered the soft sounds around them.

"Are there any more?" Cadwyn asked, trying to arrange her so he could see in her mouth.

Basheba cried out, short and sharp and laced with pain.

Cadwyn stilled, "Where does it hurt?"

"My ribs," she choked. "Buck?"

"Buck's fine. He's right here," Cadwyn assured as he lowered her to sit on the stone. With his adrenaline fading, he felt the pain in his leg for the first time. The spike of agony made him crumble the last of the distance, and they fell to the ground.

"Sorry," he grumbled, reaching for the soggy hem of her flannel shirt.

In his exhaustion, he was almost pushed from the rock entirely as Buck nudged past. Basheba expertly avoided the spikes of Buck's armor to draw him into a hug.

"Hey, beautiful." Basheba's voice rasped as if she had inhaled fire, but her smile was bright and full. Buck's entire hindquarters scattered about with his excitement. "Sorry I worried you. I'm all right."

"We're okay, too," Mina said, a smirk pulling at her lips and seeping into her voice.

"I was getting around to asking." Basheba coughed hard, gasped in pain, and added, "Don't be jealous."

Balling the shirt up at the side, Cadwyn spotted the scratch marks. Four clean slashes that thankfully didn't cut to the bone.

"Why does my chest hurt so much?" Basheba asked.

"It could be the CPR. You have to be a bit rough," Cadwyn said.

Ozzie loomed over his shoulder. "It could also be the ridiculous amount of snakes you just spewed."

"Snakes?" Basheba asked.

"It doesn't matter," Cadwyn said. "Let me tend to these."

"Do you need my shirt off?" Untangling herself from Buck, she quickly worked the line of buttons, opening the wet material without a hint of embarrassment.

Cadwyn released a grateful sigh. Having never seen Basheba bashful, he had no idea how to handle that particular scenario. Mina inched her way closer, his med-kit cradled between both hands, watching intently and waiting for instructions. The waterproof, heavily padded bag had protected its contents well.

As if responding to his internal pleading for more light, dawn cracked over the horizon. The thick canopy had canceled the gradual shift, making the change all the more startling, leaving him concerned by how much time had passed. Mina gasped, a shocked little sound that surprised everyone. Basheba raised an eyebrow.

"Sorry," Mina said sheepishly. "I just didn't know you had that much scar tissue."

Basheba gave the girl a thumbs up and forced out, "Brilliant bedside manner."

"I'm going to be a surgeon. My patients will be unconscious."

The soft chuckle brought a sharp spasm of pain. Cadwyn took the opportunity to sink the needle into her skin, knowing the painkillers would take effect soon enough. Of course, Basheba was impatient, and insisted he start stitching her up straight away. As hard as she tried, she couldn't keep in her first gasp of pain. It took Basheba, Mina, and Ozzie working in unison to keep Buck from taking his head off.

"Did I drown?" Basheba asked.

Cadwyn forced himself to hold her gaze. "No, just hit your head."

The lie hovered between them, known by both sides and welcomed far more than the truth.

"Thank you," Basheba whispered.

She didn't say another word while he stitched up her wounds and wrapped her in long lengths of gauze, hoping to give her bruised ribs some support. All the while, she patted Buck, soothing the dog as much as herself, and watched the sun rise. Cadwyn didn't buy it for a second. Knowing how much pain she was in, when the time came, he refused to put up with any argument.

"Piggyback or bridal carry?"

Basheba's brows furrowed. "Say what now?"

"If we're going to keep going—"

"Why wouldn't we?" Basheba cut in.

He ignored the distraction and continued. "You're going to need to rest. I'll carry you until we get there."

She arched one eyebrow. "Are you in any condition to do that? Your leg."

His own chuckle surprised him. "A Chihuahua would weigh more than you. So pick a style, Bell, and let's get a move on."

The following moment of contemplation had way too much mischief in her eyes for his liking.

"Piggyback. That way I can still shoot arrows. You did save my bow, right?"

Seeing how happy she was to be reunited with it, he decided to add, "But you lost your bag."

It hit her like a lightning strike. She started patting her pockets, drawing out each ring to hurriedly count and recount them.

"Twenty-six," she breathed. "Oh, thank God."

Cautiously, he ventured to ask if she was okay, knowing how limited her possessions were. *She doesn't keep a thing she isn't attached to.*

"I have Buck, I have my parent's car, I have the rings," Basheba said. "Nothing else matters. Although, it's going to be a bitch to get a new driver's license."

"We have our crosses to bear," he smiled.

Getting her onto his back was easier than he had anticipated. She scrambled up and wrapped her limbs around him as if she wasn't injured at all. Still, he was careful with her, trying to keep her from being jostled too badly.

"You better not drop me," Basheba said.

"I won't."

"Because I can die from falling from this height," she quipped. "I might need an oxygen tank. You're tall, is what I'm saying."

"Duly noted." He smiled, happy that, despite the pain and fatigue, she was at least in good humor. "Now, which way do we go?"

They followed Basheba's orders for the next few hours, each one of them keeping a careful eye for the snakes. At times, Basheba would wilt, slumping against him with her head propped up on his shoulder, hovering on the edge of sleep. Wanting to give her as much time to rest as they could, they started asking for landmarks rather than having her keep constant vigil. She knew the route like a well-worn trail.

Ozzie had been the one to put their dread into words. "She must have come this way a lot."

Cadwyn turned his head, checking that Basheba was asleep even though he could tell by her steady breathing.

"We can talk about that later," Mina said, adding a reassuring smile when the teen cringed. "Let's just focus on this first."

Their trudge was far longer than Basheba had indicated. Or they were just moving at a far slower pace now. Sunlight filtered through the leaves, turning the air green while still allowing the flowers to almost glow with their vibrance. Cadwyn caught himself stunned by the beauty of it all. Mina proved to have a talent for spotting the landmarks Basheba anticipated. *There's no way on earth that tree looked like an elephant.* When they reached the last marker, Basheba had begun to snore. Even so, she instinctively clutched her bow, her fingers clenching when Ozzie stirred her.

"Is that the cat eye stone?" Mina asked in a whisper.

"Where?" Cadwyn asked.

Mina pointed to a tangle of tree limbs that formed a vaguely oblong shape.

"Yeah, that's it," Basheba mumbled.

Cadwyn blinked. "That's not even a stone. How...?"

"Put me down," Basheba replied, tapping his shoulder in impatience. "It's just over that ridge."

A silent conversation passed between Mina and Ozzie in a single glance. Eventually, the teen ventured.

"Do we have to go through the orchard?"

Basheba stared at him. "How lost are you? No, we're coming around the back. The orchard will be on the far side of the house."

Cadwyn couldn't fathom how they had managed to pull off such a maneuver while moving in relatively straight lines, but he didn't comment on it. The Witch Woods weren't beholden to the same rules as the rest of the world. *Maybe that's why Basheba's so good here,* he thought. *She can find sanity in madness.*

He crouched low, biting his inner cheeks against the pain rattling through his leg, and let Basheba slip off his back. She stumbled for a bit but soon found her footing. All the while, the bow remained tight in her grip. A low, whooping whistle instantly grabbed Buck's attention.

"Recon," Basheba whispered.

Buck took off up the hill like a shadow, silent and swift. The moment he entered the shrubbery, Cadwyn lost track of him completely.

"What kind of training have you put your dog through?" Mina asked.

"The right kind," Basheba replied.

She hugged her ribs with one hand while she waited for the dog to return.

"How is he supposed to express any relevant information?" Mina pressed.

Heaving a slow breath, Basheba started to dig in the dirt with the tip of her bow. Making three squares, spaced a few inches apart, almost in a triangle configuration. She cut a line between her feet and the squares, and an arch over the top. Cadwyn craned his neck to study it.

"The Bell property?"

She started by her feet and worked her way up. "The ridge. Slave quarters and barn. Ranch home. Orchard."

Buck returned as silently as he left, a small tuft of fur nipped carefully within his jaws. After lavishing him with attention, she got around to taking the fur, holding it up to study the tuft carefully.

"What's that?" Ozzie asked.

"Goat hair," Basheba said.

"That doesn't sound too intimidating," Mina said.

Basheba shrugged one shoulder. "That depends on the size of the goat." Gingerly getting onto her knees, she regained Buck's attention and presented him with the tuft. "Where are they? Hey, gorgeous? Where's the goat?"

Buck grumbled for a moment then snapped his jaws about the fur. Cadwyn, Mina, and Ozzie all watched in stunned silence as Buck dropped the slobber-soaked tuft onto the ground by the slave quarters.

"Good boy," Basheba praised, vigorously rubbing his neck. "You're the best boy ever."

Out of the corner of his eyes, Cadwyn noticed Mina's mouth drop open, and he quickly grabbed her wrist. There wasn't time for the questions they all had.

Basheba was oblivious to the interaction. "Anything else?"

Buck scraped his paw in the area between the back of the slave quarters and the ridge, gouging deep grooves with his nails.

"What does that mean?" Mina asked.

"Something's there."

"What?" Mina pressed.

Basheba finally looked at her. "How do I know? Come on, we should be able to get a decent peek from the hill."

They all wordlessly followed in her footsteps, careful not to make too much noise, and dropping to the earth when she did. Crawling on their stomachs, they slipped under a shrub and reached the tip of the ridge. Cadwyn froze. The run-down Bell property stood as a dark figure embossed upon a vivid world. The lush orchard framed it, thankfully too far away for him to see the hanging corpses. His eyes didn't linger on it. The herd of goat-men instantly grabbed the full focus of his attention.

They stood seven feet tall, huge, imposing, ungodly creatures. A mixture of goat and man, their ink-black horns rose like twin spikes from their heads. Each trod of their cloven feet created a resounding thud that Cadwyn felt rumble through his stomach. *Devils.* The thought slammed into him, robbing him of his breath and leaving him trembling. They were biblical devils.

"Oh my God," Mina whispered.

It was the first time Cadwyn had ever seen the teenager cross herself and he wondered how deep her religious belief went.

"What are they doing?" Ozzie whispered.

They all watched as the devils lead a snow-white bull into a red patch of earth. Each one took a leg while another gripped the head, and they all pulled. The bovine roared in pain as its flesh severed. Cadwyn twisted, hiding his face in his shoulder, as he covered Mina's and Ozzie's eyes. There was no escaping the pop of joints, the wet tear of skin, and the sudden silence.

"Whitney gave one of Katrina's sacrifices," Basheba whispered. "Who do all these others belong to?"

Gathering his fortitude, Cadwyn turned back in time to see some of the devils dragging the hunks of meat to the barn while another led out a new bull. The process began again.

"We're going to have to get past them to light the house on fire," Basheba said.

She scurried backward, leaving Cadwyn to urge the others out of their shock. Once they were all safely within the trees, Basheba took Cadwyn's med-kit and began to rummage through it.

"They did it with their bare hands," Mina whispered. "How do we fight something that strong?"

"We survived a giant spider," Ozzie offered.

"You two aren't fighting anything," Basheba said absently. Cadwyn inched closer to see what had her attention. "Cad, Buck, and I will handle that. You guys just focus on setting the fire and burning that place to ash."

"How are we supposed to do that?" Ozzie asked. "Even your lighter will be drenched."

"That house is all dry wood. It'll go up easily enough. You just need a spark," Basheba replied.

"I don't have any matches," Ozzie said, turning to Mina. "Do you?"

Basheba passed Cadwyn a couple of small bottles of black powder. "Potassium permanganate. It's a water purifier. What of it?"

"Do you have any sugar?" Basheba asked.

Ozzie sat across from Basheba, his arms wrapped tight around himself and Mina pressed close to his side.

"Why would there be sugar in a first aid kit?" Ozzie whispered.

"If diabetics have a sugar crash," Mina replied, her voice just as soft.

Cadwyn was taken aback when Basheba beamed up at him, displaying a half dozen sugar packets.

"Your kit is awesome."

He preened, glad to have someone appreciate it.

"All right, kiddos, listen up," Basheba said. "The first rule of arson is to have fun and be yourself. The second rule is to know your chemistry. Potassium permanganate and sugar. Mix it together on a solid surface. Rub the hell out of it and you've got yourself a spark."

"What is with you and fire?" Cadwyn mumbled.

Basheba ignored him, passing the sugar packets to Mina.

"Do a few different spots—don't block the door—and run like hell. We'll buy you as much time as we can."

"What's our exit strategy?" Mina asked. "I don't think the devils are going to just let us go."

"We won't give them a choice," Cadwyn said with fake bravado, not because he felt any ounce of confidence, but because he knew the teenager needed him to.

"I've got a few arrows left. Buck's got his fangs. Cadwyn has my knife," Basheba smiled.

Mina wrestled in her still damp jeans pocket to pull out a small Ziplock bag of her salt powder.

Basheba's grin lingered somewhere between bloodlust and excitement. "What more do we need?"

CHAPTER 19

Ozzie swallowed thickly, trying and failing to slow his rampaging heartbeat. Despite Basheba's relaxed dismissal of the situation, she chose a methodical approach in preparing for the encounter. She had watched them for at least an hour, her eyes sharp and her focus unshakeable. He had never seen anyone be so still and utterly silent for so long. More than once, he had snuck a look at her chest to check that she was still breathing.

At last, she had slithered back, and another meeting had taken place. Out of all of them, Mina was both the most surprised and the most grateful for Basheba's care. He found it remarkable how relaxed Mina became when presented with a plan. Even if it wasn't a good one. It was the process that seemed to soothe her. That, and the illusion of control.

Once more using her dirt diagrams, Basheba explained her idea with brisk efficiency and a disturbing lack of sarcasm. While they knew the demons were big and strong, they had no way to account for their speed. Basheba's plan, unsurprisingly, was an ambush filled with chaos.

"I can hit a few with arrows from over here," she said, pointing to the far side of the yard, opposite the barn and the paddock holding the sacrificial bulls. "One or two. Just enough to draw interest to me, giving Cadwyn and Buck time to slip around the back of the barn and into the bull paddock. If they're anything like Whitney's, they'll be hostile enough that Buck can easily get them to stampede. Cad, all you have to do is open the gate and get out of the way."

Cadwyn nodded.

"I mean it. If you get gouged by a bull *again*, I'm going to have to laugh at you. A lot. I will say cruel things that will haunt you until your dying day. I don't want to be that person. Don't make me that person."

"I'm flattered you're so worried about me," Cadwyn said, flicking his gaze up to meet hers.

"Did you listen to what I just said?"

"For you, that's practically fussing." His smile fell a little as he added, "Will Buck follow my command? He doesn't really respond to anyone but you."

Buck sat at Basheba's side. He hadn't left more than an inch between them since they had dragged her from the river. Warmth radiated from Basheba's eyes as she looked down to find the dog still watching her. She spared him a pat.

"Just tell him to come to me. It doesn't matter if the bulls flee from him or chase him, it'll work the same. They'll come out and cut across the yard, right through the goat-men. In the chaos, Mina and Ozzie can get to the house."

"How can you be so sure that's the path the bulls will take?" Mina asked.

Ozzie glanced at her, not sure if she was serious. "The way it's all set up, the buildings will act as a funnel."

"But once they're past them?" Mina said.

"That spot is the flattest bit of earth. Cows don't stampede up hills if they don't have to."

Tapping the ends of her hair against her mouth, Mina studied the dirt diagram again. "How can you be sure? I know you're from Texas, but you're old money."

"And a lot of that money is from cattle." He was almost offended by the way the others stared at him. "Granddad still has a ranch. Several, in fact." They still looked unconvinced. "I used to compete at steer wrestling."

Basheba cocked an eyebrow.

"Okay, they were calves, but I was little, too." He hunched his shoulders defensively. "I prefer barrel racing. It's closer to polo."

"There's the posh," Basheba chuckled.

Ozzie wasn't able to decide if he was offended or not by the time Basheba moved the conversation along.

"The goal will be to get them into the woods," she said.

"For your booby traps," Mina said. Not a question, but a statement.

The blonde smiled. "*Our* traps. Ya'll gonna learn what your mama should've taught ya."

"We don't have enough knives," Ozzie said.

Ozzie didn't know what to do with the look Basheba threw him. "Aw, aren't you just the runt of the litter, chewing on electrical wires."

"Are," he stammered, his brows knitting, "are you calling me inept, stupid, or cute?"

"Yes," Cadwyn answered for her.

Somehow, the older man had mastered a tone that both placated Basheba and got her back on track. Ozzie added 'the tone' to the list of things he needed to learn.

"The vegetation is thick there. Sturdy enough to ensure their height and strength aren't such a clear advantage anymore. If they get the upper hand, I'll lure them back around toward the river."

Ozzie worriedly caught Mina's gaze, and they both turned to Cadwyn.

"Are you sure you're up for that?" he asked for them.

"Look at the way they're built," Basheba said, studying the crude map. "They're not going to be great swimmers. I can outpace them across the river and let the *Mahaha* deal with them."

Mina's concern faltered under her sudden desire for knowledge. "Are you sure they'll fight?"

"If they don't, they'll die," Basheba smirked. "There's a reason why we didn't hear so much as a bird in its territory."

For a moment, Ozzie tried to remember that bit of the hike, but it was soon cast aside for the issue at hand.

"Aren't you afraid of water?" he blurted out, hurriedly adding, "and your ribs are bruised."

"If I couldn't do it, I wouldn't have suggested it," Basheba said with an inch of ice caking her words.

"We'll hold everything down out here," Cadwyn cut in, his voice a soothing balm to Basheba's. "You two just focus on each other and setting the house on fire."

Basheba hurried on. "Reminder: secure your exit strategy. House fires spread *fast*. A tinderbox like that is going to fill with a lot of smoke. It should give you enough cover to sneak out. By that time, they should be trying to save the barn, and you'll be able to make a beeline to the ridge."

"Out of curiosity—"

"Are you motivated by anything else?" Basheba cut off Mina.

The brunette continued on, "Why do you think they'll go to the barn?"

"Because they need the carcasses," Basheba said, absently patting Buck as he nosed at her shoulder.

Ozzie couldn't stop himself from wondering, *Is he really that big of a dog, or is she just that tiny of a girl?*

"If the ritual was over," Basheba continued, "they wouldn't be storing them. Katrina wants them for something."

"Right," Mina said.

There was little to discuss after that and, soon enough, Basheba was teaching them how to set up the traps. They worked in the deeper parts of the woods and, shielded by the vibrant leaves and wildflowers, Ozzie almost forgot what was to come. Basheba kept the ones closest to the homestead for herself. Once they had returned to the ridge, Basheba had told them to be ready, and had slipped with Buck and Cadwyn into the plant-life.

Mina was close to Ozzie's side, her steady warmth offering some measure of comfort. They had divided the sugar and potassium permanganate between them—a desperate bid to ensure that either one of them could start the fire. Unsurprisingly, Basheba had snatched up the last couple of bottles.

"I didn't mean it to end up like this," Mina whispered. "I'm sorry."

"Don't count us out yet," Ozzie replied.

He reached out and took Mina's hand, giving it a reassuring squeeze. *Whatever comes, we're in it together.* She squeezed his hand back just as the first devil fell. A flaming arrow protruded from its shoulder, the flames quickly spreading across its wiry fur. It released a feral, inhuman cry. The trees shook as it fell to the grass, rolling and thrashing to put out the crackling flames. The other devils turned, snouts rippling in silent fury. The next arrow struck one in the neck. It went up in flames just as fast as the first.

Buck's bark was overshadowed by the infuriated bellow of the bulls. The ground trembled. A stream of pure white bovines exploded from between the houses, following the black blur of Buck's body.

"Go," Mina and Ozzie said at the same time.

Side by side, they burst free of the trees. Everything happened at once. Colors flashed and sound clashed together under the stench of burning flesh. Buck appeared out of nowhere. He cut through the group, the spikes of his armor slicing deep into the goat-like legs of the devils. Inhuman screams rang in Ozzie's ears. The newest bull being lead to their slaughter huffed and bellowed in the chaos before charging blindly, gouging anything and everything within reach.

Blood drenched the grass and flashed across Ozzie's vision. He caught sight of Basheba racing toward them. She seemed intent on one of the burning remains. Buck held the devils off long enough for the small woman to rip one of the horns free of the carcass. The combination of the dangerous spike and her small stature gave her an unpredicted advantage. She could duck under the devils' muscled arms to quickly strike at their fur-covered legs, finding the joints and bringing them down. Buck was on them once they hit the ground. He was just as efficient as his owner as he clamped down on their necks, squeezing until skin and bone gave way.

A bellow made Ozzie snap around. A devil charged toward them, its inhuman mouth curled in fury. Cadwyn charged to meet it. Just before impact, he ducked his shoulder and threw himself into the creature's legs. They both toppled to the ground, grappling with each other, the hunting knife flashing in the noonday light.

"Cadwyn!" Ozzie screamed, trying to get back to him while Mina kept pulling him forward.

Cadwyn curled his body to drive both of his feet into the devil's barrel-like chest. It brought just enough distance that he could swipe the hunting knife across its throat. Blood gushed from the slit. Ozzie began to shake so hard he almost lost his footing. The copper stench burned his nose and made him gag.

"Stay with me," Mina begged.

The white bull charged before them, blocking their path for a moment before a devil caught its attention. Mina's hand tightened on his until the bones felt as if they would break. They barreled through the back door into the Bell family farmhouse. Suddenly immersed in shadows, Ozzie strained to see. The situation got worse when Mina slammed the door shut and threw herself against it. Ozzie ran back, adding his weight to the wood in a desperate attempt to keep the devils out while Mina struggled with the Ziplock bag of salt.

The door turned into splinters under the creatures' hands, as if they couldn't be bothered to push their way inside. Through the gaps, Ozzie saw how much the fire had spread. It was getting dangerously close to the barn. Basheba and Cadwyn had fallen back to the forest. At least, he hoped they had.

Mina slashed the bag down like a sword, spreading the salt and sealing the doorway. The devils seemed to vanish. The resulting silence had them staggering back.

"Did it work?" Ozzie whispered. "Or are they messing with us?"

Mina blindly groped for his arm as her gaze darted around the room, trying to catch sight of where the devils had gone. "Start the fire."

The unholy creatures' first strike burst a hole through the wall. Blood gushed through the gap, splattering across the room, the brilliant red consuming Ozzie's vision. A copper stench flooded his lungs and made him gag. It left him sick and dizzy and choking on his screams. The devils began to rip the walls apart, tearing into the wood like it was soft flesh.

"Ozzie!"

The desperate cry snapped him out of his fear. Mina was next to what had once been the kitchen table, hurriedly working with her powders. He rushed to the nearest corner, fumbling with the items Basheba had given to him. It took a moment to find a broken stick to mix the substances together. He rubbed hard. Nothing happened. Horns crushed through the wall. Smoke poured inside, blacking the air until his eyes stung. Each new assault brought more blood and smoke. He couldn't breathe.

Come on, come on, come on, he chanted endlessly. Stirring and rubbing. The trembling of his hands almost made him drop the stick.

"Come on," he begged. *Basheba got this to work with an arrowhead and a rag. You can do it!* "Please."

A soft gasp and a small plume of smoke puffed out of the mixture. He leaned closer, trying to see if he had finally succeeded. The sudden flash of fire singed his face. He reeled back, staring in shock. His scream of victory caught him off guard.

"Ozzie!" Mina snapped.

"Right."

Riding the high of his success, he picked another spot. It was easier to get the second one going. Then the third. The walls trembled around him, creaking and groaning as the house began to breathe. Warm air rushed down the chimney, bringing with it a cloud of ancient ash. The air caught the fire, feeding the flames. It barely took a second for the walls to ignite. Red-hot flames raced across the walls, growling like a living beast, building to a blinding light.

The shadows pulled back to reveal the house in its entirety—the remains of a brutal history, a singular moment in time preserved within the decrepit walls. Everything was there—a table set for dinner, toys still spread out before the fireplace, a book open and waiting for its owner to return. Nothing had been packed. Nothing had been taken. *Everyone fled for their lives.* Another roar and the room became an inferno. Ozzie staggered back, his arms lifting reflexively.

"Front door!" Ozzie called to Mina.

She nodded her agreement but waited until he was halfway there before darting forward. Finally, the devils broke through the back door, charging in to hunt them down. Ozzie ripped open the front door to come face to face with another of the creatures. He screamed and fell back a pace. Mina skidded to a stop, her eyes wide, a devil looming behind her. Ozzie tackled her to the floor, crushing the air from her lungs as the devils collided into each other above them. Blood and fire filled the house, both increasing as the building itself continued to breathe.

The house is trying to kill us!

Mina crawled out from under him and latched onto his arm, pulling hurriedly until Ozzie broke into movement. Roof beams crashed down around them, gouging holes in the walls, and bringing the ceiling down in flaming clumps. There was too much smoke to see, too much heat to breathe without scorching their lungs. But Mina's grip was sure and her stride purposeful.

Fresh air struck him like a physical blow. Greedily, he gasped, only for his lungs to protest and throw him into a coughing fit. Blinking away the tears that welled in his eyes, he looked back to see the Bell ancestral home completely engulfed in flames. He staggered along behind Mina, mystified by the sight.

Cadwyn was the first to find them. Battered, cut, and huffing, he ushered them back up the ridge. Basheba stood at the peak, Buck curled around her legs. She only had a few arrows left. By the time they joined her, Ozzie couldn't walk another step. He dropped onto his knees, panting hard, head low. The screams of the beasts had faded away to be replaced by the crackling of the homestead.

"They're gone," Cadwyn said. More of a question than an observation, as if tempting anyone to correct him.

"Is that it?" Mina asked, far more excited. "Did it work? Is it over?"

"We won't know until the next Harvest," Basheba replied breathlessly.

Ozzie slumped to the side and glanced back. His stomach dropped. "Um, guys? Should the fire be spreading that quickly?"

The flames had reached the orchard, spewing a tunnel of smoke into the air that could rival a volcanic eruption.

"That's gonna draw attention," Basheba said. A smile stretched her face. "Upside, the cult's going to be way too busy to be watching my car. Easy getaway."

The wind shifted and the fire spread out like a swelling pool, steadily sweeping out to the horizon.

"Are we trapped?" Cadwyn asked.

"We're going to have to run," Basheba said. "No, not that way. We're heading to the cliff edge. The one that overlooks the river behind the Witch's Brew."

Cadwyn frowned. "Isaac's café?"

Basheba all but danced with excitement, walking backward and giggling. "Yeah. Some airborne embers are going to find their way over there. And, if there's time, it might make it over to Whitney's bed and breakfast, too. What a series of strange events."

Mina and Ozzie shared a glance, neither one knowing what to say, both just desperate to run.

Cadwyn, however, looked rather amused. He shook his head indulgently as they set off as fast as they could go, propelled by adrenaline and the need to stay ahead of the growing inferno.

"What is it with you and fire?"

* * *

THE
WITCH
CAVE

THE BELL WITCH SERIES BOOK 3

CHAPTER 1

Slow, rhythmic kicks brought Ozzie deeper into the gloomy depths. The farther he traveled, the heavier the water became, gathering to press against his chest like a stone. His breath left him in a flurry of tumbling bubbles. They rushed past his ears, creating an almost popping noise, the only sound to break the consuming silence. Drawing another breath from his scuba tank brought a slightly plastic taste to play over his tongue. When he had first started his lessons, his instructors had insisted that it wasn't so bad. He'd get used to it. Several months in and that had yet to happen.

The freshwater pool was state of the art. Specifically designed to cater to all levels of expertise, it was an all in one facility. The central pit was little more than a large cylinder piercing the earth for 131 feet. Perfect for deep water diving practice. Random gaping holes speckled the tiled walls; each opening clearly labeled and ranked. Some simulated cave diving. Others spelunking. The deeper they were situated, the harder they became. Ozzie had heard rumors that the ones on the very bottom of the tank were used solely for Black Ops training. He wasn't keen to explore them just yet and wasn't sure he ever would be.

The pressure grew against his chest, making every breath a bit harder than the one before it. Shadows crept in around him as the temperature steadily dropped. Ozzie shivered and pushed himself deeper, conscious of the speed of his kicks, counting off his breaths. Bubbles bounced off of his goggles and rolled over the hood of his wetsuit. His ears popped as he passed by one of the observation windows.

Carefully arranged along the length of the pit, the windows served the dual purpose of providing the instructors with some observation points and letting in a bit of light to break up the gloom. Ozzie always tried to ignore them. What he was training for wasn't going to give him any measure of a reprieve. But he couldn't help himself. Ozzie never felt as cool as he did when he got to wave at some awestruck kids. He was a little disappointed to find the observation room empty.

Just as he reached the edge of the light, the cord attached to his weighted belt gave a sharp tug. He returned the gesture, ensuring his instructors that he was fine. It wasn't the first time he was doing a solo deep dive. The whole point of this was to become as proficient as possible in everything he could. He needed to know he could survive on his own and be useful in a group. This time, he wasn't going to be the weak one. He wasn't going to be the one everyone needed to save. Ozzie couldn't do anything about being the youngest, or the least experienced, but he could get better. And he would. Cadwyn, Basheba, and Mina would be able to rely on him.

They had all started their training around the same time. Not together, they were too scattered about for that. But Mina had picked the locations and Ozzie had been happy to fund it. If they were going to the Witch Caves, he was going to make sure they were all as ready as possible. As determined as they all were, he knew they each still clung to the hope that none of it would be necessary. That they could follow through on Basheba's Plan 'B'—a cave diving trip in Mexico to celebrate that the Witch was really dead.

Ozzie counted out his breaths, four seconds in, four seconds out, ensuring they remained slow and deep even as his gut twisted sharply. He rolled his shoulders and glanced past his elongated flippers, back up to the top of the pit. The combination of the tunnel entrance and the azure blue water diffused the light, turning what should have been a single glowing disc into a spiked star.

131 feet. The same as a twelve-story building, Ozzie's mind unhelpfully reminded him. His stomach knotted again. *I'm only about halfway,* he thought then cringed. *Wow, that's some bad comforting skills you have there Davis-Sewall.* The hyphened version of his name still sounded strange. He had spent his entire life as a Davis, and it seemed that everyone had been happy with the arrangement. At least, no one had been in a hurry to tell him that, biologically, Percival Sewall was his father.

It had been a lot of information to take in all at once. He had known that his 'father,' Ethan Davis, had been best friends with Percival since college. And he had known that Ethan and Ha-Yun, Ozzie's mother, had married within a few months of meeting each other. A whirlwind romance. All the stories, however, had glossed over the part where Percival had dated Ha-Yun first. And, when they had realized that they only loved each other as friends, Percival had been the one to set her up with Ethan. Apparently, it had all happened so fast that no one was sure who Ozzie's father was. Instead of a DNA test, they agreed on the setup that had carried them for fifteen years. Right up until the moment when the Witch selected him for the Harvest and proceeded to try and murder him. Without the Witch, he probably never would have known that his godfather was actually his father. Or why on earth he had been named Osgood.

He snuck one last glance at the star-shaped light above before forcing himself to re-focus on the bottom. Looking back always left him with a sense of dread that he just couldn't shake. There was something about diving to the depths that left him feeling insignificant and helpless. It was yet another emotion he needed to learn to suppress. He needed to build himself into someone stronger. Because, when they finally did enter the Witch Caves, it would be the girls facing their deepest fears, not him. When the Bell Witch had tormented him with his fears, the girls had been there to pull him through. This time, they would need him. *And I'm sure as hell not going to let them down.*

Willimina Crane was notoriously claustrophobic. What was

worse, she was what Basheba referred to as a *freezer*. She clung so much to science and logic, that encountering something that existed beyond that fried her brain. Mina always froze up. Doing that while trapped miles underground, in flooded, ghost-infested caves, wasn't an option. She was going to need someone to keep an eye on her and push her into motion.

Basheba Bell was different. Her knee-jerk reaction to fear, or any intense emotion, was to set the cause on fire. *That's probably why water terrifies her so much*, Ozzie thought. Mina's voice echoed in the back of his mind. *It's clinically referred to as thalassophobia. The fear of deep water. And I don't think it helps that her namesake drowned in a shallow pool.*

Memories of the past spring flashed through his head as he drew in another deep breath. Everything had gone wrong when they decided to head back into the woods on their own terms instead of being summoned there for the Witch's Harvest.

Ozzie couldn't help the shudder that passed through him. *The Harvest.* It took place over the last days of October when the Witch selected one from each of the four families and drew them back to the historical Bell property, where all of the murder and madness had begun almost two centuries ago. Four people against their nightmares and deepest fears, pitted against time to relock the Witch's music boxes and keep the demons contained.

It had seemed like a good idea at the time. In theory, at least. Everything had gone wrong, and he worried that they hadn't achieved anything. *Beyond interrupting a ritualistic sacrifice and setting the old Bell farmhouse on fire*, he thought. He cringed as he recalled how fast the fire had spread. They had barely gotten out of the woods before the entire thing was burning. *It was haunted anyway.*

It gutted him to think that Basheba might have faced one of her deepest fears for nothing. The Witch had tried to drown Basheba on their first trip into the woods. She had succeeded on their second. Ozzie had never felt so helpless as he had when watching Cadwyn

Winthrop drag her limp body from the raging river. The nurse had instantly begun CPR, each contraction driving Basheba's tiny frame into the soft earth. Ozzie still didn't know how she had survived all of it without internal injuries. Or how she had managed to cough up more snakes than water. But he was sure that Basheba wasn't stupid enough to believe their lie. That she hadn't died, merely hit her head.

Basheba's reaction had been vastly different from Mina's. He could almost hear Basheba nonchalantly describing herself as a *fighter* type—impulsive, violent, and unpredictable. Burning down the Bell house in the hope of stopping the curse had always been the plan. Ozzie often wondered how much of the other carnage had just been Basheba working through her emotional issues.

Two more sharp tugs on the safety line broke Ozzie from his thoughts. He returned the gesture and drifted lower still. He wasn't prepared for the rope to go taut. His startled breath ripped free from his throat in a swarm of cascading bubbles that obscured his already limited view. It stopped as abruptly as it began, leaving only stirred water and a dull ache in his stomach. He floated in the murky nothingness, forcing his breathing to slow, constantly scanning the shadows that consumed him.

The observation window just above him cut a large chunk out of the darkness. Struck with a sudden, childish fear of the dark, Ozzie itched to swim toward it. Beyond the speckled bars of light loomed the entrance star. It rippled softly in the constantly shifting water. Ozzie's face jerked to the right, his brain working too slowly for him to understand why. It clicked a second later. Movement. Not a dark figure, but something more like a moonbeam. It slipped from one patch of light to another, hidden amongst the blueish haze.

Something moved behind him, close enough to stir the water and push it against his spine. He spun around, holding his breath to keep his vision clear of bubbles, his legs and arms working slowly to keep himself suspended. The world was an empty blue abyss. He was alone. Pain sliced around his stomach when his rope snapped taut, dragging him up again. A few feet flew past in a wave of disorientation and thrashing water.

Ozzie twisted his head up, desperate for a glimpse of what had snagged on his line. In the moment of panicked distraction, a presence slipped past his spine. Before he could turn to face it, there was another sharp jerk. He scrambled at the latch on his belt, the thick rubber of his gloves forcing him to fumble with the release. The water darkened around him in the wake of a growing shadow. He paused, looked up, and choked on a scream.

An enormous great white shark glided down toward him. Silent. Grinning. In his shock, Ozzie struggled to make sense of the animal's deformity. The tapered tip of its nose was aimed into the depths as it passed him, sinking fast with lazy swipes of its tail. Upside down, the contours of its cavernous mouth and powerful body created the impression of a grinning demonic face—all exposed teeth and laughing eyes. Frozen in horror, Ozzie could only watch as the shadowy second face winked at him.

Laughter exploded around him. Childish and shrill. Churning through the encasing liquid as if it was air. *The Witch.* Ozzie began to tremble. *It can't be. It's too soon!* All of his panicked self-assurances were in vain. The shark was right there before him as proof of the Bell Witch's power. *Burning the place didn't work. The Harvest is happening. I'm going to get a music box.* Dread consumed him even while the rest of his brain tried to argue. Something solid slammed against his back, jolting him forward, almost forcing him into the pointed end of a shark's tail.

He glanced over his shoulder to see another grinning face floating past him. *It touched me!* He screamed the words within his skull as his throat squeezed tight. *It's not an illusion; it's real, it touched me!*

The disembodied laughter continued as light and shadow played across the shark's face. The laughter took on an edge of sadistic pleasure as Ozzie's fear cut down to his bones. Blood surged past his ears as his heartbeat quickened, the rush distorting the laughter.

The safety protocol his instructors had hammered into him took over. He grasped his safety cord and tugged once. Instantly, his instructors began to pull him toward the surface, drawing him away from the sharks. The movement caught their attention, and the once mindlessly drifting sharks rolled their faces to track him. As one, they gave chase.

Hyperventilating on his artificial air, he tore his eyes from his pursuers to see where he was going. The rim of his goggles and the flurry of bubbles obscured his view of the darkened and squirming shadows. He swiped one hand through the cluster, dispersing it enough for him to see what he was heading toward.

It was a frenzy of sharks. Each one large and deformed, sweeping back and forth at unnatural angles, ghostly faces in the gloom. As he hurtled toward them, their numbers grew to blot out the light. Ozzie's rubber-clad fingers scraped over the buckle. He jabbed and pushed, unable to work the release.

Air fled from his lungs in a rush as he hit the latch in frustration, driving it into his stomach. Finally, the lock gave way. The rope slipped through the gap and proceeded up without him, flapping now that it had nothing to hold it down. One of the sharks darted past him to hunt down the trailing end, jaws wide and monstrous face giddy with joy. The laughing became deafening, a hellish choir that assaulted his ears like a thousand icepicks. Ozzie longed to grasp the sides of his skull but forced his arms out, bringing himself to a suspended stop. He searched for the second shark.

It didn't take long to spot the spectral underbelly of the great white shark playing through the azure haze. It emerged almost lazily to come alongside him. Like the others, it moved unnaturally. Tail up, nose down, drifting like debris rather than a living creature. Ozzie shivered at the sight before he willfully locked every joint to keep himself perfectly still. His lithe body tried to float up, only to be hindered by his weighted diving belt. The contrast left him drifting as the white face filled his view.

Muscles twitched under the alabaster skin to make the laughing eyes move. They shifted blindly from side to side as it inched closer, a noiseless creature in a sea of mockery. Hot tears pricked Ozzie's eyes as his lungs squeezed. He risked a quick, hard swallow, hoping to keep down the pitiful sobs that longed to break free. The demonic face alone was the same size as him. And that was dwarfed by the sheer size of the beast. Ozzie couldn't convince himself that he had any chance of winning a physical fight. *It's going to eat me alive.*

He clenched his jaw to the point of pain, barely able to keep the images of being ripped apart from his mind's eye. All around him, the murky light began to strobe. Reflexes almost had him looking up. But the slightest jerk was enough to gain the interest of the shark. It floated closer still, unseeing eyes rapidly thrashing as it searched for him. Ozzie stilled. It wasn't enough this time. Not while it was close enough to take interest with the trailing bubbles of Ozzie's breath.

The shark lingered within a few inches of him, tail slowly swiping to keep it unnaturally suspended. Eyes twitching and teeth bared. Ozzie filled his lungs and held his breath. They remained there, staring at each other as the water clouded and darkened around them, each waiting for the inevitable. Ozzie's lungs pressed against his ribs, fluttering with the increasing desire to breathe. *Think!* Despite his desperate command, his mind remained blank. *What would Cadwyn do?* Cadwyn Winthrop was the level-headed one. Calm and composed with a quiet self-assurance that Ozzie could never master. *What would Cadwyn do?*

Ozzie stretched his mind, startled to find an idea pressing against the edges of his awareness. Afraid of drawing attention, he lowered his arm at an excruciatingly slow pace, his fingers angling for the latch of his weighted belt. The monstrous shadow eyes twitched rapidly, aware of movement but not certain of its source. Ozzie was sure his heartbeat would shatter his ribs when he began to map out the belt buckle with his gloved fingertips. His whole body yearned for air but he forced himself to take his time. *Think it through. Be sure before you move. Like how Cadwyn would do it.* It was impossible to hear the click, but he felt the latch give way and the belt drop. It slipped down his legs before spiraling into the pit, swirling the water as it went.

With one ferocious flick of its colossal tail, the shark shot down after it. Ozzie didn't have time to get out of the way. The tail crashed into him. A painful blow that sent him careening into the tiled wall. Transfixed on its prey, the shark either didn't notice or didn't care. Blinking the lights from his eyes, Ozzie looked down to see that the shark hadn't simply swallowed the belt. It had sunk its teeth in and was savagely whipping its head about. Sand and metal spewed into the water, the motion drawing down the others.

Clinging to the wall, Ozzie took a few deep breaths, praying to escape the interest of the mass migration. He glanced up. It didn't matter how many of the monsters came down to fight over the scraps, there were still more, their clustered bodies steadily choking off the light, oozing out to fill the tank. *Until there's nowhere left to hide.*

Ozzie squeezed his eyes shut, forcing himself to focus, to breathe. *What would Cadwyn do?* This time, he had no answer. Desperately, his mind whirled. *What would Basheba do?* Lacking both her knife and her barbaric ferocity, there was little he could do to mimic Basheba Bell. *What would Mina do?*

His thoughts took on Willimina Crane's voice as they weaved through the laughter, repeating a phrase she often unknowingly rambled to herself while lost in thought. *Observation. Hypothesis. Experiment.* His body trembled as he crowded harder against the wall. *They're fast. But they're huge.* Ozzie snapped his eyes open. *The spelunking tunnels.* Some of the paths were barely wide enough for him to squeeze through, and they were built of unrelenting concrete and metal. *If I can get to those, they won't be able to follow.*

Glancing around, he spotted the nearest entrance on the opposite wall. It was separated from him by only a few dozen feet of shark-infested water.

His first thought was to keep to the pit wall and work his way around, slow and steady. Before he could move, however, he discovered that option was no longer viable. Blood blossomed through the blue water. The shark that had taken his belt had drawn too much attention. The others swarmed, taking a bit of flesh each time they glided past it. Ozzie didn't see the strikes. His focus was on the blood.

His head spun as he watched it seep out into the dark water, a stain that spread all the faster as the feeding frenzy took over. Ozzie plastered himself against the wall. Near hyperventilating, his eyes stretched painfully wide, he watched the impossibly vibrant red spread out to consume the world around him. *It's a trick!* Whatever logic he could gather together in his panic couldn't compete with what his senses were telling him. He still saw it. Thick, red, almost incandescent blood coiled through the black water. His oxygen tank whirled and thumped in protest. The polluted liquid pushed against him and he swore he could smell it. Taste it. It was there even when he closed his eyes. Blood. Crimson and warm. *It's not real! It can't be real!* The laughter seemed to rise and fall as it spiraled around him, a distorted warning that he was close to passing out.

Don't, he pleaded with himself. *It's only blood—fake blood. It's all just a trick. I can do this.* He forced down one deep breath. The water grew warmer against his skin. A coppery tang replaced the tinge of plastic that hovered on the compressed air. *Hemophobia*, Mina had called it. *A fear of blood.* Placing a scientific name against his childhood fear helped a little. Not a lot. But he was almost able to see it as something to be studied rather than felt. Something he might be able to control.

Bile burned at the back of his throat as he began to gag. Before he could throw up the limited contents of his stomach, the water thrashed hard, creating a compression wave that battered him along the curved wall. Groaning in pain, he forced his eyes back open just in time to see a half-eaten monster flopping against the wall beside him. The ceramic tiles chipped with every strike. Another surged upon it, shredding it apart to gorge itself. The face continued to laugh as it was obliterated.

The water changed as he watched. It wasn't just that it was tainted by the blood. It became blood. And all the creatures within it were reduced to little more than shifting shadows. Chunks of flesh emerged to bob and prod at his body. *Go!* Cadwyn had shouted the words to him more than once. And now, just like then, Ozzie darted forward to obey. There was no need to hide his movements anymore.

The feeding frenzy had changed the once placid water into an overlapping series of undertows. Each one grabbed at him, carrying him up or dragging him down. Kicking as hard as he could, his arms up to shield his face, Ozzie battled against it. His heart sputtered each time something emerged toward him. Sharks swept past, sending him spiraling in their wake. Raw flesh seemed drawn to him. It slowed him down as he struggled against the thickening blood.

He never saw what hit him. Just felt the searing pain as teeth slashed across his side, cutting through the thick material of his wetsuit to open his skin. The pain forced him to curl in on himself and clutch his side. Focusing everything he had on the sole task of getting to the other side, he forced himself to keep going.

The wall emerged abruptly from the abyss. He crashed into it, swimming too fast for his raised arms to stop his head from smacking against the tiles. Pain exploded as his goggles were driven into his face. Lights danced across his eyes, breaking up the blanket of red. The impact created a fine crack in the tough plastic and the blood began to seep through it. Ozzie retched painfully, barely stifling his urge to vomit as the warm liquid welled against his skin. He squeezed his eyes shut in a desperate attempt to spare himself the sight.

With trembling hands, he battered at the wall, blindly searching for the tunnel opening. The wound on his side pulsated in time with his rapid heartbeat. The churning water shoved him in every direction. But it was the laughter that brought him to the edge of madness. All he could do was keep moving forward, his hands tapping the way until he found nothing but empty water.

The opening! He surged toward it, slithering through the hole and mapping the innards by touch. *I know this tunnel.* The realization left him breathlessly giddy. It wasn't an easy trail, but it led to an opening. He'd made the journey dozens of times. Enough that he knew bits and pieces even without sight.

Jagged obstacles rose to almost block the path, forcing him to squirm his way into smaller and smaller tunnels. The promise of air drove him on even as he was forced to contort himself painfully to weave through the gaps. The ceiling scraped against his tank while the flooring prodded at the wound on his stomach. No matter how far he traveled, the chaos of laughter and rioting beasts remained right behind him. The tumbling water made everything harder as it threw him against the peaks.

Suddenly, the walls began to tremble, the vibrations working against his gloved fingertips and pressing against him when the passage was narrow. Cold sweat pooled under his wetsuit when he realized that they weren't just fine tremors. They were impacts. *They're trying to follow.*

Large fissures snaked through the concrete, felt more than seen, as tiles broke free and rained down upon him. He surged forward through a gap but, with a sharp crack, he was held back. He forced himself to open his eyes to see what the problem was. *The tank,* he realized after several failed attempts. *The tank's too big!* In his desperation, he had forgotten the main use of this particular trail—to teach people emergency rescue situations. Meaning that those who came this way used a handheld *Scorkl.*

How much air do they hold? He struggled to remember as the tunnel crumbled around him. *Ten minutes? How long does it take to get down here? How long can I hold my breath?* Debris toppled from the crimson muck to smack against him. Ozzie yanked at the straps of his scuba tank, preferring to drown rather than be eaten alive.

The wall beside him exploded into a bloody storm of ghostly laughing faces, fractured ceramics, and teeth. Ozzie ripped the tank free and, after dragging in one last breath, disconnected the tubes and opened the valve. It shot off in a flurry of bubbles, bouncing off of unseen obstacles and, hopefully, buying him some time. He wiggled into the small gap as fast as he could, his lungs already aching.

Blood half-filled his goggles and sloshed into his eyes with every motion. He forced his eyes to stay open as he navigated the twists and turns. Desperate for even a hint of guidance. Starved for air, his body began to tremble violently and his veins felt like they were on fire. His heartbeat struck his insides like the blows of a hammer.

Keep going. It's just up here. Keep going. His stomach rolled like the ocean in a storm. He bit his lips, terrified he would lose what little air he had if he gagged. Shrieking giggles hovered around him, the only constant in the underwater maze. A fog filled his mind. The muscles of his neck squeezed and fluttered in useless attempts to get him to breathe. *You can do this.* He put everything he had into making his mental voice stronger than he felt. *You don't have a choice.*

He surged forward to find a wall blocking his path. Desperately, he pounded against the tiles, searching for somewhere to go. The walls were solid, the floor complete and undisturbed. His eyes rolled back in his head as his body thrashed with renewed force. Hot blood filled his goggles to blur his vision. Even as the last of his strength sapped away, his body fought harder, pushing against his conscious decision not to breathe. Frantic, he swung an arm up, feeling the change of sensation a heartbeat later. *Air!* His fist had reached air. A part of his brain could only stammer that it had to be a cruel trick, but he couldn't hold back, couldn't keep himself from barreling forward.

Planting his flippered feet against the ground, he leaped up, expecting the pain of crashing once more into unrelenting walls. The air that greeted him didn't feel real. For one dizzy moment, he was sure that it was just another of the Witch's games, a cruel trick to get him to take the water into his lungs. Then he blinked, and the world shifted. Gone was any sign of the monsters, the laughter, the blood. He was bobbing in the shallow pool at the end of the spelunking tunnels. The walls echoed back the dripping water that fell from him as he stood up. It did little to cover the ringing in his ears in the sudden silence. He jumped when the doors flung open and his trainer sprinted inside, a few coworkers following in his wake.

"What were you thinking? Are you okay? Why didn't you just come up?"

Ozzie blinked owlishly. Still dizzy, he couldn't pry the stream of words apart into separate questions. They all just blended into a garbled mess. And he didn't know how to answer. Gulping air, he numbly pulled his goggles off. A deep crack connected the right side of the lens with the left. Hands descended upon the cut in Ozzie's side and gripped tight.

"He's bleeding."

They helped him out of the water before he could reel away from the agonizing touch. *It really cut me.* Ozzie stared at the open wound. *But how? How did she do it? What about the monsters? Were they real?* A light touch to his knee made him jump and he looked up to meet his trainer's gaze. "Ozzie, what happened?"

"Did you see anything in the tank with me?"

"What? No. You hired out the entire area, remember?"

Ozzie could only blink slowly, his insides swirling.

"Have you found a music box? It's a cube. Wood and gold. It would probably show up where it couldn't possibly be?"

The instructor couldn't keep the frustration and confusion from his face. "Ozzie, there's no box. Now, what happened?"

Ozzie easily avoided the question by abruptly vomiting on the man.

CHAPTER 2

Willimina Crane pulled her dark hair into a tight ponytail as they entered the parking lot. The ancient building loomed up above them, its shadows deep and cold, its architecture looking completely out of place around the rundown hotels and cheap restaurants. Ava pulled the car into one of the open parking spaces and turned off the engine. For a moment, the girls simply sat there, leaning forward to stare up at the building.

"So, this is the Leviathan," Ava mumbled.

"It's bigger than I thought it would be." Mina looked at her watch. "We better hurry up or we'll miss the tour. Okay, what is it?"

"Huh?"

"It's been a five-hour drive from Penn State. I've had plenty of time to notice the strange looks you've been giving me."

"Why do you have to be so specific?" Ava said. "It's weird. Just say you've had plenty of time."

"Fine. You've had plenty of time to get to the point. Now we're under a time constraint so can we speed this along?"

After eyeing her carefully for a long moment, Ava slipped out of the car, leaving Mina to follow. The conversation was put on hold for a moment as they checked the contents of their backpacks.

"You have the EMF reader, right?" Mina asked.

Her friend waved the device in the air before putting it in the bag again.

"I have the salt," Mina assured before noticing the way her childhood friend looked at the car.

"I can't believe you just bought this thing," Ava chuckled.

"I couldn't find a rental company that did business with anyone under twenty-five," she mumbled.

"So you *bought* it."

"Ozzie bought it," Mina corrected. "I'm going to sell it when we head back and give him the money."

"Is this the same Ozzie who bought you a house?"

Mina took a deep breath. *We've been over this.* "He didn't buy me a house. I'm just the live-in housekeeper."

"But they don't live in the house?"

"Mrs. Davis is a huge baseball fan. She even follows college games. So, they only need the house during the season."

"And, for the rest of the year, you live rent-free in a gorgeous three-story stone house. That's a pretty great deal."

"They've been very generous with me," Mina smiled. "I would have been homeless if it wasn't for them."

"Because your cousin kicked you out?"

Mina bristled. "Are we finally approaching the topic?"

Ava shrugged one shoulder. "How long have we known each other, Mina? Late October to early November has always been your 'family time.' Every year. No exceptions."

Pulling her backpack onto her shoulder, Mina slammed the door shut and started walking. It didn't take long for Ava to catch up.

"Three weeks ago, you were all set to head home to California. Now we're in Virginia on a ghost hunt. I think it's kind of natural for me to have a few questions, don't you?"

"The Leviathan is supposed to be one of the most haunted buildings in America. Well, one of the ones that won't be overrun by tourists. It's our best chance for an encounter."

"True, but not what I was asking."

"I need a subject to test my theory," Mina continued as they took the stairs to the grand front entrance. "This place is probably our best shot of finding one without interference."

"Mina," Ava said in a sing-song voice. "You're avoiding the

topic."

Standing in the threshold, she whirled to face Ava. "I've been exiled."

Ava almost tripped over her own feet. "Exiled? Do people still do that?"

"My dad does. He made it clear that I'm not to contact any relatives or attend family functions without his express permission."

"That's insane."

Mina swung her arms out in a helpless shrug. "It is what it is."

"But your dad adores you."

"Yeah, well," Mina squirmed again, not sure how to explain what had happened. "I never told you that my family is cursed, have I?"

Watching her friend's eyes widen, Mina realized that she couldn't go through with it. Some things just had to stay within the families.

"Genetically, I mean," she rushed to add. "It's this rare disorder that follows our bloodline. Onset is swift and unpredictable. There's no cure."

"Oh my God, Mina. Why didn't you ever tell me?"

"I never believed it." *I thought the Bell Witch was just legend and superstition.* "There were stories, of course. But they were watered down into fairy tales. Nothing I took seriously. It's a long-standing family tradition to keep all the gory details from the uninfected. Only the infected are fully informed. And, if they survive their temporary flare-up, they're encouraged to keep all the details to themselves."

"That's insane," Ava whispered, clearly not sure how to respond.

Having gone this far, Mina found herself struck with the urge to continue. "A year ago, I was diagnosed."

Ava dragged her into a crushing hug before Mina realized what was happening.

"It's okay, Ava. I got through it. I'm all right."

Memories of the Harvest, of her return, flashed across her mind.

She squeezed her eyes shut, trying to block it all out. Ava pulled back abruptly and grasped Mina by her shoulders. This close, it was hard for Mina to hide everything that threatened to show on her face. *It's over. I'm okay.*

"Are you sure you're fine?" Ava asked.

She forced a smiled. "Yeah. The worst of the symptoms only last a few days. And there's every chance that I'll never have another attack."

If I'm not selected, someone else will be. Her gut knotted at the thought. Katrina Hamilton, the Bell Witch, wasn't above going after children or the elderly. *If not me, it could be great-grandpa. Or baby Elizabeth.* She twisted her hand in the strap of her backpack, trying not to imagine the infant receiving a music box.

"What is this disease called? What does it do?" Ava asked.

"I'd prefer not to get into it right now."

"Right, okay." Ava gave her shoulders a reassuring rub. "Wait. Why is your dad mad about this?"

"Because I told the kids," Mina said.

"You spilled the secrets?"

"To every family member who would listen. Knowing what's waiting for them might not be pleasant, but it's the truth. Ignorance doesn't help anyone. Having an understanding of the facts is the only thing that's going to save us." She trailed off as she realized she was on the verge of ranting, months of frustration boiling under her skin.

"And your dad reacted badly?" Ava pushed gently.

"Both of my parents did. Essentially, they told me to look pretty and keep my mouth shut, or don't come home." Tears pricked at the back of her eyes and she blinked rapidly to force them back. "I couldn't do it. Isn't that the whole point of family? A gentle hand and brutal honesty?"

"I guess that's one way to put it," Ava said with a weak smile.

Mina swallowed thickly and clutched her conviction. "Omitting the truth is as good as being complicit. I'd rather die than help

Katrina."

"Who's Katrina?"

Huffing a laugh, Mina shook her head. "Just the name of the disease."

Ava pouted slightly. "Is this a disease I should be concerned about? Or are we talking about something really obscure? I want to know if further questioning will bring out your inner disease researcher."

"Pathologist?" Mina offered, biting back a smile at her friend's teasing. "I think the word you're looking for is 'pathologist.'"

"Whatever. I did bio in high school, that was enough for me," Ava dismissed.

Concern still lingered in Ava's eyes as Mina shook her head.

"It's ridiculously obscure," Mina assured. "At most, only four people die of Katrina a year. I've just taken an interest in it lately. You know, research and prevention. Raising awareness. My parents think I should leave it well enough alone."

"I'll listen." Knocking Mina with her elbow, Ava added, "So long as there's no slide show presentation."

"Don't worry about it. I'll let you know if it leads to anything." She beamed at her friend. "Now, let's go hunt some ghosts."

"Are you sure?"

"I could use the distraction." She stalked into the building, checking her watch again. "Now we're going to be late."

"Don't even try it. I know you set your watch fifteen minutes early. We'll be there just in time."

"Ava, for you, 'just in time' is a kind way of saying late."

"What is wrong with you?" Ava chuckled.

Their banter stopped when they entered the main foyer. Their footsteps echoed off the marble walls and rolled up to the lofty ceiling. Mina craned her head back to examine the elaborate chandeliers. The suspended crystals cast small rainbows amongst the clusters. Before them, a small staircase lined with a brilliant blue carpet split in two. The ends then continued in opposite directions to bracket the carved arches and pillars that lined the balconies.

"Wow," Ava said, the word ending in a slight giggle. "Not what I was expecting."

Mina turned in a slow circle as they crossed the foyer. "This place is incredible."

"Thank you."

Both girls jumped at the sudden addition. A man emerged from the area behind the stairs, a warm smile on his face and his hands held up in surrender.

"Sorry, didn't mean to startle you. I'm not a ghost, promise." his brisk chuckle gave way to a professional appraisal of each girl. "I'm Stephen, the tour guide for the night. I'm guessing one of you is Willimina Crane?"

Mina strode forward to meet the man. Shaking his hand, she made the introductions and apologized for being late.

"No, you're right on time," Stephen said.

Mina ignored Ava's widening grin.

"We're going to start on the lower floor," he said. "I'll get you to sign in and then we can get started. You're the last of the group to arrive."

Once Stephen walked ahead to lead the way, Mina spun on her heel, throwing a smug smile in Ava's direction. Ava's middle finger flew up in response. Soon enough, everything was in order and they passed under the staircase on the right.

"So, you guys are ghost hunters?" Stephen asked.

"Every girl needs a hobby," Ava replied.

"It's intellectual curiosity," Mina said.

And survival. Since childhood, Mina had fought to free her family of the superstitions that held them hostage. Now she knew better. *The only way to save them is to kill a ghost.* For nearly two hundred years, the four families had been playthings for the Bell Witch. It seemed almost impossible that it could ever change but, in the coming hours, she'd learn if they had been successful in their attempt. *First attempt,* Mina corrected herself. *We're better prepared this time. And we'll be stronger the time after that.* However long it took, this was a fight neither she nor Katrina Hamilton was about to walk away from.

"Ah. So, what do you do when you're not indulging your curiosity?"

"I'm working in a hotel at Niagara Falls," Ava said. Nudging Mina with her elbow, she continued, "And Mina here is going to Pennsylvania State. She's going to be a lawyer. Or is that doctor? Oh, no, FBI agent."

Why? Mina mouthed the word to her friend with a mixture of embarrassment and annoyance.

"Wow," Stephen laughed. "Someone's an overachiever."

"And we're so proud of her for it," Ava declared, stooping a little to loop an arm around Mina's shoulders. "Oh, don't be so sour. It's our whole friendship dynamic to live vicariously through each other."

Mina arched an eyebrow.

"I get to pretend I have some direction in my life. And you pretend that you're not an obsessive bore."

They entered a hallway drenched in royal blue. The ceiling, walls, and all the doors that lined it were the same deep shade. Only the rivulets of gold that weaved through the carpet added some deviation. The color saturation made it nearly impossible to tell the true length of the corridor. Stephen paused and turned a sly smile onto the girls.

"That's a lot of hard sciences. You're not here just to laugh at the believers, are you?"

"No, of course not," Ava said.

"It's fine if you're a skeptic," Stephen said, lifting his hands. "We've just had some trouble in the past with hardliners on either side of the fence ruining it for everyone else. I have to ask."

"We're here to try and catch sight of a ghost," Ava assured.

"So, you believe in the supernatural?"

"No," Mina said, continuing when they both turned to her with questioning looks. "The human body works the same way now as it did when we were boring holes in the skull to release demons. Just because ghosts are beyond our *current* scientific understanding doesn't mean that they're mystical. It just means that we haven't figured it out yet."

An indulgent smile curled Ava's lips even as she rolled her eyes. "Remember how you weren't going to suck the fun out of this?"

Mina's brow furrowed. "The scientific method is fun."

"Right. Well," Stephen cleared his throat. "Let's get this tour going, shall we?"

They walked the rest of the way in somewhat awkward silence. Passing through huge double doors, they entered the main hall. Rows of blue velvet seats stretched out on either side to create an undulating sea. The six layers of balconies were edged with rippling gold and lined with curtains like waterfalls. Paint, silver, and glass worked together to create the illusion of water across the dome ceiling.

"I feel like I'm underwater," Ava whispered to Mina.

She nodded her agreement. They took a narrow path around the orchestra pit to join everyone else on stage. With the same swift professionalism, Stephen made the introductions and got the tour going.

"Welcome to the Leviathan. A place of music, mystery, and murder." He spread his arms out wide to bring their attention to the incredible building around them. "Fun fact, its construction was the result of a bet. In 1901, Duke Edmund Armitage became infatuated with an opera singer and, after he refused to take 'no' for an answer, they struck a wager. If he could present her with a composition she was incapable of singing, she'd marry him. If she could master it, however, he'd build her an opera house."

Mina scanned the endless pattern of hard walls and darkened

balconies. *It looks like a beehive.* Mina's skin went cold. The comparison lingered in her mind, dredging up carefully avoided memories of how Katrina had used her deepest fear against her.

"As you can see, she won," Stephen continued. "Although, many believed she had some outside help. Rumors had been swirling for years that the diva was tangled up in witchcraft."

Murmurs went through the group, and Stephen waited for silence once more before continuing, "People believed this building was cursed. It didn't help that our diva insisted on being the only one to know the floorplan in its entirety. There's nothing like hidden rooms and hallways to nowhere to make a person think something's not quite right. Just last week we found a wardrobe hidden away within a marble pillar. So, keep an eye out and don't venture too far from the group." He dipped his voice to something mysterious but playful. "The Leviathan's got a long history of unexplained disappearances and deadly accidents after all."

A few giggles drifted up from the group at the comment; he proceeded to explain how the building had been saved from disrepair by a historical preservation society and what it was currently used for. It all faded into background noise as Mina spotted the giant, gilded octopus that sat above the main entrance. Its tentacles spread out along the walls, circled the booth above it, and held aloft a sapphire-studded crown. Something clicked within her head as she stared at the silver-plated eyes.

"What's that?" she asked.

"The Leviathan was built with an Italian influence," Stephen said. "Traditionally, that'll be the royal booth."

"I meant the octopus."

"Oh, that was the diva's influence," he grinned. "She was obsessed with the kraken, so decided to put one on the booth. Because, as she put it, 'few are my equal and none are my superior.'"

It can't be. It just can't. "What was her name?"

"Bernadette," Stephen said. "Bernadette Allaway."

"Are you kidding me!" The words were out before she could stop them.

Clamping her mouth tight, she waved an awkward apology and fixed her gaze on the floor. *Basheba's ancestor.* The small blonde had told her more than once that people focused too much on the Bell line, completely forgetting that her mother's family had a history, too. *Is this what she meant?*

Glancing around the room, she felt a new sense of dread. The décor didn't scream Basheba. She was all fire and rage and raw emotion. This place was as deep and cool as the ocean floor. But there was the kraken symbol, the name, and the slightly threatening undercurrent that accompanied Basheba's presence. The building didn't look like her, but it *felt* like her. *What are the odds of having both sides of your family entangled with ghosts?* The thought had barely formed when she jolted.

"Rumors of witchcraft," Mina whispered, her insides turning to ice. "Basheba's ancestor was a witch?"

CHAPTER 3

I should call Cadwyn. Mina had kept the older man's number on speed dial since her close encounter with Basheba's more violent nature a few months ago. Time hadn't diminished the chill that worked down Mina's spine whenever she thought about it.

She never hesitates, Mina thought. The petite blonde would just as quickly try to murder someone as she would die to protect them. Mina had experienced it firsthand and she still didn't know how to deal with the implications. It would be easier if she could believe the Bell woman was a sociopath.

She fits some of it. The thought was instantly countered by the more logical part of her mind. *Everyone does to some extent. Superficially charming, manipulative, selfish.* Mina gathered up the end of her ponytail and began to tap her hair against her bottom lip. *She's also compulsive,* she argued with herself. *Driven by a deep-seated rage and has only a rudimentary understanding of remorse and empathy. Call Cadwyn.*

Her free hand went for her front pocket, feeling the solid weight of her cell phone. *She doesn't lack empathy,* her mind groused at itself. *She's obsessed with her dog and is utterly devoted to her dead relatives. Her emotions aren't shallow or fake. They rule her.*

"Which would make her all the more dangerous if she is a witch," Mina mumbled around her hair.

The urge to call Cadwyn struck her again. Always the voice of reason, Cadwyn had the rare skill of talking Basheba back from her impulses. Mina had witnessed it, she owed her life to it, but she wasn't certain how deep that bond went or how much sway the man actually had over her. *Or how much she has over him.*

The internal debate threatened to take a new turn—contemplating just how far Cadwyn would go to support a friend. *He stayed with his possessed brother, alone, for a whole year, and then put him out of his misery when all hope was lost.* Memories of the demon that had stood outside their door flitted across her mind. *It remembered Cadwyn by name. If he went that far for his brother, would it be much of an effort to ignore Basheba's activities?* Mina stilled, shame washing over her as she berated herself for such unfounded leaps of logic. *Stop making up paranoid 'what ifs!'*

"Observation and hypothesis don't equal evidence," Mina whispered to herself.

"Did you say something?" Ava asked.

Mina barely registered the question and replied with a quick shake of her head. Used to her overthinking by now, Ava didn't push the issue and wandered across Mina's peripheral vision.

Stephen had outfitted the tour group with Electro-Magnetic Frequency readers and set them off to explore the ground floor. Most of them had quickly lost interest in the stage. Leaving it for either the seats or slipping behind the painted backdrop. It gave Mina a certain degree of silence to think. She quickly tried to set her scattered thoughts into some kind of order.

Basheba has survived the Harvest twice. She's been in the body recovery groups since she was a child. She frowned. *Hypothetically, being a witch might give her some degree of protection in those situations. It's nowhere near conclusive, though.* Basheba's knowledge of plant life spoke more to her survivalist skills. And the blonde didn't need to be using her family's wedding rings as talismans to explain her protectiveness of them. *Is there even any evidence of her being evil?* A chill ran down her spine as one memory slammed into the forefront of her mind—being chased through the woods by the cult. A man held a knife to Basheba's throat. In return, Basheba had ripped his throat out with her teeth. *Long pig,* Mina recalled Basheba boast. *Her mother had taught her how to hunt long pig.*

"People," she whispered along. "Her mother trained her to be a murderer."

It was the first time she had voiced the haunting thought out loud. Her brain went silent in response. *Have you ever seen Basheba do anything that even looks like witchcraft?* Mina contemplated the self-asked question, examining each of her memories in turn.

"I've never seen her do a ritual."

"Huh?" Ava's question jerked Mina from her thoughts.

She moved her hair away from her mouth. "Sorry?"

"You're talking to yourself again."

"I don't talk to myself."

"Yeah, you do. To a ridiculous degree," Ava dismissed. "So, what's this about a ritual?"

"I didn't—"

"Okay, shut up before I get insulted," Ava cut in. "We're finally at the Leviathan and you're too busy obsessing to focus on the awesome. So, level with me. What's on your mind?"

"It's nothing. I figured it out, anyway." Mina forced an apologetic smile and added in a playful tone, "Conclusion: no evidence of witchcraft."

Ava rolled her eyes at the attempted joke and motioned her closer with a jerk of her head. They started to pace the stage, watching the little dial of their EMF reader flicker wildly within the normal range.

"How would you even know?" Ava asked abruptly.

Mina glanced up, "What're you talking about?"

"Well, think about it. Are you a witch?"

"No."

"Then how would you know what *real* witchcraft looks like?" Ava asked. "All you've got to go on are paranoid people's hearsay and horror movies *based* on paranoid people's hearsay. Wicca and voodoo are religions, not just magic, so you can't ask them. And I suppose you can't ask Satanists for similar reasons."

"So, your question is: how can someone identify witchcraft when they have no idea what real witchcraft looks like?"

"Exactly."

The small amount of comfort Mina had managed to create for herself shattered with the thought.

"Oh, no. Not your obsessive face again," Ava sighed. "Stay with me, Mina. You don't have to worry about it. Magic isn't real."

"But ghosts are?" Mina challenged with an arched eyebrow.

"Hey, you're the one who made the argument for it. I can wrap my head around them existing. But mixing a few different herbs together and saying a secret phrase to completely alter reality? That's a little far-fetched."

I've seen a witch. I've touched monsters. It's all real. The words got lost in Mina's throat. Instead, she forced a smile.

"Right. Okay, let's focus," Ava declared. "I want to see a ghost."

After pacing the stage once more, Ava decided to wander around the side curtains. Mina followed at a slower pace. Before she could slip behind the hanging side curtains, a sudden scream shattered the calm like a crack of lightning. She whipped around to look over the ocean of seats.

The stage lights glared, scattering blinding balls of fire across her vision. Beneath it, people still shuffled through the seats, a few of them looking around to try and track down the source of the scream. *It's the acoustics*, she realized. It made all the noises echo until it was impossible to tell where it had originated from.

She held her breath, tension growing thick in her stomach, her eyes searching every inch of the building that she could see. A second later, a woman excitedly waved her husband over, the podgy man hurrying to comply. Mina rubbed her forehead as her shoulders slumped. *I'm getting paranoid.* As she turned to leave, her gaze swept higher, slipping over the royal box. An ebony silhouette stood embossed upon the dim glow from the hallway beyond it. Ice cracked through her veins. An instinctual warning that something wasn't right.

"Mina?" Ava whispered excitedly. "Have you found something?"

Fixated on the specter, Mina began to move. She was jarred out of her thoughts when she suddenly lost her balance. Throwing her arms out, she looked down to find her toes had inched over the edge of the stage. She teetered on the verge of toppling into the orchestra pit.

"Mina!" Ava's footsteps hurried toward her.

Somehow managing to not fall, she staggered back a step and twisted around to reply to her friend. A disembodied face lunged toward her, screaming, rotten, and distorted. Pain exploded across her face as it crunched into her and she fell. It was a short, gut-wrenching drop. The impact drove the air from her lungs and left her gasping in pain.

"Mina?" Ava called.

She could only groan in response.

"Stephen!" Ava yelled. "Mina fell!"

Footsteps thundered closer, the vibrations echoing through the floorboards.

"I'm all right."

Pain sliced through her as she pushed herself into a sitting position. She grabbed her stomach, gasping breathlessly.

On all fours, Ava peered down over the rim of the drop-off. "Are you sure? That looked like it hurt."

"I'm sure."

"Sure enough that I should still worry? Or sure enough that I can start calling you an idiot?"

Mina braced her forearms on her knees. "Is there a third option?"

"What happened?" Stephen asked as he appeared along with a few of the other guests.

The pain was starting to ebb away, leaving her to feel the full force of her embarrassment.

"Did you see something?" someone asked with eager anticipation.

Debating if she should be honest or not, Mina tipped her face up, fake smile in place. With a sudden snap, the ground dropped out from under her. Her stomach lurched, cool air whipped at her skin, and the light around her rapidly faded. Dust exploded around her as her back struck a forgiving surface. It bowed under her weight with a flapping hiss. The first breath she managed to choke down was thick with grime. Dust coated her throat, making her choke and sputter. She curled into a tight ball while the landing pad deflated around her. In a short time, the hard floor settled against her hip, and she became aware of the voices calling to her.

"I'm all right!" The reassurance was past Mina's lips before she thought to check.

Bloody nose. Growing bruises. Nothing's broken. The good luck almost made her laugh. Sitting up, she checked her surroundings. The complete darkness of the room was disturbed only by the clear square of light seeping through the trap door. *Too high to climb out,* Mina thought as she studied it. *How far did I fall?*

"You look so tiny," Ava called down. "How did you survive that?"

Mina shrugged. "An inflatable landing pad, I think. I can't really see it, but it seems to work like the ones the fire departments use, only older."

"A what?" Impressed against the light, Mina watched her friend turn on Stephen. "Is this a prank?"

"What? No!"

"Why the hell would you have a functional landing pad down there?" Ava demanded.

"Opera stages are all rigged with trap doors. It's how they do their practical effects—"

"She fell from an orchestra pit!"

Mina groped through the shadows until she was able to find her backpack. It wasn't hard to find her pull-up LED lantern amongst the items of her ghost hunting kit. It was large and sturdy and took up way too much space, but the glow it emitted more than made up for the inconvenience. Unlike a flashlight, the beam wasn't restricted to a narrow radius. Sterile light flooded the room, shining off of abandoned musical instruments and chasing the shadows up the wall. It was almost clinical, and she felt the tension in her chest ease just a little. *Everything's easier with some clinical detachment.* She slowly turned, prepared for another lunging ghost. Nothing came for her.

"Why did you want me here?" Mina whispered.

The argument was still raging above her, so it took a few tries for her to regain their attention.

"How do I get out?"

Stephen was too far away for her to make out his facial features, but Mina noticed the way he squirmed. Ava shoved him.

"Bernadette was notoriously hard to work for," he began, speaking loud enough for everyone to hear. "She went through several contractors. In the end, she was the only one who knew the full layout and she didn't think to write it all down."

"Are you saying that you don't know how to get her out?" Ava snarled on Mina's behalf.

"I have ideas," Stephen protested. "Hey, don't look at me like that! Thousands of cleaners, tours, and performers have crossed the same floor she has without a problem! How were we to know it was there?"

Mina held the lantern aloft with one hand and drew her bag tight to her chest. Her ears rang with the memory of Basheba's laughter. *That's not an accident,* the phantom Basheba Bell mocked. *The dead wanted you down here. Alive. Are you going to sit here and wait to see why?* Mina was instantly on the move, struggling to get off of the remains of the deflated plastic. Lifting the lantern high above her head, she twisted around slowly, scanning the room in detail.

"Stephen?" she called.

When no response came, she glanced up to find the tour guide still arguing with Ava.

"Stephen!"

Her voice echoed over the wall. He jumped and looked down at her.

"I'm here."

"You said there were hidden doors."

"That's right, we'll get you out. Don't worry."

"There're musical instruments down here," Mina said. "Big, brass ones that look pretty heavy. So, this room has to be connected to a hallway by a hidden door."

"Right," Stephen called down.

Mina swept an arm out. "So, do you know which wall has the hidden door?"

"Yeah," Stephen chirped, delighted to have a plan of action. "Let me think. Um, the right. No, my right. There's a corridor that allowed the orchestra to avoid the crowds. It leads directly from the back entrance to up here. Get on that and you can't get lost."

"Right," Mina nodded and scanned the exposed brick of the aged wall. "Are there any particular things I should be looking for?"

Stephen hesitated. "There're instruments down there. That means the room might have been common knowledge at some point. Not one of the hidden ones!"

"Okay," Mina pressed.

"Oh, right. Look for an octopus. Or a pearl embedded in the brickwork. Or dogs. She was a big fan of dogs."

"Of course she was," Mina muttered bitterly.

"What?" Ava asked. "Do you have any reception? Maybe I can call you?"

"I'm going to check the wall. Don't call me yet, I need my hands."

Mina hurried to her right, leaving behind the low murmur of the conversation. The light of her lantern danced across the wall as she wove her way through the discarded instruments. Shadows clustered around her legs until she felt like she was wading through dark water. After a few minutes of searching, she discovered a small etching of a running hound tucked away in the far corner. She had to put her body weight against it to work the stone back into the wall. A sharp clack made her scurry back. Her spine struck a tuba, toppling it over into a dozen other instruments to create a deafening crash.

"Mina?" Ava and Stephen called as one.

Choking on the airborne dust, Mina looked up to find that half of the wall had peeled back.

"I found the door! I'm heading out!"

"Willimina!" Ava yelled. "If you haven't found your way in five minutes, you call me, okay?"

"And if I don't have reception, I'll blare some music so you guys can find me."

"See, I set it up, you knock it down. That's why we work as friends," Ava said.

Mina agreed again to the five-minute deadline and slipped out into the hidden hallway that ran alongside the room. The air was dank and dark, tainted with the stench of mildew and dirt. Even the illumination from her lantern seemed weaker as she assessed her situation.

Both directions looked the same—a gaping hole that ended a few feet beyond the stark white glow of her lantern. *This hallway is huge.* It was wide enough that she could spread her arms out and not touch the walls, but just small enough that her claustrophobia could kick in. Still, she took a calming breath and turned to the right.

The exposed bricks were dry and barren. Shadows gathered in the mortar, creating a steady pattern that, for the briefest of seconds, would twist into something else. A human silhouette. A screaming face. While the illusions always vanished when she turned to look at them straight on, the sense of not being alone lingered. The weight of eyes upon her made her walk faster.

The rhythmic melody of her footsteps faltered. A second pair of footfalls rushed up behind her. Mina spun, thrusting her lantern high in the air. Her movements were the only thing to stir the silence. She stared into the darkness lurking behind the light.

At first, it was the barest of illusions. But, as she watched, it seemed to thicken and multiply until it looked like a billion ebony insects were writhing before her. A noise started as a whisper, growing louder, closer. *Bees.* Fear crushed her like a vice. *They're bees!*

The light swung wildly as her hands began to shake, casting waves of light over the walls. The glow never touched the mass of twitching darkness as it swept closer.

Mina spun around and fled. Sprinting down the hallway didn't put any distance between her and the black swarm. The steady drone of bees drowned out her thundering footsteps and frantic breaths. Her heart ricocheted around her chest while a cold lump of dread formed in her throat.

Light glistened against the metal of a ladder embedded in the wall. She bolted past it only to skid to a stop when a dead-end emerged from the dim light. Unable to slow in time, she twisted her body so her shoulders absorbed the impact. The pain stunned her for a moment. Slumped against the wall, she looked up to see bees breaking from the shadows to fill the air.

Up. It was the only way left for her. Hurrying back to the ladder, she clutched the handle of the lantern between her teeth, and clambered up the ancient rails. Rust flaked off at her touch. Each bar rattled within the loose confines of the weathered stone. There wasn't room left in her head to worry about falling, though. All of her focus was on escaping the living phobia pursuing her.

Higher and higher she climbed, unable to determine how far she was going. Existence was confined to the radius of the lantern's glow. Rails emerged from the abyss only to disappear into it again; an endless loop that left her feeling trapped in time and space. Bees swarmed around her. Driving their needles into her flesh and seeking her eyes. Biting down hard on the plastic handle, Mina forced herself to ignore the pain and kept moving.

Before she could separate the trap door from the shadows, she had already smacked against it. Pain sparked in her neck and coursed down the length of her spine. She pounded at the wood, her vision blurring for a moment as the bees pierced her flesh. Their venom burned like acid. With one last, desperate swing of her arm, the trapdoor flew open. She scrambled through the gap and raked at her skin. Every swipe left her hands full of the writhing insects. Screaming around the lantern handle, she kicked wildly. The trapdoor slammed shut and everything stopped, the bees gone.

Gasping for air, she slumped against the wall, hot tears burning her cheeks. *It's too soon,* her thoughts whimpered. *Katrina's Harvest starts tomorrow. She shouldn't be able to do this now.*

As she sobbed and trembled, she saw something move across the corner of her eyes. Twin rings of radiating crimson watched her. A deep, monstrous growl vibrated through the air. Every muscle in her body locked tight as she carefully skirted her eyes to the side. Another pair of glowing eyes joined the first. Then another. The canine growling took on a sharper edge, rolling around random snaps and snarls. The darkness peeled back to expose pure white fangs. Mina's heart thudded hard against her ribs and she burst up.

She bounced off of the walls as she tried to get her footing back. The demonic hounds ran her down, effortlessly closing the distance as she bolted through the curving hallway.

There was no hope of outpacing them. She needed to find a place they couldn't follow.

Locking her eyes onto an oncoming door, she pushed herself to go faster, reaching out with grasping hands. A solid weight hammered against her back and brought her down. The lantern scattered over the floor to knock against the still-closed door. She desperately reached toward it as she flung the other back to bat away the phantom hounds.

A sharp whistle changed everything. The three dogs became one steady pressure upon her back. Flickering firelight filled the hallway and the door now stood open before her. Her fingertips brushed against the weathered suede of old hiking boots. Choking on her rapid shallow breaths, she craned her neck up to meet Basheba's pale eyes.

"Buck," Basheba spoke clearly as her fine brow twisted up in confusion. "Release."

Instantly, her giant Rottweiler slipped from Mina's back, playfully yelping as he circled for a pat. Mina scrambled back to sit on her shins. With panicked, jerking twitches, she surveyed the area. Both ends of the hallway curved out of sight, dark but still. The flickering of Basheba's torch and her own rapid breathing was all that stirred the silence. When she turned back, Buck had moved to sit beside the blonde. The combination of his humongous size and Basheba's small stature meant that he could nuzzle his master's shoulder with a bit of a stretch.

"What are you doing here?" Basheba asked.

"A ghost tour," Mina whispered on reflex. As her fear faded, she turned to the blonde with a sharp gaze. "What are *you* doing here?"

"Tradition." Basheba said the word swiftly as she closed the door behind her.

Mina caught a glimpse of something black staining Basheba's hands. Before she could ask about it, Buck had begun to lick her fingertips clean.

"Because your ancestor built this place?" Mina ventured.

Basheba tilted her head, allowing her blonde hair to sweep over one slender shoulder.

"The tour guide," she said as if she had solved a puzzle. "They've got to stop spreading rumors."

"There's no relation between you and Bernadette Allaway?"

"Oh, no, I'm her direct blood descendant," Basheba said. After a tense pause, she rolled one hand lazily in the air. "My parents always said we were rovers. Wanderers, nomads, vagabonds. Call us what you will."

"Are you quoting *Metallica*?"

Her surprised bark of laughter rolled down the empty hallways. "I'm gonna admit it, I didn't think you'd get the reference."

Is she trying to distract me? Mina's frazzled mind almost pushed the notion aside. Basheba was brutally direct. *And she's never nervous.* Mina had personally witnessed the blonde head off to fight murderous cult members with a smirk on her lips. Mina found her gaze pulled back to the door Basheba barred with her body.

"Anyway," Basheba remarked, her sudden shrug making the fire flicker. "It's still true, though. We never exactly had a brick and mortar home. Well, not one that wasn't infested with demons. This is the closest we had."

"Apart from your home in Alaska," Mina corrected.

Basheba's eyes somehow remained soft even as her gaze sharpened. "Yeah, well, after that whole thing with my uncle, child murderers, and brutal death, mom wasn't too keen on the place anymore. She preferred it here."

A ghost-riddled maze built by a witch. Mina hid the thought behind what she hoped would pass as a curious smile.

"Shouldn't you be at the barbeque by now?" Basheba cut in. "Or with your family? Or whatever it is that you Cranes do someplace other than here?"

Mina frowned. The barbeque was a yearly tradition. The only act of defiance that the four families would allow. Her father had only ever allowed her to attend one—when she was selected for the Harvest.

"That doesn't start for another day," Mina said.

"No, it's already in full swing."

Mina shook her head in confusion. "Dad left on the same day

every year when the boxes were given."

"Haven't you checked the website?" Basheba cut in. "It's just our two families sticking to the old timeline. The Winthrops and the Sewalls already have theirs."

Ice formed in Mina's stomach. "What?"

"Don't worry. It wasn't our boys," Basheba replied with a noncommittal wave of her hand.

"It's too soon."

Basheba chuckled. "Yeah, Katrina's in a snit."

"I guess we did nothing," Mina said, her shoulders slumping.

"Oh, we did *something*. Just not what we were intending."

Mina considered that for a moment before a question bubbled from the back of her mind and blurted out of her mouth.

"What's the tradition?"

The furrow of her brow served as Basheba's 'huh.'

"You said that you come here as a tradition," Mina pressed. "I'm just curious. What's the tradition?"

"Just a visit," Basheba dismissed swiftly. "We always came here before the Harvest. I'm running a little late this year."

"And you just wander around the stage tunnel?"

"Stage tunnel?" Basheba chuckled. "Oh, you are so lost. We're in the attic."

Mina glanced around the dimly lit hallway. There seemed to be a dozen narrow passages working their way through walls and between storage rooms. It seemed purposefully designed to be annoyingly inconvenient. Like a carnival funhouse. *Yeah, Basheba's ancestor definitely designed this place.*

"Why are you in the attic?"

"Who's going to stop me?" Basheba shot back.

Despite Mina's lingering fears, both of what lurked behind her and what stood before her, she was overwhelmed with relief that she could just tell the truth. Still keeping only to the important points, Mina caught Basheba up on everything. As she spoke the last of it, she met Basheba's gaze again to find barely suppressed fury.

"The dogs belong here," she said. "Everything else. That's Katrina."

"It's too soon."

Basheba bared her teeth, snarling under her breath, "How dare that bitch set foot here."

Noticing the change in demeanor, Buck growled, the low rumble making Basheba blindly reach out to pat him.

"Something's changed," Basheba whispered thoughtfully.

"Oh!" Mina's spine straightened before she groaned.

"What?"

"I didn't do my test."

"What?" Basheba repeated.

"My test. It was the whole reason Ava and I came here. Oh, right, Ava's a childhood friend, we got split up when I fell into the orchestra pit. I should call her and tell her I'm all right."

Fishing her phone out of her pocket, she found five missed calls. Two were from Ava. The rest from Ozzie.

"Ozzie left me a message," she mumbled, fiddling with the buttons.

Basheba blinked in confusion. "Congratulations?"

"We normally text each other," Mina explained as she pressed the phone to her ear to listen to the recording. "He only rings when something's wrong." Barely half of the message had played before she was on her feet. "We need to get to Black River."

CHAPTER 4

Mina stifled a long string of swear words as Basheba stomped on the gas. The walls of the covered bridge zoomed past the window in a blur, somehow never making contact. A solid lurch and they were back on the main road, barreling toward the thick trunk of a witch elm tree. Basheba tugged at the wheel and yanked on the emergency brake, forcing her hatchback car into a skid. The locked wheels slipped over the layer of colorful fall leaves that covered the road; Mina braced for impact.

She cautiously opened one eye when Basheba cheerfully pointed out, "That's the witch elm Katrina forced me into last year."

"Glad to see the experience didn't leave you with a lasting fear."

Neither girl mentioned that it was the river Basheba was afraid of crossing. The drive from Roanoke to Black River, Tennessee, had taken over seven hours. As before, Basheba had steadfastly refused to fly. Not only was her car her home, with a mattress taking up the back seat and trunk, but she would never leave Buck behind. Not many people were willing to accept the large, muscled dog as an emotional support animal.

Mina hated that they had spent the night in a dive-up motel in Nashville. *It was only seven hours*, she had argued, a simple drive between the two of them. In their four-way conference call, Mina had suggested that she and Basheba could hire a room on the town limits and get everything prepared for the boys' arrival, ensuring that they could leave for the caves the second they arrived. But Basheba had reminded her of just how well that plan had worked out last time. And how, even the option of staying undetected in the next town over wasn't open to them anymore. The cult had given up all pretext and had attacked them directly. And, given that they had set a wildfire that had threated the entire town, and personally burnt the cult master's house to ash, their presence was going to draw attention.

Since Cadwyn had still been a day's distance from town, and Ozzie's private jet would get him there whenever he wanted, it was decided that they would stick to the basics of the original plan—enter the town on the day of the Harvest, when, theoretically, Katrina would be too busy to pay much attention to them. Drawing in a deep breath, Mina forced herself to relax and answer a few texts from Ava.

"Is that your friend again?" Basheba asked.

"Just doing her safety check-in," Mina said.

"Her what?"

Mina pulled a hand through her hair. "Ava and I read about a lot of serial killers when we were kids. Don't give me that look, it wasn't weird. I wanted to be in law enforcement, and Ava had some morbid curiosity. Whatever. The point is that we scared the hell out of ourselves. So, we came up with the check-in system. Every time you stop at a place, you take two pictures. The first will include the name of the place you're at, like a sign or something. The second is a selfie with something green."

"Green for go?" Basheba cut in.

"Orange means you're a little apprehensive, and the receiver should call you immediately. Red means that something's wrong and you need to contact our parents."

"What if you don't do the selfie?"

"If you don't get one or either of the photos, you call 911," Mina said.

"Huh?"

"The idea is that, if I were to go missing, she'd be able to supply the police with a detailed account of my movements. So far, we've only had to use it to get each other out of creepy dates."

"So, she's not mad that you ditched her?"

Mina smiled. "I let her keep the car and told her that she could crash at my place for a few weeks. She's pretty happy."

Her phone buzzed against her palm and she rechecked the screen. Basheba eyed her with mild curiosity but quickly refocused on the radio.

"It's from my brother," Mina said. The text consisted of only two sentences. *I'm in Black River. I got a box.*

"It's too soon," Mina gasped.

"What?"

"I need to get to the family barbeque," Mina said. "Now."

Keeping all further questions to herself, Basheba stomped down on the gas. She weaved the old car along the winding road, sped past the endless fields plump with the autumn harvest, and into the city proper. They had reached the Witch's Brew in a third of the time it would normally have taken. Basheba jumped the curb and slammed on the brakes just before they crashed into a lamp post. The charred remains of the cafe looked raw in the morning light.

At first glance, it looked like Isaac Bell hadn't even attempted to salvage anything in the months that had passed since Basheba had set it on fire. Mina hadn't been surprised that Basheba had followed through on her threat to do it. Although, it was a bit of a shock that she hadn't made the spindly man watch it burn.

Blow up, her brain corrected her as she fought to strip off her seatbelt. Basheba had tampered with the gas line. The passing theory was that, since only the river separated the business from the wildfire, people would think that the wind had just carried some embers. The truth was that the police of Black River had learned to turn a blind eye to the families' activities centuries ago. While they'd never admit it, their policy was that the supernatural wasn't under their jurisdiction. They documented the deaths, buried the bodies, and left everything else alone. Something Basheba exploited ruthlessly.

She told herself that the details didn't matter right now. Not that it would stop her brain from dwelling. *Isaac would know.* Whatever the cover story, it was arson. All anyone needed was to spend three minutes with Basheba to know that it was the tiny blonde's favorite pastime. *What if he tells Dad?* While she wasn't bothered by the idea of being punished, she was terrified that her father would keep her from Jeremiah. *He needs to know. He's not ready.* With a frustrated scream, she finally worked the seatbelt latch and freed herself.

"Hey, careful. I like my car," Basheba said.

"Sorry," Mina dismissed.

Basheba reached into the back seat, grabbed a small, tattered duffle bag, and dumped it onto Mina's lap.

"What?"

"Call it a Christmas present," Basheba said.

Mina's hands trembled as she hurriedly worked the zipper. There was no hiding the surprise on her face.

"It's a witch hunter starter pack." There was real warmth in Basheba's smile as she continued. "Your brother's going to be fine. Yeah, the Bell line is a joke and the Cranes are pretentious, but the Winthrops and Sewalls have some competent people amongst them. It's not a lost cause."

Suddenly, she was more interested in working her necklace free of her shirt. Basheba thumbed through the collection of family wedding rings as she continued.

"Besides, we'll be working to kill Katrina at the same time. That's got to work in his favor."

Mina stared at her, awed by the attempt to comfort her. "Thank you."

Basheba shrugged the gratitude off. "Well, hurry up."

"I can't leave you alone," Mina said. She continued when Basheba threw her a disbelieving look. "Should I list the ways we've ticked off Whitney and the cult?"

"It's been months, and I haven't had any retaliation. I can last five minutes on a curb by myself."

"I'm not saying I know how the cult functions, but it's clear they depend pretty heavily upon Katrina."

"Calling her by name now, huh?"

Refusing to be distracted, Mina continued. "They wouldn't leave her protection to come after us. Now, we're in their backyard. Just last night you were telling me that we need to be careful."

"Full disclosure? I just wanted to stop at that burger place we had dinner at last night. They have the best onion rings."

"Even if you don't see a physical threat, Isaac might have persuaded my father to interfere. You're not that good at handling the politics of the family dynamics on your own."

"Which family?" Basheba asked.

"All of them."

Basheba shrugged, "You have me there."

The fear that her father might actively, openly start supporting Isaac had left Mina sick for months. Logically, Isaac would try to build support within the four families. Her father had admitted to her a certain degree of agreement with his ideology. He had even suggested other elders felt the same. That kind of corruption weaving its way through the families terrified her. *I can't leave Jeremiah to face that alone.*

"Mina, I'm right behind you and I have Buck with me. Go find your brother."

Mina clenched her jaw but kicked the door open and ran out, the duffle and her own backpack grasped tight.

"Hey!" Basheba yelled after her. "My car!"

Music and laughter drifted from behind the elaborate pile of ash and stonework that had been the Witch's Brew. Enough of the brick walls remained that it was impossible to see the yearly party from the street. The barbeque was designed to be a morale booster for the doomed and the survivors alike. Everyone's last chance to make a pleasant memory together. It didn't seem as if a whole year had passed since she had been forced to admit that the Witch was far more than superstition and mass hysteria. All of the confusion and fear were still heavy in her chest. *Now Jeremiah has to face it.* Her jaw clenched painfully. *He won't face it alone.*

She reached the back of the building and saw the party. Streamers of bright colors flapped in the morning breeze. Already, the scattered barbeques were filled with grilling meat, and the tables were stacked with snacks and drinks. Children raced around the massive bonfire and chatting adults, some of whom were already showing signs of hitting the beer a little too hard. While the crowd had spread out far enough to reach the stony banks of the Black River, no one entered the water.

Her eyes instinctively went to the far bank. Sheer, pale stones jutted out of the liquid onyx stream. She had to fight to find any sign of the wildfire that had ravaged the woods. New growth and the vibrant autumn colors concealed the few blackened tree trunks and patches of scorched earth that remained.

We failed. Panicked tears threatening to fall down Mina's cheeks. The forest's recovery rate quashed any doubts she might have harbored. *It was all for nothing. Katrina is still out there, still just as powerful as she was, and she's going to kill Jeremiah.* Tightening her grip on the bags until her arms trembled, she corrected herself. *Try. She'll try. She won't succeed.*

Scanning the crowd, she spotted dozens of her relatives. Luckily, they all seemed too preoccupied to notice her. Entering the Witch Woods had irrevocably altered her relationship with just about everyone in her life. Exile had tested what remained. It was an alien sensation to be separated from them, physically and emotionally. It hurt. With time, she knew she could forgive her parents for keeping her willfully ignorant, for backing up Isaac in whatever deal he had forged with the Witch's cult, and even for cutting her off when she refused to obey him.

Logically, she understood why they had done it. Generations of fear and sacrifice had taught them silent compliance was integral for their survival. By going against that, by challenging Katrina, she was putting the entire family at risk. She understood, but she didn't agree, and she couldn't back down. And now that she knew just how easily they could put her aside, choose the status quo over even listening to their options, she'd never be able to trust them the way she had before. *Or even look at them the same,* she thought as she moved. *Everyone has to learn that their family isn't perfect sometime.*

Ducking her head to avoid being spotted by one of her uncles, she worked her way through the crowd. Surrounded by the festivities, she realized what aspect of the whole nightmare hurt the most. *Dad has never been selected.* Nor had he ever gone into the woods to collect the bodies afterward. Very few Cranes had done that. *Still, he wouldn't listen to me.* Looking around now, it occurred to her that none of the families actually listened to those who survived. War stories about the brave and the valiant they would listen to on end. But no one wanted to hear about the scars left behind.

After her first time in the woods, she had been treated like a returning hero. Everyone had bragged about how she had faced the Bell Witch and returned with barely more than a scratch. For a while, she was seen as more than daddy's little angel. It didn't matter how often she insisted that she hadn't earned the praise, that she wouldn't have survived a day without the others.

Dad had been so proud, Mina recalled, drowning in her conflicting emotions. *Right up until the moment I started telling everyone the brutal truth.*

Mina's thought stuttered into silence when she spotted her brother. "Jeremiah!"

Not even a full two years separated Mina from her older brother but, when he turned to the sound of his name, he looked ancient. Haggard and worn, clutching the intricate music box between his hands like it was welded to his body. *I guess some traditions do change.* Last year, when she had been selected, her father had taken the box from her almost instantly. *Was that just for me? For girls in general? Had Dad changed his mind?* Not knowing why such a drastic shift had happened within her own family came with a sharp ache.

Her brother glanced up, his eyes widening when he spotted her. Releasing a broken sob, Mina sprinted the distance separating them and flung her arms around his neck. The bags thumped against her back, but she didn't protest being drawn into a tight hug.

"What the fuchsia are you doing here?" he whispered harshly.

Mina pulled back and forced a smile. "Do you think we'll ever outgrow using colors as swear words?"

Jeremiah's face darkened. Clearly, he wasn't going to abide by any attempt to break the tension. Instead, he glanced rapidly around the yard, checking to see if they had drawn attention.

"You texted me, Jer," she said. "What did you think? That I'd just ignore it?"

"No. But—"

"But nothing."

He wet his dry lips and skittishly looked around again. Hurriedly, he hunched his shoulders and coaxed her to do the same. They pushed close together to try to get a small measure of privacy within the center of the crowd.

"Mom and Dad are going to freak out if they see you here," he whispered.

"I'm a Crane by blood. You're my brother. This is where I belong."

"Yeah, well, they say that you don't want to be a Crane anymore."

"*They* exiled *me*," Mina protested, trying to fight down the cocktail of emotions that had become crushingly familiar. "Apparently, when they said 'family is forever,' they were exaggerating."

Jeremiah shifted uncomfortably, "You did go against the family."

"Everything I have done has been for the family," she corrected. "It'll *always* be for the family."

"Then you might have to do some things you don't want to do."

She bit back her response and smiled again. "Look, none of that matters right now. You matter. How are you holding up?"

"You know," Jeremiah pushed his dark brown hair from his face and attempted a nonchalant shrug. "It is what it is."

Mina caught her brother's gaze.

He almost choked on his confession. "Actually, I'm terrified, Mina. I can't do this."

"Yes, you can," she soothed. "I know you can."

"You told me what's in there. Why would you do that? How am I supposed to walk into those woods knowing what's waiting for me? This is why Dad never told us. You get that now, right? This is why." Each rambled word chipped away at his righteous indignation to expose the raw dread that lay underneath.

Fine tremors shook his body as Mina pulled him into another tight hug, the cursed music box crushed between them. Jeremiah melted against her with another broken sob.

"I just wanted you to be better prepared than I was," Mina whispered. "Ignorance won't help you. It'll only leave you vulnerable."

Her brother released the box with one hand and looped the arm around her shoulders. "Maybe I'd prefer not knowing."

"The prepared survive, Jer. You're a survivor." Pulling back, she forced a smile. "I brought gifts."

The abrupt shift left him silent; he watched her pull items from her purse with a furrowed brow. Mina first held up two Ziplock bags, one full of sugar packets, the other containing the dark powder of potassium permanganate.

"Mix these two together in equal measure, and they'll self-ignite."

"Okay," Jeremiah said slowly. "They teach you that at Pennsylvania State?"

She gave his attempt at a joke a smirk. "Strangely enough, my criminal justice program doesn't really cover how to create chemical fires."

"I'd think that would fall under arson."

"Well, that's probably why I learned it from Basheba," Mina replied. She produced an extra pair of thick socks.

"You know I'm going into the woods, not the snow."

"The fog," she reminded, adding ski gloves to the pile in his arms.

"It's really that cold? You weren't exaggerating?"

"Katrina's goal is to make you hypothermic—" She cut herself off when she saw him violently flinch. "What is it?"

Jeremiah stooped down slightly and whispered, "You just called her by name."

Licking her lips, she nodded once and straightened her spine. "I decided that I would no longer feed into her propaganda. It's a fear tactic, Jeremiah. To make her seem like this unstoppable force of pure evil."

"She is."

"Katrina Hamilton was human once."

"A witch," he corrected. "Now she's a ghost."

"And ghosts can be stopped." Mina threw every ounce of determination she had into the words.

Jeremiah shrugged, "Yeah, I heard you say that once before. I still have a box."

"Serial killers are rarely caught on the first attempt," she shot back. "And I'm tenacious."

"Is that what you're going to do in the FBI, Mina? Hunt down paranormal serial killers? Is there a division for that?"

"I'll make one." Warmth flooded her chest when her small smile was met with one of his own.

"Okay, okay. What else have you got for me?"

She opened her own bag and produced a metal cone.

"What the hazel is that?"

"It's my untested theory," Mina stressed before continuing.

"When I was researching, I came across this idea that the perception of ghosts is influenced by geomagnetic fields."

"What?"

"It's the natural magnetic fields the earth produces," she said, watching his eyebrows rise. "Okay, bare basics. Higher geomagnetic intensity correlates with more ghost sightings. My theory is that ghosts feed off of the energy to gather power."

He heaved the shiny cone in his hand. "And this will block it?"

"No, you can't block the earth's magnetic field. But you can *bend* it. I'm hoping that, by doing so, you'll either weaken the ghost or disorient it. Maybe cause enough confusion to get away."

Once more, he studied the cone skeptically.

"Iron has always been said to repel ghosts, right?" Mina asked.

"Mina," he sighed. "You're not the first to try iron against these things. Remember the stories? It doesn't work all that well."

"But I'm not trying to *repel* them. I'm trying to *bend* them. My theory is that we've had minimal results with iron in the past because it's a metal that can be used to bend magnetic fields. The cone takes what was possibly functional about iron and amplifies it. At the same time, it emits its own magnetic field that will further disrupt the ghosts' energy."

"So, they'll be there but wavy?"

"They'll be there but weakened," she said. "Theoretically, while you still might see them, they won't be able to physically touch you."

Jeremiah tipped the cone back and forth, studying it with hesitant interest. "How do you switch it on?"

"You don't."

He frowned. "Then how do you get it to work?"

"It's a magnet, Jeremiah. It's working right now. It should be that the cone's presence alone will interfere with the ghosts to a certain radius."

"Right."

"I know it doesn't sound like much. But, trust me, when you're trying to sleep with only a thin tent for protection, it'll feel like everything."

"So, I just set it down and let it do its thing?"

"Pretty much."

"It's worth a shot, I suppose."

"Just remember, I haven't tested it yet."

Consumed by the conversation, they paid little attention to the crowd, not noticing their parents' approach until their father grabbed Mina's arm and yanked her around.

"What are you doing here?"

A lifetime of obedience to her parents was a hard habit to break, even now. Mina supposed there would always be a part of her that wanted their approval above all else. Suppressing the emotion, she calmly met her father's furious gaze.

"I came to see my brother."

"We've been over this," he growled. "You can't be half committed to the family."

Mina bristled. "I've never been anything other than dedicated."

"Yet I can give you a long list of examples to the contrary."

Glancing to her mother for help didn't achieve anything.

For better or worse, they're always a team. The dynamic had always been something Mina had revered. She'd never been on the other side. Swallowing thickly, she forced the words out of her throat.

"Disagreeing with you isn't going against the family."

"So you're only against me?" her father almost taunted.

A flash of annoyance steeled her spine. "Only when you're wrong."

Anger twisted up her father's mouth before he could smooth it out.

"All I'm asking is that you listen to me." Mina pressed. "Why can't you give me that?"

Her father's brow darkened, but he kept his voice to a private whisper. "Mina, I love you."

"I love you, too."

"I'm asking you to prove it." With an encouraging smile, he added, "Do what I say."

No one who really loves you would ever use it against you. Cadwyn's passing words flashed across Mina's mind, bringing with it a sickly feeling to fill the pit of her stomach.

Noticing her hesitation, he tightened his grip. "Do as you're told or leave."

"Dad," Jeremiah said softly. "Please, I want her here."

Their mother shushed him with a gentle touch to his shoulder. "Come on, let's go get some food and let them speak."

Mina caught her brother's gaze, trying to let him know that it was okay to leave. *Don't risk getting ostracized, too,* she silently told him. *Not now. You need the family, now more than ever.* Jeremiah took a deep breath and shifted to stand shoulder to shoulder with Mina.

"I'm not that hungry, mom," he said. "I think I'll stay."

"Jeremiah," their mother warned.

"I'm not saying she's right about everything. It's just that, if we all have to live by these family rules, shouldn't we all have a say in what they are?"

"This isn't a democracy," their mother said.

Jeremiah's brow furrowed. "It's a *family*."

"It's a kingship," Mina corrected. "Yeah, I didn't know either until someone pointed it out. Mom and Dad are the queen and king of the Crane family. Congrats, you're a prince."

Jeremiah stared at each of them in disbelief before he began to mutter about the insanity of it all. Mina hadn't taken the news much better when she had learned about the hierarchical dynamics of the family. But a lifetime of being shielded and pampered leads to a certain degree of naivety. She'd been blind to how deep the Witch had affected them. Battling a murderous evil for centuries had led the four families to cling to what they knew. Mostly, that meant a very strict dynamic, one that didn't work well in her favor as an eighteen-year-old female.

"Our ways have seen us through this danger for generations," their mother said.

"That's easy for you to say when you're not a Crane by blood," Mina said.

The harsh words caught them all off guard. Guilt gnawed at Mina's stomach like a wild animal. A childhood need to please screamed at her to take it back, make it better, be the good little girl she was expected to be.

"I love you, Mom, you know I do, but this doesn't concern you," Mina forced herself to say.

"I'm not part of this family now?"

"You married in. No matter what happens, you'll never be on Katrina's list—"

Her sentence broke into a pained gasp as her father's hand crushed her arm.

"You will not say that name," he snarled.

"I will," Mina said with a matching ferocity. "Nothing will ever change if we keep making her into the boogieman. We need to educate our children, not scare them with campfire stories and myths."

"When you have your own children, you'll understand why things are the way they are," her mother said smoothly.

Mina glanced between her parents. "You know, I'm thinking of not having any kids."

Her mother scoffed, and her father's grip loosened slightly.

"Do you see now?" he asked his wife. "I told you that nothing good would come from spoiling her."

Her mother nodded, "You were right."

"I think we can both agree that this has gone far enough."

She nodded again, and their father turned back to his children.

"Willimina, I am your father. And, as such, I think you owe me some respect."

"I do respect you."

"Good. I've arranged for you to meet with the son of a coworker. He's handsome enough, from good stock, intelligent, and has a promising career in a private law practice in Los Angeles."

"I don't understand," Mina stammered, refusing to follow his line of thought.

"You're on the wrong track."

"I'm in the top three percent in all of my classes," Mina cut in. "I'm already on track for law review and have begun to build the reputation and connections necessary to ensure my acceptance and success in med school. And Mrs. Davis has introduced me to a friend of hers in the FBI, so I'm already networking. Dad, I'm on track to the FBI. How is that the 'wrong track'?"

"You have a more important destiny before you."

"Getting married and having kids?"

"You are my daughter," he snapped. "The women of the family look to you for how to act. You need to set a better example."

"Highly educated and dedicated to law enforcement is a bad example?"

"Running off from the family. Disobedience. Scaring the children—"

"Teaching them survival skills that *you* should have taught them by now," Mina cut in.

"Relying on another of the four families for financial aid."

"I am not!"

"So you're not living off of Ozzie's money."

Mina clenched her jaw until it hurt. "I have a free ride at Penn State. I earned that. You were the one who insisted I live with the cousins. You were the one who insisted I shouldn't get a job so I could focus on my studies. And *you* were the one who had them kick me out. Was I supposed to be homeless? No, that's right. I was supposed to come running back to you, wasn't I?"

"What did you do to get Ozzie to buy you a house?"

Rage drew Mina up to full height, as minimal as it was. Not that her father was a towering man.

"We survived the Witch Woods together. You wouldn't know what kind of bond that forges."

She had never seen the level of fury that now settled upon her father's face. His hand tightened, crushing her arm, digging his nails through the layer of her thin denim jacket.

"How dare—"

His words were cut off by a sudden, joyous scream. "Which one of you morons is gonna die?"

CHAPTER 5

It seemed that all eyes locked onto her. Not that it could dampen Basheba's mood. Nothing could right now. Everything was happening earlier than the norm. Katrina usually at least waited for nightfall to make her selections. But the website for the four families had sent her an alert. A Bell had received a box, and it wasn't her. *My uncle or my cousin?* They were equally delightful options. She tingled with excitement, absolutely giddy, and fought the urge to spin around like she was singing in a green mountain meadow. Buck still bounced around her feet, yelping with delight.

"Oh, come on," Basheba laughed when no one answered her. "I deliberately didn't check for the name so this would be a surprise. Tell me, tell me, tell me!"

"People may die, Basheba," someone in the crowd said sharply.

She stopped her pleading long enough to roll her eyes, "Oh, how completely unexpected for this time of year."

"Is it possible for you to show even an ounce of respect?" a Crane family woman sneered. An agreeing murmur washed over the crowd.

"Elizabeth, last year, when it was my head on the chopping block, you got completely hammered and did a striptease with a volleyball net," Basheba said, her voice hovering perfectly between threatening and dismissive. "Call me crazy, but I'm not going to come to you for advice on respectful behavior."

One of the many Zachariahs that filled the family trees stalked forward. His mouth was set in a grim line even as he glanced at the people around him with barely concealed amusement. It was an obvious 'step back and watch how it's done' kind of look, annoyingly similar to her uncle's neutral expression.

"I think it's time that you and I have a heart-to-heart, Basheba."

"Can you give me a moment to check on the fire extinguishers first?"

Basheba had to search for Mina in the crowd before she could believe that the preppy princess had actually spouted off. Chuckling, Basheba perched on a picnic table, her feet on the seat and Buck by her feet. With a whistle, the massive Rottweiler ran off to fetch her a beer. He was back with the bottle before she had time to get comfortable.

"I was talking to you," Zachariah said.

"Well, that explains my crushing boredom," Basheba said while using the edge of the table to pop off the bottle cap.

Red splotches formed on his neck. "Now, you listen to me—"

"Oh, dear Lord in heaven," Basheba flopped dramatically. Holding up one finger, she took a few mouthfuls of her drink before continuing. "Zach, I lack the vocabulary needed to adequately express how little I care about you and your opinion."

Clearly not used to being dismissed or interrupted, Zachariah bristled. "It's about time someone educated you, little girl."

"I get it. You want to show off for your family," Basheba replied. "The problem is, I am physically incapable of acting dumb enough for you to look smart by comparison."

"You bitch."

"Sticks and stones will break my bones, but first you have to throw 'em," Basheba muttered into her beer bottle. "Look, you're boring me now. So, I'm just going to ignore you and look over in *this* direction." She swiveled barely an inch to the left. It seemed more insulting that way. Before he could sputter a response through his anger, Basheba smiled. "Oh, hey, Mina. Are you here to help them beat morals and virtue into me?"

"No. I'm trying this new thing where I don't relentlessly pursue lost causes."

Basheba took a sip from her bottle. "What are you gonna do with all your free time?" Before she could come up with a response, Basheba's attention shifted to the man standing beside Mina. They had the same tawny skin, dark hair, and doe eyes. A Filipino influence they inherited from their mother. *Her brother.* "You're Jeremiah, right?"

The boy nodded.

Basheba saluted him with the bottle. "My condolences with the sucky path your life has taken."

Jeremiah's gaze shifted to Mina before answering, "Thanks."

Letting her excitement take over once more, she leaned forward, "Do you know which Bell is going in with you?"

Again, Jeremiah looked to his sister for guidance, as if she was some kind of expert on the ways of Basheba Bell. Taking another sip of the beer, she tried to decide if she should be insulted or fascinated by this development.

Basheba watched the siblings have a conversation by looks alone. It wasn't that she thought she'd figure out what they were thinking. She just wanted to exploit the excuse to purposefully ignore everyone else who was still watching her. Noting the metal in Jeremiah's hand, she asked,

"Hey, what's with the cone?"

A murmur went through the crowd, drawing her attention back just in time to see her cousin working her way to the table. Basheba grinned.

"Who got it?"

Claudia lifted her chin. "I was selected. I suppose you have something horrid to say to me about it."

"You?" Basheba clarified.

"Me."

A fit of giggles bubbled out of Basheba's throat. "Oh, you're so going to die!"

"How can you say that to me?" Claudia asked, her arms wrapping tightly around her slightly chubby frame.

"You just acknowledged I wasn't going to be pleasant."

"But how can you be so cruel?"

Basheba choked on her beer as she laughed. "Oh, good Lord, you're serious! That's hilarious, Claudia. Or are you just too stupid to realize why I don't like you? Hmm, that's a hard call to make."

"I've never done anything to you," Claudia insisted.

Basheba's eyebrows jumped toward her hairline. "Say again."

"Name one time when I have ever tried to hurt you."

Leaning her weight back on one hand, Basheba shook her head in astonishment.

"If you know someone's getting steadily poisoned over the years, and you do nothing, you're not an innocent bystander. You're a participant."

"No one ever tried to—"

"You knew what your daddy was up to," Basheba cut in, her flash of rage simmering down quickly. With a sickly-sweet smile, she continued. "You were happy to sit back and let everyone else be led to the slaughterhouse in your place. What's wrong? Is Katrina not playing anymore?"

"Don't call her by name," Claudia hissed on a low breath.

Basheba ignored her. "I'm guessing she's pretty upset with Daddy right now, huh?"

Her smile grew as Claudia tightened her grip around herself. Neither of them vocally acknowledged who was responsible for Isaac's current failure, but Basheba preened all the same. He had promised to deliver Basheba and the others to the cult. It still baffled her that one man could be so delusional. *And now he's facing the consequences.*

Ignoring the murmured reprimands of their audience, she lifted her bottle to Claudia in a toast.

"To Claudia. May you get everything you deserve."

"You're enjoying this, aren't you?" Claudia said on a breath.

"Well, aren't you bright. Picking up on all that nuance," Basheba chuckled.

"You're truly evil."

"And yet I've never made a pact with a witch," Basheba mused. "Guess I'm ahead of the game."

"Pact?" someone asked, the question provoking a low rumble to course through the crowd.

Claudia swiftly turned to reassure them. Basheba's interest wandered back to Mina and her brother. *What is with that cone?*

"Basheba, what did you do this time?"

Basheba huffed at the laughter that weaved through Cadwyn's soothing voice. While she wasn't about to admit it out loud, Cadwyn was probably the only person in the world she'd like to hear talk more. Part of it was just nature picking favorites, giving him a voice that was both deep and smooth. The other half was likely a side effect of his occupation. *I doubt being a loud jerk would go over well in a mental asylum. Especially if you're a nurse.* As such, Cadwyn had developed this tone that drew attention while rarely ever getting loud. He was the only person she knew who could make a whisper sound intimidating.

The table trembled as Cadwyn walked over the back of it, most likely to avoid the restless crowd that was still somewhat gathered around, and dropped down beside her.

"Why do you always assume it's me?" she asked.

"Past experience?" he replied, his leather biker jacket crinkling as he plucked her beer bottle out of her unsuspecting hand.

"Hey! That's mine!" she protested.

She swiped for the bottle, but it was a pitiful attempt, given all the extra length Cadwyn had to his advantage. All he had to do was lean out of her way while taking a few gulps from the bottle. Preoccupied with this, he limited his response to an arch of one eyebrow and the presentation of his left hand. The light flicked off of the golden wedding band, making it completely unavoidable. She would have been annoyed if it wasn't for the displeased murmurs that ripped through the families like wildfire. *Well, this might be interesting.* Wanting to let that stew for a little while, she continued as if she hadn't noticed the reaction, shoving at his shoulder.

"That doesn't mean that we have to share food!"

He almost choked on the beer as he laughed. "You put it in our vows."

"Yeah. That *you* had to share with *me*," she argued, yanking the bottle back. "There's no obligation on my side."

"Sorry, wife. You said the vows. Now you're stuck with it."

"You're married?" Claudia shrieked, somewhere between mortified and enraged.

It burst the dam and all the questions, accusations, and curses began to fly. The commotion drew more people in, spreading the outrage. Basheba abandoned all attempt at keeping a straight face when she spotted her uncle's enraged face amongst the crowd. Then she burst out cackling.

"You can't," Claudia stammered.

Basheba held up her left hand, wiggling her ring finger to draw attention to the tarnished silver octopus that encased the base of her finger. It held a single black pearl in its tangled tentacles, the orb so rich that it shone like an oil slick.

"Aw, you wore it," Cadwyn said.

Basheba shrugged, "It's a special occasion."

"That's not even a wedding ring!" Claudia protested.

Rolling her head, she threw a smug look to Cadwyn, "I told you we should have gone for the mood rings."

"You can't do this!" Basheba wasn't quick enough to catch who had spoken.

She snorted over the rim of her beer bottle. "It's already done."

Claudia stomped forward a few feet, shrugging off Isaac's attempt to hold her back. "You live entirely off the grid. How could you legally get married?"

"That's the whole point of living off the grid," Basheba said, rolling her eyes. "I'm so far off everyone's radar that no one cares what I do."

"I do," Mina's father growled.

"That's sweet. I don't give a damn, but it's sweet."

When Mina's father fixed her with an icy glare, it suddenly made more sense why the girl was the way she was. Even Basheba had to admit it was kind of intimidating.

"We have rules and order," he said, slow and crisp. "For generations, they have protected *all* of us. You don't get to pick and choose what you follow."

It took her a second to shake off the fatherly disapproval and shrug. "Those rules also say that you need to stick in your own lane."

"Isaac might be too kindhearted to force you into line, but I'm not. I am head of the Crane family; you will give me the respect that position demands."

A slow smile stretched her lips. "I'm already giving you every ounce of respect you've *earned*."

"She's far too young for you!" The sudden shriek broke the brewing tension and made Basheba flinch. While she couldn't quite place exactly who the speaker was, Basheba knew it came from a cluster of Winthrops, so she choked down her automatic, snide response. *The things I do for my husband.*

"It's okay, Aunty," Cadwyn soothed.

"She's barely in her twenties," Aunty continued.

"Twenty-one, as of last month." Basheba offer was met with a very wrinkled frown.

"He's thirty-one."

"Aunty, please," Cadwyn said calmly. "It's just so she can use my health insurance."

"*Arkham Asylum* has surprisingly good healthcare," Basheba backed him up with a nod.

Cadwyn closed his eyes and took a sobering breath, "For the last time, stop calling it that."

"It's an asylum for the criminally insane. Those shouldn't exist anymore."

"If you ever meet some of the residents, you'll have a very different opinion."

Basheba perked up. She opened her mouth, but he cut her off.

"No, I'm not taking you to work. They'd never let you out. Although my boss has invited you to the company Christmas party this year. December 20th, if you can make it."

"If I'm not dead, I'll be there."

"You can't be married!" Claudia screamed, the sheer rage in her tone cutting off the steady stream of mumbling protests.

"Claudia," Basheba said. "If all you're going to do is repeat yourself, maybe consider silence."

"He's a Winthrop! The families can't intermarry. It's a rule! It's...incestuous."

Cadwyn's jaw dropped a moment before he replied. "We're not related."

"You know what I mean," Claudia dismissed. "All our lives are intertwined. She can't become a Winthrop."

"The Witch will count her as one," someone unseen argued.

They were almost instantly countered with, "No, she won't. It goes by blood. Basheba's a Bell."

"We don't know either way," Cadwyn's aunt replied, scowling at her nephew. "No one's ever done this."

"Isn't it about time we do something new?" Cadwyn said.

"The old ways have served us well," Mina's father stated.

"The old ways have made us compliant," Mina corrected, the muscles in her jaw working as she faced down her father's glare.

"We're in public," he told his daughter. "Try to have some dignity."

"A dead woman has ruled our lives for two hundred years. Where's the dignity in that?" Mina shot back.

"I'm going to have to side with her," Basheba said, jabbing her thumb in Mina's direction.

Claudia scoffed. "You lose your right to an opinion when you start inbreeding."

"Not related," Cadwyn argued.

"Not having kids," Basheba added.

"It doesn't matter. You can't do this," Claudia pushed out through clenched teeth. "Daddy!"

Isaac squeezed his daughter's shoulders and moved slightly in front of her. The sight put Basheba on edge. Isaac would never attack her physically. He was too much of a coward to risk personal injury and thought himself above such 'primitive' things. *I'm not,* Basheba thought as her hand twitched toward the hunting knife hidden by the side of her thick jacket. Subtly, Cadwyn leaned closer to her. Just enough that it would be awkward for her to retrieve the knife. She huffed. *You ruin all my fun.* Cadwyn only gave her a thin but amused smile in return.

"Cadwyn," Isaac said sharply.

The man waited with his chin raised for the younger man to give him his full attention.

Cadwyn's smile grew into something polite and professional.

"Yes, Uncle Isaac," Cadwyn replied.

The term of address made Isaac bristle.

"This marriage is illegal."

"I can assure you that all the paperwork is in order," Cadwyn replied swiftly.

His voice was as placid as a cool lake but as hard as iron. Too polite for anyone to take offense at. Too unyielding for there to be any argument.

Isaac's eyes narrowed. "No one in the Bell family can marry without the consent of the family elders. That's me. And since I didn't walk her down the aisle, you can be assured that I didn't give my consent."

"And yet, we're married," Cadwyn said. "That would seem to suggest that you don't have the power over her that you think you do."

Isaac bared his teeth, his hands trembling as he fought to keep his composure. "Basheba is mine."

"Isaac, calm down," Cadwyn's uncle said as he crossed over to the enraged man. Basheba had never seen anyone look so self-satisfied. "What's done is done. She's still a Bell. She's just also a Winthrop now."

"You moron," Isaac hissed. "She's not going to be any more loyal to you than she has been to me." He locked his spiteful gaze onto Cadwyn. "You think she'll listen to a damn thing you say?"

Cadwyn's smile took on a razor's edge. "She already does. Just like I listen to her."

The earth shook violently as an explosion ripped from the ground. Basheba gripped the edge of the picnic table with one hand and reached for Buck with her other. The Rottweiler nuzzled at her palm as he struggled to keep his footing. Panicked screams rose up from the crowd as the bonfire erupted. Flames shot into the sky, crackling wildly and filling the clearing with blistering heat. It cut the group in two, with some of them retreating behind the picnic table and the others crowding along the water's edge.

With an audible hiss, the searing heat met the chilled October air and created a mist. The white haze settled down upon them and reduced people to shadows. Giant flares set off another round of screams, and the scattered barbeques turned into fiery geysers.

Some people screamed for everyone to get to the water, while others commanded the group to the road. Basheba and Cadwyn leaped to their feet, with her gripping her knife and him protectively clutching his ever-present medical bag. Buck snarled and snapped as he pressed against Basheba's legs. Mina crashed into the table, doubling over with a pained gasp but refusing to release her death grip on her brother's arm.

"We need to find Dad," Jeremiah wheezed through the steam.

Mina met Basheba's eyes just as the trembling stopped. The flames died and the world grew quiet. Sweat made Basheba's fingers slick as she worked her grip on her knife. She stepped onto the tabletop to get a better look through the murky air. The shifting shadows had stilled. Everything went silent. A small breath of wind stirred the trees on the far bank, making them whisper as they brushed together.

"Oh my God," Jeremiah whispered.

Basheba's jaw dropped when she caught sight of the flaming circle. It floated upon the clear center of the river. A clear, crackling disk. The water within it began to drain.

"Mina?" Jeremiah said.

"I see it, too," Mina assured.

A slight gushing sound became a waterfall—a constant, impossible draining. Family members stood in dumb silence as they watched twin horns rise from within the pit. The horns were long and thick and sharpened to a deadly point. They gave way to a bull's head, a thick neck, and a man's shoulders.

Cadwyn tensed as they watched the minotaur rise, one hand absently pressing against his chest, spreading his fingers wide to cover the scar that lay beneath his shirt.

"Why is it always bulls?" Cadwyn said through his clenched teeth.

The minotaur stared at them from within the ring of fire. Its arms broke free of the flames, clawing and grasping at the water. The flesh charred and blistered. The gates of Hell had opened in Black River and Basheba was surprised by how stunned she was to see it.

"She can't do this," Jeremiah said. "How can she do this?"

He probably would have continued his rambling had the childlike voice not broken out across the area. *Katrina.*

"Welcome home," the phantom voice giggled. "Come play with me."

"Why don't you come out here and play with us?" Basheba bellowed, throwing her arms wide.

Cadwyn grabbed her forearm, holding her in place as he slowly rose to his feet.

"What's the matter, Katrina? Ya having a bad day?" Basheba continued.

"Shush," Mina hissed at the same time that Cadwyn asked her to stop.

She couldn't. Not when the possibility was lingering just out of her reach, begging to be confirmed. The minotaur slowly turned to face her. She could feel its rage like ice within her skin.

"Do you remember me?" Basheba grinned, dizzy with hope. *Come on. Show me. Prove it!* "You might not. I did melt your brain, after all. Good times."

The minotaur's bellow cracked over them like thunder. Fire erupted in its wake, spontaneous blazes that ignited and spread. The colored lights popped as the flames followed the length of the decorations. Ice coolers, grass, the toys left abandoned on the ground were all consumed.

Cadwyn's grip shifted on her arm. One hard yank and he dragged her over his shoulders, lifting her from the picnic table just before the fire began to lap at their table. Refusing to put her down, he ran to join the stream of people fleeing out onto the street, pausing only to make sure that the Crane siblings and Buck were close behind.

It didn't take long to have everyone accounted for. And the residents of Black River took even less time to begin fighting against the flames. If anyone saw Katrina's work, no one mentioned it. *Not that they would.* The thought rolled around her head, finally breaking the seal that had kept her laughter from escaping. A slight giggle turned into a cackling fit while Cadwyn dropped her onto the hood of her car.

"What is wrong with you?" Anger was in his voice, but his tone remained pleasant. "Why would you taunt her?"

"I taunt everyone," she gasped between laughing fits.

"Why are you laughing?" Mina demanded, dragging the straps of the bags she still held higher onto her shoulder.

"Because this has never happened before."

Rage clouded over Mina's pretty face. "You find it amusing that my brother is going in when she's this enraged?"

Perched on the car, she was almost eye to eye with Mina. "Oh, she's going to be more dangerous than ever. But I don't think it's because she's enraged." Her smile grew until her cheeks hurt. "If I'm not mistaken, our Katrina is scared. And I'm, oh, so keen to find out why."

CHAPTER 6

Ozzie leaned through the gap between the front seats of the sedan to stare in dreaded wonder at the chaos that had consumed the small town of Black River. The smoke had been unmissable from the air. A dark disc that blotted out the sun and shrouded the town in early twilight. They had almost been able to convince themselves that it was a mundane forest fire. Seeing it from below left no room for denial.

Townsfolk and firetrucks choked the streets, forcing them to circle the outskirts of the town, unable to get close to Main Street. Ash fell like snow. The tiny flakes joined together to cover the rustic buildings in a dreary blanket. Ozzie had only been to Black River twice. Both times, the thing he noticed the most was the color. Everything was always far brighter than it had any right to be. It made everything vaguely uncanny. Everything was real, but nothing looked quite right. The falling ash robbed it of all of that. It covered the world in a monotone filter.

Percival Sewall turned on the windshield wipers as they slowly crept down the street. Through the smeared glass, Ozzie watched as the tower of smoke rose above the buildings as a single pillar, only to impossibly split into twin pillars.

"That's coming from the river," Percival said softly.

"Does that look like horns to anyone else?" Ozzie's father added from the front passenger seat. "In the clouds there?"

Percival pulled the car to the curb but kept the wipers working. Leaning against the steering wheel, he craned his neck to get a better look.

"Yeah, those are horns," he said absently.

Ozzie watched his mother's shoulders tense.

"You can find anything in clouds. They're like Rorschach inkblots."

When her husband turned to catch her eye, she threw him a stern look and tipped her head toward Ozzie. A clear sign that she didn't want the men scaring him.

Percival had missed the exchange and continued. "The Witch's Brew is over in that direction. That can't be a good sign."

Ozzie's mother reached across the backseat, blindly searching for her son. Ozzie felt oddly ashamed as he took his mother's hand and squeezed her fingers. The original plan had been to keep her out of this. Neither of his parents had a part in it. They weren't Sewalls. *They could stay away from all this*, Ozzie thought. *They don't have to know.* He forced a small smile when his father twisted around in the front passenger seat to check on him.

Cadwyn would have kept them out of it. The fact laughed at him. Over the weeks of planning and days of practice, he had convinced himself that he could handle anything thrown his way. Fifteen minutes with the Witch and he was right back to where he had started. A scared little boy in need of his parents.

"Is this normal?" Ozzie's father asked, shifting his gaze to Percival.

"No, Ethan. The river doesn't normally catch on fire."

Decades of friendship ensured that neither man took offense. Instead, they only seemed amused by each other. In the back seat, Ozzie bit his lips to keep himself from saying anything stupid that might break their good humor. He focused on rubbing the back of his mother's hand, trying to reassure her that everything was going to be okay.

"What did you mean that it wasn't a 'good sign'? What's happening?" she asked.

The question was clearly for Percival. With a heavy sigh, he turned in his seat, softening his tone but keeping a certain degree of sass.

"Your guess would be as good as mine, Ha-Yun."

Not as easily appeased as her husband, she narrowed her eyes, "You're the one who does this every year."

"As stated before, this is new."

"Maybe we should just leave," Ethan suggested. "Neither you nor Ozzie has a box."

"That's not the point. Now that Ozzie's been formally introduced to the family, it's expected that he make an appearance."

"Do you see this?" Ethan declared, slamming his hand against the window. "What do they expect him to do?"

Percival looked between both of his old friends like they were morons. "It's more about moral support."

"I promised them I'd be there," Ozzie stammered. "They were here for me when it was my turn. I can't just ghost them now."

Ha-Yun wasn't having any of it. "I don't like this idea of yours. This is obviously a bad omen."

"Mom, it was never going to be easy."

"You're a child. You shouldn't be involved in this."

After the events of their failed Spring attack, Ozzie knew better than to keep his parents in the dark or argue the finer points. He wasn't stupid enough to think they would be okay with him cave diving in the hopes of murdering an undead witch if they thought too much about it. The trick was to distract them by mentioning the others they knew.

"I promised Mina I would help. They're counting on me."

Ha-Yun had taken a liking to Mina in particular, admiring her unrelenting drive, even if it did border on unhealthy obsession a lot of the time. As an only child, his parents had never had anyone to compare him to. Now that they knew Mina, they had been making up for lost time. Grades, manners, general room tidiness. All the sibling rivalry stuff that would have made parenting a little easier on them.

He might have been annoyed if it didn't mortify Mina. Seeing her cringe took the edge off.

"I'm sure she has good intentions," Ha-Yun said. "But you're both too young to see the danger."

"You're not invincible," Ethan added.

Before Percival could cut in, Ozzie went for Plan B.

"Cadwyn's been involved in every step of the planning. He doesn't expect that we'll run into trouble, but he's prepared for it."

Whenever mentioning Mina doesn't work, mention Cadwyn. The arch of Percival's eyebrow made it clear that he knew what Ozzie was up to. Mercifully, he kept silent. Out of his little group of four, Cadwyn was the only one his parents believed to be a legitimate 'adult.' His age helped the perception along, of course, but it was mostly his personality. The psych nurse's thoughtful composure, wit, and warm smile had utterly charmed them in a few minutes flat.

"I'm sure he has," Ethan said, his voice a little less solid.

While Ethan shot some meaningful looks to his wife, Ozzie sought out Percival's gaze. *Don't mention Basheba!* He mentally screamed the words and was a little surprised when Percival smirked. *At least he gets it,* Ozzie thought. Experience had taught him that his parents more or less thought of her as they would a savage guard dog. Not exactly something they want in the house until a bigger bad guy is banging at the door.

A car horn blared, making them all jump. Ozzie had been so distracted that he hadn't even noticed the hatchback pulling up alongside their car. Just enough copper paint peaked out from under the smeared ash for Ozzie to recognize the vehicle as Basheba's.

Percival used the master switch to roll down Ethan's window, allowing the flecks of ash inside along with Basheba's cheerful voice.

"Hey, I thought that was you," she said. "When did you guys get in?"

"What's happened?" Percival demanded in a crisp, professional tone.

Resting her elbow on the window frame, she sighed wistfully. "A lot, actually. It's been one hell of a year."

"Why don't we stick to the highlights then?" Percival said, his voice a little tenser than it had been. "Perhaps we could start with why everything is covered in ash?"

She shrugged. "Katrina's chucking a tantrum."

Cadwyn swiftly leaned over from the front passenger seat to add, "No one's been physically injured, and the radius of real damage seems to be confined to the barbeque area."

"Thank goodness," Percival said.

"Your family is going to be very happy to see you." Cadwyn smiled warmly before shifting his attention. "Mr. and Mrs. Davis, lovely to see you again."

Ozzie watched with slight fascination as that token bit of politeness worked to ease the tension within his car. *I've got to learn how to do that.*

"Where is everyone now?" Percival asked.

"Most are heading to that roadside diner about twenty minutes out of town. The one with the big clown on the sign."

"Chuckles," Basheba cut in, side-eyeing Cadwyn with disapproval. "How do you not know that?"

"It's clearly a fault of my upbringing," Cadwyn said.

"Clearly," she mouthed, exaggerating the motion so much that even the people in the other car understood it.

A flash of annoyance crossed her face as Cadwyn gently pushed her back into the seat, making room for himself to lean further across and continue the conversation.

"Take the southbound highway out of town. It's the second exit. You can't miss it."

"You're not heading over there?" Percival said.

"Time is of the essence," Cadwyn said with an apologetic wince. "I'm guessing that Ozzie has got you all up to date on our plans?"

Ozzie sunk into his seat as his godfather replied. "He was light on a few of the details. But I have the basics."

"Tours run out of the cave entrance we need," Cadwyn continued. "We want to make sure that we get in before they close it due to..." He paused as he looked for the right word.

"Weather?" Basheba offered.

"We'll go with that."

Seizing the opportunity to get away with minimal arguments, Ozzie threw himself into motion. He quickly kissed his mother's cheek, gave his dad and Percival simultaneous one-armed hugs, and leaped out of the car. It only took him a few seconds to gather his bags out of the sedan's trunk and toss them into the back of Basheba's car. It was still time enough for the ash to gather on his skin and invade his mouth. Trying to work the taste off of his tongue, he climbed onto the makeshift bed that took up two-thirds of the vehicle and almost ended up headbutting a stranger.

"Oh," Ozzie sputtered. "Um, hi. You're new."

"This is my brother, Jeremiah." Mina finished the introductions while trying to hold Buck.

Regardless, the massive dog steadily worked his way across the car to give Ozzie a slobbery welcome. It considerably slowed Ozzie down and destroyed his clean getaway. All present parental units slipped past him before he was able to work the trunk door down. They lined the left wall, each looking equally awkward and determined. Percival's dark brows knotted together.

"Why am I sitting on a mattress?" Percival asked.

"I'm curious about that, too," Basheba noted, casting a glance over to Cadwyn.

He tipped his head to the side and heaved a sigh. "Does it matter if they come along?"

If Ozzie hadn't been there when Cadwyn had been forced to cut Basheba's eye out, he would have thought the fine lines were just some early wrinkles. Now, as her eyebrows rose to her hairline and the skin pulled taut, they looked like silver Sharpie marks.

"Please drive," Cadwyn said.

"I've got four hitchhikers in my car," Basheba spoke like Cadwyn was the only one that could hear her. Mindlessly, she swept a hand out to indicate the back. "It's like my grandpa always said. Any more than two hitchhikers per trip can only end in shallow graves."

"Excuse me?" Ha-Yun cut in only to be ignored.

Cadwyn barely hid his amusement as he playfully glared at the small blonde. "Stop teasing the tourists."

"You don't let me have any fun," Basheba said. She shifted into a more comfortable position and stomped on the gas.

Buck was the only one prepared for the sudden jerk, so he was spared the painful slam against metal and flesh.

"And for the record," Basheba noted to Cadwyn. "That was one of Grandpa's favorite sayings."

"Oh, of course. Just think of all the situations you could use that saying for," Cadwyn replied.

Basheba took the snide comment as agreement and preened. "He was a very wise man."

Mina opened her mouth, clearly intent on adding her perspective to the argument. Ozzie reached out to stop her but he needn't have bothered. The brunette snapped her mouth closed and turned her efforts to comforting her brother, leaving Cadwyn to handle the continued negations. Catching her gaze, Ozzie gave her a gentle smile. He was pretty sure that it physically hurt her to keep her silence.

"So, how is this working? I'm dropping them off at Chuckles then looping back around?" Basheba asked, blindly reaching over her shoulder.

Buck closed the distance to nuzzle her fingertips.

Cadwyn kept his tone light, "Or, we can take them to the cave." He continued while she was groaning. "If we take them with us, you'll have someone to drive your car back."

Disgust distorted her face as she gasped in horror. "Let someone else drive my car?"

"Were you planning to leave it in the Witch Woods with the cultists—watch the road—or the tourist parking lot where it'll get towed? I'm pretty sure we just ran a red light."

Basheba ignored the jabs against her driving skills. "For the record, I was planning to park on a back road. It'll be safe there."

"You're right. Far better than leaving it in the care of a multimillionaire who would feel compelled to compensate you for any damages that might happen."

Basheba narrowed her eyes on him, "I know you're trying to manipulate me."

"Does that stop it from working?" Cadwyn asked with an unrepentant smile.

After a moment, she huffed, muttered a 'fine' and rose her voice for the others to hear. "If you promise not to give my car to any of my family members, I'll bring you along. Only to the mouth of the cave. We part ways in the parking lot."

"Agreed," Ethan answered hurriedly.

The falling ash thickened as they made their way through the town. Ozzie barely caught a glimpse of the graveyard as it passed his window. It was little more than a few random shadows in a dull fog. The lack of visibility reminded him too much of being in the tank to leave breathing an easy task. Buck butted his head against Ozzie's hand, offering the teenager a distracting task. While he scratched behind the Rottweiler's ears, he was dimly aware of Mina explaining what had happened at the barbeque.

Good thing she's the one telling that story, Ozzie thought as the explanation continued.

Mina had a skill at keeping to the bare facts, and the unemotional delivery eased the blow to his parents. His mother still reached out to wrap a protective arm around his shoulders as Ethan kept casting worried glances at Percival. Ozzie wasn't sure which one of them he should try and comfort first. In his hesitation, he noticed Jeremiah again.

The guy had a way of being so quiet and still that it was easy to forget he was there. All he did was stare at the music box in his hand, watching the small, gilded clogs churn. *A ticking clock*. Ozzie racked his brain for something that would make Jeremiah feel even a little better. The tension shattered in the wake of Basheba's abrupt giggle.

"I fail to see what part of this is funny," Ha-Yun said in a frigid voice.

Cadwyn tipped his head back slightly to explain. "She believes that this is a good sign."

"Damn straight it is," Basheba chirped.

"The Pompeii levels of ash?" Percival asked.

"Don't exaggerate," Basheba scoffed. "All of this is one big sign that she's scared."

"What would she possibly have to be scared of?" Jeremiah's voice cracked as he clutched the sides of the box, his nails scraping over the smooth sides.

Basheba's tone was somehow the perfect representation of rolling her eyes, "How about the fact that she was human once?"

Jeremiah's head shot up. "What?"

"She was human once. Not a witch. Not a ghost. Just a dumb, ol' boring human."

Jeremiah glanced at his sister. When she couldn't give him the answer he was searching for, he turned to Ozzie, who could do little more than awkwardly shrug. *I've got no idea where she's going with that.*

"She wasn't born with her powers," Basheba broke the silence.

Mina jolted with sudden realization. "You think that someone, well *something*, gave her these abilities?"

"Duh," Basheba said. "If 'dying while pissed off' was the only criteria to make a vengeful, killer ghost, we'd have a lot more running around the place."

"I suppose," Mina said thoughtfully.

"And if there's one thing that's always constant in this world, it's that the powerful don't do the weak favors for nothing."

Ozzie shook his head in rapid, small motions. It was enough to keep his parents from arguing the point.

"Your grand theory is that the Bell Witch made a deal with the Devil?" Jeremiah scoffed. "What a startling insight."

"So, being annoying is like a family trait for you Cranes?" Basheba replied, taking a sharp corner and narrowly avoiding a pedestrian. She didn't slow down.

Cadwyn braced his arm against the door. "Oh," he said slowly.

"Oh, what? What does 'oh' mean?" Ethan asked.

"I think I get what you're aiming for," Cadwyn told Basheba before continuing. "Most of the time, when people consider deals with demons, they think of one-off transactions. Wealth in exchange for your soul, for example. Basheba's theory is that Katrina has an ongoing debt."

"You're calling her by her name, too?" Jeremiah whimpered, half in pain, half in frustration.

Cadwyn shrugged. "Hang around her long enough and you'll pick up the habit, too."

"An ongoing debt," Mina said thoughtfully. "The bulls. The ones the minotaurs were sacrificing at the Bell ancestral home. You're thinking that they weren't her tributes. They were for her... benefactor."

"And I doubt that he'll be happy that she stiffed him." Basheba bit her smile and took another sharp turn. It was now almost impossible to see anything more than an inch away from the glass. How she saw the road at all, Ozzie didn't know. "Even if I'm wrong, they were for *something*. If they weren't intended for a benefactor, then they had to be for her. Why would she need that many?"

"So, she's either ticked off a more powerful being and needs to get things right quickly, or she's personally weakened," Cadwyn finished the thought.

Jeremiah barked a bitter laugh and slammed a fist against the window. "Does this look 'weaker' to you?"

"Duh," Basheba stared at him for a moment, clearly confused that he hadn't come to the same conclusion. "Life lesson, Crane. You don't need such a blatant show of force if you're the one in control."

"I'm sorry," Ethan cut in, slightly stammering as he tried to steady himself in the swerving car. "I'm rather new to all of this, and I'm sure you'll think this is a stupid question—"

"Not at all," Cadwyn assured.

"If it helps, there's a fairly good chance that I already think you're an idiot," Basheba said, her voice light and cheerful.

At Cadwyn's urging, Ethan ignored her to ask, "What has any of this got to do with the caves?"

"Nothing," Basheba said, taking another turn that Ozzie couldn't see. "We just want to get our hands on her corpse."

Percival shook his head as if he could physically jolt the words into making sense.

"The rumors are that she *haunts* the caves but there's no debate that she's buried in the graveyard. You've personally destroyed her headstone several times, Basheba."

Taking one hand off of the wheel, Basheba loosely gestured to Mina. "You figured it out, so you take it from here."

"Katrina was convicted and executed for witchcraft in 1817. In those times, they never would have permitted her burial in consecrated ground."

"Yes, yes," Percival grumbled. "We all know that. She had a pauper's grave on the outskirts of town until about a century after her death. Did you forget the end of the story? How word spread far and wide about Black River, the nowhere little town still ignorant enough to hang women for witchcraft. The town was desperate to save face and relocated her coffin to the town graveyard."

"Yes. Well, no, actually," Mina said in a rush. "I've been scouring through the town archives—"

"Do you think you're the first to do that?" Percival cut in. "There's nothing in the records that contradict the story."

"Not in the official ones, no. The undertaker was meticulous with his notes. The undertaker's cousin's wife's diary, however, mentioned her relative committing a blasphemy. Now, most of her belongings were lost to time. But it was a different matter for her friend, Christina Riches, the renowned poet. Her paperwork was archived upon her death and, within them, I found some of the undertaker's cousin's wife's letters along with some of Christina's replies that hadn't been sent for various reasons that don't need to be explored at this moment."

"Can you say that again?" Ethan asked.

"Maybe a bit slower," Percival added.

Ha-Yun rolled her eyes and rattled off at a pace similar to Mina's. "A woman from Black River wrote to her friend about the insanity happening in town. Said friend kept the letters. Mina read the letters."

Mina's shoulders slumped slightly. "That's exactly what I just said. Is no one listening to me?"

"Ignore them, dear," Ha-Yun said. "Do go on."

Percival and Jeremiah looked about as shell-shocked as Ozzie had felt when he had first heard Mina's theory. It seemed his mother, however, had decided to bypass shock for now and got straight into protective mode. She listened intently, hanging on Mina's every word as the girl continued.

Mina perked up, took in a deep breath, and continued. "Once I tracked down Christina's personal correspondence, it became clear that the undertaker had refused to put the Bell Witch in holy ground. Instead, he and his assistant disposed of her in a cave. There are only a few caves in the area. Mostly small ones that are often used by hunters."

"I told her that one," Basheba cut in. "So I helped and deserve half the credit."

"So acknowledged," Mina said. "Plenty of unaccounted-for skeletons show up in the Witch Woods, but none of them could have been Katrina."

"How would you know that?" Ha-Yun asked.

"The documentation of her death recorded her height and that she died at the drop, basically of a broken neck. None of the Jane Does have matched on both accounts," Mina dismissed. "They must have hidden her in the underground catacombs. The Witch Caves are the easiest entrance point."

Percival gaped at her for a moment.

"Admittedly, I'm not that great of a witch hunter, but research is my jam," Mina said.

"It's been two-hundred years. There won't be anything of her left." Percival protested.

Mina faltered for the first time. "There are numerous stories of witch's corpses refusing to rot. I don't know if there's any truth to that, but something's tethering her to the cave."

Ha-Yun choked on her words while searching for the best way to finish her sentence. "All of this hinges on the theory that, centuries ago, two men refused to do their job."

"The Winthrops have a few traditions we brought over from our tiny town in the old country. One is that you always bury a witch with a silver crucifix in her mouth." Arching in his seat, Cadwyn sought out Percival's eyes. "It wasn't in either grave."

"And how would you know that?" Ethan asked.

Basheba snorted, "Because I have a shovel and determination."

"You dug up her grave?" Percival's nose scrunched up with disgust.

"*Graves*," Basheba stressed the plural while Cadwyn shook his head in bemusement.

"It was a weird honeymoon," he noted.

CHAPTER 7

Cadwyn ran his thumb across the smooth gold of his wedding ring before twisting it around his finger. Not willing to reveal any personal information to his patients, there were few occasions when he got to wear it. So few that it still felt a novelty months into his marriage. He liked the way the gold warmed to his body like a second skin, the constant weight of it, and the way it allowed him to indulge in a rather subtle nervous habit.

The conversation continued in the back of the car. Once it had shifted from the overall plan, he decided that it didn't need his input anymore. Mina and Ozzie could handle the finer points on their own. It gave him time to dwell on their marriage reveal. It hadn't been as bad as he had expected. Even Percival had taken it in stride. Keeping the ring in motion, he watched Basheba from the corner of his eyes. She waved through the forest more by muscle memory than by sight. Completely undisturbed by both the fog and the chaos they had left behind.

While he had been prepared for a few of his relatives to treat the marriage like he had somehow secured the queen from Isaac's chessboard, he hadn't been ready to see them revel in it. He knew that look. He had seen it in Isaac's eyes the night Katrina's cult came for them. Isaac had stood boldly beside the mob, demanding Basheba's surrender without a hint of hesitation or shame. *Because he's done it all before. And people knew.* Mina's father had confessed as much, not only that he knew Isaac had been making deals with Katrina for his own safety, but that the Crane elders approved of it. What had cut Cadwyn the deepest was the man's implication that they weren't the *only* ones who knew and turned a blind eye.

The families were supposed to rely on one another. It was a belief so ingrained within them that the Sewalls used it as their unofficial motto. *And no one said a word,* Cadwyn thought with bile rising in his throat. *They saw the Bell line being carved down to nothing. They saw Basheba being selected twice for the Harvest while Isaac and his daughter remained blissfully safe. They saw him eroding the bloodline, and they said nothing.* It was enough to leave a thick sludge of dread coating his stomach.

Tapping his nail against the ring, he made a mental list of the relatives he'd seen with that same glint in their eyes. Each one undoubtedly saw Basheba as Isaac did. More a war dog than a young woman. Something dangerous to send charging at your enemies. Something useful and, ultimately, disposable. The list was longer than he was comfortable with. Anger bubbled through his veins as he resolved to pull each one aside and clearly explain the situation to them. Basheba wasn't their weapon, nor their collateral damage. She was *his wife.* No one else had a claim to her. The thought made him jolt. He wasn't exactly sure how well Basheba would take to him running around snarling that at people. *I might need a phrase that sounds a little less possessive.*

"What?"

Basheba's whisper pulled him from his thoughts.

"Sorry?" he asked.

"You're the one that's staring."

"I'm just thinking," Pulling a hand through his hair, he worked his bangs off of his forehead. Not wanting to deal with the topic seriously, but sure he couldn't avoid it entirely, he added with a smile, "I feel like you only married me to infuriate people."

"Don't sell yourself short." Reaching over, she patted him on his knee. "You're a great trophy husband."

"I'm pretty sure you have that the wrong way around."

"Nah, I don't."

"You're a pretty, younger woman with no money to speak of."

Basheba opened her mouth, froze for a moment, then ended her thoughts with a 'huh.'

Leaving the town proper thinned the ash once more into something akin to a snowstorm. Cadwyn fell into silence, still restlessly spinning the ring. *Katrina's desperate, and we're going into a giant underground water pit.* The idea played on the edges of his awareness, refusing to leave him entirely. *This is going to hurt.*

He spun the ring again and ordered himself not to think about it anymore. Worrying wasn't going to change the situation. Basheba and Mina were stubbornly set on their course of action. Nothing short of an act of God was going to stop them. He smirked, *Basheba would just take that as a personal challenge.*

There was a chance that he could keep Ozzie from coming. *He'll try and catch up with us*, Cadwyn reasoned. *It's better that he's with us from the start rather than alone for most of it.* The notion didn't sit well with him. Nothing in this situation did. They were better prepared this time, yet it still felt as much like a suicide mission as Mina's first idea.

You know you're not going to leave them to face it alone, his internal voice taunted him. Lost once more in thought, he was stunned by how short the trip was. Soon enough, Basheba was pulling into the gravel parking lot that served both for a hiking trail and the Witch Cave tours. A few scattered cars speckled the parking lot, all of them gathered haphazardly around the small tour bus. The thick layer of ash hadn't fully covered the bright purple paint job or logo.

Haunted Black River Tours was sprawled under their logo of a witch riding a broomstick. Cadwyn hated that logo. Not because it was stereotypical. He just didn't want to think of the woman who brutally murdered generations of his family as a voluptuous, sexualized, or any way attractive individual.

Basheba followed his gaze to see the bus. "Ugh, not that company. They hate me."

"What did you do to them?" he asked, a smile curling his lips despite himself.

Basheba smirked and slipped out of the car. "Nothing they can prove."

While he'd never admit it out loud, he did get a vicarious thrill out of hearing about her outbursts. It was almost charming, in its way. The raw honesty of her reactions. The completely unashamed way that she wore her emotions on her sleeve. Sometimes, he could convince himself that he had once had the potential to be like her. *If it hadn't been for...* He cut the thought off before it could fully form. Nothing good ever came from dwelling on that year.

The time came to hand over the car keys, and Cadwyn made sure to linger a little closer to Basheba's side. It had taken him far too long to realize why the crappy old vehicle meant so much to her. It had belonged to her parents. The whole family had traveled the country in it. It was all she had left of them. After long contemplation, she grudgingly handed the keys to Percival.

"You'll need to head off soon," Cadwyn said as gently as he could. "People will be wondering where Jeremiah is."

For a moment, everyone eyed the music box. No one mentioned it.

Seeking out Mina's gaze, Percival vowed to take good care of the terrified teenager. He added with a smile, "And Buck, too."

Basheba jolted, blinked, then broke into a fit of giggles.

"You're not taking him anywhere."

Ethan's brow furrowed. "You intend to take a dog into flooded caves with you?"

"He'll drown," Ha-Yun added as if her husband hadn't made the point clear enough.

Pushing past them, Basheba unlatched the hidden compartment under the mattress and pulled free an oddly shaped glass dome.

"Doggy scuba gear," she declared with a grin.

Percival was the first of them to recover, mumbling, "That can't be a thing."

"It works surprisingly well," Cadwyn said. "He can go down just as deep as I can."

"How?" Percival asked.

"There's a place in the Florida Keys that makes them and offers a training course," Basheba explained while gathering up the rest of her belongings.

"Of course, Florida," Percival mumbled.

Cadwyn chuckled as he took the emergency medical kit Basheba passed to him. After their last few trips into the Witch Woods, he had had to replace the outer pack. The new strap still felt strange against his shoulder.

"He loves to chase turtles." Basheba's delicate brow scrunched up, and she leaned her hip against the car frame. "Although, I've got no idea what he thinks he's going to do if he catches one. Oh, Jerry, I left you guys a pair of spiked collars in the back. Necks and wrists. For the record, I just sharpened them and take no responsibility if you end up impaling yourself or others."

Buck excitedly nosed at each new item Basheba pulled from the numerous hidden compartments that she had squirreled about the car's innards. It was a vast amount given her tendency to live out of a single tattered backpack. A tense stillness settled upon them, allowing their group to disperse somewhat.

Percival and the Davis couple circled Ozzie, alternating between building up his self-confidence and trying to get him to come back with them. Mina and Jeremiah slinked to the far end of the bus. Just far enough away to make their whispers inaudible.

On reflex, Cadwyn glanced over his shoulder, instinctively seeking out whoever was vying for his attention. It took him half a heartbeat to realize that no one was. A few stray people hurried to catch the tour group, stirring the ash and autumn leaves. None of them so much as glanced in his direction. *It's different without the family around.*

He shoved his hands into the deep pockets of his leather biker's jacket, and absently shifted his weight between his feet. Traveling with his new wife for a month had been an eye-opening experience. They had bred independence into her, and she guarded it with particular ferocity. When it came to setting up campsites or preparing for a hunt, it was better to stay out of her way.

Left to idle, his thoughts rippled to the forefront of his mind. *Having lunch with the family.* That's what Basheba had called eating in the graveyard, surrounded by her relatives' headstones. It was one of the few times he had ever seen her completely serene. Sitting in the sunlight, Buck's head on her lap, in a field of death and loss. *Alone.* Cadwyn clenched his jaw hard enough to feel his partial dentures shift against the scarred ridges of his gums. *She's a Winthrop now. She's got me.*

It was a small comfort. Just enough for him to realize that this was possibly the last moment of peace he was ever going to have. Suddenly, he really wanted a cigarette. A bit of shuffling and he found the mangled remains of a pack in his inner coat pocket. His training snarled in the back of his head as he pried open the box, but it counted for little. Cancer seemed like a distant mirage when the Bell Witch was lurking so close. *The Harvest brings out your best and worst.* It seemed almost pitiful that his worst was smoking.

He had one pinched between his lips and was in the course of lighting it when he recalled that Basheba hated the smell. Catching Ozzie's gaze, Cadwyn tipped his head to the side, signaling that he was going to the edge of the parking lot.

While it only took him a few strides to cross the gravel, the falling ash had already gathered over his cigarette and Zippo by the time he made it to the bin. He tossed the cigarette, retrieved a new one, and wiped his lighter off on his biker pants. *Should have changed earlier.*

The glow of the steady flame glistened off of his Zippo's siding. Taking his first draw, he rubbed the last of the ash off of the mother-of-pearl version of Guido Reni's painting, *The Archangel Michael.* He studied the lines of the stoic angel poised to slay the monster crushed under his foot. If he had been expecting a gift from Basheba, it wouldn't have been this. *Although, the fact that it makes fire wasn't a shock.*

It had become a tradition to contemplate her reasoning each time he used it. *Archangel Michael protects from evil*, he reasoned. *Is she trying to offer comfort? Honestly thinks it will keep me safe? Just wanted me to have a lighter on hand? Does she believe in angels?*

Drawing in a deep breath, the hot smoke mingled with the gathering winter chill. Autumns in Black River always gave way to early, bitter winters. He let his thoughts swirl without answers as the smoke slipped from his lips. Once he had safely tucked the Zippo back into his zippered pocket, he turned to study the mouth of the cave. A low fence of hanging chains set up across it acted as a makeshift massing point for the tourists. They milled about, chatting amongst themselves or taking snapshots of the falling ash.

Tipping his head back to release the lungful of smoke, Cadwyn froze. The teenager's image entered his head as broken segments rather than a singular whole.

Soft brunette hair flopped across the edges of the boy's forehead. A slight stir of wind was enough to force it to slip down and catch on the corner of the boy's familiar blue eyes. A simple motion that forced a thousand memories to surge forward with physical strength. Breathless, Cadwyn studied the long straight nose that hovered over thin, wide lips. The strong jawline and high cheekbones. The shoulders that, had he lived long enough to grow into them, would have become as broad as Cadwyn's own. He had forgotten how much he looked like his older brother.

"Abraham?"

Cigarette forgotten, it slipped from his fingers to burn the top of his boot. Abraham, forever frozen as a teenager, cocked one corner of his mouth into a smirk. Reason fled Cadwyn on a broken breath. He started up the small incline. Abraham shrunk back, disappearing within the crowd. Static filled Cadwyn's head as he broke into a jog. He craned his neck, searching the people around him with growing desperation, unable to catch sight of the Winthrop features.

"Abraham!"

People turned to glare at him when he jostled them aside in his search. A few of the bolder and more irritable shoved him in retaliation. None of it mattered. Not when his brother re-emerged. Lingering at the entrance of the caves, Abraham tipped his head in a silent invitation to follow.

"Cadwyn?"

He didn't know who called for him. All that registered was that it wasn't Abraham. *Abraham.* Cadwyn broke into a run, unceremoniously shoving his way free of the group and easily hurdling the low chain-link fence.

"Hey, steady on, big guy." With a wide, forced smile, the tour guide blocked Cadwyn's way.

Frustration clawed at the inside of Cadwyn's chest while the tour guide pressed a hand against his sternum, forcing him back a step.

"Relax, we're not set to go in for another fifteen minutes. Oh! Hey, I know you."

"Let go," Cadwyn snarled between his clenched teeth, his eyes locked on his brother.

Abraham turned on his heel and started into the depths of the cave, leaving Cadwyn behind and forcing him to watch as his brother entered the darkness alone. Cadwyn surged forward only to have the prattling tour guide shove him back once more.

"Cadwyn!"

The small part of his mind that responded to Basheba's call was quickly squashed. Destroyed and dismissed by the knowledge that it wasn't Abraham's voice. In that moment, only his brother mattered. Shadows swallowed his retreating figure like a wall of oil. Trembling with manic energy, Cadwyn staggered forward a step.

"Abraham!"

A static roar filled his ears. An almost physical force that hollowed him out and destroyed all thought and reason. It left him with nothing but the desperate need to join his brother. Cadwyn pushed forward again. The guide shoved him back.

Pain sparked along Cadwyn's arm, the only proof his brain would accept that he had swung at the man. Echoes of startled cries worked on the edges of his awareness, along with the vague image of ash-speckled dust billowing out from around the guide's sprawled body. A slender cut split the man's lower lip, allowing blood to seep from his mouth. The sight struck something within Cadwyn, churning his stomach as the haze began to lift from his mind.

"Cadwyn!"

Not Abraham, a dark voice whispered within his skull. He shook his head, fighting against the haze that had consumed his thoughts. His reality had narrowed down to his brother so swiftly that the idea of anyone else being important baffled him.

"Cadwyn! Stop!"

Basheba? Blinking rapidly, he started to turn, intending to go back.

"Cadwyn," Abraham called from the darkness. "Over here."

The static rose to a deafening roar that consumed the other voice. There was only Abraham, calling for him, leaving him. Cadwyn hurried after the retreating specter.

Rotten leaves squished under his feet, threatening to trip him as he fled from the light. In time, the squish of leaves gave way to loose pebbles then, at last, hard stone. As he thundered deeper into the darkening world, the air became dank and tainted with the combination of rot and stale musk. After about a quarter of a mile, the walls opened up, transforming the tunnel into a vast, hollow chamber.

He left behind the well-trodden path that lined the walls to slide down the sharp slope to the water's edge. The underground lake was little more than a polished sheet of ebony. It sat perfectly still, without a single ripple to stir its surface. Voices and motion followed him. All of it was easy enough to ignore as he searched the clustered shadows.

"Cadwyn."

After so many years, hearing Abraham's voice again broke him. Choking on a sob, Cadwyn turned to the right and began to scramble over the uneven stones surrounding the water.

"Abraham," he called softly.

He swooped under a jagged stone that protruded over the water and stopped. A few small pebbles toppled into the water, the soft splash the only noise left to break the silence. Abraham stood before him, no longer as Cadwyn wished to remember him, but the brutal reality of what he had been forced to become.

Withered and frail, reeking of early decay, his body a grotesque patchwork of gangrene and necrotizing fasciitis. The flesh-eating virus had ravaged him, devoured him from the inside out, carving out little tunnels that a variety of insects had infested.

Tears blurred Cadwyn's vision as he lowered his gaze to his brother's right leg. The battered, shredded stump where it had once been. Twelve years old, frightened, and alone, Cadwyn should have never attempted the amputation.

Why did I follow? His self-preservation instincts raged at him, cursing him for depriving them of such a slim kindness to hold onto. If he had just stayed where he was, he could have kept the image of Abraham as he had been.

"It was a lie," Cadwyn whispered, forcing himself to meet the ghost's eyes.

"Cadwyn," Abraham said, his voice distorted by the damage that ravaged his mouth and throat. "I don't feel so good."

He reached out for Cadwyn. Bloody pus broke free of the limp flesh that dropped from his bones. The droplets fell to the stone in a soft pattering.

"Help me," Abraham pleaded.

Cadwyn gasped. Everything screamed at him to go to his brother. To stay by his side, protect him as best he could, shield him from the evil that threatened them both. Without conscious thought, he lifted his hand to the remains of his brother, inching closer even as Abraham's flesh slopped away to expose muscle and bone.

"Abraham," Cadwyn sobbed, a small reassuring smile pulling at his lips. "It'll all be okay. Just rest."

The skin around Abraham's jaw chipped away as he worked it, drawing his rotten lips into an answering smile. "God, have mercy on us."

The words slashed into his soul, forcing him to buckle in half as a dark shape loomed in his peripheral vision. Cadwyn spun to see the putrid, yellow eyes of the demon blazing in the darkness. He swung blindly, feeling flesh give way under his knuckles. Pain flashed across the back of his knees, driving down hard enough to work the joint and force him to kneel. The demon's laughter filled him, threatening to crack his skull from within. The sound brought with it the echoing remains of a year spent as its prisoner. Agonized screams, both his brother's and his own. Broken sobs and desperate prayers that never seemed to be answered.

Gnashing his teeth, Cadwyn threw himself at the demon in a blind fury. They crashed to the unforgiving ground. It thrashed under him but he managed to throw a leg over and straddle the beast. It never stopped laughing. The mocking cackle shook the walls and forced stones around them to tremble. It fueled his rage. He wanted it to hurt, wanted it to feel the fear it had inflicted upon him. Snatching up a rock, he drove it down into the gleeful, monstrous face.

Fire slashed along his thigh, tracing the scar the sacrificial bull had given him months before. He bellowed in rage and agony and rose the stone to strike again. Fangs latching onto his wrist, the thick leather of his jacket barely managing to spare his flesh from the attack. Rearing back, he found himself face to face with Buck. The colossal Rottweiler whipped his jaws about before dragging him back and off of the body below him.

"Cadwyn!" Mina screamed.

He bared his teeth in a feral snarl and threw himself at the creature again. Only it wasn't there. Basheba was. Her blue eyes dazed and blood bubbling from her mouth.

Basheba lurched up, unprepared for the world to ripple and slosh across her vision. Her stomach roiled under the force of it. She braced herself against the cold stones, almost missing the copper tang that drenched her taste buds. As the blood welled in her mouth, she pressed a hand against her tender jaw, trying to force her brain to function. Everything inside her felt loose around the edges. Soft and pliable and rubbing against each other with every breath. The only part of her that remained solid was her grip on her hunting knife. It served as an anchor, allowing her something to hold onto while angry words and low growls dug into her pounding skull.

Lurching to the side, she spat out a mouthful of blood, confused by the soft clatter that accompanied it. Her blurred vision cleared just in time to see a stray tooth topple across the stones, coming to a stop on the last rock before the obsidian water. Carefully, she leaned forward, her fingers wavering as she reached out. Tinkling drips of water rose over the noise behind her. Basheba jolted, her trembling hand hovering in place, as a tentacle slipped from the depths. *It's one of Katrina's tricks,* Basheba told herself before deciding to blame the blow to her head. *It won't be here.*

Her stomach clenched tight as a single memory emerged from the scattered haze of her mind. *The Leviathan. Mina interrupted me before the tradition was complete.*

The tentacle coiled out over the rocks, incandescent blue at one moment, rich blood red the next, seeking the pool of fluid Basheba had shed. Snow white suction cups quivered with anticipation as the tip of the tentacle looped around her broken tooth. Then, as silently and swiftly as it had emerged, it returned into the lake with its prize.

Basheba flung herself back, retreating over the rocks with her knife raised and her free hand reaching for Buck. He didn't come to her. Abruptly, the sounds tormenting her took on new meaning. She whipped around to see Cadwyn stomp on the joint of Buck's hind leg and strike at the hinge of his jaw in the same moment. The dual attack was just enough for him to rip his arm free of Buck's fangs. The shredded remains of Cadwyn's leather jacket hung around his bleeding arm as he rolled up into a crouch.

The two circled each other, chests heaving and damp with blood and sweat. Saliva flung from Buck's jaws as he snapped at the air. Cadwyn's bangs had swooped down to shield his face, drawing more attention to the way his lips curled back in a snarl. Basheba stared unblinkingly at the rare sight.

Percival shattered the moment by rushing forward. It was only a few steps but more than enough to have both primal figures fix their attention upon him. The older man readjusted his grip on the cattle prod he was holding.

"Hey, that's mine." Basheba's protest became an unintelligible gargle as blood rushed past her lips.

Cadwyn brought up his hand as he growled, "Don't."

"He's going to kill you," Percival argued.

"Basheba will kill me if I hurt him."

Any protest was left unsaid as Buck charged, barreling down upon Cadwyn with bared fangs, lunging at the last moment. It was just enough room for Cadwyn to roll under the airborne dog and turn around in time for the next attack. Basheba's slight smile faded the instant Cadwyn's foot slipped back into the water. Hurriedly, she pursed her lips to whistle, but the combination of blood and pain choked off the sound.

Swearing and spitting cleared out her mouth enough that she was able to shout. "Buck! Release!"

Buck instantly lost all interest in Cadwyn, breaking away mid-attack to gallop over to Basheba. She welcomed him with open arms, laughing as he alternated between licking her face and nudging her with whimpering concern. It was hard to keep a solid hold on him as his rump wiggled around in excitement.

"I'm okay," she cooed, rubbing down his sides as she soothed him and checked for wounds at the same time. "How's my gorgeous boy? Huh?"

"Oh, God. Basheba," Cadwyn whimpered, all ferocity gone to leave him shaking and stricken.

"Get away from the water."

The horrified expression didn't leave his face as he obeyed. "I wasn't going to hurt him. I swear."

"But you have no problem attacking *her*?" Ha-Yun shot back.

Basheba tried to scoff but, once again, her damaged mouth turned it into a sharp hiss. With Buck now safely tucked under her arm, her adrenaline dwindled, allowing pain to rear up inside her like an angry beast.

"Basheba?" Cadwyn rushed toward her, stopping short when Buck released a threatening growl.

Covering her mouth with one hand, she tried to soothe her pet with the other.

"It's all right," she said.

"No, it's not," Ha-Yun shrieked.

"I didn't see her," Cadwyn said.

"You were beating her with a rock," Ethan cut in, starting for Basheba's side.

Buck lowered his head, his hackles raised and his lips curling back. A clear threat that Ethan headed.

"I didn't see *her,*" Cadwyn snarled. "It was the demon!"

"Hold up." Catching sight of Ozzie, Basheba decided to swallow the blood in her mouth rather than force him to see it. "So, you saw a demon and your first instinct was to *tackle it*?"

Cadwyn stared at her helplessly for a moment before he

shrugged one shoulder. Her first burst of laughter was a shock to everyone but herself, which only made the whole situation funnier to her. As the cavern echoed her giggles, she met Cadwyn's gaze. He managed to hold on for a moment longer, shoulders trembling and his face flushed red. They laughed until her sides ached and her blood seeped between her fingers to drench her flannel shirt.

"You're such an idiot," she gasped, flicking the blood off of her fingers.

He sucked in a breath. "It seemed like the thing to do at the time."

The whole group backed toward the entrance of the cave when thudding footsteps sped toward them. Searching beams of light slashed across the shadows, drawing ever closer.

"That would be the guide," Percival said sharply.

Basheba gulped down another mouthful of thick copper blood. "Ozzie, take your parents and cut them off. Percival, go with them. Throw a little weight around if you have to but keep them away from us."

Before Ha-Yun could ask, Basheba elaborated.

"Everyone in this town knows that Katrina has called dibs on us. Since interfering with us runs the risk of crossing her, we can get away with a lot more than anyone else can." Testing her jaw with a gentle touch made her flinch. "I have no idea why more don't exploit that little fact."

"A cult is trying to kill you." Ha-Yun's tone suggested that this was one detail Ozzie had been downplaying quite a bit. "Why would you ever come back here?"

"It's not the *whole* town. Just a few people in it," Ozzie said sheepishly.

"That's more than enough, Osgood," Ha-Yun scolded.

Mina cut in, "The plan was to stay with the safety of the families until we could slip in here."

"Isn't that what you did?" The sweep of Ha-Yun's hand chastised her more than screaming could.

"We underestimated how bold the cult was. Last time, they only attacked at night and in isolation. I thought the threat of tourists would make them hesitate."

Ha-Yun heaved a sigh, her maternal instincts softening her tone. "It wasn't safe."

"Where in Black River is?" Basheba's dismissive snort ended in a pained gasp. "Now, can you guys please go and stop the tourists before we're the attraction?"

Ethan looked between the lights, his friend, and Basheba. At last, he locked his gaze on Cadwyn. "I don't think we should leave you alone."

"I've lost a tooth," Basheba noted. "*Heaps* of blood. Might be a good idea to keep your blood-phobic son away from me for a bit."

Parental protection kicked in for all three concerned and they quickly began ushering Ozzie back toward the entrance. Ozzie himself hesitated, glancing over his shoulder and slowing his pace. Basheba smiled behind her hands, hoping that her eyes would convey the gesture without making him sick.

"It's okay. We're good."

"But," Ozzie stammered. "Cadwyn doesn't do well with missing teeth."

"That's why Mina's staying back with us," Basheba said, hurriedly swallowing a mouthful of blood as her brow furrowed. "And Jeremiah, I guess. Not gonna lie, Jerry, I honestly forgot you existed."

Jeremiah shuffled slightly more behind his sister and kept his mouth shut.

"I'm okay now," Cadwyn assured. "We'll be up in a second."

Even though he was the one they were worried about, Cadwyn had no problem placating the crowd. He waited for them to move away before trying to get closer to Basheba again, Buck's warning grumbles not enough to make him give up.

"I'm so sorry," Cadwyn said.

"You should be," Basheba snapped. "You run off to do something asinine and didn't bring me along? That's my whole thing, Cad!"

Cadwyn's lips jerked into a small smile despite himself. "I'll remember to extend an invitation next time."

"That's all I ask."

Fighting against Buck's attempts to keep himself as a furry shield, Basheba got to her feet and walked over to the cave wall, as far from the water as she could get without risking exposure to the general public. There wasn't any point in drawing more attention. Cadwyn matched her stride for stride, never coming closer nor taking his eyes off of her.

"I think I'm going to need some stitches," she said.

The pain had grown enough to throb along her nerve endings. She hid it as best she could as she settled onto a large boulder. One that would let her lay down on a slope. Buck rested his head on her stomach, whimpering softly. He settled once she began scratching him behind his ears.

"There's a dentist in town," Jeremiah said, his eyes narrowing as he watched Cadwyn pull his medical bag free from his shoulders.

"It's all right," Basheba said. "Mina knows how to do stitches."

Cadwyn flinched and twisted around to stare at Mina. She stared back at him, looking helpless and guilty.

"What is that?" Basheba asked, waving a hand between the two. "What's going on with your faces?"

"Nothing," Mina blurted out.

"I'll assist her," Cadwyn added meekly, "if you'll let me."

It clicked, and Basheba laughed. A short sound that soon turned into a pained gasp. "Right. I'm punishing you by not letting you repeatedly stab me with a needle."

"I only want to help you," Cadwyn mumbled.

"Blood, mouth, teeth. Not a good combo for you, idiot," she shot back, enduring the spike of pain it took to roll her eyes. "I don't care about the attempted murder stuff. Throwing up on me, however, is grounds for divorce."

The sorrow remained in his eyes even as the corner of his mouth jerked again. "In sickness and in health, Basheba. I'm afraid you're stuck with me."

"Hey," she snorted, the sound slightly distorted by the blood pooling in her mouth. Stripping off her backpack, she used it as a pillow. "You vowed to love, honor, and *obey*. I didn't see you doing much of that at the mouth of the cave."

Mina had been quietly bustling around them, checking the contents of the medical bag and coordinating with her brother to get the most out of their combined phone lights. Jerking, she cut back into the conversation.

"You vowed to obey?"

"So did she," Cadwyn said.

Mina's eyebrows shot up her forehead. "Really?"

"Yeah, but it was more of a suggestion for *me*," Basheba said, her words trailing off as the last of her adrenaline faded and the pain took hold.

A small whimper escaped her, and Cadwyn was kneeling beside her, ignoring Buck's growls. It was rare that Basheba got a chance to see him in full 'professional mode,' and she took a moment to enjoy it. There was a laser focus to his eyes that played in fun contrast to his utterly relaxed posture. With swift efficiency, he stripped off his jacket, sanitized his hands and battered forearms, and snapped on a pair of gloves. All while conducting his visual examination.

"Does it hurt anywhere else?"

"I've got a bit of a headache," she admitted.

"Do you know who I am?"

"It's barely a mild concussion, Cadwyn Octavius Winthrop," Basheba said, pausing to swallow the accumulating blood. "I'll be fine with an aspirin."

"Octavius?" Jeremiah repeated in a whisper, throwing a look at his sister.

"It was my grandmother's idea," Cadwyn sighed.

"You think Jeremiah is any better?" Basheba said at the same time.

While Jeremiah sheepishly retreated behind his sister, Mina lifted her mobile phone high, training the light on Basheba's mouth.

"I need you to let me look," Cadwyn said.

She settled a little more against the stone and looped her arms around Buck's neck. "This isn't going to be pleasant for you."

"Let's focus on you right now."

Even Buck's growl didn't disturb his serene, encouraging smile. *He was born for this,* Basheba thought with a small swell of pride. *A natural caregiver. He's as rare as a unicorn.*

"Let me know if you need a break," Cadwyn said gently.

She nodded once, snuggled Buck a little closer, and opened her mouth as wide as her aching jaw allowed. Cadwyn sucked in a sharp breath and flicked his gaze to the side. When Mina and Jeremiah closed in to trail their lights on Basheba's mouth, he rallied enough to look at the damage.

"How's your leg?" Mangled by the welling blood and motionless jaw, Basheba's question became a series of gargled bubbles.

"What was that?" Mina asked.

"The cut's clean and shallow."

"You're cut?" Mina asked, the question ignored in the wake of her brother's question.

"You understood her?"

"I'm a psychiatric nurse, Jerry," Cadwyn replied with a distracted smile. "I'm fluent in all kinds of gibberish."

A gentle touch swiped over a tender spot, making Basheba jump. She gagged on the blood that had pooled in the back of her throat until Cadwyn's fingers retreated, letting her sputter and swallow. During this process, he kept his attention riveted on his medical kit.

"You're going to need a few stitches."

"So we need to get to the dentist," Jeremiah huffed. "Like I said before."

Basheba craned her neck to catch Mina's eyes. "Can I hit him?"

"I'd take it as a favor if you don't."

"You owe me," Basheba grumbled.

"Cadwyn," Mina said. "You said something about your leg?"

He handed Basheba a water bottle and instructed her to wash her mouth out before answering. "Basheba's such a drama queen. If I had had time to change out of my biker pants it would have been a lot worse."

Slightly offended, Basheba sloshed the water around her mouth a little too forcefully. Pain exploded along her nerves.

"Careful," Cadwyn soothed. "I know. It's the worst part of getting your teeth ripped out. Hurts more than the initial pull."

"That doesn't seem accurate," Jeremiah said.

Cadwyn didn't look at the teen as he readied a syringe.

"Adrenaline takes the edge off during the main event."

Checking for the siblings' reactions, Basheba saw Mina throwing a lot of wide-eyed looks at her brother.

Jeremiah spoke like he had forgotten Cadwyn was in earshot. "The stories about the demon are true? But he has his teeth."

"They're fake," Cadwyn said, and Mina cringed. "I'm lucky that I was too young for my wisdom teeth to have fallen. They now get to act as anchors for my plates."

"If he loses another one, his dentist is going to give him full dentures," Basheba said, adding quickly to ease the tension in Cadwyn's shoulders. "It'll make it a lot harder to argue that I wasn't manipulated into marrying a cradle robber."

"I think everyone knows by this point that I'm simply an enabler." He checked the syringe for air bubbles and continued before she could counter. "I want to give you something for the pain."

"I can't be groggy."

"It's a local. There'll be no mental effects, but you might drool a bit."

She nodded her consent, and he began to explain each step of the process. The drug of choice that she couldn't pronounce, the possible side effects, how he calculated the dosage for her weight. At first, Basheba brushed it off as him offering up another lesson. But there was something different about it this time. An undercurrent of anxiety that Basheba didn't like. Then it hit her, *he doesn't trust himself anymore.* Whatever Katrina had done had cut deep. *Three hours,* she decided. She'd give him three hours to handle the emotional baggage himself before interfering. For now, she settled back as Cadwyn leaned into her personal space.

"This won't hurt," he promised. "Just let me know if you need a break."

Without conscious thought, she looped her arm under his to keep it out of the way, before folding it back to rest her hand on his shoulder blade. His muscles twitched under her splayed fingers, offering a small early warning for the majority of his movements. It was soothing. But there was no way to suppress the slight flinch that came with the needle entering her ravaged gum.

"I've got you," he whispered as Buck whimpered in concern.

A swift slide of steel, a little pressure, and it was over.

"It'll take a few minutes to kick in," Cadwyn said. "Bite down on this."

He put a small wad of cotton into her mouth, forcing her to speak through her clenched teeth.

"You're really good at that."

"I've had a lot of practice," Cadwyn said.

Jeremiah's brow furrowed, "They do a lot of medication that way at your work?"

Mina jabbed her elbow into his ribs and hissed under her breath. "His brother."

Realization seemed to dawn on Jeremiah as he colored red. *At least he has the decency to look embarrassed*, Basheba thought. The kind thought died as, in true Crane fashion, he couldn't leave it well enough alone.

"What did you inject him with?"

Mina, while looking mortified, still closed ranks with her brother, casting worried glances in Basheba's direction. *Like I'm in any position to attack,* she thought, idly rubbing at Buck's scruff. *Although Buck could put a swift end to this awkwardness.*

"Tales of demonic possession always mention a physical toll," Cadwyn said, threading his curved needle and collecting the tweezers that he would use to manipulate the metal through her gums. "But they always neglect to express just how agonizing the process is. Most of Abraham's care was pain management. I did what I had to."

The drug spread swiftly, and the conversation was pushed aside for the work to be done. Basheba tried to relax. It was a hard task now that she couldn't see the water's edge. Laying there, she strained to hear even the softest shift of water. She fanned her fingers out across his back, squeezing slightly. It always surprised her how soft the leather was. *Shame Buck ruined it.*

"Are you sure your leg's all right?" Basheba asked to occupy the time.

"We can't understand you," Jeremiah said.

"Cadwyn can," Basheba argued around the working fingers and metal.

Jeremiah's brow furrowed, "What?"

"She's asking about my leg," Cadwyn replied, clearly distracted. "It's fine. You keep that thing as sharp as a scalpel."

Basheba had the strangest urge to preen at the unintended compliment.

"Stay still," Cadwyn said with a small smile.

Mina lowered her voice to whisper to Cadwyn, "You remember what she uses that thing for, right? Are you sure you shouldn't be more worried about infection?"

I knew she wouldn't let go, Basheba thought. With Cadwyn so close, it was hard to let her thoughts roam where they should. Self-preservation was a natural instinct. One Basheba listened to regardless of anything else. Mina, however, leaned more toward the righteous moralizer side of things. *We're going to clash again eventually. It's best to be prepared for it.* Cadwyn paused and leveled her with a disapproving scowl. She squeezed his back to signal for a break. *Is it possible for someone to be psychic?*

Basheba rolled to the side and spat out the clustered blood. It seemed that Cadwyn's natural talent for reading body language only sharpened with prolonged contact. Their honeymoon-holiday had given him enough time to learn her habits. To worm his way deeper into her head. *Which he must have known was a stupid idea. And now we both have to suffer.* Because she could read him, too. And the expression he wore now was his 'I'm not mad, I'm just disappointed' face. *Passive-aggressive jerk,* she thought as she let him finish off the final stitches.

"Better than being aggressive-aggressive," Cadwyn whispered.

How! With a slight chuckle and a final pull, he cut the thread. She could feel the moment when the flood of blood stopped and flicked her tongue curiously over the stitches.

"Don't play with them," Cadwyn said as he pulled off his gloves.

Mina crouched beside him, careful to keep her voice soft. "We really should have a look at your leg now."

There was a certain degree of stiffness in his movements as he flopped down next to Basheba and stretched out his long legs.

"Guys!" Ozzie's breathless cry and a small landslide of stones announced his return long before he swooped around the hanging ledge and into sight.

Basheba's stomach dropped at the sight of him. *Something's wrong.* Buck felt it, too, and was up in an instant, growling furiously at the shadows chasing Ozzie. Lurching to their feet, Cadwyn and Basheba shuffled back toward the Crane siblings. The minimal light from their phones glistened off of the handguns the coming mob clutched. It was a tight squeeze for Whitney, the new leader of the

Witch's cult, but she shuffled through. Like a living flood, large bodies filled every possible exit, trapping them on the small patch of stones between the cave wall and the water.

Whitney's painted lips pulled back to show her pristine teeth. "I promised we'd meet again."

"You know I come here every year, right?" Basheba noted, struggling to properly work her half-numb jaw. It must have been clear enough because she got to relish the way the woman's face went splotchy with rage. "I see you've upgraded from pitchforks and torches. Doesn't have quite the same aesthetic, does it?"

"But it's far more effective when dealing with you." A wiry figure slipped up behind Whitney, the light catching his wire-rim glasses.

"Uncle," Basheba said tensely.

Isaac's grin stretched his face as he loosely gestured to the darkened depths of the cave. "Start walking."

CHAPTER 9

Mina grabbed Jeremiah's wrist, subtly tugging his hand behind her back, obscuring the cult's view of the music box he was still clutching in a death grip. Of the numerous cautionary tales she had been told over the years, none of them had ever mentioned a use for the box beyond its intended purpose. *But they had a demon with them last time.* It opened up too many possibilities that she couldn't stomach to contemplate. *If they can work with a demon, we can't put another one in their possession.* Jeremiah glanced to her in confusion before inching a little nearer to her side.

Moving slowly, Cadwyn lifted his hand and motioned Ozzie closer with a rapid flick of his fingers. The teen cast one frantic look over his shoulder before all but running the short distance to Cadwyn's side. A few of the high-perched cult members shuffled as if they were going to stop him. Basheba was quick to draw everyone's attention back to herself.

"You have to be kidding me," she laughed. "We're really doing this? A death march? Are you guys new to murder or something?"

Isaac's face scrunched up with barely contained rage. "Shut your mouth, or I will sew it shut."

"Hey, I'm trying to be helpful here," Basheba shot back with mock offense. "You guys didn't exactly do too well last time. Anyone recall that?"

Fear and anger simmered through the group in equal measures. Holding her breath, Mina hoped that Basheba would find a way out of this. The blonde had a particular knack for violent creativity that Mina lacked. Panic welled in her chest as she watched Basheba cast a look at Cadwyn, a slight arch of the eyebrow that, to her, clearly asked if he had any ideas.

Mina might not have been able to read his expression, but the body language was enough. He had worked Ozzie into the minimal space between himself and his wife. It was a protective stance that had Mina tightening her grip on Jeremiah's wrist.

"Walk!" Whitney's scream rolled off of the walls and made Mina flinch.

"To where, you cockalorum?" Basheba shot back. "We need a direction!"

Whitney bared her teeth as the hand holding the gun began to shake. "What did you call me?"

Basheba waved a hand about airily. "Cockalorum. A boastful or self-important person."

"*You* stole my word-of-the-day calendar?" Cadwyn accused.

"Who brings that on a road trip?"

Mina's shoulders tensed painfully as she carefully watched the mob. Some looked caught off guard, slightly flustered, but none looked ready to break free of the group. Goading people into making a mistake was Basheba's favorite defensive tactic. On occasion, Mina had seen her use her innocent, almost childlike appearance to lure people in. But she shone when it came to nurturing blind rage. Anger had worked on these people before. *That's the problem,* Mina realized.

Whitney had been there to witness the deadly fallout. *I'll bet it's how she got to be the leader to begin with.* Mina struggled to keep the memories of that night from her mind. Bile burned her throat as the phantom scents of burning flesh and blood pricked her nose.

They know how dangerous Basheba is. They're not going to get lured in again. No sooner had the thought crossed her mind than Whitney lifted a handgun, training the sight between Basheba's eyes. Cadwyn slipped between the two.

"Do you think I won't shoot you?" Whitney laughed.

"There's no reason to keep up the performance for us," Isaac said. At Whitney's glance, he continued. "They've entered into a sham marriage."

"She's not a Bell anymore?" Whitney asked.

Isaac scowled, "She'll always be a Bell."

"But she's not under your control anymore," Whitney pressed.

Smelling blood in the water, Basheba cut in with a bitter laugh, "Are you still trying to sell them on the idea that I give a damn about you?"

"I recall you threatening him before," Whitney said. "Yet here he stands—unharmed."

"Ha!" Basheba reached across Ozzie to playfully shove Cadwyn's shoulder.

"What is she doing?" Jeremiah whispered.

Mina shushed him, hurriedly checking that they hadn't drawn any attention. Basheba's gloating had kept their focus.

Cadwyn growled. "Fine. Yes. You win."

"Told you I would," Basheba taunted.

Out of the corner of her eyes, Mina noticed the confused, frightened looks Jeremiah cast her way. *Don't say anything, please, be quiet.* A relieved, silent sigh slipped from her as her brother heard her mental plea and kept his mouth shut. Isaac, however, didn't have the same capacity to refrain from taking the bait. Disgust curled his lips as he snarled.

"What are you two blathering about?"

"She bet me that, one day, I'd regret not letting her kill you," Cadwyn said, his voice devoid of all emotion. "I thought it would take more time to lose that one."

"Well," Isaac smirked. "It is a shame that she didn't, isn't it?"

"There's still time," Cadwyn replied, the calmness in his voice chilling.

"Enough of this," Whitney snarled. "All of you, turn around and start up that path."

"Can't you just kill us here? I'm already bored," Basheba grumbled.

"I've been struck with a whim to see you die in a particular location." Whitney's carefully painted lips curled into a sickening smile. "And today, you live and die at my whims."

"Yeah, yeah." Despite her dismissive tone, Basheba's gaze was sharp as she took in the armed people surrounding them.

Her fingers twitched as they drifted slowly toward the hunting knife tucked into the back of her jeans. Buck braced his front legs and lowered his head, coiled tight as he waited for his master to give the order. Menacing growls filled the tense silence, forcing new floods of adrenaline to course through Mina's veins.

Unable to work any of it out of her body, Mina could only twitch and pant, desperately searching her hazed mind for a solution. *There has to be something I can do!* Frantically glancing around didn't offer her much hope. Outnumbered by the cult, and at a lower position, there were only two directions open to them. The narrow pathway Whitney had ordered them down, or the water.

"Now!" Whitney's shout cracked over them like thunder.

Basheba rolled her eyes, her seeking hand pausing when Cadwyn shot her a look. Keeping one hand on Ozzie's shoulder, he held Basheba's gaze and nodded slowly. Mina studied the barely-there motion carefully but couldn't decipher its meaning. *He's encouraging her to obey,* she decided before changing her mind. *He's agreed to follow whatever she does.* Either way, they turned around, keeping Ozzie positioned between them. Buck reluctantly followed, pressing close to Basheba's thigh.

In the gloom, Mina caught Basheba's gaze flick down to Jeremiah's hands. The siblings took the hint and made sure the box was carefully hidden from sight as they progressed toward the path. The glow of a dozen flashlights trailed along with them as they made their way over the shifting stones.

"Can we know where we're going?" Basheba asked.

"You'll find out soon enough," Isaac replied.

The pathway curved up along the wall to delve far beyond the reach of daylight. As they trudged along, it soon became clear that this wasn't an area frequented by tourists. Narrow and brittle, the ledge chipped away under their feet to topple into the abyss.

At first, Mina used the sound to gauge how high they were climbing. But she soon lost track of the soft tumble over the rising rush of churning water. There was something off about the sound. Something almost hollow. The darkness became an almost physical shroud upon their shoulders, cold and encompassing, broken only by the thin trails of flashlight beams. Occasionally, Mina angled her mobile around, trying to make the light glisten off of the guns surrounding them. They weren't shy about displaying them since there wasn't anything she could do even knowing how many of them were armed. It just felt like something she should do.

A small gasp escaped her when she took a step and only found air. Jeremiah grabbed her shoulder, yanking her back, her shoulder thumping into the wall. Stones scattered, but their sound was soon lost under the gushing water.

"Single file," Whitney ordered. "We don't want you dying too early."

The roaring water grew louder. They were forced through a cut in the rock and the ground suddenly evened out. As they all gathered, the combined glow fought back the shadows, allowing Mina her first proper look at her surroundings.

They were in a small chamber; the ceiling low enough for Cadwyn to reach without much effort, and a gaping hole devouring most of the floor. Pushed to the edge of the precipice, she swung her arm out, training the beam downward. Her head spun at the sheer size of the drop. Deep below, wild rapids surged past in a frothy blur.

Basheba abruptly burst into near-hysterical laughter. The sound covered both the rush of the water and Isaac's demands for her to stop. The deafening crack of gunfire made Mina jump, reflexively lurching closer to Jeremiah. Whitney had put a bullet into the stone at Basheba's feet. Still, the blonde took her time wiping a tear from her eye and sucking in a sobering breath.

"The Cauldron? Really?" Basheba asked.

"It seemed fitting," Whitney replied with a smile. "It feeds out into Bell Brook. That little bit of water where your namesake died."

Rolling her eyes, Basheba dismissed, "Yeah, I know."

"Do you think that I don't know your greatest fears?"

Basheba's eyes flicked from Whitney to Isaac. The wiry man only smirked in return.

"You've always known you were going to die in that water, haven't you?" Whitney continued.

"Actually, I was picturing this thing with a bathtub and a disgruntled rubber ducky, but this is fine, too."

"Keep laughing. I can taste your terror." Whitney trained the barrel of her gun at Basheba's chest. "Perhaps I'll follow your lead. Do to you what you did to our men. Paralyzing instead of killing you outright. Leave you unable to move as the water fills your lungs. Helpless. Consumed in darkness."

Basheba flinched. It was a small motion, but one that screamed volumes when expressed by the normally unflappable blonde. The moment passed as quickly as it came, and she took in a deep breath, hiding her raw fear under a condescending smile.

"I guess Katrina got bored of failure. This seems like a pretty dull way to end it, though. Guns? Seriously? And here I thought she hated me more."

Pebbles clunked together as the people around them shuffled.

Mina gaped as the thought struck her, "Katrina didn't order this, did she?" Suddenly having the full focus of everyone around her left Mina breathless. She forced herself to continue. "From the beginning, she's always lured us back to die in the Witch Woods. Why change that now? We're not that far away. It would just be a short drive."

"The Cauldron is one of the few spots that feed into the Witch Woods," Cadwyn said.

"If they're hoping our corpses will appease her, it's the best spot to put us in," Basheba concluded with a somewhat impressed shrug.

"All of you, shut up!" Whitney hissed as the first tendrils of fear slithered over the group.

The small sign of weakness had Basheba almost beaming with glee.

"The Witch demands you!" Whitney insisted with a snarl.

"Yeah, but come on. Like this? Hardly seems sadistic enough for her, does it? No, I think Mina's onto something."

"It doesn't matter. You'll die," Isaac retorted.

"But not on sacrificial grounds," Basheba noted, her eyes lighting up as she ran with her hypothesis.

"You're still in Black River—"

"But not in the Witch Woods," Basheba cut her uncle off.

Whitney's scoff barely smothered the discontent that rose around her. A dozen hushed voices and shuffling steps. Whitney refused to look at the mob, instead straightening her spine and lifting her chin to announce, "That isn't important."

"Oh?" Basheba beamed. "The *ritual* part in *ritual sacrifices* doesn't matter? Have I been doing it wrong this whole time?"

"What?" Isaac cut in.

Basheba ignored him. "If you don't hit the important notes just right, it doesn't count."

"Katrina has killed in numerous ways," Cadwyn whispered to her, his voice weaving through the growing anxiety around them.

"Yeah," Basheba said, sweeping her arm out toward him. "So, the *location* has to be the focal point. Oh! That's why she broke up the party! Why the selection has already happened. She wasn't trying to scare us away."

"She's bumped up the schedule," Cadwyn said. "She wanted more time with less experienced people. She's staking the odds in her favor."

"Exactly," Basheba giggled.

Reaching across Ozzie, she grabbed the front of Cadwyn's jacket and tugged rapidly. The amused gesture rattled the cult more than it did the man himself.

"I knew she was scared! She's desperate to settle her debt with her benefactor." Making no attempt to hide her amusement, Basheba waved a hand in a gesture to the cult before her. "And now you morons are going behind her back and robbing her of a potential sacrifice! Oh, you are all *so* dead."

Whitney twisted around just enough to roar at the people behind her, "You idiots! She's merely blabbering."

"But, Whitney," a voice in the darkness stammered.

"She's trying to get under your skin again. If any one of you fall for it, you'll answer to me."

"Did Isaac forget to mention something?" Basheba cooed. "Like who our sweet little new face is?"

Mina tensed as Basheba jabbed a thumb toward Jeremiah.

Isaac's eyes widened slightly before he blurted out, "He's just a Crane."

Releasing her grip on Cadwyn, Basheba reached across Mina to latch onto Jeremiah. Mina froze in horror as Basheba wrenched her brother's arm in the air. The music box reflected the dim light with the strength of a lighthouse. Lunging forward, Mina desperately tried to break the grip. As if she could somehow undo the damage. But the whispering had already begun to spread amongst the group. Rocks clattered together and harsh whispers rose over the sound of the water crashing far below.

"Katrina wanted him, and you decided to bring him into a cave instead," Basheba crowed with victory. "I wonder what she'll think about all this. How do you think she'll thank you?"

"You knew about this?" Whitney whispered sharply.

"It doesn't matter. We'll just take him back with us," Isaac replied.

"Right. So, what's your plan to explain all of this to the families? I'm still curious about what you did to Ozzie's parents. Someone want to clear that up for me?"

"Percival got a phone call from the families while Mom and Dad were trying to talk down the tourists," Ozzie said softly. "They snuck up on me."

Basheba's hum carried a staggering degree of mocking contempt. "Not sure who I'm more disappointed in right now."

"Jeremiah, is it?" Whitney said gently as she lifted her free hand. "Come over here, handsome boy."

Basheba tightened her grip on Jeremiah's wrist. "Nah, I think he's gonna stay right here. I want to see how this plays out for you guys."

"You won't be seeing anything," Isaac hissed.

Basheba's smile only grew broader. "I have to admit it, Uncle. For a while there, I honestly thought that I wasn't going to be the last one standing. But now you've killed yourself *and* your daughter. All in one day! That's pretty impressive."

"Claudia won't die," Isaac snarled. "And neither will I."

"Neither one of you is getting out of this."

He lifted his chin. "You've said that to me before."

"Cadwyn convinced me that keeping you alive would be crueler. I mean, imagine having to live with the knowledge that everyone you love is dead because of you? Because you were too much of a coward to fight."

"I was too smart to die."

"And now the Bells are dead," Basheba replied. "What a strange coincidence."

Anger distorted Isaac's face. "That's your fault!"

"Dad. Uncle, the good one I mean. Both of your parents," Basheba rattled off.

"If you had just listened to me! If you had known your place!"

Still clutching Jeremiah's arm, Basheba's lips pulled back in a sick smile. Buck felt the shift in her demeanor and began to growl again. Not letting go, Basheba used her free hand to pat her lower stomach.

"Remember all those men that you sent to rape me? Well, they admittedly affected me. I mean, learning that your uncle saw you as nothing more than a baby factory? It leaves an impression. So, the second I was able, I asked a doctor to tie my tubes."

"You would have been too young for that," Isaac dismissed.

"That's what she said." Basheba hooked her thumb in the waistband of her jeans and peeled it back, exposing a small strip of scarred flesh. "It hurt like hell to make sure I cut deep enough to shred my womb. But I did it. They had to take it all out. Womb and ovaries."

The color drained from Isaac's face. "No."

"All your little plots and plans. You were *never* going to have what you wanted. I destroyed any chance you had days after your first attempt."

"No!"

"Do you get it now? My mom and dad were your best hope out of this. All you had to do was swallow your pride and follow them. But you couldn't take that, could you? You just had to be the King."

"Your father would have told me! He would have said something!"

"And betray his young daughter's trust? Did you know him at all?"

Isaac shook his head rapidly, his brow furrowing and his eyes growing wide.

"No," he whispered over and over. "You're lying."

"I went through menopause before I finished puberty," Basheba laughed. "Oh, Uncle. What did you do? How much did you offer up for Katrina's promise of another Bell? Or was it someone like my mother you wanted? Deadly and dangerous and all yours to command." Laughter spilled out from around her words. "Nothing in this world would make an Allaway kneel to you. How did you not get that?"

"Stop!"

"How long did she drag you along, dangling babies like keys in front of your face? How many plans did you build on the foundation that I'd someday be popping out some demon-spawn?"

His murmured words became sharp, panicked pants.

"She lied from the beginning, Isaac." Basheba released Jeremiah to innocently fold her arms behind her back. Leaning forward slightly, she grinned. "All you did, all you sacrificed, was for nothing."

"No!"

"And now there's no one left to go to the pyre except you and your daughter," Basheba declared. "Which one do you think will go first?"

Isaac charged the minimal distance separating them, his clenched grip tightening around the gun until his whole arm quaked. Cadwyn moved like a ghost, slipping between the broken man and the cackling girl, his shoulders squared and his teeth bared. Buck clawed at the ground, desperate for Basheba to let him free. Chaos ripped through the minimal space—shouts and orders and threats. Suddenly, Basheba hugged Cadwyn's back, sweeping an arm around his side, reaching for her uncle. Isaac jolted. His jaw went slack as he slowly lowered his face to look at his stomach. Unstable silence settled over them.

Basheba coiled around her husband, nuzzling his side as she twisted the knife to open up Isaac's stomach just a little more. She smiled as she watched her uncle gasp.

"What?" Isaac asked.

Mina followed the stunned man's gaze down to his bloodied fingertips. As if she had been waiting for it, Basheba lurched forward and drove the long blade of her hunting knife between the ridges of his collarbone. The knife clicked against the two bones, wedging between them and allowing Basheba to pull him closer. Blood rained down upon her, staining her blonde hair and dripping over her skin. An agonized scream tore from the man as Basheba ripped the blade free. Three more quick strikes came before the man had time to aim his gun. The attack only took a few seconds but the sudden brutality left them all in stunned immobility. They all watched as Basheba kicked her shredded uncle forward, making him teeter over the edge of the drop.

"Take him! He's yours now!" Basheba screamed into the pit.

Isaac rolled, trying to get his hand up, to aim the gun. Basheba's last strike drove the knife into his ear. His eyes bulged, and his body jerked. Then he was falling. Mina sucked in a gasp, but it was someone else who screamed.

"Get the boy!" Whitney ordered.

The fear of killing Katrina's chosen one kept them from using their firearms. Instead, they rushed forward like a wall of flesh. Basheba hurled herself at Jeremiah, coiling around him like a snake, to use him as a human shield. Placing the knife at his throat made them hesitate again. Just a split second. Long enough for her to grin at Whitney.

"I can help you," Whitney said, her voice suddenly calm and serene.

Basheba pulled back a little as Whitney inched forward, her knife nicking into Jeremiah's skin in warning.

"You're the Bell Elder now, Basheba. I can help you survive. I can give you everything you desire. All you have to do is give me the boy."

"Seriously? Please tell me my uncle wasn't stupid enough to fall for that."

"So you gave Isaac to Katrina," Whitney dismissed harshly, her facade slipping. "So what? Do you think that'll save you? You stupid little girl, she'll never be content with just him."

"There are things older and *hungrier* than whatever playmate Katrina has." Basheba scrunched up her nose playfully to add, "You might just get to meet them."

"Give me the boy!"

Basheba braced one foot on the rocky earth. "Come and get him."

With that, she pushed off, throwing herself and her captive over the edge. A small whistle had Buck lunging after them. Mina watched it all in stunned horror until Ozzie grasped her hand. He leaped just as Cadwyn shoved them both hard, and they all toppled together.

CHAPTER 10

Within a split second, every molecule of air disappeared from Basheba's reality. Icy water filled the place it had once been. The rapids took them instantly, toppling them endlessly until it was impossible to tell which way was up. Light extinguished. All that remained was the crushing darkness. Basheba coiled tighter around Jeremiah, trying to contain the panicked man. Even brushing against the rocks wasn't enough to stop him from thrashing. Burning coals ignited within her lungs as her body strained for air. At random, they dropped. Sharp waterfalls that took them deeper and sent them spiraling faster. Jeremiah dug his sharp elbow into Basheba's ribs, breaking free of her grip to rear up for air. The push of his ribs said that he managed to choke down a gasp. A second later, they dropped again, stopped by an unrelenting stone.

Water pelted Basheba's back, pinning her in place with the water's surface bombarding their faces. Grinding her teeth, she fought against the push to grapple with Jeremiah.

"Don't lose the box!" Basheba ordered, half drowning on the water that rushed into her mouth.

"Get off of me!"

Bloody Cranes! Basheba snarled to herself as she grabbled along his arm, trying to find the box herself. Jeremiah's resistance had them both slip back into the raging current. Basheba clutched her knife, her other hand desperately searching the frothing liquid for the Crane. He brushed against her fingertips but was never close enough for her to get a decent grip.

Something unseen looped around Basheba's ankle. Before she

could fight, she was dragged down, further away from everything but the raging current. Battered by the water, she coiled down on herself, trying to slash at whatever had latched onto her. Pain sliced across her ankle. Her blood seeped out to warm the water. She could almost smell the copper tang and knew she wouldn't be the only one. It fed her desperation. Her body quaked with the need to breathe. She pulled her leg up as best she could and struck out again. Pain radiated up her leg as the knife cut into her flesh. A scream ripped from her clenched teeth in a series of bubbles, leaving her achingly empty.

Something battered against her spine. She twisted, realizing half a second later that it was too soft to be a stone. Hands grappled over her arms and legs, digging into her flesh as they wrestled to keep their hold. The darkness shrouded her attackers. Unable to see, to breath, she slashed wildly. The knife raked across her skin. Each spike of pain fed her panic until she soon lost all thought of anything beyond cutting herself free.

Blue light broke through the darkness. A brilliant radiance that pulsated from the tendril that snaked around her waist. The hands upon her grew desperate, shredding at her skin in their attempt to keep her in their possession. *No!* Basheba screamed it within her head, begging for it to be heard beyond herself. *Not for this!* The idea that Isaac's death would only buy her a bit of trivial assistance threw her into a panicked rage. *I should get more for him! Not this!*

A sudden rush left her breathless. She broke free of the water's surface, was tossed a short distance, and came to an abrupt stop against a slick stone. A bone-deep ache radiated out from her chest. She gasped for breath, the tip of her knife scraping against the rock as she tried to push herself up. The force of the water bore down upon her as she sucked in short, quick breaths. A few hard tugs and she worked her backpack from her shoulders. Unzipping one of the outer pockets, she pulled free a glow stick and cracked it. The darkness amplified its light until she was able to see a few feet around. There was little more than the frothing, spitting water.

"Buck!" Basheba screamed over the roar. "Cadwyn!"

Neither answered her. Crawling higher onto the stone, she shoved the glow stick as high as she could. It did little to expand its radiance. Rotten hands emerged from the rapids, grasping and searching, the current stripping the flesh from their bones.

"Cadwyn!" She searched the writhing masses for a sign of him.

The torrent broke as she saw Ozzie's head break through the uneven surface. He clung to an exposed stone and crawled his way free, Mina close behind.

"Where's Jeremiah?" Mina cried out the moment she spotted Basheba.

Her shout was answered by a gargled call from the shadows. They turned to see Jeremiah clinging to the broken ridge that jutted over the bend in the river. Each attempt to wave to his sister sent him sliding downstream a few feet. Pulling her legs out of the water, Basheba swung her arm back and forth, searching the twisted limbs.

"Cadwyn! Buck!"

Blood and water filled her mouth as she screamed. The dead hands clawed at the stone beneath her. Their numbers had increased to take over the stream. Turning it into a streak of writhing dead limbs that threatened to drag them all back under. She couldn't fight back the images that invaded her mind. Of the disembodied hands holding Buck and Cadwyn under the water, keeping them there while the last of their life trickled from their bodies.

"Cadwyn!"

In the corners of her awareness, she knew the others were trying to get her attention. But her eyes were locked on the black, writhing mass around her. *They're down there! They're dying!*

"Not like this," she gasped.

Grasping her knife, she shoved the damp cloth of her shirt sleeve aside. A broken scream ripped from her chest as she peeled a strip of flesh from the back of her hand. Blood rushed free as she hurled the hunk of flesh into the water.

"You'll have more!" she promised, her voice breaking into a shriek.

Voices screamed her name. None of them were Cadwyn's tempo and tone and all easily ignored.

"I've never failed to pay my tribute!" she pleaded. "Help them! Give them back!"

Her blood trailed down her fingers in rivers, only to be smeared into the stone by the questing fingers.

"I'll give you more!"

Electric trails of neon blue crackled like lightning bolts along the river of writhing flesh. A thousand screams assaulted her ears. The limbs twitched and spasmed, parting as a dark figure broke through the surface. Cadwyn crawled out onto the ledge Jeremiah clung to, his long limbs trembling as he rolled out onto the stone.

Without thought, Basheba flung herself back into the water, pushing through the torrent to reach the ledge. The electric light fizzled and faltered, allowing the hands to move again, the clasping hands reaching for her once more. Stone slid along her aching hand. She clutched onto it, the motion stretching her shredded skin. Pain carved through her arm, making it tremble and loosening her grip. Before she could get dragged away, a solid hand latched onto her forearm and dragged her out. She clambered out and flung herself at Cadwyn. Her arms wrapped around his neck as they toppled back.

"Hey," his breathy laughter eased the tension in her chest. "It's okay. I'm okay. Watch the knife."

Basheba flipped the knife so the flat of the blade pressed against his shoulder but only loosened her grip when she heard him choke.

"Basheba," Cadwyn said, his hands gently working to pull her arms back. "We have to help the others."

She gave him one last squeeze and forced herself to let go, shoving the knife back into its sheath and raising the glowstick high. Jeremiah still clutched the very edge of the rock rim. But now, Mina and Ozzie scrambled for purchase beside him. All three of them clashed together as they tried to break free of the stream. The blue light had faded, allowing the hands to resume their task. Jeremiah lost his grip first and, if it wasn't for Cadwyn throwing himself down onto his stomach and latching onto his wrist, he would have been lost to the tide. As he dragged Jeremiah back, his shoulders gave Ozzie a better grappling point.

Basheba focused on Mina. Dropping onto the stone, she planted her feet, grabbed Mina's forearm with both hands, and flung herself back. Putting every ounce of weight and strength she had into the action didn't earn them much. Her muscles strained to the point of tearing. Agony radiated along her body, spiking anew every time Mina's hectically moving fingers brushed against her wounds. Blood slicked their grip. Basheba clenched her teeth and, with one final lurch, Mina was wrenched free from the rotting clutches.

The two girls slammed back against the stones. The impact made the glowstick slip from her fingers. It scattered away, dimming the light further. Mina and Basheba scrambled up in unison to help Cadwyn and the others. The stone blocked her view, making it hard to tell who she was grabbing hold of but, with time, blood and sweat, everyone was brought up onto the ledge.

Cadwyn cupped the side of Ozzie's face, forcing the stunned boy to meet his gaze. "Are you okay?"

Ozzie swallowed and gave a dazed-looking nod. Twisting, Cadwyn repeated the process with the Crane siblings. When, at last, he turned back to Basheba, she flung herself at him again. With her arms secured around his neck and her legs around his waist, there was little he could do to get rid of her. Warmth pressed from his body into hers, chasing away the cold and easing her nerves. But, without those distractions, she had nothing to distract her from her gnawing fear. It clawed for freedom, slashing her insides to shreds and battering itself against her ribs. Her senses screamed that she was still in the water, surrounded by darkness and fighting for air.

"Basheba," Cadwyn whispered. "You're bleeding. Let me help."

"Did you see Buck?" she whimpered.

"We'll find him," Cadwyn rubbed her back as he spoke, but she couldn't tell if he was trying to soothe her or looking for damage.

Basheba couldn't breathe. All she could summon were soft, tiny gasps that rattled around her trembling body. Slowly, she pulled back to meet his eyes. It carried all the gentle compassion she had expected to find there, and it broke her.

Cadwyn shushed her as he cradled her closer. "You're okay. You're safe."

Her fingers curled in his jacket. A sharp bark made her jerk.

"Buck!"

She twisted around. Her eyes had adjusted to the weak light of the glowstick. Just enough that she was able to spot Buck bobbing up and down over the stone's edge, struggling to get out of the water. Basheba smacked a hand against Cadwyn's face and pushed, using him to stagger back onto her feet. Buck yelped as she approached. His long tongue lolled out to lick at her forearms even as she pulled him out. Just as with Mina, the struggle against the hands ended with a sudden jerk. His heavy weight bore down upon her, crushing the air from her lungs and leaving her twitching in pain. It didn't stop her from hooking her arms around Buck's neck. The hands continued to break the surface in search of them but didn't venture out.

"Good boy!" she beamed, sobbing with joy. "Such a good, smart, handsome boy!"

"I was her favorite for a second there," Cadwyn muttered, barely audible over the constant flow of water.

She pressed a few kisses to her dog's forehead before scrambling out from under him. "Cadwyn! Hurry! He's got a cut on his paw!"

"You look like you've been through a woodchipper," Cadwyn shot back, peeling the strap of his medical bag off of his shoulders as he lumbered over. "I'm helping you before I help the dog."

"But—"

"No, Basheba," he said sternly.

She scrunched up her mouth as he crouched down in front of her.

"Fine." Eyeing the medical kit, she added, "Wow, you never give up that bag, do you?"

"Yeah. So strange," he dismissed. "Don't suppose you have any more glowsticks in your backpack."

Basheba smiled slightly, searching the pockets again as he carefully coaxed her to stretch out her legs.

"Mina," he called over his shoulder, direct but carefully without alarm. "Do you have a free second?"

All three teenagers hurried over, their faces illuminated by the orange haze of a freshly cracked glowstick. Basheba found a few more, shaking them up to mix the contents faster, expanding their little bubble of light.

"Jeremiah," Basheba said in a rush. "Do you have the box?"

The guy's mouth moved constantly, but he barely made a sound.

"The box," she insisted.

Mina placed a comforting hand on her brother's shoulder as he whimpered.

"Use your big boy voice," Basheba said. "This is kind of important."

Mina threw her a sharp look. "Yes, it's right here. What is your sudden obsession?"

"They want it, so now I want it. A lot. Put it in my bag, please."

Jeremiah stood motionlessly while his sister pried the music box from his fingers. A strangled cry escaped him the moment he lost contact with the polished surface.

"She killed him!"

"We were all there," Cadwyn snapped.

His sharp dismissal instantly drew everyone's attention. It was the first time that Basheba noticed the full extent of the damage she had created. The numbing cold had dulled the sharpest edge of the pain. Cadwyn had cut away her jeans, exposing her legs, letting her watch with relative indifference as her blood seeped out through a dozen cuts.

"Hey, Ozzie," Basheba said. "Can you collect everyone's stuff and see what we have to work with?"

Grateful to get away from the blood, Ozzie hurriedly set about the task of collecting everything but Cadwyn's bag. The waterproof casing had protected all of the items within, allowing him to wrap lengths of dry gauze around her calves. It was still cold, but she was starting to feel the warmth return to her extremities. Pain blossomed along with it.

"She killed him!" Jeremiah screamed. "She stabbed, over and over!"

"Shh," Mina soothed, torn between calming him and moving closer to help Cadwyn. "It's all right."

"How?" he screeched, hopping rapidly from one sentence to the next. "How is any of this all right? The river—there were hands—and eyes. It glowed! She skinned herself!"

"What?" Cadwyn's head snapped up. "Where?"

"In the river."

"Obviously not what he's focusing on, Jerry," Basheba said, too busy patting her sulking Rottweiler to meet Cadwyn's accusing glare. "It was just a little bit off the back of my hand."

Cadwyn pushed up onto his knees and drew her hands into the light. "Oh, God. Basheba."

"It's okay. It doesn't hurt too bad."

His movements were rushed but still carried a practiced grace. Within moments, he had examined, treated, and wrapped the wound. It wasn't that big by her reasoning. Barely bigger than a stamp and not too deep. *It just looks bigger because my hands are so small.*

Her body seemed to wake up under Cadwyn's careful manipulations. The trembling stopped, her breathing deepened, and the pain grew. It forced first a gasp then a whimper past her lips. Cadwyn's gloved hand cupped her cheek.

"I'm okay," she assured. "I can take it."

His lips tipped into a half-smile. "I'm not going to hold out on you. I just wanted to make sure that everything was working right before I started numbing things."

"Suffer for my own good?"

"Something like that." Preparing a needle, he added, "And I'm not just bitter because you like the dog more than me."

Jeremiah's cry cut off Basheba's reply.

"She killed a man!"

"He wasn't my first," Basheba shot back before reasoning that it probably wasn't helpful. *Dark, limited space. Possibly trapped. Hunted by a murderous cult and the demons it panders to. Maybe it's best not to provoke the clearly unhinged man.*

Basheba frowned and wondered exactly when her voice of reason had started to sound like Cadwyn. "He was trying to kill us. I did what I had to."

Jeremiah looked around the group before fixing Basheba with a dark glare. "I'm not an idiot."

"Debatable," Basheba said before she could stop herself.

Cadwyn arched an eyebrow but didn't find it worth commenting on. Not when he had to recheck the dosage by the light of a handful of glowsticks.

"I don't idolize you like Ozzie and Mina."

"Mina idolizes me?" Basheba scoffed.

Jeremiah continued as if she hadn't spoken. "And I don't love you like Cadwyn does. I'm not blinded to what you did. I saw you."

"I wasn't trying to hide."

"Jeremiah," Mina whispered. "Let this go."

"Are you insane? She didn't just kill the man. She *sacrificed* him. She peeled her own flesh off and fed it to get Cadwyn back."

Cadwyn raised an eyebrow as he slipped the tip of the needle into her skin.

"And Buck," she added. "It wasn't all about you."

Instead of him placidly returning to his work, he stilled, mouth opening slightly.

"What?"

"Something older and hungrier," Jeremiah quoted. "What were you talking about?"

"Nothing."

"It listened to you!" he roared. "Whatever you offered it, it accepted. You gave it a human sacrifice, and it accepted!"

"Right. Let me rephrase. It's nothing *you* have to worry about."

Jeremiah pushed forward a step, shoving past his sister, only stopping when Buck got to his feet. The Rottweiler's deep growl mixed with the rushing water as the orange light glistened off of his slick fangs.

"You made a deal with something. You promised it more. Who do you intend to feed it?"

"Did you miss the mob of people trying to kill me? Obviously, I'll go after them first. Just stay out of it."

"We have a right to know what you got us into!"

"Oh, my God! My head is pounding," Basheba griped. "Can you just shut up?"

Her bravado faltered when she felt Cadwyn pull away. There was a look close to betrayal on his face, and she didn't know what to do with that.

"Basheba," he asked in a whispered. "What did you do?"

CHAPTER 11

Cadwyn braced one hand against the cool, damp stone beneath him, trying to hold onto some semblance of reality as everything else seemed to fall away. Only Basheba remained in full focus. Her and the bubbling pit of dread that churned his stomach. *Basheba summoned something.* No matter how many times the thought swirled around his reeling mind, he still couldn't believe it. *She'd never give herself up.* But the argument faltered in the wake of her silence.

"Basheba?" he pressed.

Her soaked hair still shone in the muted light of the glowsticks, highlighting rather than hiding the defiant set of her chin.

Everyone jolted as Jeremiah's sudden shriek cracked the silence. "What did you do!"

Buck rumbled low in his throat but didn't bother to lift his head from Basheba's lap.

"Answer me!" Jeremiah demanded.

Cadwyn glanced at Mina, silently telling the girl to intervene. The shell-shocked teen only stared straight ahead, leaving it to Cadwyn to lift a placating hand.

"Yelling isn't helpful right now, Jeremiah."

"Oh, I'm sorry," Jeremiah spluttered, the words slightly hysterical through shrill laughter. "Am I upsetting her? Heaven forbid I disturb the demon-summoning-murderer!"

"Actually, that *does* sound like a bad idea," Ozzie whispered to him.

Jeremiah's jaw dropped. "Am I going mad? I can't be the only one who has a problem with this!"

"You're giving me a headache," Basheba noted.

She rubbed her temple with the butt of her hunting knife, ignoring the steady stream of blood that worked its way to the length of her forearm. The cherished blade caught and magnified the weak light. Cadwyn took it as a subtle warning to keep his distance.

"You murdered a man! Why is no one else upset about that?" Jeremiah countered, looking lost for a moment before flaring. "You've provoked a cult, infuriated the Witch, and separated me from the others!"

Basheba snorted, pulling her head back slightly as Buck licked at her jaw. "Yeah, I'm sure they're really missing your input, Jerry."

Jeremiah's narrow chest was heaving as he stared at her, his hands balling against his thighs. "What's that supposed to mean?"

"You're useless," Basheba said. A small pout curled her lips. "How did you not get that?"

"I am Jeremiah Crane. Heir to the Crane name—"

"And the woods would break you in a hot second," Basheba scoffed.

Mina stirred enough from her shock to place a hand over his. He gaped at her before returning his attention to Basheba.

"Do you have any idea what will happen if I don't lock this?" Jeremiah snarled.

Vibrating with rage and fear, he awkwardly pulled the music box from the damp material of his jacket pocket and brandished it before him. For a moment, Cadwyn was sure he was going to hurl it at Basheba like a grenade. A subdued click changed everything. They all sat silently as the first metallic notes radiated from the box. The fight fled Jeremiah until he was trembling.

"Do you know what it will do to me?"

"I do," Cadwyn answered.

It took the younger man a moment to recall the full implications of Cadwyn's announcement. When it sunk in, Jeremiah deflated a little, his hand slowly sinking back to his side.

"Then you understand why I'm not exactly calm at the moment," Jeremiah muttered.

"We're going to take care of you," Cadwyn soothed. "But we need you to work with us."

"On what, exactly?" Jeremiah said once he had gathered himself. "Don't you get it? Whatever plans you had are nothing more than burning wreckage at this point."

"Then we need to think of something else," Cadwyn said, his voice calm but curt.

At last, Mina rallied enough to try and reign her brother back in. "Help us—"

"Help?" Jeremiah cut his sister off. "Mina, Basheba just killed us all, and you want me to *help* her sell our souls to the Witch?"

"You are such an idiot, it's physically painful to be around you," Basheba retorted. "Why on earth would I pick the losing side?"

Jeremiah balled his fists, his nails scraping along the shifting edges of the box. "Then what did you pledge your allegiance to?"

"Allaways don't bow to anyone," Basheba hissed through her teeth. The flash of rage dwindled as she went back to rubbing her temple.

Jeremiah bristled. "Then what would you call it?"

Resting harder against Buck, Basheba cast a casual glance in Cadwyn's direction. He wasn't sure which of the churning emotions showed on his face, but it wasn't what she wanted to see.

A bitter smile twitched the corner of her mouth. "*Et tu*, Cadwyn? *Et tu*?"

"You're comparing yourself to Caesar now?" Jeremiah scoffed.

"I'm the most competent one in the room, and my death would lead to all ya'll's destruction, so... yeah?"

Cadwyn reached out, wordlessly requesting her hand back so he could finish bandaging it. She seemed confused to realize that she had taken it from him in the first place. As an afterthought, she switched the knife between her hands again and offered the wounded limb up. Inching closer, he gently resumed his work, glad to have something practical to focus on. It steadied him somewhat.

"In your scenario, I'm more Mark Anthony than Brutus." He kept his voice light, gently luring her into the conversation that loomed before them.

"It's going to be so weird when you hook up with my widow," Basheba noted absently.

A slight chuckle escaped Cadwyn as he carefully cleaned the pristine cut. Scalpel-sharp, the blade hadn't met any resistance when cleaving through her flesh.

"Seriously, though." He caught her eyes before continuing. "We all need to be on the same page."

She snorted.

"*I* need to know what you did."

"I panicked, okay?" she yelled, flying one arm out so fast that her knife created a silver streak through the air. "I got a little concerned and may or may not have acted somewhat impulsively."

He cocked an eyebrow. "*You* panicked?"

"What? I'm not allowed?"

"It's just hard to picture."

"I couldn't find you or Buck."

The 'casualness' of her shrug was destroyed when she jarred her arm in his grasp and hissed.

"You made a deal with a demon for *him*?" Jeremiah exclaimed.

"And Buck." She pulled her dog closer, letting him nuzzle her shoulder. "It was mostly about Buck."

Cadwyn lowered his gaze to her arm. "Of course it was."

"Don't look so pleased," Basheba whispered sharply at him.

"No, I think I will."

"It's just, well, people annoy me. It's nice to have one person I can share a bemused look with before I roll my eyes."

There were so many things wrong with this situation that he

couldn't even begin to list them all. But there was some dark, twisted part of him that took particular delight in the idea that she would go so far to safeguard him.

"What is wrong with you?" Jeremiah shouted in exasperated fury.

Cadwyn schooled his features before he turned his gaze to the petulant young man.

"Every time you open your mouth, we get a little further away from the answers you apparently want. Perhaps silence would be the best course of action?"

"I do like him a whole lot better when he's quiet," Basheba said almost wistfully.

Fastening the bandage into place, Cadwyn rechecked the wounds on her leg, reassuring himself that nothing had slipped his attention.

"Basheba—"

"Cad, it's irritating when you take that tone," Basheba cut him off.

He threw her a disapproving look through his lashes. She avoided it by fussing with Buck.

"You only use that tone when you fixate," she said.

"There is something on my mind," he replied.

She huffed. "Look, all you need to know is that I've got this. I know what I'm doing."

"You made a deal with a demon!"

"Jerry," Ozzie hissed. "Shut up."

"Fine. You guys want to have this conversation, we'll have this conversation. Nothing like brewing some panic while in a dangerous situation." Basheba clapped her hands together and grinned. "Crash course kiddos. Any supernatural creature that's willing to make a deal with you will try to screw you over in one of two ways. Either they'll go all jinn on you, or they'll get you into their pyramid scheme."

"What?" Mina spoke so softly she more mouthed the word than said it.

Cadwyn's brow furrowed in thought. "Jinn are supernatural creatures in Arabian mythology. Think evil genies if it helps. In some stories, they'll offer a wish, but you never get what you bargain for. There's always some unforeseen consequence. Like a cautionary tale for greed."

"Or, the Jinn was just super bored and messing with humans is fun," Basheba offered.

Cadwyn contemplated that with a loose shrug. "In any case, the most common example I know of is that story of the man that wished for wealth. It's granted when his parents die and he gets their life insurance. Although that's a pretty modern adaptation and probably strays pretty far from the source material."

"Are you generally a fan of Arabian mythology?" Jeremiah asked.

"There's a woman on my ward blames her actions on a deal she made with a Jinn." Cadwyn skirted his gaze over to Jeremiah, not wanting to take his attention off of Basheba for long. "She did some things in a nursing home that I'm not going to elaborate on."

"The goal is to prey on people's egos," Basheba picked up again. "Everyone likes to think that they're smarter than evil things. They get stuck in this loop of trying to find the right wording and win it all. But no one ever wins."

"And the pyramid scheme?" Ozzie asked.

"The only way to get anything out of a pyramid scheme is to drag people down under you. That's what Katrina's done. Most of her power comes from her subordinates, not herself, or her benefactor. Without the cult and their sacrifices, it all falls apart."

"You *think*," Jeremiah stressed. He glared around in the darkness. "Why is everyone taking her speculations as fact? She hasn't got any evidence."

"But she has experience," Mina countered.

There was something in her tone that spiked Cadwyn's concern. A strangled bitterness that brought her just shy of defending the blonde. He wasn't the only one who noticed and, with a reluctant sigh, Mina admitted, "I've recently heard rumors that one of Basheba's relatives might have been a witch."

Startled murmuring raced through their small group. Not quite forming into questions but creating enough tension that the air thickened.

Basheba's mouth twisted into a scowl. "That damned tour guide."

"You're a witch?" Jeremiah demanded.

"No, I'm not. My ancestor was a couple of hundred years ago—before even Katrina was born—and the information died out after only a few generations."

Jeremiah's eyes narrowed. He rocked forward and jabbed a finger toward her as he seethed, "But you know how they work."

Basheba cocked her head to the side. "Oh, yeah. We fill out the same 401k."

"Can you do spells?" Ozzie asked timidly.

A real smile lightened the gloom on Basheba's face. "Yeah, I can do magic and have access to an army of the damned, but I've decided, meh, I'll just let my entire family die."

"I wouldn't put it past you." Jeremiah's mumbled words instantly grabbed Basheba's attention.

Cadwyn lunged forward, latching onto Basheba's wrist and pulling her back before she could get to her feet. It didn't matter how careful he was to avoid her wound. The short scuffle was enough to reopen some wounds. She flopped down, letting Cadwyn hold her in place while she restlessly spun her knife with nimble fingers.

"Are you threatening me now?" Jeremiah laughed the words, trying to sound brave. It fell a bit flat as he coiled behind his sister.

"I want you to know that I mean this literally." Basheba's words were slow but carried all the heat of a blazing inferno. "If you mention my family again, I will gut you like a deer and eat your still-beating heart."

Rushing water broke the chilled silence that followed. No one dared to move, as if the slightest flinch would have Basheba follow through on her threat. Cadwyn blinked away the water spray that gathered against his skin. It left him cold as it seeped into the non-existent space between him and Basheba, slickening his grip on her arm.

Ozzie was the first to clear his throat. "I feel like we're just going in circles, so, why don't we let Cadwyn ask all the questions for a while?"

The Crane siblings twisted around to stare at him in the haze of the glowsticks. The youngest boy lowered his voice, but there was no missing his whispered explanation.

"We know that she won't hurt *him*."

Cadwyn bit the inside of his cheek to stifle his smile. The comment threw his frazzled mind back in time. Back before Abraham was taken from him. Before the year of torment had carved him into something that he never thought he could be. Almost two decades had passed since he last thought on some of the things his mind conjured up now. The abrupt shift made him chuckle. Sharp glares fixed upon him, anchoring him to the present, and he refocused on the task before him.

"Basheba, you ruined my work. Let me check you over again."

"What exactly about this do you find funny?" Jeremiah asked.

Ozzie instantly elbowed him in the ribs and shushed him.

"Nothing," Cadwyn dismissed, his mind shifting through the past while he surveyed the damage Basheba had done to herself. "This thing you," he couldn't force the words out so skipped them altogether. "Is it connected to fire?"

Basheba studied him for a long moment.

Cadwyn huffed another short laugh. "I remember the day I met you."

Basheba's face scrunched up. "I don't."

"Yes, well, you never existed without me in the world. I had a good ten years before you came along." He decided that the bandage on her hand wasn't up to his standards anymore and started to rework it. "You were a hideous baby."

She nudged him in a way that could almost be seen as a playful kick.

"Like if E.T. and a prune had a love child," he elaborated, only to make her smile. "And you *shrieked*."

"Lies."

"From the moment you woke up to the second you fell asleep. Just a constant, ear-splitting screech. It got to the point where everyone just wanted to shake you. So, you were often left in a playpen by yourself. We could still hear you over the noise of the party."

Basheba was caught between being insulted and finding it amusing. Her hesitation gave him the moment he needed to organize his thoughts. He might only get one chance to ask this, one chance to know, one chance to slip through her defenses and get an actual answer. *Mess this up, and she'll shut you out.* A dangerous prospect given their current situation.

"You know how kids in the families go through their rebellious stages early? I decided to take up smoking when I was ten. You were the perfect cover." He threw her a quick smile. "You cleared out a room for hours so there was no chance of me getting caught."

She opened her mouth, but her comment halted as she flinched.

"Sorry," he soothed, taking greater care with where he put the bandage.

Color was coming back to her fingertips. It wouldn't be long until she thawed enough to feel the pain. In the back of his mind, he started calculating what exactly he could give her that wouldn't react poorly with her local anesthetic.

"Before you start, I'm not proud of exposing a newborn to secondhand smoke. It clearly stunted your growth."

She nudged him again, and he chuckled.

"I remember staring down at you. This shriveled little bit of nothing with the lungs of an air horn. I went to light my cigarette—and then there was silence."

Out of the corner of his eyes, he watched confusion shift across Basheba's face.

"It was the lighter," he explained. "That little flame transfixed you. The second it went out, you started screaming again."

"Okay, now I know you're messing with me."

Cadwyn ignored the comment to continue his story, the memory playing out in his mind's eye. "I took you into the Witch's Brew kitchen, turned on the gas burner stove, and we just sat there together, for hours, watching the flames. Somehow, that earned me the title of 'Basheba Whisperer,' and I was stuck with babysitting duties every year after that."

"Claudia was right," Jeremiah muttered.

Mina and Ozzie both shushed him, but he protested, leaning toward his sister.

"What? He recalls a time when he *babysat his wife*. That's sick."

"It was mostly carrying her around, actually. Every time her podgy little feet hit the ground, she'd be waddling her way into the nearest bonfire," Cadwyn fastened the rearranged bandage into place, looking only at Basheba. "It didn't matter when you singed your hair. Or when you burned your hand. Not even when you got near enough to the coals that your baby skin melted."

Basheba squirmed. "You were a horrible babysitter."

Cadwyn decided that it was time to ask the question he had been skirting around.

"You never had any fear. Your mother was terrified of anything bigger than a campfire, but you, you wanted to be in the flames. I sometimes thought that maybe you saw something in them. Heard something." He swallowed thickly. "Is that where you see *it*?"

Basheba chewed on the inside of her cheek as she weighed her options. Eventually, she pulled Buck a little tighter against her chest. The dog melted into the touch rather than protested it.

"No. I don't think so, anyway." She rubbed Buck behind his ears and continued more meekly than Cadwyn had ever heard her. "It's in the water."

Cadwyn's first impulse was to latch onto the fragment of a confession and tug hard, hoping to bring everything else out with it. But that's not how Basheba worked. She'd rather destroy something than have it taken against her will.

"Is that why you're afraid of the water?" he asked gently.

"It doesn't help that my namesake drowned in a puddle," Basheba reminded him dryly. Once more, she chewed softly on her inner cheek, calculating. "I've never seen it. Not all of it. I saw its eye once when I was little. We were swimming in a dam. My siblings and I were jumping off a ledge into the deep freshwater. I don't remember how long we had been doing it, but I know it wasn't my first jump. All I remember of that day is opening my eyes to see that everything had turned red."

"What?" Ozzie squeaked before he could stop himself.

She shrugged one shoulder, trying to look casual. "It was an eye."

"An eye?" Cadwyn pressed, drawing her attention back to him.

Sheepishly, she fluttered her left hand in his field of vision, brandishing her wedding band.

"It was an octopus' eye?" Cadwyn asked.

"A brilliant, blinding red, with a bar of ebony right in the middle. It was so bright that I could see it right to the edges of the dam." She sucked in a sharp breath and forced a smile. "There's no way a creature that big could fit in that space."

"What did it do?" Mina asked.

Cadwyn tossed her a sharp look, and the brunette offered an apologetic wince.

"Nothing," Basheba said, returning to her default smartass setting. "Or at least, I didn't wait around to find out. I got up on a pontoon, sat right down in the middle of it, and refused to move an inch until my dad came out with a canoe. Huh, I must have been around five. I remember mom saying that we normally do the family history lesson on our sixth birthdays."

"Did she teach you any witchcraft?" Jeremiah asked.

"Oh, my God, Jerry! Do you ever shut up?" Basheba bellowed to the stalactites.

Cadwyn regained her attention again by patting Buck.

"The Allaway line is rather... colorful. Yes, way back when, a couple of people dabbled in the dark arts, but there was really only one witch. She was the one who made deals with *it*."

"The Leviathan," Mina offered.

A smile tipped Basheba's lips. "It's had a lot of names to a lot of people. Leviathan. Kraken. The Abyss. Most recently, The Bloop, which is kind of my favorite."

"The Bloop?" Ozzie mouthed.

"These scientists recorded *It* in, um," Basheba spun her knife casually, "I want to say 1997. You can listen to it on YouTube. I like to think *It* was bored and wanted to mess with people." She chuckled and muttered to herself, "So many conspiracy theories."

Since Mina was nearly vibrating with the need to ask the question, Cadwyn decided to get it out of the way. "What is it, exactly?"

"How would I know? A monster? A demon? A god? A creature from another world? It just... is."

"And your ancestor made a contract with it?" he asked.

"It took generations to get out of it. Mostly, we've whittled it down to paying to be left alone. *It* still checks in from time to time. I suppose to see if we changed our minds."

"Oh God," Mina gasped.

Cadwyn's annoyance at yet another interruption dwindled when he looked at the teen. All of her pretty features were distorted, doing their best to display the sheer horror she was feeling.

"The Leviathan," Mina whispered.

Jeremiah nudged her, the gesture somehow worried. "She

mentioned that."

"No, the opera house built by an Allaway." Mina shook her head and refocused on Basheba. "What was behind the door?"

"Nothing that concerns you."

"You 'pay it off'? You're talking about human sacrifices, aren't you? Did you murder someone in that room?"

Basheba snorted. "Damn, you're dramatic." She twiddled her fingers. "*Murder*."

"What would you call it?" Mina shot back.

The response came without hesitation and with a small smile. "A hunt."

"He was a *human being*."

Jeremiah's outburst only made Basheba's brow furrow. "Why do you automatically assume it was a man?"

"You're as bad as the cult," Jeremiah said.

Basheba snorted.

"How can you think of yourself as any different?" Jeremiah seethed.

"Well, I'm not actively trying to kill you. So, there's that," she replied. "And we don't use human souls as currency. It's not like we just head off into the night with a knife and a bad attitude. Everyone is carefully selected. They ask for it, really. You could even call it a mutually beneficial relationship."

Jeremiah cocked his head. "The people you murder—"

"Hunt," Basheba corrected.

"They benefit from this?"

"Didn't I just say that? If you can't keep up, maybe take a nap."

"When did this start?" Cadwyn asked, once more wrangling back control of the conversation.

Within a breath, her body language and focus fixed on him like there was no one else around.

"Long before I had a say in it," she said. "Are you okay?"

Deliberately keeping his thoughts away from working the

numbers of how many people she had 'hunted' over the years, he smiled. "It's just a lot to take in."

"Seriously? You were born cursed, too. Neither of us is stranger to dipping into morally ambiguous territory to get through the day."

"This is a bit more than 'morally ambiguous.'"

"Only if you decide it is," she replied. "Oh, come on! It's not like I'm running around racking up supernatural debt for a new car or a hot girlfriend. This is the first deal I've ever made, and it was for you."

His lips jerked into a half-smile. "And Buck."

"Mostly Buck."

The roaring water raged around them as Cadwyn tried to avoid the knowledge that reared on the edges of his mind. *Only if you decide it is.* The prospect that morality was a novelty to manipulate as he pleased was not new to him. He had first encountered it in a dingy room of an abandoned mental asylum, with a needle in his arm and his brother's broken body strapped to a rickety table before him. When he had so easily pushed his guilt away that it had scared him. It was a part of himself that he had buried along with his brother.

There has to be a line. There has to be something that people can't come back from. Mentally, he curled around the thought, trying to convince himself that he truly believed them.

"Cadwyn?" Basheba's blue eyes pierced him. "Are you angry with me?"

"You killed your uncle! You murder someone every year!" Jeremiah groused. "We're all disgusted with you."

You can't come back from that, Cadwyn told himself. Basheba didn't look at anyone but him, waiting for his response, the first tendrils of fear coursing across her face. *There's a line.*

"Cadwyn?"

The truth clawed its way out of its shallow grave. *I don't care.* It didn't matter to him what she did to survive, so long as she survived. *If there is a point of no return, a bit of ritualistic murder didn't bring her close to it.*

Basheba's voice dipped into an almost meek whisper, "Cad?"

He blinked rapidly, sucking a breath through his nose, and flashed her a smile. "We need to get organized and move out fast."

Basheba grinned, her features lighting up with a combination of relief and gratitude that stripped years of horror and grief from her face. It was an expression that was impossible not to return.

"What?" Mina asked, patting her brother's arm to keep him from butting in. "I think we need to discuss this a little more."

"We're here to destroy Katrina's bones in the hopes of killing her," Cadwyn reminded her. "And now Katrina's cult knows we're here to do just that."

"You don't know that for sure," Jeremiah offered.

"They did know to find us here, Jer," Mina noted.

"Yeah, but—Well, no one *said* we were looking for her body."

Basheba raised her eyebrows. "We did dig up her grave a bit back. That might be a hint."

"Right. But—"

"And we tried to kill her a few months ago," Basheba cut in. "Oh, and we're in the Caves! During the Harvest. While she's most distracted."

Jeremiah squirmed, but his jaw was set. It gave the impression that he didn't believe his own argument anymore, but he *wanted* to. It was probably easier for him that way.

"Yes, well—"

"Pro tip?" Basheba cut in once more. "The paranoid survive, and she's survived a long time. She's not going to start taking risks with her wellbeing now. Either they're going to hunt us down, or move the body," Basheba added with a tip of her head. "Or both."

"While attempting to get Jeremiah into the Witch Woods to act as a sacrifice," Cadwyn noted.

"And they might be a little annoyed that I killed my uncle."

"So, we need to navigate a catacomb of hypothermic waters and crawl spaces while avoiding Katrina, the Leviathan, and a homicidal mob," Cadwyn concluded.

Basheba smiled, sliding the last bit of distance separating them to swing an arm over his shoulders. "Today is going to be a fun day."

CHAPTER 12

Ozzie did his best to avoid everyone, needing some time to process what had just happened. At the same time, he wasn't a complete idiot, so he made sure to keep close to the safety of the group. It was a hard balance to strike. Sorting through the contents of their few bags to survive the trip helped.

Cadwyn kept a tight grip on his med kit as he tended to the few cuts and scrapes the Crane siblings had. So that left him with Basheba's backpack and Mina's ghost-hunting kit. With everything that had happened, Mina had completely forgotten about the bag until Ozzie had pulled the strap free from her shoulders. Carefully, he pulled each item out and set them deliberately into a broken ring of glowsticks. As hard as he tried, he couldn't focus on the items for long. It all came back to Basheba and her Leviathan.

The information sat like a stone against his chest, crushing the breath out of him and making it almost impossible to think. *Thinking is fine,* he corrected himself. All he could do was think. *It's the conclusions that are the problem.*

Once more, he snuck a glance at Basheba. Almost from the beginning, the slight blonde had dragged him through this nightmare, whether he wanted it or not. Where he stood with her had never been specified, but he had always kind of assumed it was like a hurricane taking him in as a pet. She was a force of nature. Neither good nor evil. But, no matter what she did to everyone around her, he had felt somewhat protected. *Human sacrifice.* It changed everything. Turned her from Pompeii to Chernobyl. Less of an Act of God and more of a man-made disaster. He couldn't stop a single question from bubbling up over and over. *Was I ever an option?* Was there ever a time when she looked at him and thought, 'he'll do'?

He tried to focus on the task, pulling the items out, separating what they could use from what the water had destroyed. It didn't stop his thoughts. All this time, he had thought that Basheba somewhat cared for him, or at least found him amusing. *Was I ever an option?*

"Your face is all squidgy."

Ozzie would have been embarrassed for yelping like a kicked dog if he hadn't also leaped wildly. He ended up sprawled over the damp stones, staring up at Basheba.

"Where did you come from?" he gasped.

She pointed over her shoulder to the bloody patch of rock she had been sitting on since they washed up. He blinked at her, the stone, and back.

"Are you okay?" she asked.

"Yeah," Ozzie squeaked, cleared his throat, then repeated himself.

Basheba knelt and plucked up a glowstick, waving it back and forth to better inspect the scattered items. A metallic cone spiked her interest. She began to wiggle it around with a finger placed upon the tip.

"You know what I like best about you, Ozzie?"

"I know to stay the hell out of your way?" he offered.

"That you're a horrible liar," she smiled. "There's something to be said about a certain measure of honesty, in other people, of course. People don't tend to react positively when I start spouting off hard truths."

Ozzie hunched his shoulders, quickly reassuring himself that Cadwyn was close by. "It's still better to know."

"Is it? Let's test that theory." She lifted her finger, letting the cone wobble. "We can start with you asking me whatever the hell keeps making your face go all scrunchy."

Ozzie could only stammer, not sure how to reply to that. She tipped closer to nudge him with her shoulder.

"Oh, come on." Basheba straightened and nodded once. "I won't get stabby. Scout's honor."

He laughed louder than her joke warranted, earning him some strange glances from the others—more from Mina and Jeremiah than Cadwyn. *I guess things are easier when you know you're on 'Buck' levels of affection.*

"Ozzie," Basheba sang.

He whipped around to face her, thick eyebrows climbing up to his hairline.

"Come on," she whined. "We should bond, you know?"

His voice cracked a little as he studied the wide-eyed woman. "Um—"

She impersonated a clock with a few clicks of her tongue. *Is she messing with me?* That, after everything, she was still dismissing him as a child helped to solidify his voice.

"How do you do it?"

"Stay a happy little ball of sunshine despite being surrounded by the crushing disappointment of humanity?" Basheba steepled her fingers pensively. "Dogs. Well, Dogs and food."

"No, I meant—"

"This is my natural hair color."

"The murders," Ozzie blurted.

Shock widened her eyes and dropped her jaw, "Someone's been murdered?"

"The sacrifices," he tried again, balling his hands and surging forward, determined to make her take him seriously.

"Oh." She dragged the sound out, then seemed to get distracted by pursing her lips like a fish.

His brow furrowed, "Basheba?"

"Huh? Those are *hunts*, not murders. Completely different things."

"Are they?"

"When you murder someone, the whole point is to get a corpse. You don't *do* anything with it. Well, some do some pretty sick things, but they don't *use* it." She tried to both speak and resume her fish lips. "It's such a waste of meat."

He opened his mouth but all the questions he dreaded to ask got lodged in his throat, allowing her to cut back in.

"What was the question again? Oh, right. How do I pick 'em?" Basheba chuckled and dumped herself down on her rump. Pain sparked across her face, turning her breath into a hiss. It passed before she had carefully stretched out her legs. "Broad strokes or details?"

"I don't think we have time for details." *And I don't think I could stomach them.*

Buck trotted over, seeking out her attention, and she folded herself around the massive dog. Half smooshed against his neck, Basheba blinked heavily, her lids falling slowly then opening far too wide.

"Are you feeling all right?" Ozzie asked.

"There's no real outline, you know," Basheba mused. "We're not pushing virgins into volcanos. So long as someone ends up dead, we're *allllll* good."

What did Cadwyn give her? He decided to quickly ask a few more questions before he called the nurse over. *I'm sure he's paying attention. And when else am I going to get another chance?* "How do you pick them?"

She shrugged loosely. "How do you pick someone for a job?"

Ozzie frowned. "You look at their resume and measure it up against the current needs of your company."

"Huh."

"You've never had a job before, have you?"

She snorted like he had just told her a dirty joke. "Actually, that kind of works." Thrusting a hand into the air, she declared loudly, "We check out their resumes!"

Cadwyn's head popped up. A slight bit of interest that could quickly shut this conversation down.

"What do you look for exactly?" Ozzie asked hurriedly.

"Grandma used to set the criteria," Basheba sighed wistfully. "Then it was mom's job. I'm the last one, so it falls to my pet peeves."

"Pet peeves?"

He clamped his mouth shut as his brain screamed, *You murder over pet peeves?*

"Yeah." This time, her strange blink was met with a slight sway of her body. The motion confused her. She went slack, starting at the mid-distance, before suddenly jerking back to life. Dragging a hand through her damp hair, she continued as if nothing had happened.

"Grandma was big on rapists. Mom preferred child abusers. Hey, do you taste purple?" She smacked her tongue against her teeth a few times. "I taste purple."

"Um, no, I don't," Ozzie said. "So, you guys only go after bad people?"

"We go after the ones no one will miss. I mean, yeah, people will *notice* they're gone, but come on, who would *care*? Well, that's the theory. Sometimes people just won't let it go!"

It was Mina's turn to have Cadwyn's attention. Jeremiah chose that moment to insert himself into the conversation "That surprises you?"

"It's been—what? Fifty years? And they're *still* making Zodiac Killer movies. *Let it go.*" She made the words wobble like a ghost in Scooby-Doo.

"*You* killed the Zodiac Killer?" Jeremiah asked.

Basheba gaped at him. "Math isn't your strong suit, is it? No. *I* didn't. My relatives did. He was a bit of a jerk anyway, and my great-uncle had this thing with the law, so they thought—hey, two birds, one stone." She burst upright, her words suddenly coming at a rapid pace. "Then it turns out that sacrificing a serial killer to a sea monster doesn't count as part of your court-ordered community service! What the hell? Am I right? Pick up some garbage along a highway, and everyone sings your praises. But putting an end to a giant tax drain and giving the cops a night off is apparently a bridge too far."

"What's your pet peeve?"

She nuzzled into Buck's side until the dog was the only thing keeping her upright.

"Jerks, mostly. Didn't I just say that? I could have sworn my mouth moved." Her brow furrowed as she clicked her tongue again.

Ozzie had reached his limit of how long he could put this off and turned to call Cadwyn over. He needn't have bothered. The nurse was already kneeling beside Basheba before Ozzie could get the second syllable of his name out. How well anyone could use the limited light of a glowstick to check pupil response, Ozzie didn't know. But Cadwyn put in a solid effort. What followed was Cadwyn asking a series of general knowledge questions. Basheba answered them correctly when she could be bothered to pay attention.

"Is she okay?" Mina asked, inching closer.

Cadwyn cupped Basheba's jaw, his fingers gently probing. The blonde took that to mean that he was now in charge of holding her head up. She flopped against his palms with a wide, dreamy smile. Buck shuffled restlessly, offended at suddenly being ignored, and propped his head on top of his owner's.

"She's fine," Cadwyn said with a tight-lipped smile. "Just a little high."

Jeremiah choked on his breath. "Great. If there's anyone I want hallucinating while we're trapped down here, it's her."

Cadwyn and Ozzie snuck a glance at Mina. Basheba was far less subtle about it, twisting her entire torso to stare at the younger girl. Although it looked like she was simply mirroring their body language, Basheba's exaggerated movements seemed to be what made it click for Jeremiah. Ozzie watched the color drain from under his tanned skin as he remembered that his sister was claustrophobic. With the combination of the wide burrow they had washed up in and the array of distractions, Mina had survived so far without any signs of panic. Ozzie had kept a close eye on her, though. *People can only take so much.*

"Not trapped," he hastily said. "I didn't mean trapped. You know, we're more..."

"Mildly inconvenienced?" Basheba's words slurred as she remained caught between Buck and Cadwyn.

"Yes. That."

"Ha!" Basheba blindly swung an arm out in Jeremiah's general direction. "You agreed with me! No takebacks!"

Cadwyn rearranged Basheba until she was propped up against his chest.

"I like him a lot better when he agrees with me," Basheba noted.

"I'm not surprised," Cadwyn said, his response ending with a grunt when Buck flopped across their laps.

"I feel fuzzy," she noted.

"It's okay. It'll pass soon," Cadwyn said. "Enjoy it while it lasts."

"Did you have to give her so much?" Mina asked.

"She lost a tooth, skinned herself, and slashed open her legs," Cadwyn noted.

"I'm not saying I want her in pain."

Cadwyn arched a disbelieving eyebrow.

"I don't," Mina insisted. "Whatever she's done, I believe in justice, not torture."

"That's just because you're bad at it," Basheba dismissed, lazily jabbing her index finger against Cadwyn's chin.

Cadwyn ignored the touch while Mina ignored the comment.

"Are you going to turn her in?" Cadwyn asked.

"All that's on my mind right now is saving our families," Mina said earnestly. "Our odds of survival are a lot better if she's got her wits about her."

"I dulled her pain. And her verbal filter will be down for a while. But she's with us." He swatted away the blonde's hand and asked,

"Aren't you, Basheba?"

"Sure!" Basheba chirped. "I'll kill everything for you guys. But not puppies! I draw the line at puppies. But just about everything else sucks so, you know, game on."

"Aw, that's sweet," Cadwyn smiled.

Basheba wiped a fake tear from her eye. "I got it from a poem."

"Are you sure she's okay?" Mina asked.

"We just need to get her through the next hour or so, and she'll be fine. I didn't give her a lot." Catching their worried expressions, he offered, "Just pretend she's drunk."

"I always saw her as a violent drunk," Mina remarked.

"Really?" Ozzie asked, quick to pounce on the thin slither of humor as it presented itself. Last year had taught him that he was a lot braver after a laugh. "I always assumed she was more like the 'breaking into a golf course and running through the sprinklers naked' type. Can't you just picture her stealing a golf cart?"

"She's a grog-gorgon." At their confusion, Cadwyn elaborated. "Sorry. It's a term my friends and I used in college. A few drinks in and she turns into a snake. Either she's draped over someone's shoulders, or she's on the floor. And the only time she's known to talk, it's to tempt people to do something stupid."

"Vegas was fun," Basheba giggled.

"So, what have we got?" Cadwyn asked, jerking his chin toward the scattered items.

Most of Basheba's kit still looked useable. Whatever wasn't already waterproof had been sealed away in Ziploc bags. The problem was, Ozzie didn't know what most of it was. Very little of it was still in their original packaging. Cadwyn picked up a bottle of white powder.

"Yes! We should totally make fireworks!" Basheba popped her lips as she tapped a finger on the lid. "Boom!"

Ozzie dropped the bottle before scurrying back. "Why boom? What goes boom?"

It wasn't comforting that both Cadwyn and Basheba broke into a fit of giggles.

"Nothing, yet," Cadwyn said. Grabbing the bottle, he held it up for Basheba's inspection. "I'm guessing this is the leftover saltpeter?"

"Yep."

Mina's brow wrinkled. "You carry around potassium nitrate?"

"I'm sentimental." Basheba heaved the words with a deep sigh.

It only made Cadwyn chuckle more. "After the wedding, we went into the desert and set off some fireworks."

"Started matrimony with a bang." Thrusting her arms out, she flopped more against her husband.

"And you've been making some on your own," he commented, studying the white powder again. "This is a lot more than what I left you with."

Her blonde hair flopped around her as she nodded sharply. "Every girl traveling on her own needs the means to cure their own meat and blow stuff up."

"Do you have more than one way to blow things up?" Jeremiah asked.

Basheba just popped her lips and smiled.

"Okay." Clearing his throat, Cadwyn spoke with a tense serenity. "Later on, we're going to have a long talk about not using potassium nitrate on your food. But, right now, Ozzie, do you remember where everything went?"

"Um, yeah," Ozzie said.

"I think you should put it all back. *Carefully*."

Ozzie took twice as long to put everything back in the old backpack than he had done to take it out, carefully plucking them from Mina's scattered possessions.

"Are those wick fuel chafers?" Cadwyn asked, staring at a cluster of small silver tins. "Did you steal them from a warm buffet station?"

Basheba opened her mouth, and Cadwyn changed his mind, insisted that he'd rather not hear the answer.

"What exactly is our plan?" Jeremiah asked. "We can't get far with just this stuff."

Ozzie perked up. "I did manage to toss some of the scuba stuff down before the cult grabbed me."

They all turned to him, and he shrugged.

"I didn't know what else to do," he protested. "They were already around my parents. I only had a few seconds. And there was a pit right there—"

"Where, exactly?" Mina asked.

"On the edge of the parking lot."

"I need more details, Ozzie."

Basheba slid down Cadwyn, stretching out her leg until she could nudge her backpack's side pocket with her foot. "Waterproof paper."

Ozzie moved as fast as he dared to stow the rest of the items away before he used the paper to scribble out a crude map. *My memory sucks!* After a few questions, it seemed to be enough for Mina. She alternated between staring at the sheet and squeezing her eyes closed.

"What are you doing?" Jeremiah whispered.

"Shh." She waved a hand toward him and started to work on the back of the sheet. "I've got to concentrate."

A few minutes later, Mina grinned.

"There, that's it, I think."

She displayed the paper as if everyone would know what she was talking about.

Her smooth brow wrinkled. "Did no one else try to memorize the tunnels?"

"There are no maps of the tunnels," Cadwyn said.

"Maybe not complete ones, but the historical records—" She cut herself off when she looked around the group. "A lot of the tunnels interconnect."

"We can get to the pit Ozzie used?" Jeremiah asked.

A burst of laughter escaped her lips. "Oh, God no. Not without the gear." She sobered quickly when Jeremiah scowled. "But the rapids on that side of the caves feed into an underground lake. Not the main one, but a smaller offshoot that I think we can get to. Not everything we need will wash up there, but some of it should."

"Is there a way to get to Katrina's body from here?" Cadwyn asked.

"You don't know where she is for sure," Jeremiah noted.

Cadwyn sucked in a deep breath through his nose and continued. "There's no point in backtracking if we don't need to."

"If there is one, I don't know it," Mina said reluctantly.

Cadwyn glanced first to Ozzie then Basheba.

"Does your path keep us out of the water?" he asked.

"Mostly," Mina said. "Of course, I'm working off of centuries-old information. There's no way to know for sure."

"Let's get started then," Cadwyn sighed. "Which way?"

Mina looked at her map then held up one of the glowsticks, searching their surroundings.

"We have to work our way upstream a bit."

"All right." Cadwyn reached into Basheba's bag to retrieve a small bundle of narrow rope.

"I want to be tied to Buck," Basheba chirped.

"We'll all be tethered together," Cadwyn replied. "And we'll work our way around the edges as much as we can."

"What about the Leviathan?" Jeremiah asked.

Still slouched, Basheba almost hit Cadwyn's shoulder as she flung her arms wide. "If you see something, say something."

Cadwyn bit back a smile. "Excellent idea. Shall we?"

As the only one who knew where they were going, Mina took the lead position, threading one end of the rope through the belt loops of her jeans before doing the same to Jeremiah. Ozzie was next. After that, it got a little more complicated. Cadwyn, still in his biker pants, had Basheba on his back and Buck constantly circling his legs. Hiking Basheba up higher, he exposed his waist.

"I've got belt loops," he said. "If there's enough left over, give Basheba room so she can walk when she's up to it. If not, keep it tight."

Ozzie didn't understand why Jeremiah looked so uncomfortable at first. *Oh, right. Personal space.* It had to be a little awkward to see your sister getting that close to a guy's waist. *Surviving the woods together twice bonds you, I guess.* It hit him then. No matter what else he did with his life, or whom he shared it with, he'd never bond with anyone else the way he had with Cadwyn, Mina, and Basheba. *No one else will ever understand.* He just hoped that it didn't drag them all down in the end.

CHAPTER 13

Stones shredded the water, forcing it to spew up into a wild, icy mist that slicked the rocks. A thick layer of moss covered every still surface. It squished under Mina's shoes, threatening to send her toppling back into the water. It hadn't taken long for the wide ledge they had washed up upon to narrow. At times, it was barely a few inches wide, with the moss hiding any sudden break or loose stone.

The group had used the thin lengths of twine that came with the glowsticks to turn them into necklaces. The minimal light they emitted swooped restlessly around them as they moved. Time ceased to have any meaning as they worked their way through the canyon. Mina kept her crude map clutched in her hand even after the thick paper began to crumble and tear. Having it gave her something to focus on other than the fear that threatened to consume her.

It was the darkness. It hid the walls, allowing her brain to play tricks. When she couldn't take it anymore, and her position allowed, she would swipe her arm out and up. Her fingertips never found the ceiling or far wall, so she could breathe a little easier. At least for a while.

Backtracking, they discovered a point where a half dozen streams merged into one. Barely able to see beyond the reach of the glowsticks, which was a few feet at the most, the old channels dictated on the historical maps looked the same as the newly carved paths. It made navigating with any degree of certainty an impossible task. All she could do was make an educated guess.

Her selected pathway curled up the wall. Soon enough, they had to plaster themselves against the rock face and shuffle onward in tiny, awkward movements. Mina refused to look over her shoulder once they left the river behind. Without it, there were no markers. No walls or ceiling or ground. Just a vast abyss as cold and dark as a grave. Her vision narrowed to the width and breadth of the green haze of her glowstick. Fear twisted around her lungs as the last whispers of the river faded away, leaving them in crushing silence.

She flinched as Basheba's slightly slurred voice pricked her ears.

"Just hear me out. Just—Just hear me out."

"I'm listening," Cadwyn said.

The stillness amplified her whispered response. "The Bigfoot Experience."

"Oh good Lord."

"No, no, no, no. Hear me out. Cadwyn, just hear me out," she prattled. "It's a hotel, okay? That gives you a Bigfoot Experience. Guaranteed."

"How?"

"Talking is not listening," Basheba chastised. "Okay, so, we take their money, right? Then we refuse to admit that they ever existed. If they cause a fuss, we demand scientific evidence that they're real people and then declare any proof they present as a hoax."

"That's illegal," Cadwyn noted.

"No, it's letting our guest experience what Bigfoot endures every day. *Bigfoot Experience!*"

Mina could almost hear Basheba sweeping her arms wide with the declaration.

Cadwyn chuckled. "It's going to be another no from me."

"You have no head for business."

Mina craned her neck to glance past Jeremiah and catch Ozzie's gaze. The arch of his thick brows made it clear that this conversation had been going on a lot longer than she'd been able to hear it. There was an odd comfort in that. Cadwyn and Basheba were their canaries in the coal mine. *If they're relaxed, we're not in danger.* At least, that was what she told herself as they continued through the never-ending abyss.

Pebbles shook free from the walls to scatter down around them. Every so often, Mina would strain her hearing to keep track of them. They always faded away before they hit the ground.

The moss grew thinner, sparing them from potential slips but leaving their skin to the mercy of the broken stones. Without warning, the smooth rock became rough, grating her skin till droplets of blood slickened her grasp. Mina bit her lips, killing her gasps of pain before Jeremiah could hear her. It briefly dawned on her that he was either doing the same thing or had found a better way to navigate the cliff face.

The thought slipped from her mind when she spotted something pushing against the reach of the glowsticks. Mina wordlessly slowed her pace, trusting that Jeremiah would notice the change without being told. Peering into the murky gloom, Mina traced the outline of the shape before her. It stretched beyond the limits of her light source and her stomach dropped. *Please don't be a dead end.*

A thin object careened into her limited field of vision. She jerked her hand back, narrowly avoiding contact with the swinging pendulum that knocked against the stone wall with a dull thump.

"What was that?" Ozzie whispered.

No one answered as Mina slowly extended her arm again. The dangling glowstick spun, splashing its glow across the still swaying object. *A Rope?* Another strand slashed across her peripheral vision. Mina plastered herself against the wall, ignoring the way its rough edges cut into her stomach and cheek. Swinging wild, the rope struck her back, the loop at the end hooking on her shoulder.

"That's a noose," Jeremiah said as Mina untangled herself.

Her blood smeared across the rough material as she pushed it away, leaving it to swing once more. Transfixed by the sight, she didn't notice the next one coming until it stuck the side of her head. Stunned by a jolt of pain, she clung to the stone wall, her nails splitting as she tensed. Another noose struck her back.

Jeremiah's gasp made her snap around to face him. He was staring into the abyss beside them. Swallowing hard, she reassured herself of her grip and twisted a little more, following his line of sight. Thick lengths of rope swung through the minimal light. Dozens of them. Set out in perfect rows that extended beyond their limited sight.

Mina's stomach lurched. Even as the rocks and shadows remained as they were, she *felt* the world roll around her. The spirally swell of vertigo left her unable to tell up from down and, for one paralyzing moment, she was sure Katrina had them pinned to the ceiling. Random cracks signified more nooses joining the others. It was a heavy sound. As if there were bodies to weigh them down.

"Mina," Cadwyn's voice caught her attention.

Basheba finished the thought. "Go!"

Mina flicked her wrist, wrapping the glowstick's twine tighter around her palm. The map crackled between the cord and her skin as she returned her hand to the ledge. Locking her eyes on the distance, she scurried along the wall as fast as she could. Her damp sneakers slipped at random, forcing her to tighten her grip. The stones cut into her fingers while stray ledges jutted out to slash across her stomach. Over and over, the silence stirred with the whack and thump of the falling nooses. Solid drops cut short, leaving only the slow creak of the ropes swaying.

The sound alone threw her back to her first time in the woods. The corpse in the hanging tree. Bloated with decay and hollowed out by a swarm of bees. A new sound emerged from the rhythmic thumps. It, too, was hauntingly familiar. A sound she had only heard within the Witch Woods. Mina froze. She held her breath, straining to catch a trace of it again. *The laughter of the Mahaha.* Even the possibility that the monster had followed them here was enough to have her veins frost over. She twitched her head to the side. Just far enough for her to glimpse the pit.

"Mina," Jeremiah pleaded. "Keep moving."

Before she could answer, laughter burst around them, cackling, delirious laughter that cut her to the bone.

"It's not supposed to be here," Mina whimpered.

"Mina!" Jeremiah cried out.

She tried to look past him, seeking out Basheba. "You said the *Mahaha* never leaves the Witch Woods."

"I'm not its nanny," Basheba said in a harsh whisper.

"Keep going," Cadwyn urged.

Since he had never asked for them to slow, Mina hadn't been concerned with how he had managed to wrangle both Buck and Basheba at the same time. Now she saw it. How weighed down he was. His long limbs created enough space for him to strap the Rottweiler to his chest and still navigate. It might have helped to tip his center of gravity forward and compensate for Basheba's weight pulling him back. *He can't move fast like that,* Mina realized with growing dread. *We'll never outrun it.* Memories of the *Mahaha* flooded Mina's mind: a twisted, emaciated, withered creature with talons as long as her limbs, the scars it had left scattered over Basheba's ribs; it's taunting, manic laughter. *We only survived it last time because of the river. Because we made it out of its territory. Where do we go now that we're already buried miles under the earth?*

"Mina." Ozzie's voice slithered through the demands to move, and she caught his gaze. His nod was more a jerk of his chin to indicate the feeble path before them. "You've got this. We're right behind you."

Behind me. Joined in mutual destruction. My failure dooms them. The knowledge didn't free her from her fear, but it propelled her on. *They need me.* She clung to the thought and sucked in a deep breath. Readjusting her weight, she began to shuffle again. Terror still gnawed on the edges of her mind. Each bite made her joints want to lock. *Don't freeze up.* Shrouding herself with clinical detachment, she retreated from the brutal edge of her fear. She kept a sharp eye, looking for both the monster and the means to escape it. But there was nothing to see. No matter how far they went, everything remained the same. A narrow ledge suspended in a pit of nothingness; the shadows disturbed only by the hanging nooses.

The monster's laughter continued. It rolled off of the cave walls as much as it bounced within her skull, tormenting and torturous, chipping away at her resolve. Grinding her teeth, Mina forced herself on, thrusting her glowstick out before her when she could.

A stream of severed pebbles cascaded down between Mina and her brother. They shared a glance before turning their faces up. The *Mahaha's* unblinking stare penetrated the darkness, highlighted all the more by the dark, matted tendrils of its hair. Ghostly skin emerged from the shadows as it scurried along the edges of the green hue. Its glistening talons broke easily into the rockface, creating another miniature avalanche. Catching their eyes, the *Mahaha* grinned, its lips peeling back from its bones to create the ghastly expression.

Jeremiah screamed and threw himself forward. The tether snapped taut, dragging the others along behind him. Ozzie's foot slipped. He dropped like a stone, taking Jeremiah after him. With both men off, Mina had no chance to hold on. Her stomach lurched as she fell, plummeting away from the *Mahaha's* reach and into the darkness. The rope cut into her waist as the slack ran out, and she was sent arching back toward the wall. Pain exploded along the entire length of her body as she smacked against the hard, rough surface. She felt the vibrations as the boys struck, too. Then Cadwyn slipped and there was nothing left holding them up.

She clawed desperately at the rock face, the nooses, anything that brushed against her fingertips. Someone had better luck than her, and she was suddenly barreling into the stone wall again. It cracked apart like drywall. All of the water that had been eroding the rock for years spewed free in a torrent. Desperately, she shoved herself into the narrow gap, hoping her body might wedge into place long enough for the others to get their footing. The yank of the rope was like a punch to the gut. It took everything she had to fight the instinct to curl in on herself and instead brace as best she could against the smooth stones. Water rushed around her, shoving her out while the weight dragged her down.

Hold on, she commanded herself while her body trembled. *Someone else found a foothold. They must have. I couldn't hold them all. Just hold on until they get their footing.* She repeated her thoughts like a mantra. Screaming it over the pain of her trembling muscles, the icy push against her spine, the pain in her gut, and the way the walls closed in around her. Most importantly, it fortified her against the approaching laughter. *Hold on. Hold on!*

Water bombarded the glowstick coiled around her hand, making its light scatter and dance. By its glow, she saw the pale face peek over the top of the fissure she had wedged herself into. The *Mahaha's* eyes shone with mirth as it scurried around the rim. A new fear tore into her soul. *It's going to cut the rope!* Images of the others falling to their deaths slammed to the forefront of her mind. A surge of water startled her from her frozen state. She slid a few inches before she could lock her elbows against the walls. Her scrambling feet found a small ledge to brace against, and she pushed back, fighting the deluge to hold her position. The *Mahaha's* face tipped to the side. Its smile grew wider, and its laughter took on a sharper edge.

Deliberately, making sure it had her full attention, it turned its face once more toward the rope. Frothing water covered most of her torso, hiding the knot from sight. Still, the creature found it easily and reached one long talon into the waves. *No!* She tried to kick at it, almost losing her footing in the effort. The *Mahaha* cackled with delight. *Keep its attention,* Mina told herself. *Don't let it cut the rope. They need more time.*

She felt the tug when it hooked its nail around the slender cord. An insignificant little pull that made Mina's heart stammer. *How much more can Basheba's rope take?* It was a miracle it hadn't broken already. Mina decided that the rest was up to them. Driving her elbows out until the rocks cut through her jacket, she braced one foot, took aim, and kicked with every ounce of strength she could summon.

Her heel caught the *Mahaha's* jaw but didn't dislodge it as she had hoped. The monster barely reacted to the blow at all, except to refocus its attention upon her. Wide eyes studied her as she desperately tried to regain her position. *Hold on. Hold on!* Its shoulders rattled with demonic giggles as it crawled over the rim. There was barely enough room in the fissure to accommodate them both. It loomed over her, blocking the light. Water struck them both, frothing and churning, the crush almost covering the delicate click of its talons upon the rocks. *Hold on.*

It seemed to swallow up the air as it leaned toward her. Close enough that she could feel its laughter vibrating within her chest. *Hold on.* With spider-like ease, the *Mahaha* found its footing, allowing it to lift one hand. It trailed the needle-thin points of its nails across her face. One tip followed the curve of her lower eyelid. *Hold on!* She hurled the desperate thought against the flood of memories surging toward the front of her mind. There was no stopping them. Images of Cadwyn removing Basheba's eye filled her head, dragging her toward blind panic. Mina clenched her jaw. *She did that for me. I can do this for her.*

"Mina!" Cadwyn called.

She trembled, unable to answer. Barely willing to breathe in case the motion made the blade sink in. The *Mahaha* cackled gleefully.

"Mina, stay where you are! We've almost got it!"

There was some delight that came with knowing she had been right. *Hold on, and they'll live.* Trembles rattled her body, from the fear and the cold and the strain of muscles pushed to their limits. Fire ignited in her cheek as the *Mahaha* pushed its nail in. Laughter merged with Mina's scream as the nail sunk deeper, methodically pulled down, severing her flesh. Blood rushed into her mouth. The tip of the nail clicked against her teeth.

"Mina?" Cadwyn bellowed, his voice taking on a strained edge.

She tried to silence herself and failed miserably. The nail continued its trail through her flesh. Agony exploded within her. The sight of her screaming and choking on her own blood made the creature giggle in amusement. *Hold on. Just a little longer. Hold on.*

"Now!"

Instantly, her body reacted to Cadwyn's command. She dropped her feet, flattened herself against the stone, and let the deluge take her. The back of the *Mahaha's* talon brushed against the side of her face as she slid out from under it. The fissure's rim scraped the length of her spine, and then there was nothing. No water, no stone, no monster gouging at her skin. Just open air and a sudden, gut-wrenching drop. Arms latched around her waist, bringing her to a bone-jarring stop, and she was abruptly sent into a new direction. Cradled against Cadwyn's chest, they skidded down at a sharp angle. Small bits of stone came out at random to smack against them. Each one cracked apart under the force of their descent, barely slowing them down. In the darkness, she couldn't see the tight turn or the last sudden drop. Cadwyn coiled around her to steal most of the impact. It took a moment for her brain and innards to catch up with what had happened.

"Guys!" Ozzie's panicked voice broke through her stunned daze. "Guys?"

"We're coming to you," Cadwyn grunted.

Gentle but persistent hands pushed at Mina's shoulders. Her skin felt too loose. It allowed her bones to rattle around as she forced herself back onto her feet. The severed end of the rope tangled around her legs, ensuring that her first step sent her slamming into the far-too-close wall.

Blinding pain pulsated from her cheek. She was only half-aware of the hot blood that gushed down her neck and face, countering the Arctic chill that had ravaged her skin. She was only vaguely conscious of the thin tunnel before her or the light at the end. Cadwyn knelt beside her. She caught a glimpse of Basheba's hunting knife and, after a jerk, the rope fell away. He still had to loop an arm under her shoulders to get her moving.

There wasn't enough room for them to run side-by-side. They crammed tightly together and lumbered on. Laughter followed, swelling in the air, drawing closer.

"Hurry-hurry-hurry!" Ozzie chanted.

Mina could hear him smacking the rocks, but she couldn't catch sight of him, of anyone. Between one blink and the next, the walls fell away and Mina found herself in a circular space. Small holes speckled the cave ceiling far above her head. They allowed just enough light for her to catch the shadows and shapes of things. The ground was an unstable mix of sand and stone. She barely got a few steps before she tripped on the uneven terrain. Cadwyn took her weight, tucking her under his arm and carrying her to the center of the cave.

The *Mahaha's* laughter filled her skin. Her head swirled, and her limited vision blurred. Hard strikes against stone made her lift her head. Only then did she realize she had fallen flat against the sand at some point. Ozzie and Jeremiah stood on a ridge just above the tunnel opening. Ozzie struck ferociously at a cluster of boulders, trying to jar them loose. The resulting landslide would seal the tunnel shut and separate them from the giggling monster. Malicious laughter rolled into the circular room like waves. Mina choked on her scream as she saw a pale figure emerge from the tunnel's shadows.

"Jeremiah!" Ozzie yelled, still striking the stones.

Jeremiah hesitated.

"Hurry!" Ozzie pressed.

Still, her brother remained motionless. Mina saw him stagger abruptly to the side. She was just about to lunge up when she spotted Basheba behind him. The blonde took Jeremiah's place and, together with Ozzie, they worked against the piled rubble. The *Mahaha* broke into a run. Mina scurried back over the sand before Cadwyn's body blocked her view, his shoulders braced for a fight.

Thunder crashed overhead. The ground trembled as the pile of stones gave way. They toppled against each other, making the world rumble and kick up a choking cloud of dust. By the time Cadwyn slunk back to her side, a wall of boulders filled the tunnel's entrance, thick enough to smother the *Mahaha's* laughter.

"What the hell is wrong with you?" Ozzie roared. Fury dripped from his voice as he whirled on Jeremiah. "We had a plan!"

"I was thinking!" Jeremiah protested.

"Of what? We almost had that thing in here with us!"

"And now we're trapped." Jeremiah stumbled down from the ridge only to have Ozzie stalk after him. "Everyone keeps telling me how deadly Basheba is. And she's proven that she's not above murder. Surely it would have been a better idea to simply let her and Buck handle it."

"Are you kidding me?" Ozzie screamed. "She's one person. She's *injured!* We decided—"

"And your ideas have been brilliant so far."

While his fists balled, his voice calmed. "We don't survive this by ourselves, we work as a team."

"So you say."

Ozzie's mouth opened but nothing come out for a good long while. "Ever since I learned I was a Sewall, I've hated how useless I am. I'm not as smart as Mina, or as competent as Cadwyn, or as fearless as Basheba. Even Buck does more than I do." He took the last step separating them and jabbed his hand against Jeremiah's chest. "I might be useless, but at least I'm not a jackass."

"How dare you—" Jeremiah's sentence stalled as Mina called for him.

Pain and blood distorted his name until it was little more than a gargle. Cadwyn rolled her onto her side, the position both letting the blood drain from her lips and giving him a better view of the wound. He pulled back, turning his face away to try and suck in a deep, sobering breath. When he turned back, he had retreated into a purely professional demeanor. She barely noticed any of it. Pain radiated through her body. A searing agony that made her jolt and whimper.

"You girls need to remember that my painkillers are a finite resource."

The warmth in his words eroded her fear. The steady weight of his hand on her shoulder helped more than she thought it could. Neither thing diminished the pain but, somehow, they made it endurable. Jeremiah suddenly filled her tear-blurred vision. His glowstick swung wildly as he dropped onto his knees before her and snatched up her hand.

"Are you okay? What happened? What did it do to you?"

Basheba rested her forearm on the top of Jeremiah's head, pushing up on her toes to peer down at Mina.

"Yeah, I don't think she's going to be answering you any time soon."

"Get off of me!" Jeremiah snarled and thrashed like a wounded beast.

"This isn't helping Mina." Cadwyn's voice drifted from somewhere out of sight. "Keep her calm for me, Jerry."

Jeremiah slid down beside his sister, positioning himself so they were face to face, clasping her hands between his.

"I'm sorry," he whispered, choking on a sob. "I'm so sorry, Mina."

She tried to shush him but the world lurched around her. The sand between them darkened. *That's a lot of blood.* The thought slowly slid across Mina's brain, unconnected to anything else, and left the niggling suspicion that it was somehow important.

Jeremiah tightened his grip on her fingers. "I'm supposed to take care of you. You're supposed to be able to lean on me. But, Mina..." He lowered his voice to a private whisper. "I don't know what to do."

She rubbed his knuckles with her thumb, hoping it conveyed all she couldn't say. *It's okay. You're here. That means the world to me. Don't cry.* It didn't work, and he broke down into a series of body-rattling sobs. He curled closer, kissing the back of her hand as if it could wipe away everything else. His confession came on a whimper.

"I'm so scared, Mina. God, I'm so scared."

The sharp point of the needle was barely felt amongst the agony ravaging her body. Its effects worked swiftly, however, leaving her only seconds before she felt unconsciousness looming over her. Unable to speak, she squeezed her brother's hand, willing him to understand. *It's okay. You're here. Just hold on a little longer.*

CHAPTER 14

Apparently, Buck had put their earlier misunderstanding far behind them and was content with Cadwyn's company again. At least enough to use the man's thigh as a pillow and demand ear rubs. Drool kept a patch of his scuffed-up biker pants uncomfortably damp while the rest of him dried.

Basheba had lit a few of her stolen chafer fuel tins. Since they were designed to keep food warm, their steady blue flames didn't give off much light. They were surprisingly warm, though, and Cadwyn warmed his hands over the nearest one every so often.

Azure light danced upon the walls and welled in pools upon the sandy floor. Mina hadn't regained consciousness and, since she was the only one who knew where they were going, they decided to rest awhile. After sharing a few granola bars from Mina's pack, they had settled in.

Ozzie and Jeremiah moved as a pair, circling the limits of the room and generally trying to find some common ground. Basheba decided to jerk all responsibility and curl up with Buck's stomach as her pillow. No one begrudged her it. Although Cadwyn did feel a familiar pang of jealousy. She had the remarkable talent of falling asleep on demand. It didn't matter where they were or what was trying to kill them. The moment she decided she wanted to sleep, she was out, leaving him to stare at the walls and listen to her and Buck snore. The bandages covering his palm snagged his hair as he slicked his bangs back. *This whole situation shouldn't have a sense of déjà vu.*

With Buck nuzzling at his left hand for attention, and Mina

curling against his right side in search of his body heat, Cadwyn hadn't been able to move for a while. He suspected it had been a few hours, given how uncomfortably numb his legs were. Although, it could simply have seemed longer since Ozzie and Jeremiah refused to sit still. Side-by-side, the boys circled him again on yet another loop of the room. *At least it's easy to keep an eye on both of them at once*, he thought as he squirmed, seeking a more comfortable position while stretching for Basheba's bag. She always had snacks.

Mina grunted, her bandaged fingers grasping at his knee. He stilled, which let her settle but left Buck rather disgruntled about being squished. Basheba, whom Cadwyn had personally witnessed sleep through a cup of water to the face, stirred at the dog's first grumble.

"What's wrong, handsome?" she slurred against Buck's fur.

"Just a bit hungry," Cadwyn replied.

Basheba jerked up only to stare blankly down at her pet.

"Basheba," Cadwyn slowly asked. "Did you think Buck spontaneously learned how to talk?"

"No," she scoffed, settling back down against her dog's side. "But how cool would it be if he did? I'd have an interesting conversation for once."

"I'm not insulted. In case you were wondering."

"I wasn't."

Buck mirrored Basheba's yawn. That, of course, earned the dog a few minutes of praise, which Cadwyn spent once more reaching for her backpack.

"How long have I been asleep?" Basheba abruptly asked.

He lifted his wristwatch. "It broke somewhere along the way."

Basheba kissed the top of Buck's head before rolling onto her back. Far above, through the small gaps in the cave roof, she studied the patchwork of the night sky. She stuck one hand up and looked down the length of her arm, using her thumb as a gage. For what, he had no idea, but it all seemed conclusive enough for her.

"It's between ten and midnight."

"How?" he asked.

Studying the cave ceiling again didn't help to clear anything up. He was ninety percent sure that she was messing with him.

"Do I question your encyclopedic knowledge of narcotics?" she huffed.

"Fair enough."

He settled a hand on her forehead.

"What ya doing?"

"Checking for signs of fever."

Her skin was clammy and warmer than it should have been, especially given the chill of the space. He used the back of his free hand to compare their temperatures.

"Ninety-eight," he mumbled.

"Not bad," she smiled with pride.

"If we ignore your blood loss. And the unsanitary conditions—"

"It's not that bad in here."

"Mildew-infested caves aren't recommended for people with open wounds, Basheba."

"Oh, right. That. But you stitched them. So, they're not open anymore."

"And, given our swim in near-freezing water and the ambient temperature, we should all be running a few degrees lower than normal at the moment." He traced his fingertips along her forehead and cheek, searching for any trace of fever sweating. "If you knock up one more degree, I'm giving you antibiotics."

"See how I'm accepting that without questioning your competence? Like a good friend."

He let that go with little more than a weary sigh. "How are you feeling?"

"Fine. Apart from the turmoil of my existential crisis."

He smirked despite himself. "Any chance of a serious answer?"

"What? I could be having one."

"You want me to believe that you'd ever doubt your life has meaning?"

Her brow furrowed under his fingertips. "That's what that means?"

"What did you think—"

"Yeah, never mind. I don't have time for that kind of nonsense."

Cadwyn closed his eyes, gripping the last threads of his patience. *I'm way too tired for this.*

"I ache all over, my hand is on fire, and I'm working on one hell of a headache," Basheba smiled. "I guess that means the painkillers have worn off, huh?"

"I can give you a little more."

"I don't want to deplete your stash."

He brushed her hair back before reaching for his med kit. "I learned a long time ago to always have more than you need."

By the small, steady flame, he saw a strange expression flicker across her face. She hid it quickly, and he didn't comment on it. His last months with Abraham had been educational. While he was willing to share the knowledge, he never discussed the actual lessons. He flinched as decrepit walls and empty hallways pushed at the corners of his mind. *That place holds a lot of secrets.*

Basheba resisted wiggling her shoulder out of her jacket but didn't bother to question what he was giving her. Once he was done, she snatched up her backpack and, after a bit of rummaging, pulled open a hidden compartment. Barely giving him a heads up, she tossed a bag his way and cracked open a bottle of water.

"Are you sure that's not anything combustible?" he asked with a smirk.

"No. Just water. Although I do keep snake venom in an identical bottle."

"You should probably label those."

"Why? *I* know what everything is."

Lifting the little bag to the light, he examined the contents, having to tip it back and forth to move all of the accumulated sugar out of the way. "Jelly?"

Basheba gasped in horror. "Cactus candy."

"Sorry," Cadwyn smiled.

"That's the good stuff. It's handmade in a little shop in Arizona."

"Right."

Her lips pressed into a tight line. "Give it back."

"No, no. I'm grateful and going to eat the candy."

He hurriedly popped one of the overly sweet treats into his mouth before she could snatch them away. Dusting the sugar off of his fingertips, he heard Mina release a bitter moan.

"I can't feel my face." The ravaged skin of her cheek slurred her words.

Cadwyn shot Basheba a look before the blonde could respond. She rolled her eyes but let him answer.

"It's okay," Cadwyn soothed. "You're safe."

Mina struggled to get her eyes open. The boys reappeared beside them before Cadwyn had a chance to call them over. Jeremiah shouldered his way to his sister's side and took her hand.

"Mina, can you hear me?" Jeremiah asked softly. "Are you okay?"

She blinked slowly and winced. "I'm okay. Are you all right?"

"Don't worry about me." He sniffed and forced a grin.

"I have to." She squeezed his hand. "You're my brother. It's my job."

Unshed tears muffled his light chuckle.

"Do you still have the box?" Mina asked.

He swallowed thickly and forced a smile. "I gave it to Cadwyn. He's keeping it in his med kit."

She smiled slightly, the motion little more than a twitch of the unnumbed side of her face. "That's a good idea. Help me up?"

It was a pleasant surprise when Jeremiah shrunk back to give Cadwyn enough room to handle the task himself. It wouldn't have been the first time concerned loved ones had dismissed Cadwyn's medical training. Under stress, certain people start to think that doctors can solve all problems and nurses are just glorified laymen. Since Mina had passed out, Cadwyn had prepared himself to use force to keep the twitchy boy at bay. *Push too hard, move too fast, jerk at just the wrong angle and everything goes to hell.*

Carefully, Cadwyn drew Mina upright, his well-trained hands searching for any sign that something was wrong. Her fall had been a bad one and, given the array of bruises covering her ribs and hips, he suspected she had chipped a bone or two. It was something he was acutely aware of and conscious about, ever since his first day on the job. A little boy had been brought into the hospital. Barely more than five, he had simply fallen off of his scooter. No one knew his femur had chipped until his mother had tried to comfort him. *Push too hard, move too fast,* Cadwyn thought grimly.

The sudden jerk had applied just enough pressure to the shard of bone. It had ruptured the boy's femoral artery. He bled out internally before anyone knew what was happening. Cadwyn pushed aside the image that lurked on the edges of his mind and refocused himself on Mina. He didn't know why that boy haunted him the way he did. It hadn't been his first time seeing a dead body, even one of a child. *It had never been an accident before,* a voice whispered in the back of his head. *No murder. No madness. Just bad luck and good intentions.*

Eventually, he was satisfied and allowed Mina to lean against him for support. She quickly set herself to the task of assessing their situation, unintendedly leaving Jeremiah to flutter about nervously a few feet away. The boy might have started screaming if Ozzie hadn't given his shoulder a reassuring squeeze.

She jerked. "The *Mahaha*?"

"It hasn't shown up," Ozzie said. "We still hear it moving about now and then. I don't think it can find a way in."

Mina nodded, the motion sending her eyes rolling back in her head. Carefully, she cupped the left side of her face. Delicate, trembling fingers traced the line of sutures that started just below her cheekbone and ended at the corner of her mouth.

"It's not that bad," Jeremiah assured.

"You're still hot," Ozzie added, pointedly avoiding the glare Jeremiah threw his way.

Mina rolled her head to catch Cadwyn's gaze. "It'll scar?"

She barely moved her jaw as she spoke.

He smiled sadly, "I'm sorry, but at least it'll be thin."

Taking his hand, she shook her head as much as she dared. "Thank you."

"It'll be a cool scar," Basheba noted, using Cadwyn's distraction to snatch the candy back. "Makes you look tough. People might take you seriously when you're planning your SWAT hits."

Mina pursed her lips to keep from smiling. "I want to be a profiler."

"Yeah, but profilers get to use SWAT teams."

"Not really."

Basheba made a noise in the back of her throat. "Yeah, okay. I'm sure the desk-jockeys that came up with the Unabomber profile were the same ones busting down his door."

"What?" Mina mumbled, struggling to keep ahold of the conversation. "SWAT are highly trained for infiltration. They wouldn't need a profiler... Are you envisioning that I'd be sending them off to do my bidding like flying monkeys?"

Basheba popped a piece of candy into her mouth and offered Mina the bag. "Well, not anymore. You ruined it."

Furrowing her brow, Mina reached for the bag, "Maybe we both shouldn't be drugged at the same time anymore. It's too confusing."

"Hey, I'm fine right now," Basheba dismissed with a roll of her eyes. "Just eat your candy."

Mina hesitated.

"They have the consistency of Turkish delight," Cadwyn said. "Remember to suck rather than chew."

Selecting a piece, she ripped off tiny pieces that she could push between her lips.

"It's good," Mina said tightly. "Thanks."

Basheba scooped out a handful of candy then placed the bag in the sand beside her. "You can have the rest."

Drinking from the offered water bottle was harder. After several failed attempts and a few pulled stitches, she got the hang of it. They gave her time to orient herself before gathering their belongings and addressing the question before them. *Where do we go now?*

"Can we climb out?" Ozzie asked, eyeing the holes in the lofty cave ceiling.

Jeremiah tilted his head up. "Does anyone have a grappling hook?"

They all turned to Basheba.

Looking somewhat offended, she wiggled her bandaged fingers. "Lift your hand if you think you can hold up your own bodyweight right now."

"Okay, not the best plan," Ozzie said. "There are a few openings that the *Mahaha* hasn't come through. So, I guess we can try those routes."

"And, yet, you offered rope climbing first," Basheba said.

"They're a bit narrow." Jeremiah tried to subtly sneak glances at his sister as he carefully chose his words. "We'll have to crawl."

Being far more careful with her wound, and self-conscious of the saliva that kept seeping from her numbed mouth, it was getting progressively harder to understand her. The full-body shudder said enough, though.

"What was that?" Ozzie asked.

Mina drew a breath through her nose. "Now's the time to go."

"But—" Jeremiah began.

"I'm still a little loopy." She tried to keep her smile to the uninjured half of her face. "Might mellow me out."

Jeremiah took her hand. "Only if you're sure."

At her nod, Basheba slapped a bunch of maps down before the brunette. Handing her the notebook and pencil, she grinned.

"So, where do you suggest we go, Crane?"

"A map of Black River and the surrounding area?" Jeremiah asked.

"It's all guesswork," Basheba admitted. "But from where we started, and given what I can see of the stars, I'm guessing we're in this general area." She used the pencil to make a messy circle. "Does this help?"

Mina nodded slowly and took the pencil. Seconds ticked by with little more than her staring at the map.

"Educated guesses are acceptable," Cadwyn encouraged, drawing one of the chafer tins closer to give her more light.

"But correct answers are preferable," Basheba added.

Cadwyn knew giving her a withering glare wouldn't do anything, so he snuck one of the candy pieces she had piled in her hand instead. Eventually, Mina leaned forward and scribbled just southeast of the Witch Woods.

"I think we're on this side. But I don't know."

"It's okay." Cadwyn placed a warm hand on her shoulder. "You're doing great."

"And it's not like any of us can do much better," Ozzie grinned.

It coaxed another lopsided smile from her. Basheba half-sprawled back to snatch the map.

"We have no idea where any of the tunnels go, anyway," she mumbled. "This'll probably be trial and error. At least we have a relatively safe place to retreat to."

"Are you talking about here?" Jeremiah asked.

Ozzie smirked slightly and nudged the boy with his elbow. "You miss the 'relatively' part?"

The boys used the dim light to cast playful glares at each other.

"Hate to interrupt," Basheba cut in. "But do there happen to be any tunnels in, we'll say, *that* general area?"

She waved her hand about, loosely gesturing to the far wall, and broke into a long string of profanity.

"No need for that language," Jeremiah bristled.

"Screw you! That hurt." She sat back on her knees to hug her arm to her chest. "I thought you drugged me."

Cadwyn carefully pried her hand away to get a better look at it. "I did. But you can't go around flailing skinned limbs and expect nothing to happen."

"Isn't that the whole point of drugs?" she hissed through her teeth, wincing when she clenched her injured jaw a little too tightly.

"You wanted to keep your faculties." A few specks of blood seeped out to stain the new bandage. "Just be careful and you'll be fine."

Shoving another candy in her mouth, she pouted as she chewed. "Well? The wall? Tunnels?"

"Oh, right," Ozzie said before quickly pointing out a few of the shadows that were actually cuts in the stone.

There were three options in the direction Basheba had indicated. Two of them were big enough for Cadwyn to fit through.

"So?" Jeremiah asked gently. "Which one do you guys think?"

Basheba pulled a long chain from around her neck. Over the years, it had fallen to her to collect the wedding rings from the corpses of her relatives, and she now kept the collection with her like a personal totem. One she was insanely protective of. In the entire month Cadwyn had traveled with her, he had only ever seen the collection in its entirety a handful of times. And he had only ever been allowed to touch them when she had been selecting which one to use as the wedding ring. Without taking them off of the chain, she hid two rings from view as she put one in each palm and then held her fists out into the middle of the group.

"Ruby; we take the tunnel on the left. Diamond; we take the right."

CHAPTER 15

Mina couldn't breathe. She gulped for air, but it never seemed to reach her lungs and only left her body quaking. Pain radiated along her nerve endings, bursting anew each time she clutched and dragged herself over the dusty earth. It pulsated within her head in time with her rapid heartbeat. Whatever Cadwyn had given her, it was only enough to take the edge off. To muffle her thoughts rather than silence them. There was still enough of her left to know that she was essentially buried alive.

They had been able to stand when they first entered the tunnel. The walls closed in quickly, allowing the tiny flame of the buffet chafer to paint the walls a light blue. Mina had found herself longing for light of a standard color. Ozzie didn't seem too keen on it, either, but kept his protests to random bouts of squirming. Then the ground crept up toward the ceiling, and they were forced onto their hands and knees. Another squeeze and she was on her stomach, slithering forward, her terror sparking within her bones. All she could see was her backpack that she shoved before her. Her backpack, the dirt floor, and the walls closing in around her.

Squeezing her eyes shut, she forced herself to take a sobering breath and tried to refocus. *Plan for what's coming.* Plans soothed her. They also gave the most beautiful illusion of control. *Jeremiah would be the first to see what's coming.* He had insisted on going first. As he had put it—he was the biggest coward, so he was sure to scream the loudest if anything happened and they needed to retreat. The idea didn't sit well with Mina, but she wasn't in a position to argue. Her brother needed to have confidence in himself. And this was how he chose to do it, how he was trying to earn his place amongst the group. She couldn't deny him that.

Ozzie had picked up on her anxiety and, with a smile, had offered to go next in line. It was comforting to know that someone knowledgeable and relatively uninjured would directly have Jeremiah's back.

Cadwyn brought up the end of the line. He had told Basheba that it was to protect them from the back but, in truth, Mina was sure he just wanted to make sure the injured girls didn't fall behind.

Jeremiah will see any danger first. Then Ozzie, she repeated in her head, shoving her bag over the sandy floor. *Me, Buck, Basheba, and Cadwyn. All our physically dominant ones are at the back. Great. That's just great.* Coughing hard on the dust-filled air, she reminded herself that, while Ozzie wasn't much of a fighter, he was fast on his feet. *And he has proven to be resourceful. Both things not to dismiss out of hand.* Her stomach churned with shame when she acknowledged that he had proven himself more useful than her on numerous occasions.

Focus, she told herself sharply, refusing to let her anxiety fester and grow. It only made her feel the crush of the walls and the thickness of the air. *Think. Plan. If these paths don't lead to anywhere, what do we do next?*

Slowly, methodically, she began to sort through what she knew. Plucking the ideas from her sparking, irrational mind and shoving everything else away. The top of her head scraped across the roof. Instantly, everything within her shattered, leaving only one thought behind. *I'm buried alive!*

"Mina?" Ozzie asked.

Buck nipped at her foot, the pressure against her sneakers doing more to stir her than Ozzie's voice. It chilled her to hear someone crying. It was even worse to realize that she was the one making the pitiful sound.

"It's okay, we're okay," Ozzie assured her.

There's no air. I can't breathe! Trying to smother the sound turned it into something gut-wrenching and shrill.

"Let's play a game," Ozzie suggested with a bit too much enthusiasm. "Something to distract ourselves. What do you like to play?"

We're going to get stuck. We'll rot into each other, and no one will ever find us. Her whole body shuddered with broken, terrified sobs.

"Mina," Ozzie persisted, his voice encouraging and strong. "What game do you like to play? Mina!"

"Periodic Chain," she managed to blurt out, dragging herself forward a few feet.

"I don't know that one," Ozzie said.

"I do," Cadwyn chimed in. "Someone says an element on the Periodic Table. The next person has to use the last letter as the first letter in the next element. I'll go first. Manganese. Ozzie?"

"Pass. How about you, Mina?"

E. She latched onto the thought, trying to drown out the pain in her limbs and the internal mantra that she was suffocating.

"Erbium," she pushed out through her tears and teeth.

"Mendelevium," Basheba spouted. "What? I'm awesome at chemistry."

It's dry earth. You might mummify rather than turn to sludge.

Basheba prompted, "It's your turn, Mina. You need another one starting with 'M,' or I get gloating rights."

The sandy earth streamed between her fingers as she pulled herself forward. It was too hot. The walls scraped against her trembling shoulders. A heavy thud shook the narrow passage. Dust fell like rain, stinging her eyes and coating her throat. She cupped a hand over her nose and mouth, trying to lessen the effect. Another thump and they all fell silent. Still. Her heart hammered against her ribs as the next thunderous boom fell upon them, and she realized that they weren't strikes. *Footsteps.* Something heavy was walking just above their heads.

The group stilled instantly, each one holding their breath as if the slightest noise would give away their position. The booming footsteps stalked across their concealed tunnel. Loose stones shook free with each impact, the resulting dust thickening the limited air and coating Mina's throat. She stifled her urge to cough, turning it into a series of sporadic bone-wracking spasms. Each convulsion rattled her injured cheek. Pain coursed through her, bringing fresh tears to her watering eyes. All the while, the thunderous footsteps walked over their spines. Clawing at the last shreds of her self-restraint, certain she couldn't take it all for a second more, silence descended.

The blue chafer light elongated the shadows, twisting and distorting them into snarling faces. Mina squeezed her eyes shut, her trembling fingertips snagging against the tight sutures that protruded from her flesh. She cowered, certain she couldn't take much more, when footsteps began again. Not where they had last left off. They were behind her again; starting where the last had and retracing the path above them. The process repeated, over and over, until her frazzled mind could make sense of it. *There's more than one.*

Cracks snaked through the stone above their heads. The ground trembled. A roaring bellow severed the silence an instant before shrapnel rained down upon her.

Mina scrambled back, butting against Buck as she tried to protect her face from the pelting stones.

Jeremiah screamed; the sound drowned out by the chaos around them. Through watering eyes, Mina caught sight of what was bearing down upon them. The curved, alabaster horn of a colossal bull shattered the top of the tunnel. The Minotaur drove itself down harder, searching for flesh, thrashing its head in an attempt to shred the boy's back.

Mina shrieked as thunder boomed and the tunnel shook. A kiss of pain slashed across her shoulder blade. Latching onto her bag, she shoved it up, trying to use it as a shield. It barely got a foot off of the ground before it hit the ground above her. The bull lunged again, shredding the ceiling. The tattered remains bombarded her head, her legs. Buck growled and snarled, all of it lost under the enraged bovine screams.

The tunnel rattled, throwing her helplessly about the minimal space, leaving her broken and bloody against the crumbling rock. Mina felt the sand beneath her slip only a second before the slight pull became a sinkhole. Thousands of hands reached out to grab her, their moist rotting skin reflecting the blue light. Grasping the bag with both hands, she swung it into the hole. The hands distorted before her eyes. Suddenly, they weren't solid anymore, leaving the growing pit gaping before her. The ground lurched, and shifting sand dragged her down.

***

Basheba curled against the slab of concrete, desperately protecting her head while the deluge of sand left her gasping for breath. The weight bore her down, pushing against the injuries she had sustained in the short fall. The downpour trickled away. She waited for a moment longer before pushing off of the ground. The granules slid off of her, adding more airborne dust to the lingering fog.

Coughing hard sent new spirals of pain coiling around her ribs. *Bruised, not broken.* Landing on her backpack hadn't helped. She wrapped an arm around her waist to brace herself for the next coughing fit.

"Buck?" She cleared her throat and croaked out. "Cadwyn?"

"I'm here," he groaned.

Turning her head, she found him just behind her. Exactly where he had been in the tunnel. But when she looked before her, Buck was missing.

"Buck!" she screamed before attempting a whistle, having to fight back a spike of agony to complete the task. His answering bark never came. "Buck!"

"Ozzie?" Cadwyn called. "Mina? Jeremiah?"

"Buck!"

Cadwyn suddenly hushed her. It took a heartbeat for her to realize why. The narrow tunnel had been replaced by a wide hallway of brick and hanging lights. A few of the metal light fixtures swayed in an unfelt breeze, creating a slow, repetitive creak. They were alone.

"Do you know this place?" Basheba asked when she saw the horror on Cadwyn's face.

"It's the death shoot."

"Say again?"

He cautiously stepped out into the middle of the hallway.

"Cadwyn?"

"It's the tunnel once used to transport dead patients from Dalton Ridge to the crematorium."

"Dalton Ridge," Basheba mouthed, the name sparking a distant memory.

"It's an abandoned insane asylum in Massachusetts," Cadwyn replied numbly.

"Right. Dad and I went ghost hunting in there once." She inched closer, studying his face closely. "How do you know this place by sight?"

"I know every inch of this building," he replied. Recovering from his daze, he looked down at her with wide eyes. "This is where I kept Abraham for eight months."

"I thought you were in a motel."

His laugh was bitter and sharp. "Yeah. I kept a possessed guy in a generally public area."

"The families seem to think that you did."

"And you're going to let it stay that way."

Taken aback by the sharp edge in his voice, she took half a step back. "I keep your secrets, you keep mine."

The promise seemed to soothe him somewhat. While the volatile anger seeped from his face, leaving him chastised and apologetic, he still trembled with pent up energy.

"Sorry."

"I don't need apologies," she smiled. "I'd love some exposition, though."

His laughter was short. "Abraham was losing the fight. It was just a matter of time before the demon took possession of his body. I needed somewhere safe, out of the way, where I could control who came near him. Dalton Ridge was just sitting there. Still stocked with gurneys and straitjackets and restraints. A building designed to keep people in. It seemed perfect."

"You got him here by yourself?"

Cadwyn shrugged one shoulder and resumed his survey of the space. "All I needed was a wheelchair, some heavy narcotics, and the will to make it happen."

"Katrina doesn't have the power to actually transport us to Massachusetts," Basheba said, trying to draw the conversation away from painful topics. "This has to be another trick. Maybe to get us to walk off a ledge or something."

He gave a noncommittal grunt.

Biting her lip, she huffed. "I can't just stay here. I need to find Buck."

"Yeah, I figured you'd say that." Turning to her, he looped the strap of his med kit over his head and stretched his arms wide, indicating their two options. "Hospital or crematorium?"

"Hospital."

His hands fell a little bit.

"Hey, that's just my kneejerk reaction," she defended. "I'll follow your lead."

Cadwyn looked back and forth once more before he dropped his hands altogether. "It seems like we're doomed whatever the choice."

"That's the spirit," Basheba chirped.

Without a word, he stalked off down the hall, not realizing that he was forcing her to jog to keep up with his much longer stride. She didn't call him on it. Just trotted alongside him, cursing her short stature and shrugging into her backpack. She tugged the straps until the pack was flush against her spine and pulled her hunting blade free from its sheath. Having the familiar weight in her hand helped her to feel centered. Alert and silent, they followed the hallway up into the belly of the dilapidated building.

From what she could recall, Dalton Ridge had been rather impressive in its day. A sprawling Victorian-style building of red brick and white trimmings. Three stories with random towers poking up to offer a fourth floor. Time and neglect had gutted it. What few walls that remained intact were covered in peeling wallpaper and spray paint. She read a few of the sentences that previous explorers had left behind. Most of them were meant to creep out anyone who followed; there were mentions of the devil and hints of enraged ghosts. Above the double doors that opened up to an examination area, *'People taste like chicken'* was sprayed in red paint. She rolled her eyes as they passed under it.

"What cuts are you eating?" she mumbled.

Cadwyn turned around to look down at her, his brows knitted deep in thought.

"What?" she asked.

He continued to study her in silence, his lips slightly parted but silent. Basheba knew what he wanted to ask, why he hesitated. And she willed him to leave it alone, at least for now. A flash of movement made them both jerk around bringing their stalemate to an end.

"Did you see what that was?" she asked.

"Monty," Cadwyn said, half-talking to her, half-calling to the retreating specter.

Sparing Basheba a glance, he sprinted forward. They had crossed the room and worked through a maze of hallways before he finally slowed enough for her to ask some follow-up questions. Their panted breaths rolled off of the cracked tiles that lined the room. Grimy bathtubs stood in long rows.

"You need to stop chasing ghosts, Cadwyn."

She hooked one finger around the thick material that curved over the end of one tub, making the attached metal hooks clatter against the porcelain.

"Hydrotherapy," Cadwyn told her absently. "Although, they're also useful for stopping patients from drowning themselves. Don't touch that one!"

Basheba jerked her hand back from the third tub in the row. He shrugged almost apologetically.

"Doris is protective of that one." He caught himself. "Although she's not really here, is she?"

"You made friends with ghosts?"

"Not exactly friends," he said, still paying more attention to their surroundings than her. "They needed someone to take care of them, not a playmate."

Basheba studied him as they stalked around the room. He surveyed the area with quiet, professional confidence. Nothing close to the blind hysteria she had seen in the cave earlier. *Because he's looking for his patient, not his brother.*

"You've spent most of your life in mental asylums," she noted.

He turned to her. "I haven't exactly done the math."

"That wasn't judgment in my voice," she said. "It was awe."

"Because of my poor life choices?" Cadwyn smirked.

Because you've dedicated your entire life to lost causes. "You never give up on people."

They rounded the last tub and came to stand before each other.

"You can't save everyone."

Tipping his head to the side, he studied her closely. "I'm not trying to. But a little company can make even hell a lot nicer."

"I should have been here to help you out."

"You were two," he noted with a smile.

"I was a little snake," she shrugged. "I was born with enough venom to kill."

A low tremor rattled through the walls. Hard enough to dislodge the fractured tiles, leaving them to shatter upon the floor. Cadwyn pushed in closer to Basheba's side, one hand coming up to hover protectively over her back. She could see how hard he was struggling to keep the fear from his eyes. The room darkened. Mold and rot crept out from the doorway like a thousand searching fingers crawling toward them. Hands slithered through the splintered doorframe.

Flesh hung loosely from the bones, dragged further down by gravity as the limbs twitched across the ceiling. Basheba could hear its skin pop against the broken plaster. Putrid blood splattered against the floor, the dark lumps squirming with maggots. The stench of decay invaded the room before the creature had slithered its way inside. *Abraham.* Even half-eaten away, there was no mistaking the features that were echoed in Cadwyn. *This is what a demon can do when set loose.* A terror she had never felt festered within her bone marrow.

The living remains moved in broken twitches. Each abrupt motion sent a flurry of insects scattering, making its skin heave like a rolling tide. Cadwyn tensed and crowded closer to Basheba. She couldn't tell if he was seeking comfort or trying to protect her. *He never had to protect anyone from this,* she realized. *He was alone here with it. A decomposing sack with his brother's face.* Perched upon the ceiling like a squatting bug, Abraham twisted his head, the bones of his neck clicking loudly, to grin broadly at them.

"Welcome home, little brother."

Basheba latched onto his hand and broke into a run. He staggered behind her, his attention fixed on the monster looming above them. Its teeth ripped free from its gums, and they scattered against the floor as it taunted them and offered a thousand promises to destroy him inside and out. Basheba tried to block the words out before they could construct images in her head. She couldn't think of Cadwyn enduring any of it.

Suddenly, a hand had grabbed her, dragging her into a tub before she could stop it. Porcelain cracked against the side of her head. Her vision blurred. Sudden heat brought her back to her senses. She jerked up as steaming water sloshed around her, covered her, dragged her down. Far beyond the depths of the tub into a burning, blistering darkness. She gulped for breath but only found the scorching water. Cadwyn's grip on her arm remained solid. She dug her nails in as she was sucked deeper still. Holding on even as her lungs burned, her skin blistered, and her blood began to boil within her veins. Katrina dragged her down, and Basheba took Cadwyn with her.

CHAPTER 16

A damp flick against her cheek made Mina's eyes pop open. Buck grumbled a protest as he skittered away from her flailing hand but, when she refused to get up, he came back to lap at her again. Pain rattled along her bones as she pushed herself onto her hands and knees. Buck nuzzled her, urging her on until she rocked back onto her knees and took her first good look around. A cut in the lofty cave ceiling allowed a barb of moonlight to brighten the shadows. She knelt on a strip of sand nestled between two undulating walls of stone. Trailing her eyes up the uneven surface, she spotted a half dozen ledges that could have once been the tunnel they had been climbing through.

Buck whimpered again and bumped his wet nose insistently against the side of her neck. Pushing him away stirred her enough from her fixation to realize that they were alone. Hurriedly, she checked the sand for footprints. *Nothing.* Carefully studying the wall again, this time searching for a hint of where the others had ended up, she caught a small flicker of light. The sudden, grateful lurch of her heart left her dizzy. All warmth in her died when she heard Buck's low growl.

The scruff on the back of his neck stood on end as he emitted another rumble. Heeding the warning, Mina scurried back. She was barely on her feet before her heels struck something and she was sent toppling onto her back. Her breath caught. Far above, the shifting glow grew larger, approaching the rim of the ledge. In her haste to get up, her feet kicked the object again. *My bag.* She lurched forward to snatch it up. Before her fingers could hook around the nearest strap, the sand bulged. A dozen tiny hands shot up from the unstable earth. Searching for her. Their nails twisting up in the tattered sleeves of her jacket.

Choking down her screams, she forced herself to surge forward again, pushing past them to desperately snatch up the strap. The hands dragged her down and would have taken her under the soil if it wasn't for Buck. The Rottweiler swooped in, wide jaws easily snapping through tendon and bone. Severed limbs twitched upon the ground before turning back to charge at her again. Heart pounding, Mina flicked her gaze up. Voices had joined the approaching light. She almost froze upon hearing Whitney's voice amongst them. *Get away! Hide! Move!*

Clenching her jaw, she slid the backpack toward her. Suddenly, the hands faltered. They spasmed once before slithering out like an oil slick, still undeniably there but no longer solid. She wrenched herself free of their now feeble grip, clutched the bag to her chest, and sprinted for the safety of the shadows, Buck at her heels.

Her blood thundered through her veins, weakening her knees until she half fell into the shadows that crowded against the base of the wall. The contents of her bag dug into her stomach as she clutched it. Buck's black fur camouflaged him with the shadows, allowing him to venture back out a little and remain unseen from above. Fixated on the reforming limbs, he ignored her whispered pleas for him to come back, even after the hands thickened and latched onto his paws. His first savage growl echoed off of the walls.

The golden light swept down from above like a search beacon. Mina lunged forward, anticipating a fight to free the animal, only to find that the grasping hands collapsed in on themselves once more. Looping her arms around Buck's neck, she dragged him back against the wall just as the light hit the sand. The beam trailed slowly back and forth before being joined by another. The combined glow washed over the sea of flailing limbs poking out from the dull bronze sand. They watched as the creature recreated itself, drawing in the airborne oil to return to solid flesh. *Are they toying with me? Why don't they just grab me already?* The hands continued to squirm around her, a writhing swarm that never made contact, leaving dread and anxiety to eat away at her mind.

Smothering her whimpers against Buck's scruff, she froze. The light ghosted through the canyon, inching closer to her feeble hiding place with every pass. She searched with them, both hopeful and terrified that she'd catch sight of Jeremiah and the others. There were only ghostly limbs and sand. The voices above became a steady hum; melting together until it was impossible to tell how many humans stood above her. *If they're all human.*

Mina jumped when Whitney's shrill voice sliced through the other voices. A command was given and heeded. The lights lifted, and booming footsteps worked their way along the ledge, rattling the wall against her spine even as they grew distant. It was proof enough that Whitney had borrowed some extra demonic muscle from Katrina.

Prized hogs or workhorses. Basheba's words echoed through her mind, lifting the shroud of mindless panic. Memories and observations clashed within her skull, birthing a new theory.

After her death, Katrina channeled her pride in her livestock into her cult, cultivating them over generations to better suit her purposes. Muscle or fat, they're too big to move easily down here. Watching the golden light of the torches drift through the ebony light made her stomach drop. *They know where Katrina's corpse is, and they have an easy pathway to get to her.*

Smothering her gasp, she looked around her again, desperate for one of the others to appear. *I have to find them.* A stronger thought exploded into the forefront of her mind. *If they get to Katrina first, all of this was for nothing!* She coiled in on herself, choking Buck and pulling her bag closer. Its contents rattled together at it slid along the sand. The ghostly hands reared like cobras but dissipated before they could clutch onto the material. Mina's breath caught; her panic momentarily pushed aside by the possibilities that flooded her mind.

Experimentally, she tightened her grip on the bag and pushed it to the side. By the light from above, she watched the phenomenon repeat itself. The hands showed interest in the bag but none of them could make contact. Fingers latched onto her ankle. She bit down a scream as she whirled, already swinging the bag. The hand disappeared. *They can't touch the bag?* With shaking fingers, she tore open the zipper and checked inside, half expecting to find some strange talisman amongst her belongings. But everything was as Ozzie had left it.

The cult rounded a corner in the path above her, shifting the light. Something gleamed within her bag, and she snatched it out. *The cone. It worked?* Memories of the *Mahaha* almost made her laugh at the thought. *But they weren't ghosts*, the analytical side of her mind whispered. *That's a monster or a demon. Something made of flesh, not energy. The magnetic cone can only bend energy.*

Trembling, she drew Buck closer still to her side, gripped the cone with her free hand, and thrust it out. Once more, the phantom limbs broke apart, only to reform again when she drew the cone back to her chest. *I was right? Magnetic fields bend ghosts.* Her flush of victory cooled within her chest when a noise drew her attention back up. Back to the cult. She realized then that she wasn't pinned in place. If the cone did work, she could flee. *And I can follow.*

"Come on," she whispered to the dog.

He cocked his head, watching her get to her feet. Squeezing her eyes shut, she forced one foot forward, testing her new theory. Nothing touched her and, when she pried her eyes open again, she found the twisting tendrils swirling around her. *One foot.* The cone's effect radiated out for about a foot. The hands relentlessly tested those boundaries.

"We have to follow them," Mina told Buck, as if speaking the words would somehow give her the courage to do it.

I have to do this. I'm the only one left. Sucking in a deep breath, Mina fought down her terrified tears and called the dog to her side.

They moved forward, keeping to the shadows, trailing behind the stream of murderers and demons.

***

Snow exploded up around Ozzie as he hit the ground. The flurry danced around him as airborne crystals before toppling back down to bury him. He jerked upright, dislodging them again as he hurriedly took in his surroundings. The dank confines of the caves had been replaced with a sprawling wilderness. Evergreens dominated the landscape, their branches heavy with snow, glistening as the sunlight struck the ice that encased them. Somewhere out of sight, a woodpecker worked against a trunk. Its rapid rat-a-tat drifted through the space, stirring the relative silence.

"Where are we?" Jeremiah asked.

Consumed with relief not to be alone, Ozzie didn't realize at first that it was *only* them.

"Where is everyone?" Ozzie asked.

Jeremiah was halfway through his response when he realized the rest of their group was absent. He snapped back around with wide eyes.

"Where's my sister?"

Ozzie could only shake his head helplessly.

A tree trembled in the distance, and they surged to their feet, preparing themselves as best they could for the unknown. It was rather anticlimactic when a lone moose lazily lumbered out to pass them, its long stride making easy work of the deep snow.

"Mina!"

"Jerry, shut up," Ozzie hissed.

"They're not going to find us if we keep quiet."

"Yeah, okay. But what else might find us?"

The moment it clicked, he lunged forward, the color draining from his face and his hand grasping onto Ozzie's sleeve.

"What do you think's in the forest?"

The last time Ozzie had ventured into the Witch Woods played through his mind. Goat headed satyrs ripping sacrificial bulls apart with their bare hands. He gagged at the memory of blood sitting stark against the scattered pieces of the alabaster bovines.

"I don't know," he decided to say. *Why put all that in his head?* "But let's not find out, yeah?"

Jeremiah's throat bobbed as he swallowed thickly. "Has anything like this happened to you before?"

Hiding his mounting panic behind a smile, Ozzie tried to play it off. "Katrina's pretty creative. You never really know what you're going to get."

"But we're not in the woods? How can she be this strong?"

The sheer desperation in Jeremiah's eyes caught Ozzie off guard. It was like looking into a mirror, seeing himself only a year ago. Untested and raw, pleading with someone to make it all better. Cadwyn had been there for him at his weakest point. Had held him when he cried like a newborn and told him that everything was going to be okay. *Cadwyn had made me believe I could make it.*

"We'll figure it out. But not by standing around here. Let's go find somewhere warm, all right?"

"But—"

"One crisis at a time," Ozzie grinned, lightly thumping Jeremiah's shoulder with his knuckles.

The small smile Jeremiah gave him in return made Ozzie feel like he had achieved the impossible. He might have just made this nightmare a little bit more bearable for someone else. Before he could savor the moment, a bellow rocked the forest. Birds took flight, fleeing from both the noise and the blonde girl that sprinted across the clearing. A man stampeded after her, tearing apart the evergreens in his pursuit, quickly closing the distance the child was struggling to create. Watching it unfold struck Ozzie with the strangest sense of déjà vu. *A little girl chased through the woods in the dead of winter.*

"Basheba?" Ozzie stammered.

"What am I missing?"

Ozzie hesitated to reveal a secret that wasn't his own. *But Isaac's dead now.*

"Do you remember what Basheba told Isaac?"

"Before she stabbed him to death?" Jeremiah spat before going stiff. "Something about kids? About him forcing her to have some. Ozzie, what did he do?"

Ozzie was already moving, trying to chase down the fleeing pair. He couldn't shake the feeling that he was running right into Katrina's trap, but he didn't see any other way to get out. *If she wants Jerry and me to see something, she's not going to let us go until we do,* he reasoned to himself. It was hard to ignore the little voice that reminded him that she might never let them go. As they struggled against the snow, he told Jeremiah as much as he knew about it. Just after Basheba's first period, her parents had been called away, leaving her alone with her brother in a small cabin in rural Alaska. Isaac had used the internet to essentially put a hit out on her. *Do whatever you want with the girl, so long as she can still bear the child you put in her.* Ozzie had barely been able to force the words past his lips without the contents of his stomach following. *She was only a kid. Alone and scared.*

"Isaac really did that?" Jeremiah asked breathlessly as they ran. His face darkened as he spat out with ferocity. "The guy got off easy with just a stabbing."

There might be some hope for him yet, Ozzie thought.

As they ducked under a low hanging branch, Jeremiah asked in more of a whisper, "Why would the Witch bring us here?"

A few final yards and their panted breaths were covered by broken weeping. Ozzie latched onto Jeremiah's wrist and yanked him along with him behind the nearest tree. They peeked out from their hiding place to watch what they had been brought to witness. The child version of Basheba sat curled at the base of a pine, her arms looped around her shins and her forehead pressed against her slender knees. Ozzie had only ever known Basheba as she was now—a slight figure with fire in her blood. But like this, as barely more than a child, she hadn't grown into her ferocity. She looked so small that he was struck with the sudden need to go and help her.

He must have jerked forward to do so because Jeremiah's hand clenched around his wrist, holding him in place. The snow crunched under the man's boots as he stalked closer to the weeping girl. *See.* The disembodied voice made both Jeremiah and Ozzie jump. They hurriedly checked their surroundings, but they were still alone. Standing on the edges. Waiting for horrors to unfold. *See.*

They turned back as the man's growled words rolled over them. There wasn't an ounce of warmth or regret in his voice as he demanded Basheba to stand. She wept louder. A gut-wrenching sound that made Ozzie long to race forward again. Jeremiah tightened his grip until the sharp edges of his battered nails dug into his skin.

"There'll be a whole lot less pain if you do what you're told," the man warned.

Basheba lifted her flushed face and released a pitiful hiccup.

See.

Like a ghost, a slender figure crept upon a branch. Ozzie didn't even notice it until it swung down to loop a length of rope around the man's shoulders. Physically superior in every way, the man easily shook the figure free. Still, it was too late. Basheba was on her feet. The blade in her hand caught the daylight as it arched up and severed the man's throat. Ozzie's stomach roiled as blood gushed out from the wound. It bathed Basheba. Staining her pale skin as readily as it did the snow. Spilling into her open mouth as she gasped. Eyes bulging and mouth twitching, the man wheezed for breath. Whatever he could draw into his body whistled through the severed skin, making it twitch and flap.

Ozzie longed to look away but forced himself to watch. The

limited contents of his stomach worked its way up his throat when Basheba spat out the deluge of blood that had welled in her mouth.

"That makes eight," Basheba chirped.

The boy that must have been her brother rocked down to sit upon the branch. The man was still gasping his last breaths against the snow as the siblings talked.

"You don't get to claim that one. He's mine."

"Who did the cutting?"

"All you did was fail to cry convincingly," he snorted.

Basheba slicked blood-drenched hair off her forehead to better show the roll of her eyes.

"It's my kill, Baba," the boy insisted. "I get to pick which cut we eat."

Flipping the kitchen knife in the air, Basheba caught the blade between slender fingers, presenting him with the handle.

"Fine. But no more eyes. They're way too salty."

See what she is.

The boys spun once more. This time, the disembodied voice came with a body—a small child Ozzie instantly recognized, although he had only glimpsed her once before.

"Katrina." The name slipped past Ozzie's lips as he pushed Jeremiah behind him.

See what she is. Katrina's voice surged around them like crashing waves yet somehow remained a whisper. *Say it.* At their silence, the witch fixed her dark, dead eyes upon Jeremiah. *Say it!*

Jeremiah spat out the words as if he couldn't stand to have them on his tongue. "She's a cannibal."

The words struck Ozzie to the core, and he spiraled helplessly into the darkness that reared up to swallow him.

CHAPTER 17

Shadows danced off of the broken walls of the cave, dipping and churning in accordance with the bonfire's lapping flames. From their hiding places, Mina and Buck had watched the cult assemble the blaze upon the sandy bank. At its base lay the remains of Katrina Hamilton. The conditions of the cave had preserved the Bell Witch to a certain extent. Calcite covered the bones; tiny little crystals that caught the light and scattered it as rainbows across the sand. It was a protective coating that spared her from the ravages of time the way the grave wouldn't have.

Mina braced herself against the boulder she hid behind and craned her neck, trying to get a better view. There was no doubt in her mind that she had heard the presence of Katrina's monstrous creatures, but she had yet to catch sight of them.

Townsfolk clustered on the limited sand. Their excitable chatter filled the space as they ate and drank, having brought with them a seemingly endless supply of alcohol. Some were already too intoxicated to stand. Others stumbled amongst the dancers in exaggerated masks. Gilded bull horns caught the light like liquid steel. Bee wings trimmed with gold created a kaleidoscope of colors. And men wearing goat masks seemed content to ram each other until their skulls cracked. *Whatever they're here for, sobriety isn't a necessity.*

Men with biceps bigger than Mina's head carried a gigantic wooden barrel into the middle of the festivities. Rambunctious cheers met its arrival, and they quickly gathered around it. The music ebbed away, leaving the cave to the pop and sizzle in the flames.

Mina cast a quick look at Buck. He lay by her feet, silent but alert, watching the scene unfold—a perfect hunting companion. The look only took a second but, by the time she lifted her head, Mina found that the burly men were now heaving Whitney onto the top of the barrel. Adorned with a crown of grapevines and dressed in lengths of sheer cloth, she opened her arms over the gathering. One of the men presented her with an ax before retreating with the others.

"The Witch has gathered us all here today for a purpose."

Whitney's calmly spoken words created a slight stir amongst the cult members. On the night they had first come for Mina and the others, Basheba had hypothesized that very few of them had ever had to get their hands dirty. Mina found herself convinced of it now. *The kills were in the privacy of the Witch Woods, far from their sight. All they ever saw were the good harvests and rowdy parties.*

"I know the last year has been difficult for all of you," Whitney assured, her painted lips glistening like wine in the play of shadow and light. "The Witch weeps for all of us, for the horrors the Four Families have visited upon our beloved town. She reminds us to be strong, for each other, for our home, for her. And she offers us this gift."

With that, she tapped the top of the barrel with the tip of her ax. It was enough to break the crowd into an ecstatic cheer.

"Drink!" Whitney called over them. "Be happy! It's all she asks of us!"

One swing and the ax head cracked clean through the aged wood. Red wine gushed free, bubbling and spouting, filling ready cups and open mouths. Mina sunk back slightly as the crowd drank with wild abandon. *Two hundred and six bones in the human body.* Mina rolled the number in her head. *Even if I can get to them, how will I carry them all?*

The first scream snapped her out of her thoughts. She ducked down next to Buck, who restlessly scraped and pawed at the sand. Carefully, she leaned to the side and snuck another glance. Bodies hit the ground, kicking up dust as they convulsed, wine and froth spewing from under their masks. Tendons pulled, and eyes bulged and rolled back in their skulls. Screams gargled as more fell. The golden firelight wasn't enough to hide the molten blush that claimed their skin. From her perch, Whitney watched the carnage unfold with a small smile upon her lips. In moments, she was the only one left alive.

Shocked, Mina barely felt the tremors, not until the shadows split and a pair of minotaurs entered the ring of light. Seven feet tall and sheathed in muscle, they blocked Mina's sight of the goat-headed satyr that followed close behind. Whitney beamed at them and lifted one arm in command. One of the minotaurs stalked forward to obediently lift her down from the barrel.

"Their blood is for Katrina, as agreed," Whitney instructed them. The beast turned to comply, pausing only when she added, "But their flesh is mine."

Steam puffed from the minotaur's snout. It turned its massive bull's head just enough to regard its companions with dark eyes.

"I only promised Katrina the blood. And there's enough here for her to be strong again. I even have another gift for her." Whitney pulled herself to full height and tipped her chin higher still. "It's more than I promised. She has no right to interfere with my sacrifice."

Both minotaurs clawed at the sandy ground with their human feet. The goat man seemed more content to watch with something bordering on amusement. For the first time, Whitney hesitated.

"Will you be telling our Master that he won't be receiving his gifts because Katrina had to play her games?"

The beasts shared one more glance before slowly beginning their work. One by one, they dragged the bodies of the poisoned cult members over to Katrina's skeleton, then proceed to rip them apart. The sickening sound of tearing flesh made Mina gag, and the copper scent of blood mingled with smoke and wine. They only ever let the blood splatter upon the bones. The flesh and all the innards were thrown onto the bonfire.

Whitney's a witch. Mina didn't care about the stitches on her cheek or the pain that touching them caused. She clamped a hand over her mouth, desperately holding back both panic and bile. *A living witch. Katrina's minion is making a grab for power. We're screwed.*

The desire to do something raged against the knowledge of just how weak she was. Alone, no weapons, nothing but the shadows and underground lake to hide in. Even with Buck to create a diversion, she wouldn't have time to collect the bones.

The fire crackled as the beasts scattered body parts over its embers. *Gifts for Katrina's benefactor.* Mina froze, a hand still covering her mouth. Slowly, she inched up far enough to watch the scene for a moment more. The process was the same. Drain the blood and feed the flames. *The sacrifices aren't alive,* she thought, her gaze sliding from the fire to the sparkling bones. *So, is it possible to sacrifice a ghost?*

The hypothesis was still forming when the ground rumbled again. Mina dropped, looping her arms around Buck's throat, clutching her bag when she heard its contents click together. The thunderous crack of breaking stone quickly covered the sound. Even from her hiding place, she saw the rock wall open like a gaping wound. Four bodies tumbled out. They hit the ground hard and barely had time to stand before the beasts were on them.

"Careful with them," Whitney ordered, delight dripping from each word. "They're my special gifts."

The satyr only needed one hand to pull Basheba off of the ground. *Jeremiah.* Mina shifted forward on her knees, desperate for a sight of her brother. Movement streaked across her vision. She threw herself back, landing hard on the sand and sliding away. As the spike of fear faded, she saw what had been discarded. Cadwyn's med kit and Basheba's pack and knife. They sat in a tantalizing pile far beyond the reach of her hiding place. Buck caught Basheba's scent and started forward to meet her. It took all of Mina's weight and some quiet coaxing to keep him down.

"Wake up," Whitney demanded.

Buck pushed forward again, dragging Mina with him until they could both peer around the stone. The satyr still held Basheba off of the ground by her arms, its large goat head twisting to follow Whitney as she prowled around them. Mina's heart skipped a beat when she couldn't find the others. A flash of movement brought her attention to the water's edge. She chased it, hoping to catch glimpse of the boys. It was hard to see them from where she was. The boulder blocked most of her view, and the minotaurs took the rest. She caught quick glimpses of hair—Cadwyn's dark blonde and Ozzie's midnight back. Her heart refused to beat right until she saw the brunette shade so similar to her own. *They're standing. They're alive.*

Her moment of relief soon wilted into despair. A part of her wished to be a little more like Basheba. Just enough that she could storm out there to help them. *But she wouldn't do that*, she corrected herself. Basheba had once described herself as playing by 'killer doll' rules. She relied on ambushes and stealth. *She knows her limitations and strengths.* Mina turned back to the pile of bags laying discarded on the sand. *And I know mine.*

Cupping Buck's muzzle, she directed his line of sight to the bags. There wasn't a doubt in her mind that Basheba had taught him to fetch such things. What that command might be was anyone's guess. Still, she pointed to the bags, whispered 'fetch,' added 'quietly' as almost a plea, and released him. Buck looked to her before tipping his head into the air, black nose twitching as he scented Basheba.

"No," she mouthed. Pointing sharply at the bags she ordered, "Fetch."

Buck crawled forward on his stomach then paused to check over his shoulder. Not at Mina. His attention was taken by Basheba, who had just begun to stir. Whitney's hand made a resounding crack as she drove it across Basheba's face. Buck's answering growl was lost under Cadwyn's own. Whitney couldn't let the reaction slide without a bit of mocking, and so, the attention remained away from Buck.

Not daring to clap, Mina almost soundlessly tapped the tips of her fingers together. The movement caught Buck's attention, and she thrust a hand toward the bags. He wiggled forward again.

"Why is it that, when I wake up, there's always a fifty-fifty chance I'm going to be surrounded by murders?" Basheba's voice was groggy but light. Almost as if she found it all rather amusing.

Whitney hit her again.

"Can you just get your monologue over with?" Basheba replied. "Or better yet, make it a soliloquy, so we don't have to hear you."

"Always so brave. So defiant." Whitney put one finger under Basheba's chin and forced the blonde to meet her gaze.

Mina quickly checked on Buck, sure that the woman would see the massive dog in the corner of her eye, but his dark fur bled into the shadows. Slowly, he closed his mouth around the bag straps.

"I guess it's easy to be like that when you have a demon backing you." Whitney paused to look over at the dark water. "Although, he doesn't seem to be helping you all that much right now."

"I don't know. I'm still alive."

Whitney's teeth were stark white pillars between her crimson lips. "Not for long."

Once more, Mina tore her attention away to check on Buck. The dog held the bags in his front legs as he lay flat upon the earth. His dark eyes were on Basheba. In jerky little motions, he opened and closed his jaws around the bag straps, torn between Mina's order and Basheba.

"Why don't you just let us, what's the word?" Basheba popped her lips casually, but the last word was said with force. "Go."

Tumbling into mocking laughter, Whitney didn't notice as Buck shuffled forward on his belly, obediently following Basheba's command and returning to Mina.

"Let you go?" Whitney said. "Oh, no, my dear. You're dying here today."

Mina reached out for Buck the second he was within reach. She pulled him back to her, making sure he was concealed once more.

"Why don't you just *stay* away from us?" Basheba asked.

Obediently, Buck's rump hit the sand. His tail nervously flicking back and forth, as if he was waiting for Basheba's praise and was unsure why he wasn't getting it. Mina bit her lips and gave him a quick pat before tearing into the packs.

"And people called you quick-witted," Whitney smirked. "Now, explain to me what you were hoping to achieve with Isaac's death? Is this how you've survived Katrina for so long?"

Mina blocked out the interrogation, pouring all of her concentration into the items before her. Cadwyn always boasted that his kit was well-stocked—the man was a walking apothecary. It didn't take her long to find the bottles of medical chemicals deep in the bottom. *Sulfur for skin conditions. Charcoal for poison absorption.* A scalpel made quick work of shredding the bag's metallic inner lining. She dumped everything else out onto the ground and turned to Basheba's pack.

The blonde's scream almost shattered her resolve.

Where is it? Where did she put it? Her fingers trembled as they closed around the bottle of saltpeter.

Dread boiled in the pit of her stomach, agonized screams pierced her ears, and the stench of rotting flesh bombarded her nose.

Don't freeze.

Hot tears burned the corners of her eyes when she saw the music box amongst the scattered objects.

Don't freeze.

Grinding her teeth, she knocked aside the music box to snatch up the crumpled pack of cigarettes underneath it. She never thought she'd be so happy Cadwyn was a smoker. *Sulfur, charcoal, saltpeter.* She mixed them together with the tip of the scalpel, fearful that a stray static charge, or any unlucky strike against a hidden stone, would cause a spark. All the chemistry books warned that this recipe for black powder was notoriously unstable.

Her breath shuddered in her lungs as Basheba's shrieks came again. Buck whimpered and pawed at the ground while Mina filled the cigarette papers with her mixture. The thin paper ripped in half with her first attempt, spilling the powder out over the sand. Mina squeezed her eyes shut, feeling a few fearful tears drip down her cheeks. *If you're going to be a surgeon, you better be able to roll a piece of paper.* The thought was cold and calm within the fevered frenzy of her mind. She clung to it, took a deep breath, and began again. While she felt as if her whole body was shaking apart, her fingers worked swiftly. The paper remained intact, and she capped the ends with the strips of the thin metallic lining she had cut from Cadwyn's med kit.

Cradling the small pile of cylinders in the palm of her hand, she pulled the strap of Cadwyn's bag over her shoulder and eyed the distance to Basheba's knife. Buck's eyes followed her. Waiting. *Don't freeze.* Mina pinched the top cylinder in two fingers and tossed it toward the bonfire. It dropped into the sand. *Goddammit!* In frustration, she threw them all, praying that at least one would find the flames.

The explosion blindsided them all. Instead of the small pop and crackle Mina had been anticipating, the fire roared, embers shot out in blazing tendrils, and a shock wave rattled the stones. Trapped by the walls, the blast was driven back in on itself, amplifying the force until stalactites cracked free from the roof and fell on them. *Note to self,* Mina thought wildly as she scurried back up onto her feet. *Never put makeshift gunpowder into a witch's sacrificial fire.*

She glanced down at the dog by her side. "Kill!"

Instantly, Buck bolted forward, throwing himself over the boulder rather than run around it. White smoke billowed out, obscuring Mina's vision and choking her. A tower of stone crashed to the ground just before her. It wedged itself deep into the earth, toppling over when another burst rocked the cave. Buck's snarls joined the howl of chaos. Mina ran straight for the knife. The moment Basheba appeared from the smoke, bloodied and soaked, eyes wild and teeth bared, Mina shoved the knife into her grasp.

"Keep them off me until I can sacrifice Katrina."

"What?"

"Just do some gratuitous violence."

Basheba flashed a bloody smile and unsheathed her knife. "All right."

They sprinted for the ancient corpse. The smoke had thickened to the point that she could barely see Basheba within it, but Mina never doubted that the woman was there, guarding her back. Keeping all the lurking monsters at bay.

Even in the mist, the bones sparkled. Mina fell into a skid beside them, scraping them up and dumping them into the bag. She clawed at the sand, searching for the sharp crystal peaks that covered even the smallest bones. *Don't miss one. Can't miss one.* Cadwyn broke free of the fog to slam into the ground beside her. The minotaur followed, its blood-soaked horns leading the charge. Buck appeared as a black streak. His momentum and weight forced the minotaur to stagger to the side. Only a few paces and Mina lost sight of him again. Cadwyn glanced at Mina. She nodded rapidly.

"I'm okay. Go."

He was up and gone before she finished the sentence. *Two-hundred and five. Two-hundred and six!* Clutching the bag to her chest, she shot to her feet, and almost right into Whitney.

"What have you got?" the woman snarled on a raspy breath.

Bones dug into Mina's stomach as she tightened her grip. She took a step back, but Whitney charged forward, keeping her in sight as a string of words tumbled from her lips. The meaning was lost on Mina. The effect wasn't. It only took a second, but that second was agony. One second and the opening of the bag had melted into Mina's skin. Trying to tear it free was like ripping off a limb.

"Stupid child," Whitney hissed.

Another few words and the smoke began to lift. Mina ripped at the seams of the bag as she retreated closer to the bonfire. She saw Buck hanging from a minotaur's neck, blood covering them both. Cadwyn had the second minotaur by the horns, leveraging it back while Basheba shredded its stomach. They were soon shaken free and scrambled to close ranks as the minotaurs circled. By the water's edge, Ozzie and Jeremiah had a cult member's ribs as their defense against the charging satyr. All they could do was get out of its way as it forced them back toward the water. *We're going to die here.*

Whitney seemed to hear Mina's thoughts. She smiled, holding one hand up to beckon her closer. "Make the smart choice, and I'll spare them. I have the power to do that now."

She didn't finish the sacrifice. She's using Katrina's power. Blood soaked the sand. Jeremiah screamed. She clawed at the bag, feeling the bones rattling around in their impenetrable case. *If the Witch is gone, all of this stops.*

"Don't you want to save your family?"

Mina sobbed a broken breath. "It's all I ever wanted."

Don't freeze. Wrapping her arms around the bag, Mina flung herself into the flames to burn with the Bell Witch.

Epilogue

A voice drifted through the dark haze, looping around Mina like a comforting hand and dragging her from the dark depths. It was a struggle to open her eyes. She would have given up on the task altogether if the voice hadn't been so insistent. The lights were too bright. Her eyes couldn't focus.

"Willimina?"

Stark white light blinded her. She tried to flinch away only to find that she couldn't move. Fear spiked inside of her. Swiveling her eyes around, she searched her surroundings. *Dad?* The word pushed through her numb lips in a muffled grunt.

"You're okay, Mina," her father said. "Just rel—"

Jeremiah shoved their father aside before he could finish and took his place.

"Hey, welcome back," he smiled brightly. "We're all okay, don't worry about that."

She wanted to reach for him, but her hand would do little more than a twitch. The original voice spoke again. Warm but crisp.

"I'm Doctor Patel. You're in Guardian Saints Hospital. I need you to look at me again for a moment."

Mina flicked her eyes back, her gaze swept back over her family and the vast room. Her brain struggled to handle both the speed and motion and, for a while, everything blended into a kaleidoscopic blob. Doctor Patel rechecked her pupils.

"You've been in an accident. Do you recall that?"

"Yes." Mina's voice was rough, and her throat felt like sandpaper.

"Take your time," Doctor Patel said. "You've been in a medically induced coma for a month. You're going to feel a little groggy for a while."

A series of questions followed, along with a number of small tests and some equipment checking. Mina would have been interested in observing everything were it not for her present situation. Whenever she managed to get control of her mind, a thousand questions swirled in her head. After a small eternity, the doctor finished her examination.

"Can we have a moment alone with her?" Jeremiah asked. "I think she'll react better hearing it from us."

"Ten minutes only. The FBI is going to question her tomorrow morning. You can all return then for a longer visitation."

The angle of Mina's bed didn't allow her to watch the doctor all the way to the door. She could see far enough to know that Ozzie's family was paying the hospital bills. The place looked more like a hotel suite than a hospital. *Danat Al Emarat,* her brain sluggishly offered up. Vaguely, she recalled reading about how the Danat Al Emarat hospital was creating an all-female staff, and how she had then spent a great deal of time mesmerized by the photographs of the 'royal suite.' An insane amount of luxury meeting practicality. If she hadn't had her life plan all set, she might have tried to get a job there.

"Am I in Abu Dhabi?" she asked on a breath.

A few people chuckled, but she didn't see who. The moment the door closed, Jeremiah regained her attention.

"You're still in America, Mina," he said. "Ozzie's parents are just insanely rich."

"This is a hospital?" She felt the need to check.

"Yeah, apparently Ozzie's dad, I mean Ethan—not Percival—was terrified of Ha-Yun having complications with her pregnancy. So, before Ozzie was born, he bought a hospital and just went nuts outfitting it. You get a butler with this room."

Wait. His voice flooded into her ears too fast for her sluggish brain to make sense of it. *Where am I?* The question got lodged in her throat, and Jeremiah continued.

"This place is so great, I think that's why most of these guys are here to see you wake up."

A sharp voice protested behind him. Jeremiah half-turned to insist that he was joking.

"Everyone's been counting the days. Some of the kids are a little annoyed that the doctors decided to bring you out of it on a school day, so they couldn't come and skip school. We have a lot of cards for you."

The information poured into her brain like warm honey. Slowly coating her thoughts and sticking them together. The more she tried to pry them apart, the worse it became, until everything within her was a single, jumbled mess.

"Hey," Jeremiah said softly. "Hey, I'm sorry, I didn't mean to overwhelm you. Are you still with me?"

"Yes," she mumbled. "What happened?"

"You didn't respond to Ava's safety check."

"What?" *Are you kidding me? The safety check worked?*

Jeremiah chuckled like he couldn't believe it either. "When she couldn't get in contact with you, she called mom and dad. Of course, that didn't go very far."

"Jeremiah," their father growled.

Jeremiah bristled. "Leave it alone, Dad. I'm talking to my sister."

"Don't speak to your father like that," their mother interjected.

Mina jerked with surprise when Jeremiah whipped around to face them. "If I have to get security to see you off the property again, I will."

Their father's face darkened. "You have no right—"

"She's a legal adult, Mr. Davis owns the building, and the doctor said not to stress her out," Jeremiah cut him off. His hands were shaking, but his voice stayed strong. "Either play nice or leave."

Mina instantly recognized the tension crackling between the two men. She had experienced it herself right before she had been cast out of the family. Jeremiah had been through the Harvest, although not in the conventional manner, and he had been altered by it. Not just by the horrors he'd witnessed, but by the truths he'd been forced to confront. And now he'd have to learn to walk through a world alien to everything he had ever known. *Hopefully, Dad will be a bit more understanding this time around.*

Unable to hold their father's furious gaze, Jeremiah turned his attention back to Mina. His voice softened as he continued. "So, she called Ozzie's parents. After what happened with the cult, Ha-Yun called some senator friends and got the FBI involved. I didn't even get back to the surface before I ran into a search and rescue team. They had you evacuated in a few hours."

The safety check worked. Mina couldn't get past it.

"Are you still with me?"

"Yes," she managed. "But I'm getting dizzy."

"Okay, here're the bullet points. Whitney and the others got obsessed with the legend of the Bell Witch. They formed a cult that attacked us because of our ancestors."

"Okay," she said when he paused.

"Whitney poisoned the group. We all fought back. In the chaos, you ended up in the fire, and Whitney escaped."

The door burst open. With an ecstatic yelp, Buck raced across the room and leaped onto the end of Mina's bed. The jolt brought far less pain than it should have. Buck's back legs wiggled about as he swooped down to lick her. Jeremiah's quick reflexes kept his tongue from making contact. The fur on his head was splotchy and charred, exposing glimpses of red skin. The panic that coursed through her family shifted into an uneasy murmur when Basheba sprinted into the room with Cadwyn, Ozzie, and his parents close behind.

"Look who got up," Basheba smiled. "A month-long nap. That decimates my record."

"Do you mind?" Mina's mother hissed. "This is a *private* occasion."

Basheba held up her left arm, displaying the burn scars that covered her hand.

"Buck and I *literally* pulled your baby out of a fire."

The way her mother clamped her mouth shut suggested that this wasn't the first time Basheba had used that to win an argument. She slid onto the end of the bed and called Buck onto her lap.

"Thank you," Mina croaked.

"Has anyone told you what the forecast is here?" Basheba said, wiggling one hand out to indicate her body.

"We were working up to it," Jeremiah whispered.

Her growing anxiety distorted her joy at seeing everyone alive and well. *What happened? Someone tell me!* Her mental pleadings went unanswered as arguments flared over who should break the news. Silent as a ghost, Cadwyn slipped up to her side, not so subtly positioning her chart so she could read it. *Third-degree burns requiring skin grafts. Possible nerve damage to the right hand. Surgery recommended for both legs. Oh God. They might take my legs!* Hot tears choked her, leaving her gasping for air. *My legs. My hand. I might lose them all.* Cadwyn pulled the chart back and offered her a reassuring smile.

"Don't get ahead of yourself. You haven't even started rehab yet."

Mina barely heard her father's roar. "You told her?"

"Seems more like she read it somewhere," Basheba remarked.

"Shut up." Pushing his way to her side, her father leaned over her until Mina could barely see anything but his face. "Don't you worry about anything, angel. It doesn't matter what the cost is, we'll take care of it. You'll be beautiful, you'll see."

"My legs. My hand." Mina gasped, barely having the energy to work out the words. "My life plan. It's all ruined."

"You're still young. You can do other things—"

"Wow," Basheba cut in. "So, you get a bad burn, and everyone just signs up for your BS?"

"How dare you!" someone protested from the cluster of relatives.

"It's just a hand," Basheba declared. "Yeah, you might not be a *surgeon*, but you can still be a doctor. Nurses are the ones that do most of the schlepping anyway."

"She's not wrong," Cadwyn noted.

Ozzie angled his beaming smile at the Crane siblings as if trying to soothe them both. Mina was endlessly grateful for it.

"The FBI won't take her," someone said.

"Not as a field agent. But she wanted to be a profiler. That's a glorified desk jockey," Basheba dismissed.

"And, hey, you've managed to kill a dead witch," Ozzie said. "Everything's got to be easier compared to that, right?"

"She's gone? The box?"

Jeremiah's smile was blinding. "It disappeared. All of it did. The three others just walked out of the forest. I think it's over, Mina."

Warmth blossomed in her chest before a dark thought crept in. "Whitney. She's a witch. What happened to her?"

"The FBI's searching for her now," Cadwyn said.

So, it might not be over, Mina thought. The door opened before she could voice her concern, and in walked Doctor Patel who stopped short to stare at the Rottweiler.

"He's an emotional support animal," Basheba said.

"He has to leave," Patel said before regaining her professional edge. "You all do, I'm afraid. She needs her rest. No complaining. You can see her tomorrow."

Fatigue had almost dragged her under by the time the farewells were over with. Buck managed to sneak one kiss before running off.

"See ya later, burn sister," Basheba called over her shoulder before disappearing.

Cadwyn lingered a heartbeat longer to offer her a smile in the descending silence.

"It might not be over," he said in a whisper. "But, for now, close your eyes and enjoy your freedom."

Mina did just that. Letting sleep take her with a smile on her face.

* * *

If you enjoyed the book, please leave a review. Your reviews inspire us to continue writing about the world of spooky and untold horrors!

Check out these best-selling books from our talented authors

Ron Ripley (Ghost Stories)
- Berkley Street Series Books 1 – 9
  www.scarestreet.com/berkleyfullseries
- Moving in Series Box Set Books 1 – 6
  www.scarestreet.com/movinginboxfull

A. I. Nasser (Supernatural Suspense)
- Slaughter Series Books 1 – 3 Bonus Edition
  www.scarestreet.com/slaughterseries

David Longhorn (Sci-Fi Horror)
- Nightmare Series: Books 1 – 3
  www.scarestreet.com/nightmarebox
- Nightmare Series: Books 4 – 6
  www.scarestreet.com/nightmare4-6

Sara Clancy (Supernatural Suspense)
- Banshee Series Books 1 – 6
  www.scarestreet.com/banshee1-6

For a complete list of our new releases and best-selling horror books, visit www.scarestreet.com/books

See you in the shadows,
Team Scare Street

Made in the USA
Middletown, DE
24 September 2023

39258395R00358